Duncan Sprott

THE PTOLEMIES

Duncan Sprott is the author of two previous books, *The Clopton Hercules and Our Lady of the Potatoes,* both historical reconstructions, published in the United Kingdom. He lives in Ireland.

THE PTOLEMIES

THE PTOLEMIES

Duncan Sprott

Vintage Books
A Division of Random House, Inc.
New York

FIRST VINTAGE BOOKS EDITION, JUNE 2005

The Library of Congress has cataloged the Knopf edition as follows:
Sprott, Duncan, [date]
The Ptolemies / by Duncan Sprott.
p. cm.
1. Egypt—History—332–30 B.C.—Fiction.   2. Ptolemaic dynasty, 305–30 B.C.—
Fiction.   3. Egypt—Kings and rulers—Fiction.   I. Title.
PR6069.P75P78 2004
823'.914—dc22
2004005305

Vintage ISBN: 1-4000-7510-6

Book design by Anthea Lingeman

www.vintagebooks.com

Printed in the United States of America
10 9 8 7 6 5 4 3 2 1

Man decays, his corpse is dust, all his kin
have perished; but a book makes him remembered
through the mouth of its reciter.
Better is a book than a well-built house,
than tomb-chapels in the west;
better than a solid mansion.

Papyrus Chester Beatty IV

Plunge into a book as you plunge into water.
Poverty awaits him who does not go there.

Egyptian wisdom

To speak of the dead is to make them live
once again.

Egyptian saying

Contents

Part Three: **PHARAOH**

Part Four: **ARSINOË BETA**

Main Characters

THE HOUSE OF PTOLEMY

Ptolemies

PTOLEMY SOTER (Saviour)—son of Lagos and Arsinoë

PTOLEMY KERAUNOS (Thunderbolt)—eldest legitimate son of PTOLEMY SOTER and EURYDIKE

PTOLEMY PHILADELPHOS (Sister-Loving)—son of PTOLEMY SOTER and BERENIKE; called MIKROS

PTOLEMY EUERGETES (Benefactor)—son of PTOLEMY PHILADELPHOS and ARSINOË ALPHA

PTOLEMAIOS (of Telmessos)—eldest son of LYSIMAKHOS of Thrace and ARSINOË BETA

Others

ANTIGONE—daughter of BERENIKE and Philippos of Macedon

ARSINOË ALPHA—daughter of LYSIMAKHOS of Thrace; wife of PTOLEMY MIKROS

ARSINOË BETA—daughter of PTOLEMY SOTER and BERENIKE; wife of LYSIMAKHOS of Thrace; and of PTOLEMY KERAUNOS

ARTAKAMA—daughter of Artabazos, Satrap of Baktria

BERENIKE (ALPHA)—3rd wife of PTOLEMY SOTER; mother (by Philippos of Macedon) of MAGAS and ANTIGONE

EIRENE—daughter of PTOLEMY SOTER by THAÏS of Athens

EURYDIKE—daughter of Old Antipatros, Satrap of Macedon; 2nd wife of PTOLEMY SOTER

LAGOS—father of PTOLEMY SOTER

LAGOS—son of PTOLEMY SOTER by THAÏS

LEONTISKOS—son of PTOLEMY SOTER by THAÏS

LYSANDRA—daughter of PTOLEMY SOTER by EURYDIKE; wife of Alexandros (V) of Macedon; then of AGATHOKLES of Thrace

LYSIMAKHOS—Son of ARSINOË BETA and LYSIMAKHOS of Thrace

LYSIMAKHOS—son of PTOLEMY SOTER and ARSINOË ALPHA

MAGAS—son of BERENIKE and Philippos of Macedon

MENELAOS—son of LAGOS and Arsinoë; younger brother of PTOLEMY SOTER; called UNCLE MENELAOS

MELEAGROS—son of PTOLEMY SOTER and EURYDIKE

PHILIPPOS—son of ARSINOË BETA and Lysimakhos of Thrace

PHILOTERA—daughter of PTOLEMY SOTER and BERENIKE

PTOLEMAÏS—daughter of PTOLEMY SOTER and EURYDIKE; wife of Demetrios Poliorketes; mother of Demetrios Kalos

THEOXENA—daughter of PTOLEMY SOTER and EURYDIKE; wife of Agathokles, Tyrant of Syracuse

THE ROYAL HOUSE OF MACEDON

ADEIA-EURYDIKE—wife of PHILIPPOS ARRHIDAIOS

ALEXANDER (III) (the Great)—son of PHILIP of Macedon and OLYMPIAS

ALEXANDROS (IV)—son of ALEXANDER and ROXANE; King of Macedon

BARSINE—mistress of ALEXANDER

KLEOPATRA—daughter of PHILIP and OLYMPIAS; sister of ALEXANDER

OLYMPIAS—wife of PHILIP; Queen of Macedon

PHILIP (II)—father of ALEXANDER; King of Macedon

PHILIPPOS (III) ARRHIDAIOS—elder brother of ALEXANDER; King of Macedon

ROXANE—wife of ALEXANDER; mother of ALEXANDROS (IV)

HIGH PRIESTS OF PTAH AT MEMPHIS

ANEMHOR—High Priest in the time of PTOLEMY SOTER; called OLD ANEMHOR

ESKEDI—son of OLD ANEMHOR; husband of NEFERRENPET (Rempnophris)

PADIBASTET—son of ESKEDI; husband of NEFERSOBEK (Nephersouchos)

ANEMHOR (II)—son of PADIBASTET and NEFERSOBEK; called YOUNG ANEMHOR

Chronology

All dates are approximate

Map of Alexandria

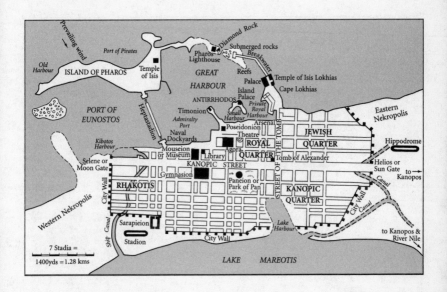

Prevailing wind

Old Harbour

Port of Pirates

ISLAND OF PHAROS

Temple of Isis

Diamond Rock

Pharos Lighthouse

Submerged rocks

Breakwater

Reefs

Palace

Temple of Isis Lokhias

Cape Lokhias

GREAT HARBOUR

ANTIRRHODOS

Island Palace

Private Royal Harbour

Eastern Nekropolis

PORT OF EUNOSTOS

Heptastadion

Timonion

Admiralty Port

Naval Dockyards

Small Harbour

Poseidonion

Arsenal

Theatre

JEWISH QUARTER

Hippodrome

Kibotos Harbour

Mouseion or Museum

Library

Agora

ROYAL QUARTER

Tomb of Alexander

STREET OF THE TOMB

Helios or Sun Gate

to Kanopos

Selene or Moon Gate

KANOPIC STREET

RHAKOTIS

Gymnasion

Pantion or Park of Pan

KANOPIC QUARTER

City Wall

City Wall

Canal

Western Nekropolis

Ship Canal

Sarapieion

Stadion

City Wall

Lake Harbour

to Kanopos & River Nile

7 Stadia =

1400yds = 1.28 kms

LAKE MAREOTIS

Map of Alexander's Empire

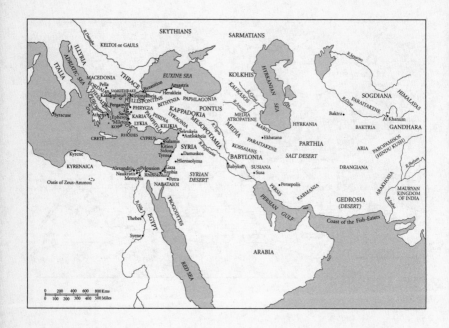

Greek Pharaohs of Egypt

THE HELLENISTIC PERIOD
332–30 B.C.

Macedonians

Ptolemies

THE HOUSE OF PTOLEMY

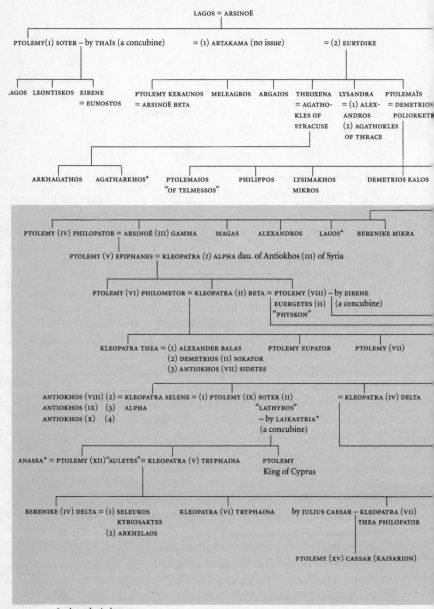

LAGOS = ARSINOË

PTOLEMY(I) SOTER – by THAÏS (a concubine) = (1) ARTAKAMA (no issue) = (2) EURYDIKE

.AGOS LEONTISKOS EIRENE = EUNOSTOS PTOLEMY KERAUNOS = ARSINOË BETA MELEAGROS ARGAIOS THEOXENA = AGATHO- KLES OF SYRACUSE LYSANDRA = (1) ALEX- ANDROS (2) AGATHOKLES OF THRACE PTOLEMAÏS = DEMETRIOS POLIORKET♦

ARKHAGATHOS AGATHARKHOS* PTOLEMAIOS "OF TELMESSOS" PHILIPPOS LYSIMAKHOS MIKROS DEMETRIOS KALOS

PTOLEMY (IV) PHILOPATOR = ARSINOË (III) GAMMA MAGAS ALEXANDROS LAGOS* BERENIKE MIKRA

PTOLEMY (V) EPIPHANES = KLEOPATRA (I) ALPHA dau. of Antiokhos (III) of Syria

PTOLEMY (VI) PHILOMETOR = KLEOPATRA (II) BETA = PTOLEMY (VIII) – by IRENE EUERGETES (II) (a concubine) "PHYSKON"

KLEOPATRA THEA = (1) ALEXANDER BALAS (2) DEMETRIOS (II) NIKATOR (3) ANTIOKHOS (VII) SIDETES PTOLEMY EUPATOR PTOLEMY (VII)

ANTIOKHOS (VIII) (2) = KLEOPATRA SELENE = (1) PTOLEMY (IX) SOTER (II) = KLEOPATRA (IV) DELTA
ANTIOKHOS (IX) (3) ALPHA "LATHYROS"
ANTIOKHOS (X) (4) – by LAIKASTRIA* (a concubine)

ANASSA* = PTOLEMY (XII) "AULETES" = KLEOPATRA (V) TRYPHAINA PTOLEMY King of Cyprus

BERENIKE (IV) DELTA = (1) SELEUKOS KYBIOSAKTES (2) ARKHELAOS KLEOPATRA (VI) TRYPHAINA by JULIUS CAESAR – KLEOPATRA (VII) THEA PHILOPATOR

PTOLEMY (XV) CAESAR (KAISARION)

* = hypothetical name.
Note: *The House of the Eagle* comprises the stories of those appearing above the shaded area.

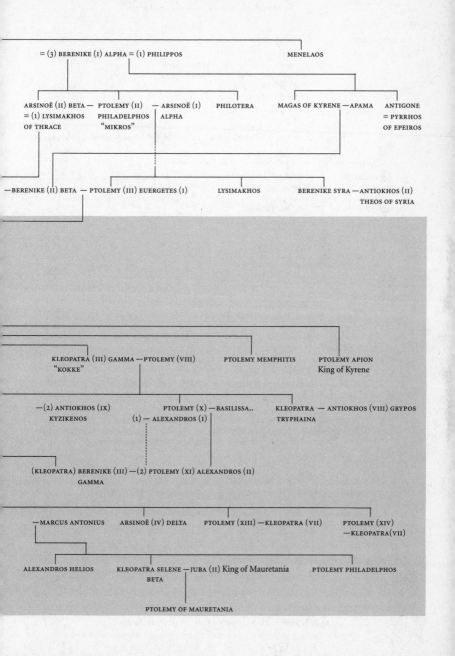

= (3) BERENIKE (I) ALPHA = (1) PHILIPPOS   MENELAOS

ARSINOË (II) BETA —   PTOLEMY (II)   — ARSINOË (I)   PHILOTERA   MAGAS OF KYRENE — APAMA   ANTIGONE
= (1) LYSIMAKHOS   PHILADELPHOS   ALPHA   = PYRRHOS
OF THRACE   "MIKROS"   OF EPEIROS

— BERENIKE (II) BETA — PTOLEMY (III) EUERGETES (I)   LYSIMAKHOS   BERENIKE SYRA — ANTIOKHOS (II)
                                                                                       THEOS OF SYRIA

KLEOPATRA (III) GAMMA — PTOLEMY (VIII)   PTOLEMY MEMPHITIS   PTOLEMY APION
"KOKKE"   King of Kyrene

— (2) ANTIOKHOS (IX)   PTOLEMY (X) — BASILISSA..   KLEOPATRA — ANTIOKHOS (VIII) GRYPOS
KYZIKENOS   (1) — ALEXANDROS (I)   TRYPHAINA

(KLEOPATRA) BERENIKE (III) — (2) PTOLEMY (XI) ALEXANDROS (II)
GAMMA

— MARCUS ANTONIUS   ARSINOË (IV) DELTA   PTOLEMY (XIII) — KLEOPATRA (VII)   PTOLEMY (XIV)
                                                                               — KLEOPATRA (VII)

ALEXANDROS HELIOS   KLEOPATRA SELENE — JUBA (II) King of Mauretania   PTOLEMY PHILADELPHOS
                     BETA

PTOLEMY OF MAURETANIA

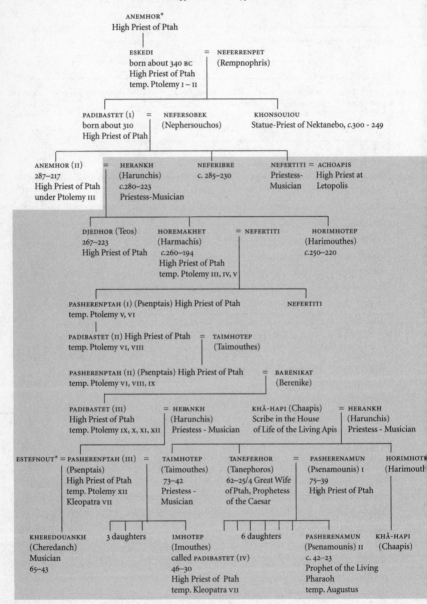

HIGH PRIESTS OF MEMPHIS

(Greek names appear in parentheses)
All dates are approximate. * = *hypothetical name.*

ANEMHOR*
High Priest of Ptah

ESKEDI
born about 340 BC = NEFERRENPET
High Priest of Ptah (Rempnophris)
temp. Ptolemy I – II

PADIBASTET (1) = NEFERSOBEK   KHONSOUIOU
born about 310 (Nephersouchos)   Statue-Priest of Nektanebo, c.300 - 249
High Priest of Ptah

ANEMHOR (II) = HERANKH   NEFERIBRE   NEFERTITI = ACHOAPIS
287–217 (Harunchis)   c. 285–230   Priestess- High Priest at
High Priest of Ptah c.280–223   Musician Letopolis
under Ptolemy III Priestess-Musician

DJEDHOR (Teos)   HOREMAKHET = NEFERTITI   HORIMHOTEP
267–223 (Harmachis)   (Harimouthes)
High Priest of Ptah c.260–194   c.250–220
High Priest of Ptah
temp. Ptolemy III, IV, V

PASHERENPTAH (I) (Psenptais) High Priest of Ptah   NEFERTITI
temp. Ptolemy V, VI

PADIBASTET (II) High Priest of Ptah = TAIMHOTEP
temp. Ptolemy VI, VIII (Taimouthes)

PASHERENPTAH (II) (Psenptais) High Priest of Ptah = BARENIKAT
temp. Ptolemy VI, VIII, IX (Berenike)

PADIBASTET (III) = HERANKH   KHÂ-HAPI (Chaapis) = HERANKH
High Priest of Ptah (Harunchis)   Scribe in the House (Harunchis)
temp. Ptolemy IX, X, XI, XII Priestess - Musician   of Life of the Living Apis Priestess - Musician

ESTEFNOUT* = PASHERENPTAH (III) = TAIMHOTEP   TANEFERHOR = PASHERENAMUN   HORIMHOTEP
(Psenptais) (Taimouthes)   (Tanephoros) (Psenamounis) I (Harimouth
High Priest of Ptah 73–42   62–25/4 Great Wife 75–39
temp. Ptolemy XII Priestess -   of Ptah, Prophetess High Priest of Ptah
Kleopatra VII Musician   of the Caesar

KHEREDOUANKH   3 daughters   IMHOTEP   6 daughters   PASHERENAMUN   KHÂ-HAPI
(Cheredanch) (Imouthes)   (Psenamounis) II (Chaapis)
Musician called PADIBASTET (IV)   c. 42–23
65–43 46–30   Prophet of the Living
High Priest of Ptah Pharaoh
temp. Kleopatra VII   temp. Augustus

Note: High Priests in *The House of the Eagle* are above the shaded area.

Prologue

On the road out of Egypt, into Egypt, there will be, all of a sudden, the whirling storm of sand that turns the world yellow, and it is the sandstorm, the engulfing hurricane of sand, that is also the sands of Time. Out of the yellow fog there emerges at length a dark face, black as night, golden as the dawn, and it is a dog face with pricked ears, wet nose, the bristles and slobber of a real dog, a living dog.

Look closer and you will see that the dog head is fixed to a man's body, and yes, under the mask is a priest of Egypt, dressed in his white robes—his once white robes, yellowed now, as if he is a man made of sand and stained from his travelling, for he has been a long time upon the road. His sandals have been stolen. His bare feet are cracked and bleeding. He is poor. His hands are no longer the soft smooth hands of the scribe, but rough. His right hand is held out to you in the begging position, and he begs not only for your coins but also for your ears—for you to listen to what he has to tell.

The Dog Face carries a knapsack or bag and a staff, and in the bag are the last of his possessions: four great rolls of papyrus, close-written, the ink faded, that he may, or may not, have written with his own pen. Who is this Dog Face? He is the man of many masks who has been two thousand years upon the road, and he has no occupation upon earth but to unroll his books and read them to you.

Who is the dog mask if not the dog god of the Egyptians, Anubis, the Dog Almighty, the companion of Thoth. Yes, he is the Lord of the Desert, who has the power to see with his eyes both by day and by night. He has seen every thing. He has not his youth, but he has better things than youth: he has age, he has experience, he has wisdom. He presides over the mysteries of the night. He symbolizes the victory of life over death. He howls like the jackal. He barks like the dog. The Dog Face: he is the keyholder of this book; he is the guardian of the gates of this writing, watching over both the beginning and the ending of it— Anubis. He seems still to keep watch, imperishable, like a beast that is moved by nothing. He waits for your own civilization to turn to dust and be blown away by the storm of sand that is Time. Anubis is the one who speaks the Judgement of the Gods, for Thoth to write down. He is the Arch-Teller of Stories—the sto-

ries of men's lives. For the moment, though, this Dog Face must put off his dog mask and wear instead the mask of a bird. It is time for the Dog Face to become the Ibis. He is the Master of All Secrets. He has been a long time upon the road, looking for you to tell you this story.

He howls the howl of a dog now, and his howl turns into the harsh cry of a bird.

He grabs you by the arm, and he is no longer the dog. His hand is gnarled, scaled, sharp, digs into the flesh, like the claw of a bird.

You are in my power, *he says.*

Hail, Dog Face, *you say.* Hail, Anubis, Pharaoh of the Underworld.

Let the darkness depart, *he says.*

Part One

PTOLEMY SON OF LAGOS

The Fingers of Thoth

HO! Stranger! OHO! Ignorant One! YOU have been such a long time a-coming! You are so very late in time! YES! It is YOU I am speaking to, Reader, YOU. Because I think YOU know *nothing* of Ptolemaios—Ptolemy—the Greek who was Pharaoh of Egypt, or of the terrible tragedy of his House. You do not know who Ptolemy is, do you? You have never heard of him, have you? You cannot so much as pronounce his name (do not say the *P*, Reader!). Truly, what you deserve just now is a beating upon the soles of your feet.

Yes, I think you have forgotten every last thing about the Black Land and the Red, the Two Lands that I called Kemet—the land the Greeks are pleased to call Aigyptos, that *you* may have heard called Egypt. You have forgotten Ra, the Sun god. You have forgotten Anubis, the dog-headed god, who is Pharaoh of the Underworld. You have not a clue who is Sobek, the crocodile god. Your ignorance is disgraceful—disgraceful—and the only Pharaoh you have ever heard of is the feeble Tutankhamun! Truly, THOTH will have to teach you everything. But do not fear. Be not afraid. Calm yourself, Reader; we shall save up the beating for later. Thoth will be pleased to be your guide. For you must know that I am THOTH.

But, idiot that you are, you do not know who is Thoth either, do you? You have forgotten even Thoth, the Great Magician, Thoth the Ibis-headed god, Thoth the Dog-headed Baboon, Thoth the Ape, who is the Greatest of Scribes; who is the Memory of the Gods; who writes down the gods' every word.

Thoth: he knows every thing. There is not one book about Egypt that Thoth has not written himself, with his own pen. Behold, then, Thoth, the Teller of Stories, for there is no man left upon earth who could unfold for you the whole horrid story of the Ptolemies, a story that men have been afraid of, that men have wanted to forget, because

of its horrors—a real donkey-upon-the-roof of a story. But Thoth—
Thoth has not the ability to forget; Thoth can only *remember*.

For you, however, since you pray and entreat me, Thoth will tell this
great forgotten story of how the Greeks were Kings and Pharaohs of
Egypt for ten generations. And thou shalt weep, and thy hair shall stand
up upon its ends, if thou hast any hair, Reader, for this story drips with
blood from end to end: it is like a shower of blood, horrible and marvellous at the same time.

Read then, Reader, and be horrified. *Read,* and be delighted.

But first, before Thoth tells of Ptolemy, he must tell of Thoth. Because
you, Reader, are Pupil-of-Thoth. You are He-Who-Wishes-to-Know,
and you can know nothing if you do not know who and what is Thoth.
For yes, I am THOTH, GREAT GREAT GREAT, THREE TIMES
GREAT.

Oho! Pupil-of-Thoth, it is I who have learned the Nineteenth
Instruction, the Teaching of Making the Speech Calm. I am Thoth,
Cool of Speech. Sweet-of-Tongue is my name. I am Thoth, Mighty in
Dread, who bathes in the blood of his enemies. I am Thoth, Great in
Slaughter, god of the dead. I am One Who Knows How To Repel Evil. I
am the Peaceful One.

Oho! Oho! I am the Beaked One, the one with the claws and wings.
I am the Moon god. I am the Trickster. I am the Thief of Time. I am
THOTH.

Know that I am Thoth who swallowed the Two Lands, who knows
every thing that can be known about Egypt. I am Thoth the Preten-
tious, Thoth the Pedantic, Thoth of the convoluted speeches.

Know that it is Thoth who makes special pleading for every man
with the Judges of the Dead; that it is Thoth whom you shall meet in
the Afterlife, when I weigh your dead man's heart in the Scales, the Balance, against the Feather of Maat, the Feather of Truth, and that it is
Thoth who shall write down the Judgement of the Gods. May your
heart be light in the Balance, Reader! For it is Thoth who shall weigh
YOUR heart when it is your turn. Is that enough to make you sit up and
listen?

Thoth I am to the Greeks, or Taautos. To the Egyptians I am Djehuty or
Djedhuti or Tehuti, author of the Forty-two Books that are called the
Tehutica, and have in them All the Wisdom in the World. Some have in

them Laws of Egypt, of which Thoth is the guardian. Some are books of Magic, for Thoth is the Great Magician, rivalled only by Isis, Lady of Many Names; and some are books of History, for the annals of every reign are written by Thoth. The book you are holding in your two hands, Reader, is a book of History, the Forty-third Book of Thoth. It will fix your eyes upon the page until you are done reading, Thoth promises you. Every word of it is true. There is no place for fictions in the writing of Thoth.

Thoth! Some times I take the shape of the ibis, and I fly upward. Now, though, I take the shape of the ape, and squat upon the shoulder of the writer. The Ape of Thoth chatters in every scribe's ear. The Ape of Thoth stares hard at every word. Every scribe, before he begins his daily work of writing, must pour out his drop of water upon the ground, out of the pot into which he dips his brush. It is his libation to Thoth, to *me*, Patron of Scribes; to Thoth, who is the greatest scribe of all.

Thoth hears you, Pupil-of-Thoth. He knows even what are your secret thoughts. You do not believe a word? Thoth waxes angry, then. May I remind you, Pupil-of-Thoth, that I am the Tongue of Ptah, the creator god, and that Ptah created every thing. I am the Master of Chronology, Thoth, who reigned seven thousand seven hundred and twenty-six years exactly. Believe me, I am the All-Knowing One. I am Lord of Khemmenu, the Most Mighty God. I am the Heart and Tongue of Ra. I am the Lord of Books. I am the Author of Time. I can read the secrets of men's hearts. I have the power to cross every barrier.

I am the very *inventor* of hieroglyphs, the *inventor* of reading and writing. I am the Lord of Kind-Heartedness. I am the Lord of the Stars. I am the Measurer of the Earth. My words take effect. I am Mighty in Speech. When I put on the mask of Thoth, I *am* Thoth, I *am* the god.

And so I begin to write. Thoth watches over me. The ape is heavy upon my shoulder. Will you not believe me? Listen, Pupil-of-Thoth, it is the truth.

Thoth beseeches you: Believe!

YEA, Thoth has written these chapters with his own fingers.

1.2

Nobody

Thoth asks, then, So who was he, this Ptolemy, this Greek, this yellow-haired Macedonian? Of what father was he the son? Where did he come from? And what did he want with Egypt?

Ptolemy: was it not the truth that he was Nobody—Nobody, from Nowhere? Was it not true that this was a man who did not so much as know the name of his grandfather?

Ptolemaios they called him, and his name meant Warlike, and there was never more fitting name for a House than the name of Ptolemaios.

From the very start there were questions asked about his parentage. Some said the father was Lagos, an army commander of King Philip of Macedon or, at least, some soldier of his, and the mother Arsinoë. Lagos, his name meant Hare, after the creature that sleeps with his eyes open and is, above all things, fast. Because of it, some have always called the House of Ptolemy the Lagids or Lagidae. As for Arsinoë, it is all Greek to Thoth, but, Reader, you must say *Ar-Sin-OH-ee* or *Ar-ZIN-oh-ay.*

Others swore, by Zeus, that Ptolemy was the son of Arsinoë but that his father was King Philip himself, and Arsinoë the victim of a rape— that rape is the privilege of kings, and Ptolemy was born a bastard.

Who was he? A boy of noble birth? Or a boy of no birth? Even Thoth shrugs his shoulders. What if he was, indeed, a peasant boy from Eordaia in Macedon, a herder of sheep and goats, the next best thing to a barbarian? What did it matter? For the fate of the boy was to be a king, and a god in his own life time, and to be called *Aionobios*—Living for Ever, and Son of the Sun.

At the moment of the birth the women screamed the ritual shout of joy, and the midwife made her examination to see that the child had the proper number of orifices, the proper number of fingers, his toes not joined up, his palate not cleft, his eyes both the same colour: blue. If such things were in order, the Greeks would rear the child, and if not, they would not, but cast him out, and the birds might peck his eyes and the dogs eat his flesh while he lived for all that anybody cared what became of him. Such was the habit of the Greeks, who would have no children but perfect children, beautiful like the immortal gods, every son handsome as Apollo, every daughter beautiful as Aphrodite.

There were many stories told about the origins of Ptolemy, and they said that, yes, he was cast out, exposed on the hillside, because of the rape of his mother. They said he was rescued by an eagle, and that the parents took him back in again, for that the child fed by eagles must grow up to be a king, and it was an omen from heaven.

Myth, or history? Thoth laughs. The Greeks!—they love to paint themselves grander, wiser, more generous than they really are. The Greeks are pretenders, actors, lovers of lies, and their stories are full of lies, because a story full of lies makes a better story—Thoth swears it.

All the same, if it was the truth that this Ptolemy was Philip's son by his concubine, then he was half-brother to Alexander, and his blood was royal blood. It would suit the House of Ptolemy to let the world believe that it was true.

On the first day of his life Lagos and Arsinoë made the proper offerings to the Fates: of bread, and salt, and drachmas.

On the third day of his life they placed a honey cake beside his head, and a mirror of bronze, and silver drachmas under his pillow—gifts for the Fates, who must come that night to bestow upon a child his destiny in life.

The Fates are three old women: Lakhesis, who sings the past; Klotho, who sings the present; and Atropos, who sings the future. Ptolemy would have time only for Klotho—for the present only—or so he liked to say; for the past he did not want to remember.

Arsinoë swore by Pan and all the gods that she saw the old women that night, shadowy figures: the first spinning her thread, the second writing down her record of what was to come, the third waving the scissors that must cut the thread of Ptolemy's life upon the day he died. But every Greek mother swore such things.

All the same, Ptolemy was in the hands of his fate from the moment he was born, and there was not a thing he could do to change it. Whatever happens to a Greek, it is the will of his gods.

Thoth says, Greek nonsense, all of it. The only gods are the gods of Egypt, but the Greek will persist in his folly.

Arsinoë, to be sure, fed this child of hers with milk from her own breasts, for to suckle the child is proof of a mother's devotion. It is the duty of every good woman to perform this service. Sure, it is tiring, but it will increase her affection for the child, and affection is a thing the Greeks do not possess in great measure. More important, the Greek child is influenced by what milk he drinks, or so they believe. A Greek child must never be fed upon the milk of the cow, for fear that he will drink in her spirit and grow up timid, obstinate, stupid, delighting to stand in his own filth.

For the Egyptian the cow is sacred, imbued with the spirit of Hathor the Golden, the Divine Cow, Lady of the Turquoise, and she demands respect, and worship. Hathor suckles the Pharaoh himself, and what is good enough for Pharaoh is good enough for his people. The Egyptian does not hold such backwards and barbaric ideas about cow milk.

For the same reason the Greek will have nothing to do with the milk of sheep or goats, and so Ptolemy sucked at his mother's breast. Nor was he handed to the wet nurse, who might pass on to him an undesirable character with her milk. No, Arsinoë did every thing according to the custom of the Greeks: to do otherwise would be to tempt the revenge of the gods.

Even so, Thoth knows, the time would come when the women of this family got so vain, so proud, so rich, and yes, so stupid, that they would hand their children to the wet nurse, and feed their breast milk to the dogs, because women's milk will stop the dogs' going mad.

Every Egyptian knows that to do such a thing is as fatal as climbing into your wife's dirty bathwater.

Thoughts of Thoth: In the House of Ptolemy the madness would lie not in the dogs but in the humans.

Wisdom of the Egyptians: The wise man knows the good from the ill action. Devotion in a mother is a goodly thing.

And yes, they bandaged this child, wrapped him in bandages so that he was bound fast, arms and legs and body, and the head also: he was tied up for the first forty days of his life, then for a further twenty, so that his limbs grew straight.

Ptolemy howled, as every Greek child howls, a prisoner in his swaddling clothes. It was as if these parents wished their son to grow up angry, which was, of course, the truth. They brought up every son to spill blood, to be a warrior. In this, at least, they were successful. By the end of it all, his story—the story of his House—would be spotted, splashed, then drenched in blood, like the papyrus of the apprentice scribe who has unthinkingly spilled his red ink.

From his first day Ptolemy wore not only the bandages but the right eye of a seal, wrapped in a scrap of deer skin, to make him desirable. On his right arm he wore the tongue of a seal, to bring him victory in war. On his left wrist he wore the heart and whiskers of a seal, to guarantee success in every thing he did.

The Luck of Ptolemy began at once, for the parents hung around his neck the charms that guard against ill luck, bad diseases, and the Evil Eye. He wore them all his life, and never took them off.

In the sixth month Arsinoë began to chew up solid food in her own mouth, then spit it out and put it into the mouth of Ptolemy, much as a mother bird will feed worms to her fledgelings.

When the time of the bandaging was done, she unwrapped his right hand first, so that he should not grow up with the disgrace of holding the sword in his left hand. A Greek must wield the sword with his right hand, the shield in his left, or he will be useless in the phalanx.

Thoth says, It is the first sensible word of the Greeks.

Ptolemy—this peasant, this nobody—he dresses in the skins of sheep against the cold. By night he huddles up to the beasts for warmth. Always he will feel the cold.

But he grows. By the age of six he is watching his father's flock on the hillside, in all weathers. His ear is acute, his eye is sharp. He is ever on the watch for the wolves and bears and eagles that carry off his lambs. He throws stones at the crows. He is skilled with the sling, and it is his fate to be a great warrior.

At twelve he catches a gecko in the *nekropolis,* and wears its right leg tied to his right forearm, for it brings charm, and endless victory in battle.

At thirteen he straps on the *phallos* talisman that will guard against the Evil Eye, and he fingers it for Luck twenty times a day for the rest of his life.

Aye, he is lucky, lucky, for it is not in the nature of the Greeks to leave such important things to Automateia, goddess of Chance.

At fourteen he walks to Pella, capital of Macedon, and is a pupil at the School of Pages, for this is the court of King Philip, the man who might be his father, and they mock him because he cannot tell his grandfather's name, because he has called him always *Pappos.*

This boy Ptolemy arrives stinking of stale milk, and with the dung of sheep and goats still upon his sandals. Some even swore, by Zeus, that he had nothing upon his feet, but arrived in the city barefoot, and they laughed at him for it.

Ptolemy hunts now with the King, and waits at his table. In return, he is given his training in the arts of war, and learns the *alpha beta,* and it is his privilege to be beaten by the King's hand and no other.

When he scrapes his cheeks for the first time with the razors of bronze, he dedicates the golden fluff to Hermes, the Thoth of the Greeks, after the Greek custom, by way of thanks for having survived so long as to enter manhood.

In honour of Hermes, Ptolemy now hangs up his *kausia*, or felt beret, and the scraper he used in the *gymnasion* to remove the sand and oil from his skin, and his sweat-soaked *khlamys*, or cloak; and the leather ball that he never tired of throwing about he presents to the god, as memorials of a well-conducted boyhood.

To be sure, Ptolemy son of Lagos did not shine at this age as a lover of books and learning. He was not then, or ever, Thoth in all things. By no means. Nor did he stand out as one whose fate it was to be a leader of men, for he was better at being told what to do than at giving orders.

Nonetheless, he was blessed by Tykhe, goddess of Luck. Ptolemy was above all things lucky. Assuredly, Alexander was lucky also, famous for his Luck, but the truth of it was that Ptolemy was *luckier*.

What of the rest of this family? Were there no brothers and sisters? No relations to speak of? And what became of Lagos and Arsinoë?

Pupil-of-Thoth, if the god were to tell you every thing, you would not be able to pick this book up in your two hands. Let it be enough for you to know that Ptolemy had one brother, Menelaos by name, who marched beside him all his life. Some times Menelaos was useful, some times not. Menelaos, at least, survived. Of any other, Thoth knows not one thing—No, not one word.

And as for the parents, nothing but darkness—dark, dark, dark— and whether they lived to be old or died before their time—even Thoth who knows every thing does not possess such knowledge.

It was when Ptolemy was eleven or twelve years old that Alexander was born, the son of King Philip of Macedon and Queen Olympias, so that Ptolemy was, perhaps, half-brother to this great prince, and perhaps he was not.

Alexander would have been two or three years old when Ptolemy first set his foot in Pella. Was Ptolemy given the task of caring for this prince? Was he the personal bodyguard of Alexander? Did Ptolemy himself teach Alexander the art of horse-riding, the elements of wrestling and boxing? It may have been so.

What Thoth does know is that Ptolemy was, before long, Alexander's Eater. He was the taster of Alexander's food, and yes, it was because his tongue was soft, his stomach iron-hard, and it was his skill to sniff out poison like a dog.

At all events, fate had bound up the history of Ptolemy with that of Alexander, without whom Ptolemy would never have dreamed of setting his eyes upon Egypt, and the Book of Thoth that you hold heavy in your hands would never have been written.

Time passed. When Alexander reached thirteen years old, his schooling began in earnest, with the famous Aristotle as his tutor. The Greeks said always that Ptolemy himself sat at the feet of Aristotle, in spite of his being ten years older than his classmate.

But Thoth asks, Why was Ptolemy *still at school* if he was twenty-three years old? Could this man not already recite Homer by heart from end to end? Was he so backwards that he needed extra lessons in geometry, mathematics, astronomy and botany?

Thoth spreads his hands, his wings, baffled.

What Ptolemy gained as a result, though, was the Memory Theatre of the Greeks, intricate in detail, exquisite in design, with upwards of twenty thousand seats of stone, and upon every seat some object such as raven, eagle, lion, antelope, bear . . . and the sequence of objects was so drummed into him that he could recall every last moment of his past, and at the end of his life—when, to be sure, he did not want to remember—he would write it all down, his history of Alexander, just as it happened.

Nobody should doubt his memory of what took place. He was with Alexander in the beginning; he was with Alexander at the end. As Alexander's Eater he sat beside the King at every meal. There was nothing that Ptolemy did not know about Alexander of Macedon.

But at the same time as he knew everything, he understood nothing. Nobody understood Alexander. Not even Thoth. Alexander would be a mystery for all time.

1.3

The Past

Thoth hears you, Impatient One. Sure, you want the story, sure you want the future, Pupil-of-Thoth, but Thoth says it: You cannot have the future without first having the past.

Thoth hears you, He-Who-Wishes-to-Know, saying Ptolemy had only time for the present, that he wanted nothing to do with his past. Thoth hears you saying you want to know the future, to move quick.

But Thoth says, Take your time. To be sure, Ptolemy wished to forget that past of his, but he could not forget it. Thoth wants you to know what was in the past of Ptolemy. Thoth is most interested in the past. Thoth *will not* leave out the past of Ptolemy. Thoth waxes angry. Do not forget that Thoth is Great in Slaughter, Mighty in Dread. Do you not wish to know what Ptolemy did? How can you not yearn to be told of his early years? Do you not wish to know what wickedness the Greeks did in Asia, of their manifold crimes of war? How can you not desire to hear of the horrible past of Ptolemy? How can Thoth leave out the founding of the illustrious and most illustrious city of Alexandria? Or the story of how Ptolemy came to eat his dog?

No more nonsense, Pupil-of-Thoth. The god would have you know every thing. Thou shalt be like Thoth himself and know all things. Turn the page and turn the page. Forget not that what you hold in your two hands is the Book of Thoth, written by the labour of his own fingers; that it shines in the dark; that it holds a reader prisoner until he is done reading.

Aye, Ptolemy would have liked so much to forget his past, but Thoth thinks different. Thoth knows that *the past is more important*.

If a man spoke the word Khaironeia to Ptolemy, he would shut his eyes and screw up his face. He remembered too much about this battle.

The Greeks say that killing the first man is the worst. Ptolemy feels sick in his stomach still when he thinks of it: the light behind the man's head, and he is a Greek, not twenty years of age, with a wife, and a family, and a farm, and he has thrown away his helmet, and his death will be the fault of Ptolemy.

He screams the *Alalalalai*, the battle cry of Macedon, driving the sword home, and he does not stop screaming as he drives the sword into the man's mouth, and he screams as he withdraws it through the man's shattered teeth, and he is drenched by the jet of black blood from his howling mouth. He drives the blade through the stomach, then rips upwards, so the entrails of the man tumble out over his—Ptolemy's—feet, like a string of bloody sausages. He jabs the sword through the man's neck, so that he is skewered, like a joint of beef, because he must make sure the man is dead, so that he does not stagger to his feet behind him and kill Ptolemy instead.

Ptolemy vomits up his breakfast, for he has killed his first man, and it is his first battle.

In the quiet afterwards he seeks out the man and hacks off his extremities—the smooth feet, the perfect hands, the *rhombos* that will father no more sons, the ears that the light will shine through no more, the nose that does not breathe—and he strings them upon a rope around the dead man's neck and under his armpits, because that is what he must do, to stop the ghost haunting him ever after.

It was a useless business, though, for the ghost would haunt him anyway.

Yes, he wept as he killed for the first time, he shat his legs like a perfect coward, for terror that he might bungle his first killing. But his comrades said, *Always it is like that, the first time you kill a man.* It was really no disgrace to feel as Ptolemy felt, they said. They said, *The second time a killing is more easy . . .*

And it was true: after that he was nothing but a machine for killing men, and he thought little of what he was doing. He was a soldier of Macedon. Death was his trade or profession. Yes, he hated it, but he also felt good about it. He was good *at* it. There is nothing like death for making a man's heart beat high; nothing like death for making a man feel *alive*.

Khaironeia. After the victory King Philip held his usual great feast, and he drank too much wine, as usual. Then he made the tour of the field, helped along by his senior officers, laughing at the piled-up dead, and speaking many coarse and insulting words. But when he came upon the Theban Band, the famous battalion of male lovers, one hundred and fifty pairs of them, lying dead in their lines, just as they had fought, Philip wept.

The Greeks, for all their faults, are not men utterly lacking in feeling. They do not have complete hardness of heart. And Philip, as hard a Greek as ever lived, now put up a great stone lion to guard the grave of these warriors, saying that none braver than these would ever wield the sword.

Ptolemy—what does he remember? So long as the wounded could move, the birds kept off; but when they stopped moving, the crows took their eyes. And the vultures swooped down out of their trees by the thousand. The last thing a man knew was the birds' circling. The last thing in a man's life was the beat of great wings, the yellow talons, the great yellow beak coming straight down at him. Then the darkness, and the screaming, and then the silence, and it was the road to Hades, from which no traveller returns.

The boys who were too young to fight—the pages from the Page School—Philip employed to scare the birds, but a battle might attract up to twenty thousand birds, and who could scare off so many?

Ptolemy vomited when first he saw it, but a man may become used to any thing, almost, and the time came when his guts did not churn. And no, he had no idea, then, what part the vulture was fated to play in his life. He did not know that his House must *love* the vulture, that the vulture would be his *god*.

If a man spoke the name of Philippos to Ptolemy, he would *not* screw up his face at the memory, though divine Rumour said this man was Ptolemy's father.

The day King Philip was murdered was the day of his daughter Kleopatra's marriage, so that her wedding feast became the funeral feast of her father, and the wedding torches served to light his funeral pyre. Ptolemy saw all: the blood upon the ground, the blood upon the King's white garments, the trail of blood as they dragged this great King lifeless away.

And Ptolemy felt nothing.

The diviner had declared it an Auspicious Day, though as it turned out the day was auspicious only for Alexander, who became King, and for Olympias his mother. Alexander, though, had done his duty, and handed the diviner over for crucifixion, for failing to forecast an Inauspicious Day, and the crows had his eyes, and he deserved it.

Ptolemy saw that Olympias was guilty of her husband's murder—Olympias, who went so far as to put a crown of gold oak leaves upon the murderer's head where he hung, nailed to the public gibbet. She even went so far as to dedicate the murder weapon to Apollo—proof enough, surely, of her guilt.

But Alexander was King, and would rule jointly with his mother, so that Olympias kept her power and influence.

Worse things happened, then: Olympias wanting to punish the dead man's new wife, and her infant son, the half-brother of Alexander; and the story went that she had these two dragged on to a great bronze dish, lit a fire underneath it and roasted them to death.

Alexander began his reign with the bath of blood. His half-brother Karanos he murdered. His other brothers and half-brothers also—all were got rid of, so that Alexander might sit easy upon his throne. The only kinsman to be let to live was Arrhidaios, his crazy brother, who presented no threat to anybody.

Such were the civilized customs of the Greeks.

As for Ptolemy, Philip never singled out this son of his for special treatment of any kind. He had not allowed him quick promotion from the ranks, but having called him to Pella he ignored him for seventeen years, as if he was not his true father at all.

Such a man it was difficult to mourn.

At the burning the wind blew the smoke up every man's nose, so that they coughed, and their eyes ran as if they wept real tears for the dead man whom nobody had loved in all his life time.

The smoke made them sneeze also, giving even the approval of Zeus for what they had done: the murder of a king, a husband, a father, and a mighty general of Macedon.

1.4

The Memory of Cruelty

No, Pupil-of-Thoth, be not deceived. Ptolemy remembers every thing, good and bad, but he pretends otherwise.

In the midst of his marching he will remember how it was. Now the heavy infantry hold the *sarissa* upright, then they lower them for the attack, swing them from left to right, and repeat the manoeuvre over and over again, upright, down, to the left, to the right. Then comes the signal of Alexander for the entire phalanx to move forwards, to wheel left and right, to about-turn and march backwards, and to execute the drill rehearsal of the parade ground just where they are—in the plain on the borders of Macedon and Thrace, surrounded by the barbarian.

Yes, the barbarian is amazed, awed, shaken to the core of his being by the perfect discipline and perfect symmetry of Alexander's phalanx. He creeps closer in order to see better what is going on. The barbarian is spellbound, like a rabbit surprised by a lamp, frozen by his surprise, and then Alexander screams the signal without warning, and the phalanx screams the *Alalalalai,* the terrible battle cry, and they charge the barbarians, and slice them up, to ribbons, butchered every one of them.

Ptolemy laughs, Ptolemy smiles his broadest smile to think of it. For yes, it was Alexander's favourite trick, performed in total silence. Such a thing no man that saw it ever forgot.

Yes, Thoth knows very well their cruelty—how they put down the revolt at Thebes. No sooner had Alexander arrived before the Elektra Gate than the famous sweating statue of Orpheus began to drip, making the citizens panic, for it was the worst of ill omens. And then the Thebans would not let Alexander inside the city, because of the sweating, and refused also to surrender to him.

What did the wonderful Alexander do? He lost his temper and laid siege to Thebes with every weapon he could lay his hands on. To be sure, the Thebans deserved, in part, what they got, for chanting *Tyrant, tyrant, tyrant* at Alexander from the battlements; but it was not the right thing to shout at this proud King of only twenty-one years old.

Alexander cut them up. Thebes he set on fire. Every house he razed to the ground, leaving only the priests alive; and only the house of the poet Pindar, whose works pleased him, was left standing.

Ptolemy, thirty-two years of age, looted and burned and raped and slaughtered with the rest of them. A soldier's work is to obey orders without question. A soldier's purpose is to kill or be killed.

The blood was, then, upon the hands of Ptolemy, as it was upon the hands of every Greek. Ptolemy had not forgotten Thebes, where Oidipous had ruled, where Teiresias had prophesied. Thoth knows, *Ptolemy did not forget any thing.*

Thoth, inventor of mathematics, keeps his tally. At the crossing of the Hellespont, which marked the start of Alexander's Persian Campaign, there were thirty-one thousand foot soldiers in his service, and five thousand one hundred horse. This was the army that marched away with Alexander, nearly forty thousand men. They would kill, murder, massacre, rape, slaughter, put to the sword, execute or crucify, in the eleven years of their wild progress, tens of thousands, hundreds of thousands of men, women and children, for the simple reason that they had thwarted the will of Alexander, dared to oppose him, or defied his wishes. By the end of the campaign he had one hundred and twenty thousand troops under his command.

Thoth asks, How many men came home to Greece?

But there is no answer. No Greek can answer this question and hold up his head. It is the great shame of Macedon. On the one hand, Alexander is the greatest hero, the greatest general, since the legendary

Achilles, since the beginning of Greek history, a man whose deeds will never be outdone; and yet, on the other hand, he is the man who led away the flower of an entire generation. For the thousands of widows of war, and the thousands of fatherless children, Alexander was no hero, but a demon, who snatched husbands and fathers and failed to return them. Greece was never the same again.

As for the mighty Empire of Alexander, there was nothing left of it after his death but quarrelling.

Thoth knows, too, about the Siege of Tyros, that Ptolemy likes to say he cannot recall.

For yes, Alexander came, saying that he wished above all things to sacrifice to Melqart, the Herakles of Tyros, which meant that he must set his foot inside the city. But the Tyrians knew very well that Alexander meant to overcome them and defeat them, and refused to let him in.

What, then, did Alexander do? He created land where once was the sea, building a great mole so that he could reach the island that was the old city of Tyros, and all the while he was under attack from the Tyrians.

The gods of Greece sent their omens. A tidal wave threw up a great sea monster into the middle of the Macedonian works, where it was stuck half on land, half in the sea, and then swam off again, which the interpreters of omens said meant that Poseidon would indeed help Alexander.

For Alexander thought that, yes, he could even get the better of Poseidon, and he did so, for although the Siege of Tyros lasted some eight months, he bridged the channel at last, and began his assault.

Hard pressed, the Tyrians heated large numbers of bronze shields in a furnace, filled them with hot sand and boiling excrements and threw them down without warning from the top of the city walls, on to Alexander's men. Nothing they did caused the Greeks greater fear than this, for the hot sand would fly between a man's breastplate and his flesh, and there was no way he could shake it out, and it burned through any thing it touched. The men then threw down their weapons, tore off their armour and all of their garments, and so exposed themselves to the Tyrian archers.

But what made Alexander most angry was how the Tyrians treated their prisoners, who were dragged up on to the battlements and had their throats slit in full view of the Macedonians, and then were dropped into the sea.

Alexander inflicted a terrible slaughter upon Tyros. By the end of the siege the Tyrian dead numbered ten thousand, thirteen thousand were enslaved, thirty thousand more were sold into slavery. And Alexander crucified two thousand men along the huge expanse of beach.

What does he remember, then—Ptolemy? He remembers the screaming, the screaming. He remembers how, in sight of the crucified men, Alexander now made great sacrifice to Herakles, and staged his great parade of troops in full armour to celebrate his victory, and held athletic sports, torch races, and gymnastic contests, and made a great feast of one hundred oxen upon the shore.

He remembers the crows. He remembers the vultures' frenzied feasting. The sky at Tyros was black with clouds of birds—black—and the clamour of the birds was with him always, and the stench.

Now Alexander marched his men south as far as the stronghold of Conquest of the Ruler, which the Syrians call Gaza. It was the last town before the desert that separated Phoenicia from Egypt and stood at the head of the Spice Road, and for that reason Gaza was rich. Alexander, therefore, could not bring himself to march by, but needs must take the city for himself, if necessary by beating it into surrender.

The Governor of Gaza, Batis, a Persian eunuch, believed his city to be capable of withstanding any assault, and he refused to give in to the demands of the Greeks. But like every man who refused to co-operate with Alexander, Batis now found out what it meant to arouse the wrath of Macedon.

The Greeks laid siege to the city, and Batis held out for seven months, with a population of ten thousand Philistines and Sand Dwellers, who threw boiling-hot sand and scalding dung, and made use of every kind of engine of war.

Gaza fell at last, and Alexander ordered these barbarians to be cut to pieces to the sound of the trumpet. The women and children he sold as slaves.

As for Batis, the eunuch, whose high-pitched, squeaking voice even Alexander had mocked, he was questioned by the King himself, but refused to speak one word.

Alexander often admired courage in an enemy, and he had been known to show mercy, but Batis was a giant of a man, dark-skinned and ugly, and Alexander disliked ugliness. He preferred a man to be handsome, like the gods to look at, like himself. Alexander was hot, and he was angry, and he had Batis's ankles pierced so that leather thongs could be passed through them, and he had this man dragged behind a chariot, round and round the walls of Gaza, until he was dead.

In doing this Alexander imitated the behaviour of his hero, Achilles, who dragged the body of Hektor round the walls of Troy. Ptolemy, among others, shook his head to see this, knowing that Hektor had at least been already a dead man before such treatment, whereas Batis was still alive.

Some laughed to hear the shrill cries of Batis, a man who had only been doing his duty to King Darius, but many could not watch, and thought ill of Alexander for behaving like a regular tyrant.

So much for the great King. So much for his greatness of spirit.

Ptolemy remembered it. This was not the way Ptolemy would treat others.

And Thoth. No secrets can be hidden from Thoth, the All-Knowing One.

1.5

Greek Demons

Wherever Ptolemy marched, the vulture followed him, like his shadow, waiting for the next battle.

At Gaugamela in northern Mesopotamia the vulture flapped his wings upon every tree, perching even upon the baggage wagons, impatient, before ever the first arrow was fired.

Some saw Zeus and Hera his wife in the vultures. But no, the truth of it was the thought of blood, the promise of feasting. The birds know the signs, such as the sharpening of weapons, the troops forming up in their lines. The vulture knows what an army is for, and yes, the campaign of Alexander was nothing but a prolonged and movable feasting.

Before Gaugamela Ptolemy watched the total eclipse of the Moon, terrified like every other man that the gods of Greece had deserted them, and they shed tears, and sat upon the ground with their cloaks over their heads, offering the prayers of last resort.

Ptolemy watched the Moon lose brightness, as the darkness fell across it, and at last glow red. He shivered with the rest of them, for it was a dreadful omen of bloodshed, and like every other man he feared it would be his own blood.

But Aristander of Telmessos, the seer, urged the men to stay calm, saying that the blood that must be shed was blood of the Persians, and that the eclipse meant a great victory for Macedon, and the conquest of all Asia; and Aristander was right.

Ptolemy liked to forget that he had been *afraid*.

Of the battle itself he remembered only the confusion, the great clouds of dust kicked up by the soldiers, so thick that no man could see more than four cubits in front of his face. He remembered the Paian of Victory echoing in the plain, and the Macedonian claim of thirty thousand dead. Before nightfall the vultures were out of their trees, and Alexander's men, like vultures themselves, stripped the armour and valuables from the Persian dead. They took their bloody trophies—ears, fingers, gold—the rewards of war, and in the morning Alexander hurried the men on to Babylon, if only to escape the stink of death and the sight of thousands of gorging birds.

Not long after Gaugamela, Darius, the great enemy of Alexander, met his end. A short time before he had ridden in his chariot and received divine honours from his people. Now he was taken captive by his own slaves and dragged about in a wagon covered with filthy skins. The Great King was bound hand and foot with fetters of gold, and his own people ran him through with their spears, their swords and javelins, and left him for dead.

Alexander came to look upon the face of Darius, and covered him with his cloak of purple, and ordered for him a royal burial. It was the duty of a king to show mercy, to show generosity to those he had defeated.

Ptolemy saw, then, the rise and fall of kings. He saw what it meant to be a king, and how to be a king, and he wanted, just then, none of it for himself, but was content to be what he was, a common soldier.

But he did not forget Darius dead. Every man had abandoned the corpse, but Darius's dog sat by his master's body, howling, and refused to be led away.

For the Egyptian, the dog—every dog—is Anubis, Pharaoh of the Underworld, a creature faithful above all others in life, and faithful even beyond death. Anubis, guide of the dead in the Afterlife—it is he who takes the dead man by the hand and leads him through the unknown.

Thoth knows. Next after the death of Darius came the trial and execution of Philotas, guilty of plotting against Alexander. The torturers first laid out their instruments before this man's eyes. They blindfolded Philotas then, and stripped his garments from him. Philotas called upon the gods of Greece and the laws of humanity, but his torturers had stopped up their ears with plugs of papyrus, and were deaf to his cries. They racked Philotas with tortures, with ordeal by fire, with beatings upon the soles of his feet, until he confessed himself guilty.

Some say that Philotas was shot to death with javelins, others that he was executed after the usual custom of Macedon, by the throwing of many stones. But Ptolemy, seeing how Alexander punished and tortured, vowed to be merciful if he could.

It was Ptolemy himself who captured Bessos, the murderer of Darius, and he handed this man over to Alexander, naked, wearing nothing but a wooden collar about his neck, and held upon a rope, like a wild beast. This man Alexander tortured also, cutting off his nose and ears, and he hung him upon a cross. The barbarians fired arrows at him and then he was taken to Ekbatana for public execution before the Persians, his own countrymen.

Some told the story that Alexander had Bessos tied between two bent trees, which he then released like a spring—a barbarity copied from Greek legend. Those who had not seen this trick before and stood staring in the wrong place were spattered with blood and guts; and those who knew better laughed.

And it was the thought of Ptolemy, some times, that Alexander—even Alexander—was nothing but a barbarian himself.

Thoth the doctor watches Ptolemy. Thoth knows his every thought. Thoth is the memory of the gods.

In his hot fit Ptolemy feels like he is on fire, burning. He thinks then of Babylon, of Susa, where it was so hot that a lizard could not so much as cross the road at noon without being fried alive.

Now he thinks of the scorching sand, of the road that burns his feet, and he loses himself in his past.

The Greeks, burned by the sun, their blood-stained garments in shreds, haggard and unwashed—the Persians called them the Demons with Dishevelled Hair of the Day of Wrath. And there was much wrath. Others compared them to a beast, terrible, dreadful, and exceeding strong, with great teeth of iron; a beast that broke every thing to bits and stamped upon the bits with its feet. The beast went on marching, and was unbeatable.

He thinks now of Persepolis, city of lilies, where the Macedonians went mad, indulging in an orgy of looting and slaughter, putting to the sword every man they met. And with the women they did whatsoever they pleased.

He sees the Persepolitans standing upon the battlements of the city, dressed in their best clothes. The men are hand-in-hand with their wives and children, and they jump off the edge of the wall like this, rather than face the violence of the Greeks. Others set fire to their houses and burn themselves alive inside.

But what did Alexander do? He feasted here at Persepolis, with many days and nights of feasting, and since there was no water at Persepolis they drank their wine undiluted, which had always been the prelude to disaster.

In his hot fit Ptolemy sees it clear. After the eleventh bowl of wine some person unknown shouted for the *komos,* the victory dance, in honour of Dionysos, god of Wine, god of Frenzy, and the procession of hundreds of men formed a line, with pipes and flutes and drums and torches, and they danced their way round the triple walls of the citadel. These men had drunk to excess, even by Macedonian standards, and were beyond the power of reasoning, for nobody in his right mind would have done what they did next.

Ptolemy sees clear: it is Thaïs of Athens, the famous whore, who is his own possession, and she hurls the first torch, squealing, laughing, laughing, and then one after another every man throws his torch, and the Palace of Persepolis, even the vast *apadana,* or audience hall, of Darius, that could hold ten thousand people, much of which is of cedar wood, burns all night, until nothing is left but a smoking ruin of blackened stone.

Thaïs, they said, forgot herself, was possessed by Dionysos, by the god. It was good, some times, to blame a woman for what went wrong. It was good, some times, to blame someone other than themselves.

But Ptolemy does not remember this.

For whatever reason, this woman would not make her appearance in Ptolemy's history. He would leave out all mention of Thaïs. He did not speak of the burning of Persepolis. He would say nothing about it.

Thaïs was his great shame, his great embarrassment. Thaïs, the high-class whore, the gold-mirror whore, with gold heels, and the words FOLLOW ME written in nails upon the soles of her sandals; Thaïs, who had a ring of gold in her nose, *like a little cow,* as Alexander said, the Alexander who had too many other women, and who, in truth, liked boys better, *and who gave her to Ptolemy.*

Thaïs, who pointed her slippers at the stars; who played the lioness so well; who straddled her man and rode him like a horse, and did the *amphiplix*, the snake coils, like no other woman. She was the best and most expensive of whores.

Somewhere, though, between Babylon and Memphis, Thaïs got lost.

No man knows what was the fate of Thaïs of Athens, and no god, not even Thoth, Great in Magic.

In his hot fit, Ptolemy thinks of Persepolis, and of Thaïs, and the memory of her causes him pain.

Thoth speaks. In his cold fit, his fit of shivering, he is at once in Paraitakene, in torrential rain, and he relives the electric storms, the hailstones and the ice, where two thousand men froze to death or died of pneumonia, not having the luxury of winter clothing. And he feels guilty for being alive, guilty for surviving.

He shivers, and he is once again on that range of mountains called Paropamisos, or Hindu Kush, on the northern borders of India, over which mad Alexander dragged his entire army with its trailing camp-followers, traders, grooms, scientists, clerks, cooks, muleteers, wives and whores, one hundred and twenty thousand persons, so many that it took them ten days to tramp through the pass.

Madness it was to try to get across, for the skin round every man's eyes burned up in the sun, and many suffered frostbite in the severe cold, and the food ran out, and the mountain was too high for grass to grow, so that there was no fodder for the beasts. Vultures perched upon every crag. The wolves and leopards crept close, sensing a meal to be had.

But the only meal for the Greeks was to eat the horses' harness, then the pack animals, and then the horses themselves, eating the flesh raw, because there was no fuel for cooking.

Up on this hateful mountain Ptolemy came close to starving to death, along with the entire army of Alexander, and it would not be the last time.

On the other side, down in the valley, Alexander, who had given his guarantee of safety to the Indian hired soldiers, their wives and children, put seven thousand of them to the sword, because they refused to join him in fighting against their own countrymen.

So much for the word of this wonderful Greek King.

Ptolemy would not, he promised himself, be like *that*.

1.6

Dog Food

Thoth's thoughts: Worst of all his memories is the memory of India, where they did battle against the elephants of Poros in monsoon rains, at that time of the year when every thing of metal—helmet, sword and spear alike—rusted within hours of polishing, and every thing made of canvas or fabric sprouted a disgusting green mould and rotted away within weeks.

Every man suffered here from marsh fever and dysentery and foot-rot and rashes caused by the heat, and every man was bitten by insects and plagued by snakes like rods of bronze, so that they were fearful of sleeping upon the ground by night (which was in any case a swamp of mud), and must instead sleep in hammocks slung between the trees. Ptolemy, like every other man, yearned to go home to Macedon, for they had been eight years on the march, some three thousand days, and they were exhausted.

The Indian campaign lasted three years, but by the end of it the army was close to mutiny. They hated India, where snakebite brought a bloody sweat and sudden death; where the dogs were half tiger, with teeth like saws; where the rain never stopped falling for seventy days in a row.

No man hated India more than Ptolemy, who was wounded here by a poisoned arrow, and suffered sharp pains, numbness in his limbs, convulsions and violent fits of shivering. His skin turned cold and livid. He vomited bile. A black froth oozed from his wound and gangrene set in, which would spread fast and give him a horrible death.

Ptolemy, loved for his gentle character and his kindness, looked death in the face and made himself ready to die. But they told the story that Alexander dreamed a dream, in which he saw a snake carrying a plant in its mouth, and showed where it might be dug up, and what must be done with it to cure Ptolemy of his wound. When Alexander woke, he hunted for this plant, found it, ground it up, plastered it upon Ptolemy's leg and made him swallow an infusion of it.

Ptolemy was restored at once to perfect health.

Out of India Ptolemy brought his own memories: elephants of war, the Indian bird that spoke with a human voice, ferocious dogs. But the misery of horses' hoofs worn thin by marching, and the damp that rotted his boots and clothing, and the non-stop rain—he wanted to remember none of it.

Thoth speaks it, because Ptolemy will say nothing. He has sealed up his memory, saying, *Yesterday is of no importance. What matters is today, now, the sensation of the passing moment . . .*

But Thoth *knows*. It was Ptolemy that plundered the seaside country of the Oreitai, looting and burning, leading the pillage, in the district next before the Desert of Gedrosia (which some call Makran), through which, for whatever crazy reason of his own, Alexander was so keen to march.

A column of eighty-five thousand soldiers tramped into this desert, with the wives and children, whores and camp-followers, carts, wagons, pack animals, horses, and every man's boots filled up at once with burning grit; and the wagons sank into the shifting dunes.

Disaster came upon disaster: the mules chewed poisonous shrubs, foamed at the mouth, and dropped dead. Many of the men were blinded by the juice squirted by prickly cucumbers. Others choked to death after eating too many unripe dates.

In the extreme heat the men were struck down by sunstroke, dehydration, hyperthermia and exhaustion. Those that were not fit to march were left behind in the sands to die.

A violent storm of sand filled every man's ears, eyes and nostrils, and wiped out every landmark, so that the leaders lost their sense of direction and the column wandered on, unable to find a way out of the desert.

Stores, equipment, wagons, carts, weapons—all were lost or left behind. When the food ran out, they ate the pack mules, then the donkeys and the horses.

What of Ptolemy? What did Ptolemy not want to remember? He survived by sucking pebbles, and by his iron will, and by prayers to Zeus, and by repeating over and over that he was not yet ready for Hades.

In the Desert of Gedrosia Ptolemy ate whatever he could find: goat droppings, donkey dung, vulture flesh, rotten lizards, snake slough, spiders, rat, thistles. He was Ptolemy of the iron stomach, that would eat any thing. He drank his own urine. He ate dog's flesh. He ate his own dog.

It should be no surprise that he did not want to hear the word Gedrosia ever again.

At the end of this expedition only twenty-five thousand men were left. Sixty thousand lives were lost. Of seventeen hundred crack troops, the Companion Cavalry, seven hundred perished, and it was the worst disaster of Alexander's career.

Did they blame Alexander, for having led them almost to their deaths? No, they did not. Every thing that happens is the will of the gods. They simply thought they had done some thing to make Zeus angry. No, they loved Alexander, this tyrant, even more, for having managed to keep himself alive. Alexander was *lucky.*

Those that lived sang to keep up their spirits: the Crow Song, the Swallow Song, the Paian of Victory to Apollo, and they hummed the marching tunes. If they had not sung, they would have wept, and when they did at last stop marching and were able to drink their fill of water, they did weep.

After Gedrosia things could only get better. Because of the very great numbers of dead, those that were left had their promotion. Ptolemy was raised to the rank of *strategos,* or general, and wore for the first time the purple cloak that marked him out as one of Alexander's most favoured courtiers.

Out of every bad thing comes some good.

When Ptolemy stumbled out of that desert, he was forty years of age. If he had perished, he would have left no sons, no heirs. Now, however, he made sure that Thaïs had no supply of the crocodile-excrement prophylactic, and it was not long before her belly began to grow stout.

Better bastard sons, Ptolemy murmured, *than no sons at all.*

In due course three children were born to Thaïs of Athens by Ptolemy, and they were called: Lagos, after his father's father; and Leontiskos, meaning Little Lion—two sons, then; and also a daughter, whom Ptolemy, weary now of war, called Eirene, or Peace.

1.7

The Persian Wife

Alexander, when he reached Susa, in Persia, the city founded by the first King Darius, took the thought into his heart that every Greek must have a Persian wife. He said it would result in more Greek sons, more

Greek soldiers, and the thinking behind it was that the men were thousands of *stades* from home, starved of *aphrodisia,* tired of whores and boys, and in need of some new thing to take their thoughts off mutiny.

As it happened, though, he could only lay his hands upon ten thousand Persian women, so that only one man in ten was fixed up with a woman of his own, and the rest were told they must wait a little, must be patient. Ten thousand marriages, however, took place, and Alexander himself, although he already had as his wife the famous and beautiful Roxane, took two new wives, one of whom was Barsine, the daughter of Darius of Persia.

Ptolemy was married at Susa to the Princess Artakama, a daughter of Artabazos, the Satrap of Baktria, a woman of surpassing beauty, and in the heat of the moment he forgot about Thaïs of Athens, his personal concubine.

The men passed a morning catching crows, without which no Greek marriage can be celebrated, for it was the custom to cut out the heart of the crow and wear it as a talisman, in order to guarantee the affection of husband and wife for all time.

With his sword, which was stained black with blood of the Persian, Ptolemy sliced in two the ceremonial loaf, and he and Artakama each ate one half of it, and this wife made no complaint about being joined in marriage to her enemy.

The Greeks sang their Crow Song, in honour of the faithfulness of the crow to his mate, but although Ptolemy wore the talisman, it did not work. No, this wife fought him with her teeth and nails whenever he tried to go near her, noblewoman though she was. Her body went rigid, she ground her teeth and hammered her husband with her fists and set up a terrible wailing.

Worse, perhaps, after the custom of Baktrian women she rubbed her flesh all over with fish oil and rancid fat, the better to keep out the cold, and the better to keep out Ptolemy. Worse still, she was locked up down below, so that no man, least of all this filthy Greek, could defile her.

The Persian marriage of Ptolemy was not, then, a great success. Artakama, his bride of seven wild nights, refused to travel one *stade* along the road with her husband, and in the end he could not carry her off by force. He left Artakama behind in Susa, and went back to the *harmamaxa,* or wagon, of Thaïs, who welcomed him as before, with open mouth and eager kisses, for she was the most famous whore in the world.

Those who knew Thaïs better than Ptolemy did, however, said this woman would never love any man, and never stop pretending to. But for the moment she rode in the baggage train behind the army of Alexander, along with the other concubines of the first class.

Thaïs was no longer young, and she knew that even the most beautiful of women cannot last for ever; he would not so much as look at her after she was thirty. As the years passed, Thaïs looked into her mirror of gold less often, and she made her prayers to the divinized Helen of Troy, the goddess of Good Looks, more heartfelt.

1.8

Cold Chicken

After Susa they set out against the enemy, in spite of it being the hottest season, when the Dog Star rises, and in spite of the heat of the road itself, that made it dangerous for an army to march upon. Alexander lost so many men from heat exhaustion and burnt feet that he changed his plan, marched at night, when it was cooler, and let the men sleep by day.

At Ekbatana, not many *stades* beyond Susa, Hephaistion, the great friend of Alexander, who was recovering from a fever, ate a whole cold chicken faster than he ought to have done, washed down with too much wine, and was found dead in his bed. The result of it was that Alexander fell into the most extravagant grief that anybody had ever seen in a man, going so far as to wail like a woman, to rip at the flesh of his cheeks with the nails of his fingers, to tear his hair out by the roots, and then have it shaved off, so that he went about looking like a slave. The tears never stopped pouring down his face, he howled like a dog, and all Ekbatana stood still to listen to it. Then he rolled his body in the dung of the cowsheds, picked up the filth in his two hands and piled it upon his head, behaviour copied from his heroes in the *Iliad* of Homer, and not seen among these Greeks before or since. He also had the mane and tail cut off every horse, as a sign of mourning, and every Greek thought it the behaviour of a madman.

Alexander lay, yes, naked and stinking, upon the dead body of Hephaistion in this state, kissing and slobbering all over the man for three days and nights, until the corpse began to heave with maggots under the flesh. When Hephaistion began to turn purple and swell up, and stank so bad that no man would go near, Ptolemy himself dragged him to the bath, and ordered the eunuch Bagoas to go in and scrub him clean.

Every man but Alexander remained dry-eyed throughout all this disgraceful exhibition, for, in truth, though Hephaistion was the handsomest of men, he was disliked for his selfish, arrogant, possessive nature, and he was really no very great soldier.

Ptolemy shrugged his shoulders. Other men had loved men more than women. It was nothing unusual among the Greeks. Alexander was not the first *kinaidos* and he would not be the last; but Ptolemy liked a woman better. Yes, this Ptolemy was *mad* after women.

For the army of Macedon, though, to continue to take orders from a commander who wailed like the women, and had forgotten himself so far as to scream the women's lament for his dead lover . . . it could not be allowed to go on, and the generals worried about what he might do next. From this time there was much whispering in private about how best they might relieve him of the supreme command, for the man was not in his right mind, not in control of himself, nor of his troops either, and tens of thousands of lives depended upon his slightest whim. To tell the truth, the generals found Alexander's behaviour disgusting, and they were ashamed of him.

The excesses of this King did not stop, however, for he ordered Hephaistion's physician to be crucified, for that he had allowed his patient to die, and he had the Temple of Asklepios, god of Health, at Ekbatana, razed to the ground, because the god had deserted Hephaistion, whom Alexander loved more than any other thing in the world.

Some hinted that the death of the lover was not from natural causes, nor the death of Alexander either, when it came, but that the pair of them were removed by a group of senior commanders, among whom the names of Krateros, Perdikkas and Antipatros were mentioned first.

For the moment, though, Alexander lived and breathed. He ordered the sacred fire to be put out until the funeral was over, which was what the Persians had done upon the death of the Great King, and this order was, in itself, an ill omen: they said it foretold the death of Alexander himself.

The funeral pyre for this Hephaistion cost Alexander the unheard-of sum of ten thousand talents, and nobody had seen anything like it for magnificence, nor, as they complained, for waste of drachmas, because it was all of gilded wood, with the golden prows of two hundred and forty ships of war on top of it; and then he wasted another fortune on a ziggurat-shaped tomb for Hephaistion at Babylon.

Alexander next sent messengers to the Oracle of Zeus-Ammon in the desert of Libya, to ask whether it would be right and good to honour this man as a god; but the Oracle would not have this nonsense, and only allowed Hephaistion to be worshipped as a hero, and so it had to be, for the Oracle had spoken.

Thus, at any rate, the flesh of Hephaistion son of Amyntor went up in a wall of flame and a cloud of smoke, just like any other mortal. In Egypt they would build shrines to this so-called hero, and it became the fashion to swear oaths *by Hephaistion,* and tales of visions, cures and miracles were gabbled, until, at length, disregarding the wise judgement of Ammon, all Alexandria worshipped this man, the male lover of the founder of the city, as God, Coadjutor and Saviour.

Thoth sniffs at it, but for the Greeks the dividing line between men and gods was never very difficult to cross over, to which the history of the House of Ptolemy will bear witness.

What did Alexander do next? He stormed out of Ekbatana with a division of his army, full of the blind, mad rage that overtakes a man who has lost what he treasures most. Just as Alexander's hero, Achilles, had slaughtered Trojan youths over the grave of his beloved Patroklos, so now Alexander massacred the Kossaians, killing every man of this tribe, and he fought in the front line, leading the slaughter, slashing with his sword, covered in blood and guts, and his eyes stuck out upon stalks like the bollocks of Anubis, and he was wild, a complete barbarian.

Thus he lightened his grief a little by killing, and it was blood for the ghost of Hephaistion. Blood spilt, however, did not pacify this ghost, for whenever he managed to sleep, the ghost came to him, in every way the image of the living man—in size, and voice, and lovely eyes—and the ghost stood over him, whispering in his ears, so that he knew no peace but was like a man possessed.

He swore that he had seen this ghost also as a bird with a human head, that its face was Hephaistion's face, and that it fluttered about him while he slept. Then every bird he saw had the face of Hephaistion, and he would speak no word for hours upon end; and when he did break silence, his words made no sense, so that they were afraid for him, and afraid for themselves, and said openly that he was mad.

A mad Alexander the generals would not tolerate for long, and they began to be afraid not only *for* him but *of* him, and they had no wish to test his emotional strength in the heat of battle. So Alexander fought no great battle after the death of Hephaistion, and it was the generals who made sure he did not, for he was in no fit state to lead one company, let alone the entire phalanx of one hundred and twenty thousand men.

There were many reasons why Alexander might have been the victim of poison, but the great reason was that he was no longer in control of himself, and to the Greeks the loss of all self-control was the thing they dreaded the most, even more than defeat in battle, even more than Hades.

By night the howling came still from the tent of Alexander, and he was so overwhelmed by grief that he knew not where to put himself or what to do about it.

In truth, it would not be long before Fate decided for him.

Whether this man was murdered, or whether he died from some natural cause, his death was the most fortunate thing. Every man would weep for him dead, of course, but every man thought the same: that the death of Alexander was, in truth, the most convenient thing that could have happened.

1.9

Rainbow Body

Alexander now turned his face towards Babylon, and the Chaldeans, men long versed in the art of forecasting the future by means of the stars, warned him with the most severe of warnings not to enter the city. But Alexander did not like warnings: he was a god and the son of a god, and he would no longer be told what he must do by any mere mortal.

The people of Babylon crowded the streets to welcome him, and they burned incense and threw flowers, but as Alexander passed through the gates the ravens, whose guttural croaking will always make men think of death, were seen fighting each other above the battlements, and although it was the worst of ill omens, Alexander took no notice.

He settled down at Babylon to try to drown his grief, drinking vast quantities of undiluted wine night after night. On what turned out to be the last of these drunken evenings, he filled a huge golden cup in honour of Herakles, and drank it off in one draught, when he was heard to shriek, as if he had been struck some violent blow, and he collapsed.

His friends put him to bed in the Golden Bed of Nebuchadnezzar, lately King of Babylon. That was, for Alexander, the beginning of the end, and for Ptolemy the beginning of the beginning.

Afterwards there were whispers of poison, and Iollas son of Antipatros, the boy whose duty it was to taste his drinks for him, was named as the one who had been paid to do the deed, and there was talk of a poison so powerful that it was kept in an ass's hoof, because that was the only vessel the poison would not destroy. But this Iollas was never accused, and never tried for any crime.

Death by poison made a better story, but Alexander showed none of the symptoms of it—neither the spasms, nor the shuddering, nor the fixed grin and staring eyes. Every man had his own theory, and, as they always said, *Everyone who wrote about Alexander preferred the marvellous to the true* (except for Thoth), but most of it was a fiction.

Thoth says, the truth of it was that Alexander died of nothing more than a fever caught in the marshes about Babylon, and it began with a shivering, something that in the searing heat seemed almost impossible. But Alexander had always done the impossible. He suffered now alternate phases of the shivers and the sweats, pyrexia and hyperpyrexia, and it was as if he was burning up in front of their eyes, as if he was on fire.

They sponged him with wet sponges to cool his burning flesh, but he poured with water, became feebler, then delirious, raving about the beauty of Hephaistion, so that it was a relief when he lost the power of speech altogether.

All the stories of Alexander's last wishes, his last words, of handing his signet-ring to Perdikkas, and giving his last orders about the fate of his empire, were nonsense. Thoth says, A man in a fever does not talk sense. A man who has lost the power of speech does not speak one word.

Ptolemy watched Alexander in this illness, thinking that he must at any moment sit upright in the bed of gold, end the jest, smile the smile that made every man's knees melt, because they had all of them, in truth, loved him enough to follow him to the end of the earth. But Alexander was tired out, tired to death, and he fell into such a deep sleep that they panicked at the thought of him dead and were afraid about what they would do without him. Somebody suggested the remedy of last resort to restore a man's consciousness, which meant tipping hot urine up his nostrils, a treatment that had often proved a sure restorative in hopeless cases; but Alexander did not return spluttering to life, and they stood around the bed in silence. The only noise was the urine dripping on to the golden floor.

And so the physicians performed next all the unbeatable tests for whether a man is dead or not, trying to make him breathe upon a mirror, trying to see if his eyes might reflect an image, and so forth, ending up with touching his eyeball with the finger, which is the surest of all the sure tests for whether a man is, or is not, in the land of the living.

There was not a flicker. His eyes just stared, blank, like a dead man's eyes, and the physicians shook their heads and said, one after another, that he was dead, dead, dead, dead.

The fact of the death of Alexander was made public upon the twenty-eighth day of Daisios at about sundown. He had reigned over Macedon just twelve years and seven months, and he was a few days short of his thirty-third birthday. Every man was head on knee, and no man among them knew what to do for his eyes flooding with tears, for it felt like the end of the world, the end of time.

Thoth asks, What would they do with a dead Alexander? Philip, his father, they had burned upon a funeral bonfire, after the custom of the Greeks, and washed his cold bones in sweet wine, and wrapped them in soft purple cloths and placed them in a *larnax,* or box, of gold, inside a tomb of stone, with his golden armour and a heap of gilded furniture and luxury goods for his delight and pleasure in the Afterlife of the Greeks. On top of Philip's tomb they had piled a mound of earth, and had a sacred grove of trees planted round about.

Alexander would have none of that. No, he had learned the great lesson of the Egyptians: that to destroy the body is anathema, because if a body is not preserved intact, there will be no life for a dead man in the Field of Rushes, no Afterlife whatever. So he had ordered that in the (unlikely) event of his death he must not be burned up, but dealt with Egyptian-style, and for this reason a wagonful of embalmers travelled with him, men skilled in the art of hooking out a dead man's brain through his nasal passage; men expert at pulling out a dead man's guts through the narrowest of slits in his stomach wall; men who would embalm Alexander and wrap him in four thousand cubits of best linen bandage, and preserve him for all time in an anthropoid coffin of beaten gold and the blue stone called *sappheiros,* with the golden image of his own face upon it, as the Pharaoh of Egypt—dead, but Living for Ever.

To the Greeks it was, yes, shocking that a king of Macedon should not be cremated, for they had no tradition of embalming. But, as it happened, they could just then neither burn nor embalm this man, for although his death had been noised abroad, he did not behave in death as a dead man should.

The days and the nights went by and the dead Alexander did not smell. Ptolemy watched close. He swore that he had seen the dead man's chest moving, that his eyelids fluttered, that his hair and fingernails were still growing, and for a long time it looked as if he was merely asleep. Indeed, Alexander had always been good at sleeping. They had always had trouble waking him up. But now he did not wake up.

Ptolemy had not slaughtered alongside Alexander for ten years and more without breathing in the sour-sweet stench of rotting flesh. Yes, it would flood back to him for the rest of his life, in his dreams—the smell of the ghosts, the memory of the blood splashing in his face, the stench that made a man gag in the throat.

Thoth says, A dead man really *stinks*.

In Babylon at midsummer it is hot enough to fry an ostrich egg upon a stone, and a dead man will bring the blowflies humming at once. Before the rising of the next moon even the handsomest of dead men's flesh will heave with maggots. Before the second dawn his skin will turn blue. By the third morning his face will be green as the face of Osiris, and his corpse impossible to shift without spilling vile liquids.

Thoth says, Yes, a dead man *decomposes*.

Ptolemy himself tried to *live for the day, for the moment,* because he had seen what it meant to die. He had looked death too many times in the face, and it was his thought to ignore death as much as he could. But Alexander, with his soul six days flitted away to Hades, looked very like a man still alive, and his bronzed face, his battle-scarred flesh had still their healthy tautness. Moreover, there were no flies, no maggots, and still no smell but the old Alexander smell—sweetish, like some costly perfume, as if to announce that, yes, he was indeed the god he claimed to be, for a god did not—could not—smell of the armpit smell that made common soldier and general alike—including Ptolemy, who was not (yet) a god—stink, sometimes, like a herd of goats. The official story was that they dared not touch this King, at first, for he seemed to be still alive, but that in the end they cleaned out the body.

Thoth says, The truth is always different.

After ten days of being dead Alexander was still hot; and yes, he had turned into that most unfortunate, that most inconvenient thing that no man knew what to do with: one of the living dead.

What, then, had happened? Had his spirit just gone away out of his body? To be sure, he had passed many hours with the wise men of India, the sages of Babylon, the priests of Ammon in Egypt, asking his questions: *Is it true that a man may suspend his life? Is it the case that a man may sleep one hundred years, be buried below ground and yet wake up at the end of it?* And the wise men had said unto him, *Sure, it is possible. You like to try?*

Thoth asks, Is that what he was doing?

Some said that Alexander had learned much from these wise men of India, who had tried to change his violent character; that he had heard even of the man called Buddha, and they said that what Alexander had arrived at in death was the state called *Rainbow Body,* in which a man's consciousness may stay after death, in absolute meditation, resting in great calmness.

He showed, indeed, all the signs. Although he had long since stopped breathing, there was heat in the chest area, and there was no decay, and he smelled like some wonderful perfume.

Thoth says, What, then, did it mean? They said he radiated the great blessings of enlightened mind, like a great wave of purification, sending out equally powerful blessings to everyone. *And he did not go anywhere,* they said. *He is more alive today; or just as alive as he ever was.* And they said it was a great joy.

Thoth says, Really, this does seem most unlikely. This murderer, to be sure, was in need of the purification himself.

All the same, at length it would be forbidden upon pain of death to speak of this man as a dead man, so that he was, indeed, Alexander the Ever-Living.

1.10

Body-Snatcher

As soon as the death—the un-death—was made public, the awful ululation of the women of Babylon started up, and it went on without cease all that night and into the next day, on and on. Every man's tears flowed, of course, but there has also to come a time when the weeping and wailing must stop. For Ptolemy and the other generals of Alexander, who became known as the *Diadokhoi,* the Successors, it was not, in fact, the finish of anything, but the start.

First, they formed the Council of State, so as to decide who must be

king, and the weightier matter of how the Empire must be sliced up
and which general was to have charge and control of what bit of it, and
there were twelve of them: Perdikkas, Antigonos called Monophthalmos, or One-Eye, Antipatros, Seleukos, Leonnatos, Menander, Lysimakhos, Philotas, Eumenes, Peithon, Arkhon and Ptolemy.

Twelve strong men sat under arms through the night, unshaven
men, haggard of face, sweating in the heat so that they stank like goats,
arguing about what to do and what not to do, and the non-stinking body
lay between them. They drew straws, they diced, they bargained, and
they carved up his territories like a turkey, quarrelling over who
deserved the choicest piece, the largest portion. While Alexander lived,
they had been his subordinates: now that he had gone from them, they
were equals, and they fought over the scraps for many hours.

At length the decisions were made, and Antipatros, who had been
Regent of Macedon while Alexander was away fighting in Asia, became
Satrap of Macedon.

One-Eye—a great giant of a man—was confirmed as Satrap of
Greater Phrygia with Lykia and Pamphylia, and he was the father of the
famous Demetrios Poliorketes, then a boy of thirteen years. And One-
Eye was the strongest power in Asia.

Menander was confirmed as Satrap of Lydia; Lysimakhos became
Satrap of Thrace; Philotas was Satrap of Kilikia; Eumenes went as
Satrap to Kappodokia and Paphlagonia; Arkhon was to be Satrap of
Babylon; Peithon was Satrap of Media; and Leonnatos had Hellespon-
tine Phrygia.

Thoth says, Yes, this may be boring, but it is important. Be patient,
O Wise One. Thoth guarantees excitements later. Thoth gives his word.
Thoth promises.

For the time being Seleukos stood apart. He wanted Babylonia,
which was not available, though he would get his hands upon it later.
Foreseeing trouble ahead, he remained with the army, and was named
as the right-hand man of Perdikkas, in command of the Companion
Cavalry, the crack troops of Macedon.

Ptolemy alone of all these men knew what he wanted. He had been
cold crossing the Paropamisos, very cold. Egypt was the richest of all
the satrapies, and the best, and the most easy to defend. It was also the
warmest place, and the least warlike. None of the other generals
wanted Egypt, which was too hot, too foreign, too un-Greek, and too
strange, with its animal-headed gods. They thought only of the insuffer-
able heat, the poisonous snakes, the bite of scorpions, the clouds of bit-

ing insects, the endless dripping sweat, the ever-present storm of sand, and they were delighted not to have to go there.

Thus the quarrelling began and thus it would go on. These men would fight among themselves and wage war over the legacy of Alexander for fully fifty years after his death—for the rest of their lives—and still there would be no peace.

Of all of the Successors, Ptolemy son of Lagos would be the only one to die in his own bed, of old age.

Over all the Successors would be the new King of Macedon; but who could be king after Alexander? It was the duty of the army to elect the king by a show of hands, and the army wanted mad Arrhidaios, the elder brother of Alexander, who was then about thirty-six years of age.

Ptolemy voiced his objection to this man as king, saying that his mother, Philinna of Larissa, had been nothing but a dancing-girl, little better than a whore. But there were more serious objections to Arrhidaios, who was some times taken for little better than an idiot, and it was Ptolemy's fear that, if Arrhidaios was king, it would give Perdikkas the chance to exercise power on his behalf, which is what did happen.

Nobody had taken much notice of this Arrhidaios in the past, but he had marched with Alexander halfway across the world. From time to time he would fall to the ground, foaming at the mouth. His tongue did not fit behind his teeth. His hands twitched about his face when he tried to speak. How, Ptolemy asked, could a man who was unable to hold a sensible conversation fill the office of king without help? It would be an absurdity, he said, to make such a man the king.

But for the troops this man was Philip's son, Alexander's brother, full of the divine blood of Herakles and Dionysos, and they shouted for Arrhidaios, because, above all, there was no malice in this man, who never showed ill temper, and when the fit was not upon him, he would smile and smile and be every man's friend.

The friend of an idiot, Ptolemy said, *is an idiot.* But his thoughts were ignored, because, no, the army would have no king but this king, mad or not mad, and he was to rule jointly with the new Alexander, Alexandros, the son born to Roxane after Alexander's death, who was not yet thirty days old. The regent for these two kings was to be Perdikkas—proud, harsh Perdikkas—and Ptolemy saw that it would mean trouble, nothing but trouble.

Thus Arrhidaios became King, as Philippos Arrhidaios, and

Perdikkas tied round this madman's head the diadem, a strip of white cloth that was the sacred sign of the kingship of Macedon. The army cheered him, and he was hoisted upon the shoulders of the royal body-guard and carried round the camp, and Arrhidaios loved it, and never stopped showing his teeth for one moment.

The infant King Alexandros wore also the diadem over his swaddling clothes, for he passed the first months of his reign strapped to a board, bandaged from head to foot, and the horoscopists said his life would end as it began, with many tears, and much screaming.

The new arrangement seemed to work, at first. Perdikkas told Arrhidaios what to do, what to say, what to think, and where to place the royal seal on documents of state, and it was indeed most useful, for a change, to have a king who would take advice and do as he was told; he hauled Arrhidaios with him wherever he went, like a dumb character from the drama, and he would stand quiet at Perdikkas's shoulder, grinning, as if he were nothing but Perdikkas's shadow, Perdikkas's faithful hound, and the rightful way of doing every thing was reversed.

Thoth asks, What was the truth about Arrhidaios? Had he been fed mind-destroying drugs by Olympias his mother? But the answer is no, he had been merely let to fall asleep with the moonlight across his face, and had suffered from fits ever after. There was no cure for the moon-struck, but Olympias had made some experiments of her own, and it may be that her cures had done more harm than good.

Now that Arrhidaios was King, it seemed proper to Perdikkas that he must marry a wife, and maybe beget a son and heir, and the woman Perdikkas chose for him was his half-cousin, Adeia-Eurydike, a grand-daughter of King Philip.

Thoth speaks: Reader, call her name *Yoo-rid-EE-kay* or *Ur-rid-EE-Ki*.

This girl had an unusual upbringing in that she had learned to ride, hunt and fight with the short sword like a man, and she had been taught these things by no other person than her mother, the Princess Kynane of Illyria, who was herself said to have killed some enemy queen in armed combat, and so was the first in a long line of rather masculine women.

Upon her marriage this Adeia-Eurydike was only fourteen or fifteen years old, but she proved of the greatest help to her husband—in some ways. For when Arrhidaios's fit was upon him, his body would go rigid, bent backwards like a bow, and his feet might even touch his head.

When this happened, Adeia-Eurydike would pin him to the ground with his arms behind his back (for she was strong), ram an apple between his teeth to stop him biting off his tongue and comfort him in his distress. He had bitten his tongue so many times that his speech was slurred, and it was this that made men call him a half-wit, which was not really the whole truth.

While the illness of Arrhidaios was worrying, his fits were short-lived, and he had all the vigour of his body. The moonstruck were often shunned, as if they lived under some divine curse, but this man was regarded with even a kind of wonder, as if he was in touch with the world of the gods to which his brother had returned. Arrhidaios was lucky, the living talisman of Macedon, just as his dead brother would be the talisman of Alexandria. Arrhidaios, then, might have thrived; the trouble lay with his wife.

Ptolemy often told the story of Adeia-Eurydike, the girl who was like a boy—who trained as a soldier, who rode into battle fully armed, dressed as a man. She had looked with dismay, he said, upon the swelling up of her breasts, and even asked her mother whether she might have one of them cut off, like an Amazon, the better to draw back the bowstring; but her mother had refused to let her do it.

Adeia-Eurydike was strong like no other Greek woman, carrying her sword, shield, spear—half her own body weight—and she ran about wearing a breastplate of bronze, screaming the *Alalalalai,* just like one of the men.

Moreover, she refused to hide away in the *gynaikeion,* the women's quarters, and found more useful things to occupy her than tapestry. She wanted to prove that a woman may be as good as a man. She wrestled and boxed, ran and jumped, rode horses and raced chariots. Adeia-Eurydike was so very like a man that they said of her *She must have walked under the rainbow,* because any girl who did this would be turned into a boy.

The only disadvantage was that, as they said, she was too much of a man to have any children by Arrhidaios. As for swift Rumour, *she* said that these two brought forth none but monsters, who were exposed at birth as an affront to the gods, and a terrible omen of what was to happen to them both.

Indeed, upon her marriage Adeia-Eurydike cast the Lovers' Oracle, which meant taking the broad petal of a poppy in her left hand and striking it hard with her right. If all was fated to go well, the petal would make a loud crack. But there came only the dull thud of her two palms clashing together, and Adeia-Eurydike knew in her heart that every thing would go wrong for her as the wife of King Philippos Arrhidaios.

So much for the splitting up of Alexander's Empire; so much for the succession to the throne of Macedon. What concerns Thoth is Egypt, and Ptolemy son of Lagos.

All of Egypt, then, together with that part of Africa called Libya, and part of Arabia, fell by lot, or by the luck of the gods, or by reason of nobody else wanting it, to Ptolemy.

Egypt, he thought, was the next best thing to paradise: a place where rain did not fall, where there was no snow, no cold, no winter season to speak of; a land where the sun shone for month after month and was worshipped as the greatest god. Egypt was rich beyond any man's dream, a place where a satrap might have everything he desired, and he would go there as soon as he could.

For the moment, though, he lingered at Babylon, waiting to see what might happen with regard to the kingship, and what they would do with the body of Alexander that was dead but not dead, and lay still unburied.

As a temporary measure they embalmed him in honey, because honey that was so sweet to the living must be bitter to all creatures of the Underworld, where everything is reversed: honey would, therefore, keep away ghosts, demons and evil spirits from this most distinguished of corpses.

Ptolemy it was that oversaw the embalming, and he had the royal ears stopped up with the best Hymettos honey to keep out the earwigs and larder beetles. He had honey stuffed up Alexander's nose, and into his every other orifice, to keep out the woodlice, to prevent the moths from effecting an entry; and he put Alexander in a wooden box with a lid while they awaited the finishing of the golden coffin and the gorgeous funeral chariot that must carry him home to Aigai, in Macedon, because tradition said that if he was buried anywhere else, his dynasty would be finished. Ptolemy never again ate honey in all his life time.

On the thirtieth day of the long sleep, Aristander the seer announced that the word of the gods was that Alexander was the luckiest king that ever lived, and the soil that received his bones need never fear the invasion of any enemy, but would itself be lucky for ever.

Ptolemy heard him, and he wanted above every other thing all the luck in the world, and while the other generals argued, he helped himself to this corpse and set off with it for Egypt, and his brother Menelaos went with him and was his partner in this crime.

Some said that when Perdikkas found out what had happened, he galloped after Ptolemy with his troops, because he wanted the luck of Alexander for himself, and that when he caught up with Ptolemy they fought a bloody battle.

Others spoke of a gigantic funeral car with a golden cornice, festive garlands and tassels from which hung large bells; with Ionic columns decorated with silver and ivory, and pulled by sixty-four mules, one pair for every year of the dead man's life. The procession, they said, was escorted by a gang of road-menders, mechanics and soldiers, and drew crowds of onlookers, but such a vehicle could never have been dragged through the desert from Babylon to Memphis, however many mules pulled it; the truth of it was that the famous funeral car of Alexander was the invention of the historians, a fiction. All the same, many men swore this was the carriage that Perdikkas captured, and that he set off with this vehicle for Macedon.

Only when Ptolemy had been gone some days did Perdikkas take the trouble to look inside the coffin of gold, and find an Alexander made of wax and straw, with a radish nose and sticky dates for eyes; the real Alexander had gone ahead in the back of a plain *harmamaxa,* one of the covered four-wheel carts in which the whores rode as part of the baggage train, and it moved not with a great escort, but almost unattended, and very fast.

It was harvest time when Alexander left Babylon for the last time, and the farmers were bringing the corn into the city on wagons, and sneezing from the dust as Ptolemy hurried the body past them. For the Greeks a sneeze is a sign of the approval of Zeus himself, the best of all possible omens, and Ptolemy knew then that he had done the right thing.

Thoth asks, Where is the truth to be found? Thoth knows only that they said Ptolemy took the body with him to Egypt, and that on the road they met with the usual storm of sand, so that the living spent day after day sucking the grit out of one anothers' ears. The truth was that the dead man returned to Egypt with less pomp than anybody could have imagined.

Ptolemy took this corpse as far as Memphis, where it would rest for some years, until the priests of that city refused to give it lodging any longer, saying that Alexander's body brought not good but bad luck, and that any place where it lay would have bad luck for ever after.

The Satrap himself thought different. He was quite sure that dead

Alexander would bring success to Alexandria, and watch over the city, and guard it from assault, and be its talisman for ever; and whether Alexander was, in fact, dead or alive, the *prostagma* went forth from Ptolemy himself: *Alexander lives and reigns*, and it was an offence to speak of this King in the past tense.

The good people of Alexandria never stopped half-expecting that Alexander would stir, as if from a good night's sleep, and go back to being Pharaoh of Egypt, Lord of Crowns, Beloved of Amun, Son of the Sun, Alexander the Ever-Living; but for the moment normal life must go on, and until the miracle of all miracles could be made to happen, a new man must rule Egypt in place of Alexander, and the new man was Ptolemy, the Satrap.

Ptolemy stole not only a corpse, but also the royal journals, which he meant to use in order to write his own history of Alexander, though he would put off the writing of it for nearly half a century.

He took also Alexander's sword, and the True Shield of Achilles (which Alexander had himself stolen when he was at Troy), as well as Alexander's plumed helmet of bronze, his greaves of gold, the gilded breastplate, and his spare manuscript of Homer, in its golden box, which Alexander had stolen from the treasury of Darius at Persepolis.

Whether the royal journals were a forgery, or the helmet not Alexander's helmet, his sword not his sword, his shield not his shield, and his Homer not his Homer—such things did not trouble Ptolemy. What mattered was that men thought he told the truth.

Some men even muttered that Alexander's flesh was so badly decomposed in the heat of Babylon that he was impossible to embalm, and that nothing whatever survived of the great man—not so much as a lock of hair.

At all events, if Ptolemy was not a thief, he was a liar; but the truth of such things is beyond even the wisdom of Thoth.

Such, then, was the character of Ptolemy son of Lagos. He was unreliable, wily, shrewd. He would steal what he could get away with, and boast of his thieving afterwards. But even Zeus, the greatest of the gods of Greece, has the reputation of a thief.

As for Alexander, some worshipped him as a living god; others saw him as nothing but a tyrant, an aggressor, a foreign autocrat, who imposed his will by violence alone. Some said Alexander was not a man, but an absolute dream. Others complained of nothing but the unending nightmare.

To be sure, they had all of them loved him, but they had hated him as well. In spite of the great adventure, the riches beyond imagining, the *kudos,* they would have quite liked also to have had the chance to live at home with their wives and children; to have been present at their daughters' weddings, their sons' coming-of-age ceremonies; to have buried their fathers; to have passed normal lives, winter and summer, seedtime and harvest, on their own farms, and not to have traipsed halfway across the world.

Alexander's great crime was that he had taken their lives away from them. He was a demon, a monster, the bringer of death. His rule was based upon nothing but fear, and they were afraid, every man, of his power, afraid of his filthy temper, and, to be sure, it was a great relief to them all when he died.

Yes, the expedition of Alexander was nothing but a useless waste of time and energy; the Greeks might just as well have stayed at home for all the good it did them. This was the opinion of Ptolemy, although he seldom spoke it; but when he had taken a bowl of wine too many he would shake his head and say, *We might just as well have passed twelve years counting the stars.*

What, then, *was* the truth? It was that Alexander would bring bad luck upon the House of Ptolemy in Egypt, three hundred years of bad luck. But just then, at the start of it, Ptolemy did not see how it could possibly be so, and his future stretched out before him, golden, all golden.

The one man with any sense among all the Successors was Ptolemy. He alone understood why Alexander had not flourished. Fate had made Alexander a god himself, but the gods had led him into a trap, snatching back every thing they had given to him. The gods of Greece are, indeed, jealous of a man's success.

Ptolemy had no great wish to be a king. He did not want to stir up the envy of the gods by having too much good fortune.

A man can be too lucky, he said. *A man can easily bring upon himself his own downfall.*

He had, after all, seen it happen to Alexander.

The Satrap now took up, all the same, his residence in the Land of the Pharaohs, and the shower of wealth that he both did and did not want began to fall upon him. He felt almost like an unwilling Midas, as if every thing he touched had turned to gold. A lesser man might have drowned in it, but the first Ptolemy did not drown: he floated upon the river of gold, the flood of gold, the engulfing tidal wave of gold, laughing.

Part Two

SATRAP OF EGYPT

Lucky Alexandria

On his journey into Egypt Ptolemy says not a word. He would be pleased to forget yesterday, but he has been taught too well the art of memory. He looks in the direction of Alexandria, and it is eight years, or three thousand days, since the founding of the city.

To be sure, they had the approval of the god for the founding of it, west of what the Greeks were pleased to call the Delta, as if it was their own invention and not the thought of Thoth, where there was nothing but an ancient harbour and the fishing village that they now called Rhakotis, or Building Site, which is what Alexandria had become.

Alexander had sacrificed oxen with gilded horns. He had burned incense. He had offered the proper prayers to the gods. He had done every thing according to Greek custom, so that his city might be successful, lucky, overflowing with good fortune, like a horn of plenty.

He stared at the entrails of the oxen, and the soothsayers said the omens were good, and Alexander was allowed to mark out with chalk the plan of his city, trapezium-shaped, *khlamys*-shaped, like the military cloak of the Greeks, for it was a Greek city first, Greek always, and tried not to be an Egyptian city. But Alexandria was so large, or the chalk supply so small, that there was not enough to finish the circuit of the walls, and it was agreed, so as not to be unlucky, to borrow the ration of pearl barley from the soldiers' knapsacks, and to mark out the city plan with grain instead.

Ptolemy remembers well. In the middle of this operation he heard the beat of many wings, so loud that every man looked up, only to see the birds—thousands of birds—fall upon the barley and eat it up, all of it. With the birds came the patter of bird droppings all around and upon some of their heads, which in itself (to be shat upon by a bird) was supposed to be lucky, and half the plan of Alexandria was eaten up, and shat upon at the same time.

What meaning? Alexander asked the soothsayers, worried, for it could be no good omen for this to happen to a city upon the day of its founding.

The truth was that these Greeks would not last long in Egypt, in Alexandria, without unspeakable things happening; events that would horrify men until the end of time.

What meaning? he asked, afraid, wondering what he had done to deserve such treatment by the gods.

The seers eyed each other in silence. They could not tell him that the gods themselves had shat upon Alexandria; that it would be the unluckiest, unhappiest, most ill-fated city that ever stood.

At length Aristander spoke: *It means,* he said, *that Alexandria will feed the whole world.* Which also turned out to be true.

Alexander breathed easy, and the rituals continued; the city was founded, and there was no turning back. The Greeks sat up all night, feasting, trying to stop time and make the day of the foundation of the greatest city of all time last for ever.

They woke with sore heads, and added vomit to the bird droppings that marked the site, and it was an ill beginning.

Thoth knows, bird droppings and vomit were nothing compared with what was to come. Alexandria was fated to be stained with blood, its soil, as it were, a bloody paste, like the field of battle in which Alexander so rejoiced. Above all, Alexandria would be a city of blood.

But Alexander himself knew nothing of that. He ordered temples and shrines to the gods upon every street.

Men might live happy lives in a new city, he said, *so long as the gods are made happy first.*

He ordered every ingredient for the finest city ever built, but he was too impatient to wait and attend to any detail. He was in too much of a hurry to sit down and think about what he was doing.

His advisers reminded him of the words of Plato, who said that grave dangers would arise if a city was built beside the sea. Alexander took no notice. He was pleased to ignore all warnings. He had the approval of the gods; there was no need to take the advice of a mere mortal such as Plato. Alexander had chosen the best, the only site, and although the forecast of the soothsayers had been that half of this great city would sink into the sea before even one thousand years had passed, he could not be persuaded to listen. For the moment, every man showed his teeth, and the column of men marched away from Egypt, singing the Greek songs of war, on their way to conquer the rest of the world.

No, nobody thought that the opposite of what Alexander wanted might come about: that Alexandria might become a city where everybody was unhappy.

In those days they took little thought for the future. Even Ptolemy did not want, just then, to see Egypt again. He had passed one hundred and eighty days plagued by biting flies. He had spent six months with the sweat dripping into his eyes. His flesh was burned almost black by the sun. He had suffered the usual derangement of the bowels that every stranger who comes to Egypt must suffer. It would not be too much to say that, just then, Ptolemy hated Egypt.

Thoth asks, What is in his memory? And the answer is, yes, he has been here before, and his thoughts are of Alexander, and the past.

For Alexander could not found his great city of Alexandria without first asking the gods, Was it the right place? Was it the right time to found a city? And above all, would this city be a lucky city? For there was little point in planning a city that was *un*lucky.

So Alexander had gone in person deep into the desert of Libya, to the oasis where was the Oracle of Zeus-Ammon, thousands of *stades* west of the River. The journey was hard, but the Oracle was the greatest oracle in the world, after Delphi, and famed for sound judgement.

The priests of Egypt had warned Alexander of the dangers: tempest, severe thunderstorms, violent storms of sand. They had warned him not to forget the fate of the fifty thousand soldiers of Kambyses the Persian who had gone missing in the Great Sea of Sand.

It was the punishment of the gods, they said; but Alexander took no notice of the warnings, and said he was going to *honour* Ammon, not to rob him. Alexander did not like waiting. Moreover, he was unbeatable. He could not be defeated by a storm of sand.

Even so, they had come close to death. The water ran out. They had lost the road, engulfed by the storm of sand, until a pair of crows appeared, and they followed the road of the crows to the Oracle.

Ptolemy, who never in all his long life was known to tell a lie, in spite of being a Greek, told a different story: that they were shown the way by a pair of talking snakes.

The Priest of Ammon had hailed Alexander as Son of Zeus, and it was all Alexander wanted to hear. The Oracle had identified him with the Sun god of the Egyptians, and Zeus, in the shape of a serpent, was indeed his father.

He had put his questions to the Oracle and no man knew what they were, for he had never revealed the answers to anybody, saying it was private business that he would tell only to his mother, Olympias, when he came home. But Alexander never did go home.

Some years afterwards Ptolemy himself paid for an altar at the shrine of Ammon, for this god had been good to Ptolemy also. Ptolemy, too, had asked his questions of the god, standing naked before the god in his shrine. And yes, his flesh crept, and yes, the hairs stood up upon the back of his neck. And yes, the statue of the god *moved* for Ptolemy, the ram-headed god, whose image was decorated with the *smaragdos,* the costly green stone. Ptolemy shivered, trembled, before the god who delivered to him knowledge of the future. Ptolemy pissed himself before the god, and when he emerged into the sunlight, he was shaking.

Ptolemy remembered the desert, pink at sundown, the fires of camel dung, the shimmering lakes of water that were not water, the travelling by moonlight because the sand was too hot by day. He remembered the men singing, the echoing shouts, the silence of the desert.

He remembered the image of Ammon in the forecourt of the temple, carried in his boat of gold upon the shoulders of eight men, and in answer to the Greeks' questions the boat had lurched from side to side, or spun round in circles, going now backwards, now forwards, followed by the procession of eighty chanting priests of Ammon, playing the savage music of conch and cymbal.

Ptolemy's own question was answered, about the future: *Ptolemy, too, will be a god,* the Oracle said.

Thoth knows, it was far worse than the histories suggested. They had nearly died from lack of water, and when the heavens at last opened they ran about like madmen, screaming, trying to catch the rain in their open mouths.

At the Oasis of Ammon, Hephaistion and Alexander had gone through some ceremony of marriage, male to male, husband to husband, for this was the only place in the world where such an abomination was allowed. It was, surely, the real reason why Alexander took himself to such a remote quarter, and it would be a secret ever after, the secret that he never told his mother.

Ptolemy had not joined himself in marriage to another male, but spent the nights hunting women. He had been bitten by fleas and kissed by women wherever he walked. He remembered the shimmering water above the salt swamps. He remembered the fires by night to keep off the wild dogs. He remembered the howling of jackals, the camels sliding upon the wet track. If he could remember such things, why did he speak of *two talking snakes,* when every other man who wrote about this journey said they were guided by talking crows?

Thoth says, If Ptolemy's snakes spoke, what tongue then did they speak in, that Ptolemy could understand—this Greek who spoke a Macedonian dialect? Did the snakes of Libya speak Greek?

By no means. This was, surely, but the idle story of a Greek, without meaning, and full of untruths, like every other story of the Greeks. On the other hand, perhaps the snakes did mean some thing.

In Egypt every word is a picture, a symbol. In Egypt every thing means something else—Thoth swears it. On the surface the snakes mean one thing; underneath, a different thing. To the intelligent, to the initiated, light; to the uninitiated, or the ignorant, darkness, confusion, mystery.

On the one hand the Greeks swear that Ptolemy never in his life told a lie. On the other hand Thoth warns you, Pupil-of-Thoth, that the Greeks like to play games.

2.2

The Roads of Horus

Ptolemy rode into Egypt the second time, past Gaza and Raphia, through the desert, and along the wet sands of the beach between Gaza and Pelousion, in order not to be swallowed by the shifting sands; and then along the Roads of Horus, the Roads of War, as far as the border fort, where he was welcomed by Greeks, the Greeks whom Alexander had left behind to govern Egypt for him.

He sacrificed at once jet-black bulls to Zeus, Patron of Travellers, and to Poseidon, Lord of the Earthquake, as a thank-offering for his safe delivery, because of the gods' great goodness.

Ptolemy had with him, of course, a detachment of troops and, of course, his brother, the faithful Menelaos, and his three young children by Thaïs, who had barely begun to walk, and had only their nurse to care for them, for their mother would not go with Ptolemy to Egypt any more than Artakama, that Persian wife of his, would go along the road to Ekbatana, so that Ptolemy lacked, for the moment, a woman at his side. He was in the forty-fourth year of his age, in the prime of his life, and at the height of his capability. But he was weary of walking, and ready—more than ready—to live the soft life of a satrap. He had had more than his share of hardship, but now, as Homer put it, *Zeus, son of Kronos, poured down over him a miracle of wealth.*

Ptolemy turned his face first towards Heliopolis, City of the Sun, where the High Priest of Ra greeted him dressed in the garment of constellations that was his alone to wear, and with words that sounded like words of welcome but might have meant anything, for this proud Egyptian refused to address the Greek in Greek, and what he said was indeed like the twittering of the swallows to Ptolemy—yet another barbarian tongue. Ptolemy's interpreter did his best, making signs with his hands, and the priests—some of them—smiled their mysterious smiles as they murmured words that meant *Indeed, may the donkey copulate with your wife and children,* for at this time not every priest was pleased to look upon the foreigner with kindness.

But even here, when his thoughts might have been Egyptian thoughts only, Ptolemy worried also that he had neither legitimate sons nor legitimate heir, and he thought day and night about what woman he should make his wife.

While it might have been a goodly thing for Ptolemy to marry a wife of the Egyptians, an Egyptian princess, perhaps—some relative of Nektanebo, the last of the native Pharaohs—and some said that this is what in fact did happen, the truth was that when Ptolemy raised the subject of such a wife, the priests of Egypt spread their hands and said there was no such woman to be had, for Nektanebo had left no family to speak of.

And while a marriage to some Egyptian princess would have given Ptolemy a greater claim to rule over Egypt, he desired this not at all, but wanted only a wife from among his own people. He was a Greek then, and a Greek always, and had no thought to dilute his Macedonian blood by fathering a son who was half Egyptian.

Ptolemy rode onwards, and the body of Alexander travelled with him and never left his sight, and he set his face towards Mennufer, which the Greeks persisted in calling Memphis, the most ancient and most illustrious of cities, the capital of the Pharaohs.

All Memphis stood on the streets to see this Ptolemy, who was to rule them in place of the Persian, in place of Alexander, and the welcome for a satrap was only a little less keen than for a king. Before the great Temple of Ptah, the creator god of the Egyptians, stood the High Priest of Ptah, the High Priest of Memphis, whose title was the Great Chief of the Hammer, the Master of All Craftsmen, and he wore the spotted leopard skin of his great office, and his head was, as usual, shaved but for the side-lock of hair that it was his special privilege to wear upon his head.

Anemhor—Old Anemhor—was the name of this man, and he had begun his training to be a scribe at five years old.

At fifteen years, in the days of Nektanebo, he had entered the service of Ptah as a *wab* priest, a pure priest, which was the lowest rank of the priesthood.

At nineteen he had become a Father of the God, a priest of the second rank.

At twenty-five he had been raised to Third Prophet of Ptah.

At thirty he had been promoted to Second Prophet of Ptah.

At the age of thirty-five, when the Persian ruled the Two Lands, he had been appointed to the office of First Prophet or Servant of the God, as High Priest of Ptah, High Priest of Memphis, and he would hold that office until the day of his death. Now Anemhor was forty-seven years of age and his wisdom was as that of no other man in Egypt.

The High Priest had very many titles. He was Father of the God, and Beloved of the God. He was prophet not only of Ptah but of his wife, Sakhmet the lioness goddess, and of their son Nefertum—the blue lotus out of which the Sun rises. He was Prophet of the Window of Appearances, and Master of Secrets. He was Prophet of the Living Apis, the Sacred Bull, and Director of the Wardrobe. He was Overseer of the Prophets of Every God in All of Upper and Lower Egypt. He was Master of the Secrets of Heaven, Earth and Underworld, Who Knows the Secrets, Who Sees the Secrets of Ptah. There was no priest or scribe in all Egypt to whom this man was answerable, for he was first of them. He knew all of the past, and he had the ability to foretell all of the future.

It was made plain to Ptolemy on this day that there was no priest more useful to him in Egypt than this man, for there was nothing that he did not know: Anemhor was Thoth in all things.

Ptolemy called this man Leopard Spots, because of his robe of office, that had fixed to it even the head of the leopard, hanging upside down at his waist, with eyes glittering, and teeth bared.

At the first meeting there was a little suspicion, with Ptolemy wondering what it might be that the High Priest truly wanted of him: whether it was his purpose to be his friend; whether in truth he wished Ptolemy dead and gone away. Though Anemhor spoke Greek, there were some difficulties of understanding, because Ptolemy would speak quick, or because Anemhor would speak Greek as it was wrote, not as it was spoke; and there was a lack of smiles. For a Greek to smile, aye, it is a sign of submission. The Greek thought is that the face of a man is meant to impress, not to charm, and the High Priest saw the unsmiling face of Ptolemy as a mark of hostility, not sure whether it was his purpose to abolish the priesthood or to support it. Anemhor knew well that for the Greek *to laugh* means also *to deceive*. He saw the distrustful eyes of a stranger, his tense look, his harsh stare, prolonged, probing, and it was the soldier's stare, the look of the man who has blood upon his sword and murder in his heart; that of a man whose hands were unclean, a man who had killed, aye, and delighted in killing.

The smile of the Greek, then, must be earned.

Ptolemy—what did he see in the face of this High Priest? He looked into the black eyes. He gazed upon the brown face, and he found there not one thing that he could understand. The Master of Secrets gave no secret away. Ptolemy sensed, though, the goodness of this man, was aware of his unblinking regard. Perhaps, he thought, Anemhor could be trusted after all.

Anemhor began then to make his demands and give his instructions: how Ptolemy must go on, what he must and must not do, as if the Satrap was not the Governor of All Egypt, but a child who knew nothing. But, indeed, Ptolemy did know nothing, nothing. Truly, compared with the High Priest of Memphis, Ptolemy knew nothing. No, not one thing.

As for the High Priest not smiling, he knew well Kleomenes the deceiver, Kleomenes the thief. His thought was that Ptolemy might be, like Kleomenes, more keen to take what he could from Egypt than to give back. It had to be proved to Anemhor that this was not so, before he would allow himself to wear that smile, the half-smile that it was the custom for every priest of Egypt to wear.

Anemhor went out of his road to make some things difficult for Ptolemy. He put, some times, obstacles in his path, saying, *Must do this, or the people of Egypt will rise up in rebellion against you.* And even at the first meeting the words were so often upon his lips, *If the Satrap does not do such and such . . .* that Ptolemy wearied of hearing it.

At the end of ten days of questions and answers, ten days of warnings about what might go wrong for Ptolemy in Egypt, and how to stop things going wrong, the High Priest smiled his mysterious half-smile that meant everything and nothing at the same time—the smile that, in due time, Ptolemy would copy and learn to wear himself, the smile of the man who knew all the secrets of the Universe, the secrets of both Earth and Heaven; the smile of the man who has seen the gods of Egypt face-to-face.

Ptolemy allowed himself to smile back at this High Priest, who saw that there was no guile and no malice in the character of this Satrap, but much goodness, much kindness. And Anemhor thought in his heart that he might be able to do useful things for Egypt if this Greek were to be in charge.

Why, though, should Ptolemy have respect for this man? Because Anemhor showed to Ptolemy in these first days that he was a man of power, who might do any thing he pleased.

On the first day of questions Anemhor threw down his staff of office before Ptolemy, in the time-honoured manner of the high priests of Egypt, and his staff became a snake, writhing upon the floor of the Satrap's Residence, a real snake that hissed, and darted out his fangs. Ptolemy flinched, as any man would flinch, and was astonished, as any man must be astonished; and Anemhor picked up the snake and held him fast, and turned him back into a stick.

It was, indeed, the oldest of old tricks, and the easiest. The Greeks, to be sure, did not know one thing about snakes, or that by pressing the thumb into the back of a snake's head he might be forced to go rigid, sticklike, or that when the thumb was released his paralysis would come to an end. No, Ptolemy marvelled, and every Greek marvelled, for they had never seen such a thing in Greece, or any place they had marched with Alexander, not even in India.

Another time Anemhor showed that he had power to turn the River to blood, and it was one more clever thing. Ptolemy did not know that every year when the Flood of the Nile began, the River ran red like blood with the red earth from up-River floating down to Memphis, or that a day or two afterwards the River would run green again.

Above all things, Anemhor showed his authority, for he had command even over the Egyptians who served Ptolemy in his Residence, making them rise and sit as one, or speak with one voice in praise of Ptah; whereas Ptolemy had no power over those who did not speak Greek except by shouting at them words they did not understand; except by beating them upon the soles of their feet.

In Egypt we speak of the Ideal Man. He is content with a humble position in life. He has few belongings. He is modest rather than boastful. He is self-controlled, quiet in his speech, kind to all people. He is humble before the gods. He is not perfect, because only the gods are perfect. He lacks all warlike characteristics, and is before everything else a man of peace. Anemhor was such a man as this, though his office was a high office, and he possessed great riches. Truly, the Ideal Man of the Egyptians was a man like Anemhor.

In these first days Anemhor went also out of his way to show kindness to the infant children of Thaïs, performing for them the best of his showy tricks. He took a dead scorpion and threw it upon the floor to show that it was dead, not just sleeping. Then he smeared this creature with white hellebore, and that dead thing moved, stood up on his four legs, came to life and scuttled about the room, to the astonishment of the Satrap's children.

Further, Anemhor, choosing his day with some care, announced that by using words of power he would make rain fall, and to be sure, out of the sky that was blue like *sappheiros,* with never a cloud in sight, the thunder rolled and the rain fell, and Lagos, Leontiskos and Eirene rewarded Anemhor with their smiles, and Ptolemy learned that Anemhor had power even over Zeus, Lord of the Thunder.

The High Priest showed the Greek who was master. He showed that the power of a high priest was worthy of the highest respect. If Anemhor could bring dead things back to life, there was, surely, no thing that this Egyptian could not do.

Ptolemy believed that Memphis meant, above every other thing, magic, and for that reason he had brought with him to that city the corpse of Alexander. Also, of course, it was because Alexandria was not yet complete, not yet safe from marauders from the sea, for whom it would be a simple thing to snatch back the body for Perdikkas, so that some other place should enjoy the Luck of Alexander.

Yes, at Memphis it seemed there would be every chance that the High Priest might wake Alexander, just as he had woken the dead scorpion.

Anemhor agreed to employ his skills, and he spoke over this King the spells that might bring him out of his slumber. He spoke many words into Alexander's ears, talking to him for hour upon hour, saying, *If he has been bewitched, this will bring him out of it . . .*

He chanted over and over. Some times he whispered. Some times he shouted:

> *Wake! Wake! O Alexandros! Wake!*
> *You have come into being complete as any god . . .*
> *Your head is Ra . . .*
> *Your face is Wepwawet . . .*
> *Your nose is as the jackal . . .*
> *Your ears are Isis and Nephthys . . .*
> *Your tongue is Thoth . . .*
> *There is no member in you which lacks a god . . .*
> *Raise yourself, Alexandros! . . .*

For, to be sure, there was no man possessed of greater sleight of hand or tongue in Egypt than Anemhor. He was great of magic, like Thoth himself.

But though he had the power to raise scorpions, and it was not unknown for the dead to awaken in Memphis, Anemhor could not bring Alexander back to life. Nor, if the truth were told, did either Ptolemy or any of the Greeks really wish him to do so, for they feared nothing more than a dead man who returned to the land of the living.

Alexander looked still as if he might sleep for all time. In any case, the truth of it was that the spells for waking the dead in the Afterlife are not of much use for waking a dead man here on Earth, and it was a hopeless exercise.

Even so, they gave Alexander no funeral rites in Egypt—none—because they simply could not believe that this man was dead.

2.3

The Prison-Builder

When Ptolemy returned to Egypt as Satrap he was in the forty-fifth year of his age, and it was nine years since the founding of Alexandria.

When he had quit Egypt after Alexander's conquest, there was nothing to be seen upon the site of Alexandria but fishermen's huts and the remains of a great harbour of the time of the earliest Pharaohs, that was now sunk beneath the sea.

Kleomenes of Naukratis had orders from Alexander to build here a Greek city divided into four quarters called Alpha, Beta, Gamma, Delta, after the first letters of the alphabet, with every thing that a Greek city should possess; to lay the foundations of a city to be built all of white marble and limestone, that would sparkle in the sun of Egypt and be the envy of the entire world.

Alexander had asked for thousands of Corinthian columns, with the main streets lined with colonnades so that a man might walk from one end of Alexandria to the other in the shade, sheltered from the heat of the sun.

Kleomenes began the magnificent Temples of Zeus, of Apollo, of Artemis, of Poseidon, ordering vast quantities of white marble column drums to be loaded on to ships at Paros and brought across the Great Sea, and it was one of the greatest feats of engineering ever undertaken.

Kleomenes also took upon his shoulders the burden of building the

Heptastadion, a bridge seven *stades* long, that was to span the harbour and join the mainland to the island of Pharos. He used here the same principles as at Tyros, sinking piers into the sea bed, pouring rubble into coffer dams, keeping up Alexander's tradition of doing what seemed to be impossible by building out into the sea. When the Heptastadion was finished, with a road and a canal of water along the top of it, Kleomenes began to think about the Temple of Isis that must grace the Pharos island, but the great Pharos, or Lighthouse, was a wonder as yet undreamed of.

While Alexander marched away to conquer Asia and the rest of the world, Kleomenes had charge of all the finances of Egypt. Kleomenes it was who set up the mint and coined the silver tetradrachms with the head of Alexander upon them, wearing the ram's horns of Zeus-Ammon his father, and Alexander was well pleased with them, and with Kleomenes.

Without the skills of Kleomenes, his energy, his devotion to duty and his eagerness to see a city that was worthy of its founder, there might, perhaps, have been no Alexandria to look upon and wonder at when Ptolemy came back as Satrap. In truth, Ptolemy owed a great debt of thanks to this man for all that he had done.

Ptolemy rode on horseback with Kleomenes along the street called Kanopic Street because it led to the town of Kanopos, that lay east of Alexandria, on the coast—a city devoted to pleasure, and luxury, and the worship of the gods—and this street was as much as one *plethron* wide, so that it could be used for chariot racing, and paved with cut stones, and lined with columns from the Gate of the Sun in the west to the Gate of the Moon in the east. Some thirty *stades* in length it was with a canal of drinkable water flowing down the middle, and statues of Alexander and Philip, and every god of Greece from Athene to Zeus, and a statue also of Kleomenes himself.

Kleomenes showed Ptolemy the *agora,* the market place, with shops that sold every kind of sea fish, river fish, and freshwater fish out of the great lake called Mareotis, that lay behind the city, and every kind of meat and drink, and every Greek thing that was necessary for the Greeks to be happy, such as olives, and honey, and bread, and moussaka, and wine.

He showed Ptolemy the underground cisterns of vast size that held the fresh water supply, and the fountains of fresh water that could be made to run also with milk, or wine. He showed off the temples to Zeus and Apollo, Asklepios and Poseidon, the Greek *gymnasia,* the public baths, the hippodrome for horse races, the *stadion* for athletic contests, the *odeion,* or council chamber, the treasury and the prison: every ingredient of the most perfect Greek city, and all of these things were begun, some half made, some barely knee-high, but none of them was finished except the prison.

Ptolemy showed his teeth. He smiled with his eyes also, his blue eyes, and he ordered the work in progress to go on as before, just as Alexander had commanded. He saw that every thing Kleomenes had undertaken was of the highest workmanship—that Alexandria would be the finest of cities—and his heart swelled for pride.

Ptolemy thanked Kleomenes for his great labours, for his careful attention to every detail, and he shook Kleomenes by both his hands and kissed him upon both his cheeks, as if he was his friend.

Then he had Kleomenes arrested, shackled with iron and thrown into the brand-new prison, accused of manifold crimes against the state, for that he had looked only to his own personal enrichment, helping himself to the taxes and revenues, as if he were not just the *hyparkhos* and financial administrator but the monarch himself.

Ptolemy had heard stories of the colossal wealth amassed by Kleomenes. He had heard how the soldiers had been cheated of half their pay; how at the time of famine Kleomenes had placed the entire grain surplus under his own control, and sold it at a great profit, for himself. Worst of all, he had heard from Anemhor how Kleomenes had threatened to close down every temple in Egypt if the priests did not pay what he demanded in return for his protection.

Kleomenes was hauled in chains before the Satrap to answer questions, and Ptolemy did not stop himself from using the *hippos,* or horse, upon his prisoner, in order to twist his thumbs, and bend him in two, and force him to speak the truth.

From his dishonesty this man had amassed a fortune of eight thousand talents. His care and attention to the new city had won him recognition as Satrap in all but name, and the pardon of Alexander, also, for the excesses of his period of office. Kleomenes had truly thought that he would be made Satrap of Egypt himself.

But the settlement of Babylon made Kleomenes the junior of Ptolemy, subject to the orders of Ptolemy, and Ptolemy set out to humiliate Kleomenes for his hubris, seeing him as his rival, and his enemy, a man who must be punished.

Kleomenes had, after all, made evil his good. He was hated by every man with whom he had dealings in Egypt, and he confessed his guilt, saying that it was all as Ptolemy had heard.

The prison of Alexandria had been built according to the plan and the precise orders of Kleomenes, out of Paros marble, with Corinthian columns upon the outside, and gates of iron, and locks and chains of iron upon the inside, so that no man, Greek or Egyptian, might make his escape from it. This prison of Kleomenes was a very excellent prison, a most handsome building, and Kleomenes of Naukratis was its first prisoner.

On the day that was named for the execution of Kleomenes Ptolemy had the colossal pink granite statue of this criminal taken down from its plinth upon Kanopic Street and ground up into a pink powder, and he made Kleomenes swallow as much of it as he could.

Kleomenes did not reside for long in his prison, for the order of Ptolemy was that he must drink hemlock, and Ptolemy watched as the *hyparkhos* grew cold in his limbs, and the blood of this man congealed, and he retched up the contents of his stomach and died racked by horrid convulsions.

Ptolemy now made ready for the expected invasion of Perdikkas, mobilizing all his troops to the border forts of Egypt. He took the wealth of Kleomenes for himself, so that these ill-gotten riches became the basis of his own fortune. Asked why he did not merely take away Kleomenes's wealth and send him home to Macedon, or just fine him, Ptolemy said that wherever he was a free man Kleomenes was bound to rise up and take his revenge. It was far better for Kleomenes of Naukratis, he said, to be a dead man, for a dead man cannot cause trouble.

2.4

Barbarians

Upon the arrival of Ptolemy, Anemhor had stood with the Satrap upon the balcony of audiences of his great Temple of Ptah at Memphis, watching the unending column of Greek soldiers marching into his city. For the whole of that day Anemhor heard nothing but the tramp of soldiers' boots, the jingle of harness, the rumble of carts and wagons, and the shouted orders of the officers, and the voice of the Greeks raised as one voice, singing the Battle Paian to Apollo, and the marching songs in praise of Athene, goddess of War, Nike, goddess of Victory, and Zeus, Lord of the Thunderbolt.

Anemhor watched the dawn, and he thought of Ra, the Sun god, of Anubis, Lord of the Underworld, of Ptah, the creator god, and the tears fell down his cheeks—tears of relief, perhaps, that Egypt had not returned to Persian rule; or tears of anger, that the rule of the foreigner was renewed—as if there might be no end to foreign rule, as if the gods of Egypt had indeed deserted the Two Lands.

At Memphis Ptolemy spoke easier with Anemhor, for the truth was that this man could speak Greek as naturally as pigs squeak, and though it was convenient for him to pretend that he did not understand, there was little this man did not know about the language of the invader.

Ptolemy asked many things, but most often he asked what must be done to gain the sympathy of the people, and how the government of Egypt should best be undertaken.

Anemhor, he told Ptolemy much, though he did not tell him all. Anemhor worried about many things, but most of all he worried about the infant Alexandros—the Pharaoh who was a child, who stayed in Greece with Perdikkas—and about the absent Arrhidaios, who did not come to Egypt either. Anemhor worried because it was the presence of the Pharaoh that guaranteed such things as the rising of the River.

If the River does not rise at the right time, he told Ptolemy, *there will be famine. And if there is famine, there will be also revolts . . .*

Ptolemy learned, then, that the rise of the Nile and the fertility of the land were bound up with the person of the Pharaoh, who was directly responsible for the prosperity of Egypt.

How, Anemhor asked, *may an absent Pharaoh make the gods happy and put off a crisis in Egypt? How can the Pharaoh act, if he lives in Greece? How can a king who is a child be a useful king?*

It was Anemhor's thought that Ptolemy would have to do his best on the Pharaoh's behalf. It was the Satrap who would have to sacrifice to the Sacred Bull, Apis, and thus make known his goodwill.

Ptolemy made the proper offerings. He ordered the repair of temples at Waset, the city the Greeks called Diospolis, or Thebes of the Hundred Gates, and he did not so much as look at what needed to be done, for he had more pressing business at Memphis.

Ginestho, he said, *make it happen,* and he knew the power of a satrap, then, and the thrill of his power, for everything this man wished for could be realized upon the instant, or so he thought.

Ptolemy played the visitor, and he made the visitor's proper procession to look upon those monuments the Greeks chose to call *Pyramid*, with his train of fan-bearers, camel-drivers, donkey-boys, and attendant priests who would, or would not, answer his every question; and Ptolemy was dazzled, as every man is dazzled, by the glare of the white stone casing, blinded by the sun reflected off the stones, and awed by the bigness that was bigger than any thing made by man that he had ever seen before.

How old? he asked, as every man asks, and the High Priest spread his hands, for it was the one question that was impossible of answer, except to murmur, *Older than memory, Excellency, older than time.* At least, it was one of those things that Anemhor did not wish to tell the Satrap, who could not be allowed to know every thing.

He asked next about the Third Pyramid—was it true that this monument was haunted by a beautiful naked woman who drove all men mad? Was it the truth? And Anemhor said, *Yes, Excellency,* and Ptolemy, who had an interest in women, naked women, but no interest in becoming mad, had no cause to make the journey to look upon the Pyramids after that, and the priests were pleased. They had no wish for Ptolemy to know the secrets of Egypt. He was the foreigner, the Greek Dog, to be viewed with suspicion. True, he was better than the Persian, perhaps, but he did not belong in Egypt. He would *never* belong: they would make sure of it. And surely, there were many men, many priests, who, welcome him though they did, would have been just as happy— only too happy—to see him march away again.

Ptolemy received, nonetheless, the polite applause of the people of the city of Unnu, or On, which the Greeks call Heliopolis, City of the Sun, and these folk threw flowers, as they had been instructed to, and showed their teeth a little, and Ptolemy, having looked, rode back to Memphis.

His army, in the meantime, marched on up-River, or commandeered ships and sailed up-River, where, unable to speak any of the names of the places in Egyptian, unable to remember what place was which, and unable to understand what any of these names signified, they thought up, with the permission of Ptolemy, names of their own, so that every city in Egypt became a *polis*: Krokodilopolis, City of the Crocodile, for example, Herakleopolis, City of Herakles, Kynopolis, City of Dogs, Lykopolis, Wolf City, Apollonopolis, City of Apollo, Hermopolis, City of Hermes, the Thoth of the Greeks, and so forth, so that the Egyptian became almost a foreigner in his own land. To fight back against the indignity of such things no Egyptian would let himself speak the name of Alexandria, the city of the Greek invader, but they persisted in their stubbornness by calling it Rhakotis, Building Site, even after it was finished.

As for Anemhor himself, he shook his head, wondering how it was that the Egyptian had managed not to fight the Greek, to repel him from Egypt, instead of welcoming him like some beloved friend, for this Anemhor was truly no great friend to the Greeks, but made things difficult for them wherever he could.

Sure, Ptolemy was made welcome, after a fashion, but he was, for all that, still a barbarian to Egyptian eyes, and his army an unwashed army, stained with blood, with the marks of rape and murder upon their garments. And however much the Egyptian might hope for it, and pray to the gods of Egypt for it, and affect not to understand what it was that the Greek said or wanted, the Greek did not go home. The Greek would never go home to Greece, for he preferred Egypt, where, as he liked to say, there was gold dust even in the streets, even if the gold dust was only *sand*.

No, the Greek was here to stay, and though there were things he hated about the Two Lands, he loved it more.

Yes, the soldier of Ptolemy liked most of the things he looked upon. He saw for the first time that bird which he called *struthion,* or ostrich, which was bred on the royal ostrich farms, and kept for her feathers; and he was pleased to ride and even to run races while seated astride this bird, and nobody lifted a finger to stop him. The Greek soldier was allowed to enjoy his pleasures. It was easier to let the men of Ptolemy do what they would, for to resist would mean that the sword would be drawn out of the sheath, and the sword would kill in thousands, as it had killed at Tyros, at Gaza, and in one hundred other places. Egypt had had her warning—what she must expect if she did not show her teeth to the Greek. Egypt knew well what would be the price to pay for not smiling, for not letting Ptolemy and the soldiers of Ptolemy do whatever they wanted.

In truth, Anemhor thought that the new city of Alexandria was a goodly thing. Memphis was no fine place to station ten thousand Greek soldiers. Apart from any other thing, the Greeks' favoured practice of *aphrodisia,* man upon man, this was forbidden at Memphis, as an impurity in this purer than pure, this purest of pure cities. And for another thing, to bring Greek gods to the illustrious and most illustrious city of Memphis, the ancient religious capital of Egypt, where every thing is concerned with Ptah of the Beautiful Face, and the greatness of Ptah—it was a thing that was most unfit to be done. Ptolemy—he should have a city of his own, where the Greeks might do as they pleased, a city, if they wished it, that was impure, where every thing was allowed, where nothing that a man might imagine to do would be forbidden, and without the gods of Egypt being offended by their every act.

Anemhor, yes, urged Ptolemy to think of Alexandria as his capital city, which would be an utterly modern city, with its proper supply of fresh water—instead of drinking the River, as a man must do at Memphis, and every place else in Egypt—with its proper Greek baths, hot and cold, and every proper Greek thing, yes, a city the Greek could be proud of, that did not smell of musty antiquity, like Memphis; that did not stink of drains and filth and camel dung. To take the Greeks out of Memphis, yes, yes, it would be a goodly thing, a fine thing, and in Memphis it might seem as if nothing had changed; as if the Egyptian was still in control of the Two Lands.

But the illustrious and most illustrious city of Alexandria was not yet finished according to the satisfaction of Ptolemy, not yet ready to be a satrapal Residence, and Anemhor could only encourage, and give his best help in the way of Egyptian workmen, and he prayed to Ptah and to all the gods of Egypt for the day when the column of Greek soldiers would march north, and leave Memphis in peace. In his turn Ptolemy urged the building programme onwards, sending his daily messages of encouragement to the overseers of workmen.

For his part, Anemhor asked often *How goes the building?* as if he would be pleased for the Satrap to quit Memphis just as soon as possible.

Anemhor, the High Priest of Memphis, was a broken man, a man broken in spirit, and yet he was a man stronger than all men, who had power beyond limit. They said that, like Thoth, he had swallowed the Two Lands, for there was nothing that he did not know about Egypt.

As well as wisdom and knowledge, he had riches greater than any other man in Egypt, after the King. He had his house in Memphis, and his gardens, his servants and slaves by the score, his fast chariots and his horses without equal. He had even two great ships, which he would sail up-River and down-River upon his priestly business.

In the past, this man would have been Director of All the Works of the King, if not also the Vizier of the King, part of the governing of

Egypt. He would have been Architect to the Pharaoh, with charge over the building and repair of every temple. But the Persian had cut his power in half. Anemhor was not Vizier of Egypt, and it was as if he had been denied the use of his right hand. Under the rule of Alexander, under the hyparchy of Kleomenes, Anemhor contented himself with being half a high priest, with being Master of the House of Gold, overseeing the making of all objects in gold and precious metal.

All of his priestly titles he kept. He remained a prince and a noble of Egypt. He did not cease to be Prophet of Horus of the Window of Appearances. He did not stop being Prophet of the Living Apis, the Sacred Bull of Memphis. But under Ptolemy Anemhor tried to get back his full powers. He would not be kept at arm's length, but put himself about, seeking to advise Ptolemy upon every matter. At the same time Ptolemy kept the governance of Egypt in the hands of his own ministers—Greeks, men in whom he put his absolute trust—and it was the purpose of Ptolemy to leave the high priests of Egypt to take care of religious matters, and not to let them meddle in state business.

But it was the thought of Anemhor to make Ptolemy unable to survive without his help.

Always there would be tension about the power of the priesthood, so long as the House of Ptolemy ruled Egypt: always Ptolemy would worry whether the priests in general, and the High Priest of Memphis in particular, was not plotting to overthrow him.

On the face of it, Anemhor's business was the festivals of Memphis, the Festival of Sokar, in which the boat was hauled round the circuit of the city walls; and the visit of the statue of Ptah to Hathor, Lady of the Sycamore, Hathor of the South, when the god would take ship and sail up-River. Yes, it was his first task to safeguard the temples; to attend to the well-being of the gods—of every god.

Thus, Anemhor made sure that Ptolemy knew that all things connected with the temples, whether carvings in the stone, or furniture, or vessels of gold, were guarded by the most powerful magic. And he said, *Any man who raises his hand against these objects, against the Temple itself, or against any of the priests therein, he will perish beneath the sword of Amun; he will perish by the fire of Sakhmet, the lioness goddess.*

Ptolemy spread his hands, as if to say, *I had no thought of . . . It had not so much as crossed my mind to . . .* But he said nothing, thinking, rather, of all the things that he must and must not do; about how Egypt had seemed such a great prize, the great gift of the gods of Greece, but how difficult it was turning out to control.

Indeed, Thoth says, Ptolemy and his House, they would not have an *easy* time. If they had thought the burden of governing Egypt might be light, they were mistaken.

But Anemhor saw in his heart every thing that Ptolemy imagined to do. He had the power to know Ptolemy's secret thoughts. He had always his spies in the satrapal Residence, his scouts in the unfinished city, reporting to him every thing that took place.

Was it, then, the purpose of Anemhor to work the ruin of the House of Ptolemy from the beginning? Did this man give his support to the Greeks only to help them build a house, a city, an empire, that would most surely fall down?

Perhaps it was so. Perhaps it was not. To be sure, the magic of Anemhor was powerful enough for him to do whatever he pleased with the fate of Ptolemy. Then it would be a mere matter of waiting for the collapse, waiting and waiting; for Time, to the priests of Egypt, means nothing, nothing at all.

The residence of Anemhor at Memphis was large, and its gardens were planted with fig trees, date palms, sycamores, vines, and arbours, and there were pools with ornamental fishes. There was no garden in all Memphis so large or so beautiful, apart from the gardens of the Pharaoh himself. Anemhor had also his beloved wife, his fine sons, one of whom would be High Priest of Ptah after he had gone to his tomb in the West, and his daughters, every one of them to be married to some priest of high rank.

The garden was Anemhor's paradise, where he passed his hours of recreation. Here he would play at draughts with his sons, or listen to the harp, lute and pipe, played by the women of his family. Here he watched them practise the dances they must dance before the god in his temple. His younger children ran among the palm trees or splashed in the pools; sons who would be priests, daughters who were already *seistron*-players in the temple, for yes, the whole family of Anemhor was dedicated to the service of Ptah of the Beautiful Face.

In spite of his constant and elaborate making ready for death, Anemhor was cheerful always; in spite of Egypt having again been delivered into the hands of foreigners, his laughter did not grow less, but echoed still among the palms and sycamores of his garden.

Anemhor went about his business, arms folded under his spotted mantle of leopard skin. Every day he bathed himself three times in the Sacred Lake of Ptah, so that he was the purest of the pure ones. Every third day he had his body shaved from head to foot, up to the eyebrows, down to the feathers. There was no hatred in the heart of this man. He did always what was good for Egypt, what was best for the gods. He had no personal dislike for Ptolemy, who seemed to be a good man—as good a man as could be found among the Greeks.

Did this Anemhor make it possible for the House of Ptolemy to destroy itself, so that the rule of the native Pharaohs might be restored? Did he, Pupil-of-Thoth? Did he?

Some have thought so.

No, the High Priest of Ptah was not cast down by events. His smile did not grow less. On the contrary, his smile grew wider.

2.5

Egyptian Wisdom

In the year that Ptolemy came to Egypt as Satrap the boy called Anemhor—and also Esisout, and also Nesisty, but who was most often addressed as Eskedi—the elder son of Old Anemhor, High Priest of Memphis, reached his sixteenth year, and the end of his days at the School of Scribes in Memphis. Like his father, he too had begun his studies at the age of five years, and for the last months of his schooling he had had charge of the horse-breeding stables at Memphis, for he was a boy marked out for high office, one who, if the gods willed it, must succeed his father.

In his first days at the scribe school he had learned the art of reading, when the whole class of boys would read aloud from the papyrus with one voice.

He had progressed by learning long passages of the Wisdom of Egypt by heart, for his father set great store by the ability to remember. It was more important to remember than to think fresh thoughts. Fresh thoughts were not needed by the scribe, for in the world of the Ptah temple every thing must remain as it has always been. For yes, in Egypt the most wondrous thing is that there is nothing new; that every thing stays the same as it was at the beginning of the world, at the First Time, when the gods were young.

Old Anemhor encouraged this son of his, saying to him, *Learn to write, for this will bring you more benefit than any other thing.* Anemhor said to him, *Your schoolwork will last you for ever, like the very mountains.*

Eskedi learned. Eskedi remembered. He had, before long, the ability to foretell the day upon which the earthquake would take place. He could forecast the failure of crops and the outbreak of epidemic diseases.

From the age even of four years old Eskedi was encouraged by his father to take thought for Apis, the Sacred Bull of Memphis, who was the Living Image of Ptah. And if he did not yet have the office of Keeper of the Living Apis, he soon would, and until his appointment he would go every day to see the bull, in order to learn the art of foretelling the future from the movements and reactions of this wondrous divine beast.

If the Apis flicked his tail, it meant so and so.

If the Apis licked his left-hand nostril with his great grey tongue, it meant such and such.

If he licked the left and the right nostril together, it meant something else.

Eskedi was a master of the signs of the Apis. Soon he would be named as the special scribe with responsibility for the food of the mother of Apis, who, upon her death, would become the Isis cow.

Eskedi learned how the sick could be healed. He learned the properties of every medicinal plant. He learned the art of making rain fall. He would be a scribe of the House of Life, a man of whom the people of Egypt might ask any question they wished, and be sure to receive from him a satisfactory answer.

Now, at sixteen, this boy sat the examination that every young scribe meant for the priesthood of Egypt must sit, and the examination was in the grammar and writing of the hieroglyphic and hieratic script of Egypt, and in knowledge of the gods, their titles, characteristics and history, and in the manifold complexities of the temple ritual. All of these things were difficult, most difficult, but in truth there was almost nothing that Eskedi did not already know, and he was successful, and Old Anemhor his father rejoiced.

This great scholar now had his garments taken off, and was bathed three times in the Sacred Lake of Ptah. He was shaved with the bronze razors from head to foot, down to the last hair upon his body, and his flesh was anointed with perfumes. Then they clothed him in the robes of the priestly office, and he was admitted to the horizon of Heaven for the first time.

Eskedi, struck with awe at the thought of the majesty of Ptah, could now draw near to the god himself in his sanctuary, for he was now and at once a *wab* priest, a junior priest, and there was no word to describe the happiness of his heart, and the happiness of his father and mother also.

Eskedi would enjoy a life free from physical labour. He would have all his days the soft hands and clean clothes of a scribe. He would bathe himself in the Sacred Lake three times every day. The thoughts of his heart would not be encumbered by bodily weariness. Eskedi was a boy who would give orders, check results, take records, and grant or with-hold his permission; he would be a man highly equipped for making every last decision about the temples of Egypt.

In the School of Scribes of the House of Life the young Eskedi had learned the magic that was so great a part of the knowledge of every priest. From time to time this pupil forgot that the most important thing for a scribe to learn is the art of self-control, the art of controlling his feelings, so that his master reminded him: *Be attentive and hear my speech. Forget nothing of what I say to you.*

And when Eskedi forgot again, the master said, *The boy who hears will become someone distinguished.*

And he said, *A boy's ears are upon his back. He hears when he is beaten.*

When Eskedi did not hear, he *was* beaten, and he learned his lesson. He was not so bad that they had to tie his legs together so that he could not run away.

In the mornings he copied texts of wisdom, such as:

> *Do the good and you will prosper . . .*
> *Do not dip the pen to injure a man . . .*
> *The Ape dwells in the House of Khnum,*
> *His eye encircles the Two Lands . . .*
> *When he sees one who cheats with his finger,*
> *He carries off his livelihood in the Flood.*

In the cool of the evening Eskedi practised with his fellows the skill of crocodile riding, sitting astride the back of the Face of Fear in the Sacred Lake, a sport that was without very great danger, for the mouth of this beast was tied fast with papyrus rope before any boy was allowed upon the water.

Riding the crocodile—it was the great skill of Horus, the falcon god. If a boy could do this, he might have no fear of any thing.

And yes, Eskedi, like his father before him, was master even of the crocodile.

In the margin of his papyrus this boy wrote, *I mastered every magical art. There was nothing thereof which escaped me.*

When he had mastered the art even of translating hieroglyphic into hieratic writing, the most difficult of all the scribe's tasks, he wrote in the margin of the papyrus, *There is nothing at all which Eskedi does not know.*

He learned that the wise man will prefer silence to empty talk. He learned how to use the secret name of every god, so as to change the order of things.

For yes, if Eskedi should speak the sacred name of Shu on the edge of the River, the River would dry up. And if he should say the sacred name of Shu upon the land, the land would catch fire.

Eskedi had such power over the crocodile that if this beast attacked the magician, the south would turn into the north—yes, the world would tilt.

Long ago he had learned to write and speak automatically the formulaic wish for the Pharaoh's *Life! Prosperity! Health!* whenever he wrote or spoke the word Pharaoh.

Eskedi was indeed a scribe with clean fingers. Knowledge and virtue were inseparable. No boy could become a scribe without them both, and his behaviour was beyond reproach.

Above all, Eskedi learned the respect due to a parent. *Make libation for your father and mother,* he wrote, *who are resting in the valley. Do not forget the one outside. Your son will act for you likewise.*

But, for the moment, the father of Eskedi lived: Old Anemhor, High Priest of Ptah, than whom there was none wiser in Egypt. Old Anemhor was indeed Thoth in all things, but Eskedi his son was not far behind him in wisdom. He wrote in the margin of his papyrus, *Behold, I am a very excellent scribe.* A little boastfulness is natural in the young. But what Eskedi wrote happened to be the truth.

2.6

The Shower of Nuts and Figs

Having laid his hands upon the eight thousand talents from the Treasury of Egypt, Ptolemy saw no reason why he should hold himself back where expenditure was concerned. He began to hire, then, soldiers by the thousand from all over the Greek world, so that he would be able to resist the attack of Perdikkas, when it came.

Vast numbers of troops now left their military commanders and deserted to the camp of Ptolemy, on the one hand because he had a reputation for fairness, but on the other hand also because the wage he offered was far in excess of what the other Successors could afford to pay. Soldiers who had never been friends of Ptolemy before became great friends of Ptolemy now, so that Memphis filled up with rough-looking men who spoke nothing but the roughest Greek dialects, and the city was so empty of Greek women that Ptolemy was obliged to import not only soldiers, but shiploads of whores, in order to keep these men happy, and in order to preserve the honour of the Egyptian women of Memphis.

Ptolemy himself should, perhaps, have been happy at this time, because he now had, surely, every thing that a Greek may desire. But Ptolemy was not happy, for he worried about Perdikkas; he worried about the future.

Ptolemy knew that he could not survive for long without allies, and yet he had, just then, no allies. He needed some other ruler who would help him to resist Perdikkas and the rest of them. His great need was to protect himself from Antigonos Monophthalmos—One-Eye—who might invade Egypt from the east. He also wanted to have control of Syria and Phoenicia, so that he could keep open the trade routes for frankincense, and for cedar wood from Lebanon, with which he must build his ships of war—for there was no ship's timber in Egypt, in fact, no wood at all, apart from the useless wood of the acacia and the date palm.

Ptolemy did, in every thing, just what he thought Alexander would have done. He would put up with no resistance, and the world should know that Ptolemy, Satrap of Egypt, would have what he wanted.

However, just now he did not have what he wanted, which was peace. In spite of owning Syria and Phoenicia he slept badly, for worrying about Perdikkas, who he knew was about to do every thing in his power to take Egypt from him by force. Ptolemy not only lacked an ally, he lacked also a legitimate heir, and he kept thinking the thought that he must found his dynasty, so that the satrapy should pass to his son, and the son of his son, and remain in the family.

Ptolemy sent ambassadors, then, to Old Antipatros, the man left in Macedon by Alexander to be the regent while he was away conquering the world. Old Antipatros had the reputation of being the wisest of all the rulers of his time, a man who did not break his word as the other rulers did, and who would not try to play tricks upon his friends.

The ambassadors suggested a Grand Alliance of true and everlasting friendship and total military co-operation, and Antipatros expressed his interest. Ptolemy knew also that Old Antipatros had a daughter called Eurydike, who might be used to seal the treaty in the time-honoured manner by becoming his wife, and he made the ambassadors ask some discreet questions about whether such a match would be agreeable to him; and Antipatros expressed, a second time, his interest.

In due course the alliance between Ptolemy and Antipatros was made public, and then made binding by the exchange of the usual luxurious gifts that were the visible signs of the friendship: Antipatros sent bowls of Siphnos gold, and the finest cavalry horses from Thessaly; and in return Ptolemy sent racehorses from Kyrene, chariots inlaid with ebony and ivory, and a beast that was called camelopard, whose immensely long neck stuck out of the crate in which he travelled to Greece, and drew crowds of onlookers.

Antipatros agreed to part with Eurydike his daughter, who was then fifteen years of age, and he told the ambassadors to tell Ptolemy that her breasts were three fingerbreadths high, like little pumpkins, and that she had yellow hair and was ripe for marriage. If Eurydike had any thoughts of her own about this match, they were ignored, for a father knew what was good for his daughter. A Greek father, they say, always knows what is for the best, and whatever Antipatros chose to do with her, she needs must put up with it.

Even so, when Eurydike learned the fate that was being made ready for her, she wept. She was young for her age, and would rather have stayed at home in Macedon with her waiting-women, and not have to give up her coloured ball of leather, or her earthenware dolls with wired-on arms, or her days at the loom; and she said that she feared the thought of journeying to Egypt all on her own.

Antipatros wrote to Ptolemy: *Our daughter knows nothing of life. She has grown up under the most restricted conditions. She has been trained from childhood to see as little as possible, to understand nothing. She will ask the minimum of questions* . . .

Ptolemy was satisfied. He did not wish any wife of his to poke her nose into his affairs of state. He wrote back to Antipatros: *Eurydike your daughter will want for nothing. She will live a life of ease and luxury* . . . And in due time the two satraps swore with the usual form of words: *If I remain faithful to the oath, may women give birth to children who resemble their parents. And if not, let women give birth to monsters.*

Eurydike now made herself ready for her sea voyage to Egypt, still fearful, for she had never in her life time sailed upon any sea in a boat before, never having set one foot outside the *gynaikeion* of Pella. She was given all manner of necessary things for her baggage, such as the seasick remedies, the indigestion remedies, magic remedies against all her enemies, real or imagined, and dress upon dress in every colour of the rainbow.

Eurydike watched the making ready with ever-widening eyes, and on the day before she said her farewells the family sat up all night with her, trying to stop time, which is the Greek manner of sending a bride upon her way. It was in the middle of this farewell party that Eurydike blurted out that really she had no wish to travel so far as Egypt, no wish whatever to be any man's wife, or the mother of children, but that she would much rather stay a maiden and live at home, and she shed many tears for the unknown future that lay ahead.

The mother of Eurydike, however, spoke firm: *Every thing has been arranged,* she said. *You have to go to Egypt. It is the one great chance of your life time, and you must take it or you may regret it for ever. Ptolemy is a kind man. He is not going to eat you . . .*

And Old Antipatros told his daughter that she was a most important part of his alliance with Egypt. She was helping to keep the peace. And so Eurydike had really no choice but to do as she was told. In marriage a Greek woman is nothing but an object to be exchanged between men. She might just as well have been a cabbage, or a donkey, she thought, for all the sympathy she was given.

But Eurydike would do well. She was not utterly lacking in female charms. She was accomplished at the loom and the lyre, and she was, mostly, of even temper. Moreover, she was in the best of health, and she came with the guarantee of Antipatros and his physicians that she was fit to bear as many strapping Greek sons as Ptolemy might care to sire upon her.

The tears of this bride-to-be at length stopped falling, and at last she stopped her sniffing in response to a sharp word from her mother. All the same, Eurydike had caused them such alarm with her nervousness about sea travel and about sailing alone to Egypt, that they sent with her an older woman who had seen something more of the world, and this woman passed for her aunt, or, as some said, her cousin, and her name was given out as Berenike, which meant Bearer of Victory.

Thoth says, it is all Greek . . . but, Reader, call her name *Ber-en-EYE-ki* or *Ber-en-EE-kay.*

The history of this so-called Aunt Berenike was that she had been married at a young age to one Philippos of Macedon (but *not* the King), a man of no very high-up family, nor of any great personal distinction, about whom nobody knew, or nobody would say, one thing, whether he was alive or dead, or whether he had just run off and left Berenike, or whether he was such a monster that she had left him. At all events, Aunt Berenike was now alone in the world but for her two small children, a wild boy called Magas, who liked eating, and a calm, thin girl called Antigone, and the two children went with her and Eurydike to Egypt.

Some asked whether Berenike was not just a whore who had got herself into trouble, whom Eurydike wanted to take under her wing. But nobody knew for sure. Certainly though, this aunt was running away from somebody, and some thing had gone very wrong with her life, for in all her years in the land of Egypt she did not utter one word about her late husband. Berenike had then a fresh start. She lived only in and for the present, and she erased her history so cleverly that nobody could say one thing about it, except to give the name of that husband of hers whom she could not bring herself to mention.

Eurydike and Berenike duly took ship for Egypt, and it was winter, the season that was not even the sailing season, when the seas were rough, and the captain of the *trieres* leered at the bride, saying, *I wish you Luck, Kyria, you are setting sail upon a real sea of trouble.* And he laughed, *Not the Libyan Sea, nor the Aegean Sea, nor yet the Sicilian sandbanks where three ships, perhaps, in thirty may avoid shipwreck . . . but the Sea of Marriage.* And he roared with laughter, as if he had been drinking. *In marriage,* he shouted, *no survivor has yet been known.*

And he might have continued like this, had not the aunt proved worthy of her hire and slapped this man upon the cheek, for there was no doubt that this woman was a tough woman who had suffered much, and her own marriage most likely had not been sailing upon calm seas either.

Tough though she was, when Berenike landed in Egypt she looked so dreadful—whether from the *nausiasis,* or from the shipwreck of her own marriage, and the sinking of her own emotions along with it—that no man so much as wanted to give her a second look. Berenike had no possessions, not one obol in her purse, not so much as a whore's mirror, and no more clothes than what she stood up in. Aunt Berenike was wholly dependent upon Eurydike her niece, and it was clear that Berenike herself needed to be looked after just as much as Eurydike did—so that, indeed, these two women of Macedon bound for a strange land swore now a solemn oath that they would take the greatest care of each other in Egypt. Eurydike even promised that she would find her aunt a fresh husband to support her, a fresh father for her children, but, having not the skills of foresight, she had no idea, just then, who such a man might turn out to be. Had she known who the new husband was fated to be, why, she might have sent Berenike back home to Greece then and there, for the day was most surely coming when Eurydike would curse herself for ever having wanted to bring her aunt to Egypt in the first place.

For the truth of it was that of these two women it was indeed *Berenike* whose fate it was to be the survivor.

The marriage of Ptolemy to Eurydike was, at any rate, celebrated at the Full Moon of Gamelion, a month sacred to Hera, queen of the gods of Greece, and patroness of marriage, because this was the lucky time to marry, or so the Greeks thought.

The Satrap's Residence at Memphis was decorated for this occasion with branches of laurel and olive, and lit up by flaming torches. On the wedding eve the women of the bride's family should, by rights, have walked to the public fountain to fetch the water for Eurydike's ritual bath. But since she had come to Egypt without her family, it was Aunt Berenike who carried the water, and she bathed her niece and spoke words of comfort, in order to calm her nervousness.

In the morning Ptolemy made his appearance, garlanded with crimson flowers, and wearing a wreath of red flowers upon his head, and he was dressed in a fresh white *khiton* and was plastered from head to foot with myrrh. He should, by rights, have walked with his family and the groom's friend to the house of the bride that afternoon, offered the sacrifices to the gods and then sat down to the wedding banquet with Eurydike's family. But the family of Eurydike were not present, and she had no house to walk to, and so the sacrifice and the banquet were held at the house of Ptolemy instead.

This Greek bride should, by rights, have been surrounded by her friends, but Eurydike had no Greek friends to support her except Berenike, and so they sat alone, just the two of them, looking about. Eurydike was dressed in rich fabrics, and Berenike had smeared her body with expensive ointments and anointed her drop by drop with costly perfumes. She was veiled with a red veil and wore the wreath of crimson flowers upon her head, and these two women sat quite apart from the men friends of Ptolemy, who stood staring at these women of Macedon whom they did not know, eating olives and holding their usual contest to see who might spit the pips the farthest, and saying nothing—only jeering and cheering on the spitters of pips—so that Eurydike, who had started out nervous, felt now thoroughly uncomfortable, and her hands shook, and her entire body trembled from fear at what was to happen to her that night.

From the landing in Alexandria and through all the trip up-River by barge to Memphis, Berenike had kept Eurydike covered up, according to Greek custom, so that nobody in Egypt had seen this woman's face; even Ptolemy himself had yet to look upon the face of his bride, and although he had made his welcome, he had yet to address a second word to her.

Where it was possible, yes, everything was done according to Greek custom. At the banquet they ate sesame-seed cakes, Greek wedding food, that was the symbol of fertility, while a naked Greek boy offered the guests Greek bread, and spoke the words of the ritual Greek formula: *I have avoided the worse; I have chosen the better.*

But throughout the wedding the hands of Eurydike kept on shaking, and the tremor was so bad that she brought the sesame-seed cake to her mouth only with difficulty, and she could think only, *I have chosen the worse, I have chosen the worse,* and she wished herself back home at Pella, in the *gynaikeion* with her mother and waiting-women, and she missed the dolls that she had been forced to dedicate in the Temple of Artemis to mark the end of her childhood and the beginning of her new life as a wife—and, though she did not wish it, a mother herself.

At this marriage there was dancing, of course, because this was a Greek wedding. Ptolemy danced, his usual elephantine dancing, every Greek danced and showed his teeth, and there was much merriment; and so it went on, until everybody had danced except for Eurydike, and somebody shouted, *Will the wife of Ptolemy not dance for us?*

Eurydike, horrified, shook her head.

But they shouted, *Dance! Dance! Dance! Dance!* so that Eurydike had to stand up, and she was still trembling.

She murmured to Berenike, *I cannot do it* . . . But Berenike nudged her, saying, *You have to. You must.*

The Greeks whistled and roared. They had been drinking wine all day.

Eurydike stepped forth. She gathered herself. She raised her arms above her head. She spun herself round once, twice. The pipes and the lyre started up, and the *kitharistes* strummed his instrument; but the music went fast, too fast for Eurydike to keep up with it, and she stood still.

The men fell silent, staring at her, and they did not now show their teeth. Then a slow clapping of the hands began. Eurydike lowered her arms and fled from the room, followed by the men's loud laughter. The laughter was not unkind, but the Greeks had laughed. Even Ptolemy had laughed, and then sent Berenike to drag the bride back again.

Take no notice, Berenike said later. *It does not matter.* But Eurydike could not help but notice. She was ashamed of herself, and she knew that nobody would forget her failure. It was not the best beginning.

As darkness fell upon Memphis the father of this bride should, by rights, have given this daughter of his to the groom, but Old Antipatros was in far-off Macedon, and so it was Ptolemy who lifted the red veil from the face of his wife to the only mildly disappointed applause of his assembled friends.

The face of this wife was, then, uncovered only when the rings of gold had been exchanged, and there was no turning back for Ptolemy, though in truth a change of heart was not possible, for the alliance was of such import to him that he had gone so far as to swear to marry the woman without troubling to make sure what she looked like.

Sure, Ptolemy was not utterly downcast by the facial features of Eurydike, but he did find himself thinking that this wife he had ordered up and promised to wed without so much as viewing her first was a *plain* girl. Yes, she lacked the glamorous good looks of Thaïs of Athens. Really, compared with Thaïs, he thought, Eurydike was nothing, nothing, a woman he would not have picked had not Fate, and military requirements, made her an absolute necessity.

Her demeanour was quiet, he thought, but he did notice the tremor. *She does not smile much,* he thought, and he caught once or twice the look he had seen one time in the eye of a madwoman. But he took Eurydike all the same by her trembling hand and helped her to the chariot that would take her in procession to his house. As they were already in Ptolemy's house they drove through the streets of Memphis in a circle, and came back whence they had started out, and Eurydike held all the while the sieve and the gridiron of bronze, symbols of every Greek wife's household duties, which, as a satrap's wife, she would never have to perform, not once, for it was this woman's fate to be waited upon even down to the nails of her fingers and toes, and to pass all the rest of her long life doing nothing.

There was no procession of singing relatives to follow her by torchlight, and no father of the groom wearing a myrtle wreath to welcome the chariot back, and no mother of the groom holding up a flaming torch, but it did not seem to matter that in all these things the Greek custom was changed, or ignored. Ptolemy welcomed his wife to the

Residence himself, and his friends showered her with nuts and figs as she walked through the double doors of cedar and gold, so that her face stung, and her arms were bruised black and blue, and she thought, *It is an ill omen.*

Once she had stepped over the threshold Eurydike was offered the wedding cake of sesame seeds, a date and a quince, symbols of fertility, and Ptolemy led her by the hand to the bridal chamber and slammed the door. His brother, Menelaos, stood guard outside it, and the wedding guests sang the wedding hymns, loud, to ward off evil influences, and to drown out the screams of the bride as Ptolemy held her down and did what every husband must do upon his wedding night.

For a start Eurydike did not like it, and since she had never done this act before, she had no idea what to do, and she was like one of her own dolls, with movable limbs, yes, but cold, like earthenware, unyielding. No, Eurydike did not excite Ptolemy as Thaïs had excited him. She aroused no great passion. She bit her lips and let Ptolemy do what he would, and kept her eyes shut, and her jaws did not let in the tongue of her husband behind her teeth, for he smelled of wine, and the truth was that she did not want his spit inside her mouth; she was a little disgusted by this man who was almost as old as her father, forty-six years of age, while she was a mere girl of fifteen.

To be sure, Eurydike was not Thaïs, and she did not behave like Thaïs. Eurydike would never do the *amphiplix,* wrapping her legs around his body to squeeze him. She would never ride Ptolemy in bed like a horse, or touch his *rhombos* with her tongue. These were unseemly activities for a wife, and unfavourable, anyway, to conception. Eurydike was not the most famous whore in the world, and, to be sure, a good Greek wife was not supposed to arouse excitement in a Greek husband, nor to indulge in a whore's acrobatics in the bedchamber.

In their love-making Eurydike would rarely smile. She would never wail the nightingale wail as Thaïs did. And she would never enjoy one moment of it. Her one duty was to bring forth legitimate heirs, sons who were brave, noble, Greek sons, the eldest of whom would be, surely, Satrap after his father. Eurydike's marriage was a political marriage, a dynastic marriage, a business arrangement, and it had nothing to do with Eros, or with love, and her heart did not beat faster when she saw Ptolemy—not then, not ever—but if anything it sank with dismay.

As for Ptolemy, he would repeat to himself, *A whore is for love; a whore is for aphrodisia; a wife is for the legitimate ploughing of children.* His nights with Eurydike would ever be tame and mechanical. It mattered not whether she pleased him, so long as she produced a son. To be sure, Ptolemy called his wife Dove, Pigeon, Duckling, as a Greek husband ought, as every other Greek husband did, and he sent her flowers on the day of her birthday, and so forth; but he had still his whores, his concubines by the dozen, just as he had before his marriage—his scores of other women of the night, of whom Eurydike was supposed to know nothing, shepherded by Lamia, his plump and comely Lamia, who kept a house full of beautiful Greek girls, towards whom Eurydike turned a blind eye.

From time to time Ptolemy looked hard at Eurydike and thought of her brother, the peace-loving Alexarkhos, who had founded a community beside Mount Athos in Greece and called it Ouranopolis, Heaven City, and had withdrawn into it, forsaking what he called the mad, mad world of wars and sieges and endless fighting—her crazy brother Alexarkhos, who had given up speaking Greek and invented his own language, and was rumoured to have identified himself with the Sun, even with the god Helios.

To give up speaking Greek—well, it was the next best thing to becoming a barbarian. But Ptolemy put Alexarkhos from his thoughts. It was Eurydike he had married, not her brother, and so far the girl showed no sign of madness herself.

Eurydike, however, was not quite as other girls. She had been drilled by her mother into hiding the less attractive aspects of her character, so that Ptolemy should not learn, for example, that she liked to eat earth. He did not know that Eurydike herself could speak Ouranopolitan, or that this was merely the childhood language of the children of Old Antipatros.

No, the madness of Eurydike would not show up until later.

In this marriage, then, there was no love, for no Greek loves his wife. Love he will reserve for his concubines. To fall in love was, in any case, the next best thing to going mad, for it meant the loss of self-control, and Ptolemy had no more wish than any other Greek man to feel the arrows of Eros. This wife of his was rather like a new purchase, and he felt towards her much as he might feel if he had bought a pair of sandals.

In spite of all this, Ptolemy did what every Greek must do upon taking a wife: he worked the spell of keeping a wife faithful, and because he was in Egypt he sought out the Egyptian spell, courtesy of the High Priest of Ptah.

He fashioned the crocodile out of mud from the River. He placed this beast in a small coffin of lead. He scratched the Name of Power and the name of his wife, Eurydike, upon the lid.

The crocodile, the High Priest said, would stop any lover coming near her, so that Eurydike was bound to be faithful—to this man who, assuredly, did not love her then, and never would.

As for Ptolemy, he was as free as any other Greek husband to pursue his other women, his handsome boys, if he wanted them, and it was normal behaviour for the Greeks, but different, very different, from the way of the Egyptian.

The Egyptian respects his wife as the mother of his children.

For the Egyptian there is no thing more important in the world than his wife, his beloved, his lotus flower.

Eurydike was innocent, untouched, pure. In truth she was very like the animal brought in for the sacrifice, which must be perfect, without blemish. Eurydike did everything that was required of her. She spoke only when spoken to. Her replies were respectful. She had every reason to look forward to her new life not with joy but with fear, for Berenike had unthinkingly told her countless horrible stories about what may go wrong for a woman in the ordeal of childbirth.

On the one hand, Eurydike was filled with a kind of pride to be, oh, a satrap's wife; but upon the other hand she felt also an awful dismay. She trembled often. She did not know what she should say to her husband. She wept often for not being at home with her mother in Macedon.

Berenike did her best, giving words of advice, and she hired even a maker of jests to come along and try to make Eurydike smile; but the jest-maker said it was the hardest work of his life, for that Eurydike really did not want to laugh, and his jests succeeded only in having Berenike and the waiting-women screaming with mirth, whereas Eurydike managed nothing but a straight face. The truth of it was, perhaps, that Eurydike had no sense of humour, and suffered from melancholia.

Aunt Berenike was all Eurydike had, and she told Berenike so. In the night time, when Ptolemy stayed away from her, and she woke in the darkness, terrified of the scorpions and poisonous spiders and snakes, and every creeping thing that scuttled across the floor of her bedchamber, she would run to Berenike's bed, climb into it with her, and cling to Berenike to be comforted, and sob for the loss of her untroubled life, her old life at Pella, in Macedon.

On the morning of the Satrap's marriage Old Anemhor came to Ptolemy wearing his leopard spots, and he wished him the best of his best wishes for the marriage, and presented him with a bowl of alabaster of the most exquisite Egyptian workmanship, a two-handled cup, with some words written upon it in the hieroglyphic writing of the Egyptians. And when Ptolemy asked what the pictures signified, Old Anemhor told him:

> *Love your wife ardently,*
> *Feed and clothe her.*
> *Fragrant unguents are good for her body.*
> *Make her happy all her days.*
> *She is like a field that brings benefit to its owner.*

Ptolemy smiled his best of smiles, showing the teeth, sparkling the eyes. He gave Anemhor his best of thanks, and had Eurydike see the bowl of alabaster also. But what did Ptolemy think? The words upon the bowl, they were words of Egyptian wisdom, but they made Ptolemy think of ploughing, work that he had undertaken in Eordaia as a boy, before ever he walked to Pella in bare feet. And Ptolemy thought only of the ploughing in which he was himself the plough, and the field was his wife, Eurydike.

Alas, the truth of it was that this Eurydike did not pass a very happy time in Egypt.

In the third year of the satrapy of Ptolemy son of Lagos, the son of Old Anemhor, who was called Eskedi, or Young Leopard Spots, by the Greeks, then aged about nineteen years, was married to a wife called Neferrenpet, a name that means Beautiful is Isis—a name that the Greeks, in their stubbornness, would insist upon calling Rempnophris.

Neferrenpet was indeed a beautiful young woman, a little younger in years than Eskedi her husband. She would pass her days bringing up her children, in organizing the household of this young priest and in performing her duties at the Temple of Ptah, as a musician, as a priestess, as one of the players of the sacred rattle, or *seistron,* that kept away every evil spirit from the domain of the god.

Unlike the young Greek wife of the Satrap, who was hardly older than she was, Neferrenpet smiled. Neferrenpet was happy. Eskedi loved his wife ardently. He gave her every fragrant unguent. He clothed her and fed her. He made her happy all her days. Thoth says, How different was the marriage of this Egyptian husband and wife from the strange marriage of the Greek Satrap, of Ptolemy and the tearful Eurydike.

The love of Eskedi for Neferrenpet his wife was just as true and real as the love of Old Anemhor had been for Eskedi's mother. The Egyptian is not ashamed to declare love for his wife. He does not flee in horror from love as do the Greeks. By no means.

When Eskedi first cast his eyes upon Neferrenpet he wished at once for her to be his wife, and he besought Hathor, the goddess of Love, to grant him the girl of his choice. Yes, even Hathor the Cow, the Lady of Love and Joy and Beauty, Hathor the Golden One.

And in her turn Neferrenpet begged the goddess to appoint her as her lover's bride.

Day after day Eskedi sent to this girl lotus flowers, that are the symbol of love, a sign of his love for her.

He would go and stand beneath her window in Memphis and sing even the love songs of the Egyptians:

> *Her hair is black,*
> *blacker than the night,*
> *blacker than sloes.*
> *Red are her lips,*
> *redder than beads of jasper,*
> *redder than ripe dates,*
> *Lovely are her twin breasts . . .*

There was delight in the heart of Eskedi the scribe. The lips of his beloved he compared to a lotus bud, her arms to the curving boughs of young trees:

> *What says the pomegranate tree?*
> *My pips are like her teeth;*
> *My fruit are like her breasts.*

Truly, the happiness of Eskedi and Neferrenpet knew no bounds.

He called this wife of his Lotus Bud, and it was a mark of his great affection for her. The Egyptian husband does not continually argue and quarrel with his wife, as the Greeks do. By no means.

Nor, when he had married her, did he ever cease from loving, but he spoke poetry often to this wife of his:

I inhale the sweet breath
that comes forth from thy mouth . . .
I contemplate thy beauty every day.
It is my desire
to hear thy lovely voice
like the whiff of the north wind . . .

Truly, the thoughts that Eskedi spoke to Neferrenpet were not mere empty words. And truly, Ptolemy did not sing poetry to that new wife of his—no, not one word of it. Ptolemy was a warrior, and his thoughts were not thoughts of love but thoughts of war.

2.7

Marsh Fever

Each morning Anemhor the High Priest would present himself before Ptolemy in his Residence, dressed in the spotted leopard skin, and engage him in the ritual of question and answer.

How did the Satrap sleep? he said.
Well! said Ptolemy.
And the Satrap's wife?
Also well, Ptolemy said.
And the three children of the Satrap?
Well also, Ptolemy said, as if he knew.
And Menelaos, the brother?
Like a snake, said Ptolemy.
And did you see some dream? Anemhor asked.

And Ptolemy would tell his dream, when he could remember it, and Anemhor would stand and think a while, and tell him then the meaning and significance, for the interpretation of dreams was the special gift of Anemhor. So Ptolemy knew, or thought he knew, what might happen perhaps the next day, and was enabled to see into the future.

Satrap and High Priest exchanged their courtesies, but Anemhor knew that Ptolemy did not sleep well. In every chamber of the Satrap's

Residence, upon earthen floors, upon papyrus mats and makeshift beds, the Greeks lay half-awake all night, motionless, bathed in sweat, or tossing and turning, listening to the armies of the night: the spiders and cockroaches, crickets and ants, to all the slithering of unseen creatures that crept out of the cracks in the mud-brick walls and clung and tickled and pinched and bit every man, woman and child of the Greeks throughout the hours of darkness, Ptolemy included, so that proper sleep was impossible.

Mennufert, Mennufer, the Good Place, that the Greeks had to call Memphis because they could not pronounce any word in the tongue of the Egyptian. What did Memphis mean to Ptolemy?

Memphis: it was the balance of the Two Lands, at the apex of the Delta. Here, in this most revered of cities, the good god Ptah, and the Sun-Eye, Hathor-Sakhmet, reigned supreme, but Ptolemy saw none of it. He saw only the lake in front of the city, and his palace, which stood upon a height. He saw the ibis and the stork upon the Sacred Lake, and he saw the gold piled up in his treasure house. The Temple of Ptah, the Temple of Isis, the Temple of Ra—all of these were forbidden places to him and meant nothing to him. About the gods of Egypt he understood nothing. No, not one word.

Slowly, slowly, Ptolemy would learn to call the quarters and streets of the city after their proper names. He learned who is Ra, god of the Sun, and who is Horus, the Falcon. He learned that Isis, Lady of Many Names, is the greatest goddess. He showed his face at the different festivals of the city, and he showed his teeth a little. He could never forget that he was a foreigner, a usurper, or that the customs of Egypt were not his customs. Every thing was strange to him, but this Satrap was better than the satrap of the Persians. He was better than Kleomenes.

Ionian Dog, Anemhor called him, some times, but not to his face, and not in any spirit of malice, for there was no malice in the heart of this priest. Greek Dog though Ptolemy was to some, his heart was kind. He did not delight in unpleasantness.

Some mornings Anemhor found Ptolemy not in the best of health, and he voiced his concern, his genuine concern for the Satrap's welfare. But on these mornings, although the High Priest stood before him, Ptolemy did not speak, but stared at the man from his chair, or from his bed, and he saw not this man's face. He saw only the blur of leopard spots swirling before him.

The first sign of the fever returning would always be the feeling of anxiety that came upon him out of nowhere. Yes, he would think, some man has put this curse upon me, and the anxiousness was like some evil spirit entering his body. He felt then the dullness, the weakness in his four limbs, and his feet heavy like blocks of stone. Everything made him feel anger, but most of all he hated the light, and the voices of other people; and the smell of Memphis, all camels and decay and musty antiquity, seemed now disgusting to him.

Then the shivering began, and it was a cold like the terrible piercing cold of the Paropamisos, and the shock of the cold made him gasp. He trembled, he thrashed about, and the tremor and the convulsions felt as if they were tearing him to pieces. Trying to save himself, he would start to say his prayers, to beg the gods for help, all the gods of Greece, one after another: Zeus, Apollo, Asklepios . . . and then all of them together, because the fear took hold of him.

In the evening his hot fit might flare up without warning, when he would feel, yes, as if his bones were white-hot, on fire, and he would lie in the pool of his sweat, dizzy, nauseous, exhausted, able to move neither hand nor foot, and it was impossible for him to sleep, but he lay awake, looking at the green lizards walking up the walls in the lamplight, and he was like a man with no muscles, a man with no bones; and afterwards he could read no dispatches for days, because the letters were blurred, swimming about upon the papyrus as if rocked by the waves of the sea.

What could Anemhor, this great physician, do for Ptolemy in his hot fit, his cold fit, in his terrible sweating and shivering?

Anemhor simply spread his hands, for there was, as he said, no means of curing this ailment.

And the leopard spots blurred and swirled and disappeared until the next time.

As for the Greeks, they gave him, first, talismans to wear about his neck and wrists, or to hold in the hand, for ordinary medicines were just about useless in such a case as his.

From time to time Ptolemy was induced to eat such things as the hearts of swallows with honey.

He ate also swallows' dung.

He consumed an entire swallow.

He took an asp's skin, in small doses, with an equal quantity of pepper, that had been known to cure Parthian tribesmen. But these things had small effect.

Ptolemy refused to try only one thing that the Greek physicians suggested. He would not eat of the flesh of the crow, for it made him think always of the number of dead men's eyes that bird had eaten. At the best of times he would hear the clamour of the crows and shudder, remembering. The Satrap had always his horror of crows.

Some days his physicians would smear the soles of his feet with the flux of a menstruating woman, a remedy supposed to work well if done by the woman herself, without the patient's knowledge. And so Eurydike his wife joined in the treatment of her husband.

Most often they rubbed his flesh with the grease of frogs boiled in oil at a place where three roads meet, the flesh first having been thrown away. But, truly, none of these cures made him much better. The ague always came back, and every time it seemed to be worse than before.

What was the cause of the fever of Ptolemy? The Greeks said it was caused by black bile, and they called the depressed state of mind that came with it *melancholia*.

Anemhor was a frequent visitor. He expressed his sympathy for the Satrap, in that the ague gave him no peace. He sent sometimes the best of Egyptian medicines that were supposed to make the fever less troublesome, but he said over and over again that no man had any cure for the fevers. And so at length Anemhor, who did not himself suffer, merely observed that divine displeasure might be experienced as illness. And then he lectured the Satrap a little as to what he must do to find divine approval: *The Satrap must build more temples,* he said. *Must make more offering to the gods. Must make bigger sacrifice . . .*

The next time Anemhor showed his face the leopard spots were not blurred, for Ptolemy's fever had left him, and he saw that Anemhor carried in his arms the plaster model of a temple *pylon,* or gateway, and he asked whether Ptolemy might be pleased to make a contribution to putting up this building in the city of Apollonopolis, because the old *pylon* had fallen down in this last earthquake.

Ptolemy, weak in every limb, nodded his head.

The time after that time Anemhor carried the model of a new temple chapel for Hermopolis, City of Thoth; and then the model of his projected new underground gallery for the mummified ibises; and then the model of a complete new Temple of Horus at Apollonopolis, because the old one was crumbling.

Ptolemy agreed to help with the *pylon,* with the underground ibis galleries, vast though they were, and expensive beyond belief, and with the chapel at Hermopolis. As for the whole new Temple of Horus, he said he would think about it, consult the *Dioiketes,* his Finance Minister, for that a whole new temple was most expensive—too much money, he said, for a mere satrap.

Anemhor bowed, and the leopard spots had gone away again.

Ptolemy was, to be sure, more interested in the building programme at Alexandria, where his new Greek theatre, his new Greek *gymnasion,* his new Greek *agora,* were designed to make ever more glorious the name and House of Ptolemy son of Lagos.

Anemhor, however, persisted. He knew that, at length, if he kept asking, he must have what he wanted. He believed there was no thing that he could not make this Ptolemy do for him if he persevered. In truth, Ptolemy was not so secure in his satrapy that he could say no to the High Priest of Ptah at Memphis over and over again—this man who was the Great Chief of the Hammer, the controller of every craftsman in Egypt; the man whose boast was that he could *make Time itself run backwards;* this man who might make a satrap into a king and a pharaoh and a god in his own life time.

2.8

Crocodile Food

Although Ptolemy had now his private life arranged more or less to his liking, he still fretted over foreign affairs. To be sure, Antipatros was his ally, but to have stolen the corpse of Alexander was, really, just as good as inviting Perdikkas to invade Egypt and take the coffin back if he dared.

And Perdikkas did now march upon Egypt with his army, because he wanted to rule every thing by force, and because he wished to teach Ptolemy a lesson; but most of all it was because he desired so much the talisman that was the dead King's body, which was, as they all of them thought, lucky to whoever possessed it.

Perdikkas tramped through Syria as far as Gaza, and then through the desert, along the Roads of Horus into Egypt, moving fast in order to save water and rations, and the word of the scouts was that his army was so great that it could not be beaten in the open field.

Ptolemy, still not ready to fight any kind of battle, turned in his alarm to the High Priest of Memphis, fearful that he would have to mobilize the native Egyptian militia, about whom he knew only that they hated war, and were not much good at fighting, and were very like to turn round and run away from the enemy.

Anemhor smiled his mysterious half-smile, his infuriating smile, and said, *Nothing to worry about . . . the gods of Egypt will keep the Two*

Lands safe from disaster . . . Have faith, he said, *take more heart, increase number of sacrifice.*

Ptolemy sent thirty pair of geese to the gods, and raised the sum for temple building, and he sacrificed half a dozen oxen; but he garrisoned his border forts all the same, and equipped them with every kind of Greek missile: mechanical catapults, stone-hurlers, siege engines and the machines designed to throw boiling hot sand, hot filth and metal bolts with the name of Ptolemy scratched upon the shaft.

Perdikkas set up his camp of leather tents at the eastern edge of the Delta in sight of the border fortress of Pelousion, and passed the night in peace. However, the scouts and spies of Ptolemy used the hours of darkness to slip past the guards and offer bribes in excess of one talent for each man, so that many of Perdikkas's brave hired soldiers found themselves tempted to desert him.

Worn out by the heat, this enemy next chose to march south all night at high speed, and he pitched his tents anew opposite to the place called the Fort of Camels. At sunrise Perdikkas ordered his army to cross the River: elephants first, then shield-bearers, ladder-carriers, infantry and cavalry, meaning to take this fort for himself.

When Perdikkas was halfway across the Nile, Ptolemy and his army appeared in the distance, and with much shouting and blowing of trumpets they took up a defensive position in the fort. Undeterred, Perdikkas set up his scaling-ladders; his men swarmed up the walls like ants, and his elephant troops tore down the palisades of wood and pulled apart the parapets of mud brick.

Ptolemy himself stood on the top of the outwork, leading his men from the front as a Greek general should, and doing in all things just what Alexander would have done. He showed the greatest courage, striking out at the stream of armed men, many of whom he sent crashing down into the River. He put out the eyes of the leading elephant with his *sarissa*, slashing at the flesh of the Indian rider with total disregard for his personal safety.

When it was too dark to see what he was doing, Perdikkas gave up the siege and retired for the night, but the next evening he regathered his strength and force-marched his army south as far as Memphis. Here the River divides into two, making an island that Perdikkas saw was large enough to house his camp, and here he thought he would set up his headquarters, for it was his purpose now to launch a great attack upon Ptolemy in the plain beside the Pyramids.

Perdikkas son of Orontes was a skilled and experienced soldier, a distinguished general of Alexander, but he made now a terrible error of judgement, for there is no means of getting across the River just here other than by wading through it at a ford, as nobody could swim across while wearing his heavy armour and carrying all the gear needed for battle as well. Perdikkas, though, was suffering from the heat, and also from the usual derangement of the bowels that hinders every visitor to Egypt. Because of this, perhaps, he seemed to have forgotten all of Alexander's clever tricks, such as floating an army across a river by stuffing the leather tents full of straw, or by building a bridge of boats, or by fixing together a number of rafts. But, to give Perdikkas his due, there was no straw to be had, no wood for rafts, and he had no boats—no, not one. For want of any better idea he gave now the order to wade through the River, which was already up to the height of a man's chin, and rising fast, for it was the time of the Flooding.

The men who went first got across without trouble, but the elephants churned up so much mud on the river bed that the men who went after had difficulty finding a footing, and because of that, the rest of the men could not cross the River at all. The problem now was that the soldiers on the far bank were not strong enough by themselves to face Ptolemy in battle, and the men on the near bank could not cross to help them.

What, then, did Perdikkas do? Alas, he did the wrong thing, and it was the stupidest decision of his life time, for he changed his strategy and ordered, by shouts and signals, the men who had crossed the River to wade all the way back again.

The stronger swimmers managed to swim over, but in doing so they threw away all their gear. The weaker swimmers, non-swimmers and veterans were in deep trouble, however, and Perdikkas stood on the near bank looking at the heads of his men, hundreds and thousands of them, bobbing in the water; and when he saw what was happening, he hid his face in his hands and wept.

The poor swimmers were washed away by the current. The non-swimmers sank out of sight. Some were landed upon the wrong bank of the River, and thus delivered into the hands of Ptolemy, but one thousand men were drowned, and another thousand were unfortunate enough to become the luncheon of the crocodiles.

The army of Ptolemy, drawn up on the west bank, laughed and jeered and whooped, and sang the Paian of Victory to Apollo, for a battle won without the striking of a single blow was the best kind of victory.

Some said that the High Priest of Memphis himself had had the presence of mind to open the sluice gates of a canal farther upstream, in order to make the water flow deeper and faster, but whatever the truth was, the High Priest had good reason to smile, and the crocodile, already a most sacred beast in Egypt, found that he was worshipped and revered more than ever before.

Ptolemy fished out of the Nile what severed limbs he could find, and he gave them honourable burial, which was the duty of any Greek commander. All that night the camp of Perdikkas was loud with lamentation for the loss of so many fine men, and the rage of those who lived was loud also against the incompetence of their general. Before the sun rose the next morning the senior officers surrounded Perdikkas in his tent and stabbed him to death with their knives, and they threw his corpse into the Nile, so that this man of blood shared the same fate as his lost troops, being the crocodiles' breakfast.

When Ptolemy heard the news of the murder he showed his teeth and punched the air with his fists. At dawn he crossed the River in his satrapal barge and was carried into the camp of his enemy under heavy guard. He inspected the depleted Macedonian ranks, greeted many old friends with tears, and cursed the wickedness of the crocodile and the senseless war of friend against friend, fought only to satisfy the ambition and greed of a tyrant like Perdikkas.

Ptolemy wept the crocodile tears, then he ordered for his enemy a full Greek breakfast of porridge and sausages and bread and undiluted wine—and it was their first square meal since leaving Gaza. When they had eaten their fill, he offered to double their wages if they would fight for Egypt and himself. There was a pause while they thought, but the hands began to go up, one by one, until every man's hand was up, and then they cheered their new commander and swore everlasting loyalty to Ptolemy, and every man threw his *kausia,* or felt sun-helmet, into the air.

In this way lament turned into rejoicing, and no man rejoiced more than Ptolemy. Unlike his late enemy, Ptolemy enjoyed a reputation for generosity and fair treatment, and his heart beat high because of his great success.

As for Anemhor, High Priest of Ptah, Great Chief of the Hammer, who knew all of the past and all of the future—what did he think? He knew what nobody else knew: that no foreign army would now set foot upon Egyptian soil for one hundred and fifty years.

Anemhor did not allow himself the indulgence of showing any teeth, but kept up at all times the mysterious half-smile of the man who is Thoth in all things.

The rule of the Greek, he thought, would be good for Egypt. The coming of this foreigner was not the disaster it might have been. And so he shook the hand of the Satrap, looking him in the eye with his unblinking stare, utterly inscrutable; and Ptolemy suggested, without prompting, that he might make a further offering for the Temple of Ptah, by way of saying thank you to the gods of Egypt in general, for their help, and to Sobek, the crocodile god, in particular.

Sobek, the High Priest said, *he is the policeman of the River. If he eats a man up, it is only what he richly deserves. Sobek will never eat those who do not deserve death anyway. A good man has nothing to fear from the crocodile.*

Yes, Ptolemy made great gifts now to the smiling crocodile god, whose eyes glittered always.

2.9

Birth of the Thunderbolt

In the exhilaration of victory Ptolemy the husband turned his thoughts to begetting an heir, for although Lagos, his eldest son, was a fine son, it was his father's thought that the son of Thaïs of Athens should not be Satrap of Egypt after him. A base-born boy could not succeed him.

He looked at the works, then, of Aristotle, seeking what was the right season. He asked his soothsayers about what were the most favourable weather conditions. He asked about the Egyptian Calendar of Lucky and Unlucky Days.

He gave orders for Eurydike his wife to eat roast veal; he made himself eat the rocket-leaf aphrodisiac, and he tied up his left-hand testicle with the papyrus string after the custom of the Greeks, in order that he might beget a male child, and set to work.

It was as near to winter as Egypt ever gets: the wind was in the north, and every omen, from the flight of the lapwings to the alignment of the red planet in the heavens, was favourable, most favourable, or at least, Ptolemy had been led to think so.

The pregnant Eurydike passed her nine months of anxious waiting in sending offerings to the shrine of the deified Helen of Troy at Pella, in Macedon, for it was in her thoughts to make sure the child in her womb was blessed by the goddess of Good Looks.

For reasons of safety Eurydike placed herself under the guardian-ship of Maiden Artemis, goddess of the Hunt, goddess of the Moon, the Lady of Wild Things, who was the patroness also of young lovers, and she sat day after day staring at the statue of Artemis that stood in the corner of her bedchamber.

Eurydike took care to do every thing that was right, according to the advice of Aunt Berenike. She ate once a month the testicles of a cock-erel, so that her child might be a male child. She avoided lifting heavy weights. She did not run or jump. She rubbed her flesh with ibis oil and goose grease to prevent miscarriage; she employed Berenike to anoint the parts of her back that she could not reach herself, and she chattered about the perfect, perfect son that kicked and kicked within her belly.

In the eighth month, thought to be the most dangerous time, she lay in her bed, waited on by black eunuchs, who brought all the foods she craved: black olives, raisins, prunes, dates—all the black fruits. And she kept by her a supply of black earth in a gazelle-skin bag, and every so often she put a little of it into her mouth.

The child of Eurydike was indeed a boy, a most handsome boy, who could not be called by any other name than Ptolemaios. He was born, though, feet first, upon the most unlucky day in the calendar, and in the middle of a thunderstorm, and even Eurydike knew that these were the worst of omens. The new Ptolemy got his nickname at once, for they called him Keraunos, Thunderbolt, saying that it was lucky for a birth to be marked by the activity of Zeus. And yes, it was a name that was fit-ting, most fitting, for this boy, for it signified the power of Zeus.

For yes, yes, the Satrap had made up his mind, of course, to rear this son, in spite of the bad omens, for there was really no question of expos-ing, after the manner of the Greeks, a legitimate son. Ptolemy took no notice of the fact that the eyes of this son were a little too close together. He ignored, for the moment, the undoubted fact that a boy born feet first must live an unillustrious and calamitous life, and he was delighted by this son of his but for one thing: that Ptolemy Keraunos did not have the yellow hair of his father, nor yet the yellow hair of his mother, but the dark hair of a stranger.

How could two fair-haired parents produce a dark-haired son? It was a mystery to everybody but Berenike, who knew from of old that Eurydike was an earth-eater, and that the black diet must influence the colour of a child's hair, but she had said nothing, nothing. So had Berenike designed this outcome? Was this dark child the result of Berenike's meddling? Some, in later days, suspected that it must be so.

After the birth Eurydike underwent the proper Greek rituals of purification. She bathed herself in seawater brought from Alexandria. She had herself drenched with the blood of a piglet. And the Residence of the Satrap was fumigated from top to bottom by burning incense and sulphur.

Before Ptolemy Keraunos, the Thunderbolt, was one month old, the Satrap asked the High Priest of Memphis to have this child's horoscope drawn up, according to the observations of the Egyptian watchers of the stars, for he wished, like any other Greek, more than any other thing, to know what would be the future.

But the horoscope of Ptolemy Keraunos was so bad that Anemhor did not dare to tell the Satrap the truth of it: that this boy was born not just unlucky but three times unlucky; that he would die an untimely death in a foreign land; and that it was his undoubted fate to be dogs' meat.

The bad luck of Ptolemy the Thunderbolt began at once, for the mother did not wish so much as to touch this child of hers. Eurydike declined the discomfort of feeding him at her own breast and handed him over to the wet nurse, a Greek woman chosen for her good character, and for the fine quality of her milk, which both Ptolemy and Eurydike approved of, for they tasted it themselves.

Keraunos was then strapped to a board, with each leg and each arm bandaged after the custom of the Greeks, and his head and body also; and the bandages were tight, so that he should grow up with straight limbs. The parents then passed the next sixty days listening, not listening, to his distant howling, and the result of it was that he grew up *angry.*

This nurse was made to put her mark to a two-year contract of wet-nursing, and to speak aloud the terms of it: *I swear to give Ptolemy milk from both the breasts. I swear that I shall not drink wine. I swear that I shall not take this child into my own bed* . . .

Keraunos was denied nothing. When he cried, the nurse picked him up. When he was hungry she pushed her *tithos* into his mouth. In all things she let this child do as he pleased, for he was a satrap's son and heir. She did not teach him the difference between what was Right and what was Wrong. She did not teach this boy one thing about what he ought and what he ought not to do. And the result of it was that they murmured, in after years, that Ptolemy Keraunos had his manners spoiled for him by this nurse of his.

From the prison of his bandages the cries of this infant sounded like nothing so much as the creaking of pine trees, which was a strange thing, for there were no pine trees at Memphis, not one, just the palm trees of Egypt that clacked in the sweet breath of the north wind, or were bent double under the storm of sand that whirled in from the desert.

The nurse, however, knew better. *He has the pines of Greece in his blood,* she murmured, *and will grow up to be savage, and a great warrior,* and as if to prove she was right, this child began to bite her, so that she cried out herself.

As Keraunos grew bigger, he began to bite hard, and she would pinch him to make him stop; but as she pinched, he bit all the harder.

As he grew bigger still, Keraunos did worse things than biting, that the nurse complained of to the Satrap, but the Satrap merely smiled, and did nothing. He had all the affairs of Egypt upon his head, and he had no time for family troubles. To be warlike was, in any case, how a Ptolemy was meant to be, and he would have this son of his no other way. He did not wish Keraunos to grow up wanting to try on his mother's clothes. He did not wish Keraunos to turn into another Alexander, but he must be a proper man, interested in war, in siege-craft, in swordplay, in violence, for Ptolemy would never forget Alexander's slobbering over the dead Hephaistion, an exhibition that was a disgrace to Macedon.

To be sure, the nurse wanted Keraunos to be warlike also, and when his lip started to crumple and he looked like to cry, this Greek nurse would shake her charge and tell him: *Herakles never wept.* And Keraunos would sniff, and control his emotions, and his lip stayed firm. He was from a young age very keen to be like Herakles, a warrior and a hero. He was keen to be as great a general as Alexander. From his earliest years he wanted also to be Satrap of Egypt, like his illustrious and most illustrious father.

For two thousand one hundred and ninety days and nights Ptolemy Keraunos sucked the tainted and impure milk of his drunken nurse, and he drank in, they said, her bad character with her milk, and the parents found out only when it was too late.

A whore, Ptolemy said, when they found her kissing the Captain of the Residence Guard. *No better,* he said, *than the sow that rolled upon her piglets,* for they found her squashing him as she slept, and they found also her private supply of wine, and *booza,* the beer of the Egyptians.

Eurydike, who knew nothing about how to rear children, seldom set her foot in that part of the *gynaikeion* set aside for the rearing of the children, and Ptolemy—he kept always to the men's side of the Residence.

So they threw the nurse out of Memphis, without paying her the one hundred and sixty drachmas of gold or the thirty-two *kotylai* of oil that they owed her.

To speak true, it felt good, some times, very good, to blame some person other than themselves.

Swift Rumour said that the rejected nurse left Egypt screaming with rage, and that she cursed this child and all his House, down to the twelfth generation. True or false, some would say that the family of Ptolemy looked very like a family that lived under the most terrible of curses. Others saw things different, and said that the House of Ptolemy was blessed by the gods of Greece with every goodly thing, and that wealth and power were the only things that mattered. But, to be sure, in the long run of things, what the House of Ptolemy would lack was happiness. Yes, indeed, it would look like they had been cursed for the rest of time with the curse of Unhappiness, but for the moment—they knew nothing of it.

Ptolemy Keraunos, as soon as he could stand up, began to break things: drinking-cups, earthenware jars, chairs of ebony and ivory, Egyptian things that his parents did not value highly, so that they did not take steps to stop him. He broke things not, perhaps, on purpose, at first, but nobody could say that this boy did not delight in the noise of glass being dropped upon a mosaic floor, or that to smash a bowl did not give him pleasure.

Indeed, Keraunos would grow up to be so very violent that some would think he was almost the Living Image of Seth, the Egyptian god who is the embodiment of disorder and chaos.

As soon as he could run, Keraunos began to charge about the Residence like a miniature centaur, and his father's friends smiled upon him, for that he must succeed Ptolemy as Satrap. Keraunos began to kill things: flies and beetles at first, then scorpions, and the giant orange cockroaches that found their way into the Residence. Some praised Keraunos for ridding the house of unwanted creatures that did much harm, but as he grew older, the size of his victims grew accordingly. When Keraunos strangled one of the Residence cats, his father beat him, hissing that if a single Egyptian heard what he had done there would be revolution in the Two Lands, for the cat of the Egyptians was sacred above all other beasts.

Keraunos was, to be sure, old enough to shrug his shoulders, but he did not understand the meaning of Wrong. Nobody had bothered to teach him that the cat was sacred. He had been brought up by Greeks and Greeks only, learning about Greek customs and Greek gods, and Egyptian things had not been allowed to enter his thoughts.

In this way the seeds of trouble were sown, and Ptolemy Keraunos would go on just as he had begun, except that, as time passed, he would become worse. The Satrap had no moment to spare for his children, unless some great misdemeanour came to his ears, when he would chastise, or beat, or pace up and down the mosaic floor and raise his voice, so that Ptolemy the son came to identify Ptolemy the father with punishment. The kinder side of the Satrap this boy seldom saw, so that there was, in truth, from the start, a distance between the Satrap and Keraunos that could grow only larger. After his education began in earnest, at the age of thirteen, Keraunos would see his father only when he had done some wrong thing, and was in trouble. His father always said to him, *Do your best to be a good boy, and pray to the gods for good fortune.*

But Keraunos did not want to be good. He thought prayers were a waste of time.

Those who knew Ptolemy the Thunderbolt better than did his father would look at this boy and shake their heads, saying that he would go far in wickedness.

And Yes, it was what the horoscopists had forecast at his birth, and the horoscopists would be proved right in their every prophecy.

As for Eurydike, his mother, she knew the Satrap hardly any better, because he lived all the days of his life in the Hall of Audiences, talking to his ministers, or with Anemhor, or reading the dispatches of his foreign agents. He would dine or feast with his generals and admirals, always apart from Eurydike, whose place was the *gynaikeion,* with her waiting-women, and he slept, when he did sleep, in the *andron,* the men's part of the Residence, or with one of his numerous concubines. Ptolemy was too much occupied with the running of his satrapy to give much thought to the needs of his wife.

Eurydike he visited for the ploughing of children only, as if she were nothing but a machine for ploughing. And while he was not unkind, he was a Greek, and behaved as a Greek, and treated his wife like a Greek wife: no word escaped his lips, only the grunts and sighs that went with the ploughing. No, a Greek does not expect to love his wife, or to address her with words of sweetness as the Egyptian does. Ptolemy some times remembered to call his wife Pigeon or Dove, but he was a soldier, used to spending his days with the men. His thoughts and con-versations were of weaponry and siege warfare, of ships of war, of the supply of corn, of the balance of power and the balance of payments, and the military strengths and weaknesses of the other Successors—things of which Eurydike knew nothing whatever.

In truth, Ptolemy had few words to speak to any woman, and in her turn Eurydike did not know what to say to her man. When necessity demanded that they have speech, Ptolemy would send a messenger, and because Eurydike had not the skills of reading and writing, Berenike would tell her what Ptolemy said. In return Eurydike would send a message back with this Berenike, who thus began to have more contact with the Satrap than did his wife.

In the *gynaikeion* Eurydike did not throw herself into the women's work of spindle and loom, although she was more than capable of the finest tapestries, and had been raised to see the needle as her whole life. No, she was the wife of a satrap now, and she thought herself above needlework. It was her waiting-women, led by Berenike, who worked the loom and spun thread, and wove wool and sewed garments, and the mistress of the house did nothing but watch, and criticize. No, Eury-dike had not so much as been taught the *alpha beta*. She could not pass the time in reading. She knew only the hard labour of doing nothing, and her hands were empty, twitching, and she did not know what to do with them. She lived a life of enforced idleness that was self-imposed, by reason of her pride.

To be sure, Eurydike did not lack charms, but she would flinch when her husband touched her flesh. Ptolemy was pleased by the half-smile that she would some times wear. He was pleased by her modest glance and lowered eyes, eyes that were like black olives, glistening; but to tell the truth, this husband and wife had nothing to say to one another. No, not one word.

It happened that the eldest son of Eskedi, son of Old Anemhor, and Neferrenpet, his wife, was born at about the same time as Ptolemy Ker-aunos, and there was great rejoicing in Memphis, for the child was the first grandchild of Old Anemhor.

When this son was born the women held him upside down by his ankles, which was the custom, and they spoke the wise women's words about his fate:

> If he cries ni, he will live;
> If he cries ba, he will die.

This child cried *ni,* and did not die, but sucked at his mother's breast, and grew in stature every day; and there was no question of this son of Neferrenpet being handed to a wet nurse, but the mother fed her son herself, like any other Egyptian mother.

This son of theirs they called by several different names. Some times they called him Nesqed, some times Nesisty, some times Esisout, but the name they used most often was Padibastet.

Padibastet he was, and he did not stop crying *ni,* and when the father cast the horoscope of his son he learned that it was his fate to live for sixty-six years, four months, and five days.

It was long enough, he thought. It was a good life. It would neither be too long nor too short.

2.10

Half a Million Ibises

Ptolemy asked very many questions of the Egyptians and, in time, the governance of Egypt seemed to him, yes, to be under his control. He had his men of wisdom in every department of governing—for River business, for city business, for foreign business, and also, of course, for the business of war.

When Ptolemy questioned his Egyptian advisers, the high priests, about the fleet, he asked, *How many ships of war? How many sailors?* And he saw before him then a sea of blank faces, as if the high priests of Egypt had no answer to questions like these questions.

Ptolemy asked again, louder, saying, *How many vessels?* Perhaps, he thought, he had been misunderstood, mistranslated. But no, the Egyptians sat silent all round him. Ptolemy heard the chattering of the baboons, the twittering of caged birds, the screeching of the *psittakoi* he had brought from India.

At last the High Priest of Heliopolis said to him, *Excellency, there is no fleet. There are no ships of war. There is no tradition of battle at sea . . .*

Ptolemy scratched his head under his *kausia.*

We are bad sailors, the High Priest said. *The Egyptians hate the sea,* he said. *We have no sea god, no equivalent for your Poseidon.* And he told Ptolemy the truth: that the Egyptian likes better to stay at home with his wife and children, with the beasts of the field, having no need to go abroad, except for trading.

The Egyptians are River sailors, Excellency, said the High Priest. *Really, the Great Sea—we do not like to sail upon it . . .*

Ptolemy frowned, at a loss for words, and then he spoke of other matters, and he sent for the Greek admirals, and the Greek builders of ships of war, with orders to *come running.*

For some time afterwards the lack of Egyptian ships of war was the cause of much jesting, and for Ptolemy to say *Send the fleet* came to mean *Do nothing.* In the Residence at Memphis Ptolemy and his Greek friends would laugh aloud whenever a man spoke of Egyptian ships of war.

Ptolemy himself did not do nothing upon this matter. He had inherited the better part of the fleet of Alexander, and he made for Egypt a fleet where before there had been none. He would fight Egypt's every battle for her. He would push forward the boundaries of Egypt in every direction. He would defend the sea coast of Egypt with the savagery even of Sakhmet, the lioness goddess. Ptolemy swore that it would be so.

Truly, there was no goodly thing that Ptolemy did not promise to do on behalf of Egypt. Truly, this Ptolemy would be the great friend of Egypt.

This fleet of Ptolemy was, to be sure, just then of the highest importance and urgency, for his great enemy, Antigonos Monophthalmos, had a first-class knowledge of seafaring, and his son, Demetrios Poliorketes, the Besieger of Cities, was a brilliant master of the sea, without compare in his design of ships of war of the most modern kind. These two, father and son, had set out to match the ships of Ptolemy, and outdo him. Now it was that the great race began to build ever bigger and better ships, giant galleys of war with three banks of oars, some twin-hulled, but ever longer and longer, and with ever larger crews, until some of these ships needed upwards of one thousand men to sail them.

Aye, it was not long after Ptolemy came to Memphis that One-Eye launched his *hepteres,* a seven, which was a reference to length, not to the number of banks of oars, for to be sure a ship with seven banks of oars, one above the other, would be impossible to row anywhere.

In the next ten years Demetrios the son would build an *okteres,* an eight, as well as the *enneres,* the *dekkeres,* and the *hendekeres*—the nine, ten, and eleven; and he would add a *triskaidekeres,* a thirteen, to his fleet before long—ships so very large that they were only with difficulty manoeuvred in the water; but in spite of being slow they had great power, with a heavy iron-clad ram in the bows that was of the greatest use in smashing another ship to bits.

From time to time Old Anemhor would urge Ptolemy to make the journey up-River, in order to see the progress of the temple-building that he had agreed to help finance out of the tax revenues, and to look also at what further might be done.

Ptolemy disliked the heat up-River, and the thought of hostilities and disease, but he went, in one of his smaller oared ships, and with him went a detachment of soldiers, enough to protect him from any uprising, but not so many as to make uneasy the native population.

At Krokodilopolis he made the proper offerings to Sobek, the crocodile god. At Herakleopolis he made sacrifice to Herakles. At Kynopolis he made offerings to the Dog, Anubis of the Egyptians, and he sailed onward, and the heat grew more intense.

At Hermopolis he saw that the ibis flapped and perched everywhere in the city, scavenging in the butchers' shops, preferring offal and carrion, and leaving his mark upon every street. The ibis some condemned as a foul, disgusting bird, that lives upon filth, that loves filth, and pokes his beak into everything, no matter how repulsive. But the ibis is Thoth, and the embodiment of Thoth, a sacred bird, the cleaner of the streets, the eater of snakes, and the ibis received the offerings of Ptolemy.

Anemhor told him, *These embalmed birds, they are capable of transmitting the prayers of the pious pilgrims who have brought them, who wish to petition the god Thoth, or offer him thanks for favours already granted.*

Ptolemy could not but make the face of disgust.

The bird, Anemhor said, *provides direct access to the god.*

Aye, he asked about the ibis, that they bred in the Lake of Pharaoh at Hermopolis, and along the city dyke that was sacred to Thoth, god of the scribes, the god of Wisdom. He asked about the ibis: *How many?* And he asked, *Why do they murder them?*

And the High Priest of Thoth, whose title is the Great One of the Five, said unto him: *Twenty-nine ibises each day; two hundred and ninety ibises each week; eight hundred and seventy ibises each month; ten thousand four hundred and forty ibises mummified in one year.*

So that Ptolemy said, *Many ibises.* And he said, *But why?*

Offering to Thoth, the High Priest said, *Thoth, the Great God.*

In the entire time of this Ptolemy in Egypt, until his death, some five hundred thousand ibises would be strangled, or drowned, disembowelled, and embalmed, wrapped in millions of *stades* of bandages of the finest linen, and stacked in earthenware pots in the underground ibis galleries of Hermopolis—City of Hermes, City of Thoth—that stretched for hundreds of *stades* beneath the desert.

Ptolemy learned much about the ibis upon his visit to Hermopolis: he learned that the intestines of one single ibis, if stretched out, would measure ninety-six cubits long.

Kataplektikos, he said, Amazing, and he smelled the smell, the nauseous stench of decayed birds, and he was sick in his stomach seven days.

He sailed onward, to Lykopolis, Wolf City, and to Koptos, City of Min, or Pan of the Greeks, and to Diospolis, the Egyptian Thebes, that was the City of Amun, and to Hierakonpolis, City of the Falcon, Horus.

At Apollonopolis they told him it was the custom for every citizen to eat of the flesh of the crocodile, and even Ptolemy ate crocodile steak in the City of Apollo, god of Happy Landings, and he sacrificed to Apollo, who knows the count of the sand grains and the measure of the sea—to Apollo, who of his divine knowledge will tell a man, when he is unsure, when he is anxious, what to do; Apollo, the god who knows the rules of the complicated game that the gods of Greece play with men; Apollo, the supreme *alexikakos,* or averter of evil.

For no, no Greek could do without believing in the oracles of Apollo, not even the Satrap Ptolemaios, and he consulted the god here, and ate crocodile to excess, and was sick in his stomach ten days.

He sailed onwards, visiting the thirteen fortresses that lie between Elephantine and Semna at the southern end of the Second Cataract— the Downcrash, as the Greeks called it—fortresses with names such as Repelling the Tribes, and Curbing the Deserts, vast structures with thick mud-brick walls.

Ptolemy made the tour even of the Gold-Bearing Country, sailing up-River past the date palms, past the mimosas, the broad-leaved banana trees, the oleanders and lemon trees, in the shade of which scuttled golden beetles that are the embodiment of the god Khepera, the Beetle of Ra. And in the intense heat he was ill.

He looked upon the island of Philai, where the priests of Egypt had great plans for new temples, many many temples, but where, just then, there was almost no building. Ptolemy looked, and he thought of the cost, and said, *Later, later.* And then he came down-River in short stages, stopping to visit the temples of the Egyptians, every one of them built in yellow stone, every one of them covered with bright-coloured paintings of the gods of Egypt, and wherever he stopped he was allowed to look at little more than the outside walls, to set his sandal no farther than the First Pylon, the First Courtyard, and then he must stop, where he was invited by the High Priest to make his offering of many drachmas, which he did, so that his ship returned lighter than it had set out. In every thing he must do what had always been done, they told him. He must follow the custom, the tradition, for everything in Egypt must continue just as it had always been. It must be as if there had been no change.

Ptolemy learned, yes, that the total journey time of the whole length of Egypt was fourteen days by River, without stops, and that from the Great Sea, the Inner Sea, the Sea of Osiris to Thebes was three thousand six hundred and ninety-six stades exactly. Always Ptolemy learned some new thing, but he was never allowed to learn every thing. In this way the high priests sought to keep this man, Satrap though he was, under their own command.

2.11

Fake Gods and Lucky Snakes

Back home at Memphis Ptolemy sought the coolness of the store-rooms of his Residence, where, among the lumber of the Pharaohs he came upon the great *sarkophagos* of pink granite from Syene, and Old Anemhor told him that this had indeed been made ready for that Nakhthoreb whom the Greeks called Nektanebo the Second, the last Pharaoh of the Egyptians, who had been ousted by the hated Persian. But Nektanebo had not been buried in his *sarkophagos*, because he had not died in Egypt, but had fled the country, or been allowed to flee.

Ptolemy asked Anemhor, then, *Where is this Nektanebo now?*

The High Priest spread his hands. It was one of his questions that have no answer.

He is dead? He is alive? Ptolemy asked, wondering when this man might reappear, whether he might yet become his enemy—yet another enemy—and whether Anemhor was working for him to be reinstated.

The High Priest pursed his lips and looked long into the eyes of Ptolemy. He both knew and did not know where was this King of Egypt, who might one day return to sit upon the throne of his ancestors once more.

Such a sarkophagos, Ptolemy murmured, *it would suit Alexander. The coffin of a Pharaoh would indeed serve, as a temporary measure* . . .

And Anemhor found that he could not think of one reason why Ptolemy should not lay his friend to rest in this box of stone; so they put the golden coffin of Alexander inside it.

Thoth that knows the future knows that thousands of years later this same pink granite *sarkophagos* would be used as a drinking trough for beasts of burden, all covered in hieroglyphs as it was, the sacred writings that should have preserved Alexander from all evil in the Afterlife. But where was Alexander? Aye, the *sarkophagos* would indeed *eat the flesh* of the king that lay inside it, a coffin meant for another king altogether.

So often the thought of this Ptolemy was: *Nothing lasts . . . Live for the day.* Even the corpse of Alexander, which was the lucky talisman of the city that bore his name—they would lose it.

In those days Alexander *had* been lucky, a man blessed by Tykhe, goddess of Luck, so lucky that every Greek wore the image of the dead man pinned to his cloak, and touched it for Luck, tens and hundreds of times every day, for the Greeks were obsessed by Luck at that time, having begun to forget their old gods, or, at least, to think of them as of less account.

The Greek suspected that the gods of Olympos did not listen to him; that the gods were tired of helping men, and were really of not much use. The Greeks were pleased to turn a man, a hero such as Alexander, into a god.

Every year, year after year, Ptolemy kept the birthday of the dead, or not quite dead, Alexander, marching in solemn procession with the Greeks to the tomb on the desert edge, with the eponymous Priest of Alexander, and the *Kanephoroi,* or Basket-Bearers, and the proper offerings of honey, and milk, and undiluted wine.

In spite of some men's doubts about the gods of Olympos, Ptolemy made outward show of piety. In all his concern to keep happy the priests of Egypt he did not quite forget the religion of the Greeks.

When time allowed he gave his attention to the design of the Heröon at Alexandria, in loving memory of the dead Hephaistion son of Amyntor, whom the Oracle had forbidden to be worshipped as a god (for there were limits) but allowed to be worshipped as a hero.

The statue of Hephaistion he at length set up in the *agora,* and Hephaistion was, of course, naked, more youthful than his actual age at death, and somewhat androgynous; and he stood beside the gilded statue of Alexander, unclad also. Between them stood the golden statue of Tykhe, who had withheld from these two men the Luck of long life, but granted instead the favour of undying fame.

The Greek thought it was better to live a short life full of glory than to put up with a miserable old age. Those who died young stayed young for ever, had attained everlasting youthfulness.

Ptolemy had given his word. In spite of his distaste for Hephaistion, he put up the statue all the same. He did not, to be sure, encourage the cult of Hephaistion much, and yet the number of visitors to his shrine remained steady, and then grew—as if he was, after all, some kind of new god. Hephaistion would not be forgotten in Alexandria, not yet.

To the immortal memory of Alexander, Ptolemy was more faithful. He made his regular visits to the corpse, had the stone lid dragged off the *sarkophagos* and the top taken off the golden coffin, and he looked hard at the length of the dead man's hair, and the state of the nails of his fingers. He poured again and again the milk and the honey, food and drink for the dead man's soul in the Afterlife of the Greeks; or food for the living, lest he should wake during the night.

Ptolemy behaved towards this man as if he were still alive, half afraid that whatever he did in Egypt might be subject to his scrutiny when he returned to the land of the living. And in his moments of crisis Ptolemy asked himself always *What would Alexander have done?* The answer was always the same answer: Alexander would have shown anger, violence, his usual savagery. He would have taken lives first and asked questions later. He would have shown no mercy.

Always he tried to be like Alexander, but he showed also his kindness, his gentleness. He was no tyrant, but a man with feelings, who woke every day at dawn, the hour of burying the dead, with his face wet with tears, thinking of his dead comrades: the men that had fallen at Gaugamela, the men left to die in the desert, to whom he had not said *Fare thee well, even in the House of Hades*.

In Egypt they did not stop being Greeks just because they lived in a foreign country. By no means. They brought their Greekness with them, kept it alive, and Alexandria, the new city, would be more Greek than Greece.

Nevertheless, Ptolemy began to think that a different god might be a fine thing, an extra god, who would be good to Greeks and Egyptians alike; who might bring the two peoples together, and stop riots and revolts and stone-throwing. He wanted Egypt to be one nation, not two endlessly hostile nations: for there were times when the Egyptians—even the peaceable Egyptians—threw stones at the Greeks.

To break down hostility Ptolemy had the thought of inventing a fresh god, out of the bits and pieces of other gods: half Osiris and half Zeus, perhaps. A saviour god, perhaps. A healing god, a god for trusting, for every man to believe in, because, for once, this would be a god who did not have an animal head, but would be all human, a real man as well as a real god.

He took advice. He asked the opinion of the High Priest of Ptah, and his thought found favour with Anemhor, for the new god would be very like the Osorapis of the Egyptians.

They called the new god Sarapis, and the Egyptians called him Osorapis, and he looked very like the Zeus of the Greeks, for he had a full beard, and yet the Egyptians might recognize their Osiris in him.

In the end they forgot whose idea Sarapis was, even saying, some of them, that Sarapis had been Alexander's idea. But most men said that he was the thought of Ptolemy, working in league with the High Priest of Sebennytos, Manetho, and with the Greek called Hekataios of Abdera, and that between them they had thought up this kindly god with a beard, who wore upon his head the *modios,* the tall cylindrical basket that was the corn measure of Egypt.

Ptolemy ordered then the giant chryselephantine statue, the statue all of ivory and gold, from Bryaxis, the most famous of Greek sculptors, and he gave his precise instructions: that the eyes of Sarapis must be costly stones that would glitter in the darkness of his shrine, the great new temple that he planned for Rhakotis, the native quarter of Alexandria, to be built upon an artificial hill, so that Sarapis's temple might be seen from afar, like the Parthenon at Athens.

Sarapis, then, was a fake god who lived upon a fake hill—a hybrid god. Would the people believe in Sarapis? Ptolemy wondered. He rather thought they would, because Sarapis was a fine invention, as good as Zeus, as good as Osiris, if not better, because he was under human control. Whether they believed or not, at first the Greeks flocked to the Sarapieion at Alexandria, and to his temple at Memphis also: the sick, the chronically ill, the disappointed in love, the dying, the barren women, the lunatics, cripples, and even the impostors, who showed off their stumps and suppurating wounds; and in return for a small payment Sarapis was meant to cure them all.

The practice was encouraged of sleeping all night in the Sarapieion when the god was supposed to show himself in a vision, and to prescribe in a dream the course of treatment that must be followed, and in one or two cases the cure was complete by morning—so long as the god was gracious enough to lean his ear to the petitioner; so long as the petitioner had faith.

Ptolemy smiled, because his false god seemed almost too good to be true.

Sarapis seemed to be a success at Alexandria, where he was treated like a Greek god, and had a Greek priesthood. His temple was a Greek temple, with Corinthian columns and a pedimented roof.

Outside Alexandria Sarapis was not so popular. The Egyptian had already two thousand gods. Really, he had no need for more. But outside of Egypt Sarapis did better, and they made excuses for his indifferent reception in Egypt, saying that he was meant for export more than for home use, and that he was the patron god and ambassador for the whole of Ptolemy's empire. And Sarapis was indeed the god of foreign traders—hence the corn basket upon his head—and the great guardian of all sailors.

Ptolemy looked about and looked about, to see what other gods he might think up, and then, behold, more important even than Sarapis, almost, there was the cult of the little female house snake, which the Greeks called *Agathos Daimon,* the Good Spirit, the Lucky Spirit, and Ptolemy had found a second fresh deity, whose purpose was to keep the city of Alexandria safe from every danger.

Ptolemy, he smiled some more.

Agathos Daimon made her appearance, then, in mosaics and carvings, coiled around poppy flowers, or entwined about the club of Herakles, or wrapped around the trunk of the palm tree. But most often she was shown twining herself round the *kerukeion,* or wand of Hermes, the Thoth of the Greeks, Lord of Books and Prince of Scribes.

The Lucky Snake of Alexandria haunted every house, every street. Since the Alexandrians could not rid themselves of her presence it was just as well they turned her into a goddess, but once this was done, nobody wanted her to go away, for the little snake guaranteed the prosperity of the metropolis and every person who lived in it. Agathos Daimon was a snake, moreover, who did no harm. She was the snake of all snakes, because, wondrous to report, she was not poisonous and never bit anybody.

Alexandria loved Agathos Daimon, at length. She caught Alexandria's imagination to such an extent that they built for her a temple all of her own, and gave her priestesses. Better still, the Lucky Snake corresponded with the Egyptian Shai, or god of Fate, who also was snake-shaped.

The little snakes they called Thermouthis, and thought of them as messengers of Isis, the great goddess of the Egyptians, and Thermouthis was Isis herself, deserving the greatest honour and worship, for she was the *Lucky* Snake of Alexandria.

In these ways Egypt and Greece at last intertwined in certain matters of ritual, rather like the snake and the stick, the one wrapped round the other.

Whether it was the truth or not, they *thought* that Alexandria was the Lucky City, and the famous Luck of Alexandria drew more Greeks than ever to live there, seeking always the riches that Zeus would pour down upon a Greek man's head if only he would go to Egypt, where even the dust in the streets looked like gold.

Alexandria got, then, her population. Ptolemy lived at Memphis a little longer, beset by troubles; by wars and swift rumours of wars.

2.12

The Syrian War

From Triparadeisos, in Upper Syria, there came rumours that the other Eurydike, Adeia-Eurydike, the wife and queen of Philip Arrhidaios, had been pleased to meddle in affairs of state, and that she was working much mischief against the best efforts of the Guardians, who had taken the place of the late Perdikkas in charge of the remains of Alexander's empire. Worse, the Macedonians seemed to be taking orders from Adeia-Eurydike, and it grew so bad that the Guardians even resigned because of her, and the Macedonians elected Old Antipatros as Guardian instead, with full powers.

When Antipatros arrived at Triparadeisos he found that Adeia-Eurydike was indeed trying to stir up trouble and turn the Macedonians against him as well, and the result of it all was a great disorder and unrest in the army.

Antipatros called a general assembly and he put a stop to the tumult of shouting by speaking to the crowd, and by thoroughly frightening Adeia-Eurydike, who was still not yet twenty years old.

He told this girl to keep her mouth shut, to keep quiet, to leave matters of business to the men, and to stop poking her nose into things she did not understand, and he went on and on criticizing her until she burst into tears and fled from the meeting.

Then Antipatros distributed the satrapies all over again, the details of which Thoth will leave out, as of lesser importance. Sufficient to say that to Ptolemy was confirmed what was already his, for it was by this time anyway impossible to dislodge him from Egypt, which he held by virtue of his own prowess, as if it were a prize of war.

Four years after the death of Alexander, in the heat of summer, Old Antipatros lay sweating upon his own deathbed. He was eighty-eight years old, and he remembered above all other things his bitter struggle with Olympias, mother of Alexander, when she had held the *prostasia,* and also his struggle with the headstrong Adeia-Eurydike, and he gave his last words of advice to the Macedonians for the future, the prophetic last words of a dying man, and what he said was: *You must never allow a woman to take the first place in the kingdom.* For it was his thought that government is really no business for women.

And did they take his advice, these Macedonians? Thoth asks it. Did they heed these words in Egypt? Did they? They did not.

In that same year of the death of Antipatros his father-in-law, Ptolemy marched his army out of Egypt along the Roads of Horus, across the desert to Gaza, and invaded Syria from Lebanon southwards, the region that was called *Koile*-Syria, or Hollow Syria, because it was nothing but one great valley.

Having defeated Perdikkas, Ptolemy saw Egypt as his by right, but he worried still about the security of Egypt's borders. Indeed, he could see that Phoenicia and Koile-Syria were very like to launch an all-out attack upon him, and it was his thought now to invade Syria before Syria invaded him.

Some while before this, he had tried to *buy* Koile-Syria from its Greek governor, Laomedon of Amphipolis, by offering him as much gold as he cared to mention. But Laomedon sent his messenger to tell Ptolemy that Syria was *not for sale,* and that as he did not own it himself, he was not in a position to sell.

Unable to buy, then, and unwilling to wait any longer, Ptolemy resorted to theft, and sought to steal Syria for himself. He was, after all, a Greek, and thieving was what a Greek was expected to do. So he gave the order for Nikanor, one of his finest generals, to march upon Phoenicia.

General Nikanor hurried from Pelousion direct to Gaza, with the fleet sailing alongside, as usual, with water and rations. From Gaza he marched north to Tyros, and then on to Sidon, and still farther north. He took the Satrap Laomedon prisoner, and put down the region he had orders to put down, and installed Egyptian garrisons in the cities of Phoenicia and secured their allegiance to Ptolemy.

Nikanor's short campaign was a famous success, and he marched his troops home singing the Paian of Victory to Apollo, the great god, and the city of Memphis went wild in welcome, in spite of the fact that his army was a Greek army and his victory strictly a Greek victory, but the rejoicing was on account of the preservation and enlargement of the borders of Egypt.

Ptolemy held banquet after banquet at which the honoured guest was General Nikanor, who was given every possible reward, such as free seats in the theatre for life, vast tracts of land in Upper Egypt, the purple cloak of the First Friends of Ptolemy; and the sacrifice of jet-black bulls to the gods of Greece went on for many days.

Within five years of Ptolemy taking charge of Egypt and helping himself to the territory of Kyrene in the west, a revolt blew up there against his authority. The good people of Kyrene, the city, attacked the citadel and were on the point of ousting the garrison of Ptolemy, when envoys from Alexandria ordered them to stop.

What did the people of Kyrene do? They answered by putting the envoys to death, and they continued to attack the citadel with renewed vigour.

Hearing what had happened, Ptolemy showed anger, as Alexander would have done, and he sent another of his generals, Agis, with a land army supported by a fleet of ships of war under the command of Epainetos, to crush the revolt.

General Agis took Kyrene by storm, bound the rebels hand and foot, and sent them to Memphis for punishment. And Ptolemy did punish them, by crucifying their bodies upon the beaches of Alexandria, just as Alexander had punished those who defied him at the Siege of Tyros.

Memphis, then, was not defiled by bloodshed, Kyrene was restored to Ptolemy's governance and peace broke out once more.

It was about this time that the famous Seleukos fled from Babylon to Egypt and took refuge with Ptolemy, for he knew of the kindness of this man's heart (crucifixions notwithstanding) and of his friendly treatment of all those who sought asylum in his capital of Memphis.

Seleukos proved most useful to Ptolemy, who put him in command of the Egyptian fleet, and he became a particular friend of Ptolemy's family, notably of his young son and heir, Ptolemy Keraunos, the famous Thunderbolt; and all the while the High Priest of Memphis knew that the fate of Seleukos was to die by the hand of this boy, and all the while the High Priest said nothing of it to anybody, but waited and watched.

Ptolemy, then, was the great friend of Seleukos, and later he would help Ptolemy by commanding at his side in battle, for which his reward was to be installed once more in his lost territory of Babylon, as satrap once again.

Friendship however is not always repaid with kindness, and this Seleukos, friend though he was, he and his House were fated to be the bitter enemy of Ptolemy's descendants, fighting battles without end over the disputed regions of Syria and Palestine.

What one thing did Ptolemy learn, as Satrap, that he passed down to his sons and to the sons of his sons, that would be of most use to them? Thoth asks it. It was that a ruler may trust nobody, not even the men who seem to be his best friends.

Trust not a brother, Anemhor would say. *Trust not a friend,* he said, and it was Egyptian wisdom. For even a satrap—especially a satrap— has many enemies.

Some, at least, of the family of Ptolemy learned this lesson; some did not. Seleukos, alas, did not.

As for trusting his brother—Menelaos, younger brother of Ptolemy, was still resident in Egypt, where he made himself more or less useful most of the time, and proved himself loyal, and, yes, even trustworthy above most other men.

Menelaos did whatsoever he was asked to do without complaint, and every thing he did was done to the best of his ability.

But Ptolemy thought about rivals, about usurpers, more and more often, and the day came when it seemed to him safer to send Menelaos away from Egypt, where he could not put poison in his brother's food, or stir up rebellion in the Residence.

And so Menelaos went to Cyprus as *strategos,* or governor, where he could not plot his overthrow. He had at Cyprus every good thing, such as slaves, women, his palace, and he was allowed to do, within reason, more or less as he pleased, so long as Cyprus continued to supply Egypt with timber and copper, for it was Menelaos's first task to safeguard the regular dispatch of these valuable materials to Egypt.

He collected the taxes of the island and sent shiploads of drachmas home to his brother. A lesser man might have kept them for himself, as Kleomenes had done, but Menelaos knew very well that his brother would attack him if he did.

Menelaos liked a peaceful life, and, to be sure, every thing was well for him until his island was invaded by Demetrios Poliorketes, when Menelaos would fall into disgrace. But for the moment the trust between the brothers remained as before. As for the rest of the Greek world—there was little trust, as may be seen from what happened next in Macedon.

2.13

Macedonian Matters

Only six years after the proclamation of Philippos Arrhidaios as King of Macedon and Egypt, he was a dead man, and his wife, Adeia-Eurydike, fulfilled the forecast of her bad end.

For, alas, this Queen was not happy just to be a queen and sit upon her throne doing nothing. This woman had never done nothing. She had the spirit of a man and had to be always up and doing some thing. And now she had taken it upon herself even to try to rule through this tame husband of hers, aligning herself with Kassandros, the man who Rumour said had poisoned Alexander. Adeia-Eurydike could not stop herself from interfering in political matters, for she had, after all, been brought up to behave like this.

Adeia-Eurydike thought she knew just as much about military matters as Kassandros son of Antipatros. She thought she knew better than Olympias, the mother of Alexander, about foreign policy. She thought herself the equal of these people who had year upon year of experience of careful government, and waging war, and conquering other kingdoms.

She stirred up, as might have been foreseen, the wrath of Olympias, who was utterly determined that neither this girl nor her husband should be a threat to her grandson, King Alexandros, who was now just six years old.

In her exasperation Olympias declared war upon her own stepson, Philippos Arrhidaios, and upon his wife, Adeia-Eurydike, and the two armies met at a place called Euia, in Macedonia, where Adeia-Eurydike made her proud appearance upon horseback, dressed in the full golden armour of a King of Macedon, and she screamed the Paian of Victory to Apollo herself, and all her troops echoed her, shouting in strophe and antistrophe, as they headed towards the clash.

Opposing her, Olympias rode into battle at the head of her army, and she was dressed in fawn-skins and accompanied by the beat of the drums of Dionysos, the god of Frenzy, and she was angry, very angry.

The two queens now screamed the same battle cry, the terrible *Alalalalai* of Macedon, and their hair flew in the wind, and had they come close enough they would most surely have used tooth and nail to tear each other's hair and eyes out, for no two women ever hated each other like these two women hated: Olympias and Eurydike surpassed all hatred.

However, at the Battle of Euia a most wondrous thing took place. The Macedonian troops saw Olympias, their old queen, advancing to the fight. They heard the clamour of her drums and trumpets, and they were struck by her majesty, which was so like the majesty of her son Alexander, and they recalled that she was, yes, the widow of King Philip, and to a man they deserted Adeia-Eurydike, and joined instead the army of Olympias, who was, as a result, victorious.

As the Paian of Victory rang out, Olympias placed her stepson, Philippos Arrhidaios, and Adeia-Eurydike his wife, under strong guard, and had them bound in chains like a pair of criminals, and gave orders for them to be shut up in a confined space, and she gave them only what food was needed to keep them alive, pushed through a single narrow opening in the wall.

They endured this shameful treatment for a long while, until the behaviour of Olympias so scandalized the Macedonians that they were moved to express their pity for the King and Queen. But at length Olympias grew tired of the whispering, and the petitions, and the deputations of courtiers, and she paid some Thracians to stab Philippos Arrhidaios to death.

Throughout her ordeal Adeia-Eurydike showed never a sign of fear, but she now sent a message to say that she, Adeia-Eurydike, was the Queen of Macedon, not Olympias.

By way of a reply, Olympias sent her three objects: first, a dagger; second, a length of rope; and third, a bowl full of hemlock, as if to offer her a choice of self-murder, because the time had come for her, too, to die.

Adeia-Eurydike, alas, could see no way out of her trouble. No man had come to rescue her. Her friends had stayed away. Her husband the King was dead. But Adeia-Eurydike was a king's daughter, and she was determined to die a noble death. She cursed Olympias before the messenger who brought her the order to kill herself, and she prayed that Olympias would receive the same treatment.

So, Adeia-Eurydike now wiped the blood from the wounds of Philippos Arrhidaios, and wrapped his body in a cloak of purple. She would not hang herself with the rope. Nor would she die a coward's death by drinking the hemlock. She took off her own girdle, the gift of her husband, and she hanged herself from it, without, they said, so much as shedding a tear for her own fate, but with her pride unbroken; and she was just twenty years of age.

Kassandros buried the corpses and honoured them with funeral games, and much good it did them.

As for Olympias, she had just two years left to live.

At Thebes, in Egypt, there was built by Ptolemy, but in the name of King Philippos Arrhidaios, a pink granite shrine for Amun. The reliefs on the inside walls showed a pharaoh whose features were quite regular, and whose tongue did not loll outside his mouth, making offerings to the god under a blue ceiling spangled with golden stars.

On the outside walls of this shrine there were reliefs showing the coronation of this man as Pharaoh (an event that, to be sure, never took place) as well as the welcome of Thoth, and the goddess Amunet giving suck to the young king, although this man was, upon his death, forty-one years old.

The protection of the gods of Egypt had not done this Greek Pharaoh much good.

In that year the third disastrous flooding of the city of Rhodes by the Great Sea caused much loss of life and destruction of property. Great storms of rain marked the start of the spring season, and hailstones fell that weighed upwards of one *mina,* so that many of the houses collapsed under the burden.

Such things were always seen as a very bad omen by the Greeks, but as usual, as always, there were far worse things than murder to come; far, far worse things lay ahead than hailstones the size of ostrich eggs.

2.14

Crocodile Racing

As for the other Eurydike, Ptolemy her husband bore in mind the words of Homer:

> *Never be too gentle with your wife.*
> *Never show your wife all that is in your mind.*
> *Tell her as little as you can.*
> *Women are not to be trusted.*

In a family of Greeks violence is not an uncommon thing. A wife may expect to be beaten if she does not do whatever her husband tells her, or for some impertinence. A daughter, likewise, might be slapped in the face by her father for some careless word. But really, the family of Ptolemy was not like this. No, such things did not happen at Memphis.

For the most part, though, Eurydike did not so much as take one step outside the Residence, being afraid of foreigners. Housekeeping and silence were most fitting for Greek women, and Eurydike's housekeeping was taken care of by her steward and an army of servants and slaves, so that she had only the silence. She might, perhaps, have been allowed to visit her relatives in a different quarter of the city, but she had no relative in Memphis or, indeed, in all Egypt, but for her Aunt Berenike, who lived under the same roof. As for strolling in the street or riding in a chariot—these were not pastimes for wives, and only whores got away with looking out of windows.

So Eurydike lived what the Greeks call the *tortoise life,* trapped inside a shell that she could neither take off nor escape. The tortoise is an attribute of Aphrodite Ourania, the symbol of domesticity; and the life of Eurydike was indeed closed in, shuttered, and very very slow.

Yes, she found Egypt hot beyond all imagining. She dripped with perspiration—suffered from an uncontrollable dripping, day and night. Either that, or she sat shivering as the fog of Memphis came down, and during the thunderstorm and the storms of sand, her tremor returned.

The winter she spent trying to warm her hands at the brazier. Sure, Eurydike shared the Satrap's life of limitless luxury, and the most obvious aspect of luxury was a plentiful supply of every goodly thing to eat. But Eurydike did not much care for eating. She would pick at her food like a bird, then push the plate away, saying, *It is too hot to eat in Egypt,* and she grew, in consequence, very thin.

On the other hand, Aunt Berenike benefited greatly from Ptolemy's generous table. She delighted to eat the dates and bananas and figs and melons that grew in Egypt, and she put on weight and began to smile. Berenike was quite free, as a waiting-woman, to walk about the city of Memphis on behalf of her mistress, buying dresses and materials, and every article that the Satrap's wife needed. For, yes, a Satrap's wife was far too grand to step outside the *gynaikeion* door. Eurydike had to remain hidden, except upon state occasions, such as some trip up-River on the satrapal barge.

Berenike also now began to take better care of how she looked. She learned again the habit of painting her face with white lead and rouge, and she attended to her hair, whereas before she had hardly bothered.

Berenike inherited the cast-off garments of her niece. She recovered, bit by bit, from whatever the unspeakable ordeal of her past had been. Whereas before she had been haggard of face, and indeterminate of age, ignored by every man, she now put the flesh back upon her bones, blossomed into a handsome woman again, and looked, surely, as if she must still be only in her twenties. Berenike was most attractive, with eyes that sparkled, and she had that luxuriant yellow hair of Thracian women. Men's eyes followed her figure as she walked about the Residence, and they noticed that Berenike had a pleasant, low voice. Nor was she without education or accomplishments, for she had the skill of reading and writing, and was able both at the loom and the lyre and in the kitchen. It was not long before Berenike caught the eye of Ptolemy himself, who was, it must never be forgotten, *mad* after women, and he began to see in this woman attractions that his wife, Eurydike, really did not possess.

Eurydike bore Ptolemy a fresh child every year for five years, so that she was hardly delivered of the one before she was swelling up with the next: two more sons she bore after Keraunos, called Meleagros and Argaios, and three daughters, whom they called Theoxena, Lysandra and Ptolemaïs.

When the Satrap entered her bedchamber after the birth of the first of these daughters, Eurydike lowered her eyes, turned her face to the wall for shame, and wept the tears of a wife who has failed. To be sure, Ptolemy had wished for sons, more sons, as many sons as could be, and she had given him, yes, what he did not want; but he spoke, all the same, a few words of comfort.

A daughter, he said, *is by no means useless. She will make a fine marriage. We shall not expose her . . .*

For he thought less of the waste of money that paying this girl's dowry would involve than of the brilliant alliance that marrying her off—in due time—to some foreign ruler would bring, as a result of which he might, perhaps, sleep easier in his bed, and worry less about the everlasting threat of war.

Meleagros, Argaios, Theoxena, Lysandra and Ptolemaïs were fair-haired children, for their mother had given up eating earth, for the time being. The sons would grow up to be strong, brave Greek warriors—generals, perhaps, in their father's armies, at least until he died, when their future must be less certain. As for the girls, they grew up silent, placid, wide-eyed, and pale of face for the rest of their lives, for it was forbidden to girls of such high station to walk out of doors; utterly unthinkable that they might walk out into the sun of Egypt uncovered. They would, yes, live the life of all Greek girls of satrapal rank, behind the bolted and barred doors and shuttered windows of the *gynaikeion,* that strange, dark world of the women, where it was forbidden even to look down on to the street below. They would pass their days doing little but weaving and tapestry, for they were above carrying water from the well, too exalted to spend a morning slapping octopus upon the rocks, and they never so much as went near to the River to bathe. The girls were prisoners in all but name, waited on hand and foot by black eunuchs from the Land of Punt, men half their height, who waddled about on short legs—miniature men who had the shrill voices of women.

The girls had, even so, their pleasures: their pet monkeys, their dogs who sat upon the knee, their yellow birds in papyrus cages. The girls were not unhappy in their lot and upon rare occasions they too might sail up-River with the Satrap as far as Apollonopolis, or to Krokodilopolis, in order to see the feeding of the sacred crocodiles; and they talked about their outings for months afterwards. But for the most part nobody much set eyes upon the daughters of Ptolemy, so that a glimpse of them caused among the Greeks some excitement.

Ptolemy's younger legitimate sons were quieter than Ptolemy Keraunos. Meleagros was a boy about whom nobody had anything to say, who seemed almost to have worked the Spell of Invisibility. His horoscope forecast that he would be a king, but he was not the eldest son of his father. He would never be the Satrap, unless some disaster befell his brother, or unless some wonder made Keraunos fall from favour. Neither a madman nor a military genius, Meleagros was ignored. He would survive, as Eurydike his mother survived, by remaining quiet, by not drawing too much attention to himself.

As for his younger brother, Argaios—he was quieter still, so that in latter years nobody could say one word about how he had lived, or what he had done with his life. There were, perhaps, good reasons for not knowing anything about Argaios. What happened to this son only Thoth would remember, and Thoth would weep.

There was also a fourth son, who was so quiet that nobody, not even Thoth, had any record of his name; there is even a doubt in Thoth's heart about this son's very existence, and it may have been that this boy died at a young age.

Ptolemy had, to be sure, his other bastard sons and daughters, of his body, as well as the bastards of Thaïs, who lived, all of them, and had their food and their tuition, under the Satrap's roof. But these were sons and daughters of the second rank who, as possible usurpers of his satrapy, must of necessity live out their lives in fear of the assassin's knife, of the caller in the dark. They must think always of poison in their moussaka, or that they might be murdered as they slept, according to the Greek custom whereby every claimant to a satrapy must die, in order that the Satrap himself might live.

For the moment, though, all these children of Ptolemy played and fought together, learned the *alpha beta* at the feet of the same tutor, and were brought up to be more Greek than the Greeks of Greece. The girls bettered their skills in weaving, sewing, embroidery, tapestry, in the *gynaikeion,* from which the boys were firmly removed upon their seventh birthdays, to live from then onward in the *andron,* with the men, where they learned how to be warriors, soldiers, expert horsemen: and in the *gymnasion,* where they began to acquire the famous and perfect Greek physique, and the hard muscles of Greek athletes.

On their birthdays the High Priest of Ptah would send to these children of the Satrap, legitimate and illegitimate alike, his gift: a painted crocodile egg to hatch out in the Egyptian sun. His meaning was, on the one hand, a genuine gesture of goodwill to the House of Ptolemy; and upon the other hand, it was his sincere hope to rouse up real devotion to Sobek, the illustrious and most illustrious crocodile god of the Egyptians, whom the Greeks, who managed to change every Egyptian name, called Souchos.

The ninety days between the laying of the egg and the hatching of it were counted with impatience and mounting excitement, as the children listened for the tap-tapping within the shell, which meant they might at last help the infant crocodile to escape from his prison into the world of the living.

Theoxena, Lysandra and Ptolemaïs liked to decorate the ears of their crocodiles with earrings of gold, and they fastened bracelets of gold around the four scaly ankles, just as the priests of the crocodile did up at Krokodilopolis. The girls fell quite in love with the white teeth, and the snapping jaws, and the glittering eyes of the baby crocodiles, and they kept them in the great bath, or dragged them about the Residence upon a leash, feeding them daily upon the raw flesh of pigs and upon honey-cakes; and they laughed to see the terror of Eurydike.

As for the boys, they held crocodile races across the echoing halls of the Residence, and passed the suffocating hot afternoons of Memphis arguing about which creature was fastest, handsomest, fiercest, or which had won the most races.

However tame these beasts grew, the day always arrived when they would be declared too big for any house, too fearsome to be kept indoors, and they would be sent back to the Temple of Sobek, to live in the Sacred Lake there; and the girls would then sulk, and the boys bang doors, until they were promised a new crocodile egg at the next birthday, for, indeed, no crocodile lasted in the Residence so long as one year, because Eurydike complained always that a crocodile one cubit long was too much for domestic comfort.

What, though, was the real intention of Anemhor? Why did this man choose to fill the Satrap's house with crocodiles? Some saw the truth of his purpose, saying that he was responsible for something of the spirit of the crocodile entering these children, and perhaps they were right. Whatever the reason of it, fierceness and ill temper were things that the Ptolemies of future generations would possess in large measure.

The Satrap, all the same, wanted his sons to follow the best aspects of Alexander's character, and be not a plague and a great disease but a healing force, a force for good. But the High Priest, this Anemhor—had he not sown the seeds of discord among these children? Had he not done this on purpose? Perhaps. Perhaps not. Thoth shrugs. On the other hand, everybody knows that Greek children never needed very much encouragement to start quarrelling.

In the same year that the youngest daughter of Ptolemy and Eurydike was born, the Satrap ordered the founding of a fresh city in Upper Egypt, that he meant to be his Capital of the South.

Ptolemy was at this time of the opinion that it would really not amount to very great hubris if he were to call his daughter Ptolemaïs, after himself, and that the gods of Greece would surely not see it as hubris if he were to call the fresh city Ptolemaïs also.

In any case, he sent to the gods to seek their approval, and the Oracle of Zeus-Ammon made no objection, and so the daughter was called Ptolemaïs, and the city was called Ptolemaïs, and the city was near Diospolis, the Thebes of the Egyptians that was the religious capital of the south, a place that swarmed with Egyptian priests.

Ptolemaïs, though, was to be a thoroughly Greek city, like Alexandria, the southern capital for trade with Upper Egypt and the Land of Punt, and the spice country of Arabia. It was to be a city run by Greeks, with Greek temples, a Greek council, Greek theatre, *agora,* hippodrome, and so forth, and settled with Greeks, in the midst of the country of the black-face.

It was a city more suffocating even than Memphis, a place where the storm of sand was more troublesome, but it was here that Ptolemy might send men he wished to get rid of, where the Greeks would complain of being cooked alive.

The Oracle promised that Ptolemaïs, the city, would be indeed a lucky place, in spite of the heat. As for Ptolemaïs, the daughter of the Satrap, the Oracle spoke only in the vaguest of terms, and the horoscopists could provide Ptolemy with no sure forecast for the future, but spread their hands, saying that the gods did not seem to want to make known the fate of this child.

Only Thoth knows, and just as the fate of Eurydike was unlucky, so the fate of her youngest child would be unlucky also. Ill-starred Ptolemaïs—her future held nothing but tears and waiting, and she was for the first eighteen years of her life lucky not to know one word about what the gods had in store for her.

2.15

_____

The Bringer of Victory

Aunt Berenike, the Macedonian widow—it had been her task to shield Eurydike from the attentions of her husband when they were unwelcome. When Eurydike had a pain in the head, or the stomach, or the derangement of the bowels, or her time of the month, it was Berenike who told Ptolemy of it, and made Eurydike's excuses for her.

When Eurydike was heavy with her sixth and—as it turned out—her last child, it was Berenike herself who the Satrap called to his bed. She was, to be sure, older than her niece, but not much older, and she had, he thought, better looks than his wife, bigger breasts, and he told her she was _kallipygous,_ that he liked best of all the ampleness of her hinder parts. Berenike made Ptolemy think of Thaïs, and he began to have the thought that Berenike might also make a better wife.

For the moment, however, Berenike was his concubine, and after some months of Berenike's curious disappearance from the _gynaikeion_ during the dead hours of the night, Eurydike noticed that Ptolemy had given up all pretence of calling her any more his Pigeon, his Duckling, and that he no longer called her Polycharidas, his Dearest. In fact, he had stopped using all his terms of endearment, which he had never, perhaps, meant sincerely in the first place.

Eurydike wondered, in her innocence, what she might have done wrong, what she could have done to deserve such treatment. But the truth of it was that she had done nothing wrong. She had merely continued to be herself. All that had happened was that Ptolemy had begun to prefer Berenike, and he was starting to forget about his wife.

Some days Eurydike, feeling panicky, would send Berenike out to the _agora_ to purchase the newest style of _sminduridia,_ the fashionable women's shoe. She ordered up the latest kind of Klytemnestra _peplos,_ scarlet in colour, and she would hitch up the hem of it to show her ankles when she was near Ptolemy. But Ptolemy did not notice. He hardly looked at this wife of his, and had no idea that she was wearing some different thing.

From time to time Eurydike broke the rules that confined the women to the *gynaikeion,* dressed herself in her finest dress, and asked the way from the *gynaikeion* to the Hall of Audiences, and made so bold as to address her husband upon some pressing household matter. She would touch the sleeve of his tunic, or tap upon the arm of his chair with her fan; but Ptolemy seemed deaf to what she had to say about slaves, kitchen servants, eunuchs, pet monkeys, parrots or the size of the household crocodiles, and he stared into the distance, his thoughts taken up with Egyptian affairs, things of international importance.

When Eurydike pulled hard at the sleeve of her husband's *himation,* he looked through her, as if he did not know who this woman was—as if, really, she had nothing to do with him—and when he clapped his hands together, or nodded towards his Macedonian guards, Eurydike would be led gently away.

What was the truth? Yes, it was that Ptolemy now reserved his affectionate words for his wife's aunt. It was Berenike whom he now called his Polycharidas, his Dearest, his Sweetest. It was Berenike who filled his thoughts, and Berenike he sent for in the middle of the night when the pressure of state business weighed so heavy upon his spirits that he could not sleep. And Berenike went to him without making any complaint, without anger at the time of the night. Berenike walked swift through the vast halls and courtyards of the mud-brick fortress that was this man's official Residence. Berenike *ran,* and her hair flew out behind her, and she did not stop even to put on her shoes.

Eurydike, she saw nothing. She suspected nothing, because she was asleep, snoring. In the morning she was some times surprised to see the bed of Berenike empty, but Berenike often went out early, visiting the market of Memphis, buying all manner of goodly things to tempt Eurydike to eat for her breakfast. Eurydike knew nothing of what was going on. No, not one word.

Eurydike never dreamed that Ptolemy might want to have *aphrodisia* with her aunt, but that is what happened. When Eurydike did find out, she ran about the *gynaikeion* screaming, and she tore at her hair, and she beat her two breasts with her fists, and howled like the wolf of the desert, as if somebody had died, and it was herself.

Thoth shakes his head in dismay. What Eurydike had done by bringing her aunt to Egypt—it was as good as committing a slow self-murder.

As for Ptolemy falling in love—this went against every Greek scruple, for the Greeks hold that to fall in love, why, it is the next best thing to madness. But Ptolemy was beyond help. The arrows of Eros the Boy were stuck fast in his flesh, and kept him awake at night, and distracted his thoughts from business during the day, because in truth he could think of nothing but Berenike and the breasts of Berenike that were like two great pink melons, and of her ample flesh, and the sparkle, the sweet sparkle of her blue eyes.

He thought of her name—Berenike, that meant Bringer of Victory—and he had the thought that Berenike was lucky, lucky, lucky.

As the star of Berenike rose—soared even—so the star of Eurydike fell. She told herself, Yes, she was tired of the Satrap, that he was old, that she had never loved him, and she thought of the fact that he was more than fifty years of age, and of his weight, pressing down upon her, and that she did not like any of these things. That Ptolemy seldom came to her bed was, in truth, a relief, and yet, at the same time Eurydike minded very much, and there were times when she thought that, Yes, yes, she did perhaps love this man who was her husband and the father of her six children after all.

When the truth was told to her—that Ptolemy was in love with Aunt Berenike—Eurydike screamed some more; but when she calmed herself, she thought that this love of his need not bother her very much, for that she would now be left alone, and that her eldest son, Ptolemy Keraunos, would still be the heir of his father. Nothing had changed. Things might go on just as before.

One time Eurydike felt coming over her the desire to destroy her aunt by poison, but she banished this thought upon the instant, for she could not seriously think of killing an aunt, her beloved aunt, because a murder within the family carried with it dreadful, dreadful consequences, that she really had no wish to bring down upon her head: such as the whole of the rest of her life being haunted by the dead woman's ghost. And so, no, she could not, she did not, do it.

Eurydike told herself that she could bear the humiliation of being ignored by her husband so long as she might keep the title and position of Satrap's First Wife. And then she made up her mind to be beautiful—to get for herself the radiant beauty of Berenike—and she plastered her face with white lead, and with rouge, and did outlandish things with her hair to grab the attention of the Satrap, piling it up high, and dyeing it blue, or green, or red. But Eurydike ended up looking ridiculous, and her efforts came too late. Berenike had the beauty of maturity. Eurydike had been a plain girl, and all her efforts now with cosmetics did not manage to make her anything but a plain woman, and yet she was still not thirty years of age.

Desperate, Eurydike made trial of eating the Greek herbs that were supposed to bring back a lost love. She even crept up to touch Ptolemy with the magic herb called *anakampseros* while he slept. But the truth was that Ptolemy had never loved this wife of his in the first place. There were no dying embers to fan back to life: the flame of love for Eurydike had never been lit.

All might yet have been well, but Aunt Berenike now began to grow stout round the waist, and the day at last came when the looseness of her garments failed to hide the fact that she was big with child.

Eurydike screamed worse than ever when she saw the belly of her aunt and the full truth of what had been happening was made clear to her. She wept in private, and berated Berenike for a whore and a concubine, but her public face, when she got a chance to show it, was untroubled. For no, there was no question that her son Thunderbolt would forfeit his place as Ptolemy's favoured son and heir. Since Berenike was not married, her child must be a bastard child, without any right whatever to his father's high office. And if it turned out to be a girl—well, they might expose her. Yes, Eurydike reassured herself, the pregnancy of Aunt Berenike was nothing but an accident, and her own position was still secure.

Really, Eurydike had no fears for her future or for the future of her son either, until Ptolemy put the fox among the chickens by telling her that he was to be married to Aunt Berenike, and then—then Eurydike's feelings of security were as if made all of glass and dropped upon a floor of stone and smashed to pieces.

On the eve of the *wedding* of Berenike to Ptolemy, when the truth had still to sink in, Eurydike overheard one of her own waiting-women saying, *It is a real love match,* and the words shot through her as if it was she who had been struck by the arrows of Eros. She found it hard to catch her breath, and when the women asked after her health later that day, she did not know—she really did not know—that she had fainted away from the shock.

What, then, had happened? Old Antipatros, the father of Eurydike, had died only a few years into her marriage and so the grand alliance had ground to a stop. There was now really no very good political reason for Ptolemy to take an interest in the welfare of Eurydike his wife, or in her children either, apart from the fact that they were his children also. Even so, he still had no thought to divorce Eurydike. All he meant to do was to take a second wife, which was nothing very unusual for a satrap of the Greeks, for these men were men of such power and had such a high opinion of their own worth that they thought that they might do just exactly as they pleased. In truth, no man upon earth had more power than a satrap, and there was nobody in the world to tell Ptolemy what he must and must not do, apart, perhaps, from the King of Egypt, who happened to be that Alexandros who was but a boy, and who, in any case, had his residence far away, in Greece.

At the time of the Full Moon in the month of Gamelion, when the pupils of the cats' eyes grow very large, Ptolemy and Berenike celebrated their marriage, and it was done with very great pomp and ceremony, far exceeding that of the marriage to Eurydike. At the wedding banquet Ptolemy himself sang the Crow Song of the Greeks, and the Swallow Song also, and the members of his household threw nuts and figs at Berenike as she walked through the door of the Residence, but not so hard that they stung her face or arms, and Berenike did not for one moment stop from smiling.

At this banquet the men called for Berenike to dance, as the men at every Greek wedding call for the bride to dance.

Berenike stood up at once, and the pipes and the lyre and the *kitharistes* started up a slow tune, and Berenike moved slow in time to it, arms above her head, arms stretched out at her sides, and her feet moving up and down. As the music went faster and faster the arms of Berenike waved above her head, hands clapping, and she stamped her feet ever faster and faster, and the music went faster still, and the men whistled and cheered, and clapped in time with the music, and in the beginning Berenike was good, but in the end she was brilliant; the men shouted that Berenike was wonderful, that she was surely the embodiment of Terpsikhore, that Berenike would be a goddess.

Berenike danced, smiling, pink-faced, like a lobster upon red-hot coals.

And Berenike *would* be a goddess.

As for Eurydike, she did not grace this happy occasion with her presence, but pleaded her time of the month one more time, and shut herself up in a clothes press in a remote part of the building and howled with jealous rage, raising her voice like the jackal of the desert.

When she found herself alone, which was often, or when she believed she could not be overheard, Eurydike began to talk to herself once more in Ouranopolitan, the language invented by her mad brother, Alexarkhos.

This, perhaps, was harmless enough, but it was at about this time also that Eurydike went back to her old habit of eating earth, and her waiting-women began to be worried about her state of mind.

Under the new arrangement, however, there could be no conflict. Berenike and Eurydike were not only relations, but truly the best of friends, and to be sure, it would be a tribute to Ptolemy's diplomatic skills that he did not manage to turn these two women at once into the bitterest enemies, but that they lived contented—more or less contented—lives under the same roof, in the same *gynaikeion*.

Did Ptolemy feel some small guilt at what he had done to that wife of his, to whose father he had made his solemn promise that he would look after her, whatever might happen, for all the days of her life? Perhaps. But he had not, after all, sent her away. At least, not yet. All the same, as if to justify his actions, Ptolemy would sometimes murmur, *In truth, Eurydike was quite unfitted to endure the summer heat of Egypt*. And the fact was that he now spoke of his first wife in the past tense, the aorist, as if she no longer existed.

Sometimes he would say, *In truth, Eurydike was quite unable to keep at bay the smell of sweat that assailed her day and night*.

It was an excuse. It was one reason among many reasons, but the greatest reason was the true fact of his love, his very great love, his real, true, and overpowering love for Berenike.

As he lay in his satrapal bed beside Berenike, he would murmur into her ear, *In truth, Eurydike was very like a dove, totally without brains . . .* And it was odd but true that he would often sneeze in the middle of saying something of this sort, as if Zeus himself confirmed the truth of what he said.

Yes, the spirits of Eurydike plunged, but it was the hour of Berenike's flourishing, and from the very start of her second marriage she set out to get what she wanted, and not to be told in every thing what to do, for she had found, now, if the truth were told, a new and very great determination.

Berenike knew how the Satrap's household worked, and how to manipulate it to her advantage. In the coolest part of the day she would walk about the servants' offices making sure that every thing was arranged how it should be arranged: bread, wine, beer, meat, water, sweeping, polishing—every thing must be just so. Berenike took charge, and the slaves from time to time trembled under the whip lash of her angry tongue. Suddenly Berenike had become a person of power, whose word was law, and her two children, Magas and Antigone, were no longer quite children of unknown provenance, but the stepchildren of the Satrap, who must be treated with a certain respect.

If silence had been the watchword of Berenike in the past, it was by talk that she arrived at an altogether different station in life. Where

Eurydike had been tongue-tied in the Satrap's presence, almost afraid to speak one word, but bit her lip whenever he came to her bed, or spoke of trivialities, of dresses, or jewels, or her fund for new shoes, the tongue of Berenike was, yes, the secret of her success, because she was quite capable of holding her own with the Satrap, happy to talk to him for hours about military matters, the different designs of ships of war, or of siege-engines and the art of undermining an enemy citadel, and she knew the whole of the history of Alexander. The truth was that Philippos, her late husband, had been an army officer, so that there was little Berenike did not know about war. Her common-sense advice was what Ptolemy wanted, and he began even to ask for her thoughts about the weightiest matters of state.

Thus Berenike set about making herself indispensable. She was indeed a most clever woman, and she was well aware of what she was doing. Berenike wanted power. She wanted to have children by the Satrap in order to make stronger her power over him. And she wanted also *her* son—her as yet unborn son—to be Satrap after Ptolemy, because in truth she looked at the three sons of Eurydike and thought that they were useless sons, not one of whom would make a good ruler of Egypt.

Berenike was quite sure that her own son would make a very fine satrap, and why not, she thought, Pharaoh of Egypt also? To be sure, she had got herself now in a most advantageous position. All she had to do was to bring forth a male child. But this was the thing that in all her life was to cause Berenike the most difficulty.

While Aunt Berenike grew stouter round the waist, and stouter still, her children flourished: Magas, a boy not many years older than Ptolemy Keraunos, made a suitable wrestling partner, a suitable opponent for games of dice and knucklebones, and this Magas proved to be the closest Ptolemy the Thunderbolt ever got to having a true friend.

As for Antigone, she wove and spun now at the side of the Satrap's daughters, Theoxena, Lysandra and Ptolemaïs, living the tortoise life of the *gynaikeion*, trying her best not to look out of the window. She learned to carry herself like the daughter of a woman who might, if the golden wing of Tykhe, goddess of Luck, did not desert her, be Queen of Egypt. She learned the behaviour required of a girl who might one day be married off to some high prince, for as well as her ambition for herself, her mother had the very highest ambitions also for her children.

Eurydike was still quite sure that she would herself be the mother of the next satrap, but in the eyes of Ptolemy it was his new wife who was the most important wife. His second wife was now the first wife, and she was the most powerful woman in Egypt.

Berenike herself was sure of it. Her horoscope had already told her what was to come: *Wife and Mother of Kings,* it said, and while such things were beyond the dreams of any ordinary woman, Berenike was no ordinary woman. She was Berenike, Bringer of Victory, and she felt now that even the impossible might be made to happen.

2.16

The Daughter with Claws

Berenike, in her great eagerness to bring forth the best of sons for Ptolemy—though she told him not a word of her secret thoughts— dosed herself thirty days and thirty nights together with hawk dung in honey wine, after the habit of the Egyptians. During her time of child-bearing Berenike did not crave the diet of black earth, but stuck to apricots, lemons, bananas, and she chewed the heads of yellow flowers, and had the walls of her chamber painted like the Sun. For she dreamed not of a dark boy like Ptolemy the Thunderbolt, but of a yellow-haired boy as handsome as Apollo, who might be the Son of the Sun, Pharaoh of Egypt. And really it was not an impossible thing to wish for.

Shortly before her labour was due to begin, Berenike had herself carried in a litter to the temple of the new god Sarapis, at Memphis, to sleep the night there, so that she might enjoy the blessings and encourage the cult of the god that had been thought up by her own husband.

And sure, the temple dogs came to lick her private parts, and the temple snakes came to lick her ears, but although Berenike felt lucky, and swore she had seen, oh, her vision of the bearded god in the dead hours of the night, she confessed to Ptolemy that she had seen nothing, nothing at all—that she had felt cold sleeping in the Temple of Sarapis, and that she thought little, very little, of a god who could not even manage to show himself to her in person.

When the shrieking of Berenike began, four of her waiting-women shook her up and down to make the child come forth, while—like every other Greek mother—she made her panted prayers to Artemis and

Eileithyia, the goddesses of birth pangs, and sniffed pepper to make her sneeze. Like every Greek woman in her position she chewed wolf's meat. She screamed and howled; her noise was drowned out by the women banging upon pots and pans, and at last she was delivered of a blue-eyed child one cubit in length, whose hair was indeed not dark but fair, like gold.

When Ptolemy stepped into the chamber of Berenike for the first time after this event, she turned her face to the wall in shame, for that son of hers had turned out to be a daughter—fair of face, sure, but a girl, and born upon a day that was inauspicious for the birth of girl children, most inauspicious.

Berenike, because of it, fully expected Ptolemy to say that he would expose this child, and she wept, and wailed, and apologized for her failure to please her lord.

But Ptolemy took her by both hands. *A daughter,* he said, *is a great asset. A girl child will prove most useful for some political alliance in future years* . . . though the truth was that he had now five daughters and only four sons, and that he was not pleased, for the birth of girls is never anything but a disgrace and a disaster to a Greek man. But he gritted his teeth, and ordered the child to be bandaged, so that she should at least grow up with straight limbs, and he said, *Her name shall be called Arsinoë, after our own mother.*

Strapped to a board for the first sixty days of her life, it could only mean that Arsinoë would grow to be an angry child, and yes, she would grow up fierce, not unlike her mother, a girl who would claw and scratch like the lioness; a girl who would stop at nothing in order to get what she wanted, not even at shedding blood within her own family. For, indeed, this was the illustrious and most illustrious girl who would grow up to be Arsinoë Beta, the famous Queen, and not only her hair but all her future before her looked, just then, golden.

Anemhor, High Priest of Ptah, visiting this daughter for the first time, insisted, *You must spit into her mouth, to give her good luck, long life,* and he smiled his half-smile at the two parents.

Ptolemy hesitated. On the one hand, any daughter needed all the luck she could get; on the other hand, it was really *not* the Greek custom to spit into a baby's mouth, and he said so.

But Anemhor said, *You are Egyptians now. To spit is the habit of the Egyptians* . . . *it will bring great good luck.*

So Ptolemy gathered his spittle and spat, thinking *Disgusting!,* thinking that it could hardly be lucky to do such a gross thing, and that he would *never* be an Egyptian.

Arsinoë Beta would indeed need all the luck in the world, for the High Priest had drawn up already her horoscope, and it was bad, as bad as bad could be, for it said that she would enjoy neither long life nor good fortune, but was fated to pass a disastrous and unhappy time upon earth; that she would make an ill-starred marriage, to her own brother; and that she should know horrors, many horrors, the kind of horror, yes, that makes the hair stand up upon the head like horns.

As for Berenike, she worried whether she had done the right things after all. She had had her ears licked by the sacred snakes in honour of Dionysos, god of Frenzy. She had sacrificed to Agathos Daimon, the guardian snake god of her husband's new city of Alexandria. She had even looked upon images of snakes throughout her pregnancy, thinking it would bring good luck.

So many snakes, so very many serpents—it was perhaps only to be expected that something of the snake should be born in this daughter, Arsinoë Beta. As if the snake was part of her psyche.

Poor Berenike. She had suffered much in the past, so very much that she could not speak of it. Her thought now was that she had been much too nice all her life, and it was her hope that this new daughter of hers might grow up strong, like Berenike was now, not a meek woman who would always be pleased to do what she was told. For she really did not wish Arsinoë Beta to be another Eurydike, useless for any thing but the ploughing of children. She thought a woman must do more with her life than that. And so Berenike made up her mind then and there to bring up this daughter to think that to hate was better than to love.

Believe me, she would say to Arsinoë Beta, and she said it often, *too much niceness is the best way to destruction.* And having seen what the wet nurse had done for Ptolemy Keraunos, Berenike shocked her waiting-women by feeding this child herself, so that there should be no doubt about the forming of her character.

As soon as Arsinoë Beta began to take solid food, chewed up by Berenike first and spat out after the manner of the birds, Berenike took thought for her next child, and of her great wish to be the mother of a son by the Satrap; and she began to goad him to tie up his left-hand testicle once more with the papyrus string, and set him to work.

When Berenike suffered her first miscarriage, the Greek physicians blamed the flowers, and she had the gladioli removed from her bed-chamber, and every flower of the gladiolus family was rooted out from the Residence gardens and burned upon a great fire.

All the same, while Berenike suspected the guilt of the flowers, she knew in her heart that the reason for her trouble was more likely to be the magic of Eurydike.

When Berenike suffered a second miscarriage, her Greek physicians blamed the mirrors for her trouble, and she had every mirror removed from the *gynaikeion*.

Even so, part of her wanted to put the blame upon Eurydike, and she saw in her mind's eye her niece sticking pins into a wax doll fashioned in her image, and it was, after all, what Berenike had herself taught Eurydike to do, in order to while away the hours upon their voyage to Egypt, making her learn by heart the words of power to be spoken over such a doll, and it had all been part of training Eurydike up to look after herself in a foreign land.

Was this the truth? Or did Berenike imagine such things? Thoth looks now into the state of mind of this Eurydike, this woman spurned by her husband. Was she not a bitter woman? Was she not, in truth, seeking her revenge?

Eurydike was, after all, a woman who had nothing to do but brood. She passed the days, every day, sitting in her chair fanning herself against the suffocating heat. But Eurydike, the meek girl, was changing. She discovered now how to eat, and she ate to comfort herself in her distress. She began even to say, *Eating—it is the only pleasure left to me*. She had started her married life much like any other girl to look at, but now she grew stout, and it was not the stoutness of another pregnancy, for her husband no longer came near her, but from eating too much. She started also to laugh a strange laugh, that often burst out for no reason at all.

Like the laugh of an idiot, Berenike said to her husband, *like the laugh of a mad woman*.

Eurydike would pass the morning sitting in her chair, fanning herself with a fan in her left hand, and putting olive after olive into her mouth with her right. From time to time she leaned forward to look out of her window, trying to see all she could of life in the street below, without the vulgarity of being seen, and from time to time she spat the pips out of the window, amusing herself by trying to hit those passing by below, and laughing her mad laugh.

All through the afternoon her Nubian boy servants would pad barefoot across the floor, bringing Eurydike the golden plate laden with sweet things that kept her going until supper time.

Thoth says, Boredom sharpens the appetite, and Eurydike grew fatter still, and laughed that mad laugh more often. She was not entirely unhappy. She had every thing she desired, any thing she asked for—all except the love and attention of the man who was her husband. For Ptolemy seldom visited this first wife of his, except perhaps to shout about the wayward Ptolemy Keraunos. But Eurydike did not know what she should do with this son whom she rarely saw, who after the age of seven was forbidden to enter the women's quarters, and she spread her hands and giggled, as if to say that this boy was hopeless, and even then her mouth was full of a dozen dates, so that her speech was muffled.

Ptolemy liked women with the elegant curves of a Greek statue, not the rolls of fat that Eurydike now had, that wobbled as she walked, like the *argurotrophima,* the silver delight, which they ate upon everybody's birthday, which so amused them all by the way it trembled upon its golden plate.

Upon the death of Old Antipatros, her father, Eurydike came into a great deal of money in her own right. She had still her jewellery, her costly stones, and nobody could take them from her. She liked to make remarks about her Will, as if she were planning to depart this life, or as if she wanted to exercise some power regarding inheritances and bequests, but her children were too young to understand either death or money, and if she thought to make them behave better by threatening to cut them out of her Will, she was unsuccessful, for Eurydike's children went on quarrelling as before.

Eurydike did not realize that with Antipatros dead the alliance signed upon her marriage was without meaning, and that her own importance had melted away overnight, like the snow sent from Syria to cool her husband's wine. The treaty of peace was finished, finished, and she was merely one among many women, of whom Berenike was the first.

Did Ptolemy think to divorce Eurydike? No, he did not. Did he think to send her away from Memphis? By no means. For the moment he did nothing. Always it was easier to do nothing. And Eurydike was still the mother of Ptolemy Keraunos, the boy who must be Satrap after him, and so the situation among the women carried on as it was, for the time being.

Berenike, she continued to dose herself daily with the hawk dung and honey wine, trying to bring into being the son of her own who should be a better satrap than Eurydike's Keraunos. But she would pass eight long years swallowing hawk dung and honey wine before she was successful. Yea, the Satrap tied the papyrus string for two thousand nine hundred and twenty nights before the luck of Berenike returned.

During that time Berenike was brought to bed of several infants, but every one was born dead or died within a few hours. Berenike felt she had failed in her whole being, and when she brought forth the first mis-shapen child, which had to be cast out, her husband thought of the words of Aristotle: *Children always resemble their parents. An unnatural parent will always have an unnatural child.* And he wondered what they had done to anger the gods. Neither he nor Berenike had any unnatural features. There should have been no question of their producing any-thing but a perfect child. But none of Berenike's babies lived. Only the daughter, Arsinoë Beta, survived, and the younger brother whom it was her fate to marry, the gods of Greece refused, it seems, to allow to be born.

Eurydike expressed her sorrow and her concern, and she shed many tears with Berenike in her time of trouble, but she could not help feel-ing a sense of triumph for that Aunt Berenike had not managed to give the Satrap a living son, whereas she, Eurydike, had borne four healthy sons, and in private she laughed, because her aunt was too old to bring forth any more children.

Behind the bolted door of her private apartment, where no one went but herself, Eurydike had indeed passed a night moulding the image of Aunt Berenike out of wax, and she had indeed stabbed the doll of the aunt with seven nails of lead: one nail in each of Berenike's pink ears; one nail in each of her blue eyes; one nail in her big mouth; one nail in the top of her fat head; one nail between her sagging breasts, and one nail plunged into her *bolba,* deep into her fruitless womb.

When Berenike complained of pains—pains in the head, pains in her ears, and of painful eyes, and pains in her chest—her physicians, Greek and Egyptian alike, said her trouble was caused, yes, by an imbalance of the humours, and they supplied her with potions and poultices derived from the intestines of the crocodile.

But no remedy made much difference to the health of Berenike: there could be no change until Eurydike pulled the nails of lead out of her doll of wax, releasing Berenike from the binding, because Berenike was bound, bewitched by the terrible power of Eurydike's magic spell.

Sure, Berenike had her suspicions. There was, she thought, but one person in all of Egypt who would go to the trouble of working the Spell of Binding. But search her niece's private chamber though she did, Berenike could find no wax doll, nor any sign that Eurydike was any-thing but loyal to her, because the wax doll was buried deep in the mud-brick wall, where nobody, but nobody, could find it.

As for the dead babies, Berenike buried them, each one, bandaged not in birth but in death, at the suggestion of the High Priest of Ptah, inside a golden coffin one cubit in length, and they made a row of golden dolls in the *nekropolis* of the wonderful new god Sarapis, who had let her down time and time again.

Berenike carried each one herself, in her own arms, up on to the desert plateau opposite Memphis, and for each one she brought some children's toy such as the wooden crocodile with moving jaw and laughing, painted eyes, or the wooden leopard with wagging tail, that her sons had not lived long enough to enjoy, and Berenike wept, tough woman though she was.

In public, Eurydike too shed her tears; in private she laughed.

Berenike sent now the most lavish offerings to the temples of every god and goddess of the Greeks, and even to some of the gods of the Egyptians; but the greatest offerings she reserved for Sarapis, the god dreamed up by her husband, in whose powers she still did not quite believe, in hope of a miracle.

Ptolemy was not much troubled, himself: he had his four sons, of his body. He had his heir to the satrapy, and he found no fault in Ptolemy Keraunos that was great enough to stop this son—this eldest legitimate son of his, the apple of his eye—from succeeding him.

By no means: it was the thought of Ptolemy that the Thunderbolt would make a fine Satrap of Egypt, and he was careful to train him up, so far as he could, in the way that he must go.

2.17

More Syrian Wars

Asked by Anemhor whether he would not, one day, be pleased to stop being a satrap and be instead a pharaoh, Ptolemy laughed, for he had no thought of doing such a thing. On the one hand, there would be the *kudos,* the power, and such delights as to fly to the sky upon the whirlwind and become one of the Imperishable Stars upon his death; but upon the other hand, he thought about hubris, about overweening pride. Yes, he thought of the words of Homer on this matter: *Think, and shrink back! Never think yourself a god's equal.* Ptolemy had still enough fear of the gods of Greece to be wary of the madness they could send down upon the man who was guilty of the sin of pride.

And so he said to Anemhor, *Extravagance is perilous. Hubris will most surely be punished by Heaven.*

He told Anemhor that he was quite content to be Satrap. *A satrapy is enough for any man,* he said. He did not wish to be a king. He had no thought to turn himself into a god. And surely, to have the absent boy Alexandros as king was enough.

But this was not enough for Anemhor. Egypt needed a pharaoh who lived in Egypt. To have only a satrap was not enough.

Although he was not keen to tempt the gods, Ptolemy began now to put his own head upon his coins, the drachmas, tetradrachms and okto-drachms of bronze and gold with which he paid his soldiers and his hired soldiers; and upon the reverse he stamped his badge, and it was the eagle of Zeus, and the eagle stood upon the thunderbolt that was the sign of Zeus's mighty power.

And why so? Because the eagle is the only bird that is never struck by lightning or killed by the thunderbolt. The eagle is the king of birds, who sleeps upon the sceptre of Zeus. As always Ptolemy copied Alexander, whose standard was an eagle mounted upon a pole, with a snake held in his talons.

Eagles, thunderbolts—such things were all about power. And in the struggle for leadership of the lands that had once made up the Empire of Alexander, Antigonos Monophthalmos now began to look like the common enemy of all the other Successors, who began to make special alliances with one another, in order to combine against One-Eye and take his power from him.

In the eighth year of the satrapy of Ptolemy, One-Eye swept down from Macedon with his army to invade Phoenicia and Syria, which were just then Ptolemy's own possessions, and before One-Eye Ptolemy found it wisest to retreat, because he was not ready to fight.

In Egypt, then, the word was that there would be war, and the *prostagma* went out from the Satrap to the women of Memphis and all Egypt to stop cutting their hair, but to grow it long, so that it might be twisted into stout ropes, the ropes that would fire his torsion catapults and bolt-throwers and siege-engines and machines of war, and so help to bring about a mighty victory for Ptolemy.

That same year war was declared, and One-Eye's land army triumphed wherever it marched, though his fleet of two hundred and forty ships of war was not so successful. One-Eye, like Alexander, found that he must put down the city of Tyros, but in spite of this man's hostilities, Ptolemy made no effort to resist his army, but merely garrisoned the main cities. Joppa and Gaza fell easily into the hands of Antigonos One-

Eye, but Tyros withstood yet another siege, this time holding out for four hundred and fifty days.

Ptolemy sighed and groaned as he stared at the papyrus map of Syria and Palestine with nails of bronze stuck in it to show what was his and what was not, and where was his army, and where the army of One-Eye. The heart of Ptolemy was not in this war. He was interested more in peace, for he was fifty-two years of age, and tired of fighting, weary of wasting the revenues of Egypt in endless battle.

Nonetheless, before the end of the year Ptolemy was obliged to ride out and meet Antigonos at Ekregma, on the borders of Egypt and Palestine, for talks about the exchange or ransoming of prisoners of war. Not long since, these two men had been comrades-in-arms and the best of friends. There was no personal hatred between them. They embraced upon meeting, and showed the teeth, and spoke of past times.

The following year, old friendship notwithstanding, One-Eye seized Tyros for himself, and he laughed long at the thought of his one-time friend's distress.

War now followed war, and in the heat of Egypt Ptolemy lost his temper and shouted that the fight over Syria looked fit to last ten years. For now he was pitched not only against Antigonos One-Eye but against his son Demetrios also, the boy who was to be called Poliorketes, or Besieger of Cities, and who had under his command an enormous army and forty-three elephants of war.

Ptolemy had not one elephant, having learned from Alexander to despise this beast as unreliable, for though he might sometimes do what he was told and charge ahead, he was just as likely to turn round and trample upon the men of his own army.

In the eleventh year of his satrapy Ptolemy marched eighteen thousand soldiers and four thousand horse out of Memphis to Pelousion and the borders of Egypt—Macedonians and hired soldiers from all over Greece and Asia, as well as a mass of native Egyptians, to be sutlers and carriers—and he pitched his tents at Gaza, not far from where his new enemy, Demetrios Poliorketes, sat waiting for him.

The friends of this Demetrios had given stern warning that he must not think of taking on so great a general as Ptolemy; but Demetrios took no notice, and made himself ready for a very great battle, which he rushed into without waiting for the tactical advice of his father, and with only the vaguest of orders to do what he could to keep Syria under Antigonid control. Demetrios was just twenty-two years old, and although, sure, he showed great promise, he had little experience of war, and no experience of high command. Moreover, he now faced

Ptolemy and Seleukos, two of the greatest generals of the day, who had followed Alexander as far as India, and who were, at this point, unbeaten.

Demetrios was a handsome young man, of striking stature—like a young god, they said, a young Apollo—so handsome, in fact, that both men and women would follow him along the street the better to gaze upon his near-divine beauty; his silver armour glinted in the sun, and he struck his troops, they said, with awe, and his gentleness and good manners won him the devotion of everybody, and made them think of Alexander.

But Thoth says, Good looks do not win great battles.

Among the passengers who had come to watch the war was the entire family and household of Ptolemy: both his wives, and ten children, daughters included. For it was the thought of Plato that *children should see war*, the work for which they were destined, and with this thought in his heart Ptolemy put his family on horseback, in front of, or behind, experienced riders, so that, if danger threatened, they might make their escape.

To take children into battle was, in fact, no new thing, for the royal children of the Pharaoh Ramesses the Second, for example, had looked upon the Battle of Kadesh in Syria many centuries before.

Here, then, were Lagos, Leontiskos and Eirene, and the nine-year-old Ptolemy Keraunos, and his three young sisters, Theoxena, Lysandra and Ptolemaïs, six, five and four years old, all watching the phalanx of Ptolemy in action. And Magas and Antigone were present, and the four-year-old Arsinoë Beta was held up to see her father's mighty victory.

The great battle cry went up, and the screaming of the troops and braying of trumpets; and the crash of *sarissa* upon *sarissa*, sword upon sword, went on from dawn until the hour of perfuming the mouth, and there was a cloud of dust hanging in the air, and blood all over the plain.

Berenike urged the troops of her husband onward, screaming her words of encouragement. As for Eurydike, she trembled, and she did not shout for Ptolemy and Egypt. She did not stop from trembling for one moment, and she could not bring herself to look upon the clash of war, but kept her eyes tight shut.

Of all the children of Ptolemy it was Keraunos and Arsinoë Beta who gained most from this outing to see the war. In later years Arsinoë Beta would have the control of the Ministry of War herself, but her training in strategy, tactics and diplomacy began here, at the Battle of

Gaza. She said always that this was the very first thing she could remember, and she would never forget it: Arsinoë delighted in the noise, the chaos, the violence, and it was her first sight of blood. *War, she said, is a wonderful thing,* and she did not stop talking about her war for years afterwards.

What, then, did Arsinoë Beta see at Gaza? She saw Ptolemy and Seleukos face this Demetrios Poliorketes, a mere lad, with his elephants of war and his seventeen thousand troops lined up for the fight with their helmets polished on purpose to dazzle the enemy. And what happened? Ptolemy did, as always, what Alexander would have done, for Alexander's ways were the best ways, and his spirit, as it were, watched over them.

The terror Demetrios's trumpeting elephants aroused in the troops of Ptolemy was very great, but Ptolemy hurled spiked devices among these beasts to halt their charge, and somehow the veterans urged on the beginners, and the phalanx pushed forward, and no man stopped from screaming the *Alalalalai;* the dust flew up, and the sands of Gaza turned red with blood. Many men were wounded, and many killed, but in the end Ptolemy captured all forty-three elephants of war, and took eight thousand prisoners, and the cavalry of Demetrios panicked and fled.

Demetrios lost not only his elephants and cavalry but also his leather tent, his money, and his personal belongings—every thing that he had—and it was a terrible defeat for this boy, of whose army of seventeen thousand men five thousand lay dead on the field of battle. Three out of four of the prisoners of war changed sides on the spot to fight for Ptolemy, for they were hired soldiers, who do not fight out of loyalty but for money. These men Ptolemy settled in Egypt, with their right-hand thumbs cut off so that they could never again wield sword or bow against him.

In this way the city of Gaza fell into the hands of Ptolemy.

As for Demetrios himself, he fled also, but Ptolemy now showed the most extraordinary goodwill by sending back the money and lost effects of his foe, and a polite message also to compliment him upon his bravery—which was unheard of in a battle of Greek against Greek. Yes, it was a gentlemanly finish to a fight that had really nothing to do with blind hatred—that was not a struggle for life and death, but a simple matter of honour and power, a fight about how to solve a boundary dispute.

Demetrios was pleased by the generous gesture of Ptolemy, but at the same time he prayed that he might not remain long in Ptolemy's debt, and he swore the most solemn oath before the gods of Greece that he would have his revenge.

Demetrios was by no means cast down by defeat, but behaved more like an experienced general who has already known the twists and turns of fortune. He began at once to enrol fresh troops and gather new stocks of weapons, and he threw his energy into training his army for the next battle, which he swore, by Zeus, he would win.

Ptolemy himself marched home at the head of his troops, and when they marched into Memphis in triumph, singing the Paian of Victory to Apollo, the city went mad for joy once again.

The twelve wicker baskets of right-hand thumbs Ptolemy dedicated to Sakhmet, the lioness goddess of Memphis, Lady of the Bright-Red Linen, who breathes fire against Egypt's enemies, and the priests and high priests of Egypt sent to Ptolemy their sincere congratulations.

Ptolemy was pleased now to reoccupy all of Palestine and Syria. Everywhere he marched he was generous, polite, kind, the very opposite of a tyrant; for he wanted above all things for Egypt to be a popular overlord. He wanted himself to be a popular Satrap. Everywhere he spread goodwill and fairness. He was a just ruler, loved by all who served under him.

Seleukos, the former Satrap of Babylon, and son of Antiokhos, who had been his co-commander at Gaza, Ptolemy now reinstated in his old satrapy, with Egypt's full support. Alas, this was an act of goodwill that the House of Ptolemy would regret, because goodwill was a thing that the House of Seleukos would seldom show for the next three hundred years.

Not long after this, Ptolemy sent Killes, one of his generals, through the desert with a large force, and orders to drive Demetrios Poliorketes right out of Syria.

Demetrios was ready, and launched a surprise attack, routed Killes's troops, seized his camp, captured his officers, and took seven thousand prisoners and a great quantity of treasure. This, of course, delighted Demetrios, but not because of what, and who, he had got hold of, but for what he could now give back. And he made the same gesture as Ptolemy had done, by loading Killes and his comrades with presents; and he sent all the prisoners back home to Egypt, without cutting off any man's thumb.

There was, then, little hatred involved in the Syrian wars. It was almost as if these satraps were playing games with one another, though the loss of life gave not much cause for laughter. Even so, these were times when the business of war was taken almost not quite seriously. War would not always be undertaken in such a civilized manner.

What, though, was the result of Ptolemy's defeat, apart from his troops marching home to Memphis in total silence? Why, just that; for having gained Syria and Palestine a second time, he was now forced to withdraw from Syria and Palestine a second time, and for the first time in his life he knew defeat, defeat, and he did not like it.

Ptolemy sacrificed oxen to all the gods of Greece and many of the gods of Egypt also. He shed tears, but not in public, and not for long. In due course, he too swore, *By Zeus, by Pan, by all the gods, I shall have my revenge.*

Later in that year Ptolemy made his peace with Antigonos One-Eye and the other Macedonian generals—Kassandros, ruler of Macedon, and Lysimakhos, ruler of Thrace—and Ptolemy agreed, with heavy heart, to abandon all his claims to Phoenicia and Syria.

He did not, however, make peace with Seleukos of Syria, and it was not long before war started up again, as before, with his one-time friend turned now into his enemy. Ptolemy concentrated upon making stronger his power at sea, ordering new ships of war by the hundred. Although he had lost Syria and Phoenicia, he had still the island of Cyprus, that was of the first importance in matters of strategy.

Though he fought on, Ptolemy sighed often that he was tired of war, worn out by war and the horror of war. On this subject the Egyptians agreed with him. The Egyptian dislikes bloodshed. He hates the destruction of peaceful family life that is caused by battle.

Ptolemy had seen enough pointless fighting, and he went about the Residence quoting to his advisers the wise words of Bias of Priene: *Gain your end not by force, but by persuasion.*

The enemies of Ptolemy liked to say that his tendency to retreat whenever he could was evidence of foolishness—of this man's cowardice. But Ptolemy was no coward. For him, not to fight was the wiser course of action.

He was tired also of fighting his wife Eurydike, who had been making demands for an increased allowance, and who had become strangely loud and confident about what she seemed to think were a wife's rights.

He thought of her now as the *Unlucky Wife,* for that she seemed to have brought him nothing but ill fortune and defeat.

Yes, he thought that Berenike, whose name, it is never to be forgotten, means Bringer of Victory, might change his luck, and bring him luck, and it was now that he took away the title of First Wife from Eurydike and gave it to Berenike, her aunt.

And he was right. Berenike would indeed turn out to be his lucky wife.

2.18

City of Fishes

All these years—these eleven years in Egypt—Ptolemy suffered in the heat. In the summer time, when the heat was at its worst, he appointed extra collectors of snails, extra pounders of snails, to make ever more of the sunstroke remedy that contained pounded snails and frankincense.

Ptolemy had read to him the treatise of Theophrastos, *Of Sweat,* and its sequel, *Of Dizziness,* and he looked for fresh ways of coping with the flood of perspiration that poured from every Greek in Egypt, but most particularly from himself.

He sent regular orders for the turpentine ointment that stopped or disguised the rank odour of the armpit, and he sent for shiploads of the rose powder that was supposed to dry up a man's sweat upon the instant. None of these things, however, was of much use, so that Ptolemy thought again of making Alexandria his headquarters, for this seemed to be a more bearable city, so far as temperature and climate were concerned, and the word from the north was that the new satrapal Residence there was just about fit to be inhabited.

Ptolemy laid his plans, and gave his orders for wall paintings of scenes from Homer, and thought about the last details of decoration. Meanwhile, his army continued to make ready for the invasion of Egypt by Ptolemy's enemies, drilling upon the sandy plain opposite Memphis in the scorching sun, with ostrich egg smeared upon their faces against the sunburn; and no man removed his *kausia,* or beret, except to wipe his brow with it, or to wave it above his head as he cheered the Satrap on his progress up or down the River.

Ptolemy slept ill. The intense heat, the whine of biting flies, the braying of donkeys, the barking of the jackals, the responsibility of affairs of state weighing upon his spirits—all these things kept him from proper sleep. And when he did sleep, he dreamed wild dreams, and woke up screaming, as if the Persians were upon him; or he would be woken by a cockerel standing upon his window ledge, or by the ibis tapping at the shutters with his long beak.

Ptolemy made, then, the greatest use of the Greek cures for sleeplessness: the houseleek, wrapped in a black cloth, he placed beneath his pillow; or he would eat nightingale flesh before he retired for the night. Mostly, though, he stayed awake, worrying not so much about the present as about the past, which he could not forget, and about the future: about what had gone wrong, and about what would go wrong next.

Ptolemy was, to be sure, tired, but more than physically tired: he was tired of Memphis after ten years of not one breath of wind except the whirling storm of sand, and no water but Nile water, in which the native bathed himself and washed his clothes, and into which he threw his excrement, and where, in the hot season, the water dried up into a trickle.

Like all Greeks, Ptolemy preferred to live close by the sea. Moreover, he now wished to have a more direct control over Egypt's trade with Greece that would flourish by way of the Great Harbour of Alexandria.

Memphis, in truth, stank, he said, of mummies, for the air from the *nekropolis* was not fresh air. Yes, Memphis was a place of death, that stank of death and tasted of death, and Ptolemy had had his fill of death.

The Residence there was full of three thousand years of pharaonic lumber, golden rubbish that Ptolemy had no use for, but could neither throw away nor magic out of sight: rooms stacked high with gilded furniture, and golden mummy cases, and ceremonial boxes of ebony and ivory; things that nobody would ever use again, but that were part of a pharaoh's inheritance and could not be disposed of.

Really, there were too many echoes of the past at Memphis. Ptolemy wanted a house without echoes of the past, and so he made his mind up to move to the north.

Alexandria herself, now twenty years in the building, was no longer a fishing village but a fine Greek city of the very greatest magnificence, and Ptolemy longed to live there.

His new Residence was a great white palace of Paros marble that glittered in the sun, defended by high white walls, with guard posts, lookout points, battlements, and guaranteed proof against all assault, whether by sea or by undermining. The system of drains was perfect. The underground water supply, in giant cisterns, would never fail. Above all, the city was so aligned that the sweet breath of the north-west wind blew straight down Kanopic Street into the Satrap's open windows.

Ptolemy moved house, then, taking with him the best pieces of golden furniture from Memphis, down-River to Alexandria, and as he floated his household goods towards the sea, the people of Egypt waved at him and chanted from the River bank, or sang the song of welcoming the Satrap.

With Ptolemy went also the perfectly preserved talisman, still sleeping in his coffin of gold, beneath a golden mask of surpassing Egyptian workmanship, escorted by a crowd that shrilled the funeral lament for a pharaoh, for Ptolemy took with him the unfortunate object that was the living corpse of Alexander: all the way down the Nile they shrilled the lament for a dead king, and it made Ptolemy, in spite of the heat, shiver.

Alexander he laid to rest in the noisiest part of the new city, at the crossroads where Kanopic Street meets the Street of the Soma, or Body, so that the carts and wagons and racing chariots and braying donkeys and the quarrelling population might, if it were possible, wake up the Alexander who had now overslept by three thousand six hundred and fifty nights. And it was in spite also of the Greek ban upon burying any dead man within the city walls.

Above all other reasons for quitting Memphis was Ptolemy's great passion for fish. The trouble with Memphis was that the fishes of the sea always went bad by the time they got there, and salt fish was no substitute for fresh. Alexandria, then, meant an uninterrupted supply of river fish, sea fish, and fish also from Lake Mareotis, which lay behind the city: fresh fish, and the mouth of Ptolemy watered to think of it.

He soon found, of course, that in Alexandria every thing seemed to taste of fish. Every thing smelled also of fish, and the stink of rotten fish lingered upon the air, or was blown from the harbour along Kanopic Street into the Residence windows. To Eurydike, who moved north not without protestations, even the dates tasted of fish, the meat tasted of fish, and the fishes tasted—like Ptolemy. But Berenike did not complain. The smell of fish was unimportant compared with what she had now got for herself, which was power over an entire city, where there were no Egyptian priests who must be pleased. In Alexandria she would do just what she liked.

Ptolemy, then, exchanged the stink of Memphis for the stink of Alexandria. But there was the consolation that he was a little less hot, and it seemed also possible that in the new city he might sleep better.

Memphis he had thought to leave to the priests of Egypt, though he did not escape from the High Priest of Ptah so easily, for the result of Ptolemy moving house was that Anemhor spent the rest of his life sailing his ship back and forth between Memphis and Alexandria, in order to wait upon the Satrap and give him his wise advice, so that this man seemed never to be in the right place at the right time, but was always upon the River.

Throughout all the inconvenience of his travels, however, the half-smile of the High Priest never left his face, for he was a man whose self-control was complete. A scribe does not show ill temper. And in any case, whatsoever was done for the good of Egypt did not displease this man.

Ptolemy and his family, they at once both loved and hated Alexandria, just as they had both loved and hated Macedon, for these were people who would never be wholly happy wherever they were. It was their fate, in truth, to find fault with every thing, and wherever they found themselves they wished to be some place else. When in Greece they longed to quit Greece, but no sooner had they left it than they yearned for home. Such is the paradox of the Greeks; such was their everlasting discontent.

Contrast, if you will, Reader, the family of Anemhor, High Priest of Ptah, who were happy wherever they found themselves and whatever they did; for the service of the gods of Egypt is happiness, and the office of a scribe brings contentment. Thoth swears that it is the truth.

Ptolemy himself felt more comfortable in his skin living at Alexandria. He perspired a little less, but now he was troubled less by the heat than by the damp, and he missed the beautiful Egyptian winter of Memphis. But he had not sworn an oath never again to set his sandal in Memphis: he would go there when business demanded his presence— he would go back. Meanwhile, at Alexandria in early spring violent storms undid the window shutters of the new palace and made them bang all night long, so that Ptolemy lay sleepless, thinking of his past, trying to remember how to forget.

After a beautiful month of Pharmouthi the summer would follow, and a mephitic damp would rise each evening from the sea, settling upon every dry thing in the Residence, and he would begin to shiver, and to sneeze, and it was the return of the marsh fever, and he suffered agonies until it left him.

Then, yes, the thousand palm trees planted by Kleomenes down the middle of Kanopic Street would clack in the wind so that the sleep of the Satrap was disturbed, and he threatened to have them cut down, saying he could not, in any case, have Egyptian trees in a Greek city; but Berenike talked him out of it, and the palm trees clacked and clacked in the sweet breath of the north wind that came to Egypt laden with the scent of lemons from Greece—or so they liked to pretend— and this man lay sleepless ever after.

As for the rest of the city, Alexandria teemed with people from all over the Greek world, who showed themselves quite quickly to be unstable, volatile, given to riot and rocked by the slightest rumour, moved by the most trivial of causes to stand shouting under the Satrap's windows about some imagined grievance. At the public shows, the horse races in the hippodrome, the foot races at the *stadion* and at the great Greek theatre overlooking the harbour, the crowd went wild. Worst of all were the chariot races, when the mob went quite mad, tearing up their clothes and throwing them at the horses and charioteers. These were people who would even draw swords over a donkey race.

Thoth asks, What was the reason for it? Yes, Alexandria was a city of great luxury. Her citizens were Greeks, most of them, or Syrians, men of Kyrene, immigrants from Cyprus or Palestine and Phoenicia. Some were criminals on the run from arrest and certain crucifixion, but most had set out as hired soldiers. They had come to Egypt from all over the Greek-speaking world, in search of good times, better times. Hardship and poverty they had thought to leave behind them. So that when the good time was not forthcoming, not possible, or for some reason withheld, they turned to violence.

From the start, Alexandria was trumpeted by Ptolemy himself as the city where a man might do just what he liked. It was to be a city without rules, a city devoted entirely to pleasure, a city where no thing that a man imagined to do would be forbidden him. Alas, to advertise such a thing was, in truth, asking for trouble, and could only attract large numbers of quite the wrong sort of citizen.

However, Alexandria was not, of course, a city without *laws*, and when these migrants and immigrants found that there were limits to their famous freedom, limits to licence, they felt that they had been tricked. It should have been no surprise to anybody, least of all to Ptolemy, when these people showed their displeasure by riot and revolt, and by pushing down the statues of their rulers. The Alexandrians had cut themselves off from their roots. They had, many of them, left their families behind them in order to start a new life. There were too many men and not enough women, so that it was a city with many whores, attracted by rumours of brisk business. Thus the city of Alexandria began, and thus it would continue. Nobody, as they said, could mistake it for a happy place.

Thus Thoth seeks to explain the volatile nature of this city, the fickleness, the lawlessness, the high spirits, the unfortunate moral character of the Alexandrians. Aye, and he shakes his head for what is to come: terrible things, terrible things.

2.19

The Handle Kiss

While the Satrap was away fighting his battles in Syria, or gorging upon fishes, or floating up-River on official business, his children were left under the care and control of their mothers, or their tutors, or to fend for themselves, and at the best of times Ptolemy was, because of the pressure of his work, a little distant. The result of it was, of course, that their habits of life were formed without the Satrap watching what was happening. He did not eat his food with these children of his: he ate with his Greek advisers, his Greek generals, his Greek admirals, and with the commanders of his army, or with the High Priest of Memphis. Nor did he sleep in the same part of the new Residence with his children. No, indeed, days and even months might pass by without these infants setting eyes upon their father, except to catch a glimpse of him being carried from courtyard to courtyard in some procession of officials, or receiving ambassadors from some foreign country.

You must not think, Reader, that Ptolemy *forgot* about his children. He might have been remote, but he was sent always reports of their progress, he heard always of their good—and bad—behaviour and he never forgot the anniversary of any child's birth, legitimate or illegitimate.

For his fifth birthday gift the Satrap sent his son Keraunos a blunted wooden sword, as if to show him the way that he must go, and Keraunos fought from one end of the Residence to the other, sparring with the guards in mock combat, learning from them the proper strokes: how to parry and thrust, how to disarm his enemy, how to throw the sword spinning high into the air and catch it as it came down again without hurting himself.

The Satrap was pleased with Keraunos's progress, and he looked upon this boy with great favour, as his heir. At the same time, though, wherever this boy went there was trouble, almost as if he were the embodiment of Disorder. Keraunos, Thunderbolt—sure, it was one of the titles of Zeus himself, and the bolt of lightning was his personal signature. Keraunos had become already very like the Thunderbolt, and he strove to live up to his nickname.

When Anemhor was in Alexandria, he made a point of sending for this boy, to speak kind words, to keep an eye upon his progress, for that he was the boy who should be Satrap after his father, and he brought Keraunos gifts, whether it was his birthday or not—hounds of high breeding, in which Keraunos delighted, or monkeys from the Land of Punt; or, best of all, the leopard cub whose spots matched exactly the spots upon Anemhor's leopard skin of office, which Keraunos hauled about the Residence upon a leash, or carried about in his arms, or had sleep upon his bed—until he grew too large for comfort. Anemhor noted the Greek belief that for the child whose cry was like the pine trees the future held nothing but bad things, and he shook his head, because he could see that around Keraunos the thunder would get worse.

As soon as the Thunderbolt was seven years old he was removed from the *gynaikeion,* forbidden to go there, and lived henceforth with the men. At the same time he was put on the back of a pony and taught to ride, because all Macedonian boys are meant to grow up horse-crazy, and because, really, it was not possible to start riding too young.

Keraunos learned how to start and stop a horse. He jumped walls and ditches, and often he flew right over the horse's head. At length he was allowed to canter and gallop, and though he felt as if his mount was running away with him, he behaved like his father's son, as if he had been born on horseback. He showed no fear, and he loved the horse, and the Satrap was proud of his progress.

Before he was ten years old Keraunos could perform every horse trick: fast starts, rapid turns, circles, pivots and spins. A spin is the most difficult thing, for to make a horse turn upon the spot, faster than the eye can see—it can make him lose his balance. A spin is important, though, for a horse in battle must counter attacks from all sides, and it needs a rider with nerves of iron and a horse with total obedience. Keraunos had, indeed, nerves of iron. Book-learning he had little time for, but he was very good at physical things, and they said he was a born warrior, a born horseman. Some murmured, even then, that he was also a born madman.

At dawn, before it grew too hot, the mounted troops of Ptolemy would lead their horses from the stables that adjoined the barracks, which were next to the Residence of Ptolemy, and gallop along the beaches east or west of Alexandria, or round the shores of Lake Mareotis, or into the desert towards Taposiris, riding so far into the sands that if a man's horse failed him he would die of thirst before he could walk back.

Ptolemy Keraunos, young though he was, rode with them, for his future lay with the Macedonian army, in battle, in the defence of Egypt and her empire.

From a young age Ptolemy Keraunos was encouraged by Berenike to show his affection for his younger half-sister, Arsinoë Beta, by kissing her with the *khutra* kiss of the Greeks, in which they held on to each other's ears, using the ears as handles. At first this kiss was innocent, a sign of real tenderness, and the sister would grab the brother's ears in return, and kiss him upon his lips with a sweetness that made Berenike smile—and did she, even then, foresee that her daughter might wed her own half-brother? Was this the plan, even at this early date, of Berenike? Was she, even so soon, plotting for her daughter to have power in Egypt? Perhaps.

As they grew older, however, Keraunos kissed the sister with the same handle kiss, but he would pull her ears hard, so that she cried out, and he would some times even go so far as to bite her, some times in play, some times not, but with a fierceness that startled Arsinoë and caused her to slap at him with her hands. Keraunos, though, was the older by four years, and he was stronger, and the kiss, the biting and the slapping would turn into a fight, in which the hands of Arsinoë Beta would fly into Keraunos's dark, curly hair and pull hard, and they would shout insults at each other—*Ibis-face!* and *Hippopotamus-face!*—and have to be dragged apart by whatever relative was bold enough to come between them.

In this way half-brother and half-sister would some times exchange brotherly and sisterly love for hatred.

Thoth says, This was, alas, to be the pattern for the future.

2.20

Unlucky Women

In Greece, meanwhile, the hatred went on as before, and that unhappy woman Olympias, mother of Alexander, went on putting her enemies to the sword, one after another; but when Kassandros heard about the killing of Philippos Arrhidaios and the self-murder of Adeia-Eurydike, his rage knew no bounds, and he declared war upon Olympias, and it was his purpose to show her no mercy.

When Olympias heard what was about to happen, she left Aristonos, the devoted bodyguard of Alexander, in charge of her troops and fled to Pydna, a city on the north-east coast of Greece, taking with her not only her waiting-women but the young King Alexandros, her ten-year-old grandson, and Deidameia, the young girl who was betrothed already to be married to him, and Roxane also, the widow of Alexander, and she barricaded herself inside the citadel.

Kassandros laid siege to Pydna, blockaded the port to cut off all supplies, and settled down to starve Olympias out. The Siege of Pydna would last two hundred and seventy days, and by the end of it Olympias's soldiers had eaten every beast, even the horses and mules, within the walls, and it was said that they had begun even to kill and eat each other.

Olympias herself was reduced to feeding her elephants of war upon sawdust, and she herself was said to have eaten the flesh of the elephants that died, and, unlikely though it might seem, she was supposed to have eaten the corpses of her waiting-women also.

She held out against Kassandros until she could bear the stench and pestilent filth no longer, and then she tried to make her escape by sea, for she was a woman of the greatest strength of will, who would never admit defeat.

Kassandros, however, was warned by some deserter of what Olympias was going to do, and he seized the swift-sailing *trieres* in which she had planned to set sail. And so, at last, Olympias gave herself up, and Kassandros swore his most solemn oath regarding her personal safety, but had her accused by the friends and relatives of those she had put to death, before the National Assembly of the Macedonians.

Kassandros knew what the result would be if he let Olympias plead her case in person: the Macedonians would surely be moved to tears by the sight of this old Queen, the mother of their great general, and grant her a pardon. And so Kassandros took her death into his own hands.

First, he sent a party of two hundred soldiers to murder the Queen in her palace, but she faced them in her majesty, the Queen of Macedon, so that these men were ashamed of themselves, and turned round and shuffled away, murmuring that they could not put to death the widow of King Philip, the mother of Alexander, whatever she had done wrong.

Kassandros sent next the relatives of the people Olympias had murdered, and they were not moved to tears by her royal presence, or awed by the memory of her murdering son, or sentimental about the glorious history of Macedon, but stabbed her to death.

A different story said that Olympias was stoned to death, which was the traditional manner of executing criminals in Macedon.

Nobody, however, disputed the fact of her death, or that her body was cast out unburied. Her beautiful eyes were pecked out by the crows. The scavenging dogs licked the breasts that had given suck to the master of half the world. The flies of Pydna feasted upon her flesh.

Such was the end of Olympias, who was said to be one of the most poisonous women that ever lived—at least, until the women of the House of Ptolemy rose up to take her place.

What of the rest of the family of Alexander? All this time his widow, Roxane, had survived. And she had the reputation of being the most beautiful woman in all Asia, second only to the wife of Darius, King of Persia, and she was still beautiful, for she had been only fifteen years old at her marriage, and was now only thirty-one, a woman who might, had she not married the king of all the trouble in the world, have lived to a ripe age in her native Baktria. But that was not what the Fates had planned for her.

No, Roxane, Little Star, would not glitter for long.

Her son, as King Alexandros, was still in Greece with his mother, and Kassandros, the man who had killed off nearly every other member of Alexander's family, chose this moment to turn his attention to Roxane herself.

Kassandros sent the boy King and his mother, as virtual prisoners, to the citadel of Amphipolis, where he kept them under close guard. The winter was cold, so cold that the soldiers wore fox-skin caps, and Roxane and Alexandros shivered, and were fed upon eels from the River Strymon and not much else. The cold made them ill, and Kassandros, by all accounts, offered little in the way of medical assistance.

The boy Alexandros had never known his great father, but he was by now old enough to understand why things happened as they did. He had studied Greek with a tutor, but at Amphipolis there were no lessons, for it was the plan of Kassandros that his prisoners would soon have no need to speak any language.

The existence of this boy troubled Kassandros. He thought about putting him to death, getting him out of the way, and his mother also, and yet he put off doing the deed. He did not torture or ill-treat these two, but kept them locked up, deprived of their freedom and comforts. It seemed good to him to say that he had in his train the son of Alexander, good to see the King under his control.

It was at this time that Roxane dedicated the last of her possessions, a golden necklace and a *rhyton* of gold, to Athene, but although she made her offerings and her prayers to the gods of Greece, they were deaf to her pleas and did not hurry to her rescue.

Roxane had, of course, been jealous in her turn. By sending a forged letter she had tricked Stateira, another of Alexander's wives, into visiting her, and she had murdered this woman, and her sister also, with a welcome-drink laced with hemlock, and the story was that she had thrown the bodies down a well-shaft, filled it up with earth, and danced upon the top of it. Now the sort of treatment Roxane had given to others was to be the treatment she would enjoy herself.

After they had been twelve months in their prison, Kassandros sent Roxane a bowl of wine with hemlock mixed into it. Roxane had her suspicions about the mouselike smell, but she had drunk nothing that day, and had a great thirst. And so it was that the hemlock brought mother and son out in small red spots, and chilled their bodies and congealed their blood, and they died with retching and with horrible convulsions.

Kassandros lit the funeral pyres with his own hand, and he had the good grace to bury the King and his mother properly, in a royal tomb. The bones of Roxane he placed in the usual *larnax*, with a silver hand-mirror, the gift of her late husband; those of young Alexandros he crowned with the wreath of golden oak leaves that must be placed in the tomb of every king of Macedon. Much good these gifts did them.

In Egypt the only reminders of this Pharaoh who had never set one foot in his kingdom, but was known as Rahaaabsetepenamen, or Aleksantres, were a colossal head in pink Syene granite, wearing the Double Crown, that was ordered for the city of Alexandria, and an avenue of forty sphinxes that lined the approach to the Sarapieion there, each with the young King's smiling features. The hieroglyphs described this Alexandros in the traditional manner, as Horus the Youthful, Lord of Crowns, Lord in the Whole World, King of Upper and Lower Egypt, the Delight of the Heart of Amun, Beloved of the Sun, Alexandros the Ever-Living.

But Alexandros the Ever-Living was dead, and he had not lived long enough to celebrate his thirteenth birthday.

In this way Kassandros, the most ruthless of the children of Old Antipatros, brought disgrace upon his family, who now refused to have anything more to do with him.

His sister, Eurydike, the wife of Ptolemy, devoted herself from this time to good deeds, in order to make up for and drive out the bad. She made it her duty and pleasure to defend the innocent, and she helped many poor girls of Alexandria to be married at her expense, by providing them with dowries. She did not speak the name of her brother Kassandros, but worked the Spell of Forgetting, so that she might no longer dream of the dreadful things he had done.

Kassandros now had the blood of most of Alexander's family upon his hands, and yet he still lived, and was haunted by no ghost. But the oracles forecast that he might not die too happily himself, saying that he would swell up full of water, and that the worms would breed in his living flesh. This horror would not occur for twenty years to come, but an oracle always speaks true.

There was now, then, no male heir left from the family of Alexander, no king to rule over Egypt, and only one member of his House left alive: his sister, Kleopatra, sometime wife of King Alexandros of Epeiros, but now twice widowed.

This woman's life had been far from lucky, for it was at her wedding that her father, Philip of Macedon, had been assassinated, and she was then eighteen years old. Now she was no longer young, being forty-six years of age, and near the finish of child-bearing.

Ever since her brother's death, however, ex-Queen Kleopatra had attracted very many suitors, all wanting to attach to himself the glory of Alexander, for this Kleopatra was every man's last chance of a dynastic alliance with the blood royal of Macedon.

Kleopatra, the first of many women of this name—and Thoth says,

Reader, Do *not* confuse this woman with the most famous of the Kleopatras, the seventh Kleopatra, who comes later, much later— received all messengers with haughty words, and though she heard every proposal for marriage, she rejected them all.

Kleopatra remained unmarried, and now was living at Sardis in Lydia, surrounded by treachery and plots, and fortified only by her extraordinary strength of will. In their turn every one of the Successors had sought her hand: Perdikkas, Old Antipatros, Antigonos One-Eye— all had wanted to marry her. Even Kassandros had made his offer, though she would never have agreed to marry the man supposed to be her brother's murderer.

The attraction of Kleopatra was the glamour that fixed itself to her brother's name, and perhaps no longer was it her physical attractions that made men seek her out with such diligence; but it was now that even Ptolemy began to fancy himself as Kleopatra's husband, and this hopeful bridegroom was fifty-nine years of age.

All was not well, though, with Kleopatra, whose enemies were closing in, and she now looked about, afraid for her safety, seeking an ally and a protector, and the thought of a secure marriage looked like the answer to her troubles.

When Ptolemy sent his first messenger to ask Kleopatra to be his wife, she would have none of it, knowing very well that he did not woo her, but the *kudos* to be got by marrying Alexander's sister. But when she heard that Kassandros had murdered her twelve-year-old nephew, and then, shortly afterwards, of the murder of his older half-brother Herakles, and of Barsine his mother also, she was very afraid. Now she sent ambassadors to Ptolemy to arrange a marriage, for she remembered him as a kind, fair, generous man, and it so happened that he was also the wealthiest of the Successors. Of all the satraps Ptolemy was the man whom Kleopatra wanted, and she sent word that she was about to quit Sardis and set sail for Alexandria, and Ptolemy made himself ready to welcome her.

While these things were being arranged Kleopatra was suddenly put under house arrest on the orders of Antigonos One-Eye, and it was One-Eye who sent, one night, some women to visit Kleopatra, and the next thing that was heard about her was that a body had been found upon the floor of her bedchamber, lying in a pool of sticky blood.

For many days Ptolemy paced the floor of his Hall of Audiences. For many hours he stared out to sea, and kept a close watch upon the Great Harbour, sending to ask what ships had been sunk, what ships arrived; but no word came from Sardis, and no ship, and in the end there were no festivities, and no fourth wedding for Ptolemy, because his bride was dead.

The news of the death of Kleopatra caused Eurydike and Berenike no small relief. In fact they both of them screamed for delight.

Every legitimate claimant to the throne of Alexander had now been done away with, and there looked to be no obstacle left in the way of creating independent sovereignties for the Successors. Thus, within twenty years of Alexander's death every member of his House had been brutally murdered, a total of ten people, most of them women and children.

With no king to rule over Egypt, the road was now clear for Ptolemy the Satrap to become king himself, if he wished it. But Ptolemy was a modest man. He had no desire to bring down the jealousy of the gods upon his own head. And when the High Priest asked whether he might be pleased to be a pharaoh, Ptolemy shook his head and said, *No, no, I cannot think of doing it.*

2.21

Ptolemy Mikros

In that year of many deaths there occurred also one remarkable birth: that of Berenike's second child by Ptolemy, and it had been eight years in the making.

How many dead babies had Berenike taken to the *nekropolis*? She had lost her count. Five, perhaps, or six it was. But there was much plague, much fever in Egypt, and nobody was expected to live much longer than thirty years, so that it was every time almost a miracle to live beyond infancy, and the occasion for great offerings to the gods.

Berenike had in the end resorted to Egyptian remedies suggested by the priests of Sakhmet the lioness goddess of Memphis, such as crawling seven times backwards and forwards under the belly of a camel. Another time she had been required to walk seven times round the Great Pyramid of Khufu, or Cheops, like the barren women of the Egyptians, sure in the belief that this would help her to become a mother again. But the walking had not been a success either, merely serving to make her tired and angry.

For an Egyptian remedy to work it is necessary, of course, also to *believe,* but Berenike did not really believe. She was a Greek, from Greece, more Greek than Greek could be, and to tell the truth she hated Egyptian things, the dates and camels, the palm trees and the storm of sand, the snakes and scorpions, and she despised herself for taking notice of Egyptian medicine that did not work for her.

At length, in the summer of the fifteenth year of the satrapy of Ptolemy, when many of the Greeks quit Alexandria for the temperate islands of the Aegean Sea, because of the blinding clouds of lime dust in the streets and the searing heat, Ptolemy and Berenike took themselves to Kos, island of lettuces, where the heat was less fierce, moderated by cool breezes. For yes, Kos was healthier than Egypt, and it had also the finest medical school in the Greek world, and a Temple of Asklepios famous for cures of women's disorders. On Kos there was green abundance, and quietness, and Greek physicians who understood Berenike's trouble.

On Kos they plied her with decoctions of kidney sinews and frankincense in wine, to restore a fertility lost by sorcery. Many medicines Berenike tried, but she was cured at last by eating a hyaena's eye with liquorice and dill, which guaranteed conception within seven nights of swallowing it. And the Satrap himself stood by, with his left-hand testicle tied up one more time with the papyrus string, in the sure belief that by doing this he might become the father of a fresh son.

In the cool of the morning Berenike would stroll along the temple terrace to witness the feeding of the sacred snakes. In the cool of the evening she would wander through the sacred groves of cypresses and gaze at a sea blue like *sappheiros,* towards Knidos and Halikarnassos, and she believed that Asklepios, god of Health, was with her.

At the same time Ptolemy sought the cure for his hot fit and his cold fit, the repeating fevers that had troubled him ever since leaving Greece. Ptolemy, too, underwent the cure called Incubation in the Temple of Asklepios, where he was made to eat lion's fat and rose oil, and laid himself down to sleep in the sanctuary of the god, where the sacred snakes came to lick his ears, and where, at length, the god should have come and touched him, whereupon the repeating fevers should have passed away. But Ptolemy saw no god. Ptolemy saw nothing. He did not sleep in the Temple of Asklepios any better than he slept at Alexandria, and none of the supposed cures to be had on Kos had the least effect upon his shivering fit. He stayed some weeks, however, sending messengers back and forth to Egypt, ruling by proxy, through the *Dioiketes* and his army of officials, and nobody so much as suspected that the Satrap was not at home, for in Memphis they had been told to say he was down in Alexandria, and at Alexandria to say that he was up at Memphis.

At length Ptolemy sailed for Egypt, leaving Berenike in the care of Asklepios, his holy dogs and sacred snakes, and in the month of Phamenoth following, when the poppies were just in flower on Kos, her stoutness of the stomach persisting, she experienced again the pangs of childbirth.

Berenike breathed deep, as instructed, and she held on until the twentieth day of the month, which was the best possible day, though in truth no day was unfavourable for the birth of a boy. But the boy born upon the twentieth of the month, they said, would grow up to be a wise man. Berenike's child was indeed a boy, and she screamed her thanks to Artemis for it, and for his yellow hair that was the mark of a true son of Macedon, and she dedicated to Asklepios a brace of ears cast in solid gold, that were large enough to sleep in, as a thank-offering to the god for listening to her prayers.

On the tenth day of his life this son of Ptolemy son of Lagos was given his name, as previously discussed by the parents—or, in fact, as not discussed, for he could not have any other name but Ptolemaios: Warlike. This was the Ptolemy son of Ptolemy who would be known to history as Ptolemy Philadelphos, The One Who Loves His Sister, though this title did not fix itself upon him until many years afterwards. In the beginning, since he was the last and youngest child, the *metakho-iron*, as it were, or runt of the litter, they called him simply Mikros, Small One, in order to distinguish him from all the others in his family who had also this illustrious and most illustrious name.

Mikros Berenike nursed herself, having taken to heart the wise words of her Greek physicians *not to employ the wet nurse if possible, but feed the child yourself,* Satrap's wife notwithstanding. For there was no being sure, really, what bad qualities a nurse might pass on to her charge by letting him drink milk meant for some other child, not of satrapal rank, and Berenike had no wish for her beloved son to suck milk meant for a dead baby.

Berenike, then, this mother of some determination to get her own way, refused not only the wet nurse: she refused also to have anything to do with the bandaging.

She said no, Ptolemy Mikros would *not* be strapped to the board with bandaged limbs for the first sixty days of his life, and that she did not wish her son to grow up ill-tempered like his half-brother Ptolemy Keraunos, about whom they often said that it was the bandaging that had left him angry for life. This, at any rate, was the reason for Mikros having the unstraight legs.

Nor would Berenike allow Mikros to be fed boiled mice to check the incontinence.

If he wets the bed, she said, *he wets the bed. But the son of the Satrap will not eat boiled mice.*

Berenike was, in truth, the most powerful of women, with most singular opinions of her own, which she was in no wise fearful of giving voice to, and any physician, Greek or Egyptian, who thought to tell her that she was wrong would feel the razor edge of her tongue.

The Satrap also could not but recognize the power of this wife of his. But the forcefulness was what he liked about her. She was a woman who knew what she wanted. She was not tongue-tied like Eurydike. She was not afraid to tell him what she thought about his governance of Egypt. And from time to time even Ptolemy would find that he had to do exactly what Berenike told him.

In due course Berenike took ship for Egypt with this fresh son, and on the fortieth day after the birth the Satrap held the proper Greek celebrations in his Residence at Alexandria. The days of doubt and uncertainty were at an end. Ptolemy Mikros lived. He would be raised, not cast out. He was a member of the family, and he had the same yellow-gold hair as his father, hair like the Sun, and he was as unlike his half-brother, Ptolemy the Thunderbolt (who, of course, was dark), as might be imagined.

Berenike, who had been homeless, loveless, friendless, was in truth nothing but a schemer, a dreamer of schemes, who would stop at nothing in order to have her own way. How, then, did she bring up these two children of hers? Her elder child by Ptolemy, Arsinoë Beta, the girl that should have been a boy, she had brought up already to be tough, to be like a man, not to be weak and womanly, and she even wished her to stifle her feminine feelings.

Sure, to begin with Berenike taught Arsinoë Beta how to do all the usual girl's things, how to work the loom, how to sew and embroider, how to strum the lyre—the things without which no girl could put up with the boredom of living in the *gynaikeion,* for it was work that helped the Greek women through their shuttered lives, work that was unending, and carried out in the half-dark of those rooms where no man must ever set his sandal, apart from the eunuchs, the half-men, who guarded them.

But when Arsinoë Beta had arrived at her seventh birthday, she began to receive the full education of a boy also. To start with she learned the *alpha beta,* and the art of reading and writing Greek. She learned simple mathematics and geometry, then complicated mathematics. She learned all the arts of war: tactics, strategy, diplomacy, and she had even the weapons training so that she knew very well how to defend herself, and all as if it was her fate to be some kind of latter-day Amazon, like that ill-fated Adeia-Eurydike, the wife of Philippos Arrhidaios.

Yes, this was exactly the thought of Berenike: that her daughter would need these skills if she were to be the wife of some great ruler. Berenike herself had survived by being tough, by suppressing her womanly feelings, by thinking her way into being very like a man.

Most important of all, Arsinoë Beta was absolutely forbidden to grow up to be like Eurydike: dovelike, feather-brained, completely feminine, and utterly useless to her husband for anything but the ploughing of children. For Eurydike had been a satrap's daughter, but she was brought up to rely upon slaves and servants for her every requirement. Eurydike was a woman who could hardly put on her own *peplos* without help. She hardly knew which of her hands was which, let alone how to run her husband's household. No, poor Eurydike was incapable of looking after herself, let alone of looking after others. And look at what had happened to her—the rejected wife. She was a hopeless failure, and her children would, in the opinion of Berenike, be hopeless failures after her.

Arsinoë Beta was made to promise, yes, she would try to be tough. Yes, she would try to be manlike. Yes, she would do her best to be the son that Berenike had not given birth to. And yes, indeed, by the time Ptolemy Mikros was born, Arsinoë Beta was nine years old, and it was too late to go back to being feminine: the damage was done.

At the beginning the scheme of Berenike worked. Arsinoë Beta fought just as well as her half-brothers with the short sword, and was even an example to them for fierceness. She jumped with weights and threw the *diskos* and javelin as well as any of Eurydike's sons. But while Arsinoë Beta willed herself to be like a boy, to have a heart like a stone, a heart of iron, *that felt nothing* and was not moved by feelings as other women's hearts were moved, she could not succeed in what she strove so hard to do.

For it was the fate of this girl to fall in love so intensely that she hardly knew what she was doing, and with the most tragic consequences. Though she did her best to crush her woman's nature, Arsinoë could no more banish her female feelings than any other woman. She did weep—of course she did. She did have motherly thoughts, for how could she not? She did care what happened to her children. Alas, though Arsinoë Beta was tough, in spite of herself, she was not tough enough.

What does the god of Wisdom say? Thoth says, Really, you cannot turn a woman into a man. Thoth says, Really, you cannot stop up a woman's love.

As for the son, Ptolemy Mikros—Berenike would teach *him* not to be like Ptolemy Keraunos, saying, *Do not be so warlike. Do not be always wanting to fight, for this is how the barbarian behaves* . . .

This mother would encourage her son's tutors to teach him about science, about the drama, about poetry—things of the mind—and she poured scorn upon the delight of drilling with the phalanx, and learning the best way to kill a man. Keraunos had grown up, she thought, to love war more than a boy should, and so she tried to redress the balance and teach Mikros to be interested in peace, like his father.

Mikros, then, would grow up a little soft, and it was in any case his natural tendency to be lazy, inactive, and his natural instinct to think rather than to use his body and be violent. He grew up to be more of a scholar than his half-brother, so that, really, he had few words to speak to the generals and admirals of his father's armed forces.

Thoth asks, Had Berenike in truth planned every thing this way? So that she had a daughter who was most like a man—active, warlike, with a head for mathematics and high finance, and for war—and a son who was rather like a woman—passive, a thinker, more interested in peace than war? Was all of this the doing of the powerful Berenike? But for the moment Thoth has not the answer. Perhaps, he says, perhaps.

Thoth saves up his answers for later. The plan of Berenike would not be accomplished for many years, and she would not live to see it come to fruition. But when the marriage of these two children of hers to each other took place, some twenty years and more into the future, yes, yes, the triumph of Aunt Berenike over Eurydike, the niece, would be complete.

Thus, at any rate, appeared the future to Anemhor, High Priest of Ptah, when he stared into his bowl of water with oil poured upon the surface of it, and he was not displeased by what he saw there, although he could scarcely believe that what he saw would come to be true.

In the same year that Ptolemy Mikros was born, an army commanded by the Satrap's youthful stepson, Magas, the son of Berenike and the mysterious Philippos, recovered the lost territory of Kyrene for Egypt.

Ptolemy showed his teeth, and by way of reward he made this Magas, who was only eighteen or nineteen years old, governor of Kyrene, where his mother would, from time to time, make the journey to visit her son, taking with her camel-loads of edible luxuries from Alexandria.

At first Magas had been puzzled to be sent out of Egypt, and asked, *Why may I not pass the days at Alexandria? Why may I not remain a soldier in my stepfather's army?*

But Magas had not the ability to foresee the future, as others had.

The problem was that Magas might find himself jealous of Ptolemy Keraunos, the heir. For Berenike knew very well that the moment her husband died, and Keraunos was given the power of a satrap in Egypt, her son Magas would be a dead man, for he presented a threat to security, and was one of the makers of trouble, who might oust Keraunos and take power for himself.

Unlikely, perhaps, given that Keraunos was hardly fourteen years old, but Ptolemy was nearing the age of sixty. This Satrap might die at any time, and he must think of the future, of what might happen when he was no more.

Magas, then, went happily to Kyrene. He was an upright young man, sensible of the proper way to do every thing. He did not forget that he had lived in Egypt by the goodwill of his stepfather, or that if he put one foot wrong in Kyrene he might be banished, sent back to Macedon, where he had neither friend nor relation. He did not forget that if he posed the least threat to the stability of Egypt, he might be quickly murdered. At Kyrene Magas might do, within reason, much as he pleased. He was honoured by Ptolemy's trust, and grateful for the support of his mother.

Magas liked eating, and in Kyrene, famous for fine cooking, he would grow fat. For the time being he took no wife. He had the usual concubines and boys to keep him amused. There was plenty of time to marry and beget an heir. Meanwhile, he busied himself with enjoying his pleasures, and with the governing of his province.

The horoscope of this Magas had forecast that he would be a king, and the father of a famous daughter. From the Kyrenaica, famous for horses, for fresh fish, famous for fine chariots, the future of young Magas looked bright.

2.22

Thief of Books

At the finish of the sailing season in that year when Ptolemy Mikros was one year old, Ptolemy the Satrap made at last his peace with Kassandros, brother of Eurydike, his wife, and he withdrew the Egyptian fleet to Alexandria, saying, *Really, nobody in his right mind goes to war in the winter.*

A year after this the famous Demetrios of Phaleron—Thoth says, Reader, Do not confuse with Demetrios Poliorketes, who is another man altogether, a real man—was forced to flee from Athens, where he had been some kind of ruler, upon the approach of this Poliorketes. And Demetrios of Phaleron now sought asylum with Ptolemy, at Alexandria.

This Demetrios it was who gave Ptolemy the thought of founding a great Mouseion, or Temple of the Muses, and the Great Library of Alexandria was also supposed to have been thought of by him. Some men even said that the great Pharos, or Lighthouse, was not the idea of Alexander, but of this Demetrios of Phaleron. So that, at all events, he was a figure of importance before ever he set his sandal in Egypt, and Ptolemy, kind, fair, generous man that he was, took the trouble to make him welcome.

For Demetrios of Phaleron was wise, clever, shrewd above all other men, and full of brilliant thoughts. And Ptolemy felt that he might prove most useful to him, so useful that he gave this exile upon the spot an apartment to himself in the Residence, and slaves and servants, secretaries, three meals every day and even a salary, in return for thinking fresh thoughts, and he was to have, at any hour of the day or night, the ear of the Satrap to listen to what he said.

Within ten days of his arrival Demetrios had dreamed up one dozen glittering projects that were designed to make Ptolemy and the House of Ptolemy famous throughout the Greek world, and the first of these was the idea for a Library that would have one copy of every book in the world. And what showed the great wonder of being a satrap, and the power of a satrap, was that, no sooner had the thought been had, than it was put into practice. Yes, Ptolemy agreed to the Library in the morning, and by the afternoon the librarians had been given their instructions, the rules for readers had been drawn up, and the *prostagma* sent out that said every book in the city should be carried to Demetrios to be looked at, with a view to acquiring it for the Library—which is to say that those who possessed papyri were more or less expected to *give* them to the new foundation. So that, to some, it looked almost as if Ptolemy started his Library by *stealing* books from every scholar in Egypt, and the great thing about this was that the Library did not cost Ptolemy so much as one hemiobol. All that was needed was the shelves to house the scrolls, and a building in which to house the shelves. The building already existed, for it was an unused part of the Residence, and so the Library was open for business upon the instant.

Demetrios of Phaleron, a graduate of the Lyceum of Aristotle, was famous not only for being clever, but also for dyeing his black hair yellow, and for his habit of smearing his face with women's cosmetics in order to make himself look younger than he really was. He liked both elegant women and handsome boys, banqueting as well as philosophy, and although philosophy was his first interest, he liked also to become very drunk indeed, having the same great thirst for undiluted wine as Ptolemy himself.

The other most important thing for which Demetrios of Phaleron was responsible was to urge Ptolemy to cast his eye over the treatise entitled *Upon Kingship,* and to make him think about being a king himself, for it was Demetrios's though that this was what Ptolemy must do.

Yes, it was Demetrios who sowed the seeds, saying, *There is no reason why you should not be a king,* and he shared Anemhor's thought that a resident pharaoh would keep Egypt calm, and quiet, and free from revolts.

Ptolemy began to read then, at night, when he was unable to sleep, and he dreamed of a glorious future for his descendants, and it was all the doing of Demetrios of the well-hung tongue—this man with cheeks rouged like a woman's, who had himself waited upon by naked boys, and whose great claim to fame when he had lived at Athens was the invention of a giant mechanical snail, who trailed a trail of alcoholic slime down the street behind him.

In Aristotle's work *Upon Kingship,* Ptolemy read that a kingship was hard-wearing, and unlikely to suffer destruction from without. If a kingdom fell, it would fall for one of two reasons: either because the king had tried to claim control of more than he was entitled to, or as a result of quarrelling among his family.

It was the most important thing, Aristotle said, for the royal family not to quarrel, for the children not to quarrel with each other, for the queen not to quarrel with her sons, and for the king not to quarrel with his daughters.

Ptolemy laughed as he read. How in the name of Zeus was it possible to stop a Greek family from quarrelling? For his family seemed to pass the whole day, day after day, in quarrelling. They quarrelled about everything and nothing. They quarrelled because they were Greeks, and because Greeks love to quarrel and are good at quarrelling. They outquarrelled every other family in Egypt. During meals the sound of voices raised in anger was heard always from the Satrap's dining room, for these Greeks sounded as if they were angry, as if they were quarrelling, even when they were not.

The Ptolemies—even their *name* meant Warlike.

Thoth knows it: This family was a family that would quarrel for three hundred years. And under this first Ptolemy the quarrelling had scarcely begun. Thoth swears it: Quarrelling, as Aristotle foresaw, would be their downfall.

Ptolemy, however, went on reading, and his eyes could not quit the page. After he had read, he discussed with Demetrios the art of kingship, and how to be a king. Demetrios gave Ptolemy much wise advice. He told him to think about the causes of failure. The heir to the throne, for example, might be a man whom it was hard to respect. Although the power such a man had would be royal power, not a tyrant's power, he might abuse his position.

The end of the kingship would then be in sight, Demetrios said, for when the subjects of a king stop consenting, that king is no longer a king; but a tyrant was still a tyrant even though his subjects did not want him. It was for reasons like this, Demetrios said, that monarchies were destroyed.

What, then, did Ptolemy want? He wanted his House to be Kings of Egypt for all time. How, then, he asked Demetrios, might that be possible?

And Demetrios told him that the way ahead lay in education. *Three things,* he said, *are of very great importance:*

First, he said, *you must teach the heir How To Be King.*

Second, he said, *you must teach the heir How Not To Be A Tyrant.*

Third, he said, *you must teach the heir the Art of Self-Control.*

Ptolemy paid very careful attention.

The tutor of the heir, Demetrios said, *is the most important man in the Residence, more important even than the king himself, for the tutor represents the future, even the very survival of the dynasty.*

Ptolemy could see that Demetrios spoke words of great wisdom. But he saw also that it might already be too late for a boy like Ptolemy Keraunos to be taught these things. Keraunos was already set in his ways.

Demetrios himself, he had his own private thoughts about the House of Ptolemy. In his treatise *Upon Fortune,* Demetrios prophesied that, just as the Macedonians—who had been almost unknown barbarians only fifty years before—had overthrown the Empire of Persia, so in due time the Macedonians would themselves be defeated by Fortune, and have to give up their mastery to another power. Demetrios referred, just then, to the Kingdom of Macedon, but in his heart he thought the same thought about the rule of the Macedonians in Egypt. At the very beginning of this House, then, Demetrios, wisest of Greeks, could see how it must end.

To say such things to Ptolemy, however, would have been more than his life was worth. And so Demetrios bit his tongue, that well-hung tongue of his, and kept quiet about what he really thought.

But in his cups Demetrios would speak out, and speak true, saying, *Fortune has simply lent to the House of Ptolemy her blessings, until she decides to deal with it differently.*

As for Thoth—Thoth says that a man does not need to be so wise as Demetrios of Phaleron to know that every thing must, some day, come to an end. Except, of course, Thoth himself, and the gods of Egypt, who are true gods.

And as for Ptolemy, he began to think that he could, indeed, make the rule of the Greeks over Egypt last for all time.

2.23

The Battle for Cyprus

In the spring of the year in which Egypt celebrated the sixty-first birthday of Ptolemy son of Lagos, Antigonos One-Eye sent for his son

Demetrios Poliorketes, who was now in the twenty-ninth year of his age and at the height of his powers, to take command of a great campaign against Ptolemy, and the purpose of it was to capture from him the island of Cyprus, which was still governed by Ptolemy's younger brother, Menelaos, a man believed by some to be not a very good *strategos*.

Demetrios must, of course, obey his father's orders, though he would have preferred to carry on doing what he had been doing, which was campaigning for the liberation of Greece from Macedon, which he thought was a nobler cause. But One-Eye wanted an end to the war with Ptolemy as soon as that was possible.

Demetrios tried, first of all, to bribe Kleonides, Ptolemy's general, but this man refused to accept so much as one drachma, and so Demetrios set sail for Cyprus with his fifteen thousand soldiers, his four thousand horse, his one hundred and ten swift-sailing *triereis*, and his fifty-three heavy transport ships and merchantmen that were sturdy enough to take the weight of cavalry, infantry, and the hundreds of engines of war, bolt-throwers and catapults that Demetrios needs must carry wherever he went.

Demetrios made his landing and pitched his tents upon the northeast coast of the island, then moved his troops overland, so that he could attack the city of Salamis, which was the stronghold of Menelaos.

This man was taken quite by surprise, but he gathered the largest army he could muster, and marched twelve thousand men and eight hundred horse out of Salamis to face his enemy. A short but fierce battle followed, in which Menelaos's men were overwhelmed and chased back inside the city walls by Demetrios; and Menelaos barricaded himself as best he could and sent urgent word to Ptolemy in Egypt that one thousand of his troops were dead and three thousand taken prisoner.

Menelaos made many excuses, writing, *In truth, we had not one hour to make ready for battle . . .* and he asked for his brother's help, saying that his interests on the island were in grave danger.

Some said that Menelaos had, in fact, lost as much as half his army, and that he had retreated to the citadel in utter disorder; but he now showed what he was worth, by hauling every siege-engine and any thing that might be hurled at Demetrios as a missile, up on to the city walls, and he posted soldiers upon the battlements and made his best efforts to defend Salamis against the siege.

Demetrios set his men to build battering-rams, and he built also the famous siege-tower called the Helepolis, or City-Destroyer, that stood ninety cubits high and had nine storeys, and was filled with catapults and engines of war that could fling rocks of up to three talents in weight, and it needed two hundred men inside, just to work the machinery.

This great weapon Demetrios now rolled up to the city walls, and he fired from it shower upon shower of great stones so that the battlements of Salamis were quite broken down. But though Demetrios battered at the walls, Menelaos's men resisted with such skill that for some days the battle was in doubt. Both sides suffered setbacks and severe wounds, and when at last it looked as if Salamis must be taken by storm, Demetrios gave the order to stand off until sunrise, for that it was too dark for any man to see his own hand in front of his face.

Menelaos, fearful that Salamis would be lost unless he took some desperate action, prayed to the gods of Hellas, and had in return the idea to hurl down on to Helepolis during the dead hours of the night all the timber he could find, and then he shot fire-bearing arrows into the timber, so that Helepolis burst into flames.

Demetrios slept through the destruction of his wondrous machine, and though he was enraged, he did not lose heart, because he thought Menelaos was not the brightest of commanders, but must soon be beaten.

When the herald brought Ptolemy the news, he sailed for Cyprus with ten thousand foot soldiers and his great fleet of one hundred and fifty ships of war and two hundred transports. He took also the fifteen-year-old Ptolemy Keraunos, the nine-year-old Arsinoë Beta, nine other children, and all his wives and concubines, to watch his great victory.

He cast anchor off Paphos, at the opposite end of Cyprus from Salamis, and then coasted along to Kition, from where he sent a message: *Ptolemy to Demetrios greetings. Get off my island before I beat you to a pulp.*

Demetrios replied: *Demetrios to Ptolemy greetings. I am unbeatable, and it is yourself that shall be ground to a powder.*

Demetrios then made a generous offer to let Ptolemy withdraw from Cyprus if he would surrender the cities of Sikyon and Korinthos. But Ptolemy refused to withdraw from what was his own property, and said he would give up nothing without defending it. There was no choice, then, but to fight, and the battle followed that was called the Sea Battle of Salamis in Cyprus; it was of the highest importance to every ruler in the Greek world, because the prize for whoever won was not only Cyprus but Syria also, and absolute mastery over all their rivals.

On the night before this fight Ptolemy dreamed the dream of drinking warm beer, which meant the loss of property, but his thought was that in Egypt the beer was always warm, and he took no notice of what the oneiroscopists told him. He asked his admirals, even so, for their thoughts regarding what he should do, for this Satrap was a landsman, by no means at home on board any ship at sea. Now, however, Ptolemy sent troops to Menelaos overland, and he sent Menelaos himself orders to sail out of the harbour of Salamis, if he could, with the sixty ships of war which he had by him, when the battle was at its height, for it was his plan for Menelaos to fall upon Demetrios's fleet from the rear, and throw it into confusion by performing the famous manoeuvre that the Greeks call the *diekplous,* or sailing through. Ptolemy thought that if Menelaos's reinforcements appeared in time he must surely win his battle.

Somehow, though, Demetrios got wind of Ptolemy's strategy, and he stationed just ten of his ships of war to block the channel that was the harbour exit, which was very narrow, so that the ships of Menelaos were trapped inside. Demetrios then set sail with one hundred and eighty *triereis,* among them ten *hexeres,* or sixes, and seven *hepteres,* or sevens, ships larger than any yet used in battle, with missile-throwers mounted upon their prows, and catapults capable of shooting bolts up to three spans in length; and Demetrios smiled because he knew he was going to beat Ptolemy to a jelly.

As Ptolemy made for Salamis at full speed under cover of darkness, Demetrios lay in wait for him. It was Ptolemy's thought that he could take the best position before his enemy was ready, but at first light he saw Demetrios's fleet nearby, riding at anchor in battle order, and his spirits received a jolt.

What happened? Demetrios thrashed Ptolemy, as he had promised, for Menelaos failed to arrive in time to save him, and Ptolemy, having lost all but eight of his ships, was forced to flee. The soldiers of Ptolemy floundered in the sea in their hundreds, watching their ships burn upon the water. The war trumpets of Demetrios brayed, and his men jeered and cheered and chanted abuse, such as *We fucked the enemy,* as they watched the bodies sink one by one from view, to provide food for the fishes and the nameless creatures of the deep.

Demetrios had won a most brilliant victory, smashing the Egyptian fleet to pieces. He had sunk sixty-two of Ptolemy's ships and captured one hundred and seventy, making this the most humiliating defeat of Ptolemy's life time. Worst of all, Ptolemy had been beaten by a man half his age.

Ptolemy did forget himself upon this occasion so far as to rage, and he cursed his useless brother, for it seemed that everything Menelaos had done in his life had turned into a disaster. Then he threw away the gecko talisman that should have brought victory in battle, saying it was *useless, useless,* as useless as his brother Menelaos.

As for Demetrios, he lost just twenty ships, all of which could be refitted and put back into service almost overnight. And yes, the city of Salamis and the island of Cyprus now belonged to Demetrios Poliorketes, Antigonos One-Eye, and Macedon, and not to Ptolemy and Egypt.

Almost as bad as the loss of Cyprus was the disappearance of Ptolemy's train of attendants: his friends, wives, concubines and all of his children, who had been left for safety upon the transport ships that sailed behind the fleet, as onlookers. Ptolemy feared that all of them must have fallen either into the hands of Demetrios or into the sea, and he did not yet know what had become of them, but feared the worst: that he had lost every last thing, including his heir and the future of his dynasty.

The customary Greek treatment for prisoners of war was to mutilate them, whether by cutting off the ears and lips, or by branding, and then to sell them into slavery for a handsome sum of money. But Demetrios proved once again generous in victory. He buried with full honours the enemy dead that could be fished out of the sea, and he set the prisoners free without asking for the payment of any ransom. Among them were the young Leontiskos, son of Ptolemy and Thaïs, on active service for the first time, and many of Ptolemy's finest officers. Demetrios might easily have cut off the right-hand thumbs of every one of these men, or sold them all for eunuch slaves, but he sent back his prisoners without asking for so much as one drachma.

Demetrios sent back also Ptolemy's wives and concubines and among them was Lamia, the famous whore, whose priceless beauty was now on the wane, and who Ptolemy imagined would prove much too old and raddled meat to be the delight of a young man like Demetrios, who might have his pick of the most beautiful women in the world; but it was this man's personal triumph to send Lamia home, having made full use of her services himself.

It had, after all, been the constant chant of Ptolemy's men: *We fucked the enemy,* and Demetrios thus took the sweetest revenge by doing to Lamia what Ptolemy's sailors had threatened to do to him.

But Ptolemy was quite ready to call Demetrios a *kalokagathos,* a complete gentleman, for he laid not a finger upon Berenike, and restored her to him unharmed and with the fabled sharpness of her tongue undulled, and she used it now to berate Ptolemy himself for his stupidity, and, Thoth knows, she may have been in the right.

Ptolemy now swore a great oath before the gods of Greece that he would take back Cyprus, which was his rightful possession, if it was the last thing he did, though the Oracle of Zeus-Ammon in Libya said it would take him ten years to do so.

For his part, Demetrios was surprised that Ptolemy's captured troops refused to change sides and fight for him—a thing that was almost unheard of. But there were good reasons why Ptolemy's men stayed loyal to him. He had settled these hired soldiers with smallholdings of land in the Lake District of Egypt that lay a short sail up-River from Memphis, giving them all the appearance of owning a stake in his satrapy. In this way he had secured the trust of men famous for disloyalty. Because of the grants of land, they would fight for Ptolemy again. For Ptolemy was the kindest, the most generous, the best of masters, a *kalokagathos* himself.

As for the eleven children of Ptolemy, they bit their tongues and did not dare to speak of their father's defeat, but they did not forget their adventure or the terrible *nausiasis.* The nine-year-old Arsinoë Beta had stood upon the prow of her ship retching over the side, but wide-eyed, missing nothing. It was her first *naumachia,* and the thrill of it she would recall for the rest of her life as a great lesson in how not to win.

Her sister, Ptolemaïs, aged twelve, remembered this day also, for she had seen in the distance a man of surpassing handsomeness and heroism, who would play a significant part in her future, the man who was fated to be her husband—Demetrios Poliorketes himself.

As for her half-sister, Eirene, only daughter of Thaïs of Athens, the eldest of all the daughters of Ptolemy, it was as a result of the Sea Battle of Salamis that she, too, got for herself a husband, and unlike Ptolemaïs she got this husband very quick.

After Salamis Demetrios Poliorketes became the master of all Cyprus, and he abolished the city-kings who had ruled there before him, so that these men were forced to make themselves scarce. One of them, Eunostos son of Pasikrates, who had been King of Soloi in Cyprus, fled to Egypt, where it would be his good fortune to be married to Eirene, daughter of Ptolemy.

Demetrios celebrated that great victory of his by minting golden tetradrachms that showed Nike, the winged goddess of Victory, standing upon the poop of his flagship. Nike had been good, very good, to Demetrios, and he made lavish sacrifice to her. Antigonos, his father, rejoiced to hear of the success of his son, and he assumed on the strength of it the diadem of a king, and began to call himself by the style and title of *Basileus,* or King, and to behave like a king, and he was the first of the Successors of Alexander to do so.

Ptolemy himself, he returned to Egypt in the lowest of spirits, thinking that Ptolemaic sea-power was finished, finished for ever. He had struggled sixteen years to keep a hold of Palestine, and Syria, and Cyprus, and now all that great empire of his was gone. All he had left to call his own was Egypt itself, and the territory of the Kyrenaica to the west.

He was not, however, downcast for very many days. He swore his solemn oath before the gods of Greece, and he did, as always, what he thought Alexander would have done in the same circumstances: he gathered his strength and made ready to do battle yet again for what he believed to be his by right.

2.24

The Miracle-Worker

As for the other Demetrios—of Phaleron—he became a little more famous still about this time as a result of the god Sarapis—Sarapis, that the people of Alexandria had been neglecting of late, for the truth was that the new god was a strange hybrid, almost identical to Zeus, who had already his own temple and his own cult elsewhere in the city.

In that great new Temple of Sarapis at Alexandria stood the giant cult statue of the god, blue-faced, bearded, benign, with his jewelled eyes sparkling in the darkness. His face was mild, mysterious, majestic, fitting for the god of the Underworld, and on his head stood the corn basket that symbolized the granary that was Egypt.

The statue and Temple of Sarapis were truly awe-inspiring, but until there were wonders, a new god was as good as useless, for the people just came to gape at him out of curiosity, then went away again. Few people lingered to ask favours of this god, for he granted none. Nobody left behind so much as one obol for Sarapis, who had no reputation except for his enormous size.

What, then, did Ptolemy do? He spoke to Demetrios of Phaleron, the wisest Greek in all Egypt, and asked him what he should do about the great new god that was beginning to look like a great failure.

For the first time in his life Demetrios was at a loss. He began to speak, but no words came forth from his mouth, and he just spread his hands, and Ptolemy thought about withdrawing the slaves and the salary and sending him back where he had come from.

It was while Ptolemy was still trying to think of some way to make Sarapis popular that Demetrios was, without warning, struck blind, and had his slave lead him by the arm through the *agora* to his physician.

Demetrios saw darkness by day for one month, and it was dreadful to behold, for he was led from doctor to doctor by his slave, seeking a cure. He stopped eating. His face grew haggard. He would fall down and damage his limbs, so that he was covered in cuts and bruises.

Demetrios went to every physician in the city. He had the mixture that was made up of two eyes of a pig, eye-wash, red lead and wild honey, injected into his ears, supposed to be an instant cure for blindness. Nothing happened.

He made trial of the lotion of dried myrrh in sour milk.

He tried the poultice of powdered onions.

He went about sobbing, *Thou wert better not alive than living blind.*

Ptolemy himself then made available his personal physician, who had Demetrios try even the infamous crocodile-dung eye-salve. But Demetrios continued to see total darkness, and said he was resigned to living in the dark for the rest of his life.

Then he went one day, quite of his own accord, to pass the night in the Temple of Sarapis, where he prayed to the god, and he made sure that every man knew that he was putting his trust in Sarapis and seeking a cure.

In the morning there was a commotion in the native quarter, Rhakotis, where the Sarapieion was, and crowds of people, and Demetrios was standing on the steps of the temple, smiling, and demonstrating that he could see now perfectly well. And he stood there shouting at the top of his voice that Sarapis had *spoken* to him during the night. He said that his sight had been restored, and the first thing he saw was the statue of Sarapis inclining his head towards him. He yelled, *It is the Lord Sarapis who has cured my blindness.*

From that day on, the crowds never left the temple. The sick came to sleep in the Sanctuary of Sarapis, hundreds of them, and they dedicated artificial limbs of gold and silver in return for their miraculous cures, and left offerings for the god who had made them whole again.

For the Alexandrians, then, the false god turned into a true god, and the shouts of *Miracle* echoed every morning down the colonnades of Kanopic Street, and spread across the waking city.

Some whispered that Demetrios had never been blind in the first place, but had been cured of his darkness by his own dark deception. But Demetrios saw no reason why a fake god should not perform a fake miracle. It was the reason why Sarapis had been invented: so that there might be one god at least who was under human control.

Old Anemhor knew nothing of Demetrios's falsehood, except to suspect it, and to expect it, for that every Greek was a deceiver. But the people of Alexandria *believed*. It is in the nature of the Greeks to believe in miracles.

Ptolemy, however, was puzzled. What he could not understand was that the cures effected by Sarapis were real cures, and the faith of the sick was real faith. *It was as if his invented god had become real,* and Ptolemy began, almost, to believe in the reality of Sarapis himself.

The statue was seen often now to *move,* and even *nodded his head* to his worshippers, a god as true as the truest of gods, who drew real tears of devotion from the faithful.

The people of Egypt did not know that Sarapis was a piece of trickery, a delusion, the invention of Ptolemy, and that one of the purposes of his new god was to make them part with their money.

Ptolemy himself—the success of his god made him show his teeth and rub his hands together at the thought of the money to be made, and in his private chamber he laughed until the tears ran down his cheeks to think of it.

As for Thoth—Thoth knows that there is no lie like a Greek lie; no liar like a Greek liar.

The next miracle to take place at Alexandria, some said, was the marriage of Eirene, Thaïs's daughter, who was now, to be sure, more than eighteen years old, and ripe to be some man's wife.

Eunostos it was, the sometime King of Soloi in Cyprus, who was chosen to be this girl's husband, and it was said that he hung about Ptolemy's Residence asking what woman he could be married to, and that in order to bind this man's loyalty to himself Ptolemy agreed to his proposal.

Bastard daughter or not, Eirene was not to be deprived of a husband. Eirene could marry a king, for she was as good as any other girl, and the fact that her king had been king of less than half an island, and was now no king at all, took away nothing of her excitement. By no means: Eirene was sure, as both Ptolemy and Eunostos were sure, that *in a matter of months* Demetrios Poliorketes would be beaten, that Cyprus would again be Ptolemy's own possession, and Eunostos could go back to being a king, and that Eirene should be his queen.

In private, Ptolemy said to Berenike, *To be sure, an out-of-wedlock daughter is lucky indeed to find any husband, let alone a husband who happens to be a king.*

Ptolemy was pleased to see this daughter married off, even though, for the moment, she must live under his own roof. For yes, Eirene reminded Ptolemy of her mother. She had, yes, the same husky voice as Thaïs, the same olive skin, the same yellow hair, the same matchless beauty.

Ptolemy did not just then wish to be reminded of Thaïs, of whose fate and present whereabouts he knew nothing, not even whether she was living or dead. He had sent away that woman, and all the riches of Egypt, all the fine palaces, all the glory of being a satrap, all the concubines, even the love of Berenike—none of it made up for the loss of Thaïs the whore, and in the heart of this Satrap there was a grand emptiness that was his yearning to have back his time that was lost; to retrace his steps to the spot where he had taken the wrong road.

In the end, yes, he would have preferred to go home to Macedon, to his ordinary life in the hills of Eordaia; to the simple life of a Greek countryman, minding his flocks of sheep and goats, to a life that was uncomplicated by the cares of state and the obligations of war; a life in which he was not forever forced to make himself ready for battle, or sleep with a dagger under his pillow for fear that his oldest friends and closest relations should murder him in the dead hours of the night and take from him all that was his, even his satrapy.

But Ptolemy had chosen his way of life—or his Fate had chosen it for him—and he must make the best of it. He could not turn back, but must go on, and impossible though it was, he willed himself to forget Thaïs and the past, and not to think of the future either, impossible though that was as well, but to live for the passing moment, for the pleasure of *now*.

And Eirene? What of Eirene and Eunostos? Did they live at Alexandria for ever? Did they return to Cyprus as king and queen? To be sure, the marriage of Eirene was the last that history would hear of her.

Thoth asks it: Did not Ptolemy and his House forget Eirene also? Queen Eirene? Who, in after years, could say *one word* of what became of her? What were the number and names of her offspring? What was the fate and history of this most beautiful young woman?

In Egypt nobody knew one word of it. In Egypt nobody had so much as one thing to say about her.

So much for the out-of-wedlock daughter of the most beautiful woman in the world: her fate was the same as that of her mother—to be forgotten.

2.25

The Siege of Rhodes

The loss of Cyprus was a terrible blow to Ptolemy, but there were further blows to come, for within the year Antigonos One-Eye gave orders for the invasion of Egypt itself.

One-Eye took personal charge of this expedition, and commanded the land army himself, in spite of being close to eighty years of age. He took with him eighty thousand foot soldiers, eight thousand horse, and eighty elephants. His fleet of one hundred and fifty ships of war was under the command of his son Demetrios, who boasted that he had thrashed Ptolemy at sea, and that now he would thrash him also on land.

While the equipment was being made ready, one of One-Eye's friends dreamed a dream in which he saw One-Eye running a foot-race in the *stadion* with his eighty thousand soldiers, but after the halfway mark he became weak, panting hard, and only just managed to finish the course.

But although this friend told One-Eye of the dream, and the Interpreter of Dreams said that it could mean nothing but disaster to come, One-Eye said that the forecasting of the future by dreams was meaningless nonsense, and refused to take any notice.

One-Eye was warned also by the pilots—men who should have known what they were talking about—that rough weather lay ahead. But Antigonos was a man who, once he had started a thing, never failed to finish it, and he disliked taking advice. In this he was not unlike Alexander, but he felt that this might be his last chance to teach Ptolemy a lesson, and grind this enemy of his to dust. And he said, *If I can defeat Ptolemy son of Lagos, I shall die a happy man.*

Antigonos One-Eye set out, then, from Gaza City with a great convoy of camels loaded with corn and fodder for his beasts of burden, fully expecting to win a magnificent victory and to take Egypt for himself, and he boasted that the gods of Greece looked with favour upon Antigonos Monophthalmos.

But the gods of Greece always hear boastful words. The gods do not like hubris, and every thing that could go wrong for One-Eye did now go wrong.

First, he had assembled all these troops at Gaza, but there were so very many of them that they could do nothing with any speed, and nothing by stealth, so that Ptolemy knew they were coming, and every thing about them. Next, and more serious, One-Eye had picked the wrong season of the year, having been delayed until the setting of the Pleiades, after which time the weather was sure to be bad.

It was One-Eye's plan to attack Ptolemy as soon as he could after the defeat at Salamis, while his fleet was still rebuilding, and while his troops were still low in spirits, tending their wounds and trying to regain their fighting fitness. Ptolemy had indeed lost many ships, and to recover his full strength would take some time, for ship's timber must be brought from Lebanon, and took months to fell and transport, and every thing was made one thousand times more difficult by the fact that Palestine was no longer his property.

Meanwhile, One-Eye marched through the desert, and Demetrios sailed alongside with his fleet. But, as the men of wisdom said, *Zeus, who is always upon the watch, took it now into his head to give Demetrios a rough time,* for he sent hurricane winds and towering waves that smashed Demetrios's heaviest *triereis* to bits upon the rocky shore at Raphia.

When father and son came at length to the Pelousiac mouth of the Nile, they found that Ptolemy had blockaded the entrance with boats so that his enemy could not sail through, and One-Eye's troops were met by Ptolemy himself, riding at anchor in his gilded satrapal barge, offering parcels of land to the brave soldiers who might care to change sides and fight for Egypt, and shouting the details of his bribes through a golden speaking-trumpet, to the effect that he would pay the enormous sum of two minas for the ranks and as much as one talent to every officer who would desert to his camp.

One-Eye shouted a counter-proclamation, saying that any soldier of his that dared to desert to Ptolemy would be punished with death by torture, his ears cut off, his fingernails torn out, and so forth, and he prayed to the gods that the fate of the army of Perdikkas was not about to fall upon his army also, for he could see that Ptolemy had brought half the crocodiles in Egypt with him.

Demetrios sailed the fleet on past the Pelousiac mouth, seeking for some place to make good his landing farther west, nearer to Alexandria, but he was beaten off by Ptolemy's men. And then, as they said, Zeus himself planned a fresh disaster for this Demetrios, for a second storm at sea now wrecked his largest ships of war off Kanopos, so that he was forced to turn back and join his father in camp east of Pelousion. One-Eye withdrew, then, as far as Gaza, shamed and defeated, having achieved nothing, but he swore by all the gods of Greece, who had not lifted one finger to help him, that he would be back.

Ptolemy hung up his sword and shield in the Temple of Apollo at Alexandria, and he told his sons that they could win his battles for him in the future, for that he was tired of war and the folly of war, and wanted to devote the rest of his days to peace. He made repeated thank-offerings to Zeus and the Greek gods, but he did not forget Sarapis, or Thoth, and he entertained his generals and admirals at lavish victory banquets, pressing upon them very many gifts of silver and gold.

Antigonos did not return in person to Egypt the following year, but sent Demetrios instead to lay siege to the neutral island of Rhodes. His purpose was still to injure Ptolemy in every way he could, but this time he sought to do it in a less direct manner, by doing the utmost damage to his trading interests, and by depriving him of luxury foods from Greece for that he knew from of old Ptolemy could not live without his comforts.

Ptolemy himself was at a loss to know why Demetrios had gone to the trouble of doing what he did. But the answer was not hard to find. The island and city of Rhodes was Ptolemy's great ally and friend, and had a long history of trade with Egypt. It was Demetrios's clever thought to stop all supplies from Greece reaching his enemy, for he saw that if the great market and banking business of Rhodes could be shut down, the whole of Egyptian and Levantine trade would grind to a stop, for all goods either went through, or depended upon, Rhodes. Ptolemy lay awake at night, worrying. By day he would break into a sweat when he thought of it, and he could not stop thinking of it, for it meant, to begin with, that there would be no spices in Egypt, and a shortage of incense. And yes, it was a devastating thought, because without incense no Greek could worship his gods, nor any Egyptian either.

The smile, then, of Demetrios was broad when he enlisted the help of the enemies of Rhodes—the pirates—and broader still when, with an army of forty thousand men and four hundred ships of war, he attacked the city of Rhodes, which consisted of a strong fortress encircled by triple walls and moats, with one side facing on to the sea.

The Rhodians took the precaution of bringing inside these walls every thing that was out in the fields, such as corn, cattle, sheep and goats, and they stored up meat and drink against a siege, strengthened the walls and made ready to defend their city.

They also sent messengers with an urgent appeal for help to Ptolemy, the man who, they said, could save them if any man could, for they feared very much the reputation of Demetrios Poliorketes, having heard how he had bombarded the city of Salamis.

At first Demetrios tried to storm Rhodes from the landward side, but for some curious reason he did not trouble to close off the harbour, so that Ptolemy was able to send in supplies from the seaward side, his fleet now being fully repaired. Having made the delivery, Ptolemy helped himself to the parcel of goods sent for Demetrios by one of his wives: rich purple robes, silver plate and suchlike—luxury gear that could be of no use to anybody but a satrap.

When Demetrios did try to take the harbour, he failed, and he changed his strategy then to concentrate once more upon a land assault, building a bigger and better Helepolis, one hundred cubits in height, from which he fired arrows and rocks and hot sand, and every kind of terrible missile.

The tower rolled forward upon four great wheels of oak, and she made such a noise that she aroused terror and delight at the same time in every man who saw her, for this mighty engine of war was worked by three thousand four hundred men, one thousand of them pushing from the inside.

Demetrios also built a ram that swung back and forth upon a frame in order to smash at the walls of Rhodes, and battering rams one hundred and twenty cubits in length, iron-sheathed and mounted upon rollers, powered by one thousand men. But Rhodes proved quite capable of resisting the assaults of Demetrios, who, in spite of his nickname, made not much progress. He fired greater rocks than ever, scalding oil, flaming arrows, human filth, and barrels of boiling tar for one full year of days and nights without cease, but he barely dented the walls of this great proud city of Rhodes, whose people were very keen to keep him out. No, Demetrios did not manage to set Rhodes on fire, nor did the tunnels dug by his engineers manage to undermine it. Nor yet did he succeed in starving Rhodes into surrender, for her allies, Kassandros and Lysimakhos, sent ten thousand measures of barley, forty thousand measures of wheat, and enormous quantities of lentils.

Ptolemy, he sent fifteen hundred soldiers and several shiploads of food: dates, and figs, and melons, and pigeon pies, as well as three hundred thousand measures of grain, beans, peas and lentils, and many amphoras of the beer of the Egyptians that was called *booza*.

The Rhodians could not hide their admiration for the heroic scale upon which Demetrios worked, terrible though it was for them, and they gawped at, and even applauded, his scores of vast oared galleys, *pentekaidekeres* and *hekkaidekeres,* fifteens and sixteens, as they cruised past, rowed by thousands of oarsmen, all singing in order to row in time. But they held out against this man until his father sent him a carrier pigeon with orders to return home to Macedon. Demetrios was then very anxious to find some means of abandoning his siege without losing face, but One-Eye ordered him to make terms and sign a treaty of peace before he left, and said he must leave at once.

Greatly relieved, the Rhodians signed the papyrus upon the spot, and as Demetrios's fleet rowed out of the harbour they went wild on the ramparts, cheering and whistling, and singing some very rude songs about Demetrios Poliorketes, the Besieger of Cities, whose famous Siege of Rhodes was such a famous failure.

This last expedition of Demetrios was, then, a very great waste of time and energy for everybody. For Ptolemy, however, the important thing was that trade with Egypt was restored, and that he had once again spices in his kitchens and incense in his temples in order to please the nostrils of the gods, both Greek and Egyptian, because above all other things it was a goodly thing to keep the gods happy.

2.26

The Apotheosis of Ptolemy

Such were the very warm feelings of the people of Rhodes towards the satraps who had helped them in their trouble that they were of one mind in agreeing to raise gilded images of Lysimakhos and Kassandros in the city. But they thought that even a solid gold statue would not be enough to show Rhodes's deep deep debt of thanks to Ptolemy. And so they sent ambassadors even so far as the Oracle of Zeus-Ammon in Libya, to ask whether, by chance, it might be lawful for them to honour Ptolemy as a god.

The last time Zeus-Ammon had been asked about such a matter— regarding the apotheosis of Hephaistion—he had refused the request. But this time, to the surprise of everybody, including the Rhodians, who had perhaps sent to ask a question that expected the answer *No,* and who were just making a gesture, the Oracle did indeed grant permission for Ptolemy to be honoured as a god, and so it had to be.

Rhodes had to build, therefore, the most lavish marble shrine to Ptolemy of Egypt, and they enclosed it within a sacred enclosure with marble colonnades one *stadion* long. They called the shrine the Ptolemaieion, and in it they offered up daily blood sacrifice to Ptolemy the god, sang hymns to Ptolemy the god and made dedications of golden arms and silver ears and other body parts cast in precious metals, in the hope that Ptolemy the god might cure them of their medical complaints, *which he did.*

The Rhodians awarded also to Ptolemy a most prestigious Greek title, namely, *Soter,* which meant Saviour, for that he had saved— although not single-handed—the island and city of Rhodes. They said that he must be known and called by this title in Egypt, and it was, Ptolemy thought, the very greatest honour, for Soter was a title that he must share with Zeus himself, and he would be Ptolemy Soter for the rest of his life, and, indeed, for ever after, for the rest of time.

Some men took it upon themselves to smirk at this title, seeing it as a gesture of the highest degree of sarcasm, reflecting only the fact that Ptolemy had really not sent very much aid to Rhodes, or at least, not as much as he could have done; that he had sent really not enough soldiers and not enough food; and that he had sent the dreadful *booza,* which had made every man in Rhodes burp for fifteen months without stopping.

Others recalled that the title of Soter had been awarded to Ptolemy not by Rhodes but by the citizens of Alexandria, who were good at sarcastic titles, to emphasize the fact that this Ptolemy never in all his life time saved anybody from any thing, because really he preferred the retreat to the attack, peace to war, staying at home to going abroad, sitting down to standing up, and sleeping to being awake, and because this man was really rather good at doing nothing at all.

Thoth says, Really, this was, perhaps, a little unfair.

Wherever the title came from, and whether it was sincerely meant or not, Ptolemy accepted it with the greatest of grace. He worried, of course, that he had taken for himself one of the titles of Zeus, the greatest god of the Greeks, but he did not worry for long. To be sure, he had continued to perform the Greek sacrifice all these years. And in any case, he had no thought to desert his gods while they showed every sign of being on his side. To do otherwise would have been to invite disaster.

Every night, then, Ptolemy Soter, Satrap of Egypt, would dedicate his third cup of wine to Zeus Soter—Saviour—as he had always done. To drink the third cup like this was the symbol of Good Luck, Good Fortune. The third cup, the third time, had always been the lucky time. Now, the third cup seemed to involve also the House of Ptolemy, and, strange though it was, to be called Ptolemy Soter felt lucky also.

It was, he thought, not unlike drinking a solemn toast to himself.

At Rhodes they rebuilt the destroyed Greek theatre, the damaged city walls, and repaired every thing that was broken, so that the reputation of Rhodes as the most beautiful city in the Greek world (after Alexandria) was restored.

With the siege at an end, the Rhodians made a polite request to be given some of Demetrios's engines of war as a memorial of his power, and of their own courage in resisting him, meaning to dedicate these machines in their temples.

A different story said that Demetrios simply left his Helepolis behind, as too unlucky for use in any future conflict, and too big to take away, and that he left orders for the engines of war to be sold for scrap, and the profits to go towards raising a statue to commemorate the Siege of Rhodes.

Whatever the truth was, a giant bronze statue of Helios, the Sun god of the Greeks, who was the protector of this island, was now put up, and this was the famous Kolossos of Rhodes, which was one of the Seven Very Great Wonders of the World for ever after. The Rhodians liked to boast that the Kolossos would be famous until the end of time, and that he would stand for ever. It took them twelve years to make him stand up, and he straddled—or, as some said, stood beside—the harbour entrance, glittering in the sun, dazzling and blinding sailors and landsmen alike, and utterly useless.

Cynics scoffed that the Kolossos would *not* last for ever, because no thing made by man lasts for ever, and they were right, for the Kolossos fell down in an earthquake not fifty years afterwards.

Ptolemy thought little of this statue, which was nothing to do with him, and not of him. For his part, he was already planning a much more wondrous monument, the famous Pharos, or Lighthouse, of Alexandria, of which it was his proud boast that it would stop the ships smashing into the rocks at the entrance to the Great Harbour of his capital. Ptolemy also boasted that his Pharos, built upon philosophical and scientific principles, would never fall down because it stood upon earthquake-proof foundations. His greatest boast, though, was that, unlike the Kolossos of Rhodes, the Pharos would save lives, and be a Soter itself, and be useful. In that, at least, he was right.

When the news came to Ptolemy that Antigonos One-Eye of Macedon, and his son Demetrios Poliorketes also, had bestowed upon themselves the style and title of Basileus, or King, Ptolemy began to think that it might be time to do the same thing himself.

Soon afterwards, Lysimakhos began also to call himself not Satrap but King of Thrace, and then the rest of the Successors did likewise, and really the only thing for Ptolemy to do was to follow, so as not to be left out, or left behind in glory. He worried, of course, about hubris, but Ptolemy worried about everything, and in the end he put out the *prostagma,* and the deed was done. He began to sit in his chair in a more kingly manner, as Alexander had done, and his chair became a throne, and not unlike an actor who puts on the robes of a monarch and is at once because of it a king, he changed every aspect of his behaviour—his way of walking, his speech, and his bearing.

Berenike, of course, was able to call herself, in consequence, *Basilissa,* or Queen. And there were those who said they could *see* Berenike becoming more and more puffed up, grander, prouder, more haughty, more queenly by the moment, so that she was more of a queen even than Olympias, the mother of Alexander; even than the queen of Darius, King of Persia, surpassing even the late queen of Nakhthoreb, the last native Pharaoh, so that she was ready and waiting to be quite the most *regal* queen Egypt had ever seen. Berenike became so puffed up in her heart that she began to hold the goddesses of no account. The courtiers flattered her, saying that Hera and Athena, Artemis and Aphrodite, these goddesses came nowhere near her in beauty.

Ptolemy laughed. He told his wife not to forget Gerana, Queen of the Pygmies, who became so puffed up that she boasted that she was more beautiful than the goddesses, so much so that Hera changed her into a crane, a most hideous bird.

Ptolemy was, to be sure, a king over the Greeks, not yet King and Pharaoh of Egypt, but the High Priest of Ptah noted with some satisfaction the Egyptian aspect of Ptolemy's title of Soter, for Horus, the falcon god, the son of Osiris and Isis, who was the Harpokrates of the Greeks—he himself had been a Saviour, a *Soter* also. It was entirely fitting for Ptolemy to make use of such a title, if he would only agree to adopt also the titles and dignity of Pharaoh, and agree to be the Living Horus, Horus the Saviour, a living god to the Egyptians as well as to the Greeks.

If Ptolemy were to do this, Anemhor told him, the terrible emptiness at the heart of Egyptian society, which was caused by the lack of a pharaoh—it would be at an end. Yes, the uncertainty about the Flood of the Nile would be removed and the fertility of the Two Lands would be guaranteed. If only Ptolemy would be a pharaoh, all that had been wrong in Egypt all this time would be put right.

Assuredly, to be called a king and to be a god made up, in some measure, for Ptolemy's defeat at Salamis, and helped him not to think about it, but for the moment he was uncertain whether he wanted to be a pharaoh.

We are a Greek, he said, *not an Egyptian.* And he asked for time to put his thoughts in order upon a matter of such weight.

Ptolemy's spirits were low. To be sure, he never called a defeat a defeat, but always a *Misfortune.* But he thought that Tykhe, the goddess of Fortune, must have been looking the wrong way at the Battle of Salamis, and he wondered what he had done wrong to deserve such treatment from her. Had he been *less Greek* than he ought to have been? Had he forgotten to make the proper Greek sacrifice? How much worse might things become if he became an Egyptian, a pharaoh for the Egyptians? Fortune had let him down, deserted him in his hour of greatest need, and he worried about *hubris.* He worried that he had already shown too much pride.

Living god or not, as if to prove that his doubts were not unjustified, there were more misfortunes to come for Ptolemy. At the Battle of Kos he was so badly humiliated that the engagement went unrecorded even in the Annals of Thoth, and the date of this battle remained uncertain ever after.

At the Sea Battle of Andros, Ptolemy was defeated once again, and he ordered that all reference to this *naumachia* should be struck out of the official Court Diary.

When he returned home to Egypt after these Misfortunes, he would find Anemhor, High Priest of Memphis, waiting for him upon the quay, as always, to greet him. He stood there in the leopard-skin costume, his bald head glinting in the sun, and he would look direct into Ptolemy's eyes, as if he could read there what had happened before ever Ptolemy could speak the word to tell him.

But of course, for the High Priest knew all things. He was good at fixing Ptolemy with his dark eyes, looking, looking, and Ptolemy, upon such an occasion, was unable to stare him down, but looked away, ashamed. And he cursed himself for having thrown away the gecko talisman.

The disapproval of the gods, murmured Anemhor, *may often be shown by the failure of military enterprise . . .*

Ptolemy would frown, and spread his hands, as if to say that, really, he knew very little of the gods of Egypt, which was the truth.

Failure, Anemhor said quietly, *may be a sign of the anger of the gods . . .*

Ptolemy would purse his lips and flap his leather fly-whisk at the flies, and Anemhor would think only that if this man's fly-whisk had had the alternate bands of gold and *sappheiros,* he might win his battles; and he thought again that Egypt still lacked a pharaoh.

Really, Anemhor said, *Ptolemy must build more temples . . .*

Ptolemy breathed in. He breathed out. He felt sick in his stomach. He felt he could strike the High Priest of Ptah, the Great Chief of the Hammer, upon the jaw, and Anemhor, who knew all things, knew what Ptolemy thought.

Really, Anemhor said, *Ptolemy must make more offerings to the gods of Egypt . . .*

Ptolemy took deep breaths, knowing what the man would say next.

Yes, he knew very well that, whatever it was, it would cost him a fortune, another fortune, but what Anemhor advised was usually for the best. In his heart he knew that Anemhor gave him wise counsel. And so it was that Ptolemy agreed to the endowment of more Egyptian temples, to more public works in the Delta, to more aid for the Egyptian cities up-River, and made himself a more generous benefactor to Egypt.

The Egyptian, he thought, *is quick to see signs of the divine in every thing.* Whether a man won his battles or not, all was in the hands of the gods. This time they had withheld their favours. Again. The solution to his difficulties was quite obvious. The *only* way to defeat the enemies of Egypt was by lavishing upon the gods of Egypt the most extravagant sums of money. This is what Ptolemy now agreed to do.

In return, the High Priest looked upon this man with ever greater favour. He was already, now, a Greek king, ruling over the Greeks in Egypt. It would surely, Anemhor thought, not be long before he agreed to be King of Egypt.

2.27

Nothing Too Much

At Memphis the great question among the priests of Egypt was whether they would, or whether they would not, crown this Satrap of the Greeks, this foreigner, this Greek dog who was not of royal blood, this Ptolemaios, Ptlumis, Ptolemy, as Pharaoh.

Some asked, *How may we crown a foreigner who is ritually unclean?*

And some asked, *How can we crown a Greek, who is guilty of impure acts with other males?*

But Anemhor, High Priest of Ptah, insisted that even a Greek, if he underwent the proper purification ritual, could be as pure as the purest Egyptian priest. He spoke at length of the goodly things Ptolemy had already done for Egypt as Satrap. He pointed out that even Alexander had taken the crowns. Further, he said it was his opinion that Ptolemy was innocent of impure acts. *He is not like the other Greeks,* he said, *but prefers women.*

And at last the priests decided that they would favour the proposals of Anemhor.

Ptolemy himself, he still hesitated, worrying as usual on the lines of: *Never think yourself a god's equal.*

But at the same time he told himself, *There is no thing that a Ptolemy cannot achieve.* And he thought of the words of Homer: *The gods, after all, can do any thing.*

When Anemhor came one more time to stare deep into his eyes, he said, *The Pharaoh is the embodiment of the link between the world of men and the world of gods.*

Ptolemy stared back, thinking that his Greek was not quite correct.

The King, Anemhor said, *is the keystone of Egyptian society. He holds all things together.*

Ptolemy stared, trying not to blink, thinking, *Real gods do not blink.*

It is the task of the King, Anemhor said, *to make the world function. He makes the Sun to rise, the Sun to set.*

Ptolemy twitched his cloak about his shoulders, thinking, *How may such a thing be possible?*

But Anemhor went on, *It is the task of the King to make the River flood and ebb, the grain grow in the fields . . . All these things may only be achieved by performing the rituals in the temple.*

A fly settled upon the Satrap's nose, and stood there, flexing his limbs.

Egypt must not be too long, Anemhor warned, *without a Pharaoh.*

Ptolemy brushed off the fly.

Without a King, Anemhor said, *the River will not rise.*

If the River does not rise, he said, *there will be revolts in Egypt.*

Without a Pharaoh, he said, *chaos and disorder will come back . . .*

Ptolemy blinked in spite of himself. He said he was happy to be a satrap. He had every thing he desired. He said he had no need to be king over the Egyptians. He really did not wish to raise himself so far above other men that his actions looked like an affront to the gods of Greece. He really did not want to earn the punishment of the gods by becoming himself a god in Egypt.

Anemhor begged him to agree to be Pharaoh, and Ptolemy saw even the tears in his black eyes, but still he could not make up his mind. He lay awake at night thinking about what it would mean to wear the bull's tail at all times, hanging between his buttocks; to wear the Double Crown of Upper and Lower Egypt and be the Living Horus, the Falcon of Gold.

And he sent to Anemhor to say that he was not yet ready; that he was not sure; that he would need more time to think.

Berenike, his wife, thought otherwise. Berenike knew just what she wanted, just what Ptolemy should do, and she began to bully him about the income from the up-River villages whose taxes might be diverted for the upkeep of her wardrobe. Above all others, it was Berenike that urged her husband to take the Crowns and be Pharaoh. She thought of the unlimited supply of gold that might be hers if she were Queen of Egypt, and she thought also of the fact that Eurydike would *not* be Queen of Egypt.

Aye, Berenike wanted very badly to be the Lady of the Two Lands: it was Ptolemy that hesitated, thinking of the responsibility; thinking of the great increase in his work. He thought of the already unending queues of petitioners with grievances, every one of whom he must hear; upon every one of which he must give his judgement. And he thought of ten years, of twenty years more, perhaps, of nothing but petitions. As if he did not have troubles enough already.

To be a monarch, he thought—it was to put golden shackles upon his wrists and ankles. It was to walk of his own free will into the prison with doors of gold. There would be no way out of that prison, and no ending to his imprisonment, except in his death.

Berenike dreamed again and again of the glory. She saw herself wearing the Vulture Tiara, and the golden earrings dripping with every costly stone. She longed to show herself in the costume of Isis, the Great Goddess, or dressed as Hathor, Lady of the Turquoise, and to wear the cow's-horn headdress. She said she would *love* to be a living goddess. And she was curious also to be a shaker of the *seistron,* the sacred rattle, and see inside the temples of the Egyptians, where, as a Greek, she had always been forbidden so much as to set her sandal.

Berenike, clever though she was, did not understand what any of these great and mysterious things meant, but nor did Ptolemy. Neither of these Greeks was fully aware of the burden that must weigh upon the man who was King of the Egyptians. But in the end it was Berenike's thought that began to sway her husband's heart.

Berenike, aye, she thought of what she would *have* if Ptolemy were to be Pharaoh, and she thought little of his duty. She did not think, then, of the months on end of anxiousness that must come upon Ptolemy when every last thing in Egypt went wrong—low Flood, drought, famine in the land, and then revolution, all at once—all of which things, if they happened, when they happened, were the *fault* of the Pharaoh, and the responsibility of the Pharaoh.

To be sure, this man and his wife did not know what they were being asked to take upon themselves, and upon their children, and their children's children, down to the tenth generation. For, indeed, once they were kings in Egypt, they must be kings for ever, for all time. Just then, at the start of it, Berenike was most excited, like a child at some festival, thinking of the money, thinking of jewels and of every goodly thing that must fall down upon her head like a shower of gold from Zeus himself; and Berenike laughed to think that Ptolemy might say no to it, and perhaps have to go home to Greece some day, and be an ordinary citizen again.

Berenike did not think that when a thing falls upon a man's head it may injure him. She did not think that to carry a burden for a long time might result in that thing feeling heavy. No, she thought that the burden of the kingship would be light.

So she urged him on, and in the night time she nagged at him to do what she wanted, and in the day time she could speak of nothing else but being the Queen, the Great Royal Wife, and when she thought she was out of earshot she would scream with wild laughter at the thought of what was to come: *the Lady of the Two Lands, the Mistress of Happiness.*

The next time Old Anemhor came to speak with Ptolemy about the great matter of taking the Crowns, Ptolemy voiced again his worries.

To be seen to be even like the gods, he said, *it is to a Greek the crime most sure to call down divine vengeance.*

Anemhor moved his shoulders, as if to say, *Really, it is nothing.*

The Greeks call it hubris, Ptolemy said, *insolence.*

Anemhor made some noise in his throat, as if to say, *Really, it is nothing to worry about.*

Hear what Pindar says, Ptolemy said. *He says, Strive not thou to be a god. The things of mortals best befit mortality.*

And he told Anemhor about *Nothing too much,* and about *Moderation in all things,* and *Nothing in excess,* as if Anemhor did not know all about the so-called wisdom of the Greeks already.

Anemhor pursed his lips. He reminded Ptolemy that so far as the Greeks were concerned he was already a god. Anemhor reminded him that the other Successors all called themselves King: Seleukos in Syria, Lysimakhos in Thrace, Antigonos in Macedon. They were all of them *Basileus.* Even Ptolemy called himself *Basileus,* which meant, more or less, King. What difference would it make merely to call himself King of Egypt as well?

Little by little Anemhor and Berenike brought Ptolemy round to their way of thinking. Perhaps, after all, he thought, he *should* put off Greek dress, and put on instead the Double Crown, the Red Crown and the White Crown of Egypt, or the red-and-white-striped *nemes* headcloth, the bull's tail, and the golden sandals of the Pharaoh.

To be a pharaoh, assuredly, was the only thing left for him to achieve, for that he had everything else.

But still he would not say the word.

Thoth knows what you are thinking, Reader. You are impatient. You want Ptolemy to make his mind up quick, to get on with being Pharaoh. Quit your complaining, Reader. Thoth says that putting on a crown is a weighty matter. You must give Ptolemy time to think. His decision will affect the whole of his dynasty. There will be no going back. Turn the page and turn the page. Never was the like of this story heard in Egypt before.

2.28

Greek Gods

To Anemhor Ptolemy had long since said, *My house is your house.* And Anemhor and the Memphite priests had, of course, the privilege of entering the Residence of Ptolemy in front of all the orders of the Egyptian priests of all the temples of Upper and Lower Egypt.

Anemhor did not, as High Priest of Ptah, have to stand in line, but went straight in to talk to Ptolemy at any hour of the day or night. For it was Anemhor above all who kept order among the priesthood of Egypt, and the priests who, in turn, kept the people calm and manageable.

Anemhor helped Ptolemy very much. Without Anemhor Ptolemy would not have known what to do. Without this priest Ptolemy would have been as helpless as a bandaged child.

Up-River, the High Priest of Thebes was not such a friend of Ptolemy. He did not smile when he came into the presence of the Satrap, for he had no liking for the Greeks, treating them with coldness, with hostility. Thebes did always what it could to undermine this foreigner.

Anemhor of Memphis, though, gave his best help, his best support to the Greek. He saw that Ptolemy did many things that were good for Egypt; that Ptolemy was Egypt's friend; that he was ready to fight Egypt's battles for her, even though he did not always win.

Yes, Anemhor would have the statue of himself that was to stand in the Temple of Ptah inscribed thus: *I was consulted by the ruler of Egypt, for he loved me and knew my intentions.*

When Anemhor stood before Ptolemy, looking into his blue eyes, he wondered still what manner of man this man was. When Anemhor died, his son would follow him in his high office, if the god willed it, and his son's son after that. There were forty-eight generations of High Priests of Ptah in this man's family before him; yea, twelve hundred years of High Priests of Ptah, and the heart of Anemhor swelled with pride to think of it. And yet, his heart also shrank when he thought that he might yet serve a pharaoh who was no Egyptian: that he might perform the temple ritual on behalf of this Greek, this Ionian dog, this uncircumcised one, the unclean, the Impure One, whose people copied the way of Seth, lying down male upon male after the way of a man with a woman, to the defilement of Memphis and the high offence of her gods.

Sometimes even the friendly Anemhor saw the Greeks as Typhonians, as followers of Seth, who was the enemy of Horus, the enemy of the Light—as evil made flesh.

No, not every man in Egypt welcomed the Greek with flashing teeth, though, to be sure, the Greek was more welcome than the Persian. No, as soon as the Greek had arrived there had been some who consulted the horoscopists and made their forecasts of how long it would take for the Greek to be thrown out of Egypt, and for the rule of a native pharaoh to be restored.

There was a writing written at this time that was called The Oracle of the Potter, that spoke of the Greeks destroying themselves, for that they were followers of Typhon, followers of Seth. And the Oracle forecast that even the Agathos Daimon would abandon the city of Alexandria and migrate to god-bearing Memphis. Alexandria would be deserted, and the foreigner would vanish like leaves from the trees in autumn.

Yes, the prophecy was that even the illustrious city of Alexandria would be returned to a place where the fishermen dried their nets, just as it had been before the coming of Alexander.

And yes, there were times when it seemed to Anemhor as if he was the only man in all Egypt who was ready to help Ptolemy; the only man who wanted this Greek to be Pharaoh.

At the prompting of Berenike, Ptolemy now began to send for Anemhor to question him about the Egyptian matters he did not understand.

What is *Pharaoh?* he asked.

Anemhor spread his hands. Where to begin?

The Pharaoh is he who causes things to multiply, he said.

Ptolemy nodded his head.

The Pharaoh is he who knows how to give, he said. *The Pharaoh, he is god, the King of the gods. He is Ra, whose visible presence is the disk, and who lives for ever.*

Ptolemy stared into the dark eyes, eyes that betrayed nothing about what Anemhor was thinking.

When Pharaoh sits upon the throne of Horus, he is the son of the gods. Seated upon his throne, with Horus the Falcon hovering above his head, the Pharaoh is Horus.

Ptolemy seemed satisfied. He looked as if he had understood. But then he questioned some more.

What is the Pharaoh's duty? he asked.

The Pharaoh, Anemhor said, *is responsible for the destruction of Egypt's enemies.* And then he said, *He must maintain, impose or restore Maat,* and he paused, knowing what must be the next question.

What is Maat? asked Ptolemy, and it was not for the first time. He did not understand *Maat.*

Maat, said Anemhor, *is Justice. Maat is Balance. Maat is the most important thing. It is the work of Pharaoh to drive off the opposite of Maat—that is to say, Chaos, Disorder.*

Ptolemy nodded, understood, urged Anemhor to go on.

The Pharaoh, he is absolute master of the Sun. Under the Sun he is the sole owner of the Egyptian earth, bequeathed to him by Horus, son of Osiris.

Ptolemy fidgeted now with his cloak.

In turn, the Pharaoh entrusts the care of the land to the temples. He ensures the protection of his people through his relationship with the gods. In return, the people of Egypt will give the Pharaoh their obedience, their homage, and their labour.

What, then, is a good Pharaoh? Ptolemy said.

The good Pharaoh, Anemhor said, *he will rule his flock like a careful shepherd, with a firm hand, with a just hand. The good Pharaoh will tolerate no insurrection.*

And a bad Pharaoh? asked Ptolemy.

A bad Pharaoh . . . Anemhor said, *he is the enemy of the gods. He is the man who brings back chaos.*

Anemhor knew, and Ptolemy himself knew, which kind of Pharaoh he might turn out to be. After all, the priests of Egypt had *invited* this man to be their king and their god.

Just then Ptolemy was tempted to say, Yes, yes, yes, without asking any further question. For he thought, What Greek in all the history of the Greeks, apart from Alexander, had been a pharaoh? Was not to be Pharaoh of Egypt the greatest thing any Greek had ever done?

2.29

The Sacred Bull

It was while Ptolemy still hesitated about whether he should take the title of Pharaoh, and be crowned, that the last of the children of Berenike was born. She wept once again for shame at having borne him yet another girl child, sobbing that the gods had abandoned her, wailing that she was useless, useless, a failure; and she begged Ptolemy to have the child cast out.

But he told her, *A daughter is nothing to be ashamed of; a daughter is just as much as a son,* and although this child was plain and sickly, and although the physicians shook their heads and said she would not live, Ptolemy did not order this daughter to be exposed, but gave her the name Philotera, and said that, whatever she looked like, the daughter of a satrap might yet be married to some high prince, and be part of some alliance that would mean peace in the world for a little longer.

And while it was the fate of Philotera, in fact, never to marry a husband, it was her fate also to be a goddess.

As it happened, all three of Berenike's children by Ptolemy were fated to be numbered among the gods, and Berenike herself also.

Within the Residence the children of Ptolemy called their father *Pappas,* and he had been known, from time to time, to play some game of ball with his sons, to hold polite conversations with them, and to make some show of affection. In his private apartments Ptolemy would relax his guard and be heard to laugh, and he was the old Ptolemy he had always been—kind, loving, like any other Greek father.

But Ptolemy began now to change. The burden of public affairs weighed already upon his shoulders. Outside the Residence he would seem severe, and he showed not his feelings, except perhaps his anger at some foreign intelligence. In public he would behave towards even his wife Berenike with indifference, and his children, illegitimate and legitimate alike, he often ignored utterly.

In public the daughters of a satrap must walk with measured steps and downcast eyes, and they must never run. Only in private could these girls laugh and gossip, ask riddles or make jests. In private, yes, they seemed almost to be happy, like any other family. But the atmosphere of normality was possible only when they were shielded from the public gaze. Among strangers these children would keep up a kind of impenetrable reserve.

What was happening to this family of Greeks, this ordinary family? They were people upon the road to becoming a royal family, for, to be sure, it was only a matter of time, now, before they were princes and princesses of Egypt, sons and daughters of a living god.

Some days Ptolemy would forget the growing burden, look out of his windows and shout *Thick falls the snow,* and bring his children running to see it, for they could only imagine the wonder that was cold goose feathers falling out of a grey sky.

When Ptolemy played such games, his children would smile, and smack their father gently about his shoulders for tricking them.

The sons came closest to their father through the Greek dances that they must dance at the Greek festivals, when according to the custom of the Greeks, they would show their teeth and sing, and have their arms round each others' necks, and stand in the line and make their feet go up and down in the dance, like any other Greek family, getting the steps wrong; the father would show them the right way, and they would copy his elephantine dancing, and sparkle their eyes, and it would seem that every thing was well.

But the Satrap behaved, really, more and more like a man in a dream. Even in private he laughed and jested less. He had almost stopped being the happy Ptolemy of his past, but retreated into himself, wearing often the half-smile of the High Priest, as if he was thinking himself into becoming Pharaoh. For how could he become the Son of the Sun and remain the same?

Thoth speaks true: The children of Ptolemy suffered. He spoke with them seldom. These children passed more time with nurses and bodyguards than they passed with their father and mother, and no, the parents did not notice what was happening. Slowly, their children became like strangers unto them, who dwelt in a world of their own making. They were, to be sure, children who had every thing they wanted, every thing they asked for, but they lacked the one thing that every Egyptian child enjoys: the affection of his, or her, parents.

No, the children of Ptolemy did not live ordinary lives any more. They had wandered halfway along the road to royalty without being aware of it. Lost children, they would never be the same again.

While Ptolemy lived and breathed, every one of these children was safe, but the nearer he drew to old age, the greater was the danger to their lives. When Ptolemy died, his heir must ensure that his siblings were put to death, so that he alone survived. Meanwhile, they would live strange, remote lives, removed from reality, Greeks in a foreign country, children mystified by what was going on.

Yes, their father was about to turn into a falcon.

Yes, their mother was about to wear the Vulture Tiara for the first time, upon her forehead.

Yes, their father, this Greek, this ordinary Greek, of the people, would from henceforth be carried everywhere by eight men, so that, like a real god, his foot would never so much as touch the ground.

For Ptolemy the past was, he said, of small interest. His own past he wanted to forget, although he could not forget it. What mattered to him, he said, always, was today. But at this time, from time to time he would ask a question about the history of the Two Lands, and find that nobody, Greek or Egyptian, had an answer. And when he asked for a history of Egypt that he might read, in his own language, he found, of course, that there was no such thing, and no book upon this subject but the works of Herodotos of Halikarnassos, the Greek whom many chose to call the Father of History, but many more preferred to call the Father of Lies.

Ptolemy had then a sudden desire and longing to know the names and characters of the Pharaohs who had gone before. He suddenly wanted to know about the Pyramids, and the Great Sphinx of Memphis, and when they had been made. But for all his questioning, the priests and high priests of Egypt, all of them, still spread their hands, pretending that nobody had the answers to such mysteries.

And so Ptolemy had the High Priest of Memphis send for whatever man in Egypt could best write the book of the history of Egypt, which he thought would be a proper book to have in his Great Library of Alexandria, and the man who was sent to him was Manetho of Sebennytos, the High Priest of Heliopolis, who wrote and spoke Greek as well as the best of Greeks, and Ptolemy gave the order for Manetho to start writing.

This Manetho was most learned in historical matters. He had the archives of the House of Life in the great Temple of Ra at Heliopolis at his disposal. In the Egyptian tongue this man's name was Mer-en-Tehuti, Beloved of Thoth, and it was Thoth himself that watched over the writing of his book of history.

Manetho wrote fast, because the Satrap did not like to wait.

Manetho did not write, however, every thing that he might have written about Egypt. Sure, he gave every impression of authority. He gathered his materials in the library of the priests of Ra. He named the names of three hundred Kings of Egypt. But at the same time as he wrote down what was true, he filled his papyrus also with charming stories that he thought would make Ptolemy smile, and he kept from the Greek the whole truth about the Two Lands.

Manetho repeated the tale about Menes, the first King of Egypt, who reigned sixty-two years, and was eaten by the hippopotamus.

He copied down the story of King Nepherkheres, who ruled twenty-five years, including a period of eleven days when the River flowed with honey.

In the not so distant past two Greeks, Plato and Eudoxos, had spent as long as thirteen years living with the priests of Heliopolis, learning from them, thinking to extract from them their most precious secrets. But they had met with small success, and at the end of it Plato had written, *The barbarian conceals most things*.

Of the true history of Egypt Manetho revealed, in fact, not much. His purpose was to make Ptolemy think that he knew every thing there was to know about his kingdom, but to leave him in darkness about things of great importance. Thus the secrets of Egypt stayed secret.

In this way some of the Egyptians fought back against the usurper, thinking that the day must come when the Greek Dog sat no more in the seat of the Living Horus, the Falcon of Gold. Ptolemy they saw as nothing better than a visitor. Soon he would surely return home to Greece. Soon Egypt would be restored to its rightful king. Soon, they thought, a native pharaoh would rule in Mennufer once again.

Thoughts of Thoth: For the Greek, the distant past is obscure, of no import. His history is riddled with the tragic and the monstrous. He will tell absurd stories about how the sisters of Phaethon were changed into poplar trees; how Daphne found herself turned into a laurel bush!

To be sure, more than half of his history is fiction.

What does the Egyptian think? He thinks that it is only from the truth that the reader may obtain profit. Without truth there is nothing but an empty story.

The thing that is of the highest importance to the Egyptian is the Truth of Thoth.

More Thoughts of Thoth, then: In Egypt the Persian was loathed for many reasons, but most of all because their King, Kambyses, murdered

the Sacred Bull, the Apis of Memphis. Yea, this Kambyses walked into
the Temple of Ptah and mocked the image of the god, saying that Ptah
was nothing more than a dwarf.

Kambyses was guilty also of breaking open coffins at Memphis,
seeking for golden jewellery, and his memory was repellent to every
priest because of it.

This Kambyses had said, *When I am a grown man, I will turn all
Egypt upside down.* And he had done so.

Most of all, Egypt hated the Persian because he had picked out the
handsomest of Egyptian youths and turned them into eunuchs. *Stone-
less ones,* he had called them, and laughed at their misfortune. And the
most beautiful of Egyptian girls they had taken to the Persian king to be
his concubines.

Truly, the Persian was hated more than any other enemy of Egypt,
more than any other people upon earth.

Some men of the Egyptians, indeed, hated Ptolemy also, but for the
most part, wherever he went he was welcomed with polite applause,
and bombarded with flowers, like a hero. For yes, this Satrap had been
popular with the army of Macedon, and he believed now that he was
popular with the people of Egypt. Unlike Kambyses, he was careful to
visit the bull Apis often, and to make plain his reverence for this god.

Anemhor said to him often, *Apis—there is no thing in all Egypt that
is more important.*

At this time Anemhor became again urgent in his talk with Ptolemy,
that he must take the Crowns, that he must agree to be King and
Pharaoh of Egypt, but Ptolemy hesitated still, saying he was not sure.

Anemhor did not know how he might best change the heart of the
Satrap and make him do what would, after all, only be the best thing for
the Two Lands, but in the end he had the thought to say to Ptolemy,
Why not ask the Apis what he thinks?

So that Ptolemy came to put his question, treating the Apis like an
oracle of his own future. Day after day he came in person to the stall of
Apis, which lies in the southern part of the great Temple of Ptah, in
order to know Apis better.

Apis had grown old, and he passed many of his days lying down,
chewing his grass, or as if sleeping. Apis was heavy, with great muscular
shoulders, the Living Image of Ptah, and Ptolemy watched him.

He saw the tongue of Apis lick his left-hand nostril and his right-
hand nostril.

He saw Apis lift his right-hand back foot to scratch his belly. He saw
how Apis twitched his ears and flicked his tail against the flies. He

watched for every omen, and asked Anemhor about the meaning of every last thing that Apis did, until Ptolemy knew almost as much about the Sacred Bull of the Egyptians as did the High Priest of Memphis, for in this matter Anemhor withheld nothing. It was surely not necessary for the secrets of the Sacred Bull to be kept from the man who should be Pharaoh.

And Anemhor knew more about the Apis and the history of the Apis than any man in Egypt, than any man alive. Anemhor had served and worshipped the Apis since he was a boy of five years old. There was not a time in his memory when he had not come to speak to Apis in all of his life. Aye, Old Anemhor *loved* Apis, the Sacred Bull, and *love* was not too strong a word to put upon what he felt.

But at no time during all these visits of Ptolemy—and he walked to see Apis every day, day after day—was there one sign regarding whether the Satrap should or should not turn himself into the King of Egypt, so that, at length, Ptolemy was led to ask his question of the Apis direct, to make trial of the Oracle of Apis, and approach the bull in his stall, inside the gate, and speak into his hairy ear.

Ptolemy prepared himself according to the strict orders of Old Anemhor. He bathed himself seven times. He put natron upon his tongue, so that his tongue tingled. He put on fresh white linen garments. And then he drew near to the stall of Apis, fasting, of course, since the day before, so that his belly gurgled.

In the darkness of the stall Ptolemy whispered his words into the ear of the bull, and Apis was standing, and Ptolemy felt his hot breath, heard his sigh, and Apis cast his eye upon the Satrap and looked away again. Ptolemy held the long horns and placed his hand upon the flank of Apis, and Apis was hot, and his hide was soft to the touch. And Ptolemy breathed in the sweet smell of the bull, and spoke his question once again, for luck. Then he covered up his own ears with his two hands and walked outside the enclosure of the bull, towards the sunlight.

The first words that Ptolemy heard when he took his hands from his ears—this would be the answer of the god to his question, and the words would be the words that came forth from the mouths of the Egyptian children who played on this side of Memphis, south of the great wall of the temple, where there was a sandy plain.

What did Ptolemy hear? What words might these boys shout, he wondered, these boys playing with a ball of leather? To be sure, whatever Ptolemy heard, he would not understand it. To be sure, whatsoever words were spoken would have to be translated for him by the High Priest. But Anemhor was with him, for this very reason.

Ptolemy stepped into the sun, into the open air. He took then his hands from his ears and listened. He heard the bellow of Apis behind him. He heard the trumpets of his own soldiers, drilling upon the parade ground in the distance. He heard the hubbub of the Egyptians in their market place, and the bubbling of the pigeons, and the chatter of the apes of Thoth, but he heard nothing that sounded like a word in any language.

He looked at Anemhor, and Anemhor looked at the Egyptian boys, kicking their leather ball up and down the sandy plain, when the ball passed between two marking places on the ground, which signified a victory for the one team over their fellows and opponents; and the passage of the ball over the line that marked the scoring of a point resulted in the players sending up a great cheer: *Tiw, tiw, t-i-i-i-i-i-i-w, tiw, tiw, tiw;* and to Ptolemy it sounded, indeed, very like the twittering of the swallows, shrill, like every other barbarian language; but it meant *Yes*.

And the boy who kicked the ball screeched out—all unaware of the presence of the Satrap behind him, quite unaware of what depended upon his words—*I am King, I shall be King be King be King*.

And Anemhor translated the words into Greek, and there was Ptolemy's answer: *Be King*. And so he said yes, he would take the Crowns; yes, he would be Pharaoh; yes, he would wear the red-and-white-striped *nemes* headcloth, and the bull's tail, and yes, he would be pleased to ride in the electrum chariot of the Pharaoh, Greek though he was, and in all things do whatsoever it was that the High Priest of Ptah, and all the priests of Egypt, wanted him to do.

He looked, then, deep into the eyes of Old Anemhor, and the eyes of this man shone, and Ptolemy saw the half-smile—the shy, mysterious smile of the High Priest—grow broader and broader, spreading across his face, until this man was wearing a smile greater than any smile Ptolemy had seen him wear before, and it was because, yes indeed, the High Priest of Ptah, Master of Secrets in the Secret Place, had now and at last what he wanted: Egypt safe, Egypt sound, Egypt's future secure, and Ptolemy the Greek completely and utterly under Egyptian control.

Anemhor walked back with Ptolemy to his Residence, past the stall of Apis, to greet this god, whose sweet smell made him think of his boyhood in Eordaia, with the beasts inside the house. They paused to look once more upon the great bull, who nodded his head at Ptolemy, and looked him in the eye, as if to say that he did indeed wish Ptolemy to be the Pharaoh. And Apis bellowed three times, and stamped his left front foot, and flicked his tail, and bellowed three times more; and it was just then that Ptolemy began to *love* Apis, the Living Image of Ptah, himself.

2.30

Eaters of Emeralds

On the first day after the *prostagma* went forth that Ptolemy would be Pharaoh, and he was a satrap no more, his life changed for good, and every thing that had been in the past the same was now different.

As the sun went up, the line of dwarfs stood outside the door of his bedchamber, waiting, and they were the dwarf slaves who had attended the last native Pharaoh, that Nektanebo the Second, some forty years previous or, at least, they said they were, or the children or grandchildren of the last royal dwarfs—and they said it was their duty to carry on the care of the body of the Pharaoh as before.

And, really, Ptolemy had no choice but to surrender his body to them, and be the Pharaoh that he now was.

Dwarf hands pressed him into his chair. The Keeper of the Pharaoh's Wig brought the wig that was of giraffe hair, and placed it upon Ptolemy's head, and adjusted the back and the sides.

The Keeper of the Right Foot of the Pharaoh massaged Ptolemy's right foot, and his identical twin dwarf brother did the same with his left foot.

The Keeper of the Pharaoh's Wardrobe presented to Ptolemy his clothes of the day, the *chendjyt* kilt, or loincloth, of the Pharaoh, and its whiteness was whiter than any white thing Ptolemy had seen in his life time, and the pleats of it more straight and perfect than any other pleats in the world.

The Keeper of the Pharaoh's Sandals pressed Ptolemy's feet into the sandals of gold that had the images of his enemies upon their two soles, so that he ground them to dust with his every step.

The Keeper of the Pharaoh's Jewels brought for him now also the collar of gold and every costly stone—carnelian, and *sappheiros,* and amethyst—that was arranged in the shape of the vulture head, and had upon it also the Eye of Horus, that he must wear that morning, and this collar was a thing that Ptolemy had not known existed before, let alone been allowed to look upon; but now that he was Pharaoh, many things that had been hidden were brought forth into the light.

Dwarf harpists and dwarf singers played and sang the proper music that must be played while the Pharaoh was made ready to face the day.

And so it went on. To be sure, Ptolemy would have preferred to do all these things for himself, as he had always done, but he was the Pharaoh, and he surrendered that morning his body to the servants of his body, as if his own flesh no longer was his; as if he was no longer his own master but rather some prisoner of the state. And yes, the thought crossed his mind that he had surrendered up his life also to this nation, and yes, he was brought, by the Keeper of the Pharaoh's Bracelet, the bracelet of gold, heavy, encrusted with every costly stone, that he must wear upon his wrist all that day also, and all of every day, and that was heavy, heavy, a heavier thing than he had been obliged to wear before in his life time, excepting only his breastplate of bronze in battle—heavy, yes, as if to make him think during every last moment of the day of the fact that he was Pharaoh, and that he must never forget it.

A prisoner in a cage of gold, he was, and he would never be let to go free.

So what did this man do, now that he was the Pharaoh? He began at once to issue a series of golden coins in Greek denominations: drachmas and tetradrachms and oktodrachms, and obols and hemiobols, with his own head upon the one side, wearing the diadem of a Greek king, and on the reverse, Alexander, riding in a chariot drawn by elephants.

All Alexandria wondered whether the bug-eyed, beetle-browed, worried-looking man, whose chin seemed to be trying to make contact with his forehead, was the Ptolemy they knew and loved. All Alexandria wondered whether Alexander had ever ridden in an elephant chariot, and decided he had not. But such things were of slight importance. What mattered was not the crudity of the die-engraver's art, but the fact that there were coins bearing the name of PTOLEMAIOS, that showed the face of Ptolemy, with the magical word BASILEUS, King. What mattered was that, although he had taken it upon himself to be an Egyptian king, the fact of his Greekness was emphasized also, and not forgotten. What mattered was that Ptolemy's name and face were in every man's hand, in every man's fingers, upon every man's lips, so that the Greeks might never forget the debt they owed to him.

But how would he comport himself, now that he was King, a king indeed? He asked Demetrios of Phaleron, who sent him the rolls of papyrus that contained the Greek treatises *Upon Kingship* for his further study, saying that Ptolemy might find in them the advice that his courtiers did not dare to give him to his face.

Ptolemy read late into the night by a flickering oil lamp:

A King must be a King, not a Tyrant . . .

A Tyrant is the very worst thing for a King to be . . .

*A Tyrant's purpose is his own pleasure; a King's purpose is
his duty . . .*

*A Tyrant grasps after money; a King will grasp after
nothing but honour . . .*

*The Tyrant's Army is made up of hired soldiers, foreigners; a
King's Army should be made up of his own citizens . . .*

*A Tyrant will not trust even his own people: he takes away
their weapons; he will ill-treat the poor; he will do
nothing that is not for his own benefit . . .*

*The Tyrant thinks books are dangerous, because they
encourage the imagination, and he does not wish his
people to use their imagination. No, he prefers them to
do what he tells them . . .*

*A Tyrant employs spies, and sows quarrels. He will
impoverish his subjects, keeping them busy in great
works, such as the building of useless monuments . . .*

*A Tyrant is forever going to War, so that his people are
never idle; so that they will always need a leader, such
as himself . . .*

And so on, and so forth. Ptolemy worried a little about his hired soldiers. He thought of the Kolossos of Rhodes, of the Pyramids . . . but there was really no danger of Ptolemy turning into a tyrant. He had been made a king for his superior virtue, for his deeds of valour. All would be well in Egypt, unless there should come along a Ptolemy who was not a good man, not of superior virtue, who had done no deed of valour. Then, perhaps, there might be trouble in Egypt.

Ptolemy absorbed the great lesson of the treatise. It crossed his mind that his son Keraunos was the kind of boy who might become a tyrant, but he put this thought out of his heart at once. Really, it was too soon to think about the succession.

After the decision about being Pharaoh was made, Anemhor came often to Ptolemy so that he should know something more of the beliefs of the Egyptians, about the Afterlife, the Field of Rushes, and the weighing of the heart of the dead man in the Balance against the Feather of Maat, the Feather of Truth. Anemhor explained, and Ptolemy looked blank, as if he did not understand one word of it, and Anemhor almost thought that Ptolemy was inclined to laugh, although his face kept straight; that he would not believe in an ibis-headed god any more than he believed in the gods of his own country.

Ptolemy, Anemhor thought, was not a believer in the things of the heart, the things of the spirit, but a warrior; his heart's desire was only to kill.

But no, in truth Anemhor was wrong, for it was indeed the most heartfelt wish of Ptolemy to have peace.

As for Berenike, she asked Anemhor many questions now in her own right, about her new life.

What is the proper dress, she asked, *for a goddess in her own life time?*

And Anemhor said, *A goddess must wear red.*

So that Berenike had to wear red, in spite of her thought that *red* was, for the Greeks, the colour of death.

Next she asked, *What might be the most proper food for a goddess?*

For it had been told her, by some maker of mischief, that the gods of Egypt lived upon a diet of frankincense and every costly stone, and nothing else. *How,* she asked, worried, *may I live upon incense and per-fumes, and upon the sweet breath of the north wind, and upon jewellery?*

But Anemhor reassured her. It was true that a plate of *smaragdoi,* emeralds, might sustain Berenike for some considerable time, but the human side of her—the stomach—would be content with much the same foods as before she became a goddess.

Anemhor told her that she might continue to eat olives and dates, and bread and fishes, and every Greek foodstuff.

A Queen, he said, *will only eat emeralds when she flies to the sky.*

Divinity, then, brought its own difficulties. *But how to be a god?* they thought. *How to be half-divine?* And what did it all mean, if, indeed, it meant anything?

It required many lessons from Anemhor and very great attention to the detail of the ritual.

A god, Anemhor said, *must not run, except at his Sed Festival, that is, his Jubilee, when he must race the Sacred Bull, Apis.*

For, to be sure, a god cannot move in the same way as a mortal moves. By no means. So that Ptolemy and Berenike, and the children of Ptolemy also, must now, all of them, learn even how to walk anew, and take lessons from Anemhor, who amused himself for a while by making this royal family march up and down the empty Hall of Audiences, in order to practise the footsteps of the gods.

Anemhor did not smile, no, not once. Not so much as a smirk broke forth upon his face.

The new Residence of Ptolemy at Alexandria became now a Pharaoh's Residence, guarded by saw-toothed dogs. It had its windows upon the north side, to let in only what light and air was needed. There was no window upon the west side or upon the south side, in order to keep out the choking storm of sand that flew in from the desert in the spring, but the sand blew inside, somehow, all the same, so that from time to time every object in this supposedly sand-proof Residence was covered in grit and thick dust, and it took months for the slaves to remove it by sweeping, when the storm of sand would blow in from the desert once again.

No man entered this palace without the knowledge of the *Dioiketes,* or Vizier, of King Ptolemy, and its gates were decorated with images of the enemies of Egypt, kneeling and bound, their hands tied behind their backs, so that they posed no threat to the stability of the Two Lands.

Ptolemy slept now upon a bed of gilded wood, and its four feet were the hoofs of bulls, for Ptolemy was himself now *Strong Bull.* He slept in a pharaoh's bed. He dreamed the dreams of a pharaoh. He was protected by a pharaoh's powerful magic, with every biting insect charmed to keep off his golden flesh by the best of Egyptian spells.

This Residence was his House of Millions of Years, in spite of being Greek in plan, Greek in its design, and filled with Greek servants. But now it became an Egyptian residence also. Ptolemy was content. He had his children, his heirs—of his body. He had every thing he desired. He worried about nothing. No, not one thing.

Where he could, and where he saw fit, Ptolemy was careful to observe the custom of the Egyptians, and it was the custom in the royal residences, when any dog died, for every member of the household to shave his entire body and go into mourning. They threw out of the Residence then all stocks of fine wines, all grain, all eatable foodstuffs, and the King's larder was restocked.

Ptolemy loved his dogs: his guard dogs, his hounds for hunting. When his own dog departed this life, Ptolemy shed a tear, and had this beast buried with a great bone of beef close to his nose, so that he might wake up in the Afterlife of Dogs with what was most dear to him. All Greeks loved their dogs. Even Berenike had her little dogs, who sat upon her lap in the *gynaikeion*. To be sure, at this time every thing in the life of this Greek Pharaoh was perfect. The unfortunate thing, however, about these Greeks was that, in truth, they found it difficult to love each other.

Part Three

PHARAOH

Living for Ever

The accession of King Ptolemy was timed for dawn, so that he came up like the rising Sun in his glory, to the chattering of the baboons of Thoth, and it was upon this great day that was the first day of his glorious reign that he assumed all the titles of the Pharaohs of time past:

He was Horus the Youthful.
He was Lord of Crowns.
He was Lord in the Whole World.
He was the Chosen One of Ra.
He was the Beloved of Amun.
He was King of Upper and Lower Egypt.
He was the Son of the Sun, the Son of Ra, Ptolemaios, Living for Ever.

To the people of Egypt, who could not then or ever wrap their tongues round the sounds that made the word Ptolemaios, he was *Ptlumis,* and they chanted their corruption of his name with a rhythmical chanting that went on for the whole of the first day of his reign. They would chant it wherever he went and for the rest of his life time, for above every other thing Ptolemy was popular, so popular that the priests of Egypt taught the people that he had, in fact, been Pharaoh ever since the death of Alexander, and that his regnal years must be backdated accordingly.

In spite of becoming Horus the Youthful, Ptolemy was sixty-two years old in that year, and the hair upon his head, if it had been allowed to grow, and the stubble upon his chin, were white.

Berenike, his Queen, his Great Royal Wife, was said to be forty-three years old, and it was her name that was everywhere sung and lauded, for the name of Eurydike, the wife of the second rank, was nowhere spoken, except to say that, no, she was not to have the title of Queen, nor the privileges and attentions of a queen, for she was just another wife, little better than the concubines, to be ignored and forgotten about.

Even so, the Prince Ptolemy Keraunos was looked upon by all Egypt as his father's heir. He was sixteen years of age, and he walked behind his father in every Egyptian procession, wearing the Horus sidelock that is the sign of youth, and with the rest of his head shaved, like an Egyptian. He wore Egyptian sandals, an Egyptian loincloth, and a Falcon-and-Vulture necklace studded with every august costly stone, and he hated every moment of it.

Keraunos wanted more than anything else to be King, but he nursed the thought in his heart that he would be a *Greek* king, a Macedonian king, not an Egyptian king. *Aye,* he thought, *I will close down every temple, I will drive every Egyptian out of this land.*

How did this family of Ptolemy feel, now that they were royalty? They felt strange, and they did not know quite how they must behave, or what they ought or ought not to do, now that they were set apart from ordinary children.

Ptolemy himself sent often to the High Priest of Memphis to know *Which headdress? What regalia?* Or to know whether it was a day for the striped *nemes* headcloth or some other? And whether he should show himself that day in Greek or Egyptian dress. Because it seemed now to him that, whatever way he dressed himself, he must offend either the Greeks or the Egyptians by it, and there were times when he threw his hands up for not knowing how to proceed or what to do.

Anemhor his friend, as usual, gave reassurance. He it was who brought the tail of the bull that Ptolemy must wear fixed to the back of his belt at all times as a sign of his power. He it was who taught Ptolemy how to strap on the plaited false beard of the Pharaoh beneath his chin, that he must wear whenever he showed his face in public. He it was who explained the significance of the jewelled bracelet with the *udjat* eye that was called the Eye of Horus and was made of solid gold and *sappheiros.*

The human eye and eyebrow, said the High Priest, *it means filial piety. It is a most powerful amulet against all sickness, that will even bring back the dead to life.* And as he fastened the bracelet to his wrist, Ptolemy was aware again of its great weight, of what it meant: the bracelet of Pharaoh; that he must wear it at all times, day and night.

In such ways Anemhor helped Ptolemy to be King of Egypt. Many things he arranged so that Ptolemy could not but depend upon Anemhor for help, for information, for explanations. Anemhor was often by the side of Ptolemy, listening, watching, making sure. There was no thing that this man failed to see: the High Priest was the eyes of the Pharaoh, and the ears of the Pharaoh.

Whatever Ptolemy did in Egypt, this High Priest wrote down details of it. Every journey up-River and down-River was recorded. Every last breakfast that he swallowed was itemized in the book called *The Annals of Thoth*. There was truly no thing that Ptolemy did, or attempted to do, that this High Priest did not know about. No thing did he omit to write down. He forgot nothing.

For the day of Taking the Crowns Anemhor found the most auspicious day and hour of that year, and it was the eighteenth year of the satrapy of Ptolemy.

Since the night before he had been made to fast, and his lips were set already in the serene unchanging half-smile of Pharaoh. Sure, he would have been pleased to forgo the emptiness of the stomach that he had not known since the desert of Gedrosia, but he had promised in every thing to do just what his friend asked of him. He took his thoughts from food by listening to the crowd of chanting Egyptians, who did not stop shouting his name all of that night.

Before sunrise, according to the demands of the coronation ritual, the High Priest of Ptah waited upon him in the succession of ritual baths and purifications with oil, and for the removal of every hair upon his head, and every last hair upon his body, up to the eyebrows, down to the feathers, until this man who was Satrap no more stood before the razor priests naked as a plucked turkey—except for the Greek talismans that he refused to take off for man or god—but the purest of the pure, the purest man in Egypt, with the natron tingling upon the tip of his tongue, so that he was pure within as well as pure without.

Bare-headed and barefoot, Ptolemy wore no garment but the pure white *chendjyt* kilt or loincloth of the Pharaoh. He breathed in. He breathed out, slower than slow, and his stomach fluttered like the moths, for he was a mortal man on the day he was to be turned into the Living Horus, the Falcon of Gold, a god walking the earth, a god in his own life time—and because he was hungry.

The procession of the Pharaoh moved out of the double gates of the Memphis residence, with Ptolemy seated upon a portable throne ornamented with lion and sphinx, and the throne was carried upon poles, so that he rocked from side to side upon the shoulders of the generals of his army. He was waited upon in this progress by the priests and scribes of Egypt in their thousands; by his guard of soldiers, his band of trumpeters, drummers and pipers, and by the bearers of the ostrich-feather fans of purple and gold that protected his flesh from the scorching sun;

and the crowds through which he passed did not stop from chanting *Ptlumis, Ptlumis, Ptlumis* with one voice, and the rhythm of the shout was like the rhythm of his beating heart, and his heart beat high and hard.

Greek though he was, he was surrounded by Egyptians, and could see no Greek face that day but his wife's face, and the wife carried aloft behind him was Berenike, and it was her day of glory like nothing she had known, *ever*.

In front of Ptolemy walked the Egyptian priest called the Singer, who carried the Books of Thoth that had in them the hymns of the gods, and all orders relating to a pharaoh's life.

Behind the Singer walked the *Horoskopos,* or Horoscope Priest, who carried the hourglass and palm branch that were the symbols of astronomy, for this was the man intimate with the astronomical Books of Thoth, with stars and eclipses, and every last word about the rising of the Sun and Moon.

Behind the *Horoskopos* walked the *Hierogrammateus,* or Sacred Scribe, who wore feathers upon his head and carried writing materials in his hands, for this was the man whose duty it was to understand and explain the hieroglyphs, the sacred writings of the Egyptians.

Behind the *Hierogrammateus* walked the *Stolistes,* the priest whose duties concerned sacrifices and prayers, and processions and holy days. And then there walked a long procession of priests, bald-headed every one of them and dressed in white robes and white sandals, whose titles and functions Ptolemy had been told of, but which were still to him strange in the extreme, even after eighteen years of his life in Egypt, and they were:

> The Wardens of the Gates of the Great Sea
> The *Galaktophoros,* or Carrier of Milk
> The Prophet of the Ouraios Serpent
> The Mouth of God
> The Man of Anubis
> The Superior of Divine Vestments
> The Porter of Crocodiles
> The Chief of the Brewers of Min of Koptos
> The Carrier of Baskets
> The Keeper of the Ibises
> The Scribe of the Divine Seal
> The Scribe of Memoranda
> The Master of the Nekropolis

The Servant of the White Crown
The Servant of the Red Crown
The Priest of the Dead Children of Apis
The Nurse of Bastet the Cat
The Guardian-in-Chief of the Sacred Falcon
The Master of Monkeys
The Ears of the King of Lower Egypt
The Eyes of the King of Upper Egypt
The Master of the Secrets of Isis
The Herdsmen of the Cows of Min of Koptos
The Warden of the Royal Concubines
The Keeper of Sacred Dogs
The Priest of the River
The Prophet of the Goddess Maat
The Warden of the Treasury of Horus of Behdet
The Servant of the Goddess of Gold
The Chief of Flocks
The Controller of the Royal Lands
The Master of Divine Serpents . . .

Truly, if Thoth were to write down the title of every one of these priests, Thoth's list would fill up the whole book.

In front of Ptolemy walked Anemhor himself, the High Priest of Ptah, the Director of All Works, who presided over every sacred thing, and over the great ceremony of the Crowning of Pharaoh, and as he walked he burned incense before Ptolemy, so that the smoke of it rose to his nostril, making pure also even his heart and lungs.

If Ptolemy had had one hair left growing upon the back of his neck, it would have been standing up on end. As it was, he was aware of the tingling of his flesh, and that his secret parts itched from the razoring with razors of bronze, but that he must not scratch. He bit his lip against the coming sneeze, and it was the incense up his nose; but then he gave in to it and sneezed three times, and for a Greek it meant Good Luck, the blessings of Tykhe, and the approval of Zeus.

Twenty-two priests now carried forth the great golden image of Amun-Ra the great god, upon his litter of gold, and behind Amun-Ra walked thousands more white-robed priests, and the bald heads flashed in the sunlight.

In front of Amun-Ra walked the Sacred Bull that was the protector of the Pharaoh at his coronation, Apis himself, led upon a tether, wearing his crown that was the shining golden disk of the Sun, and shaded from the sun by a purple and gold canopy. From time to time Apis sang out with his bellow, and his voice echoed across Memphis and the crowds applauded, for he was the Living Image of Ptah, just as Ptolemy the Pharaoh was the Living Image of Horus, the Falcon of Gold.

To be sure, Ptolemy had seen something of this march to the crowning before, for Alexander, but he had taken small notice of the barbarians then, being more anxious about how to satisfy his great thirst. But now things were different, and he was no longer among barbarians. The smoke of incense rose in the air, clouds of smoke, and Ptolemy saw and yet did not see the crowd, and he heard and yet did not hear the clamour of his shouted name; the god was with him, an almost touchable presence, and in spite of the heat the shivers ran up and down his spine.

As Ptolemy entered the First Courtyard of the Temple of Ptah the high priests of Egypt were with him, and nobody else, for the secret part of the ceremony went first, and as they walked towards him he saw the flocks of white birds fly upwards, released to the four corners of the earth to proclaim him as the Pharaoh.

Three priests stood before him, wearing the masks of gods: Anubis the black-faced dog god, who is Pharaoh of the Underworld; and the creator god Atum, human-faced, the first and last source of pharaonic power, wearing the Double Crown of Egypt and the plaited false beard; and Horus the falcon god, with curved beak and tall feathered crown and black staring eyes. These three led Ptolemy by his hands, without speaking so much as one word to him, to the Pylon, or Main Gate of the Temple, and performed the first rite of enthronement in the pillared hall there.

Ptolemy put his feet into the shallow pool and the gods poured over his flesh the holy water that carried divine life, out of ewers of gold, so that his body was changed, and he was worthy to show himself before the gods.

The masked ones led him next to the Hall of Jubilation that has rows of giant columns carved in the likeness of papyrus stalks, where he looked upon the faces of Nekhbet the vulture goddess, and Wadjet the cobra goddess, and upon the faces of Neith, Mistress of the Bow and Ruler of the Arrows, and Isis, Lady of Many Names, and upon the face even of Thoth, the Ibis, who is Great Great Great, Three Times Great, for these are the foremost gods of Egypt.

They laid their hands upon Ptolemy, nodding their heads, and gave to him the figure of the Ankh that is the symbol of Life, and he held it in his hands, and his hands trembled.

In words that he did not understand they promised him that his reign should be long and glorious, that he should enjoy tranquility, and certain victory over all his enemies.

For Ptolemy, then, there should be no more *Misfortune*.

When he walked into the Southern Chapel, Wadjet the snake goddess embraced Ptolemy with her cobra's hood raised, and he was acknowledged as heir to the throne of Egypt. And then Anemhor came towards him, slow, stiff, and this aged priest lifted up one by one the six crowns and lowered them upon the head of this Chosen One of Amun, enabling him to take upon his shoulders the powers and duties, the burden of the Pharaoh.

First, the Double Crown of Nekhbet and Wadjet, vulture and cobra, that was half red, half white, the Crown of the Two Lands, and its name was Pasekhemty, the Two Powerful Ones, which the Greeks would call Pschent, and it was made up of the Crown of the South, or the Lady of Dread, and the Crown of the North, or the Lady of Spells, and the two crowns put together made up the Double Crown that was called the Lady of Power, or the Lady of Flame. The Crown sat upon the head of Ptolemy the Greek, the usurper, and it felt at once both heavy and light. When the great Osiris had put on this crown, it had generated so much heat that he felt faint. Now, in his turn, Ptolemy felt the heat, and his legs felt weak, and he sensed the power of the cobra that would protect him always—the cobra, whose lidless eyes never close.

Anemhor crowned this King with also the Seshed Headband, and with the feathered Atef Crown of Ra, and with the Diadem of the Two Plumes. Last of all came the Khepresh Crown, the Blue War-Crown of leather, that Ptolemy would most often wear, his helmet of war.

Next, the Ka, the royal double, descended upon this King in a stream of light from the Sun god, Ra, his father, and the Ka took the form of a living falcon.

Now Anemhor anointed Ptolemy with fragrant oils, so that he left this chapel sticky-sweet, and the Blue War-Crown was upon his head, and the bull's tail swung from the back of his belt, and upon his left-hand wrist was strapped the archer's leather bracer with the words upon it, in hieroglyphs, *May All the Protection of Life Attend Him.* Upon the sheath of his dagger of gold was written, *The Good God, Possessor of a Strong Arm, PTOLEMAIOS, Given Life.* And upon his belt were written the hieroglyphs for *The Good God PTOLEMAIOS, Given Life for Ever, Like Ra.*

Upon his feet were fastened the golden sandals of the Pharaoh, and he walked in them to the threshold of the Third Pylon, to the shrine hewn out of a solid block of pink Syene granite, and he knelt there, with his back to the god Amun, and he felt the hand of the god touch the nape of his neck as he confirmed upon his head the Khepresh that gave him sway over all the circuit of the Sun.

The shivers ran down his spine, and he felt, yes, the majesty of this god, Amun the Hidden Wind, and the god was real to him, real.

Now they gave Ptolemy the five great names that the Scribes of the House of Life at Memphis had chosen for the Pharaoh, and his names were these names: first, his Horus name, which described the new King, and his Horus name was Great in Strength; second, his Two Ladies name, which expressed his double nature as the image of the vulture and cobra, Nekhbet and Wadjet, the guardian goddesses of Egypt, and his Two Ladies name was Powerful Conqueror, Virtuous Ruler; third, his Golden Horus name, that was the principle of good and of everlasting life prevailing over evil, and his Golden Horus name was Strong Ruler Over the Whole Land; fourth, his Throne name, for he was the earthly embodiment of vitality and dynamic energy of the god, and his Throne name was Setepenrameriamen—Beloved of Ra, Chosen One of Amun, King of Upper and Lower Egypt; fifth, his Solar name, his birth name, and his birth name was, of course, Ptolemaios, preceded by the august title Son of the Sun—his own name, which he heard faintly chanted by the people outside, for he was at the very heart of the Temple of Ptah.

Ptolemy grasped now the two sceptres of the great god Osiris, the *heqat*, or crook, of the King of the South, and the *nekakha*, or flail, of the King of the North, which were made out of alternate bands of gold and *sappheiros*, and his two hands trembled as he held them.

He walked back to the main aisle of the temple. He entered the Sanctuary of the Sun Barge. He passed the Hall of Offerings. He entered the Holy of Holies of Ptah of Memphis, Ptah of the Beautiful Face. For the first time he would perform the holy office as the Priest of All Priests, for whom even the high priests of Egypt were but humble deputies, and this he must do on his own, following the strict orders of Anemhor.

First he lit the torch and broke the clay seal upon the shrine. He slid back the heavy bolts. He stood eyeball to eyeball with the glittering god of gold, whose statue was decorated with jewels from head to foot; whose close-fitting cap was of blue-coloured glass. He stared for a long moment into the glistening black eyes, thinking both everything and nothing, and he prostrated himself before this god in awe and dread, and kissed the earth, and the tears fell out of his eyes; and they were tears of pride and relief. He dipped then the little finger of his right hand into the unguent and anointed the Beautiful Face of Ptah with the stickiness. Now he laid the plates of food before the statue of the god. He sealed the seal of the double doors of the shrine with clay. He walked backwards out of the Sanctuary, brushing away his footprints with the broom, so that the holiness of the domain of Ptah was preserved inviolate, and he put out the torch and left the god in darkness.

Ptolemy, even this General Ptolemy, who had himself been Great in Slaughter, trembled in his every movement, as he had done when he killed his first man.

The secret part of the Crowning was done, and now Ptolemy might show himself before his people, and the masked priests, Dog Face, Ibis Face, Falcon Face, performed once again, this time in the light of day, the same ceremonies all over again.

And so it went on, hour upon hour of ceremonial, until Ptolemy at last left the temple by the Great Pylon and made his appearance riding in the chariot of gold and electrum that was the chariot of the Pharaoh, and he drove back along the road of processions, where food and drink had been handed out to his people since before dawn, where they sang his praises as the King who would restore Egypt to her former prosperity. He had done every thing as it should be done, down to the usual amnesty for prisoners in the gaols. Memphis had not known such rejoicing since before the coming of the Persian.

When this Pharaoh stepped down from his chariot and entered the Residence he was unable to speak one word. In spite of the briefings of Anemhor he had understood little of what the endless rituals meant. He did not know what it was that he had done. All he knew was that the gods of Egypt seemed to be gods of power, who stirred up his heart inside his breast.

He was Ptolemy, Living for Ever. He was reborn, and he almost believed it; but just then, above all, he was hungry. After the Coronation Feast, at which he never stopped, even while he ate, smiling the serene mysterious smile of Pharaoh, he did not sleep. He was a Living God. He was the Son of the Sun. He was Horus the Falcon made flesh. The light of the sky dwelled in him. His subjects would worship him and his enemies would fear him. He was all-knowing. He was perfect. He could do no wrong, not then, not ever. He was both a god and a mortal man, both human and divine, and he was half-afraid for having done what he had done: afraid of the hubris, afraid of having offended the gods of Greece, and afraid of what would happen next.

At the same time he had relished every trembling moment. Ptolemy would be a good pharaoh, Anemhor thought, and Anemhor was right.

Outside the Residence the people sang:

> *The happy times have arrived . . .*
> *A Master has arisen in the Two Lands . . .*
> *The Flood will rise high . . .*
> *The days will be long . . .*
> *The reign of the god-man Ptlumis is absolute and*
>   *incontestable, in accordance with the ritual-books . . .*

The Egyptian would sing these words whoever was made Pharaoh, Egyptian or foreigner, because it was the custom. The chronicles of the profane saw things in a different light. The power of Pharaoh was beset by snares. No Pharaoh was ever free from intrigue, from plots, from conspiracy, from men with knives in the night. But for the moment it seemed both to Ptolemy and the High Priest of Ptah as if every thing would be well, and for the time being the people of Memphis and All Egypt continued to sing and to dance, into the dead hours of the night.

Up-River and down-River were raised statues of this Ptolemy as Pharaoh, wearing the *nemes* headcloth and plaited false beard of the Pharaoh. The cobra and vulture, his protectors, sat upon his brow. The body of this King was modelled with broad shoulders and muscular chest and arms, to express his more than human strength and power. In truth, though, Ptolemy had no more muscles than the next man, for in Egypt he had exercised his body not at all. In stone, however, he was frozen in eternal youthfulness, smiling the same faint smile of every Pharaoh that had gone before him.

In these statues Ptolemy had his left foot put forward. He looked eager. He looked a little pleased. But the truth was that he would now pass his days seated in his chair of gold, listening to petitions. The throne he sat in was cube-shaped, with a backrest that reached to his shoulders, and above the backrest was Horus, the Falcon of Gold, enfolding the head of Ptolemy with his wings. The feet of the throne were the paws of the lion. The arms of it were Nekhbet the Vulture and Wadjet the Cobra, goddesses with wings outstretched for his protection, and the throne felt hard, not soft like the chair he had sat in as Satrap.

For some months Ptolemy delighted to wear the costume of

Pharaoh, and he quite forgot about *khlamys, khiton, himation, kausia, petasos, krepides,* all his Greek gear—cloak, tunic, heavy cloak, felt sun-helmet, travelling hat and soldier's lace-up boots—that he had stepped out of upon the day of his crowning. To look at, this King gave every appearance of being the Pharaoh that he was. He walked like Pharaoh. He smiled now like Pharaoh. He asked even for a pharaoh's food in preference to the Greek olives, Greek cheese and Greek bread that he had eaten before. Some days he ate nothing but Egyptian beans, Egyptian dates, pigeon pies, bananas and camel milk, and never so much as thought about fishes, which, as a priest of Egypt, he was not supposed to eat, saying he would do no thing to distinguish himself from his subjects: *So that I may even think,* he said, *like an Egyptian.*

Not everybody was convinced by the change in this man's habits of life. Anemhor knew that this Greek would not be able to give up eating fish for long. Anemhor, friend of Ptolemy, a great friend, sometimes thought in his most deep and secret thoughts: *Once a Greek, always a Greek . . .* And the truth was that, in spite of his smile, behind his impenetrable reserve, this High Priest kept still some of his suspicion of the foreigner.

There were times, moments, when Anemhor had to tell himself that he knew the future, and that, no, Ptolemy and his House, Ptolemy and the Greeks—they would not, after all, last for ever.

3.2

The Great Royal Wife

Berenike it was, Aunt Berenike, of course, not Eurydike whom they crowned Queen at Memphis, with the Queen's Crown of ostrich feathers, and the two great horns of Hathor, the cow goddess, the Golden One, the Lady of the Turquoise, and with the great silver disk of the Moon. It was not Eurydike but Berenike who took for herself the manifold titles of Heiress, Great in the Palace, Fair of Face, Adorned with the Double Plumes, Endowed with Favours, the Mistress of Happiness, the Great Royal Wife of the King, the Lady of the Two Lands, She at Hearing Whose Voice the King Rejoices, His Beloved. Berenike it was whose Greek name the Egyptians called *Barenikat,* and it was of

Berenike that they shouted in the streets *May she live for ever and always.*

Of the other wife of Ptolemy they said nothing and chanted nothing. No, not one syllable, for Eurydike was not the Mistress of Happiness, but rather the Mistress of Unhappiness.

Overnight, Berenike changed. She took upon herself the bearing of a queen as if she had been born to it. She had long since had her slaves and waiting-women. She had the freedom of the great residences: the huge rambling maze of audience-halls, courtyards, colonnades, pavilions, nurseries, kitchens, store-rooms, private apartments, terraces and gardens that overlooked the River and the city of Memphis, or, at Alexandria, the Great Harbour and the Great Sea beyond. All of this was the domain of Berenike, where she oversaw every thing from the cooking of the Pharaoh's dinner to the hiring of sweepers of floors and groomers of horses. Berenike refused to sit idle. She took control of both households, and it was a goodly thing.

In spite of the change that came from being royal, she was the old Berenike also. She went on removing the rough skin from her face with the old Greek remedy that was oil of radishes. She still made use of the skin cure that was locust legs, macerated ants, mouse-droppings and vulture's blood, all beaten up with goat's suet. To be sure, she did not give up the daily habits of a Greek noblewoman, but her face shone with a new radiance that was the reflection of her husband the Son of the Sun, and she went about her business weighted down with as many of the jewels of the Queen of Egypt as she could bear: gold, and carnelian, and chalcedony, and emerald, and *sappheiros,* and every august costly stone.

Berenike wore the tight white sheath-dress, the almost-see-through dress of the Egyptian Queen, or the red dress of a goddess. Upon her head she wore now the Vulture Tiara that no other woman in Egypt could wear, with the head and beak of the vulture poised above her brow, and the vulture wings draped about her ears, and the vulture tail dangling down the back of her neck. The lobes of Berenike's ears became longer, from the great weight of earrings of gold that she would insist upon wearing. From time to time Berenike had occasion to put on the towering feathered crown of the Queen, and her litter would be carried through the streets of Memphis upon the shoulders of strong men to the Temple of Ptah, in order to shake there the golden *seistron,* the rattle of Isis, the Lady of Many Names; and the purpose of the rattling was to drive off the wrath of Hathor, the cow goddess, and it was of the utmost import for the well-being of Egypt, and to do this, it was the delight of Berenike.

Yes, she learned the snakelike rhythms, the hypnotic music of the temple women that would force the gaze of the Sun god, Ra, towards the King her husband, Ptolemy, Living for Ever, Beloved of Amun, Son of the Sun.

Herself, Berenike had no fear of the Sun; she had never been content to hide in the shade of the *gynaikeion*, but was carried about the city, looking into what must be done, and what should not be done, and she made her thoughts known to Ptolemy, and he did not ignore her voice, but took notice. Indeed, Ptolemy did almost every thing that Berenike asked him to do. Why, Ptolemy agreed even to Berenike's request to set up, under her command and control, a manufactory for perfumes, which would serve a useful purpose and increase the royal income. The perfume factory was a fine thing, and it gave Berenike the perfect excuse to make experiments with powders and ointments. It was also the perfect cover for this Queen's experimentation with every kind of poison. Poison was Berenike's speciality. Berenike, then, was busy, very busy.

No, it was Eurydike, the discarded wife, who sat all day in the *gynaikeion*, sitting, sitting, leading the tortoise life, doing nothing. Some days Eurydike would weep the tears of hopelessness that only an abandoned wife can weep. Some days she worked the spells of spite that were designed to take away from a rival every thing that she had, and her magic was the bitter magic she had learned from Berenike herself.

At this time Eurydike kept up all the melancholy silence of a woman possessed by Dionysos, all the rigid stare of a half-crazed maenad. Her eyes took on, at times, a wild look, as if the horror of loss or the desperate nature of her position was driving her close to madness. She took then to winding the domestic snakes of Alexandria, the Agathos Daimon that was supposed to be so lucky, into her dishevelled hair, and she took snakes into her bed, for luck, for comfort, and let them slide across her hot flesh and lick her ears. She allowed their flickering tongues even to touch her own tongue, as she half wished Ptolemy might touch her tongue. But the snakes brought her little luck. Yes, Eurydike neglected her appearance now, washed herself seldom, and stopped eating regular meals. There were good reasons why Ptolemy never set his sandals of gold over the threshold of Eurydike's apartments.

Whereas before it had been Berenike who had looked haggard, thin, ill, old before her time, now it was the turn of Eurydike, and the two of them as it were changed places: as the one rose, so the other fell, and it was a thing that would have the most far-reaching consequences for Egypt.

Everywhere Ptolemy went, he took with him the dais of gold-plated acacia wood that might be put up and taken down at will, the purpose of which was to shelter the King and Queen during open-air ceremonies in the blistering sun of Egypt. And now, when Ptolemy travelled up-River, it was Berenike who went with him, and Eurydike was left behind.

Once a year Ptolemy and Berenike would take the parts of Zeus, God of Thunder and the Bright Sky, and Hera, his wife and sister, and act out the Greek drama called the *Theogamia*, or Wedding of the Gods. The marriage of Zeus and his wife was notable for storms and quarrels, but the marriage of Ptolemy and his wife Berenike was everywhere believed to be as perfect as might be imagined, blessed with every good fortune.

Ptolemy had never played at Zeus and Hera with Eurydike. His marriage to her seemed, now, very far from perfect, and his children by her far from perfect children, for that they never stopped fighting. Really, Eurydike had never looked much like a goddess to Ptolemy, and from the play-acting his lesser wife was always missing.

But what would become of Eurydike? This was what worried Eurydike. Would Ptolemy throw her out of the Residence? Would he send her away? How might she stop such a thing from happening? She did not know. She did not know, and she bit the nails of her fingers down to the quick for worrying about it.

As for Berenike, she felt, in truth, no ill will towards the niece. By no means: Berenike had much to be grateful to Eurydike for. Berenike had no fears, none, for she had worked already the spell to neutralize all hostile magic, and was proof against every attack. Berenike was safe, very safe, in the arms of her Pharaoh, with nothing to worry about.

At first, to be sure, these two wives lived in peace, but it was impossible that they should not, at length, have some difference of opinion. Time passed and they began to fight with words. More time passed and Eurydike struck out with the nails of her fingers, and from time to time even with her fists, and it was all because the Pharaoh had not the sense to keep the one wife only, but would have two, showering the privileges of the monarchy on the one, and withholding them from the other.

Anemhor showed his concern at the fraught relations between the aunt and her niece, but his private thought was that this was a flawed family, divided against itself. The family of Ptolemy would always be like the crew of an oared galley. To move forward the oarsmen must pull all together. If not, the ship will spin round in circles and go nowhere. The family of Ptolemy would not pull all together. Their ship was fated to run aground. It was, indeed, a ship that was already leaking, and it would sink.

Anemhor was a man who knew such things. Shipwreck would not, he knew, come yet, but shipwreck would come before long. The seas ahead would be rough.

3.3

Leopard Spots

At both Alexandria and Memphis the dawn came with the barking of the palace dogs, the clamour of doves and chickens, and the chattering of the apes of Thoth in adoration of Ra. But if Ptolemy thought to escape from Anemhor by living at Alexandria, he was wrong, for most mornings, wherever Ptolemy was, there would Anemhor be also, wearing as usual his leopard-spot mantle, on some mission of the greatest seriousness for the welfare of Egypt, or full of warnings about some new thing that Ptolemy was not doing right. To be sure, there was on the one hand the delight and pleasure of being Pharaoh; but on the other hand there was a dark side, the dangerous business of being a king and a man of power, which meant there were some who had for him nothing but ill will.

One time Anemhor showed himself and said, *The body fluids of a god hold all his divine essence and creative power.*

Ptolemy looked at him, wondering, *What now? What next?*

When he spits, Anemhor said, *when he passes water, when he blows out his nostrils, or perhaps sheds some tears . . .*

Ptolemy furrowed his brow.

Either the bodily fluids of the Pharaoh must be kept for ever, Anemhor said, *or disposed of with the greatest of care.*

Ptolemy stared, bemused.

In the past, Anemhor said, *there were Pharaohs who had magic worked against them by means of their own toenail clippings, with their own hair . . .*

Ptolemy scratched the head that was every day shaved close, so that he might wear the Blue War-Crown.

In the story of the Secret Name of Ra, Anemhor said, *the saliva of the Sun god was used to poison him* . . .

Ptolemy sat in his chair of ebony and ivory, wondering whether the filth of every Pharaoh was indeed kept at Memphis, labelled and arranged upon shelves in chronological order . . . Assuredly, Memphis smelled as if it might be so . . . Ten thousand years of the Pharaohs' excrements, kept for posterity, for all time . . .

If Ptolemy had not been Pharaoh himself, he would have roared with laughter at the thought of it. But now, he wondered. Should he ignore the High Priest and his absurd demands, and have his filth thrown where everybody else threw his filth—into the River that was the drinking water of all Egypt?

But no, he did not ask. He did not wish to know these secrets. Anemhor, worker of wonders that he was—he could take care of the royal effluvia as best he pleased, against the day when, perhaps, they might prove useful . . .

Yes, Anemhor knew that the excrement of an enemy was a great prize, the very thing needed to work magic against a man, and it might be preserved against the day when magic might be required against even this Pharaoh.

When Anemhor bowed, and kissed the earth, and the leopard spots of his costume moved out of the chamber, Ptolemy did allow himself to laugh about this most serious of matters. But Anemhor, he thought only of the words of wisdom that said the Greek, compared with the Egyptian, was a child: the Greek knew nothing; the Greek understood nothing. Anemhor smiled his usual half-smile, but he did not often allow himself the luxury of laughter. A priest of Egypt was not meant to laugh too much. The service of the gods was too serious a business for laughter, and he folded his arms under the leopard spots and went about his other tasks, thinking, thinking.

Anemhor always came back though, and within the month of the coronation he brought the newest of his requests to Ptolemy.

Tradition, he said, *it says that Pharaoh should deliver geese, pigeons, swans, ducks, fattened fowl, to his Egyptian courtiers. Will His Majesty follow the custom?*

Ptolemy thought about the expense. In all things he was keen to follow tradition, for to do otherwise would be to invite disorder, chaos, disaster.

It is the most wise course to follow, Anemhor said.

And so, yes, Ptolemy ceased even to try to resist, and ordered the distribution of birds. He ordered also all leftover food from the Residences to be sent to the courtiers, or to the Ka priests, to be placed upon the offering tables for the dead.

He thought of the words of Periander of Korinthos: *Keep to old laws but fresh fish.* Change for the sake of change was not a goodly thing. Every thing must be done as it had always been done in Egypt. And he thought of fishes again, fishes, that he was no longer supposed to eat. The craving came upon him, then, and when Anemhor sailed back to Memphis, Ptolemy sent to the *agora* for fish, and gorged himself upon red mullet, and this abstention from fish had lasted all of thirty days. But Anemhor—Anemhor, he thought, need never know.

In the second month Anemhor came again with his fresh demands saying, *The Pharaoh Ramesses gave sixty geese to the temples of Egypt every day of his reign . . .*

Ptolemy looked at him, but said not a word.

Ramesses gave one thousand eight hundred and twenty geese to the temples each month, Anemhor said.

Ptolemy thought only of how much it might cost him.

Ramesses gave twenty-one thousand nine hundred and thirty-five geese every year, Anemhor said.

Ptolemy raised the flesh where once his eyebrows had been. *Many geese,* he said.

Very many geese, said the High Priest. *Total six hundred and eighty thousand geese for the divine offering.*

Ptolemy drew down the corners of his mouth.

Every Pharaoh before and since, Anemhor said, *did likewise.*

And Ptolemy saw, once again, that there would be no peace if he did not do the same, and he put his seal to the *prostagma,* so that sixty geese were sent to the temples every day of the year, for however many years he might reign. And the breeders of geese hatched more eggs, reared and fattened more geese, and the goose barges sailed up-River and down-River once again, with their burden of one thousand eight hundred and twenty-seven geese each month, as they had always done; as they had not done since the time of Nakhthoreb.

It so happened that the House of Ptolemy would keep up the goose deliveries to the temples without interruption for ten generations.

At Memphis the Horoskopos calculated that the number of geese to be given by King Ptolemy and his successors would be six million four hundred and ninety thousand five hundred geese exactly. But he told nobody of this figure, thinking that nobody would believe it possible.

Three hundred years of Ptolemies seemed far too long for comfort. And the Horoskopos himself doubted whether his forecast in this matter could be right.

All these early months the question most often upon the lips of Ptolemy was *How to be Pharaoh?* Often Anemhor had no sooner returned to Memphis than Ptolemy would send with some question that meant Anemhor had to sail north at once. But Anemhor gave of his wisdom, because it was in his interest to help Ptolemy in whatever way he could, for a stable Pharaoh meant a stable Egypt.

Beware of subjects who are nobodies, Anemhor told him, *men who will plot behind your back.*

Another time he said, *Trust not a brother, not even Menelaos son of Lagos.*

Ptolemy nodded, knowing very well what he meant. The useless Menelaos would not be given high command again.

On a third occasion Anemhor said, *Know not a friend. Make no intimates, it is worthless.*

Ptolemy knew that a king can have no friends. He saw his advisers, his ministers, his slaves of the body, and the members of his family, but he was learning to trust not at all. He had learned to be on his guard against poison, having his own Taster of Food, his *Progeustes,* just as he had himself been Alexander's Taster.

Even the Great Royal Wife did not enjoy his complete trust. Even Berenike was not privy to his most secret thoughts, for it was really not the custom for a Greek to speak much to his wife, useful though Berenike was for sounding out his new ideas. And so, no, he did not tell her all that he thought. As for Eurydike, he spoke with her very seldom.

Some times he thought again, *Strive not to be a Zeus . . . Mortal aims befit mortal men,* but he had already ignored the warning. It was too late to turn back. Whatever action he took now, the Fates must do with him what they pleased. And so he found comfort in saying to himself, *A god does not need friends . . . A god is self-sufficient . . .* He concentrated his thoughts upon being a good king. He was elect, born of the gods to pursue their work upon earth. He was the All-Knowing One. He was the source of all life. He controlled all things. He was the Son of the Sun.

He believed and he did not believe it, and when he woke in the night, sweating from the heat, or in his shivering fit, he was afraid because of what he had done, and he understood none of it—no, not one word—and because only death or revolution would release him from the burden of his duty.

Ptolemy could do nothing but continue upon the road upon which he had started, and lo! the road was long, and difficult.

So the instruction of Anemhor must continue also, and Ptolemy fell ever deeper into this man's debt, ever deeper under his control.

The first duty of Pharaoh, Anemhor said, *is to keep up communication with the gods, in order to safeguard victory, prosperity, order, peace . . .*

Ptolemy stared at the bald head, at the fly standing upon it, flexing its legs.

That is to say, Anemhor said, *you must perform the ritual. The ritual is the important thing . . .* And so absorbed was he in his explanation that he did not seem to notice the fly.

The wealth of Egypt, he said, *depends upon the actions of Pharaoh. If you do not do such and such, there will follow Low Nile, famine in the land, then revolts in Upper Egypt.*

It was but a simple thing to avoid chaos.

Next after the ritual, Anemhor said, *the most important thing is to offer Maat to the gods. Only Pharaoh can do this.*

Ptolemy stifled his yawn. He told Anemhor that he understood: *Yes,* he said, *Maat is righteousness, straightness, law, order. Maat is universal order, cosmic balance, truth . . .* But he still put more trust in Tykhe, goddess of Good Luck. He took comfort in the knowledge that Pharaoh was protected by the Falcon, Horus, whose two eyes are the Sun and Moon, whose speckled plumage is the starry sky, and he thought of the two city gates of Alexandria that were called Gate of the Sun and Gate of the Moon, as if all Alexandria was but a reflection upon the ground of the state of affairs in the heavens, just as all Egypt was a reflection of the heavens.

The Falcon even so spread his wings to guard Ptolemy, and all would be well; the High Priest of Memphis, his very great friend—perhaps even his only friend—had promised it.

Thus the strange, new life of Ptolemy began. The six dwarf body servants of the Pharaoh followed him even to Alexandria in order to continue their sole function in life, which was to present Ptolemy with his clothing for the day, to polish and clip his nails, to make ready his bath, and to dry him after it.

Ptolemy became accustomed to doing no thing for himself, but to being waited upon morning and night. He would have been pleased, sure, from time to time, to wash and dry his own hands, to shave off his own whiskers, to bathe unattended, all of which things he could do himself with more speed, but there was no escape from being Pharaoh. He had to be Pharaoh in all things, not just a Greek who was pretending to be Pharaoh, playing at Pharaoh.

He *was* the god, Living for Ever; he must *be* the god.

At times he felt like howling, confined as he was by the slowness of his dressing and undressing, and his every private ablution taken care of by the hands of strangers. It was his own choice, though. He had no cause for complaint. He had been a willing prisoner. Even after his death he would still be Pharaoh, who flew to the sky upon the wings of Thoth the Ibis. Even in the Afterlife, as one of the Imperishable Stars, he would not be able to stop being Pharaoh.

Each time the High Priest of Ptah, or the High Priest of Ra at Heliopolis, or the High Priest of Amun at Thebes, came to Alexandria, they brought for Ptolemy sphinxes of stone, obelisks, granite statues of the old-time pharaohs, with which to adorn his new city. And these gifts were made with deliberate purpose, to make the Greek city as Egyptian as could be. A gift could not be refused without giving offence. A gift meant that Ptolemy would have to ask: *What may Pharaoh do for you in return?*

And Anemhor, or whichever High Priest it happened to be, could then say, *New Temple at Letopolis*, or, *Rebuild the Sanctuary at Lykopolis*, or, *More offering for the god at Philai*. And Ptolemy would have to agree to help.

Left to himself Ptolemy would have preferred a city with nothing but Greek things in it, but the line of Egyptian obelisks soon stretched the length of Kanopic Street; colossal statues of Ramesses and Amenophis and Amenhotep adorned the Great Harbour, and the streets began to have lotus-head columns as well as Doric and Corinthian columns, and there were statues of Anubis the Dog, protector against all evil, upon every corner. Alexandria would come to love Anubis, Pharaoh of the Underworld.

The gifts came also at New Year, and upon the Birthday of the Pharaoh, and upon his Accession Day, and upon the Queen's Birthday, for there were many days upon which some gift was in order. And there were gifts as tokens of goodwill also: golden statuettes of Sakhmet the Lioness, and Ptah, and Horus the Falcon, and jewels, beautiful things that made Berenike catch her breath in wonderment.

Ptolemy, believing the High Priest of Ptah to be his friend, told him ever more of his secret thoughts, and asked his opinion about his every difficulty, and he came to rely upon his support more than he relied upon any other man in Egypt, more than any Greek. Truly, Ptolemy would not have lasted thirty days as Pharaoh without the help of Anemhor.

To know the secrets of the Greek, it was just what Anemhor wanted. For the man has power, great power, who knows all the secrets of his friend.

Under this High Priest the Egyptianization of Ptolemy and his House began in earnest, and it was done with such skill that they almost did not notice. To be sure, Ptolemy did not forget his Greekness, nor did he give up his Greek habits of life, nor did he stop from speaking Greek, for no conqueror will trouble to learn the language of a subject nation. But Ptolemy began to gather Egyptian habits as well—at first in jest, but then with more seriousness.

Time passed, and even the Greek petitioners started to copy the native habit when seeking an audience, hiding their faces upon entering the divine presence of the Pharaoh, so as not to be blinded by the light of his countenance. For, to the Egyptian, Ptolemy was Ra, the Sun god, and no man might draw near to him unprotected, because if he so much as looked at the god without the god's permission, his heart would burn up inside him; he would catch fire, and die.

When the rumble of the earthquake was felt, Ptolemy himself would murmur, *It is the corpse of Osiris stirring,* and he did not jest, but fingered the earthquake talisman that hung ever about his neck as well as the heavy Horus collar of the Pharaoh.

Ptolemy and Berenike were pleased to laugh, some times, about the ever-present gods of Egypt, who saw and heard every thing that a man said and did. It amused them to know that Ptolemy himself, as a god, had seventy-seven eyes and seventy-seven ears, and such was the obscure information they drew out of Anemhor that Berenike at least thought she knew every thing there was to know about his gods.

At first, then, every Egyptian thing made the Greeks laugh until the tears flowed, but already Ptolemy did not laugh any more.

Woe, then, to the son of his that guffawed at the procession of the Sacred Falcon up at Apollonopolis.

Woe, then, to the prince or princess who smirked during the twenty-nine days of funeral rites for the Hesis, the Sacred Bull of Heliopolis.

Woe also to the courtier who turned up his Greek nose at the stink of a badly mummified ibis.

Ptolemy began to speak, quite soon, without astonishment, of the Ram of Amun, the Ape of Thoth, the Crocodile of Sobek, all of them embodiments of the divine. It was not long before even Ptolemy came to think it quite natural that the gods should walk about Memphis upon four legs, or were to be seen perched upon every rooftop.

Sure, Ptolemy wanted to learn, and, sure, the gods of Egypt were almost too complex for an *Egyptian* to understand, but it pleased Ptolemy some times to seek out Old Anemhor and ask him the one question that reduced the great man to opening his mouth only to find that no word would come forth—to make Anemhor say *No man living has the answer to such a question.*

It kept the High Priest, Ptolemy thought, in his place. It made Anemhor realize, Ptolemy thought, who was the master.

For Anemhor, though, it was not always so much a matter of *Do not know* as of, still, refusing to tell. Anemhor had not forgotten the words of Plato the Greek, that compared with the Egyptians the Greeks were *like children.*

And the Greeks, though they were careful to pay lip service to Osiris and Horus, at bottom stuck to Greek ways of thinking about the world, holding no god in very high regard, not even the gods of Hellas.

Even after his coronation, Ptolemy would murmur to Berenike in the middle of the night, when Egyptian affairs kept him awake, *Greek ways are the best ways.*

And Berenike, of course, agreed.

3.4

_____

The Arrows of Eros

In the year of his father's crowning Ptolemy Keraunos, the Thunderbolt, reached the age of sixteen, said farewell to his childhood and hung up his leather ball and other toys in the Temple of Hermes of the Winged Sandals upon Kanopic Street in Alexandria, as memorials of a well-conducted boyhood.

This was all very fine, and the Greek custom, but the fact was that Keraunos's boyhood had not been very well conducted, for he had been allowed to run wild, and to do in all things just as he pleased.

When the feathers sprouted about the *rhombos* of this youth and a dark shadow crept across his upper lip, Ptolemy Soter held the first of three great celebrations for the *Anakleteria*, or Coming of Age, of his eldest legitimate son, who was marked out, of course, to be his heir upon the throne of Egypt.

Thus the future of Keraunos was sure, and the High Priest of Ptah sought to make it even surer by giving him, at his Coming of Age, the Egyptian necklace called *Baraka,* or Bringer of Luck, that he would wear for the rest of his life time, making him still more Lucky Keraunos. In that year also Anemhor took it upon himself to teach this youth a little about the gods of Egypt, so that he might at least recognize the names and faces of Anubis, Hathor, Sobek, Ptah, and know a little about their attributes, and to make him ready for the office that lay ahead of him; and the Pharaoh agreed that such teaching would be a goodly thing.

Anemhor came then to Alexandria and settled down from time to time to talk to Keraunos about Thoth, and about the Afterlife, and how upon entry into the next world a dead man's heart must be weighed in the Balance, against the Feather of Maat, the goddess of Righteousness and Truth.

Alas, Keraunos was not much interested in righteousness or truth, and he did not much want to think about his death. He had been led to think, in any case, that as the next King Ptolemy he would live for ever, and he thought he had no need of Anemhor's instruction.

What Anemhor said, though, was this: *Do not think that all will be forgotten upon the Day of Judgement. Do not put your trust in a long life, for the gods see life as but one hour.*

Keraunos smirked. He knew he had at least seventy years left to live.

After his death, Anemhor went on, *a man will continue to exist, and every one of his actions, good and bad, will be piled up beside him . . .*

Keraunos fidgeted with his *khiton* and eyed the door of the chamber in which they sat.

The man who comes without sin before the judges of the dead, Anemhor said, *he will walk in freedom with the lords of eternity . . .*

Keraunos laughed into his sleeve. These were surely barbarian beliefs. As for eternity, Keraunos thought only of the stink of decay from the ibis galleries upwind of Memphis, that was blown day after day through the windows of the King his father's Residence. He thought, in truth, that there was nothing but rotting away. And he said, *I do not wish to know about Thoth.*

Anemhor quoted the wisdom of Egypt at Keraunos then: *The evil that befalls a fool, his belly and his phallos bring it.* But Keraunos laughed out loud, snorted at Anemhor's nonsense, and he vowed to do his best to keep out of the High Priest's way if he could.

. . .

At his next audience with King Ptolemy Anemhor spoke again the wisdom of Egypt: *Better a statue of stone than a foolish son,* he said.

And again, *A fool in a house,* he said, *it is like fine clothes in a wine cellar.*

And again: *The fool who has power,* he said, *what happens to him is bad.*

Ptolemy stared hard at Anemhor and stopped smiling the unending smile of the Pharaoh. He did not need to be told who Anemhor spoke of, and for some hours his smile did not return.

Anemhor did his best to train up Keraunos in the way that he should go, saying to him, *When you live as one who has power, let the wrath of your heart be small.*

But Keraunos just looked at him as if he did not know what he was talking about. The wrath of the heart of Ptolemy Keraunos would never be small. He would in every thing live up to his name.

Anemhor persevered with his lessons, but the day came when Keraunos shouted even at the High Priest of Ptah, the Master of Secrets, just as Anemhor had known he would, for he tested this boy, having heard what was said of this son of the King: that he was quick of temper, that bitter wrath sat ever in his nostril.

The behaviour of Keraunos, then, did not improve under the instruction of Anemhor, but, if anything, worsened. He began to go about the Residence of Alexandria holding the cats upside down by the tail, and he liked to swing them back and forth in the air like this, some times with great violence, and he would laugh a strange hyaena laugh that was very like the laugh of a maniac.

Anemhor, when he heard of it, said to him, *The cat is worshipped throughout the Two Lands. If you ill-treat the sacred creature of Bastet the cat goddess, the people of Egypt will ill-treat you also.* For it was the truth that if one Egyptian had seen what Keraunos did there would have been revolution, and perhaps even the end of the House of Ptolemy almost before it had begun.

Anemhor said, *If you kill the cat, the people of Egypt will kill* YOU. But Keraunos only laughed the more, and he went on, when he could, swinging the cat like this, and he killed the cat also, because he needed the blood of a black cat for the spell that would upset other boys' chariots at the races, and enable him to win.

Anemhor shook his head. It was as if Keraunos had set out to be first in wrongdoing; as if he had made up his mind to be wicked in every thing he did; as if he was trying to avoid the *Moderation in all things* of the Greeks, and had devoted himself instead to Excess. And it looked, in truth, just then, to Anemhor, as if Keraunos was going to end up like the moth that flies into the candle flame, for that nobody had control over him; and he seemed to have no control over himself either, and the last person to take this son in hand was his father, who was busy being Pharaoh of Egypt and in any case loved this son of his to blindness, for that he was his heir, and had the makings of a fine fierce warrior, who would not be afraid to drink a bowl of undiluted wine. This kind of son was a credit to a Macedonian father.

And the Pharaoh *was*, in some sense, blind, for it had been asking for trouble to name this child Thunderbolt, which was one of the titles of Zeus himself. It was one more act of terrible hubris, and this father should have known better than to call his son Keraunos.

Keraunos's half-sister, Arsinoë Beta, with whom his fate was bound up, she behaved like the young girl that she was. She would weep, and show all the softness of a woman, letting her feelings run free about the death of some pet animal—her scarlet parrot that she had trained up to speak a few words of Greek, or her Greek lap-dog, who came running when she called him, or when one of the palace cats of which she was most fond had been strangled by Ptolemy Keraunos her brother.

When Arsinoë wept, her mother, Berenike, would scold her, saying, *Most women are soft, useless, unable to defend themselves. Most women are not fighters . . . But you, Arsinoë, you could be like no other woman. You should make yourself hard. You should be strong. You must show the world that a woman can be just as good as a man . . .*

And this is what Arsinoë Beta did. She trained herself up to be hard, like iron, like *nails*.

From the beginning Arsinoë might speak easy with her brothers, sit in the same room with them or play rough games without being always watched by her nurse, and it was quite different from the usual Greek way of going on, where the girls were kept separate from the boys, and it was Berenike's doing. It was Berenike who said, *My daughter Arsinoë shall not be a prisoner in the gynaikeion. We trust her to behave like a well-brought-up daughter. She does not need to be spied upon day and night.*

No, Arsinoë Beta found it easy to do just whatever she wanted within the bounds of the Residence, whether at Memphis or Alexandria, and she got what she wanted also in the way of schooling, for she demanded to be taught just what the boys were taught, such as mathematics and geometry, and tactics and strategy, and all the art and science of war, and she became very hard—much harder than the usual kind of Greek girl. And yes, it was a goodly thing to be so strong, as hard as nails. It was a fine thing to be made of iron, until a magnet walked by, and she was attracted. For this was what was fated to happen to Arsinoë Beta.

She grew fast, and she read many books, and the day came when she was no longer a child, and the one thought of her father was that this daughter of Berenike was clever, clever like a man; that she was as good as a son, *if not better.*

These daughters of his—Ptolemy looked at them hard as they grew up, and he made his calculations from the gentle swelling of their breasts that the time of betrothals was almost upon him. He had the names of his daughters written upon a strip of papyrus, and he walked up and down the mosaic, thinking about what match would bring him the best of alliances.

In due course he sent his ambassadors to the fathers of the sons he had in mind to be his sons-in-law, armed with his list of questions, and orders to ask: *If King Ptolemy were to suggest so and so, would His Majesty agree to such and such . . . ?*

He gave notice that he had six daughters left to get off his hands, and he listed their names, and asked what he might be offered in return for each, in the way of treaties of peace and alliances for war, and they were: Theoxena, Ptolemaïs and Lysandra, the three daughters of Eurydike; and Arsinoë Beta and Philotera, the two daughters of Berenike; and Antigone his stepdaughter.

The eldest girl, Theoxena, was ripe for marriage . . . while the youngest, Philotera, was not yet blooming, though it was, Ptolemy thought, never too early to be making plans.

Where a marriage was concerned, foremost in the Pharaoh's thoughts was the question of the alliance that must go with the wedding of a daughter, for marriage was a matter of politics first.

Second in importance was the dowry, and how little he could get away with paying, for although he was an Egyptian now, he was only an Egyptian upon the surface. Underneath, he was a Greek, always a Greek.

Last in importance was the feelings of the daughter herself, who would do what she was told, or take a beating.

Never to be overlooked was the fact that marriage to one of King Ptolemy's daughters, even an out-of-wedlock daughter, must be seen as the greatest honour to the bridegroom's family.

In time Ptolemy put in writing his thoughts, lining up the list of his daughters with the list of eligible husbands, kings if possible, or the sons of kings, Greek-speaking, with whole countries under their command and control:

Theoxena might marry Agathokles of Syracuse.

Antigone might marry Pyrrhos, King of Epeiros.

Lysandra might marry Alexandros, the son of Kassandros.

Arsinoë Beta might marry Lysimakhos, King of Thrace.

Ptolemaïs might marry even the great enemy of Ptolemy, Demetrios Poliorketes, Besieger of Cities, and so bring about that greatest of goodly things: everlasting peace and an end of all war in the Greek world.

The daughters, when they learned what was planned for them, were not happy. They thought only of the hatefulness of being sent away, for none of them wanted to live anywhere but Egypt, and in Egypt nowhere but at Alexandria, which was the finest city in the world. And so the daughters sulked a little, but said nothing, so that they were not beaten for making pert remarks. To be sure, not one of these girls would know the least thing about her intended husband, but they were kept in the dark about what lay ahead.

What, though, of the marriage of his son and heir? What did the Pharaoh think about that? If he was to be the heir of his father, Keraunos should not, by rights, marry a wife until he inherited his kingdom, so that the best of alliances was got, and so that his sons were born in the purple, sons of the King. All the same, Keraunos's marriage must be planned ahead, lest when the hour came there was no suitable wife to be had, and the best of all possible alliances fell to some other monarch.

As it happened, though, this son was already open in his defiance of his father, for he said that he would choose his own woman, when the time was right, and not before, and that his father would not choose for him.

Keraunos showed great interest in women. He had the run of the best whorehouses of Alexandria, his women of the city, his women of the night, and there were legends already of his feats of endurance, which made his father smile, for that in such matters this boy was his father's son.

No, Keraunos did not worry Ptolemy very much. He wanted him to be a true Greek, a true Macedonian. To be mad after women was normal, not a cause for concern. It was better than being mad after boys, like Alexander. Keraunos, Ptolemy thought, would grow up. Keraunos would see sense. He had faith in Keraunos, his heir, who showed a fine interest in argument, in quarrelling, in making ready for war, and all of these signs were good signs. Ptolemy wished above all for his heir to be warlike. Was it not why he had named him Ptolemaios in the first place?

What King Ptolemy did not then know, however, was that the Thunderbolt was showing also a too great interest in the body of his own half-sister, the Princess Arsinoë Beta, who was just four years younger than himself, whose breasts had not yet reached the height of three fingers, but were swelling even so, like quinces growing ripe for the plucking.

When her father took the Crowns of Egypt people began to call this Arsinoë Beta, and her sisters, *Basilissa,* Princess, and she was then eleven or twelve years of age. When she reached her fourteenth birthday, the slaves of the Residence and the waiting-women in the *gynaikeion* there began to call her by the title of *Kyria,* the Greek word for Madam.

All eyes were upon this quite beautiful daughter of Berenike, wondering to what great king she would be handed in marriage. And Ptolemy himself continued to eye this daughter with a keen eye, measuring the steady rise of her breasts, yes, like two round loaves of bread rising in the oven that was Egypt, for when her breasts grew to the height of three fingers, she would be ripe for a husband, and he could seal his alliance.

As for Berenike, she guarded this daughter with some care from this time, knowing that the impulse towards *aphrodisia* is strongest when it first begins, conscious of the great need for a Greek girl to keep intact her maidenhead.

Ptolemy watched, then, and Berenike watched, thinking about the political marriage with some man of high lineage and quiet temper, a man of satrapal family, perhaps, who had proved himself worthy of the title of King. But while these parents watched, they did not watch close enough. They did not see how much time this Arsinoë Beta spent with her half-brother, the Prince Ptolemy Keraunos. They did not notice that the unthinkable thing was about to take place under their own roof, beneath their very noses.

On the surface the relations between Ptolemy Keraunos and Arsinoë Beta looked quite innocent. They were children who played together, exchanging daily, hourly, the insults that every brother and sister exchange, quarrelling about such trivialities as which of them had the greater number of peas on the plate, or putting spiders in each other's beds. They enjoyed the turbulent childhood of all Greek children, voices raised in anger from dawn to dusk over some small thing, making always an elephant out of a fly.

Berenike heard, some times, the angry shouting, but she took little notice. She put such arguments down to the heat, and to the fact that all Greeks love to argue and dispute. And no, she made no move to keep Arsinoë and Keraunos apart, never thinking that the horror of horrors might happen.

This Princess Arsinoë Beta grew further still until she was a striking young woman. Her eyes sparkled. Her yellow hair she wore long, so that when war broke forth she could have it cut off, to be woven into the stout ropes that would fire her father's catapults and siege-engines, for she was determined to play her part in the victories of Egypt. She had not forgotten her father's misfortune at Salamis in Cyprus, and she was, indeed, a most warlike girl, for she had read every text she could find upon tactics, strategy, navigation at sea and the history of war. There was really not much that Arsinoë Beta did not know about Greek warfare, about the military markets of mainland Greece where an entire army of fresh soldiers might be hired. She knew how much each man must be paid, and exactly how soldiers must be managed in order to keep their loyalty. She had questioned her father close about Alexander's campaigns, and she was a credit to this father of hers, and he was proud of her, most proud.

Arsinoë Beta almost lived for war, and it was her purpose, when she got the chance, to ride into battle herself, and fight, just as Adeia-Eurydike, the queen of Philippos Arrhidaios, had done.

Now the eyes of this spirited girl were of a striking blue, like *sappheiros,* and it was the same blue that made strangers think of the Evil Eye and touch their talismans for Good Luck when they saw it, and it may have been that Arsinoë Beta indeed *had* the Evil Eye, or was the victim of it, for it seemed in truth that every thing she did in her life was troubled by Bad Luck.

These blue eyes of hers at any rate fell from time to time upon her half-brother, Ptolemy Keraunos, and caught his gaze, when they would lock glances and try to stare each other out, as all children do. But they both of them tried very hard at this game, and it was sometimes as if they could not look away but their eyes were glued fast; as if they had been struck by the arrows of the Boy, by Eros himself.

Sure, to stare into the eyes of another is a most dangerous thing to do at the best of times, but the effect it had upon Arsinoë and Keraunos was to draw them close together, and the next thing that took place was that the tongue of the Thunderbolt flickered out, like a lizard tongue, and he kissed this sister of his upon her lips, and then he fitted his tongue inside her mouth when no one was looking, and his tongue felt smooth, and his lips felt hot.

At first these kisses were short kisses, quick kisses, but then these big children became not only glued in their staring but glued also at the lips, copying the behaviour of their elders, and Ptolemy Keraunos hardly stopped to draw his breath.

Arsinoë Beta, she said, *What are you doing, satyr-boy, putting your hands under my peplos?*

Keraunos would listen to not one word of her protests, but went on doing just what he wanted. *Why are you trembling?* he said, laughing. *How timid you are.*

By Pan, she said, *I am fainting, take your hands away.*

But Keraunos did not, would not, take his hands off her flesh.

Arsinoë Beta—was she not just as bad as her half-brother? At first she resisted him, knowing that what he tried to do was forbidden, and she would say in a low voice, *Our father will have your nose and ears cut off with his cruel knife, and rip away even your privy parts to give them as raw meat to the dogs, for what you have tried to do.*

But Keraunos just laughed at her fears, took no thought for what she said, and was upon her again at once, panting, like a satyr pressing grapes. Until Arsinoë, thinking once more what she was doing, broke off the embrace and ran off to the *gynaikeion,* scarlet-faced. And no, she was by no means always accompanied by her waiting-women. Her parents did not feel the need to have her watched all day as if she might commit some crime, but trusted her, not dreaming that any harm could befall her within the palace walls.

Yes, it was easy then for the kissing of Keraunos to become a regular habit whenever he found her alone, and his kisses were hot, smouldering, like coals, and it felt to Arsinoë Beta as if his kisses would set them both on fire.

What, then, had happened? Had not the Boy, Eros, indeed arrived, unseen, in the palace of King Ptolemy, bent upon his mischief, as usual, like a gadfly setting out to sting the grazing cows? Had not Eros strung his bow and taken a fresh arrow from his quiver? Had not Eros run across the threshold, unobserved, and crouched at the feet of Ptolemy Keraunos, fitted the notch to the middle of the string, drawn back the bow as far as his arms would stretch, and fired at Arsinoë? Had not Eros sped, laughing, away, leaving his golden arrow deep in the breast of Arsinoë Beta, hot as fire? To be sure, all these things had taken place. Arsinoë could do nothing but glance at her brother over and over again, and the fire of love swept through her heart, and her soft cheeks turned from rose to white and white to rose, and she did not know what to do with herself for confusion.

Yes, Arsinoë Beta fell in love with her own brother, and he gave every sign of having fallen in love with her in return.

Eros, the Greeks say, *is forever on the loose, and no man can escape his shafts. Aye, and no woman either.*

3.5

Balance and Unbalance

Until he was seven years old the youngest of Ptolemy's sons, Ptolemy Mikros, lived in the *gynaikeion* with the women, pampered and spoilt. When he was hungry he was given sweet things such as dates and figs to eat. When he hurt himself he was kissed until he stopped screaming. When he was old enough to know who Herakles was he learned that *Herakles never wept* and how to hold back his tears.

He learned also that the purpose of woman is to give comfort. He liked the perfumes of Syria that filled the women's quarters, and he breathed deep breaths of scent when he was carried through the double doors of cedar and gold, past the black eunuch guards, into the women's place, where the scarlet-feathered birds from India perched in wicker cages, and screeched in Greek, for some of them had been taught to utter no other word but *Ptolemaios*.

At seven years Ptolemy Mikros was removed from women's government, like every other Greek boy, and sent to live in the *andron,* the men's part of the Residence, where he slept with the men, surrounded by the bronze armour, the bright breastplates, the greaves of bronze, and the bronze helmets with black ostrich feathers, in a place where the talk was not of tapestry but of war, and where there was no perfume of Syria, only the stink of sweat, the goatlike smell of men's armpits. At first this Ptolemy wished to go back to the scented calm, the rustling skirts, the comfortable thump of the loom, but he could not go back. The women's place was forbidden to him, and the boy who ran to his mother for protection was mocked without mercy. Now Mikros was governed by the *paidotribes,* the boy-trainer, who made him run and jump whether he liked to or not; whose task was to turn boys into warriors, and heroes on the field of battle.

The eight-year-old Mikros grew, and by ten years old he had the well-defined pectoral muscles, the pronounced iliac curves, of a regular Greek boy, who threw weights and ran in the boys' foot-race, threw *diskos* and javelin and did not come last in any contest. Bit by bit the women's rooms faded from his thoughts. For now, he dreamed only of the day when he might become an *ephebos,* and put into practice the theory of war, and use his short sword not against a sack stuffed with chaff but sharpened, against the enemies of his father.

However, it was not the fate of Mikros to be a great soldier. Men would soon speak of the laziness of this Ptolemy, of his glorious, voluptuous laziness, and as he grew up he found he was more interested in the art of peace than the art of war, *like his father*.

Mikros set eyes upon Berenike his mother but seldom, unless she sought him out herself, perhaps to bring upon his birthday some garment woven by her own hand in purple cloth and golden thread. Berenike kept away from Mikros, because this was what a Greek mother must do, for it was better for a son to grow up under the influence of the men rather than the women, imitating his father rather than his mother.

Did this mother love her son, this Ptolemy Mikros? Perhaps she did, perhaps she did not. How can Thoth know such a thing? All the same, if there was any affection in a Greek family, it existed between mother and daughter, not between mother and son. Sure, a Greek father almost always loves his sons, and King Ptolemy was no different from the rest. To be sure, he loved the Thunderbolt, who was almost an identical copy of himself. But the truth? What was the truth? It was that he loved Ptolemy Mikros the more, for that he was the youngest son; for that he was the child of his great love for Berenike. Yes, and it was because Mikros clambered all over this father of his, Pharaoh though he was, and made him laugh a little, whereas the other sons now stood upon ceremony, and were in some awe of their father as a divinity, and kept their distance.

And no, it was not so obvious that Ptolemy loved his daughters. The day would surely come when he must say his farewell to a daughter, and send her away to some foreign court, and thrust her into the arms of some man she had never so much as seen before, who might or might not treat her with kindness, in order merely to make good the terms of some alliance. And to be sure, it was not the way an Egyptian father carried on.

Ptolemy tried, then, not to become too attached to his girls, but kept them at arm's length, thinking of the expense of the dowry; thinking that they were the image of their mothers; thinking that before long he would be wanting to slide his fingers inside the *peplos,* and that *aphrodisia* with your own daughter was a grotesque affront to the gods of Hellas, and though he watched the rising of the breasts, he tried also not to look, not to be tempted; but in spite of himself he could not but be looking for the breasts to be three fingers high; he could not stop thinking of his daughters' breasts that were round, like rosy apples ripe for the picking.

He did not know his daughters well. He did not speak with them often, for he was weighed down under the burden of state business. He knew his sons better.

The education of Ptolemy Mikros began in earnest at the feet of the *grammatikos,* the Greek teacher of letters, who taught this child to hold the reed pen, and how to go from alpha to omega. And Mikros, like the good boy that he was, learned by heart the maxims of the wise men of Greece, from *Moderation in all things* to *Think what you are doing,* before he was eight. He had by heart the names and characteristics of the gods of Greece, and none of the names of the two thousand gods of Egypt, no, not one, not even the name of Thoth. He learned how to strum the lyre and sing, because, as his tutor said, *Without music a man must be thought a total barbarian.*

Mikros ran, then, when he had to, and he had his muscles in the right places; but to tell the truth he disliked physical exertion. Often Mikros complained *It is too hot to run,* and was beaten for saying it. Mikros was fair-skinned and burnt up easily in the sun of Egypt. After a time he was given leave not to exercise himself naked in the *gymnasion* with the other youths, and at length he was given leave to exercise himself not at all, and it was the influence of Berenike his mother, who would have her way in every thing. Alas, it was the fate of this boy to grow fat, and because he was the son of a king, he got away with it, with being a fat prince, who ate too many dates, too many sweet things.

Mikros, of all his family, saw most of Arsinoë Beta, his full sister, and it was often she who acted the part of his nurse, for she had been just eight or nine years old at his birth. Mikros preferred the company of the women. When he came to man's estate this boy would surround himself with very many women, delighting in women's flesh—like his father—and in those things that a man might do with a woman, and in truth he had been put off the kind of love for which the Greeks are famous, the love of men for boys, and men for men, because the goat-like stink of the *andron*—really, he found it disgusting.

For Ptolemy Mikros, then, there were three things: food (and to Hades with *Nothing in excess*); women (and to Hades with the *kinaidoi*); and idleness. Mikros would be famous for being lazy, famous for doing nothing. He was fated to be one of the most idle men who ever lived.

And yet, he would be famous also for riches, for glory, and for his extravagance.

But all of that lay in the future. Years must pass by before his glori-ous idleness might begin, and in the meantime he would have to train with the *sarissa* in the phalanx, and ride with the mounted troops, and learn geometry, and write poetry in the style of the better poets of Greece. Although he learned much, Mikros was useless always at mathematics, useless at the theoretical arts of war, and if he learned one thing he learned that he would all his life have to rely upon some other person to look at accounts, and finance, and taxation, and the bal-ance of payments, and profit and loss, and at the economics of hiring a great army, because when this boy looked at a page of numbers his head seemed to spin, and when he thought about addition and subtraction the mathematical signs upon the papyrus ran together in a blurred black block.

If Mikros learned one other great thing as a young boy, it was that this elder sister of his, Arsinoë Beta, possessed just the mathematical and financial skills that he lacked.

Although he would not need to think about such things for twenty years and more, he did not forget that his sister was the best at calculat-ing. Arsinoë Beta was better even than the *Dioiketes* of her father the Pharaoh at spotting the mistake in the Taxation Returns of All Egypt, which ran into one hundred rolls of papyrus. Even more remarkable, this girl was interested enough to read the pages of calculations, every one of them, from end to end.

Mikros, then—if he had a talent, it was for words rather than num-bers. Arsinoë Beta had the talent for numbers. But Ptolemy Keraunos, of all the children of Pharaoh, was already famous for having no talents except a talent for killing. Keraunos was really very good at killing.

As for the half-sister of these two, Lysandra, daughter of Eurydike—this girl was fair of face and grew up sweet of temper. She had not the fiery determination of Arsinoë Beta, nor her cleverness, nor yet her keenness to be treated very like a boy.

No, Lysandra did not draw attention to herself. She had the woman's skills with the needle. She was happy in the half-dark of the *gynaikeion,* and she wished for nothing more than to be allowed, when the time came, to bring up her children in peace, and to be a good Greek wife to some good Greek husband, whoever he might be. Lysandra did not, like Arsinoë Beta, long to be queen of some foreign land, or to have great power in her hands. She was modest, unassuming, like Eurydike her mother, but lacking the streak of madness that ran through the family of Kassandros. Lysandra did her pious duty by the gods of Greece, always making the proper offerings, the proper prayers, the proper sacrifices. In the soul of Lysandra there was neither an excess of love nor an excess of hatred. She ate neither too much food nor too little, but lived that life of perfect balance so beloved of the Greeks, whereas, if Thoth speaks true—and he does—the life of Arsinoë Beta would be unbalanced; and the life of Keraunos was unbalanced; and the life of Eurydike too was unbalanced.

What Anemhor knew, but neither Ptolemy Soter nor Lysandra knew, was that it was the fate of Lysandra, her unavoidable fate, to be married twice, and that both marriages would end in disaster, if not in the most terrible of all Greek tragedies.

3.6

Aphrodisia

Having kissed Arsinoë Beta, his own half-sister, Ptolemy Keraunos wanted, of course, more than kisses, and in the great white marble Residence of his father, that slept upon afternoons of great heat, and was quite deserted when the chariots raced in the hippodrome, Keraunos and Arsinoë might complain of some pain in the head, or a derangement of the bowels, and stay at home. It was not unusual for the children of Ptolemy to be found panting in the cool of the cellars beneath this Residence, because of the great hotness of Egypt, and down there one thing led to the next thing, until Arsinoë Beta, a maiden girl and chaste, lay with her own half-brother in secret, and committed the crime that is, for the Greeks, the crime of crimes.

Thoth himself? He shrugs his shoulders. For the Egyptians an incest such as this was really no great horror, nothing out of the ordinary, but among the families of the Pharaohs quite the normal thing to do. But, to be sure, the Greeks felt quite different about it: for the Greeks to do this thing, it meant the anger of the gods of Greece, all of them, from Apollo to Zeus, and trouble, deep deep trouble.

So what happened? There they were, in the great cellar where the wine was stored, thousands of amphoras of wine, and Keraunos pressed the nails of his fingers into his sister's flesh, round her waist, and said he would cut off her ears if she did not do as he wished. And Arsinoë Beta, really, she had no choice but to obey this madman, for he would, she knew, have done it, and his knife he pressed then to her throat, as if he might kill her also. But he kissed her, then, with that smack upon the lips of his, and it was a meaningless act, for to the Greeks a kiss is not a sign of love. *Wet,* she thought, *disgusting,* she thought, and it had hurt her, and it was her thought that her brother smelled of wine.

And then he thrust his *rhombos* into her private place and thrashed about, with the sweat pouring off him, and panted like a dog all the while, and at length he cried out, regardless of who might hear, and collapsed on top of her, and they were on the floor, in the dirt, and their clothes were stained from the floor, and there was blood, and stickiness everywhere.

It means nothing, he whispered, *nothing,* but he did not look her in the eye, and smiled with his mouth only.

As long as we agree that it means nothing, she said. But she knew that it did mean something. To have *aphrodisia* with a brother was not a deed with no meaning, and she knew in her heart that the gods could not have missed it, even though the time was after the gods' luncheon, when every god was known to be sleeping, except for Pan.

But Pan was the most dangerous of all the Greek gods, and yes, if any god had seen them, it would be Pan, Pan of the goat's feet, who was most dangerous after luncheon, at the hottest hour of the day.

Tell no one, he murmured, squeezing her throat, *speak not one word of it,* he hissed, squeezing her ripe breasts with his two hands, digging his nails into her flesh so that he hurt her. *Swear that you will tell nobody,* he said.

I swear, she said, *by Zeus and all the gods, I swear it.*

And then he let her go, and tickled her so that she laughed a little.

I swear upon our grandmother's tombstone, Keraunos whispered, *that I mean you no harm . . .*

But her thought was that he lied like a Cretan, and she knew that he meant her all the trouble in the world, and that most of all, surely, he loved to hate. And the truth anyway was that neither of these children had known their grandmothers, nor knew whether they had tombstones or not. The Ptolemies were a family lacking forebears, for Ptolemy Soter had wiped out the entirety of his past just as surely as Berenike, his wife, had wiped out hers. And here they were, in a new land with a fresh start, and it was like scraping a wax tablet clean and beginning again.

No, nothing meant anything to the members of this family except the present hour, today, now, the sensation of the passing moment, and deriving the greatest pleasure from it. Hence this *aphrodisia* upon his own sister, in spite of the grave prohibitions of the Greeks upon such a deed, in spite of his knowing very well that what he did that afternoon was, short of killing his own mother, just about the worst thing any Greek could do.

Keraunos, though, was a boy who did not know the meaning of wrong, and he boasted of it to his friends, saying that it was simple, that it was easy, that there was really nothing wrong with doing what he did; that what his sister had between her thighs was just a hole. And when Keraunos's companions suggested that an *aphrodisia* with his half-sister might be an affront to the gods of Greece, behaviour highly unwise for any Greek to indulge himself in, Keraunos laughed like the hyaena.

The gods do it, he said. *The Persians do it,* he said. *The birds do it,* he said. *Truly, there is nothing wrong about aphrodisia with your sister.* And he lied, saying that, in any case, she had wanted him to do it, she had begged him to do it, and he boasted, saying, *There is no woman in Alexandria hotter than my sister,* as if he thought now to hire her out to his friends for the same purpose and make a regular whore of her.

These companions of Keraunos smiled, but they did not laugh with him. He was, after all, most interested in girls at the age when just about every other boy in the city had time only for other boys. The electric atmosphere of the *gymnasion,* where the boys ran naked, jumped naked, wrestled naked, and honed their bronzed flesh to Greek perfection, until they looked, in truth, like nothing so much as the sculptures of the famous Praxiteles, like young gods, and fell in love with each other's manly beauty—none of this held much appeal for Ptolemy Keraunos, whose father had made certain that this son of his was not brought up to be a *kinaidos,* but that he should take delight in women, in women's full breasts, like ripe melons, and in the ripe fig that every woman has hidden between her legs. Yes, Ptolemy Soter had taught Keraunos what he must do with a woman as soon as he was old enough to do what a man must do. Soter wanted Keraunos to be a man, not a half-man like Alexander and Hephaistion. So that, in some sense, what happened was *Ptolemy Soter's own fault entirely.*

Sure, Keraunos had needed little encouragement, but now, what was he doing? He was sowing his wild oats not only within the Residence of his father, but within the confines of his own family, in the bed of his own sister, and in truth he cared nothing for the consequences, for he did not care much about any thing.

Aye, it was all part of the lesson learned from his father, the rule of the Kyrenaic School of Philosophy, which held that a man must live for the enjoyment of the passing hour, and let the past and the future take care of themselves.

What matters, Keraunos would say, *is now, today.* And it was the echo of his father's words, for the son was just like the father.

Thoth? Thoth is not a follower of the Kyrenaic School. Thoth thinks that the past is of very great importance. You cannot leave the past behind. You cannot forget the past. And Ptolemy Soter himself, although he denied the past, and said that the past was forgotten, gone—he lied, like the Greek that he was, for he had not, in truth, forgotten. He might have wanted to forget, but he could not forget. No one could go through what Ptolemy Soter went through and forget about it. By no means—this man remembered every moment, every last thing. Thoth speaks: Yea, indeed, for the Egyptian the past is supreme. Education in the hieroglyphics takes the priest back into a long forgotten world whose inherited wisdom is the final word. The priest who cherishes the writing lives in a land of shadows. For the world of today he has no vital meaning. He lives in the past. He is lost in yesterday.

This high princess, Arsinoë Beta, learned quick how to put up her legs like a whore, and how to wrap her bare legs about her brother's back, and squeeze, in what the Greeks call the *amphiplix.* And in all her life Arsinoë Beta would know only one more love that was anything like so powerful as the love she felt then for this half-brother of hers. She delighted in the hot flesh of Ptolemy the Thunderbolt, and of the far-reaching consequences of their forbidden act they were both of them quite unaware.

Arsinoë Beta, to be sure, had been given every warning about what she might and might not do so far as *aphrodisia* was concerned. Her nurse had warned her about the Horse and Maiden, because it was the warning that every nurse must give her charge, to ensure that the girl remained a *parthenos.* And yes, the story she told was of a girl who lost her maidenhead before the time came for her to marry a husband, and who was walled up with a horse in a house in some remote place, so that nobody might hear her screams, and then forgotten about.

What would happen to such a girl? Arsinoë had asked.

Why, the nurse had said, *the horse would be so hungry that he would eat the girl alive.*

And Arsinoë Beta, who was above all other things so very *clever,* laughed aloud and said, *But how may the horse eat this girl? A horse does not eat flesh, but only grass.*

And the nurse had slapped her, and beaten her with a slipper, and chased her screaming about the *gynaikeion* for her cleverness.

Arsinoë worried none the less about what might become of her if they were found out, and she had good reason to worry. She made, some times, a show of fighting off this brother, who began now to creep about the corridors and courtyards of the Residence in the middle of the night, in order to seek her out, but more often than not she was his willing partner, finding some means of escaping from the *gynaikeion* in order to meet him in secret.

The first time Keraunos made so bold as to clamber over the roofs of the Residence and let himself even into the *gynaikeion* by his sister's window, and place his hot hand over her mouth in the dark to stop her screaming, Arsinoë did indeed struggle, for he had taken her by surprise, but after that she did not even trouble to bolt her shutters against him, so that he came to her at whatever hour of the night he pleased, and the palace guards, if they saw Keraunos, merely winked at him, because this boy was every soldier's friend, because he was Ptolemy Keraunos, the marvellous boy who must be Pharaoh, and he got away with what he did, somehow, thinking always that he lived a charmed life and was lucky for ever.

Arsinoë Beta reasoned that she could not stop Keraunos from doing what he did, even if she wanted to, and the truth of it was that she longed for her brother to visit her again.

Ptolemy Keraunos—did he have no guilt for what he was doing? Sure, he knew that the *aphrodisia* with the sister was forbidden. Sure, he knew it was an unthinkable thing, a gross affront to the gods of Hellas. But no, he was pretty much untroubled. He had been raised to have no great fear of the gods. He had been brought up to have no fear of any thing. That was how Keraunos was to be such a great warrior, such a mighty Pharaoh of Egypt: he was utterly fearless, without fear of man or god, or of any thing in the world.

All the same, Keraunos knew enough of Greek theology to see that what he did with Arsinoë Beta was no different from what the great god Zeus did with his sister Hera; moreover, it was what the old-time kings of Egypt did—they even got themselves *married* to their own sisters.

What, then, was wrong with what he did? Nothing. And thus, if doubts he had, he justified his actions to himself.

Arsinoë was swayed, perhaps, by her brother's argument, but at the same time she dreaded being found out, and she was terrified that her father would have the pair of them killed on the spot.

But the *aphrodisia* went on and on, for months, and Arsinoë Beta would lie awake half the night waiting for her brother's shadow to fall across her bed. When she did sleep, she dreamed terrible dreams of being eaten alive by a horse who had lived all his life not upon grass but upon flesh, and the face of the horse was the face of her brother, with his horse hoofs trampling her body in the dark.

And when she saw Keraunos the next day she would hiss at him and show him the scratch-marks upon her breasts, or the red marks upon her neck, and say some words such as, *My mother will beat you like a polypus for what you have done to me.*

Keraunos—he would laugh, and scratch her flesh one more time with the nails of his fingers.

When Arsinoë Beta one morning sicked up her breakfast upon the *gynaikeion* floor, it was clear to her nurse what course of action must be followed.

First she made Arsinoë eat nothing but Egyptian dates. The result was a violent derangement of the bowels.

Second, she made her undergo the bath of hot water. The result was the flooding of the *gynaikeion* floor.

Third, she made Arsinoë drink deep draughts of hellebore wine, but the result of this was only drunkenness.

Fourth, she made Arsinoë eat garlic, then Egyptian grapes, then the excrements of the vulture; but none of the nurse's remedies, Greek or Egyptian, brought an end to the steady swelling of her belly.

Then the nurse fled the palace, for the truth was that she had failed to protect her charge, and that she was privy to what had been going on—for how could a boy climb into the *gynaikeion* by night and be gone before first light for months upon end without the nurse, who saw all, who knew all, finding out?

The belly of Arsinoë grew larger, and though she made herself jump up and down upon the spot, the only result was ill temper, until she could not hide her shape from her sisters, nor yet from Berenike her mother, and was forced to tell the truth: that Eurydike's son Ptolemy Keraunos had taken away her *parthenos* against her will and gotten her with child; that she had been eating earth, and that she had tried to end her pregnancy herself by eating the excrements of the crocodile.

The reaction of Berenike was to scream and shout. She railed against this daughter of hers, and beat her about the arms and legs with her hands, with her fan of gilded acacia wood, and with her fists also, and she kicked and punched Arsinoë Beta until this girl was bruised black and blue, and the screaming and shouting of Berenike, Queen of Egypt though she was, echoed all over the Residence, as she dragged the weeping Arsinoë Beta before her father the Pharaoh.

When she saw Ptolemy Keraunos, the father of her child, loitering in the distance, Arsinoë screamed at him, *Make haste and get your shoes on, for my mother has found out what you have done and she has sworn to have your bollocks for her earrings.*

Keraunos had known that some thing was wrong, for he had dreamed the dream of eating the bread of his backside, and it was bad, very bad, for it meant the complete reversal of a man's way of life.

Keraunos, then, made himself ready for the worst.

Ptolemy Soter paced the mosaic of dolphins, thinking. *Zeus and Hera did it. To be sure, the Persians and even the Egyptians did it.* What, then, was so *wrong* about an *aphrodisia* with a man's own sister? What was it, he wondered, that made him so angry, and his wife scream?

The answer was that an incest was not all right. It was the thing of all things that must not be done if a man is a true Greek. In Greece they used to say that the child of such a union would be born with the tail of a pig, and Ptolemy did not desire the disgrace of a pig's-tail grandson. Nor would he have his Greek girls eating vulture excrement, whatever the reason for it. No, his anger was wholly justified.

Ptolemy Keraunos was made to wait outside the Pharaoh's apartments for hour upon hour, while he finished bathing, while he instructed the *Dioiketes,* while he sealed his seal to scores of papyri. Ptolemy Soter knew that his son would not be able to bear even one morning of the duties of the Pharaoh, let alone the rest of his life hearing petitions. He kept Keraunos waiting on purpose, until the end of the day's business, by which time this boy was dripping from the heat, and at the limit of his temper, upon the verge of weeping tears of rage, for the guards had orders not to let him go away, but that he must stand by the door, thirsty and unfed, waiting, waiting, with his father in sight in the distance, ignoring him.

When King Ptolemy at last called Keraunos to his side, his eyes flashed and his jaw was set, and he was almost unable to look upon this son of his for disgust. But Keraunos now affected indifference, staring at the floor with its dizzying pattern of Tritons and sea-creatures, at the coffered ceiling of cedar and gold, at his father's golden sandals, and he half-expected his father to order for him the beating upon the soles of the feet that was the punishment for disgraced slaves, that was dreaded so much because they might never walk again after it.

His Majesty was upon this occasion like Sakhmet the lioness goddess in the moment of her rage. Ptolemy Soter almost glowed with anger, and his heart was urgent to hit this son of his and knock him to the ground, for that he had brought shame upon his father's House.

It was not the first time Keraunos had heard his father shout, but to hear it now made his heart bound like the antelope, and Ptolemy Keraunos, that had no fear, trembled a little. He stood before his father, clenching and unclenching his fists, with the sweat trickling down his back so that the *khiton* stuck to his skin.

Accused of this crime Keraunos showed his front teeth, the grinners, and laughed in his father's face, and it made his father shout at him all the louder. The eyes of His Majesty flashed like the panther of the south about to spring upon his prey. *Tell me this true,* he said, *did you do what we have been told you did?*

And when Keraunos said nothing, he waved his hand and the guards called to the chamber of His Majesty twenty eyewitnesses, who swore, one after another, that they had heard and seen the Prince Ptolemy Keraunos do that which he said he had not done, at times and in places when he thought himself unseen.

Keraunos bit his tongue hard, so that he should not disgrace himself by weeping, but he said only, *I will swear a great oath that I never mounted her bed and lay with her as is the way of mankind between men and women.*

His Majesty said, *Zeus withers the proud of heart.* And he said, *Your enemy is yourself* and, *Like a swift and two-edged sword, your father's curse shall sweep you out of this land.*

Only then did it occur to Keraunos that a Greek father might drive his son out of the house, but not out of his inheritance, only if he was guilty of some crime such as incest, or the killing of a brother. Keraunos had forgotten himself. He had not thought that his father's curse might fall upon him. He had truly thought that he could do no wrong.

In the end he stammered out something of the truth:

I was blinded, he said. *I listened to my heart's persuasion.*

I am not bad in all things, he said. *Arsinoë and I were alone a lot of the time . . . One must find ways to entertain oneself . . . When everybody went to the racing-track we would make some excuse . . .*

The face of His Majesty looked blacker. He could see now no hope in this son. Keraunos—truly, his fate would be worse than that of a skinned fox.

What would His Majesty do with this son? He spoke now only one word: *Ataxia*, indiscipline, and Ptolemy Keraunos was carried away by the guards to be beaten with rods.

But what should he do further? Should he cut off this boy's nose and ears and send him for a convict to Rhinokolura? Should he have Keraunos made a eunuch for this crime? Should he drive the boy out of Egypt altogether? Or should he be merciful, and forgive him?

His Majesty thought to say, *Although you are our son, we shall henceforth treat you as our enemy.* But he could not bring himself to speak the words.

He thought to say, *If I could see that boy dead and gone to Hades, I could say my heart had forgotten its misery.* But the truth was that he loved this son who was his heir, and he had not the stomach to banish him from the court, this boy who ought to be Pharaoh after him.

Ptolemy Soter worried about many things, but most of all he worried about the Furies, and he said to Berenike, *The Furies will cling to my House for ever. They will sing of the frenzy that began it all, showering curses upon the boy who trampled his sister's bed.* And although Berenike poured scorn upon such thoughts, they both of them knew that it would be so, and Thoth knows it to be true.

No, there was no basis for forgiveness or reconciliation here. Keraunos was guilty, guilty of behaviour of the deepest dishonour. The boy had sowed the seeds of great trouble for the rest of his family.

But at the same time Ptolemy Soter thought, *What does the Iliad of Homer say? Thou shalt not have a heart that does not forgive.*

Thoughts of Thoth: It is not in the nature of the Greeks to forgive anybody for anything. A Greek will always prefer revenge.

When the palace guards brought Keraunos back from his beating, he was dishevelled but defiant.

The quality needed for a king, His Majesty said, *is ataraxia—calmness, balance.*

Keraunos spat his spittle upon the floor. He did not possess calmness. He did not know the meaning of balance. Nor did he have any pricks of conscience for having done what he did with his sister. He felt no guilt. He made no apology.

And so at last His Majesty ordered the traditional Greek punishment, and Keraunos was stripped of his garments. They shaved off all the hair of his head so that he looked like a slave, and he was ashamed to show his face in public for a month.

When they burned off his feathers with a flaming torch, Keraunos that never wept began to howl. He swore terrible oaths. He struggled. He went purple in the face, but strong hands held him down.

When they rammed the radish up the fundament of this boy, he screamed, because the radish grows large in Egypt, and he made use of the direst curse he knew against the King, and the curse took flight, and the deed was done, because there is no turning back a son's curse upon his father.

His Majesty hoped that Keraunos might be taught a lesson. The curse he chose not to hear, thinking that what this boy had always said was wind and nothing.

What would he do with Keraunos now? He did not force him to take ship for some foreign land. No, Keraunos would only stir up trouble against Egypt from abroad. It was better to keep Keraunos where he could see what he was doing. And so for the time being His Majesty confined his son to the Residence, and let things go on as they were. It was early, he thought, early to be making up his mind about the succession to the throne.

As for Anemhor, High Priest of Memphis, he said to Ptolemy Keraunos, *Thou art lucky to be let to live.*

This time Keraunos did not laugh at him.

When Queen Berenike found out the full story of what her daughter Arsinoë Beta had been doing, she ran about the private apartments shouting, and she tore at her hair and garments as if somebody had died.

If my daughter is no longer a parthenos, she cried, *who will want to marry her?* For she was beside herself, at a loss to know what to do with a deflowered Arsinoë Beta.

By rights, King Ptolemy told this daughter, *you should be sold as a slave, your head shaved and your forehead branded with the mark of your deep disgrace . . .*

And Arsinoë wept, because she had been brought up to believe that she might pass her life as the queen of some foreign country.

Ideally, her father told her, *a girl who has aphrodisia before she is married to a husband should be put to death . . .*

And Arsinoë cried out, because she had thought to live longer than her fifteenth year.

The two partners in every Greek marriage, her father said, *must be spotless.*

But Arsinoë was no longer spotless. She would have to be not a *parthenos* but a *pseudoparthenos,* a pretend maiden, and she wept now for the loss of what could not be brought back.

As for Berenike, she snapped at her daughter, *What high and mighty prince will want you now?*

What man, she said, *will take you now that you have lost the most precious thing that a girl has?* Berenike shouted, *What could you have been thinking about when you allowed your brother to do such a thing?*

Arsinoë stood before her parents with her head bowed low, and in her distress she recalled what Keraunos had said to her before ever he was found out: *Tell him it was the god that fucked you . . .*

And so she tried, at first, to claim that she had been impregnated by divine, not human, means. She began to speak of the apparition of the god in her chamber during the siesta; of the heavy beating of his wings; of the sweet breath that came forth from his mouth. But her father snorted through his nose at the absurdity of it, and when she saw the look upon his face, she could not with a clear conscience continue speaking.

All this talk is bluff, her father said. *I hate like Hades the girl who hides one thing in her mind and speaks another.*

And then Arsinoë Beta wept again, and said, *I swear by the nymphs of the pool, that I never asked my brother to do what he did . . . I swear it by the waters of the Styx,* and it was the most portentous and inviolable oath that any girl could take, and Ptolemy wished to be merciful to her, because she was but a young girl, and he believed more in the guilt of Ptolemy Keraunos.

Berenike held that it would not be right to put this daughter to death, whatever crime she had committed, and she suggested that the punishment of punishments that would fit this crime of crimes was the Horse and Maiden.

When Berenike spoke her thoughts Arsinoë Beta wept a third time, and clasped the knees of her father in supplication.

Yes, indeed, Ptolemy said, *the only course is for you to be locked up in a house with a horse and no food, and the horse shall eat your flesh. This is only what you deserve.*

Arsinoë wailed. She blamed Keraunos, and said he had threatened to kill her if she told anybody. She swore that she was not guilty of any crime herself. She pleaded that the deed was all Keraunos's doing, that he had taken her by force, against her will, while she was sleeping, and placed his hand over her mouth so that she should not cry out. Thus Arsinoë Beta tried to save her skin.

At length King Ptolemy took pity on his daughter, saying, *To avoid public dishonour we shall not after all have recourse to the lawful punishment. Perhaps we shall send you away from Egypt, to Lysimakheia on the Hellespont. Perhaps Lysimakhos may be persuaded to take you to wife.*

Who is Lysimakhos? Arsinoë asked, as if she did not know already.

He is the King of Thrace, Ptolemy said.

And so Arsinoë Beta escaped death for the first time, because her father had not the heart to kill her.

Vengeance is in the hands of the gods, he said. *They may, or may not, treat you kindly.*

Since a public humiliation was unthinkable, Arsinoë Beta would be privately humiliated instead. For what she did not then know was that the marriage to King Lysimakhos of Thrace would in itself be enough punishment. She would indeed learn her lesson, and almost the greatest part of her punishment was the thought that she should never set eyes upon Alexandria again but be an exile for ever.

Before this marriage could be celebrated, the Greek surgeons of King Ptolemy brought that instrument of bronze called the *ambleterion,* the purpose of which was to smash up an unborn child inside his mother's womb, and they pulled forth from her body by means of ropes and hooks a misshapen creature, and the groans of this girl were drowned out by the waiting-women beating the cooking-pots and singing at the tops of their voices. When this deed was done the waiting-women themselves set to work upon the body of Arsinoë Beta, in order to render her a *parthenos* once again.

Some thought that this Arsinoë Beta deserved everything that was coming to her, but only the horoscopists and the High Priest of Ptah knew the truth of it: that in the future of this princess there was nothing but trouble, and that no, the gods would not be kind to her.

Ptolemy Soter sent to Lysimakhos to put in hand the marriage that he had been planning for Arsinoë Beta all along, and then he banished family troubles from his thoughts and went back to worrying about war in Syria.

3.7

Moderation

Ptolemy Soter's great cautiousness in military matters, some said, took away from his greatness as a general. They said he was guilty of making no effort whatever to get back his lost island of Cyprus. They said he bothered himself not at all to challenge the mastery of Demetrios Poliorketes on the sea either, for when Demetrios sailed his fleet from Rhodes into Greek waters, what did Ptolemy do? He did nothing, nothing, until his alliance with Kassandros and Lysimakhos and Seleukos made him think that he might be able to reoccupy Palestine, and even Syria.

Ptolemy did next to nothing in the three years after the Siege of Rhodes but enjoy his title of Soter, and turn himself into Pharaoh. For Ptolemy, to be Pharaoh was enough. He wished for nothing more, apart from the survival of his dynasty after he was dead.

No, Ptolemy was weary of war, tired of taking risks, and shocked always by the stupid loss of life in war. He wanted just to be left alone now, to grow old without having to look death in the face before his time. He said he had killed enough men, and he felt worn out by his endless bad dreams.

So, Ptolemy dedicated the cockerel of solid gold to Ares, god of War, and hung up his sword and shield in the Temple of Ares on Kanopic Street, and announced the fact of his retirement from fighting, for that he was sixty-five years of age.

More than once Ptolemy had called himself simply *The Macedonian*, rather than King of Egypt. It was the proper Greek style, but it showed—did it not?—that he disliked needless boasting. Boastfulness was un-Greek. Far better was the way of modesty, which would not bring down upon a man's head the jealousy of the gods.

Some men sneered, even so, at the way this King retreated whenever he could, even after a victory, saying that a retreat showed nothing but a lack of confidence in his own abilities. But the retreats were not the retreats of a coward, for Ptolemy was not a coward.

Moderation in all things, Ptolemy said. *Nothing in excess, and especially not killing.*

And so, mostly, they praised him for his wisdom.

In spite of his keenness to retire, however, Ptolemy's sword did not stay hanging up in the Temple of Ares for very long. Within two years of the Siege of Rhodes three of the other Successors—Kassandros, Lysimakhos and Seleukos—had talked Ptolemy into joining them in their campaign to destroy the power of Antigonos One-Eye for good, and Ptolemy found that his sword was again in his hand.

Then Kassandros fought off Demetrios, and Lysimakhos helped himself to most of Ionia. Meanwhile Ptolemy marched his troops into Palestine and took back all the cities of Koile-Syria one after another, and laid siege to Sidon.

If Ptolemy had lost his relish for war, what took place next gave it back to him, for he had the foresight to walk into the city of Hierosolyma upon the Sabbath Day of the Hebrews, when the law forbade any Hebrew to pick up his sword to fight with it, even in self-defence, upon this holiest of days, for that war was work; and so Ptolemy, who was not obliged to abide by such a law, took Hierosolyma under his command and control, and with much cheering and laughing, for the Hebrews could only stand and look on, with their mouths hanging open at the boldness of this Greek.

This circumstance, so wonderful for Ptolemy but not so wonderful for the people of Hierosolyma, enabled the wise men of the Greeks to point out the lesson to be learned: *Never to have recourse to dreams and superstitions except when all human councils have failed.*

Ptolemy deported vast numbers of prisoners of war to Egypt, and when he was forced to evacuate Hierosolyma, he was careful to knock down the city walls, so that One-Eye could not make use of it as his stronghold.

While Ptolemy was camped at Sidon, he got wind of a rumour that One-Eye had defeated Lysimakhos and Seleukos in a great land battle, and he saw no reason to think the story not to be true, for he knew One-Eye was upon his road to Syria.

What, then, did Ptolemy do? He signed a four-month truce with the good people of Sidon, secured the cities he had captured with garrisons, and set off for Memphis with his troops.

No sooner had Ptolemy settled down again in Egypt than he heard that the rumour of battle was false; that no battle had been fought, and his allies were not defeated. Ptolemy thus lost his great chance to extend the borders of Egypt's empire upon the north side, for when his allies made the final settlement after the coming battle, the Battle of Ipsos, they did not trouble to seek the opinion of Ptolemy, whom they had written off as a useless and unreliable character for that he had broken the terms of his alliance *by going home early.*

The great Battle of Ipsos, in Phrygia, came in the fifth year of Ptolemy's reign, when Antigonos One-Eye—now eighty-one years old, white-haired, bent with age, short of sight and hard of hearing—himself rode into battle, and his son Demetrios Poliorketes was with him, against the coalition of four kings: Seleukos, Lysimakhos, Kassandros and Ptolemy, only that Ptolemy did not bother, as they said, to turn up to fight.

This battle was known as the Battle of the Kings, and there were eighty thousand foot and ten thousand horse upon each side, so that the troops were fairly matched. In this fight One-Eye himself was injured by javelins, spears and rocks, and died upon the field, so that Demetrios succeeded to his kingdom, and he sailed away afterwards to Cyprus, which still belonged to him.

Ptolemy took no part in this battle, but, as those who were not his friends liked to say, *hid himself* in Egypt, waiting only to take advantage of the outcome of it. And he was indeed careful to fortify himself against the threatened advance of Seleukos by making himself very friendly towards Lysimakhos of Thrace, and his plan was to make peace with this King and to seal it by making Arsinoë Beta marry him.

Although Lysimakhos was just then happily married to a Persian wife called Amastris, Ptolemy suggested that it would be a better arrangement if he were to send this wife of his away, and be married to Arsinoë Beta instead, for she was, he said, his eldest daughter by Berenike, and was a beautiful young woman of fifteen years old, ripe for marriage, and he recommended warmly the loveliness of her two breasts that were rosy, and full, like two juicy peaches.

At length the word came from Lysimakhos, and what he said was *Yes.*

Arsinoë Beta was thus to be given away for political purposes, and under this wondrous convenient state of affairs she would be kept away from the wickedness of her half-brother.

Meanwhile, Ptolemy's other so-called ally, Seleukos, now drew himself closer to Demetrios Poliorketes, who, although he was a fugitive with no kingdom, had complete control of the Great Sea, including Cyprus and many of the lesser islands, and most of the coastal towns of Kilikia.

Ptolemy, then, had to keep looking out for new friends, and he went so far as to write a letter even to the upstart Agathokles, who was the Tyrant of Syracuse in Sicily, and he offered him the hand in marriage of the Princess Theoxena, Eurydike's daughter, in return for yet another alliance of peace.

Agathokles of Syracuse was a cold old man in search of a hot young wife, which was just what Ptolemy promised him, and he recommended the sweet character of Theoxena, and Agathokles also said *Yes* to Ptolemy's proposal.

And yes, Ptolemy rubbed his hands together and smiled a great smile, for that he was getting what he wanted.

In the pact that was agreed before the Battle of Ipsos, the territory of Koile-Syria had been earmarked and guaranteed to Ptolemy in the event of a victory. But the kings who actually did the fighting at Ipsos now felt that, as Ptolemy could not be bothered to show his face upon the field of battle, he was not entitled to any reward, and so Seleukos and Lysimakhos joined all of Koile-Syria to the Empire of Seleukos.

Ptolemy, as might be expected, refused to recognize this new arrangement, protesting that Koile-Syria was his by right, and he said he had been tricked by swift Rumour, and that his non-appearance in the battle was not his fault. But Seleukos refused to regard the original agreement as binding, and he refused also to have anything more to do with Ptolemy, who was supposed to be his friend, thus turning him into his enemy.

Far from retiring from war, then, all this aggravation roused Ptolemy to new vigour, and he gave the order to march his army into Koile-Syria a fourth time. When Seleukos arrived with his army and tried to take hold of Koile-Syria, he found Ptolemy already in possession, and that he had once again all of Koile-Syria under his command.

And so it went on. Ptolemy swore again, once again, yet again, that he would take *no further part in any war* with the rival kings, but was thoroughly sick of war, and the waste of war, and not being able to live under his own roof, and that his generals might take charge of war for the future. And he dedicated again the cockerel of solid gold, and hung up his bronze armour for what was the fifth last time, in the Temple of Ares, and sent to the Oracle of Zeus-Ammon in Libya, saying that he would be pleased to know what his future held, and that he was hopeful of an end to all fighting, an absolute end to war.

But the Oracle of Zeus-Ammon sent Ptolemy the truth, as it always had and always would: that the quarrel over who should be the owner of Syria, and rule Syria, would rage between the House of Ptolemy and the House of Seleukos for generation after generation after generation; that it would outlive both the mighty Houses of Ptolemy and Seleukos. And indeed, the final pronouncement of Zeus-Ammon upon this matter, though nobody believed it possible, was that the world would fight over Syria and Palestine and Koile-Syria and Lebanon and all the countries in this corner of the world *for ever.*

At the end of the Syrian War, and before the start of the next Syrian War, Ptolemy welcomed some thirty thousand Hebrew settlers to Egypt: traders, farmers, market gardeners, craftsmen, masons, ship-builders, men with skills that he had need of in Alexandria, which had much room for building—for this was a state of affairs which, according to Aristotle, should not be endured in any city.

The Hebrews of Alexandria were promised their own quarter of the city, called Delta, in the north-eastern sector, right by the royal Residence. They were tolerated, encouraged to keep up their own customs, and to worship their own god in the usual manner, in their own synagogues.

And yes, the Hebrews were content, apart from expressing their disapproval of the statues in the streets, which were Greek statues, of King Ptolemy, of Alexander, and of other heroes—partly because any graven image was forbidden by their religion, but partly also because they were offended by the nakedness of the statues in the Greek style. Some nights, under cover of darkness, the statues would be dressed in linen drawers by some person or persons unknown, but believed to be some Hebrew person. And this went on and on, until it was agreed that there should be no naked statuary in the Delta quarter, because of Hebrew sensibilities, and at last the Hebrews declared themselves to be completely happy.

Ptolemy told the settlers that he was their friend, unlike that Pharaoh of old who had chased the Hebrews back home to Palestine, and they agreed to stay on in Egypt, where they might be useful to King Ptolemy by lending him vast amounts of money.

In time the Hebrews would forget even how to speak Hebrew, having become speakers of Greek. They traded in corn and built ships, and helped Ptolemy to finance his temple-building projects, and public works, such as the canal that was to join the Great Sea to the Red Sea.

It was not long before the Hebrews said that they were pleased to regard Ptolemy even as their friend.

And Ptolemy said, as he always said, *We want everybody to be happy. We are happy that you are happy to live with us in Egypt.*

It was the first, and perhaps the only, instance of real happiness in the entire history of Alexandria. For the rest, it would be quarrelling, and nastiness, and unpleasant nicknames, and then, as the years turned into centuries, it would be riots and revolts and blood shed in the streets, and blood shed even also in the palace.

Alexandria began well, but grew steadily worse. At the head of it was the family of Ptolemy, about which many people would say much the same thing.

But not yet. At the start every thing was full of promise, and every member of the House of Ptolemy smiled, or pretended to smile—apart, perhaps, from Eurydike. And, just then, nobody was happier than Ptolemy himself, in spite of his not sleeping; in spite of the flies that bit the flesh; in spite of the tensions between Greek and Egyptian, he still *said* he was happy.

In the same year as the Battle of Ipsos, as if, happy though he most surely was, Ptolemy did not have enough troubles, the Sacred Bull, Apis, calf of the Cow Ta-nt-Aset the Second, died of old age, plunging all Egypt into mourning for him. Up-River and down-River the women plastered their flesh with mud, and beat their breasts with their fists and howled. At Memphis the High Priest was troubled, much troubled, by the problem of how to find the money to pay for the elaborate embalming ritual for the bull, and he went to Ptolemy and made the strongest of hints that it was the custom for the Pharaoh to make some generous contribution to the burial expenses.

Ptolemy looked hard at Anemhor. *How much money?* he said.

Anemhor was silent for some time, looking at the floor.

One thousand drachmas? Ptolemy said.

Anemhor shook his head.

Fifteen hundred? Ptolemy asked.

Anemhor said nothing.

Two thousand drachmas? Ptolemy said, incredulous.

But Anemhor said, *Not drachmas, Majesty, talents.*

And Ptolemy said, *Two talents?* which was twelve thousand drachmas—an impossible sum, he thought.

Anemhor wore a pained expression. *Much money,* he said, *very much money, very many talents.*

Five talents? Ptolemy asked, hopeless, knowing that he did not want to pay even so much as the first mentioned figure.

But Anemhor only shook his head.

And so it went on, until these two had arrived at the figure of fifty talents, and Ptolemy felt a sinking sensation in the pit of his stomach because his Treasury felt as if it had been the victim of robbers. But he smiled because he loved the Apis bull, and he called the fifty talents a *loan*, so that Anemhor should not think of it as a right, but merely a concession.

All the same, the speed with which Ptolemy moved to underwrite the expense was seen as a goodly thing, as Ptolemy intended it to be: there might, then, be further grants, further loans, further gifts, additional favours from this King. He had not done as the Persian did and shown contempt for Apis by murdering him. By no means: Ptolemy was a great friend of Apis. He only hoped and prayed that the new bull would not die young.

The mummification of Apis went ahead, then, with his bandaged forelegs stuck out in front of him, and his long gilded horns sticking up above the bandages, and they dragged Apis upon a great sledge to the burial vault of the sacred bulls that lies on the west bank of the River, on the edge of the desert of Libya, while all Egypt wept and lamented, and the funeral rites for Apis lasted twenty-nine days.

Afterwards came the rigorous search for the new Apis bull who must take the place of the old one. Up-River and down-River, it took month upon month of seeking, until the black bull-calf with the correct white markings upon his back and flanks, and the triangular white mark upon his forehead, was found, and there were twenty-nine marks of Apis in all, and he was the Bull of the Cow Ta-nt-Merwer, and Anemhor, High Priest of Ptah, installed this bull in his stall in the precinct of Ptah at Memphis, and crowned him with the Crown of Apis, just as he had crowned Ptolemy himself as Pharaoh, and the horoscopists forecast that the reign of Apis would last for twenty-two years, and that King Ptolemy would not die before him.

This amused King Ptolemy, who calculated that he must live himself, if this were true, to the almost unheard-of age of eighty-eight.

And no, Ptolemy would not die young himself, for the horoscopists were always right.

3.8

The Thracian Alliance

Five years it was after Ptolemy took the crowns that he confirmed his great alliance with King Lysimakhos of Thrace, the comrade who had served with him under Alexander and who had been first his friend, then his enemy, and who now was to be his friend one more time.

Lysimakhos happily agreed now to cast aside his then wife, his second wife, Amastris, whom he had married only the year before, in order to take into his bed instead Arsinoë Beta, that young daughter, sixteen years old, of his naval ally, the delightful, charming, beautiful-above-all-other-girls, and really most seriously clever Arsinoë Beta, fresh from the disgrace and shame of the *aphrodisia* with her own half-brother, about which, of course, Lysimakhos of Thrace knew nothing.

Yes, the ambassadors had sailed back and forth between Alexandria and Lysimakheia upon the Hellespont, praising the long yellow hair of this girl, that was yellow like the Sun, yellow like gold, that was her great glory, and at length Ptolemy swore by Zeus and Helios and all the other gods of Greece, to stick by the agreement. He swore that Lysimakhos's friends should be his friends, and Lysimakhos's enemies his enemies, and he swore *May my affairs prosper if I keep the oath, and if I forswear, the opposite.* And Lysimakhos swore the same.

The oath would be made permanent and binding by handing over Arsinoë Beta, whose great virtues Ptolemy kept proclaiming, like a typical Greek, regardless of the truth, in order to get her out of his house and seal the agreement as soon as possible. As it happened, though, every thing Ptolemy told Lysimakhos about this girl, including the beauty and the cleverness, was the truth.

Ptolemy said to this daughter, though, nothing about how old her husband was, nothing personal about him whatever, but gave her political information only, and all thought of whether she might like this man, or find him charming company, or a delight to look upon and talk to was immaterial. The one thing that mattered was the alliance, and the fact of Lysimakhos being a king, and these were, just then, the only things that mattered to Arsinoë Beta.

No, she was not being married off for love. By no means: she was married for the stability of Egypt and its empire, and for peace in difficult times. Her marriage was not a matter of love, but of the ploughing of legitimate children. All thought of love was, in any case, madness, and to marry for love was but asking for trouble. No Greek wife expected very much affection. She was more likely, in fact, to receive blows and beatings from her husband than kisses. Such, at any rate, is the custom of the Greeks, who are pleased to boast that they are not barbarians; and it was very different from how the Egyptians marry a wife.

When the happy day came for Ptolemy Soter to send away this daughter, the whole family sat up all night in order to say farewell to her, which was the Greek custom, eating roast thrushes and olives and moussaka, and drinking the fine wines of Mareotis, and trying to stop time. And the celebration was only a little less than the usual on account of the business with Keraunos, which Ptolemy tried now to pretend had never happened, and it was one good example of his ability to forget the past and think only of now, the present moment. Ptolemy, at least, shed one or two tears when he embraced this girl, because it was the custom, but in truth he did not feel sad to be rid of this daughter, who had come close to bringing ruin upon his House. No, in return for parting with her he would have the one thing that he most desired in the whole world: peace, and an uninterrupted supply of luxury goods from the Hellespont, such as salt fish, spices, peas from Byzantion, carpets of purple, sloe-eyed slave girls . . . a never-ending list of Thracian delights.

For her part, Arsinoë Beta treated being packed off to Thrace like a parcel of dates with some indifference, affecting not to care much what became of her. She had not forgotten that her marriage was her punishment, though she could not then see for the life of her what form the punishment would take, for going away to be Queen of Thrace felt to her more like a wondrous reward, and she should at length, surely, have been married to somebody, whatever she had done wrong.

Berenike was careful to drum into Arsinoë Beta that she must agree to her husband's every desire, and do whatever he asked of her, and she said, *No husband will put up with a wife who does not do what he wants.*

Berenike warned her to make herself willing, whatever might be her private feelings, and urged her to seek to be indispensable, lest Lysimakhos should send her home to her father, branded for life as the girl who had failed to please her husband in the bedchamber.

And she pointed to the example of Amastris, the previous wife of Lysimakhos, who had been very quickly replaced when found wanting.

Arsinoë Beta smiled her best iron smile. She had learned all there was to know about *aphrodisia* from her own brother, and she thought of the two of them sweating upon her giltwood bedstead, under the insect curtains made of old fishing-nets, which was the only way the Greeks knew of keeping free from bites, and she felt a pang of regret for the loss of the past; but her lessons at the hands of her brother had not, as it turned out, been altogether wasted time.

Arsinoë Beta, then, was ready. The restoration of her lost *parthenos* had not been beyond the wit of her waiting-women, who had built her a replacement hymen of rubber from the Land of Punt, that made a not unpleasing twang when fingered, like some barbaric musical instrument.

Arsinoë Beta sailed for Thrace with two waiting-women of her own and her impossibly large dowry of goodly things, more lavish than any Greek had ever given his daughter, or so it was said: slaves, ebony, ivory, jewels, spices, unguents, and, of course, gold in bars, gold in rough-hewn lumps, as well as gold in the form of coins, sack upon sack of oktodrachms and dekadrachms, every one of them bearing the weather-beaten face of her father. She took with her also her personal physician, Dion, a learned eunuch who was to act as her *apokrisiarios* or secretary, as well as give his best advice on women's complaints, pregnancy, childbirth and children's ailments, as appropriate. Most importantly, Dion would help Arsinoë to escape from Thrace if, or when, everything fell to pieces there, for at Lysimakheia, as in most cities at this time, things were uncertain, and no man could tell when even a king so great as Lysimakhos might not be toppled from his throne by revolutionists, or by some usurper, or by some wild Thracian tribe, or by the invasion of barbarians out of the north lands, or whether he might not so soon as the next month be poisoned by some member of his own dearly beloved family.

The last thing Arsinoë Beta did in Egypt was to dedicate her earthenware dolls with movable limbs in the Temple of Artemis upon Kanopic Street, and she wept as she said farewell to her childhood, but she prayed the extra prayers to Artemis Who Wields the Bows and Arrows of Might, for extra strength in the ordeal that was to come.

The giving up of the dolls marked the end of Arsinoë Beta's girlhood, and almost the end of her femininity. Apart from the unpleasant necessity of giving birth to sons and heirs, her life would from now on be devoted to men's business: to war and government, to the negotiation of alliances, to the balance of power in Europe and Asia and to hanging on to power, whether by the shedding of blood, or by engineering the disappearance of relatives in the dead hours of the night, or by murder in cold blood and broad daylight. And, to be sure, Arsinoë Beta would do all of these things better than any man, and King Ptolemy her father would be proud of her.

At the same time as being really very like a man, Arsinoë Beta needs must go on being the woman that she was, and she had packed in her baggage her face paint, her oils to keep supple the skin, her plethora of coloured veils and dresses, her sandals of gold, and the tapestry that she would never do. The jewel box of Arsinoë Beta, Princess of Egypt, was full of magnificent Egyptian bracelets, anklets, girdles and scarab rings, all of gold and studded with every august costly stone, and at the bottom of the box, underneath the jewels, was her dagger of bronze with a hilt of gold, inlaid with emeralds and rubies and turquoise and carnelian, that was the parting gift of her mother, Berenike, who said, *You never know when you might not have to make use of it.*

The most important item in her baggage, however, was the black earthlike substance, and the grey powder, wrapped in oiled cloth and tied fast with papyrus string, that was poison—poison powerful enough to dispatch half an army.

In case you have need of it, Berenike said, who knew all there was to know about poison and poisoning, for this too was the gift of Berenike.

And Arsinoë Beta *would* have need of it.

Before Arsinoë boarded the *trieres* Berenike gave her the very last of her best wise advice: about how to escape from Thrace in the event of a revolt, when a king's wife might need to do nothing but save her own flesh, and she said, *The key to a successful marriage is a wife's readiness to agree without question to her husband's rule, regardless of his qualities or defects.*

Arsinoë nodded her head, as if to say that she understood, though she had some ideas of her own upon this matter.

A wife, Berenike said, *has no feelings of her own . . . She will adapt herself to her husband's moods. When he is cheerful she is cheerful, and she is sad when he is sad . . . She will not laugh when he is in a bad temper, nor will she sulk when he is laughing.*

Arsinoë said she would do her best, though there would be small cause for laughter at Lysimakheia.

Marriage, said Berenike, *has one purpose only—the getting of heirs to the throne.* But she overlooked the fact that Lysimakhos already had his heir, though Arsinoë had some ideas of her own upon this matter also.

Unable to witness the marriage of the Princess Arsinoë Beta, her family sang the Crow Song of the Greeks on the quayside at Alexandria, so that she might cherish Lysimakhos and be faithful to him so long as they both might live.

But the truth of it was that Arsinoë Beta was a girl whose mind was a man's mind, and she knew that no man ever loved or was faithful for long.

At the last moment she did not want to step on to the frail-looking ship for Thrace, having heard stories about the tremors of the earth there. But her father promised extra prayers to Poseidon, Lord of the Earthquake. Arsinoë Beta cast then one last long lewd glance at her half-brother the Thunderbolt, who stood sulking nearby. She loved and hated Keraunos in just about equal measures, and she did not know under what circumstances she might set eyes upon him again. But Keraunos did know: he had asked the Oracle, and had been told, *Boy, you have not seen the last of this sister.*

As for Old Anemhor, all he said to this princess was: *Those who drink of the River will come back to drink it again*—as if he knew that Arsinoë Beta was fated to return. For yes, she had always drunk River water, and nothing else.

Ptolemy Soter made now the proper sacrifice of a black bull to the gods of the Sea, and the trumpet sounded, and the *trieres* moved, oars rising and falling in perfect order like the wings of some great sea-gull; the oarsmen sang the songs of the sea and hummed with one voice to keep the time, and Arsinoë Beta did not look back, but stared ahead, thinking about Thrace, thinking, thinking.

She had swallowed the green lizard seasick cure, and the ash of snails with nettle-seed and honey that promised her an untroubled voyage, but she was greenish about the face before ever her ship sailed past the Hogsback Rock that lies at the mouth of the Great Harbour of Alexandria.

Unused to the water, like most Greek women, and afraid of a drowning, Arsinoë Beta murmured the prayers to Poseidon, god of the Angry Sea, for a calm passage, and she thought of why she was doing what she did: not for herself alone was it—not for herself at all—but for the greater good and glory of Egypt, and for peace, and because it was her father's wish and her father's command.

The family watched the *trieres* speed out to sea, so light and fast that not even the wheeling falcon, the fastest thing that flies, could have kept pace with her, until she was but a black dot upon the horizon, and Ptolemy and Berenike sighed sighs of relief for the happy end to a difficult beginning. This was not, as it turned out, the last that would be heard in Egypt of this high princess, who had been compared, for temper, even to Sakhmet the lioness goddess. In truth, this Arsinoë was possessed of such hardness of tongue and such hardness of heart that her parents were not wholly displeased to see the back of her.

Waving his *kausia* in farewell to his sister was Ptolemy Mikros, her youngest brother, then in the ninth year of his age. Arsinoë Beta was almost old enough to be this boy's mother, and it was upon this boy that she had poured what motherly feelings she possessed, treating him like one of her earthenware dolls, dressing and undressing him, bossing him, and making him do whatever she told him. To be sure, if Arsinoë Beta so much as snapped her fingers, Mikros would *jump*.

As Mikros waved the beret he wiped with it the tear that rolled down his cheek. He had almost loved this sister of his, his full sister, his elder sister, but he had no idea just then that it was his fate to be married to her.

When Ptolemy Mikros saw Arsinoë Beta again, he would be in the twenty-ninth year of his age and married to some other woman; and Arsinoë Beta herself would be nearly forty years of age, with her life in ruins. But even after so long a time Mikros would still almost love her as the one person in his life who had shown him kindness.

He would have very good reason also to hate her.

Ptolemy Soter, he would never look upon the face of Arsinoë Beta again, and in his heart he knew it. For a long while his strong voice was blocked, and his eyes were damp with tears, and they were perhaps tears of regret, that he had not known this girl very well.

If Arsinoë Beta had had the power to see into her future, she might have been pleased to choose the punishment of the Horse and Maiden instead of sailing away to be Queen of Thrace. For Thoth speaks true when he says that in some ways her fate would be worse, far worse, than being eaten alive by a hungry horse.

If the tears fell down the soft cheeks of Arsinoë Beta as she left Egypt, they were not for the loss of her family life, nor for her last sight of the illustrious and most illustrious city of Alexandria. No, she wept, in truth, for never seeing her half-brother, Ptolemy Keraunos, more, the brother whom she had loved as more than a brother and hated more than any enemy. And just then she felt a little sorry for herself.

Her last murmured words to Keraunos, whose face she had not been allowed to look upon ever since the radishing, had been, *I shall not write . . . We shall not meet again.*

She was as sure of that as she was sure of anything, but as matters turned out, she was wrong. She would look into the black, glistening eyes of Ptolemy the Thunderbolt again.

Keraunos was just nineteen years of age at his sister's sailing, and he seemed to her on that day more like the gods to look at than ever.

Fifteen years, twenty years, would pass by before she saw him again, but no, neither Keraunos nor Egypt had seen the last of Arsinoë Beta, although for the moment she did her best to forget them both, to forget the past, but relish the sensation of the passing hour, just like her father, by watching the dolphins that raced her *trieres* over the sparkling sea.

3.9

Mikros the Unwarlike

At about the same time as Arsinoë Beta sailed for Thrace, King Ptolemy appointed the famous Strato of Lampsakos to be the tutor of his youngest son, Ptolemy Mikros.

Strato was the author of many books, including the interesting *Upon Kingship*, the important *Upon Justice*, the useful *Upon Dreams*, and the essential *Upon the Breeding of Animals*. His writings on physics and cosmology had got him the nickname of The Physicist, and it was his great theory that all life, every living thing, must be explained by natural causes; that living things are nothing whatever to do with the gods of Greece, or any other gods.

Thoth, of course, knows better, but it was this Strato that gave Mikros his scientific curiosity, for Mikros would show all his life a great passion for scientific knowledge and for engineering projects. He liked best of all things that were new, things that were different, and he was pleased to think that he blazed a trail ahead.

As the scholarly disposition of Mikros grew, so his interest in military matters would shrink. His father was a hard man, toughened by a soldier's training, but Mikros was going to be soft. In spite of his name, he was never going to be warlike.

Who was to blame for spawning this son with no time for war, and no wish either to make larger the borders of Egypt, a boy whose great delight was to sit in a chair reading a book?

Some said it was the mother, Queen Berenike, who devoted her days now to her perfume factory, to silks from the island of Kos, and to jewels, and to organizing lavish theatrical entertainments, or exotic and expensive processions up and down Kanopic Street.

Others said that Strato of Lampsakos, the tutor, was guilty. Strato, who so civilized his pupil that he lost utterly the Macedonian will to fight his enemies, but preferred to sit at home thinking about science, about the design of mosaics, about the Theory of Pleasure, frittering away his days talking about *ideas,* as if he wanted to be a second Aristotle, instead of a second Alexander, *and what was the use of that?*

For the Macedonians, a man of inaction, an unwarlike heir, was a disaster. The only possible heir to Egypt was the rightful heir, the eldest son of Ptolemy Soter, Ptolemy the Thunderbolt, a boy who had at least the courage to pick up his sword and fight for his country.

But Mikros—Mikros did not want to do battle even with the giant orange cockroaches that infested the Residence. He was nervous even about squashing spiders and flies. He was fearful of finding snakes in his bed, and with good reason, for the snakes were put there by the hand of his elder brother, Ptolemy Keraunos.

King Ptolemy persevered with the education of this son, his youngest son, and the rumour was that he paid the phenomenal sum of *eighty talents* to Strato for tutoring Mikros in science and mathematics, even though Mikros was not much good at numbers. This boy's education cost, then, as much as the annual wages of one thousand nine hundred and seventy-two foot-soldiers exactly, or one-tenth part of a lighthouse. Thoth swears it.

Ptolemy swore that Strato was the cleverest man in the world, and that he was worth every last drachma, and, as it happens, Thoth can reveal that the eighty talents was money well spent, the best investment Ptolemy Soter could possibly have made in the future of his dynasty.

For Mikros was clever, as clever as his full sister, Arsinoë Beta, and those who liked to whisper about the future were whispering already that Ptolemy Mikros was the future, the fresh beginning. Some people at the court of King Ptolemy even murmured that a youth like Ptolemy Keraunos would do Egypt no good, for that he was a little backward at his lessons, if not a little stupid, like his mother, Eurydike.

Really, Eurydike's children did not fare very well, and the next of her children to fare not very well was Theoxena.

At much the same time as Arsinoë Beta was sent to Thrace, Ptolemy Soter married off Theoxena, daughter of Eurydike, to Agathokles, the Tyrant of Syracuse.

The story of this Agathokles was that he had been a strikingly hand-some boy of humble origin, the son of a potter, and that he had got rich by selling his body, allowing any number of men to indulge their lust according to the habit of the Greeks. But when he reached maturity he had astonished his customers by switching his trade from males to females, and then got richer still by setting up as a pirate, thieving from every ship in the Great Sea.

If Ptolemy knew of all this—and how could he not know about it?—he said never a word to Theoxena, who was told only the tales of Agath-okles the Hero, and of his mighty victory against the Carthaginians. The murky past of Agathokles was over and done with, he was now a man of power much respected for his military skill, and he called himself King of Sicily.

Theoxena was then about fifteen years old, ripe for marriage, with her breasts not like two great melons, but rather flat, and she was keen to do something with the days of her life that was not the panorama of the city of Alexandria woven in gold and purple threads.

Ptolemy told this daughter so much about Agathokles, a man whom he had not, in fact, met, and so much about Sicily, a place where he had, in fact, never been, and so much about the high citadel of Euryalos at Syracuse, where she should live, and about that bone-dry island with its ceaseless chatter of crickets, that Theoxena almost looked forward to quitting Egypt.

As well as encouraging Theoxena, her father gave her also his wise advice and his most solemn warning for her new life in Sicily, the new world that was rich, and young, and generous.

Sophokles says, he said, *that Silence brings credit to a woman.* For he had in mind the fact that Agathokles was so fond of boys, and this daughter of his had some times found it difficult to stop talking.

Talk, Ptolemy said, *is men's business. A wife must keep to her quarters and to her work, the loom and the spindle.*

And if Theoxena had thought to say farewell to tapestry, she was mistaken, but she promised, *I shall keep silent as a block of stone.*

Ptolemy told her every thing she should know, every thing about how to do well, except the fact that this husband of hers was now an old man of sixty-one years: for he knew that if Theoxena learned this, she would most surely refuse to go to Sicily in the first place.

When the day came that must be the last day of Theoxena in Egypt, her family sat up all night eating dates and olives and roasted thrushes, and drinking the heady wines of Mareotis, and they threw the water out of the *klepsydra,* trying to stop the passage of time. Early the next morning Theoxena gulped down the green lizard seasick remedy and stepped on board the *trieres* that had her enormous dowry stashed below, and every golden dekadrachm of it bore the benign face of her father, the BASILEUS PTOLEMAIOS that had negotiated her sale.

In spite of the green lizard, Theoxena was seasick, and she set her foot upon the island of Sicily somewhat greenish about the face, and with the vomit stains yet upon her travelling-cloak. When she set her eyes upon the face of the man who was to be her husband, she was shocked to see that he looked older than her father, but she remembered Ptolemy's words about what she must do, and that her marriage was for the greater good of Egypt, and for peace in the Greek world. She knew that she must not speak of pottery, and that she must not speak of pretty boys, and she bit her tongue some times, because pottery and boys, the two great secrets of Agathokles, were the only things she really wished to know about. She knew just how she must oil the *rhombos* of Agathokles upon his wedding night. She knew that she absolutely must not ride him like a horse, woman on top, and absolutely not perform the *amphiplix*, however much he begged her to, and absolutely not look out of any window, because only a whore rode a man like a horse, only a whore did the *amphiplix*, and only whores looked out of windows, and Theoxena was to be not a whore but a wife and a queen.

Sure, Theoxena knew how to make her marriage the success that her mother Eurydike's marriage had not been. And it was Berenike, her great-aunt, who gave her the sternest orders and the starkest warnings, when Eurydike was out of earshot.

Berenike advised Theoxena that Syracuse was but six or seven days' sail from Alexandria with a good wind, and that if every thing went wrong for her in Sicily she might easily come back home again. She told her how she must effect her escape from Agathokles if things turned sour between them, and she told her not to mind her manners too much, but to fight Agathokles with her fists if she had to. She was not to put up with any ill-treatment. She must never forget that she was a daughter of the House of Ptolemy, the daughter of a king.

Under every stone, Berenike said, *beware a scorpion.*

What did they not tell Theoxena before she sailed? They said little about the political nature of this marriage of hers, that was nothing but a bribe or a reward for Agathokles in return for helping Ptolemy regain his control over the territory of Kyrene after the near disaster that was the Revolt of Ophellas some five years before, and to safeguard also the corn supply.

Before she left Alexandria, Theoxena had the good sense to send to the oracles in order to find out what her future might be. She sent questions to Zeus-Ammon in Libya, and even to the great Oracle at Dodona in Thesprotia, but she was surprised to learn from every oracle the same thing: that this marriage of hers would last but twelve years, and not a day longer.

Theoxena had hoped to find a husband who might last for ever, but she was not altogether downcast. Twelve years, she thought, might be long enough, and if she were to loathe this Agathokles—well, she would only be twenty-eight years old when her marriage came to its end, and there might be time yet for a fresh husband, more children, and a new life—if, indeed, the twelve-year marriage was not brought to a stop by her own death. Theoxena told herself not to think of the future, but to follow the example of Ptolemy Soter, her father, and live for the day, for the moment, and worry not at all.

In his heart Ptolemy thought that Theoxena would be lucky if her marriage lasted twelve days, let alone twelve years, given Agathokles's taste for hot Sicilian boys with smooth buttocks, but he wished his daughter all the blessings of Tykhe, goddess of Good Luck, and he did not worry Theoxena by telling her that Agathokles was famed not only for his victory over Carthage, but also for his evil temper, his perverse cruelty, and for his violence when drunk. He did tell Theoxena every thing there was to know about *corn*, however, for it was the bounden duty of Theoxena to safeguard his corn supply from Sicily. A daughter was not a disaster. A daughter was above all things a useful asset.

And so Theoxena was gone, never to be seen in Egypt more, or so her family thought, for twelve years was but a short marriage, and the oracles about her future must surely be wrong.

In Sicily Theoxena enjoyed the olives, lemons and oranges that were sent down to her from Aetne's fertile slopes. She calculated that the famous smoking mountain, at seven thousand two hundred and seventy-four cubits high exactly, was twenty-four times higher than the Great Pyramid of Memphis, and she was amused to see that it was the same shape.

At first she worried that the mountain should spit fire into the sky, but the Syracusans reassured her, saying that Aetne had not erupted for one hundred years, and that it was quite safe to dwell in its shadow.

Theoxena became used to the silver hair and deeply lined face of her husband. She was the Tyrant's third wife, and he had already his son and heir, but, as Agathokles said himself, *The third time is the lucky time*. This husband exchanged never one cross word with his new wife, and the evil temper did not show itself. Agathokles had long since given up taking boys into his bed, or so it was said. His heavy drinking was a myth. He had eyes only for the Princess Theoxena, the beautiful daughter of King Ptolemy, and to the great surprise of every body in Alexandria, Theoxena wrote to say that she was quite in love with her sixty-one-year-old husband, for that he looked just like her own father, and she knew exactly how he must be treated.

The start of Theoxena's famously ill-starred marriage, then, turned out to be the greatest success.

3.10

The Stepson

When the swift-sailing *trieres* of Arsinoë Beta docked at Lysimakheia the crowd that had gathered to greet her burst into song and applause for the girl who was to be their Queen, and she drew all eyes upon her face, for she refused to show herself veiled, as was the Greek custom, thinking that from the very beginning she was going to do just whatever she pleased.

Arsinoë searched the line of officials, looking for a kinglike husband, and her eyes fell first and at once upon the figure of a young man of about nineteen years old, who was dressed for a marriage ceremony, in a white *khiton,* and had a wreath of golden oak leaves upon his head, and his limbs all bronzed by the sunshine; a young man who looked to Arsinoë Beta more handsome than any man she had ever looked upon before, like the gods to look at, more handsome even than her brother Keraunos, and she imagined that this young man must be the King Lysimakhos she had been sent to marry, and she was shot through in that instant by the golden arrows of the Boy, Eros, and fell in love.

Eros, however, always did like to make mischief, and it was the *Dioiketes,* or First Minister, of Lysimakhos who led Arsinoë Beta by the arm to a different man, who stood nearby dressed all in garments of white, garlanded with crimson flowers and plastered with myrrh, who said he was Lysimakhos of Thrace and held out his hand for her to take it in the *dexiosis* of the Greeks. But the hand of Arsinoë Beta did not shoot out to take the hand of this man. Nor did her face break into a smile. Nor did her heart leap up, because the face of this Lysimakhos was deeply grooved with lines, and deeply scarred with the marks of battle, and he had a long white beard, and white hair, and was an old man—old, old—and the thought of Arsinoë Beta was that she had been tricked, tricked, and that this was, indeed, her punishment for the *aphrodisia* with her own brother.

No, Ptolemy her father had said to her not one word about the age or appearance of her husband. Ptolemy Soter was a Greek, cunning, as every Greek is cunning, and he knew very well that if he told Arsinoë that her Lysimakhos was old, upwards of sixty years old, and scarred all over his body, and that he was cantankerous, notorious for his meanness, and old enough to be her grandfather, she would make a fuss about travelling to Thrace and refuse to go there at all, and that his alliance would be worthless.

Arsinoë Beta shook a little in her limbs, then, but when she recovered herself somewhat, she asked the *Dioiketes* who, then, was the young man, the handsome young man with the golden oak leaves upon his head; and back came the answer, the terrible answer, that this was the Prince Agathokles, the *son* of the King, who was the heir to the throne of Thrace.

The shivers ran down the spine of Arsinoë Beta then, and she knew the first of the many horrors of her time in Thrace, for that the young man with whom she had, to be sure, fallen in love at first sight, was the man who, though older than she was, must be not her wedded husband but her stepson.

What did Arsinoë Beta do? What could any girl do, under such a circumstance, but take the outstretched hand of the old man, still held out to her for the *dexiosis,* and clasp it in hers. And yes, she found the hand cold, wrinkled, callused like the flesh of some Egyptian lizard, but she forced herself to speak words of politeness in reply to his welcome. And though she pulled at her hand to regain it for her own possession, because of her disgust at the touch of this old man, Lysimakhos held on to it and would not let go, for the truth of it was that, Greek though he was, old man though he was, and madness though it was, the King had fallen in love with the beauty of this young girl as soon as his eyes fell upon her face, and that Eros was having a busy day.

When at last Lysimakhos let her go, Arsinoë Beta was presented to Agathokles his son, and she held out her hand for the *dexiosis*, as she had been taught to do, and the hand she took now was hot, smooth, alive, as hot even as the hands of her brother Keraunos, and the shiver ran up the spine of Arsinoë Beta as she held and shook this hand; she looked into the sparkling eyes that were blue like *sappheiros*—she looked and could not stop looking, and her face took fire, and she did not know where to put herself for confusion.

But she remembered the words of Berenike just in time and resolved to make the best of things, for to be sure, she could not, just then, change them, because the alliance and the peace were signed and binding, and she, Arsinoë Beta, was, as it were, the strong, tough glue that must hold it all together.

The marriage of Arsinoë Beta to Lysimakhos took place that day, and the sacrifice of hundreds of black oxen with gilded horns that was offered up to the gods of Greece was lavish, most lavish, surpassing any thing she had seen even in Egypt.

Arsinoë Beta felt much as if she were the sacrifice herself. She felt as if a great part of her had died; as if it was, yes, her own blood that splashed upon the altar, her own neck that was severed by the axe, her own voice bellowing, not the voices of the murdered bulls; and she felt weak at her knees, as if she would faint. In such a state Arsinoë Beta could not dance, and when the courtiers of Lysimakhos shouted for her to stand up and move to the beat of lyre and harp, she refused.

We have hurt our ankle in stepping off the trieres, she said, and she limped for a day or two after, until she forgot what words she had spoke.

Alas, throughout the ceremonies that bound her to this old, old King that day she could not take her eyes off the golden flesh of the young Agathokles, who was but two or three years older than herself, and had, as yet, they told her, no wife of his own, and no, was not even betrothed to be married, and the iron heart of Arsinoë Beta, now molten and white hot, beat hard and high with this new love of hers that was already and again both forbidden and impossible.

Throughout the voyage to Thrace Arsinoë Beta had been unable to stop herself thinking of her brother, in spite of the parting words of Berenike that she must forget about him: *Let him not lie too heavy upon thy soul,* she had said. *Take not too much thought for him,* she had said, as if perhaps she understood what Arsinoë was feeling. But while she was at sea her heart's thought was that she could never stop loving Keraunos.

Now, however, in Thrace, she did forget him, and her heart beat now with a strange beat that she had not known even in the arms of her brother.

Alas! Thoth shakes his head and weeps for these children, for thus the seed of the dreadful tragedy of this Arsinoë Beta was sowed, and the seed would grow. The seed would not stop growing.

When Arsinoë Beta retired to her royal bedchamber that night, and the singing of the Crow Song and the Swallow Song and the Epithalamion was done, and the wedding guests had worn themselves out with showering her with hard nuts and unripe figs that bruised her flesh, and she was for the first time alone with the King her husband, she began to know his character.

Lysimakhos was a Macedonian from Pella, a comrade-in-arms of her father and a former bodyguard of Alexander. Lysimakhos had been handsome enough as a young man, but his good looks had gone. He was loud of voice, passionate, a man with still a great appetite for food and drink and *aphrodisia*. He was kind enough, but he would not stop touching her flesh. In truth Arsinoë Beta found herself satisfied with this husband in all things but the one that mattered the most: the fact that he was an aged man; for her delight was not in old men but in young men, and though Lysimakhos received divine honours, he was *not* like the gods to look at.

Lysimakhos bored Arsinoë with just the same stories about Alexander as her father told, only with a little less exaggeration. But the consolation of Arsinoë was her husband's wealth, for he had all Thrace for his province, and was overlord of all the lands of Asia that lay north of the Tauros Mountains. She thought of his great power, and of his riches, and really, she had no choice but to put up with this old man, if she could, for the good of the alliance with Egypt.

As for the reputation of Lysimakhos for tight-fistedness, from the start of his marriage he showed his love for his wife by showering her with gifts of gold and jewels.

She was wary of this strong old man, who was supposed to have rammed his fist down the throat of a lion and ripped out its tongue. She made up her mind to play the dutiful wife, for the time being. She took care to upset nobody, and she prayed three times a day to Aphrodite, Bringer of Wedded Happiness, for some change in her circumstances, such as the sudden death of her husband.

While the truth was that Arsinoë Beta had been thoroughly deflowered by her own brother, she had been enabled to preserve the illusion of maidenhood, and she said to Lysimakhos, *No one has troubled me . . . I am still the parthenos that I was at home . . .* And her husband noticed nothing out of the ordinary about her hymen of rubber from the Land of Punt, and her moment of anxiousness passed. Lysimakhos was cold, fishlike, and he aroused her disgust, for she could think now only of how Ptolemy Keraunos had done these things; and of how the Prince Agathokles might be very different from his father.

She thought of Ptolemy's words, *Is not the sweetest laughter to laugh over one's enemies?*

Now her father's enemy was to be his daughter's friend.

The daughter of Lysimakhos would *not* be a friend of Arsinoë Beta. In the palace at Lysimakheia Arsinoë Beta found that she must share the *gynaikeion* with the women of Lysimakhos—with another Arsinoë, who was his daughter by his deceased wife Nikaia, and a second girl who lived under the dark shadow of a bad horoscope; and to these girls Arsinoë Beta must now behave as stepmother, although she was only seven or eight years older. Such a state of affairs was not the best of starts. There being two Arsinoës in the same *gynaikeion*, it was hard not to muddle the one with the other. Their good relations were not helped by the fact of letters addressed to the one being opened and read by the other, so that the stepdaughter read the soft words from her father to his young wife, and the stepmother read the soft words of half the young noblemen in Thrace, who were already seeking the hand of the younger Arsinoë in marriage.

Worse, Lysimakhos decided that he would put an end to the confusion by calling Arsinoë his daughter Arsinoë *Alpha* and that Arsinoë daughter of Ptolemy must be known as Arsinoë *Beta*. This by no means pleased Arsinoë Beta, whose thought was that the wife and Queen of Lysimakhos should take precedence over his daughter, and that really she deserved the style of Arsinoë *Alpha* herself.

But Lysimakhos would hear no complaint, his word was law, and Arsinoë Beta she remained, for the rest of her life time, and, indeed, for all time.

Arsinoë Alpha was already a charming, sweet-tempered and beautiful girl, as beautiful as her brother Agathokles was handsome, and it was said of her that she must surely one day become the wife of some great Greek monarch.

Now in Greece it was the long-established custom for a stepmother to be *not* upon very good terms with her stepchildren; there was a long history of wicked or cruel Greek stepmothers, and since these two Arsinoës got off to such an ill beginning, it looked as if Arsinoë Beta was going to keep up the old tradition and be horrible.

For the truth was that Arsinoë Beta just did not agree with Arsinoë Alpha upon any thing, and one of the reasons for the tension was that they must needs share the *gynaikeion* between them; and because Lysimakhos, from his great meanness, sent the waiting-women of Arsinoë Beta straight back home to Egypt, she had to share the waiting-women of Arsinoë Alpha, whose ways were quite foreign to her, and who liked to chatter among themselves in some thick Thracian dialect that Arsinoë Beta really could not understand.

Arsinoë Beta resented very much the presence of Arsinoë Alpha in the women's quarters, thinking that a Queen of Thrace should have spacious apartments all to herself, and not be obliged to have to *share* anything with anybody, and she needs must also put up with a bunch of Thracian slaves who babbled also in that Thracian dialect aforesaid, which served only to make Arsinoë Beta think that they spoke unpleasant words about herself.

Because of these arrangements the two Arsinoës began pretty bad, and went on worse, and it was not many days before the sound of Arsinoë Beta's voice was heard to come from the women's windows, raised in anger, or shouting, and the terms of abuse flew from her lips and she was quite impolite to her stepdaughters, calling them *Ibis-face* and *Hippopotamus-face*, much as she had addressed Keraunos her brother; but through all this abuse and quarrelling that was over nothing but trifles, the other Arsinoë, Arsinoë Alpha, and her sister, spoke never a bad word against their stepmother, but continued to smile and return sweet words to her words of wrath; they could not understand why it was that Arsinoë Beta was so displeased with them, and with every last thing that they did.

Arsinoë Alpha, however, thought that the truth of it was that her stepmother simply *liked to pick a quarrel,* and that this girl should really have been placed in charge even of war, and made the Minister for War in all Thrace, for that she seemed never to stop talking about battle, and in truth was the most aggressive and poisonous woman she had ever seen in her life, who liked to find fault with and complain about absolutely every thing.

Arsinoë Beta found that her husband's capital city was not what she had been led to expect. Lysimakheia had been founded only eight years previous, and was by no means a splendid city such as Alexandria, but still in the course of construction. The streets were ill-paved, without Greek columns of any kind, and littered with animal filth. The Temples of Apollo and Zeus and every other god were still only half built, and without roofs. As for the so-called Palace of Lysimakhos, the walls of it had no fine paintings of scenes from the *Odyssey* and *Iliad*, its floors lacked mosaics of dolphins and Tritons, and score upon score of its rooms stood open to the sky, so that the rainwater stood in puddles, and the birds of the air, pigeons, doves, crows and such like, were to be found inside the house, which was not the best of omens. The Palace of Lysimakhos was hardly the well-appointed modern residence Arsinoë Beta had been promised.

She gave voice to her displeasure at the lack of every civilized comfort. She complained to Lysimakhos even about the Thracians, from among whom her slaves were recruited, and who gave every appearance of being a warlike, primitive people, resistant to Greek culture. Lysimakhos ignored her.

From time to time the air about Lysimakheia grew cold and showers of white feathers fell from the skies and caused the mules to slide about in the streets. Arsinoë learned, then, about the miracle of snow and the mystery of ice, and she complained about the bitter, bitter cold, just as she had complained of the terrible heat in Egypt. But Lysimakhos laughed at her, saying that even a king had no power over the weather.

When even the water in the amphoras inside the palace turned solid, Arsinoë declared herself convinced that she had been sent to the country of the barbarians, and she wished that she might be allowed to go home to Alexandria. Her life in Thrace felt, indeed, just as if she had been walled up in some remote place and forgotten about. She shivered, hating Thrace, hating Lysimakhos and all of his family also, apart from the handsome Agathokles, but most of all she hated herself, and she prayed to the gods of Hellas that she might be delivered from a torment that seemed worse than Hades.

But, as it happened, the prayers of Arsinoë Beta did not reach the ears of the gods, and she had to put up with her lot, for when she sent to the great Oracle of Klaros to ask whatever might happen next, she was told *To dwell there and hold on.* And so hold on she did.

At length Arsinoë Beta became accustomed to Thrace and its climate, and she found that she pleased this husband of hers. She ceased to complain and saw every thing with fresh eyes. Every thing that was wrong, every thing that was displeasing unto her, every thing that was unfinished, she saw now as a challenge, and she made up her mind to do what she could to right what was wrong. She was careful not to fight her husband but to work with him, and to be firm in her support of his every endeavour, to go out of her way to engage him in conversations, and to listen to whatever he might say in answer, so that within a short space of time he began to appreciate her cleverness, and to rely upon her help, and even to trust her judgement.

It was, after all, what Berenike had advised her to do.

Out of his thanks to this wife who was not a Persian, and who did not resist his nightly embrace, Lysimakhos started to settle large sums of gold upon this girl, in order to finance her wardrobe, and to satisfy her sudden and insatiable demand for jewels. A businesswoman from the beginning, conscious of the glories of mathematics and that she was indeed upon the royal road to geometry and perfection, Arsinoë Beta resolved to make the old man pay for every favour granted, and she played the games of the tigress, and the infatuated old Lysimakhos did everything that Arsinoë Beta told him to do, even with regard to the affairs of Thrace, so that he began to be under her complete control.

For Lysimakhos so admired the spirit of Arsinoë Beta that he gave his permission for her to be present even at his councils of state. She had, after all, the ability to read and write, unlike Lysimakhos's first two wives. She had a falcon's eye for numbers. She knew just what measures must be taken to put off a crisis in the food supply, a crisis in the army, a crisis among the palace slaves. She knew how an army must be managed, and how to put down a revolt with all speed. She knew all about how to hire soldiers from the hired-soldier markets in the Peloponnesos. Truly, there was nothing this girl did not know about the upkeep of a fleet of swift-sailing *triereis*.

Arsinoë Beta had indeed been taught the art of survival as the wife of a great monarch, and she was not sent home for complaining, but survived, so that the gifts of the grateful King of Thrace did not stop. By no means, for she came now to possess enormous wealth in her own right.

Berenike, yes, Berenike had taught this daughter all of her secrets, and she had taught her so well that Arsinoë Beta was able now to edge her way into a position of very great power, from which she would not be easily dislodged.

Above every other thing, Lysimakhos trusted this wife of his so much that when he must travel beyond the borders of his kingdom—to seek alliances with other kingdoms, perhaps, or if he must go away to fight a war—it was not even his *Dioiketes* who was left in charge of the great seal of state, nor yet the heads of the armed services, and not even his son and heir, the Prince Agathokles either, but Queen Arsinoë Beta herself.

No, this wife did not disappoint her husband in any thing: not once, not ever.

. . .

King Lysimakhos had buried, for one reason or another, fifteen of his children. When Arsinoë Beta now gave birth to three healthy sons in as many years, he was quick to invest her with the fiefdoms of three mighty cities, as a mark of his profound appreciation.

Ephesos she got for her own possession upon the birth of her first-born son, whom she insisted must be called by no other name than Ptolemaios, after her father. This was a city that Lysimakhos himself had replanned, but it was Arsinoë's city now, to use as she pleased. Perhaps, he told her, she might like to use the annual revenues and taxes of this place for the purchase of new shoes. But Arsinoë laughed her dry laugh. She preferred to save up the revenues in her treasure house. She had shoes enough. She was not interested to acquire more, and she asked for nothing but that the city must be renamed Arsinoëia in her honour, and all was done as she demanded.

Ephesos-Arsinoëia was a city built upon a swamp, and was thus subject to epidemics of the shivering sickness, so that, if the truth were told, she was not at once filled with wild delight to be the owner of it. No, when she went there, she was bitten almost to pieces by the flies, and obliged to sleep—albeit upon a couch of gold—under the fishermen's netting that was the only known means of keeping off the insects.

There were, however, things that made up for insect bites, not the least of which was that she could mint coins for this city that had her head upon one side, showing her round eyes and her long unsmiling face stamped in gold, a tribute that even Berenike did not enjoy in Egypt.

In the *agora* at Arsinoëia a larger than life-size statue of Arsinoë Beta glared down upon the business of butchers and fishmongers from the top of a gilded Ionic column, and the statue was itself of gold, solid gold, that glittered on the days when the sun chose to shine upon it.

Lysimakhos made over to his wife also four further cities that had once been the property of his wife Amastris: the city called Amastris itself, and Tlos, and Herakleia Pontike, and also the city of Kassandreia in the Khersonesos. Such things made up, to some degree, for being married to an old man with long white hair, and there were times when she forgot all about Alexandria and Egypt and the Thunderbolt she had left behind her.

Day after day, though, Arsinoë Beta rose to the overpowering stink of fish from the Hellespont. At nearly every meal she would be presented with some new fish dish. There was no prospect from the Palace of Lysimakhos but the view of the empty bay of Lysimakheia and the fishy Hellespont, its fishing boats and fishermen, and the occasional sighting of the fleet of her husband performing its manoeuvres upon the water. It was not long before Arsinoë began to hate the sight of fishes.

She hated also the fishy odour that hung about her husband, who clung to her in the sticky night, the old man from whom the heat of youth had departed; whose once bright eyes stared at her now with all the allure of a cold, dead fish.

All the same, as if to make up for his physical shortcomings, Lysimakhos gave her almost daily gifts of gold in the form of rings and necklaces and earrings, upon which the figures of Aphrodite or Eros took pride of place, and Eros held always the *iunx*, or magic wheel, that was a love-charm meant to arouse desire: things of exquisite workmanship that were tokens of his love for her.

The truth of it, however, was that Arsinoë Beta was so much taken up with men's thoughts and men's business that she took no delight in jewels of gold, but thought only of their monetary value, and she hoarded them in her private chamber, against the day when she might achieve her heart's desire and quit Thrace and this fishy husband for ever. Nor did Eros wake up Arsinoë's love for Lysimakhos in return. By no means. She could only find it in her to love his son, the handsome Agathokles.

Time and again the gifts of Lysimakhos were sent to her: gold fans, gold sceptres, gold bracelets and anklets, often bearing the figure of Ares, god of War, or Athene, goddess of All Handicrafts. Almost every thing this girl owned was made out of gold. Every present she was given was of solid gold, or plated with gold, or encrusted or inlaid with jewels, as if this husband were Midas himself.

The time would come when Arsinoë Beta and all the House of Ptolemy were tired of gold, weary of riches, worn out by unending excess, but not yet.

Gold: for the time being Arsinoë Beta could not get enough of it.

3.11

Rumours of Happiness

Having disposed of three out of six daughters, and enjoying almost for the first time the thought of uninterrupted peace as a result of his alliances, Ptolemy turned his thoughts to the art of peace with great zeal.

What should he do, he thought, now that he had no need to think always about war?

And in the heart of Ptolemy there arose at this time one great thought, which was to found a great Temple of the Muses, or *Mouseion,* that would be a Palace of Thinking, a mighty palace of fresh ideas, that would be the Greek counterpart to the House of Life of the Egyptians that formed part of every Egyptian temple.

Ptolemy—was he a man of great thoughts himself? He was not. If he had been indeed a pupil of the famous Aristotle, he had got from it no great love of philosophy. Ptolemy disliked abstract thoughts. He liked better to think of facts.

His one previous great abstract thought had been about glory won through victory in battle, a thing he had now achieved. Ptolemy had, indeed, all the glory that any human being could wish for. And yet, having gotten his glory, there was something missing from the list of his achievements. Perhaps it was the thought of Greece, of Macedon, of home, and that he was in the wrong place. Perhaps, again, it was that his glorious name might not die, but be remembered in Egypt for ever.

One solution was to make Alexandria more Greek than Greece, and so Ptolemy ordered more Corinthian columns, more Greek theatres and temples, and he dispatched pleas for more Greek immigrants to come and fill up his great Greek city. He doubled the numbers of Greek ships bringing amphoras full of Greek wine, Greek olives, Greek cheeses from Macedon to Egypt.

He sent out also a number of invitations to the Greek men of wisdom, urging them, too, to come and dwell in Alexandria: men like Menander, and Stilpon of Megara, and Straton, and Theophrastos— men who would think wondrous new Greek thoughts and make Alexandria famous for Greek learning. *Come soon,* he wrote. *Come and think for Ptolemy and Egypt . . .* And he offered so very many drachmas that these Greek scholars found his invitation difficult to ignore.

Some men insisted that, once again, the Mouseion was not the thought of Ptolemy, but of the brilliant Demetrios of Phaleron, but if it was not his idea, Ptolemy soon claimed it for his own: a foundation where Greek scholars would pursue Greek knowledge and Greek civilization, and study Greek poetry, Greek tragedy and Greek comedy, to the great glory of the name of Ptolemy.

First came the plans for the buildings, in the Greek style, with pediments and courtyards and Greek columns, and a public walk with seats where Greeks might have Greek conversations, and a common dining-hall where the men of learning might eat their Greek olives and Greek cheese and Greek-style bread, all the time thinking, thinking, without being disturbed by the traffic of chariots and the braying of donkeys in the streets, and there would not be a sphinx or a lotiform column in sight. Yes, it was to be a Palace of Creative Thinking, or Creative Disputation. For out of argument, Ptolemy thought, some goodly thing was sure to come forth, because what the Greeks were best at was disagreeing.

Some of Ptolemy's scholars came to Alexandria of their own free will. Some of them Ptolemy flattered to such a degree that they came out of thanks for being noticed. Some he poached from the courts of other Successors, from Pergamon, from Macedon, from Babylon; and he laughed, because none of his rivals had any thing to match this new thing of which he had thought.

The ceremonies and sacrifices, both animal and human, of the foundation were in due course celebrated, and the Temple of the Muses was open for business. The thinking began, and the scholars enjoyed free lodgings, and lavish wages, and scholarly independence (because Ptolemy was *not* a tyrant), and free food, and free seats at the theatre. Every necessary thing was provided for these men free of charge, because a scholar must have no worries of a practical nature to distract his mind from the thinking up of new thoughts.

Ptolemy expressed his delight, and every thing in the Mouseion was wonderful, wonderful, and utterly Greek.

And so, yes, Thoth asks it: What thoughts did Ptolemy's scholars, the wisest of the wise of the Greeks, have, who worked so hard at their professional thinking, all expenses paid, in this Mouseion?

After one month Ptolemy sent to ask the question, and the answer was sent back, at length, *No thoughts yet. No significant thoughts . . . No thoughts worth a mention . . .* Ptolemy, they said, must wait a little longer. Ptolemy, they said, must be very patient.

Meanwhile, the scholars argued about the order of their sitting down to their dinner; they argued about who should have which apartments for his sleeping-quarters; about which of them must talk less; and about the order in which they must march, when commanded, before His Majesty.

So that, as the disputations went on, and grew more rather than less, the Mouseion got to be called *The Cage of Fowls* by some, because of the mighty squawking that came from it, and because the argument made much noise but meant little, for it was the unending argument of the wise men over next to nothing.

The Great Library of Alexandria and the Mouseion also would, at length, be fine institutions, famous for all time, but they were made to look small in comparison with Ptolemy's very grandest project, the Pharos, or Great Lighthouse of Alexandria.

Was this, too, the idea of Ptolemy? Perhaps. Some thought it. Others swore that only an Alexander could have thought up a building so very grand, so very large; that it was Alexander himself who saw that what was needed to stop the ships crashing into the rocks as they entered the Great Harbour of Alexandria was a Great Light.

Others again, the flatterers, gave the first thought of the Pharos to Ptolemy Soter, and others still said it was Demetrios of Phaleron, who thought, at least, of nearly everything else.

Whoever thought of the Pharos first, there was never any question about who paid for it: it was Sostratos son of Dexiphanes who paid, and Sostratos's name would appear in great letters of lead upon the side of it, so large that perhaps the very idea for the Pharos was Sostratos's idea also.

Sostratos of Knidos was a man of very great wealth and influence in Egypt, of a family that kept four-horse chariots—which was something that only the very richest men could afford to do. He had got rich from the building of many ships, both ships of war and merchant ships that sailed up and down-River. He had got richer from the shipbuilding race between the Successors too, in which Ptolemy sought to outdo his neighbours by dreaming up ever bigger and better vessels that needed hundreds and thousands of oarsmen to row them.

The ships of Sostratos were often smashed upon the rocks on arriving at Alexandria, so that it was Sostratos who would get very great benefit from the Pharos himself. He had the least to lose from funding the building, and the most to gain from its existence. He also happened to be the owner of the Bank of Alexandria, so that it was entirely fitting that he should pay for the Pharos out of his own purse.

To be sure, Sostratos did not much *want* to pay, for like every man of riches he would have been better pleased to keep his money in his own hands, but he was the only man in Egypt, apart from Ptolemy himself, who had the eight hundred talents, or four million eight hundred thousand drachmas exactly, that the Mouseion scholars, proving their usefulness for the first time, worked out to be the cost of a giant structure three storeys high, that would tower above the city and harbour and be remembered by men for all time as one of the Wonders of the World for so long as the world might last.

Sostratos had expected Ptolemy to say *Egypt will pay.* He had thought the Pharos would be financed out of the olive-oil revenues, the profits from the late Syrian Wars, or Ptolemy's monopoly in the manufacture of papyrus. But no, he was disappointed. He found himself talked into giving the Lighthouse as a gift to Ptolemy, as a mark of his esteem for the King—as an act of homage to His Majesty—and he swore that he saw Ptolemy laughing at him for agreeing to it.

In spite of this, Sostratos of Knidos had plenty of drachmas left. His reward was surely that he would himself be famous for ever, for the fame of the man who built such a building was almost as good as the fame of a pharaoh.

It was not quite what Sostratos had intended, however, and they said always that the shock of the eight hundred talents turned the hair of Sostratos of Knidos white overnight, and that whenever his gaze turned towards the harbour he felt sick at the thought of the cost.

The Pharos was begun at once, for the great thing about being a king and a pharaoh and a living god was that whatever idea Ptolemy had, it could be made to happen just as soon as he thought of it. *Ginestho,* he said, *Let it be done* . . . Earthquake-proof foundations were laid. War was waged with the pounding seas. The prisons of Egypt were emptied and gangs of slaves, carpenters and masons toiled in the sun, hundreds and thousands of them. Some scoffed, forecasting that before ever the light could be kindled the Pharos would fall into the sea, but further human sacrifices were duly made, jet-black bulls with gilded horns were sacrificed, and the first stone was levered into position by the hand of Ptolemy himself.

The Heptastadion became now a constant procession of donkeys and mules, carts and wagons, carrying loads of stones, rubble, scaffolding, mortar and every ingredient of the finest Lighthouse. The first mason duly fell to his death upon the rocks, and Ptolemy shrugged his shoulders, saying, *Every thing that happens, it is the will of the gods.*

In spite of the numbers of workmen it would be twenty years and more before the Pharos was finished and the great light put a stop to darkness by night in the city of Alexandria. Ptolemy himself feared he would not live to see it, but he encouraged always his workmen, saying, *It will be worth waiting for* . . . and he smiled and showed his teeth, wearing his old smile that was twice the half-smile of a Pharaoh of Egypt, more of a Greek smile, as if he had forgotten for a moment such things as burden and duty, and thought merely as a Greek thinks, proud that he had done some thing that was bigger and better than anybody else had done.

At about this time, King Ptolemy gave his royal seal of approval to a programme of public lectures in the Mouseion, and it happened that the biggest crowd was drawn by Hegesias of Kyrene, a philosopher of the Kyrenaic School, whose subject was *Happiness.*

The swift rumour went about that this Hegesias had found the True Secret of Happiness, or at least that he was going to give some scholarly insight into the Nature of Happiness, whereby, perhaps, the happiness of all Alexandria might be enhanced. But Hegesias was not even a happy man himself, and he said he knew nothing about Happiness, and he could find only unhappy thoughts to speak. The result was that he got the nickname of Gloomy Hegesias, because, as he said, *Happiness is impossible.* He said that a wise man should not even try to be happy, but merely seek the avoidance of distress.

Happiness is nowhere to be found, he said, *and least of all in the city of Alexandria.* And they applauded when they heard these words, as if they agreed with him.

In the audience were many young men crossed in love, who passed their time casting spells with crocodile excrement after the custom of the Egyptians, in order to force some young woman, or some boy, to yield to their advances. Hegesias was heard also by many men who despaired of flourishing under King Ptolemy, whose levels of taxation, upon every commodity, were so very high that it was hard for any man, except a man like Sostratos, to get rich.

There was, then, already a good deal of despair in the city, but it was not long after Hegesias started to lecture that there came the first casualty of Happiness: a youth named Andronikos, who threw himself off his *trieres* into the Harbour of Eunostos, the Harbour of Happy Returns, leaving a note that said *Only a dead man is a happy man.*

More deaths followed. Some did not fall but jumped off the unfinished first storey of the Pharos, and smashed their brains out upon the rocks of Pharos island. Bodies were found washed up on the beaches east and west of Alexandria, their faces half-eaten by the fish. Others waded into the River with rocks tied about their necks, and became, according to the Egyptian way of thinking, instant gods.

For the Greeks, who hate cowardice more than any other thing, self-murder is the most extreme form of cowardice. A Greek is meant to be brave, a warrior, not a coward.

But Hegesias went on teaching his course in Practical Gloom with such success that they said he had decreased the amount of Happiness in all Egypt. He began then to be jostled and hissed and pelted with rotten fruit when he walked into the *agora,* and they called him Hegesias *Peisithanatos,* the Death-Persuader.

In the end there was so much self-murder that Ptolemy stopped Hegesias from teaching, and banished him from Egypt in disgrace. To try to restore the balance Ptolemy declared extra festival days and went about saying, *There is really nothing wrong with being happy.* But at the same time as he said it, Ptolemy knew, as every Greek knows, that it is unlucky to be too happy. To be too successful is to tempt Fate, for the gods of Greece are always jealous of a happy or successful man.

That, of course, presupposed that the gods did mean something, and there were men in Alexandria who thought that the gods of Greece counted for little. Chief of them was Theodoros, who taught that there are *no gods:* that the entire Greek pantheon is a lie and a myth. In spite of this man's name meaning Gift of God, Theodoros got for himself the name of The Atheist, and he agreed with Strato of Lampsakos that every thing that happens has a physical cause, and that no god has any thing whatever to do with it.

Theodoros, however, was *not* banned from teaching or banished from the Court of Ptolemy. Proof, perhaps, that even Ptolemy did not much care for the gods of his own country.

After Hegesias left the city the spate of self-murder did at least stop, and the level of happiness at Alexandria, insofar as there was any, went back to normal.

Ptolemy said he was happy. He was supposed to have said, *We are very happy. Our family is a most happy family,* and he said this kind of thing over and over again, wherever he went, and whoever he spoke with. *We want everybody to be happy,* he said. *There is no reason for unhappiness,* he said. *Every thing is ordered for the best.*

But, as it happened, what lay ahead in his own family was not happiness but further unhappiness, this time for Ptolemaïs, the youngest daughter of Eurydike.

3.12

Greek Manners

Ptolemy looked out of his Window of Appearances at Memphis, thinking of what he would do in his years of peace, if at last peace broke forth in the Greek world, for there was now one party left only who still regarded him with hostility, and that was Demetrios Poliorketes, his old enemy.

How, he thought, might he make his peace with Demetrios, whose delight was war, and the prolongation of war, and quarrelling for the sake of quarrelling?

It was a letter from Seleukos of Syria that reminded him of his old plan to engineer a marriage between one of Ptolemy's daughters and Demetrios; and it so happened that he had one girl left who was ripe for marriage, and she was Ptolemaïs. Ptolemy looked and looked at her, thinking of her two breasts beneath her *peplos,* rising like two round pink honey-cakes in the oven that was his Residence. If such an alliance could be signed, *Why,* he thought, *there will be peace for ever.*

Ptolemy sent, then, his ambassadors, with orders to suggest an alliance of peace that would be made binding by the marriage of Ptolemaïs; and Demetrios, they said, showed some interest, though he never stopped polishing his armour throughout the interview. Ptolemaïs herself made plain to her father that she would be happy, very happy, with such an arrangement, if it meant peace and the greater glory of Egypt, and, of course, of the House of Ptolemy, for she had heard of Demetrios, and thought she had seen him, one time, in action. And so the papyri were made ready, and dispatched for signing to wherever Demetrios was then camped with his engines of war, his bolt-throwers and catapults, and his latest Helepolis, and his battering-rams and myriad troops, and the alliance looked set to be in force.

For one reason or another, though—and even Thoth knows not why—this mighty Demetrios, who thought himself quite the gods' equal in wisdom, now declared he was not quite ready actually to marry Ptolemaïs, and—perhaps it was because he had already two other wives upon his hands, and already a grown-up son and heir to his kingdom called Antigonos Gonatas, or Knee-Cap—he managed to wriggle out of naming the day, or the month, or even the year in which he might be most graciously pleased for this new marriage to take place.

He had battles to fight, Demetrios said, and things to arrange, and the fact of it was that, just then, though he had the command and control of the Great Sea, he had no kingdom to his name, but must get him a kingdom, he said, before he got himself another wife.

To make up for the delay, and as earnest of his best intentions, Demetrios sent his young companion, Pyrrhos, the ex-King of Epeiros, in mainland Greece, off to Ptolemy in Egypt as a hostage. The curious thing about this was that Pyrrhos—whose name, on account of the striking colour of his hair, signified *Ginger*—was the most tremendous success in Egypt, for that he was handsome, well-mannered, and charming beyond almost any Alexandrian courtier, and he made a friend not only of the scholarly Mikros, but also of the really quite often obnoxious and difficult Keraunos, who lingered at his father's court, waiting to find out what would become of him, because his father could not bring himself to send him away.

Pyrrhos was everybody's friend, and he even became the personal friend of Ptolemy Soter, who admired Pyrrhos for his good nature, and for the fact that he really did not mind being beaten at dice or knuckle-bones, or draughts, or indeed at any game, and also because he was not afraid to make Ptolemy laugh, but liked to make jests, for he had that most rare thing for a Greek to have: a proper sense of humour.

Pyrrhos was also in high favour with Queen Berenike, who looked upon him almost as an extra son, and he reached such a height of royal approval that when it was suggested that he would make a most suitable husband for Antigone Berenike's daughter, Berenike most generously gave her consent and her blessing, and Pyrrhos and Antigone were betrothed.

The terms and conditions for the marriage contract were, of course, that Pyrrhos must now switch his allegiance from Demetrios Poliorketes to Ptolemy, for there was no possibility that Pyrrhos could be married to Ptolemy's stepdaughter and continue to support Ptolemy's great enemy.

Thus began the alliance between Ptolemy and Pyrrhos, who was declared to be no longer a hostage but was given his freedom, and a dowry of great value, in order to keep Antigone in the style befitting to a wife who was a Princess of Egypt in all but name.

As it turned out, Antigone would be a mother and ten years in her tomb before her half-sister Ptolemaïs ever got so much as to meet the famously missing Demetrios Poliorketes.

Antigone was married, then, and went at length to live in Epeiros as Queen of it, for Pyrrhos was in due course restored to his kingdom—but Ptolemaïs was married to nobody. Ptolemaïs was left sitting at home in Alexandria, waiting, waiting, and she devoted her days of waiting to weaving and tapestry and to sewing the household linen that she would need as the wife of a royal husband. She swore that she had caught sight of this most handsome of men just once, years before, when she was ten years old, at the Sea Battle of Salamis in Cyprus, and although she had but seen him in the distance, and there had been low cloud, and fires burning upon the water, and smoke, and a heavy sea, Demetrios had looked to her, Ptolemaïs said, like a man who had all that a girl might wish for in the way of cleverness and good looks; the kind of man a girl like Ptolemaïs might dream about. But though the name of this man now filled every sleeping hour of Ptolemaïs, and was upon her lips from sun-up to sun-down, so that her waiting-women grew really quite tired of her chatter about this man she did not know, Ptolemaïs had, in truth, long since forgotten what he looked like.

Twelve full months passed, in which Ptolemaïs did not stop from smiling, but Demetrios did not send for his betrothed, and though she sent twice daily for the list of foreign ships arrived in the Great Harbour, there was no ship bearing Demetrios or news of him to her.

Meanwhile, Ptolemaïs gathered up her belongings into a travelling trunk against the day when she might sail off to Greece to become this man's wife. Ptolemaïs waited with patience and then with impatience. But when she sent, at last, in desperation, to the Oracle of Zeus-Ammon in Libya to know just how many more days she must go on waiting, the Oracle answered her with one word, yes, one word only: *Years.*

From time to time a letter came from Syracuse in Sicily, full of the happy marriage of Theoxena and her Tyrant husband. Agathokles, she said, gave every sign of loving her most tenderly, and Theoxena said she adored Agathokles in return. The Tyrant's career as a regular *kinaidos* seemed to be at an end, and within two years of her going away Theoxena was able to report the births of two fine sons, named Arkhagathos and Agatharkhos, who might grow up, she thought, to share the rule of Syracuse between them, if not the whole of the island of Sicily.

Some hinted that the success of Theoxena's marriage was from her having had in Alexandria a thorough boy's education, for she had not wasted her girlhood in doing nothing but sewing and weaving, but had, like all Soter's daughters, sat at the feet of her brothers' tutors, learning about strategy and tactics and how to defend a city against a siege, while the boys yawned, and squashed the orange cockroaches, or dreamed about *aphrodisia*. The outcome of it was that Theoxena, too, thought very like a man. She knew nearly every thing about war—about hired soldiers, about alliances, and the manufacture of arms and armour. This kind of wife would be of the greatest use to a man like the Tyrant of Syracuse, and perhaps her military knowledge was the reason why her marriage flourished.

In the intense heat of Sicily Theoxena found it more comfortable to wear her hair cut short, like a boy's hair. Or she would grow her hair until it was very long, and then have it cut off, to be turned into the stout ropes that fired the siege-engines of her husband, and in doing so she set the grand example for the women of Syracuse, who did the same.

Theoxena was not well-rounded in the flesh like most Greek women, for she ate like a bird, and was thin, like the whippet. In short, Theoxena was very like a boy, and this may have been why Agathokles liked her so well, and why this match of hers was such a roaring success. But at the same time as being delighted, Theoxena worried, because every oracle she asked still said that her famous marriage was fated to last no longer than twelve years.

Theoxena had been given the most thorough teaching in mathematics, and she worked out the exact number of days and nights that was left to her life in Sicily, and the number of days was four thousand three hundred and eighty.

She scratched this number of notches upon the wall of her bed-chamber and crossed off the days and the nights as they passed by, living for the moment when she could, according to the principles of her royal father, but thinking always of her future—her future that was fated to come to an end sooner than she wanted it to. And all the while she spoke not one word to Agathokles the Tyrant of what the oracle said, lest he should send her away, but told him that the notches upon the wall were merely her calculation of the calendar of the year according to the Egyptians.

Six years it was after the Battle of Ipsos that Ptolemy got back his control of the island of Cyprus, which had been ten years under the rule of Antigonos One-Eye, when there was great rejoicing in Alexandria.

This most remarkable thing came about by the defeat of the forces of the famous Demetrios Poliorketes, son of One-Eye, in which the defence against King Ptolemy was handled with great energy by the brave Phila, wife of Demetrios. This Phila just happened to be the daughter of Old Antipatros, so that it was the sister of Ptolemy's first wife, Eurydike, and his own sister-in-law, who was at the last obliged to raise the white flag of surrender at Salamis with her own hand.

Ptolemy once again returned the gentlemanly behaviour of Demetrios ten years previous by sending Phila and her children home to Pella in Macedon, loaded with presents of every goodly thing from Egypt, in spite of his private thoughts, which were that he should have been pleased to have Demetrios and his entire family cut to ribbons. But no, Ptolemy's kindness got the better of him. *We are not barbarians,* he said. *We shall cut off no man's ears, nor no man's nose either, as the barbarian does. These people were once our friends . . . Perhaps they shall be our friends again . . . Phila is, after all, our wife's sister . . .*

Eurydike, sitting at home in Alexandria, had tried hard not to take the part of Phila her sister, nor that of Demetrios her brother-in-law, nor even that of her husband either. No, Eurydike made every effort to be quite uninterested in the outcome of the war over Cyprus, and how her husband fared in it. Nor, to tell the truth, did she much care whether Ptolemy lost or won Cyprus, and perhaps that was the whole trouble with this wife: she did not much care about any thing, whereas Berenike cared about whatever Ptolemy cared about, and supported him in his every trouble.

Ptolemy knew, though, in his heart, what it was that Eurydike truly thought, and which party she was supporting in the battle for Cyprus. It was one more reason why he must reject this wife who in her secret secret thoughts was *praying to Zeus and all the gods of Hellas for the defeat of her own husband.* And he was right. Eurydike did want Ptolemy to know defeat, in order to teach him a lesson for having married Berenike, her *aunt,* in preference to herself.

When the Eighth Anniversary of the Crowning of Ptolemy Soter was celebrated, with great processions of priests, and a parade of the entire army through the streets of Memphis, and free bread and *booza* for the natives, and the ceaseless chanting of *Ptlumis, Ptlumis, Ptlumis* in the streets, it was two years since Demetrios Poliorketes had still not sent for Ptolemaïs to be his wife, but ever sought to make war upon her father.

Ptolemaïs was by this time no longer just a young girl, but a young woman, with her breasts like two ripe watermelons and several fingers more than three fingers in height, and she was ripe, more than ripe for her marriage, which did not take place. Upon the very hot, airless days at Memphis, or upon the cold, grey days of winter, but most often when the storm of sand swept across Egypt like a giant yellow blanket, a kind of despair would overtake this daughter of Ptolemy, and the tears flowed down her face and she would wail that her Demetrios would never send for her, but that she had been tricked, and that if he did not marry her soon she must hang herself with her own girdle, for that she could not bear to wait for him much longer.

The waiting-women of Ptolemaïs did their best to reassure her, and they urged Eurydike, her mother, to ask Berenike to ask Ptolemy to send his swiftest-sailing *trieres* to Demetrios to find out whether it was indeed his thought to make this woman his wife, and whether his intentions were entirely honourable. At length the answer came back that, yes, to be sure, he wanted to wed Ptolemaïs, but that she must please to wait a little longer, and he asked how old she was, and for a description of her countenance, as if he had forgotten every last thing about her.

And so Ptolemaïs the betrothed went back to her sewing, and to counting the wasted days of her life, and she began to scratch notches upon the wall of her chamber, and to keep count of the number of days that this Demetrios had kept her waiting.

With his sister Arsinoë Beta sailed away to Thrace, Ptolemy Keraunos lingered still in Egypt, neither quite disinherited nor yet quite having got back the full approval of his father, but both parties eyed each other up, like two dogs that had had a scrap, and were wondering whether they must scrap again, and, as it were, *waiting to see what might happen*. And Ptolemy waited and watched, and waited, to see whether the character of his son and heir might change for the better, or for the worse.

Keraunos polished his armour and sharpened his sword, but apart from his daily drilling and training with the armies of Egypt upon the sandy plain opposite Memphis, or his riding with the mounted troops along the beaches at Alexandria, and, of course, his physical training in the *gymnasion* that kept his body like a statue of the Greeks, he had no other occupation. Ptolemy Keraunos had, in fact, nothing to do but wait for his royal father to die, so that he might be King in his place.

And did the character of Keraunos change for the better? No, it did not. There were reports of various outrages, and King Ptolemy heard them and said nothing, but watched, and waited, and watched. To go anywhere near the Pyramids of Memphis after dark was a wilful act, sure to bring down upon the visitor the wrath of the dead Pharaohs. A man of any sense will avoid a tomb by night, when the spirits of the dead walk abroad to enjoy the cool of the air. But it was the delight and pleasure of Ptolemy Keraunos, the Thunderbolt, to gallop his horse round the Pyramids after the hours of darkness, screaming the battle cry of Macedon. And when he was tired of galloping he would stop to break into the tombs of the priests of Memphis that lie upon the desert plateau, seeking what he might steal.

The High Priest of Memphis warned Keraunos not to do this, but Keraunos was a boy who was pleased to ignore warnings. He would go down into the tombs if he wished, hunting for treasures. He really did not like to do what he was told.

The words of Thoth are no secret: *Anybody who violates a tomb will have his neck broken like the neck of a bird.*

Even so, in spite of the many wrong things that Keraunos did, he still had not lost his place in his father's favour. Even now, nothing this boy asked for was refused him. In spite of his shortcomings he was gazed upon and admired by all for his physical strength and for his handsome good looks. Even for his father, Ptolemy Keraunos could almost do no wrong. He was still marked out from Soter's other sons as the boy who *must* be Pharaoh.

3.13

Love, and Madness

Ptolemaïs, daughter of King Ptolemy, celebrated her twenty-fifth birthday without one smile, for she had now passed, according to her calculation, one thousand four hundred and sixty days since her betrothal to Demetrios the Besieger and he had not yet sent for her to be his wife.

The despair of Ptolemaïs grew now, if that were possible, worse, and she thought the thought that by her age many women had given birth to nine or ten sons and had long since gone down to Hades.

She began now to make the daily sacrifice of a goose to Aphrodite, Bringer of Wedded Happiness, and somehow she kept her hopes alive. She made regular use of the remedy for perfect skin that was made up of Egyptian onions and wild turnips, in order to make sure that, however long she might wait for this husband, she might still *look* youthful even if she was not. She thought the thought also that her hair would be grey before she got to be a wife and a mother, and from time to time she worked herself up to such a degree of anger that she smashed dishes upon the mosaic floor.

After four years of her marriage it was the calculation of Theoxena that she had but two thousand nine hundred and twenty days left to live with her husband, and yet she did not know whether it was herself who was fated to die, or her Tyrant, or whether he would just grow tired of her after twelve years, and divorce her. But Theoxena had too much sense to ask Agathokles whether she pleased him or not, in case he said *not* and made her leave Sicily at once.

What, then, did Theoxena do? What *could* she do but cross off the number of days that were left, day after day, and try to forget that the end of her marriage had been foretold. Theoxena did her best to live for the present, for *now,* according to the philosophy of her father, and to pretend that the future did not exist.

If Ptolemaïs and Theoxena seemed to have brought upon their heads all the ill luck in the world, what, then, of Arsinoë Beta, their half-sister, in Thrace? What news was there out of Lysimakheia?

From time to time Arsinoë Beta would put her reed pen to the papyrus and write to Egypt. Three times she wrote to tell of the birth of a healthy son; three times there was rejoicing at Alexandria upon the birth of a fresh grandson for King Ptolemy, and the news was good news, but the truth of it, which was never told to her family in Egypt, was that all was *not* very well with the life of Arsinoë Beta.

Yes, the whole trouble of Arsinoë Beta was Agathokles, the other Agathokles, who was Prince of Thrace. Arsinoë Beta was still *on fire.* Arsinoë Beta *burned* with love for Agathokles, and she cast longing eyes and smouldering glances upon this young man every day, day after day.

In her idle moments, sitting in the half-dark of the *gynaikeion*, Arsinoë Beta would scratch upon her wax tablet some words such as these:

> *I love Agathokles*
> *I gaze upon Agathokles*
> *I am mad about Agathokles*

She felt just as if she was burning to ashes for love of this young man, and yet she could tell nobody of it. As for Agathokles himself, he had at this time no idea that his stepmother nursed these feelings for him, and he seldom spoke so much as two words to Arsinoë Beta, except to greet her when he passed her in the corridors of his father's palace.

But now, when they did have occasion to speak, Arsinoë Beta began to make her voice supple towards Agathokles, thinking to let him know what were her thoughts for the man she regarded as her lover. What did Agathokles do? He seemed to take no notice.

Agathokles, with his yellow hair, his blue eyes like *sappheiros,* his tight sinews and broad shoulders, his manly chest, his impossible beauty—all began to drive Arsinoë Beta *crazy,* for this boy was at the height of his physical powers, and indeed, his golden flesh seemed to melt under the hot glance of his stepmother, who was dazzled by the handsomeness of his body, and by the sweetness and nobility of his character, thinking that he was like the gods to look at, like a young Apollo.

Arsinoë Beta was in love. What should she do? She knew, sure enough, that the Greek standard in every activity was a sane balance, but she had lost her balance. Love was madness, and Arsinoë Beta was not in her right senses, and things would get worse for her.

What should she do? The only answer to her troubles was to forget— to try to forget—Agathokles by plunging herself into affairs of state rather than an affair of the heart, for it was only when she turned her thoughts to war, to defence, to the building of ships of war, to the hiring of soldiers, to the provisioning of the armies of Thrace, that she could give pause to her lustful thoughts about her stepson.

Even so, Arsinoë Beta could not stifle her passion, and her trouble did not stop, and she did not know what she should do about it all. This strongest of women just suffered in silence, and in secret she wept great floods of women's tears, and all the while Agathokles the Handsome knew no thing, no thing, of what she felt for him.

Assuredly, at Lysimakheia upon the Hellespont Arsinoë Beta had every goodly thing that she might desire. The only thing this Queen of Thrace lacked for was the only thing that she could not have: love—a love that was returned to her in a degree equal to that which she gave, and the love of her husband, King Lysimakhos, who *did* love this wife of his, was nothing to do with it, for she did not, could not, would not love *him* in return.

Yea, love was the only thing Arsinoë Beta truly wanted, and love was the only thing she never had.

Six years it was after Arsinoë Beta sailed to Thrace, when she was now the mother of three sons, that Lysimakhos sent Agathokles, his son and heir, off into the north lands with an army and orders to put down that ferocious tribe that was called the Getai, whose leader was Dromikhaites, and who fought stark naked but for a collar of gold about the neck, and with their hair stood up on end like spikes. *Like regular satyrs,* as the Greeks said.

Agathokles was then about twenty-four years of age, and as it was his first military campaign in sole command, his army paraded through the now handsomely paved streets of Lysimakheia, cheered on its way by the people, who fully expected a quick and glorious victory over the barbarians. Arsinoë Beta herself watched Agathokles ride away to battle at the head of his troops from her high window, and when her waiting-women asked what was the matter, whatever was wrong, she said, *I was not weeping, it is the dust in the eye, the dust kicked up by the marching boots* . . . But what Arsinoë Beta thought was, *When shall I see this Agathokles again?* And her heart was heavy in her breast, like a lump of lead.

There was a long silence from the region of war, the usual lack of any word from the front, and through many days of uncertainty Arsinoë Beta quite stopped eating any thing but the nails of her fingers, and she pulled out great lumps of her famous yellow hair, and she would wake screaming in the dead hours of the night, for that she had seen the vultures circling over Agathokles in her dream.

At length the usual herald, bloody and bandaged, staggered into Lysimakheia from the direction of the River Istros, where the army of Agathokles was supposed to have gone, and poured out the news that the Prince had been defeated in battle by the barbarian and taken as a prisoner of war by that very Dromikhaites whom he had been sent to subdue, and that there was a price of thousands of talents upon the head of this boy that was equal to the gross national product of the kingdom of Thrace for ten years.

Arsinoë Beta, not so manly now, ran to her private apartments and bit her pillow to drown the dreadful noise of her sobbing, for she thought that she had seen the last of her Agathokles.

But although she offered up the most lavish sacrifices to the gods of Greece, and did every thing in her power to talk Lysimakhos into paying the ransom, the tight-fisted King refused to hand over so much as one hemiobol to the Getai, and he told his wife that her sacrifices were, as well as a waste of money, a waste of time, for that the gods of Greece had lost their usefulness years ago.

Seven hundred and thirty days passed, during which the Getai sent ever more insistent demands for the ransom money to be paid, but Lysimakhos said he could in no wise raise such an outlandish sum, and that Thrace really could not afford the release of Agathokles.

If Arsinoë Beta could have resigned herself then and there to the fact of losing Agathokles, one of her own sons might have been King of Thrace upon the death of her husband, and the history of the world might have been different, but Arsinoë Beta could think, just then, of nothing but Agathokles, and she begged Lysimakhos to send the money, or some payment upon account, or at least to do something, and she screamed at him, offering even to find one quarter of the ransom out of her own purse, for the thought of Agathokles out of sight, a prisoner for ever, or Agathokles dead, was almost as much as she could bear, heart of iron notwithstanding.

It was only when, after much sulking and stubbornness, she at last withheld her favours in the bedchamber and would not let Lysimakhos come near her for thirty nights together, that she finally made him agree to set out in person, aged though he was, against the barbarians, and he marched across the River Istros with a great force, meaning to teach the Getai a lesson they would never forget.

But it was the Getai that taught Lysimakhos the lesson, for they took him prisoner as well, so that he suffered now the same fate as his son, becoming the personal hostage of Dromikhaites, a man whom Lysimakhos despised and had dismissed in the past as primitive, ferocious and utterly lacking the military skills of a Greek, for Dromikhaites was a man clad in *skins,* and beneath his contempt.

Back at Lysimakheia Arsinoë Beta had now occasion to scream some more, but she had been left in sole charge of her husband's kingdom, so she might at least do something to rescue her family. Even so, things looked bad, very bad, to Arsinoë Beta, for the entire army of Thrace had been captured along with the King.

All Arsinoë Beta could think was that such a train of disasters would not have happened if she had been present herself. She dispatched her messengers, envoys, ambassadors, scouts and spies. She stuck bronze pins into maps to show where it was that her husband and stepson might be imprisoned, and she came close to setting out in person along the road to the north, and Thoth knows, she would have been successful in bringing back the prisoners, for this Queen was just as smart as the fox, just as cunning as the vixen.

So what happened? The naked savages screamed for Lysimakhos and his son to be brought before them and receive their proper punishment—that is to say, their death—but Dromikhaites surprised every man by inviting father and son to a lavish feast, and instead of murdering them he treated them with exaggerated courtesy. And Dromikhaites said, No, he would not let Old Lysimakhos have control of the territory he wanted, not then, not ever, and he sent these two prisoners back home to Lysimakheia humiliated, and looking rather foolish.

The release of the King of Thrace was agreed only when Arsinoë Beta promised to pay the ransom for Agathokles, *and* to form an alliance with the Getai that would be made binding by the marriage of Dromikhaites himself to Lysimakhos's younger daughter. To be sure, for a daughter of the King of Thrace to be given in marriage to the barbarian was a terrible disgrace to his House, but Lysimakhos could do nothing but agree to it, and Arsinoë Beta was only too pleased to be rid of one of Lysimakhos's women, who crowded her *gynaikeion* and got in her way. Arsinoë Beta, who might, in other circumstances, have fought the idea of a barbarian marriage, gave her consent, urging her husband to agree to all the conditions, because it would mean that she could have her beloved Agathokles where she could look upon his face.

Yes, in her husband's absence in the territory that lay beyond the Istros River, it was Arsinoë Beta who oversaw every affair of state in Thrace. Now, while he was held prisoner among the barbarians, Arsinoë Beta had her first real tasting of power, and she *loved* power, and she did not mean to let go of it.

In due time Agathokles rode into the city of Lysimakheia with his father beside him, bearing gifts from the Getai, and with not so much as a scratch upon his body, but looking, if that were possible, more handsome even than before, so that when Arsinoë Beta saw him safe, her knees melted under her and she fainted away, and far from loving him less because she had seen him not, she loved him even more.

In her belief that Agathokles had been saved from certain death by her unceasing prayers and sacrifices to the gods, Arsinoë Beta now dedicated a gigantic pair of ears of bronze, each one six cubits high, in the Temple of Artemis daughter of Apollo, for having listened to her.

Lysimakhos, upon his return he seemed older than ever, but his gifts to his wife for having minded the kingdom while he was away were lavish, most lavish, and all of gold, bearing witness once more to the high regard in which he held this young wife of his, and also to his love for her, which she felt ever less able to return. In fact Arsinoë had no feelings now for this husband but feelings of disgust.

What, though, of the ill-fated daughter of Lysimakhos who must be sacrificed to the barbarians in the cause of peace? She was sent across the River Istros in fulfilment of her father's oath, which he dared not break, for he knew that if he failed to hand over this girl he must suffer the invasion and annexation of all Thrace by this wild tribe, and he had given his word regarding the daughter, who now left home with very many tears, heading for the northern border of Thrace, and her face was not seen in civilized society again.

To all intents and purposes this daughter was a dead daughter, one of the disappeared, whose name was not to be spoken by her family more, but who some times shed their tears in private, for that they did not know what dreadful fate had overtaken her.

However, this girl's tears dried up quick, and she went almost happily to the Getai, saying that a life with the barbarians would be better and more peaceful than a life passed under the same roof with a snake like Arsinoë Beta.

Thus it was that Arsinoë Beta got rid of one of her stepdaughters, who was so comprehensively forgotten about after this that the history of Thrace did not so much as record what was her name.

3.14

_____

The Mother-in-Law

The life of Arsinoë Beta as Queen of Thrace was not, in truth, without its pleasant moments. She had every jewel, every object of gold she asked for, and riches beyond any man's belief, and three handsome young sons of her own, whom, yes, she loved as any other Greek mother loves her sons, enough but not too much.

The one great thing that troubled the spirit of Arsinoë Beta was the matter of Agathokles, but she was content, some times, merely to look upon the man's flesh, and it was almost enough, some times, to satisfy her terrible yearning.

All this regular and more or less peaceable existence of Arsinoë Beta was, however, about to change for the worse, because the dreadful day was approaching upon which her own half-sister, the Princess Lysandra, daughter of King Ptolemy and Eurydike, would step off a swift-sailing *trieres* from Alexandria and turn her sister's love into a bitter hate that would bring disaster and utter ruin upon the House of Lysimakhos.

What was the history of this Lysandra? At about the same time as Arsinoë Beta had been married off to Lysimakhos this girl had been married to Alexandros son of Kassandros, a boy of about fifteen, who was also her first cousin. And LOOK!—Lysandra had gotten herself married to a young husband, and it was the disgraced Arsinoë Beta who had had to marry the old man.

This Alexandros was, however, a younger son, so that he had not much hope of inheriting the throne of Macedon, but his mother, Thessalonike, a daughter of Philip of Macedon, was a woman who was pleased to have her own word as law, and when Kassandros died, and then his son, King Philippos as well, only four months after, this Thessalonike insisted that her two remaining sons must rule jointly over Macedon, because she disliked her elder son, Antipatros, who was about seventeen years old, while Alexandros, the younger boy, was her favourite.

The first thought of Ptolemy was that a boy king was bad enough, but that to let two boy kings rule together was asking for serious trouble, because they would never be able to agree upon any matter. No, they would lack the foresight and military knowledge of grown men, and they would lack also the wisdom of years. They would attract usurpers and foreign invaders, who would be most sure to take every advantage of the confusion. Ptolemy thought that war was certain, and yet, under the new arrangements the Princess Lysandra his daughter would be Queen of half Macedon, and it was an alliance that Ptolemy could not let pass by him without seizing hold of it.

Lysandra was duly shipped off to Greece and married to the young Alexandros, and with regard to the two boy kings all the fears of Ptolemy turned out to be justified. They agreed, at first, to split Macedon down the middle, with Antipatros ruling the east and Alexandros the west. How their neighbours rejoiced, for the cutting up of the kingdom was seen as nothing but an invitation to every possible claimant to the throne to interfere in Macedonian affairs. Lysimakhos, Demetrios Poliorketes, Pyrrhos of Epeiros—all of them next-door neighbours of Macedon—became most excited at the thought of annexing for themselves a large slice of new territory, and sure enough, the two boy kings, who, as everybody forecast, could in no wise agree upon the slightest matter, began at once to quarrel in earnest, and they looked like an easy enemy to beat in battle.

Young Antipatros grew quickly tired of his bossy mother, who could not stop herself from meddling in state business, and he murdered her in cold blood, and then drove Alexandros his brother out of Pella, which was his capital.

Alexandros, terrified at the thought of losing his half of Macedon altogether, panicked, and sent his messengers to both Pyrrhos and Demetrios, begging for urgent military support. Pyrrhos was the first to appear, and he helped himself to a vast tract of land, as he said, in return for his services, having set aside, for the time being, his gentlemanly manners.

Demetrios set off with a great army, and his usual engines of war, siege towers and thousands of iron bolts for his catapults, every one of them with his dread name scratched upon it; but he frightened Alexandros because of his power and his phenomenal military reputation, and lurid reports filtered through to the boy of Demetrios's troops looting and burning and raping as they marched towards his headquarters.

Alexandros was very young. He had no experience of war, and little experience of diplomacy, and cherish and love his beautiful wife Lysandra though he might, he did not listen to her wise counsel, for she was a woman, and he had listened too often already to the advice of his mother. He met Demetrios as his honoured guest at the town of Dion, but the first words he spoke to Demetrios were that he no longer needed his help.

Demetrios did not turn around and march away again. He had heard some rumour that there was a plot to assassinate him at the banquet of welcome planned by Alexandros, but Demetrios did nothing, except order his soldiers to line the walls of the banqueting chamber, armed as for battle. And this alarmed Alexandros still more, because Demetrios's men outnumbered his own troops.

The banquet passed off without any trouble, but Demetrios still did not do what Alexandros wanted him to do and go away. On a second night Alexandros accepted the kind invitation of Demetrios to another banquet, and in the middle of the feasting Demetrios suddenly stood up from his couch and stamped out of the room. Alexandros, wondering what was wrong, followed him. But as Demetrios passed through the door he said to his bodyguards, *Kill the man who is behind me,* and Alexandros was a dead man upon the instant, lying in a pool of his own blood.

The screams of Lysandra echoed around her husband's camp, and somehow she escaped to the court of King Ptolemy in Egypt. Thus ended the short marriage of Lysandra, who was now a widow in search of a fresh husband.

Lysandra had been married off. She was as good as dead, and she found little sympathy in Alexandria, for a married daughter is not supposed to return to her father's house within the year. Few people shed tears for Lysandra, who was not, in any case, supposed to have any personal feelings for her husband. All the tearing of her hair, the scratching of her cheeks, the wailing, the beating of her breasts with her fists—it was merely the Greek custom, that meant nothing whatever, and her feelings were nothing to do with it.

Lysandra, however, contrary to Greek custom, had loved Alexandros, and she felt now as if the heart had been cut out of her breast by butchers' knives. At the same time, she had been trained in the school of hard women, where a girl did not put her feelings upon show, but was supposed to bottle them up and keep quiet.

While Lysandra began all over again her tapestry of the Pharos of Alexandria in purple and gold thread, her father sent his ambassadors to the men who might be pleased to take this girl to wife, but as it turned out, the only husband to be had that was of suitable rank and short of a wife was the Prince Agathokles, the young son of King Lysimakhos of Thrace, who, by common consent, was just about the handsomest man alive.

The papyri were signed, then, and the terms and conditions and reversionary clauses agreed, and Lysandra was packed off to Thrace like some parcel of nuts, to Lysimakheia upon the Hellespont, where her ill-fated marital history was set to continue upon its terrible course.

For, indeed, this second marriage of the Princess Lysandra was doomed to end in a disaster just as hideous as the first, if not worse, and the whole trouble behind it was this: that the two half-sisters, Arsinoë Beta and Lysandra, would, under the new arrangements, end up living at the same court, under the same roof, sharing the same *gynaikeion,* married to two husbands, one young and one old, who happened to be father and son.

Lysandra had agreed, as she must agree, to journey to Thrace in order to become *the daughter-in-law of her own younger half-sister*, and it was a state of affairs that any man worth two drachmas could have foreseen was bound to stir up all the trouble in the world.

How, in the name of Zeus, had such a thing been allowed to happen? The horoscopists and soothsayers of Alexandria had all shaken their heads and given Ptolemy Soter the direst of forecasts and warnings, for in the catalogue of stupid things this was surely one of the stupidest things that any father could do to a daughter, and perhaps the stupidest thing Ptolemy did in all his long life time. And yet, Ptolemy was untroubled. He had not shown his face in the *gynaikeion* at Alexandria for years, because he really did not want to meet Eurydike. He had never heard how Arsinoë Beta and Lysandra argued. He had never seen the lioness that was Arsinoë Beta with her claws out. Ptolemy, alas, had but small knowledge of his daughters, and he failed utterly to see what must happen. He was, after all, a man who liked to live for the moment only. He thought only of his alliance, his double alliance with Lysimakhos, and of the fact that when Old Lysimakhos was dead, a daughter of his would still be Queen of Thrace, and have power and influence in Thrace. Ptolemy Soter was a fine man—kind, generous, famous for his fairness—but he really did not take much thought for the future.

When this Princess Lysandra stepped off her swift-sailing *trieres* then, at Lysimakheia, her younger sister, the Queen of Thrace, Arsinoë Beta, embraced her with false smiles and crocodile tears, and it was her thought that this day, the day of the marriage of Lysandra to Agathokles, was the worst day of her life.

But Arsinoë Beta—short of committing a murder, what could she do? She was powerless to stop this marriage, for Lysimakhos had not asked for her thoughts about a matter that was private, concerning his side of the family. And in any case, Lysandra would make the best of queens, and was much the same age as Agathokles: the marriage was a perfect match, and he could see no reason to consult Arsinoë Beta about it.

And so Lysandra made the acquaintance of King Lysimakhos, that was her half-brother-in-law and her father-in-law to be, and made the *dexiosis,* and she shook also the hand of the Prince Agathokles who was to be her husband, and she met his beautiful sister, the Princess Arsinoë Alpha also, and the other members of the Royal House of Thrace—notably the three wild boys that were the children of Arsinoë Beta, the Prince Ptolemaios, the Prince Philippos, and the Prince Lysimakhos Mikros, to whom she was already a half-aunt, and these boys, aged now about six and five and four years, bowed to her, and smiled, and all of them together gave every appearance of being one happy family—though, Thoth knows, the truth of it was otherwise.

The marriage of Agathokles and Lysandra was celebrated with the greatest pomp and display, and with processions, and dancing, and one hundred oxen were sacrificed, and the whole populace of Lysimakheia feasted until dawn, for Lysandra was the young woman who would be the next Queen of Thrace.

Lysandra was delighted to find that her fresh husband was young, and that he was indeed handsome beyond all belief, and charming also, and kind, and generous—in fact the perfect husband; and these two were struck at once by the golden arrows of the Boy, Eros, and were quite unlike most other Greek husbands and wives in that they were devoted to one another from the very beginning.

But what of Arsinoë Beta, the present Queen? She did not smile and show her teeth. She did not sparkle her eyes, or rejoice, or join in the dancing and feasting at this wedding. Arsinoë Beta could do nothing but scowl, so that Lysimakhos asked her what was wrong? And she replied, *I am a little unwell . . . I have a pain . . .*

Alas, poor Arsinoë Beta—who cannot find for this woman, this most unhappy woman, some feelings of sympathy?—for that she found herself the mother-in-law of her own elder sister. And for a while the two sisters actually called each other *Mother* and *Daughter,* and laughed a little at their curious situation. But all was not well in the *gynaikeion,* where the younger sister and mother-in-law, Arsinoë Beta, fully expected the elder sister and daughter-in-law, Lysandra, to do just what she told her to do, whereas it was really the thought of Lysandra that this state of affairs must be the other way about, just as it had been in Alexandria, when she had tried, though never with very much success, to tell Arsinoë Beta what she must and must not do.

At the first opportunity, then, Arsinoë Beta began to boss Lysandra upon every last matter relating to the women's quarters—about their food, and the linen, and where she may and may not leave her shoes, and so forth—so that there was at once a good deal of trouble between them. In fact there was so much shouting and screaming that the other Arsinoë, Arsinoë Alpha, ran screaming herself, from time to time, right out of the *gynaikeion,* to take refuge with her father, crying that she could not bear to be with the two Egyptian sisters one moment more.

But why did these sisters quarrel so? Why?

The root of the tragedy in Thrace was that Arsinoë Beta *loved* the husband of Lysandra to distraction. Up till this time she had been able, more or less, to hide her feelings, but now to have her own half-sister sharing the chamber and the bed of the handsome Agathokles, and to come upon her sister kissing this man upon the lips, and to see her sister stroking the bronzed flesh of Agathokles beneath his tunic, and to see her sister looking into the glittering blue eyes of Agathokles with love, true love, and to see that her love was returned, and to think then that her sister would have the delight and pleasure of bearing Agathokles's children—all of these things were suddenly more than Arsinoë Beta could bear, and she truly thought that she must go mad from thwarted desire, and yet she must keep silent about it all, and tell nobody, for there was no one in Lysimakheia, not even her waiting-women, to whom she might speak her innermost thoughts and her most private secrets, but she must pretend that the love of Agathokles for Lysandra meant nothing to her, nothing, and that she could not care less about what had happened.

All of this was made ten thousand times worse by the fact that Lysimakhos her husband was ageing fast, was more bent, more frail, and more old and ill-tempered than ever before. And although he continued to lavish his gifts of gold and all the jewels in Thrace upon this girl, none of that made up for the fact that she must stand by from dawn to dusk and see her sister *smiling,* sparkling-eyed with her love for Agathokles, while she, Arsinoë Beta, had to endure her terrible marriage to the cold old man, sleeping at night either alone in her bed, or held tight in the arms of this fishy King.

It was for these reasons that a terrible jealousy and a terrible hatred were unleashed in the Palace of King Lysimakhos of Thrace, and to speak the truth, *nothing, nothing* had been known to match it in all the Greek world since the dreadful stories they told about Agamemnon and Klytemnestra and the House of Atreus. No, the tragedy of the House of Ptolemy would be worse, far worse, than that, with the blood trickling down over ten generations.

For some days after the wedding Arsinoë Beta would retire early to her private chamber, from where she could be heard howling, like the hyaena, like the jackal of the desert, and one night she went so far as to smash up the giltwood furniture of her bedchamber, and she smashed also upon the mosaic floors every costly bowl of glass, and every vessel of earthenware, and, indeed, every thing that would break she broke, stopping short only of smashing to bits the contents of her jewel chest, which things were too valuable to destroy.

She worked out her rage in this way until she was exhausted, and then there was a long silence from her chamber, in which the waiting-women refused to go near her, afraid they might be bitten. But Arsinoë Beta calmed herself. Now she pulled herself together and her anger went, as it were, underground. She showed her face in public and walked about the palace of her husband wearing her golden shoes and her golden jewellery just as before, as if nothing had changed, and she was seen even to smile a grim kind of smile.

Lysandra flourished in Thrace, and was healthy, fulfilled in her life, happy in her marriage, though the stars that ruled her end were bad, very bad, and it was well for Lysandra that she did not know it.

On the other hand the good health of Arsinoë Beta—unfulfilled, unhappy, unlucky above every other woman in her stars—it was something that would not last much longer.

When the men who fished in the Hellespont netted a sturgeon, they would adorn themselves and their boat with garlands of flowers, and march in procession with this greatest of fishes to the palace, for the sturgeon, sacred in Greece, must be brought to the royal table like this, preceded by a piper.

Arsinoë Beta put her hands together and clapped with the rest of them upon seeing this enormous fish, but she began now to work her spells, the terrible Greek spells that she had learned at her mother's knee, and she prayed to Artemis that a fishbone might become lodged in the slender throat of her beautiful sister and choke her to death. She *willed* it to happen.

But Lysandra had by chance divined the way things might go with her sister, her poisonous sister, and she had worked beforehand the spell that makes any spell bounce back upon the one who works it, so that whatever Arsinoë Beta wished upon Lysandra she wished upon herself.

At any rate, it was Lysandra who showed every sign of health, and Arsinoë Beta who began to fall ill rather more often than was normal, so that her suspicions were woken up, and perhaps it was because of her mysterious illness, her strange almost daily vomitings, her strange troubles with the operation of her stomach, that this woman became now very like the snake for poison.

Lysimakhos still gave this wife almost daily jewels and gold, but his most frequent gift was the gift of golden snakes, for it so happened that the snake made a perfect twining ornament for a woman's finger, for her ankles, and for her upper arms, and for the girdle round her waist, so that the flesh of Arsinoë Beta was, by chance, decorated most often with some snake or other. It was not, indeed, an unfitting attribute for this woman, who had it in her, when roused, to spit fire like the cobra of the Egyptians; a woman who had, indeed, as Queen, the power to remove the breath of a man from his nostrils with one word, or even by the wave of her jewelled hand.

She did not know it herself, to be sure, but the days were coming when this woman, this Arsinoë Beta, would have the delight and pleasure even of wearing the snake *upon her brow.*

3.15

Arsinoë Overheats

In the twentieth year of the reign of King Ptolemy Soter the second stage of the great Pharos was declared to be complete, with the finishing of the octagonal storey that sat upon the massive square base, and it was all of white nummulitic limestone that glittered in the sun with a great shining, like the Sun god himself, like Ra of the Egyptians.

Ptolemy ordered the proper celebrations so that the gods were appeased, and should not be made jealous by his monument: the sacrifice of one hundred cattle with gilded horns, public banquets in honour of Poseidon, Lord of the Angry Sea, and Zeus, Father of Gods and Men. All Alexandria applauded as Ptolemy himself condescended to set his golden sandal upon the spiral stair and climb up inside the Lighthouse so that he could look at the progress, and urge on the workers, and so that he might see the wonder of the view of his capital city. He looked, and he saw, and he marvelled, and he was well satisfied.

Ptolemy congratulated himself: no monarch had ever dreamed of any thing upon such a grand scale before, not even Alexander. No man had ever put up a building that would be so useful.

Without boasting, Ptolemy wrote in his own hand the news about the Pharos so that his daughters living in foreign lands might know of it and, knowing, be proud of their father and of Alexandria his city that they would, to be sure, none of them ever see again. And when Theoxena in Sicily read her father's words, she wrote back to him at once to praise his wonderful works. Likewise Lysandra the wife of Agathokles. But Arsinoë Beta—she screwed up the papyrus from her father, for that she could not bear to read of the happiness of her family left at home, and she threw it into the brazier, unread.

For Arsinoë Beta, the trouble was not yet over. Indeed, her troubles had hardly begun.

As Lysimakhos aged still further, it was his wife, bothered by her health though she was, who now made the most important decisions about Thrace. Nobody doubted the abilities of Arsinoë Beta, or raised so much as one question about her wise judgement, for she was always proved to be in the right.

The bringing up of her three sons she undertook herself, and only with reluctance entrusted their education to the best of Greek tutors. She by no means lacked motherly instincts, and although men would complain of her cold, hard heart, she found it in her to be warm where her sons were concerned, but not too warm. And yet, where the Prince Agathokles was concerned this supposedly iron heart would melt away altogether, and she became, yes, white-hot with desire for him. That heart of iron, that heart cold as a stone—was it not perhaps a myth, a pretence, a way of getting for herself even more power and influence than she had already, for, to be sure, in the man's world that was the Kingdom of Thrace she needs must be tough.

For years Arsinoë Beta had done nothing about her lust for Agathokles, merely nursing it, or suppressing it, too scared of what might become of her if she was found out. But as the time passed and the time passed, Arsinoë Beta's behaviour changed. She had gone to Thrace when she was but a girl of fifteen years. She was still only twenty or twenty-one years old when Lysandra arrived at court, but now she grew in confidence.

As Lysimakhos grew ever older and older, he came less often by night to the bedchamber of this wife of his, and she longed more than ever for the embrace of the young Agathokles, who was more nearly her equal in years.

Arsinoë Beta thought long and hard. What could she do? Would she pass her whole life time having done nothing about this love of hers, this great love? As she grew older herself, she began to think that Agathokles might be persuaded to return her feelings for him, and this thought so bothered her waking hours that the time came when she felt that really she had nothing to lose, for that if she did not soon tell Agathokles what she felt for him, she must surely die from the pain of her impossible love.

She also began to think that when Lysimakhos died, Agathokles, as the new King, might very well send her away from Thrace. She feared that he would surely murder her three sons, who posed such a threat to his stability as possible usurpers of his throne, and she had not brought them up to be soft, but hard, hard like she tried to be herself: boys who would be men, great warriors, generals, if not kings in their own right. She saw that if Agathokles was ever to make her his wife and her eldest son his heir, she must act without delay.

First, she began to make sure that she crossed paths with Agathokles more often.

Next, she started to make improper suggestions, offering to kiss this Agathokles upon the lips, saying that she would very much like to place her tongue inside his mouth, for that she was tired of her old, cold husband.

Agathokles was surprised, but he smiled his devastating smile that made Arsinoë Beta feel faint, as if not only her heart but her knees also were melting, and he said he would rather not kiss her.

When Arsinoë Beta forgot herself so far as to lift the skirts of her *peplos* and show Agathokles her *bolba*, like the women of Memphis on the inauguration of the new Apis bull, he turned upon his heel and walked away from her without saying a word. The behaviour of Queen Arsinoë was, then, very like that of a whore, and she was all the time the Queen of Thrace. All her lewd suggestions, however, Agathokles rejected, in the politest manner, saying that he really had no thought to make a concubine of his stepmother.

Every time Arsinoë Beta set her eyes upon this Prince she felt faint, and ill. At night she would lie awake for hours in her bed of beaten gold, thinking of Agathokles and his golden flesh. When she did sleep, her dream was full of the naked flesh of Agathokles, who would kiss her upon the lips, and fit his tongue inside her mouth, and thrust his *rhombos* into her private place, and do every thing that he had refused to do by day.

Her dream was full also of the figure of her half-sister Lysandra, who was always dead, always being carried away upon her bier in procession to her funeral pyre, and always the face of Lysandra was eaten up in flames. Then Arsinoë saw the marriage rites of herself and Agathokles, the pair of them crowned with crimson flowers, and as they passed, hand in hand, smiling, through the great cedar doors of the palace the citizens of Lysimakheia flung figs and nuts that cut like knives and were heavy like rocks, that bruised her flesh and made her bleed, and then she would wake herself up with her wailing.

For seven years, or eighty-four months, or two thousand five hundred and fifty-five days and nights Arsinoë Beta lusted after this young man, her stepson and brother-in-law, without telling him that she loved him. Now, at last, she began to do every thing in her power to make him climb into her high bed and take his pleasure with her, when all the time he was married to her own sister.

At about this time, as if the tale of these two Houses was not complicated enough already, Ptolemy Soter took it into his head to make his great friendship and alliance with Lysimakhos of Thrace stronger still by a third marriage, and he put forward the proposal, through the usual ambassadors, that his younger son, the Prince Ptolemy Mikros, now aged nineteen or twenty years, might be pleased to take as his wife Lysimakhos's daughter Arsinoë, who was called always Arsinoë Alpha to distinguish her from Arsinoë Beta, who was, of course, still Lysimakhos's queen.

The Arsinoë in question was, of course, Lysimakhos's daughter by his first wife, Nikaia, and she was now perhaps sixteen years of age, the elegant and beautiful sister of the handsome Agathokles, and ripe for marriage, with her two breasts, as her father noted, swelling like two ripe arbutus berries, and large, so that if Ptolemy Mikros was anything like Ptolemy his father he would be more than satisfied.

Thoughts of Thoth: As a result of this marriage Arsinoë Beta would become the mother-in-law, or stepmother-in-law, of her own full brother, although they would live at different courts, in different countries, and never set eyes upon each other; but nobody in Thrace or Egypt gave a second thought to any of that, because the families of all the Successors who had turned themselves into kings were so intermarried and so convoluted that by the end of it all no man but Thoth would be able to untangle the branches of the genealogical trees, and it would be utterly impossible even for the god to work out the relationships between them.

However, by journeying to Egypt the Princess Arsinoë Alpha would make her escape from the claustrophobic atmosphere of the *gynaikeion* at Lysimakheia, and get away from having to live year upon year upon year with the ill temper of Arsinoë Beta her stepmother. So that Arsinoë Alpha was more than willing to be the wife of Ptolemy Mikros. Indeed, she begged her father to let her go to live in Egypt, for that she had heard from Arsinoë Beta herself that Mikros was indeed kind, generous, good-tempered, level-headed, handsome, wealthy beyond any woman's dreams and young, and Arsinoë Beta, in a moment of truth, told her that to be married to a young husband like that was the dream of every woman, and Arsinoë Alpha saw, then, just what a torment it must be for her stepmother to be wedded to the old man who was Lysimakhos.

Arsinoë Alpha sailed away then, upon her swift-sailing *trieres,* to Alexandria, and was married with the greatest pomp and ceremony, because her husband was the son of the richest man in the world; and the other Arsinoë stayed, of course, on the other side of the Great Sea, so that, as it were, each nation held an Arsinoë hostage, as earnest of the good behaviour of the other nation, and all parties were happy with this arrangement:

Arsinoë Alpha was happy because she had escaped from Arsinoë Beta.

Arsinoë Beta was happy because she had got rid of the second of Lysimakhos's two daughters.

Lysimakhos was happy because he had made still firmer his alliance with Egypt.

Ptolemy Soter was happy because he had in sight the next generation of his Dynasty.

And Mikros was happy because his wife was guaranteed to be fair of face, even of temper, full in the breasts and well-rounded in the hinder parts—*kallipygous,* as Mikros liked to say, which was how he liked his women to be.

The only party who did not show pleasure was Ptolemy Keraunos, the eldest legitimate son of his father, who had not yet been married to a wife, and who, although he must have been all of thirty-two years of age, had as yet begotten no heir, of his body, who might be seen as the third generation of the House of Ptolemy, but had sired nothing but bastards upon the whores of the city of Alexandria—some of whom were not white of skin but *black.*

Of Arsinoë Alpha the ambassadors reported: *In face she is like the goddesses,* and Ptolemy Mikros was not disappointed, as he had taken care to write to his sister and make her promise by Zeus and Pan and Poseidon together that Arsinoë Alpha was indeed the beautiful woman that the reports said she was.

With this wife of Mikros there came to Egypt also, as part of her dowry, a goodwill gift from Lysimakhos to Ptolemy Soter, and it was caged up in a wooden crate and secured with iron chains, and had to be manhandled with the utmost care; and when Ptolemy Soter had the crate opened, he found that inside it there was a white bear for his

Beast Garden, a creature so very rare that it was supposed to be the only example of its kind in the world, and thus a most proper gift for the King of Egypt.

It was Ptolemy Mikros, however, who took the greatest delight in this present, for he was delighted by any beast that was out of the ordinary run of things—by the exotic, by the bizarre—and for a while he would go every day to visit this beast, in order to listen to his shouting, and he valued the white bear, if the truth were told, almost as highly as he valued his wife.

At the beginning of this marriage every thing was well, and the Princess Arsinoë Alpha was within the year heavy with child. She passed her first months in Egypt delighted by every new thing, delighted by her husband, and relieved not to have all of her life controlled by Arsinoë Beta, her stepmother. She was not troubled by the heat, or by the storm of sand, or by the clacking of the palm trees. She got on very well with Eurydike, and even with Berenike her mother-in-law also, and she passed happy days in the *gynaikeion* with Eurydike, for she too delighted to spit the stones of olives out of the windows on to the heads of the passers-by below, a thing that Arsinoë Beta had *never* allowed in Thrace.

Sure, Arsinoë Alpha enjoyed also a mild neglect in Egypt, but she had not, in truth, expected anything very different. She was pleased, in fact, for once, to be left alone, to be ignored, for she had suffered in silence the browbeating and abuse of Arsinoë Beta for many years, and now, thanks to some miracle of the gods, she had managed to get away from her, and she said, *Truly, it is like being free from a prison.* She did not, of course, say such things to Berenike, who was Arsinoë Beta's mother, but only to Eurydike, who laughed her mad laugh to hear it.

Arsinoë Alpha busied herself in Egypt with women's things: tapestry, weaving, sewing. Not having had the luxury of a man's education, she did not pass her hours at her husband's side, giving him advice about military matters, which were a mystery to her. And as she had not been given the delight and pleasure of learning the *alpha beta* she could not read the messages that her husband sent to her. She would not be *useful* to this husband of hers in any respect but the upbringing of her children, but Mikros wanted nothing more of this wife than that, and Mikros was happy, more than happy.

Meanwhile, Arsinoë Alpha cultivated the gods of Greece, in order that she might have the best of Good Luck, and so that she might give birth to a fine boy, who would be lucky also, and who might even be lucky enough to be King of Egypt.

Arsinoë Alpha knew perhaps better than any other person in Egypt the true character of Arsinoë Beta. She had put up with four thousand three hundred and eighty days of that woman's iron will and evil temper, living even in the same apartments, in the same room with her, and she thought of the other Arsinoë, if the truth were told, with very much the same horror as she thought of snakes.

For Arsinoë Alpha, Arsinoë Beta was the Snake Queen, and she was happy, very very happy, to think that she would *never* see this horrible woman ever again.

3.16

The Caged Bird

After eight years of Theoxena's perfect Sicilian marriage had passed by, it was her calculation that there must be only one thousand four hundred and sixty days of it left to run, but she felt no sign of ill health in herself, and she saw no suggestion of any ailment in the person of her husband the Tyrant, who continued affectionate, generous, and pleased with every thing that Theoxena did. Her two sons were now seven and six years old, and Theoxena saw to it that they learned their letters and did not dream away the lessons in mathematics, so that Arkhagathos and Agatharkhos might be worthy tyrants in their father's stead.

If Theoxena flourished, in spite of her looming fate, what of Ptolemaïs, who had now been waiting eight years for Demetrios Poliorketes to come and fetch her away to be married, and who had no sons to comfort her in her old age? Ptolemaïs had now sewed more garments for this man than he could wear out in all the rest of his life time—tunics edged with gold thread, for example, by the dozen; but now she toiled at a great web of purple cloth that would be a double cloak for Demetrios.

From time to time Ptolemaïs would send these things off to Demetrios as gifts, hoping to remind him of her existence, and to make him think of his obligation to her, but even the purple cloak embroidered with the signs of the Zodiac, the Sun, Moon and stars, that took her six years of sewing, did not make Demetrios Poliorketes name the date of his wedding day to Ptolemaïs.

In the meantime Ptolemaïs occupied herself playing the lyre, but her tunes were sad tunes, because in her heart of hearts she feared that Demetrios would never summon her to be his bride, but that she was fated to stay a maiden for ever.

She sent her questions to every oracle in the Greek world, including the great Oracle of Zeus-Ammon in Libya, but they all sent back to her the same answer: that her future was bad, very bad indeed, but without telling her *why*.

Eurydike, the mother of Ptolemaïs, she was not much happier than her daughter. Some afternoons the heat of Memphis was so intense, and the air so stifling, and so heavy with the stink of death blowing through the windows from the *nekropolis* of mummified baboons and ibises, that Eurydike would tear off her *peplos* and girdle and run about the *gynaikeion* naked, screaming all manner of rubbish about Ptolemy her husband whom she never saw, but mostly hate, hate, hate, because she could not cool down, and it was all of it Ptolemy's fault.

At the best of times Eurydike was still pleased to slam doors and smash crockery upon the mosaic floors for no very good reason.

Some days she would shout abuse at her black slaves, who understood not a word of her Greek, but thought her possessed by some evil spirit.

Eurydike lived this strange, idle life, with no useful thing to occupy her time. *What is Eurydike for?* she asked herself, but the answer was that she had no purpose. She had borne her children. She did not read. She did not write letters.

Eurydike's inner passion was for Ptolemy, the husband who never came near her, whom she thought she loved, now that she had lost him.

Eurydike would have liked also to be loved by her children, but she had screamed at them once too often, so that they were wary of her temper, and thought her a little crazy.

She wanted now above all things to be in Greece—in Macedon, at Pella. She said openly that she had never wished to go to Egypt in the first place, and now she was trapped, a prisoner, a caged bird longing to be set free. Eurydike was her husband's prisoner. Yes, the one thing she needed now was to be set free, to live her own life in her own way, for to be sure Ptolemy did not need her any longer.

Some days Eurydike would be found weeping. But at length she thought to petition Ptolemy to be allowed to leave Egypt and take up her residence in some city of Ionia—Miletos, perhaps—where the heat was less fierce; where she would not be frightened by snakes and scorpions; where she might walk in the streets without arousing the disapproval of anybody; where she might look out of the windows without being called a whore.

And Ptolemy—Ptolemy might have agreed to let her go, for in truth he wished his wife no ill, and to be sure she was of no use to him in Egypt.

But Eurydike was afraid to ask. She was afraid of the unknown. She was afraid of the future. And so, for the time being, Eurydike stayed where she was, and carried on dripping in the heat as before.

3.17

The Jaws of the Tyrant

When the eleventh anniversary of Theoxena's perfect marriage arrived, she knew that there must be only three hundred and sixty-five days left of happiness, and she began to panic, making prayers and sacrifices to every god, but all the time not knowing what it might be that would bring her happy life in Sicily to an end.

But it was in this twelfth year that the aged Tyrant, her husband, began to suffer pain in the jaws, and he was led even to seek the opinion of his physicians, men he did not trust, for fear that they might give him poison, though in truth Agathokles did not trust any man. Because of this it fell to Theoxena herself, the devoted wife, to bring to Agathokles the remedies that his medical men recommended, and to mix them with her own hand, because Agathokles trusted no one else to do it, and be the taster of his medicine, to prove to him that there was no risk of poisoning.

After eleven years and one month, when she had three hundred and thirty days left, Theoxena talked Agathokles into making trial of the whale's-flesh dentifrice.

After eleven years and two months, with three hundred days left, she made him scrape his gums with the ray of a sting-ray, that was supposed to be beneficial.

After eleven years and three months, with two hundred and seventy days left, she brought whole frogs to tie upon his jaws as a talisman.

When Theoxena saw that her marriage had lasted eleven years and six months and that there were but one hundred and eighty days left for it to run, she poured spiders beaten up in rose-oil into her husband's ears.

None of these remedies had the slightest effect, but Agathokles complained now of a terrible grinding pain in his jawbones.

He sought more desperate cures, going even so far as to pass a month of nights in the Temple of Asklepios, god of Health, in the hope of some miracle; but Asklepios was not listening to the Tyrant of Syracuse.

When only sixty days remained, Theoxena poured into her husband's ears earthworms boiled in oil.

With thirty days left, she had given the Tyrant every known remedy for pain in the jaws, but the pain was, if anything, worse. Agathokles slept not by night for pain, and in the silence of the dead hours his groaning could be heard in all parts of the Citadel of Euryalos.

When Theoxena found herself alone she would weep, because she knew now and at last what was going to happen, and because she did not know how she might further help her husband. Fourteen days before the twelfth anniversary of the marriage Agathokles's physicians spread their hands and murmured that there was nothing more that could be done for the Tyrant of Syracuse, for that he was shortly going to die.

Theoxena had loved this Tyrant of hers almost to distraction, this cruel Agathokles, who was kind enough to her but whose pleasure it had always been to punish a man by the slaughter of his entire kindred, and who had liked to exact reckoning from a city by the massacre of its entire population, from the youths upwards. Theoxena loved this man for himself, and turned a blind eye to his dark side, just as she turned a blind eye to the Sicilian boys who were visitors to his apartments, the hot boys like Erotes, who did things with her husband that no wife could do, or ever dreamed of—boys whose eyes sparkled like the stars, and whose olive skin was soft as peaches.

Theoxena had borne this man two handsome sons, who were not, alas, fated to succeed him as Tyrant. She had loved the Citadel that was her home. She had relished the life of a tyrant's wife, with jewels and gold and every costly stone, and slaves and foot-boys and every luxurious thing she could think of asking for, and her every wish granted upon the instant.

But the eldest son and grandson of Agathokles were already quarrelling over who should be Tyrant in his place, and both of them laid claim to the rightful succession, as if the old man was already dead.

Some supposed Agathokles to be the victim of a slow-acting poison; others imagined his trouble to be a cancer of the jaw. Whatever it was that was wrong with this man, he found now no relief from his agony, but lay day after day upon his bed of beaten gold, with a cloth jammed between his teeth, groaning.

Agathokles was dying, and he knew it, but he did not know what would become of Syracuse after he went down to Hades, and he had the gravest fears for Theoxena and her children in the upheaval that must surely follow his death. He had lived by indiscriminate killing, punishing the many for the crime of one, and he had made himself very many enemies, from whom his family, he thought, would receive no mercy. Agathokles was sure that the moment he breathed his last breath Theoxena and her sons would be put to the sword.

He took then the decision to send Theoxena with her children and all of his treasure, more magnificent than that of any king (apart from Ptolemy), home to her father in Egypt, where she would be safe.

Theoxena continued to nurse Agathokles as before, but she begged not to be separated from the man she loved. She said that in marrying him she had undertaken not only to share his good fortune but his ill fortune also; she had hoped, she said, when the time came, to perform with affection the last offices at his funeral, which only a wife could do, and which, she was sure, nobody else would trouble to perform for him if she went away.

Agathokles knew, however, that whatever man succeeded him would turn out to be the bitter enemy of his wife, and he shouted at her, and struck out at her with his fists, and threw what things he could lay his hands on in his sick-bed—pillows, plates, drinking-cups, his golden walking-sticks—saying that she must escape while she could.

Theoxena wailed, then, *What will become of the corn supply of Egypt, if I am to be sent home?*

But Agathokles said only, *If you value your life, you must obey our wishes without question.*

Theoxena prayed next to Athene, daughter of Zeus, that she might still save Agathokles from Hades, but the goddess did not answer her prayers, and so Theoxena made herself ready for sailing.

Twelve years *to the day*, after the Princess Theoxena first set eyes upon Agathokles, Tyrant of Syracuse, her marriage, as had been foretold by every oracle in the Greek world, came to an end.

She left the island with many tears. Her sons wept for their dying father, and the father wept for his banished sons, boys whose future would be, even in Egypt, uncertain in the extreme.

Her *trieres* was rowed out of the harbour, with the oarsmen humming the tunes that made them row in time with each other. Theoxena did not know what she would do—not then or ever—without the husband whom she loved, and she felt as if the heart had snapped in two within her breast, and she lifted up her voice in wailing.

Not long after Theoxena came home to Alexandria the news reached her of the death of the Tyrant of Syracuse, as they said, from the *gomphalgia,* or toothache, and Sicily was invaded by Carthage, and every thing there fell into the greatest confusion.

Agathokles was seventy-two years of age at his death; Theoxena the widow, who must go on living, was just twenty-eight.

Yes, the Princess Theoxena had quit Alexandria twelve years previous with trumpets blaring, and garlanded with roses. She had known that her marriage might be short, but to be returned to her father even with his dowry repaid in full and much increased—it was still a disgrace, and just about the worst thing that might happen to any woman. The failure of her marriage was, to be sure, not the fault of Theoxena, but she blamed herself, and she railed also at Tykhe, goddess of Luck, in particular. *Fickle Tykhe,* she thought, raging against her fate, and she wept for days upon end, so that her waiting-women feared she must be as mad as her mother.

King Ptolemy welcomed this daughter into his Residence, but to have her back was, in truth, not convenient. He had thought Theoxena would not be seen or heard of more, and he had no fresh husband ready to whom she might be married. A second-hand wife was always more trouble to dispose of than a first-time wife, even a wife who was the daughter of a king; even a wife who was still only twenty-eight years of age.

But no, everything had changed in Alexandria since Theoxena left home, because for ever after the ousting of her mother from the Pharaoh's bed, he had been pleased to ignore her children as much as he could.

Twelve years had gone by, and there were new faces in the Residence, women who did not know the Princess Theoxena, who were polite enough to give voice to their sympathy for her, but to whom she was a stranger, an incomer with the different habits of life of a Tyrantessa of Syracuse, for that she expected people to do things for her as soon as she asked, and she had a taste now for strange and exotic foodstuffs, and they did not understand her distress over the loss of such an aged husband—a man with such a curious reputation—but thought that Theoxena was more than a little crazy.

The question, then, was upon everybody's lips: *What will become of Theoxena? What man can Theoxena marry?* And there was the further problem of what to do with her two young boys in a family that had in it already too many males for comfort, every one of them thinking about the succession to the throne of Egypt; every one of them aware that the moment Ptolemy Soter was dead, his heir, whoever he might be, must put to the sword every one of his male relations, because that was the only way the heir to any throne might survive; that it was a matter of *murder or be murdered.*

Such was the charming custom of the Greeks.

For the moment, then, Theoxena felt insecure, and her position and her future were uncertain and Ptolemy did not know what he should best do with her.

He could not, in any case, do any thing until Theoxena's tears dried up, and for the moment Theoxena carried on weeping.

3.18

_____

The Four Thousand Seven Hundred and Forty-five Nights

Far from securing his treaty of peace with Demetrios Poliorketes, in the seventeenth year of his reign and the seventy-ninth year of his age, Ptolemy Soter was once again obliged to go to war with his future son-in-law. It was in this same year that Ptolemy and his allies, Old Seleukos of Syria, and Old Lysimakhos of Thrace, launched their expedition against Asia, and it was a massive campaign, greater than anything mounted since the time of Alexander.

As the fleets made ready to sail, these three kings formed their alliance *against* Demetrios, and sent messengers to the exiled Pyrrhos of Epeiros, who wanted to get back the empire once ruled by his father, urging him to attack Macedon as a decoy manoeuvre, so that Demetrios would have to fight battles on several fronts at once, and before he was ready to fight anybody—for although Demetrios had laid the keels of five hundred most modern ships of war, not one ship was ready to be put into the water.

Even so, later that year Demetrios launched his *hekkaidekeres,* or sixteen, a giant of a ship, which he boasted was the biggest oared galley ever built.

Ptolemy now sailed in person for Greece with his fleet, and he took most of his family with him—Ptolemy Keraunos, aged thirty-two, Ptolemy Mikros, aged twenty, who saw active service for the first time; even Berenike and the girls who were still at home went to Greece, and the grandchildren also, in accordance with the thought of Plato, that it is a goodly thing for children to see war. War was, for this family, a family affair. And Ptolemy even jested that war was his family business, for that now he was going to fight against the man who was meant to be his son-in-law, and who was then married to Phila, who was the sister of Ptolemy's wife, Eurydike.

And so, Thoth asks it: What happened? Lysimakhos invaded Macedonia, marching across the border from Thrace; Pyrrhos invaded Macedonia, marching across the border from Epeiros, and both armies laid waste the countryside, burning field after field of ripe wheat as they went, so that every man's dwelling-house was in flames, and a great cloud of black smoke hung over the land, for Macedon was on fire from end to end.

Demetrios, alarmed, left his thirty-year-old son, Antigonos Gonatas, or Knee-Cap, in charge of Greece and hurried back to march against Lysimakhos and so relieve Macedonia. On his way a messenger brought him word that Pyrrhos had taken the city of Verroia, and the news of this great disaster spread through the Macedonian ranks with such devastating effect that, to a man, they sat down upon the ground, head in hand, and wept. When they recovered themselves a little they began to sing rebellious chants against Demetrios their commander, so that he utterly lost control of his army, for the men refused to stay with him one hour more, turned round, said they were going home, and deserted, every one of them, to the camp of Lysimakhos.

Demetrios saw that his troops had no further need of his services. What did he do? He was not dismayed. He simply took off his diadem of kingship and his royal robes—the cloak of purple and gold that was the work of Ptolemaïs, the buskins of purple felt—and he put on instead a plain cloak of coarse grey cloth and the laced boots of a common soldier. He muddied his face and slipped away from the military camp, leaving all the showy gear of a king behind him, much as an actor who has played the part of a king will take off his costume at the end of the drama.

For Demetrios, indeed, the drama was almost over.

He now took refuge in the city of Kassandreia in the Thracian Khersonesos, not far from Pella, where his wife Phila, daughter of Antipatros and sister of Eurydike, found herself unable to bear the thought of her famous husband reduced to the state of a private citizen, no longer a king, a hero, or a god, and herself, alas, no longer a queen, and she swallowed poison and died, with horrible convulsions, vomiting up her intestines in a disgusting manner.

And Demetrios? Demetrios shrugged his shoulders. He had more urgent affairs to attend to than funeral rites. There were other women in the world. Most Greeks had little feeling for their wives. Perhaps, now, he thought, he might marry the rich rich rich Ptolemaïs, daughter of Ptolemy. At all events, he now announced that he was fed up with fighting just to increase his power and luxurious way of life, and he joined the camp of his enemy, Pyrrhos of Epeiros, that *Ginger* whose wife was, of course, Antigone, daughter of Queen Berenike of Egypt.

Not long after this, Demetrios Poliorketes set his face towards the city of Miletos. He was short of a wife, short of a kingdom and short of money, and it might suit him now, he thought, to make peace with Ptolemy and seal it by marrying his daughter. Yes, Demetrios put his reed pen to the papyrus and named the day for the marriage, thus bringing to an end the betrothal of Ptolemaïs that was the longest betrothal in the history of the world.

Ptolemaïs was now thirty-three years of age. She had passed much of the four thousand seven hundred and forty-five days of her betrothal in the embroidery of the largest tapestry anybody in Alexandria had ever set eyes upon, and it was the panorama of the Life and Adventures of Demetrios, Besieger of Cities, leaving out only his defeat, or *misfortune*, at the hands of Ptolemy her father, and the misfortune of Ptolemy at the hands of Demetrios at Salamis in Cyprus, and it was to be her wedding-gift to this husband, this much delayed husband, of hers.

Ptolemaïs had waited very many days, and when the papyrus was read to her by her father she jumped for joy and lost control of herself in screaming. When she came to her senses, Ptolemaïs sent, as was her frequent habit, to the Oracle of Zeus-Ammon in Libya, to find out if her future was still bad, very bad. And she was relieved to hear that the Oracle said she would be the happiest of women, and the mother of the handsomest boy that ever lived. Ptolemaïs was seen to laugh, and it was the first time in thirteen years.

Yes, Ptolemaïs went about smiling, in spite of the fact that this husband-to-be of hers was a king with no kingdom, and had lost his every last personal possession, every thing he owned, and had not so much as a roof over his head, and in spite of the fact that he was stuck at Miletos without even the means to sail to Alexandria, and would not, in any case, go there, lest Ptolemy went back upon his word, so that Ptolemaïs must journey across the Great Sea to be married, just like the rest of her sisters.

But no, Ptolemaïs cared nothing for these drawbacks. She had riches in her own right. She had the substantial dowry of a daughter of King Ptolemy. She was slave-rich, jewel-rich, dekadrachm-rich, one of the richest women in the world, and she would go anywhere to marry her Demetrios.

Alas, what the Oracle of Zeus-Ammon did not tell Ptolemaïs was that it was her fate to be the happiest of women *for one month only.* And Ptolemaïs, who had achieved the doubtful honour of setting the record for the longest betrothal of all time, was fated to hold (for a short while, at least) also the record for the shortest marriage.

Everybody said Ptolemaïs had been patient beyond all good reason. A lesser woman might have abandoned her hopes and asked to be married to some other man. But Ptolemaïs had said all along, *Demetrios Poliorketes is the only man I can marry.*

At last, then, this overgrown girl was able to dedicate her earthenware dolls with movable limbs fixed on by wires, in the Temple of Artemis upon Kanopic Street, together with their wardrobe of moth-eaten *peploi*. At last she left her long-finished childhood behind her. At last she was able to hold up her head, and for the first time since anybody could remember, she passed an entire day without shedding tears.

Eurydike and Ptolemaïs sailed in due course for Miletos, where the mother ordered thousands of pink roses and thousands of white narcissi for the marriage ritual, because Ptolemaïs was, after all, a king's daughter, and could not be married without the proper show of extravagance.

When Demetrios Poliorketes at last showed his face, and Ptolemaïs held his right hand in the *dexiosis* of the Greeks, she said to him, *There are, in point of fact, four thousand seven hundred and forty-five white narcissi and four thousand seven hundred and forty-five pink roses—one narcissus and one rose for every wasted day and every lonely night of my waiting for you . . .*

And Demetrios, overpowered by the stink of the flowers, had the good grace to say that he was sorry for her trouble, sorry that he had made her sad, sorry that he was thirteen years late; but Ptolemaïs said she forgave him for it all the same, that it had been worth the wait.

For she was delighted to see that her husband was still young, that he was still not quite fifty years of age. She was relieved to find that her marriage would be held at all, after this man's running after so very many other women, and, making up for time lost, she was relieved also to learn that she was got with child upon her wedding night, for she had been afraid, very afraid, that it would soon have been too late for her to bear a child by any man.

The Besieger had been thirty-seven years old at his betrothal, with his hair the colour of pale flames, and his body very like the famous statue of Hermes by Praxiteles, so handsome that both men and women had followed him down the street. Now he was going grey at the temples. His face was grooved deep with the lines of worry, and his flesh bore the livid scars of many battles, but only upon the front side, for he was a man who never in all his life time turned his back upon an enemy, but was brave—brave as Herakles, brave as Achilles—and the crowd of Greeks who followed him was only a little smaller now than it had been during the years of his great fame.

As for Ptolemaïs, she bore small resemblance to the girl of nineteen who had been described to Demetrios by her father's ambassadors thirteen years before. Her spirits had been quite used up by her endless waiting. Once praised for her calmness, Ptolemaïs was now more likely to show ill temper, and there were hot days when she showed a little of the craziness of Eurydike, her mother. Now, however, Ptolemaïs might begin to be a *wife*.

Demetrios and Ptolemaïs enjoyed, indeed, just thirty days of their married life, when the husband said one morning that he must return to his work, his unending war, because of his most pressing need to get back, if he could, his rightful kingdom of Macedon, and to feed his unceasing urge to spill the blood of men. As he left her, the tears fell once again out of the eyes of Ptolemaïs, because she did not know when, or if, this most perfect of husbands might return to her. But she held up her head. She did not bite the nails of her fingers, and her stomach grew daily stouter with the son and heir of the Besieger of Cities.

Nine months after this marriage—eight months of which were passed in her customary aloneness—Ptolemaïs was brought to bed of the son who would be famous for all time as Demetrios Ho Kalos— Beautiful Demetrios, the most beautiful man that ever lived. It was, alas, the fate of this boy to come to the most unfortunate end, and his beginning was not so wonderful either, for he never did set his eyes upon the face of the man who was his father.

The army of Demetrios Poliorketes just then numbered eleven thousand foot soldiers and an unspecified number of horse, and it was indeed remarkable that this man should stage his comeback from nothing and take once more his part in the great drama of public events. But although he gave, as always, of his best efforts, Demetrios was trapped in Kilikia within a twelvemonth and forced to surrender to Old Seleukos, the King of Syria.

Seleukos, they said, caged Demetrios up in a wicker cage like some wild beast, and although he some times allowed Demetrios his freedom to go hunting, under strong guard, he also gave him his freedom to drink as much wine as he pleased. In fact Seleukos gave this prisoner of his so much wine, and such very generous hospitality, that within two years the Besieger of Cities, still in his cage, and groaning, indeed, very like an animal, drank himself to death.

Demetrios was then in the fifty-fifth year of his age. His remains were sent home to his grief-stricken son, Antigonos, called Gonatas, who gave them most honourable burial, for his father was a very great man, a very great general, and the loss of his life was a terrible blow to Macedon.

Ptolemaïs had, perhaps, waited long enough for this man of hers, but now, having gotten herself married to him, she found herself waiting some more. No word was sent to Ptolemaïs from the Syrian Khersonesos about her husband, or the state of his health, or about the possibility of his release from captivity. Not one word came to Ptolemaïs about Demetrios until the news reached her that he was a dead man.

When they told Ptolemaïs, she tore her clothes and beat her breasts with her clenched fists, and she smeared upon her body the black mud of Miletos and sprinkled dust and ashes upon her head, and howled, as every Greek widow must howl. Unlike the grief of so many Greek wives, however, which was pretend grief, because they had never known the Arrows of Eros the Boy, Ptolemaïs's grief was real grief, because her love was real love, and the pent-up feelings of thirteen years of waiting for this man came flooding out, and she railed and raged and screamed and broke up the furniture, and she did not know where to put herself, or what she should do, but thought only that she would have to die.

Her waiting-women embraced her in tears, saying, *Let him not lie too heavy upon thy soul . . . Take not too much thought for him . . .*

But Ptolemaïs could not but take a great deal of thought for this man, for whom she had passed nearly half her life time in waiting. She felt as though the heart had been eaten out of her breast, and the tears never stopped falling for forty days, as if she was going to break the record not only for the longest betrothal and the shortest marriage, but also the record for the most days of non-stop weeping.

The waiting-gentlewomen, fearing for her mind, told her, *We shall find you a fresh husband,* but Ptolemaïs shook her head. She had no wish for any other man but Poliorketes. There was ever but one man in her thoughts, and there was not room for any other. No, the sweet, calm nature, the hot, firm flesh of her Besieger could never be replaced.

To be sure, the offers of marriage came to Ptolemaïs by the score, but she turned down her every suitor, saying that she had had enough of the fickle ways of men, and she put on the black *peplos* of an old woman, although she was only thirty-five or thirty-six years of age.

The truth of the matter was that Ptolemaïs was more than satisfied with the ghost of Demetrios Poliorketes, who now began to make his appearance in her bedchamber during the dead hours of the night.

No other woman set eyes upon this phantom, but Ptolemaïs swore always that her late husband was in the habit of sitting upon the end of her bed, with his hair all rumpled, and his clothes all bloody and torn, and his flesh so thin that the bones showed through, and that he smelled rather strong of liquor.

When the waiting-gentlewomen heard Ptolemaïs speak of her ghost, they shivered down the spine, and offered extra prayers to the gods of Hellas, and sent the physicians to talk to her. But Ptolemaïs was quite insistent, saying that Demetrios liked to kiss her, just as he had always done, with his tongue stuck inside her mouth, and he would do the other things that men so liked to do as well.

The great weight of Demetrios's flesh pressing upon her body was proof enough that she told the truth, and she had her bruises and the livid purple marks of his biting her clear upon her neck. And it was, of course, a well-known fact that any Greek man who died before his allotted span of years was done would come back to haunt the living until he reached at last the proper age at which all men are meant to die.

Ptolemaïs, then, looked forward to enjoying some twenty more years of nightly visitations from this ghost of hers, *Seven thousand three hundred nights,* as she said, and she was pleased to find that the number of nights she would enjoy his company dead was greater than the number of nights she had waited for him living.

By day Ptolemaïs was given to strange outbursts of screaming. By night, however, the eyes of Ptolemaïs shone with a curious shining, and she was, yes, conscious even of a certain happiness, for that she had this ghost for her own possession, and she knew for sure that a ghost was something that nothing and nobody in the world, not even Death, not even Hades himself, could take from her, but that she had Demetrios Poliorketes with her for ever and always.

Ptolemaïs lived, then, at Miletos, with the friends of her late husband, and she urged Eurydike, her mother, to make the journey to visit her, and Eurydike would come and go between Egypt and Ionia, staying with her daughter for longer and longer periods, and it was some thing of a relief to the House of Ptolemy in Egypt that she did so.

Ptolemaïs had her ghost, who stayed by her, and nothing else but that son of hers, her only son, Demetrios Kalos. By all accounts this boy was brought up at Pella, at the court of his grandfather on the father's side—that is to say, in the house of Antigonos One-Eye, where he had the Greek education proper to a prince of Macedon. So that, Thoth presumes, when Ptolemaïs lost her wits utterly and completely (and how can she not have done?) this boy was removed from her care and control by his father's relations.

A mother, to be sure, is of little worth in the Greek world without her husband. Whatever was the fate of Ptolemaïs after that, nobody could, in later times, rightly say. Aye, the world was full, in those days, of stories that had no ending; of folk who were counted among the Disappeared. Ptolemaïs, Princess of Egypt, who had some times called herself *Basilissa,* or ex-Queen of Macedon, was one of them.

Yea, Ptolemaïs was to be remembered only as the mother of the most beautiful man in the world, whose own passing would *not* be forgotten. Perhaps Ptolemaïs might have found the fact that she was remembered at all some thing of a consolation for her utterly ruined life.

3.19

Beautiful Heart

Thoth asks now a question: Was there not, in all the marriages of the children of Ptolemy Soter, one example of happiness such as the happiness of the Egyptians? And he answers, Yes, there was for, indeed, the marriage of Ptolemy Mikros to Arsinoë Alpha was a happy marriage, very happy.

Mikros had, to be sure, married his wife sight unseen, based only upon the reports of his father's ambassadors, and upon the promise of his sister, and upon his father's orders, because this was how the Greeks did such things: there simply was no choice in the matter of a wife for this son, or for any Greek son. But every thing was well for this husband and his wife. It mattered not that Arsinoë Alpha lacked the cleverness of an Arsinoë Beta, who could manage wars, and armies of soldiers, and knew the answer to every last problem, whether foreign or domestic. No, Arsinoë Beta was thousands of *stades* away, married to some other man and, so far as Ptolemy Mikros was concerned, she was as good as dead.

No, Mikros thought not of Arsinoë Beta from one end of the year to the next, save to hear, from time to time, his wife's stories of her strange behaviour in Thrace. His sister did not write letters to Egypt. She troubled Mikros not in the slightest.

Within a few months of her marriage the Princess Arsinoë Alpha began to grow stout in the belly with a child, and the thought flashed through her heart that this son of hers might some day be the Pharaoh of Egypt, for that Ptolemy Keraunos looked to be out of favour in his father's eyes, and because she saw at once that King Ptolemy spoke more often with Mikros, having words about the books in the Great Library, and how to keep the scorpions out of the scrolls, and about the great Mouseion, and how to keep the little snakes from creeping into the scholars' bedlinen, and about the Great Lighthouse, and (despite Mikros not being interested) about the army, and the fleet of ships of war, whereas he seemed to speak to Keraunos about none of these things, and engaged Keraunos in polite conversations hardly at all.

Arsinoë Alpha grew heavier. She avoided looking upon every ugly thing, in the belief that whatever she cast her eyes upon would affect the character of her child. She had no hostility to Egyptian things, and when the High Priest of Ptah brought her the broad collar of multiple strands of beads that had three Horus heads upon it, Arsinoë Alpha was pleased to wear it, because Horus the Falcon was her protection against all the forces of evil.

The birth of Arsinoë Alpha's child took place in the Egyptian manner, with the mother kneeling upon two large bricks in a makeshift tent of greenery that was set up on the roof of the Residence at Memphis, and it was the first time things had been arranged contrary to the custom of the Greeks, because this child would be the first grandson of the Pharaoh in the direct line.

The Egyptians say that there are three kinds of birth. The normal kind they call *hotep*. The difficult kind they call *bened*. The long-drawn-out kind, with much screaming and straining, and much trouble, they call *wedef*. Arsinoë Alpha's labour was of the *wedef* kind, as if this prince did not want to see the light of day. But the midwife hastened the delivery by burning terebinth resin near the mother's stomach, and the women massaged her abdomen with saffron powder dissolved in beer, and then with marble dust dissolved in vinegar, in order to lessen her pains.

Arsinoë's child was, of course, a son, for the parents had taken every proper measure, from the tying up of the left-hand testicle of Ptolemy Mikros the father, to the gulping down of great draughts of hawk dung in honey wine, and Arsinoë had always the vulture feather under her feet as she lay in her bed.

This illustrious and most illustrious of sons was the first Ptolemy to be born since Ptolemy Soter took the Crowns of Egypt, and perhaps it was for this reason that Old Anemhor took great care to draw up with his own hand the horoscope of this boy, for the day upon which he was born must determine the entirety of his fate, and every day of his future.

Old Anemhor explained how such things worked: *A boy born upon the Ninth day of Phaophi*, he said, *he shall live to be old . . .*

A boy born upon the Twenty-third of Phaophi, he said, *he shall be eaten by the crocodile . . .*

A boy born upon the Twenty-third of Thoth, he said, *he shall not live . . .* And so forth.

But it happened that this boy was born upon the luckiest of days. Old Anemhor had himself made sure of it, counting the days backwards, and telling the parents upon what days they might and might not have their *aphrodisia*.

They called him, of course, Ptolemaios—Ptolemy. From the start Old Anemhor made certain demands that had not been made before. He insisted, for example, that the afterbirth must be preserved, saying, *It is the twin brother of the newborn child, which shall go with him throughout his life, like a ghost.*

Ptolemy Mikros, the father, pulled a face, as if to say *Disgusting*, as any Greek would do.

Old Anemhor seemed not to notice, but went on: *The Ka is a descendant of the afterbirth.*

Mikros looked happier, for he knew what was the *Ka*, the Double that every man had, the Spirit Double.

The fate of the afterbirth, Anemhor said, *it will affect the future of the child. If it is destroyed, his future will be damaged also. We must therefore keep this object with the greatest of care.*

And so they wrapped up the afterbirth in a cloth, and, as it happened, this bloody thing would be carried before him upon a standard wherever he went for the rest of his life.

Mikros complied with Old Anemhor's curious requests. In private he thought, *Obscene.* And in private he complained to King Ptolemy. *We are Hellenes,* he murmured, *not Egyptians . . . Surely they do not practise such filthy rites in Hellas?*

The Pharaoh shrugged his shoulders and smiled his half-smile. *We are all Egyptians now,* he said. *When you are among monkeys, you must do as the monkeys do,* and he showed his teeth, as if he was jesting.

The Greek custom is to burn the afterbirth upon the fire, and to observe with care the number of pops it makes as it burns, for this enables the parent to forecast the future of his child. But no, the Greeks in Egypt were no longer quite Greeks, their situation was no longer quite *normal circumstances,* and from this birth onwards the Ptolemies would do many things that were according to Egyptian manners.

From time to time Mikros would voice his fears to his father, for that what he had done was against all Greek custom, and he said that he was fearful, very fearful, of meddling with tradition. But King Ptolemy, as usual, reassured Mikros. *All will be well,* he said, *all is arranged for the best,* and he smiled, and put his arm upon the young man's shoulder to encourage him.

Thus the family of Ptolemy Soter walked a little further into the dark, where they did not know the road, and there was no turning back for them. Little by little they burned their bridges and they must go on.

This new Ptolemy, that would be called Ptolemy Euergetes, did not suffer the fate of his Uncle Thunderbolt, for his nurse was made to swear by Zeus and Poseidon to suckle this prince with her own pure and untainted milk. She swore by Zeus and Poseidon that she would take proper care of herself and of her charge. She swore never to injure her health by drinking wine or *booza.* She would impart her good character to the child together with her good milk, and she would feed him six years, after the custom of the Egyptians.

After that, when the work of this *Agathon Gala,* his Good Milk, was done, Ptolemy would be suckled by the goddesses of Egypt: by Sakhmet the Lioness, by Hathor, the Cow of Gold, and by Isis, Lady of Many Names. He would swallow not only the milk of the goddesses but divine life also.

To be sure, everything would go well for this new Ptolemy, the son of Ptolemy Mikros, the grandson of the Living Horus, Ptolemy Soter. The gods would watch over him, and he would be called Benefactor, the Giver of Goodly Gifts to Egypt.

Ptolemy Mikros and Arsinoë Alpha held the proper Greek celebrations for the birth of this son, and the future of the House of Ptolemy looked full of promise, full of every goodly thing, as the High Priest told them.

For the horoscopist said that this son would live sixty-three years, four months and three days. Indeed, every oracle these Greeks consulted, and every omen, all forecast perfection, and a glorious future.

But Thoth, that knows every thing, knows that even the perfect marriage of Mikros and Arsinoë Alpha was fated to end before its time, in disaster.

The Egyptians, on the other hand, fared better.

In the fifteenth year of King Ptolemy Soter, the grandson of Old Anemhor, Padibastet, also called Nesisty, and also Esisout, like Eskedi his father, married a wife at Memphis, and her name was called Nefersobek, which the Greeks, in their stubbornness, called Nephersouchos, and her name signified Beautiful Is the Crocodile.

For yes, this Nefersobek came even from that city called by the Greeks Krokodilopolis, for her father was the High Priest of Sobek, the crocodile god. And Nefersobek had been brought up from her earliest years to honour and adore the crocodiles who lived in the Sacred Lake there. She had with her own hands adorned the ears and ankles of the sacred beasts with bracelets and earrings of gold, and was often present at the feeding of the crocodiles with pig's flesh and the finest wines of Egypt, joining in the worship of this creature as the embodiment of the god.

In spite of living in such closeness to the Face of Fear, the character of Nefersobek did not become savage. Her temper was not wicked like the temper of the crocodile. By no means: she had the sweetest of characters. She was the most beautiful of women, and in the Temple of Ptah at Memphis it was her delight to lead the players of the *seistron,* the sacred rattle that kept away every evil spirit, for this was a most important part of the ritual of Ptah, he who is Beautiful of Face.

Nefersobek, truly, smiled from dawn to dusk, and her husband Padibastet smiled upon her, and their love for each other was said to be the sweetest thing in all Memphis.

It followed, then, that in Year Sixteen of King Ptolemy, on the third day of the third month of Peret, the third month of the season of Emergence, was born the child called Young Anemhor, or Anemhor the Second, who was the firstborn son of this Padibastet, who was Padibastet the First, and Nefersobek.

Though Padibastet was at this time but a young priest, twenty years old, and held the lesser office of Prophet of the Sanctuary of Ramesses the Second, in the Temple of Ptah, it was his fate to succeed his grandfather, Old Anemhor, as High Priest.

Thoth says it: This boy was born to be the Great Chief of the Hammer, and from the day of his birth he was raised to be among the Pure Ones, trained up for this great office, brought up to love the gods of Egypt, every one of them, but above all, Ptah, the creator god.

The great-grandfather, Old Anemhor, who was then more than eighty years of age, drew up the horoscope of this child with his own hand, so that he might know the number of days of his life upon earth, and he was pleased to find, before the day of his own departure to the West came upon him, that his great-grandson would live seventy-two years, one month and twenty-three days.

The dynasty of the High Priests of Ptah of Memphis was, then, secure in its future, just as the future of the House of Ptolemy was secure. Indeed, the forecast of the horoscopists for these two Houses was that they would last exactly as long as each other, and come to an end *upon the same day.*

But just then, the thought that either House could end was an unthinkable thought.

Young Anemhor would be the father of three sons. He would be Master of Secrets in the Secret Place, and his days would be full of peace, undisturbed by horrors. This boy was born at much about the same time as the new Ptolemy, the firstborn son of Ptolemy Mikros and Arsinoë Alpha, that would be Ptolemy Euergetes. They would know each other from childhood, a Greek and an Egyptian, and there would be no hostility between them, but they would be friends. Their parents knew and respected each other. Between them they would achieve great things for Ptah, and for Egypt.

Old Anemhor, if he knew the number of the days of his life (and he did), and the name of the day upon which his life on earth must end— did these things trouble his heart? They did not. By no means. For the Egyptian sees death as but a change of residence. He looks upon death with calmness, not with fear, as the Greeks do.

Did Anemhor trouble to count down the number of days to his

departing to the West? He did not. Every thing was in the hands of the gods. Death really does not trouble the people of Egypt: they make ready for death all their lives. The Egyptians are cheerful with regard to death—Anubis, Lord of the Underworld, god of the embalming-house, he is their trusted friend and guide in the Afterlife.

The new Ptolemy they bandaged after the custom of the Greeks. The new Anemhor they did not bandage, for the Egyptians do not wrap up their children as if they are already dead, but think rather that a child's limbs should be allowed to grow without restriction. And as Eskedi, the grandfather, said, *There will be time enough for the bandaging later.*

Ptolemy Mikros would teach this son of his that as a true Greek he must learn to lie in order to live. But Padibastet taught Young Anemhor that an Egyptian always tells the truth, and his training in wisdom began as soon as he was able to understand, because this father read to his son out of the books of wisdom:

Be small of wrath, wide of heart, then your heart will be beautiful.

And yes, even before that, almost the first words this boy heard in his life were words of wisdom:

> *What good is one dressed in finery*
> *If he cheats before the god?*

And again:

> *Faience disguised as gold.*
> *When day comes, it turns to lead.*

Padibastet would teach Young Anemhor, this son that would be High Priest of Ptah—if the god willed it—just as his forefathers had been High Priests before him, the virtues of self-control, of moderation, of kindness, and generosity, and justice, and truthfulness. These virtues he must practise towards all men, all women. Padibastet did not teach his son the martial values. No, not one. Padibastet did not give this son a wooden sword to be his plaything, for his son would not be a man of war like Ptolemy—like the Ptolemies—but a man whose life time was devoted to peace.

The priestly training of this boy would start, aye, even before he was five years old. He would learn about every god. He would learn the art of foreknowledge. He would learn the arts of magic and medicine.

Padibastet, his father, would himself be the Master of Secrets.

Already he knew every thing that happened in the past, every thing that was to happen in the future. He knew what were the thoughts of a man even when he said nothing. He knew what any man would do next, without him so much as opening his mouth. Such a man was a most powerful friend for King Ptolemy and his son and for his grandson. And the new son, yes, he would be brought up to be a perfect copy of his father, just as his father was also a copy of *his* father before him, so that he might wear the leopard-spot skin instead, when the day came for Padibastet to go to the Field of Reeds, to his tomb in the West.

The family of the High Priest—four generations of them now there were since Ptolemy came to Egypt: Old Anemhor, Eskedi, Padibastet, and Young Anemhor—they loved smiling and laughter. They spoke never one word in anger to each other. Of hatred they knew nothing.

And the Greeks? They went on calling their sons *Ptolemaios*, War-like, and they went on arguing, quarrelling, fighting. The Greeks were true to their name. What was the truth? Was it that the Greeks were not happy? It was their thought that the Greek was better than the Egyptian, the Greek way of life better by far than the Egyptian. But the truth—the truth was that Egypt was older; that the sophistication of the Greeks was, at best, temporary, and that at bottom they were little more than savages, still calling their sons Ptolemaios, as if they saw some great virtue in fighting for the sake of fighting.

Padibastet taught his son quite the contrary: *The ideal man is a man of peace.*

In Year Seventeen, third month of summer, day twelve of the Lord of the Two Lands, Ptolemy, Lord of Diadems, May-He-Be-Granted-Life-Like-Ra, the sound of wailing and lamentation came from the house of the High Priest of Ptah, for it happened that Anemhor departed to Heaven to rest in the embalming-house under the charge of Anubis, that he might mummify his body.

The son and grandsons, the daughter-in-law and granddaughter-in-law wept for the old man, and the wailing of his widow rose above all other noises in the neighbourhood of the dead man's house. She beat her breast. She scratched at her cheeks with the nails of her fingers. Nobody forgot the sorrow of Anemhor's wife at the loss of the husband whom she loved.

They embalmed the body of Old Anemhor in the usual manner, removing the brain through his nostrils by means of the hook. They pulled out the entrails through the usual slit in his stomach wall.

They steeped this man's body in a bath of dry natron for the usual seventy days and nights. And the weeping and wailing of his family continued all that time.

Meanwhile there was made ready the three anthropoid coffins of cedar that would sit one inside the other, painted gold upon black, with the scenes of embalming the dead, and Anubis the jackal-headed god of embalming, and Thoth, who is three times great, and with the Weighing of the Heart that would take place in the Afterlife.

They bandaged the remains of Old Anemhor with very many cubits of linen bandage, and beneath his wrappings this great man wore the proper golden finger-stalls over the nails of his fingers. He wore solid gold covers over the nails of his toes. The entire head of this priest was gilded directly over the skin so that in death his face *shone* with gold, like the flesh of the gods. Thus Old Anemhor became one with the god Osiris, and was called, according to the custom, the Osiris Anemhor, and they made ready to set him upon his journey through the Underworld.

The wife of Old Anemhor, who herself held the great office of Wife of Ptah, saw in her mind's eye her husband crossing the dark halls of the Afterlife. She saw the weighing of his heart against the Feather of Maat, the Feather of Truth, and she knew that his heart was light in the Balance, light as the Feather. She saw in her dream Osiris the great god, seated upon his throne of pure gold, with the great god Anubis upon his left hand and the great god Thoth upon his right hand, holding up his reed pen, ready to write, while Anubis addressed the company, and she heard Anemhor declare that he had done no wrong to any man; that he had committed no crime; that he had not oppressed the poor; that he had not done any thing he should not have done in all the days of his life time. She knew that Anemhor was a good man, upright in the pursuit of his worship of the god. No, there was no spell that Old Anemhor could not chant by heart to assist his preservation from the terrors of the Afterlife. Old Anemhor had nothing to fear.

This wife saw her husband walking through the flames to the Field of Reeds, the Field of Offerings, the Field of Grasshoppers, and he was not harmed, but walked through, smiling. She saw him as one with the Imperishable Stars, enjoying his life of bliss in the sky, and she wept for never seeing him more, but she was happy for him at the same time.

For Old Anemhor dead they worked the spell to ensure that a scribe has his writing implements in the next world: his water bowl, his round blocks of dry ink, one red, one black, and his reed pen. For if a scribe has these things by him in the next world, he will know all the magical secrets contained in the writings of Thoth.

Between the dead knees of Old Anemhor they placed not the papyrus that some call *The Book of Coming Forth by Day,* that the vulgar call, wrongly, *The Book of the Dead,* but a roll of blank papyrus ninety cubits long, so that, yea, Old Anemhor might go on writing in the After-life, into everlastingness, for millions and millions of years.

Old Anemhor had not been openly hostile to the Greeks—to Ptolemy Soter—but he had not shown himself quite openly friendly either. He had kept up a reserve, a certain wariness in how he spoke with this Pharaoh who was not an Egyptian. Sure, the one had co-operated with the other, for Old Anemhor saw many goodly things in this man, and Ptolemy knew well that even he had not the power to remove Old Anemhor from his office, but that every high priest must be high priest for life, carrying the *kherep* sceptre until the day he dropped dead.

Old Anemhor—he was proud, very proud, that his ancestors, father to son, had been High Priest of Ptah going back to the days of Hatshep-sut, long before even the time of the Ramessides. He had shown Ptolemy their statues of wood in the great Temple of Ptah, a long row of them, the Great Chiefs of the Hammer, every one with the same myste-rious smile of the men who know every secret of Heaven and Earth and Underworld; all of them Masters of Secrets of the Secret Place, all with heads shaven but for the sidelock of the High Priest of Ptah; and all with the left leg striding forward—forty-eight generations of his family, spanning nine hundred and sixty years.

And yes, Ptolemy had been awed by such an expanse of time, speechless. Now, though, Old Anemhor had gone, and Ptolemy must find the priest of Ptah who might replace this great man, this man of high wisdom: some member of the priesthood who would work with him at all times, and not seem to oppose him. It happened that the new High Priest of Ptah whom Ptolemy chose was another Anemhor, who went also under the name of Nesisty, and also Esisout, but was known most often as Eskedi, who was the son of the Anemhor who had gone before, because although it was not a *right,* it was the tradition for a dead man's son to be appointed to his father's office, and Ptolemy saw that Eskedi was a man who was with him in all things; that there was no reserve, no suspicion; that Eskedi was the best man to be Great Chief of the Hammer.

So it was that Eskedi, aged thirty-five years, was led before His Majesty, and he bowed seven times and laid himself full length upon the floor and he kissed the ground before the feet of His Majesty, and he was First Prophet of Ptah, First Servant of the God, and His Majesty raised him up and spoke to him the words that must be spoken upon his appointment:

> *Thou art henceforth High Priest of Ptah . . .*
> *His treasuries and his granaries are under thy seal . . .*
> *Thou art Head of his Temple, all his servants are under thy*
> *   authority . . .*

And His Majesty presented to Eskedi the two rings of gold, and the sceptre of electrum that was the *kherep* sceptre of his office, and he was at once Head of the Double House of Silver and Gold, and Head of the Double Granary, and Chief of Works, and Chief of All Trades in Memphis, and Great Chief of the Hammer.

And the royal messenger was sent out to let all Egypt know that the House of Ptah was handed over to Eskedi, son of Old Anemhor, as well as all its property and its people.

And Eskedi praised Ptah, he of the Beautiful Face, the great god, the god who has the ability even to make Time run backwards.

Thoth speaks: The character of this Egyptian is calm. His temper is sweet. He loves his wife Neferrenpet. His wife loves him in return.

Eskedi, his heart is wide. He is small of wrath. He is beautiful of heart.

3.20

Hot-of-Mouth

Thus it came about that Eskedi the son waited upon Ptolemy in place of Old Anemhor his father, wearing the leopard-spot mantle of his august office. Eskedi did not bring crocodiles as gifts for the Greeks. By no means. He brought the best of cats from Bubastis. He brought the swiftest of hounds for hunting in the desert. He brought monkeys, saying, *Beautiful is a monkey among children*. It was Eskedi who now gave Ptolemy wise advice. And it was Eskedi who inherited now the task of instructing Keraunos about Egyptian matters, of which Keraunos wanted to hear not one word.

Ever since the crowning of his father, Ptolemy Keraunos had been looked upon by all as the heir to the throne and kingdom of Ptolemy Soter. To Keraunos alone of all the sons of Ptolemy had something of the Egyptian Mysteries been revealed, although, to be sure, he had really wanted nothing to do with Egyptian things.

When Eskedi explained to Keraunos the significance of Thoth and the Hermopolitan Ogdoad, this young man dared to yawn.

And when Eskedi asked him, *Wherefore, pray, dost thou not listen?* Keraunos said, *I am a Greek. The gods of Egypt mean nothing to me.*

No, Ptolemy Keraunos had resisted from the start any thing that was un-Greek. He was not interested to know of Anubis the Dog, who is Pharaoh of the Underworld, or Horus the Falcon of Gold, or Osiris and the absurdity of flying to the sky and becoming one of the Imperishable Stars upon his death. Keraunos—he was a Greek, and he professed to hate every foreign thing and all foreign people.

It was the same, however, with Keraunos's Greek learning, for he showed small interest in the Greek gods either. He had no wish to read Greek books, or, indeed, any book—not even Homer; not even the *Iliad* that overflowed with wars and blood shed. No, Keraunos was interested only in fighting, in the different ways of killing a man; in weaponry and swordplay. He was not interested to read of tactics, or strategy. He thought he had little need to know geography, or mathematics, or geometry. As for the lyre, he said that music was for the *kinaidoi*.

Keraunos lived, in truth, very much at random, like a barbarian. He was not unlike a slave, not unlike the animals, in that he was not ruled by *reason*.

Such a man would not, Eskedi thought, be able to bear the burden of being Pharaoh of Egypt.

No, Keraunos did not look much like the Living Image of Horus. He seemed more than ever like the Living Image of Seth, Enemy of the Light, the embodiment of Disorder.

Ptolemy Keraunos had been brought up, though, to believe that, whatever he did or did not do, he *would* be King after his father, and that this was his right as the eldest legitimate son of Ptolemy Soter, and it was this fact that made him go about thinking he might do exactly as he pleased. It should have surprised nobody, then, that when the promise of the kingship was put in doubt, and the thought was raised that Keraunos might not be the right man to be King, the thunder rolled a little. The new High Priest of Ptah foresaw trouble, great trouble, to come if Keraunos were to be King of Egypt.

Eskedi thought many days about the matter of the succession, and of the quarrel between the gods Horus and Seth, between Light and

Dark, Good and Evil, that seemed to be mirrored in the two sons of Ptolemy Soter that were rival candidates for his throne. It looked to Eskedi almost as if these two relived the ancient quarrel; almost as if the myth provided the model for history—almost, he thought, as if some person great in magic had arranged it on purpose.

If Ptolemy Mikros were to triumph over Ptolemy Keraunos, his half-brother, it would be a victory for reason. But if Keraunos were to be Pharaoh, surely, Evil and Disorder must be enthroned with him. It would be the beginning of the reign of Seth, the Eternal Troublemaker, upon the throne of Osiris, a thing that was meant not to happen. Really, nobody would leave Keraunos in charge of even a *trieres,* let alone a kingdom.

To Eskedi the choice between the two heirs looked quite simple. It was clear to him who must be the better Pharaoh—who was the *kalok-agathos,* the perfect gentleman of the Greeks.

But how to persuade Ptolemy Soter to choose the right son, the right Pharaoh for Egypt?

When Ptolemy Soter began to be very old, and even fell asleep whilst he heard the petitions of his subjects, and stumbled over the words in the temple ritual, and found it hard to attend for long to what any man said to him, his advisers, and the Egyptian advisers in particular, urged him to take the decision about his heir.

What would be the best course of action? He could not make up his mind. And so he asked for the thoughts of others, and on the day of deciding there were three parties involved in the questions and answers about his heir: Eskedi, High Priest of Ptah, and the other high priests of Egypt; Demetrios of Phaleron, who was Ptolemy's adviser upon almost every Greek thing; and Berenike, the Great Royal Wife of the Pharaoh.

On the side of Ptolemy Keraunos the loudest support came from Demetrios of Phaleron, who did his best to defend the son of Eurydike by quoting Aristotle: *Is not a boy sometimes naughty, sometimes good?* for it was his thought that Keraunos's wrongdoing was nothing but boyish mischief.

But against this Eskedi said, *Keraunos is no longer a child, but a grown man. He has had every chance to show his worth. And he is not wicked sometimes, he is wicked all the time.*

To be sure, Old Anemhor had favoured Keraunos, but Eskedi his son liked the look of Mikros better, who in spite of his being the after-pig, as it were, or runt of the litter, was not a madman like Keraunos.

Eskedi murmured even to the Pharaoh, *There is the evil man who is calm like the crocodile in the water,* and he meant Keraunos. And he said, *Greater is the claim of the mild man than that of the strong.*

Eskedi said, even to the man's father, *Ptolemy Keraunos, he is Hot of Voice. He is like the Heated Man. He is Whenever-He-Likes-He-Does. He is Whenever-He-Dislikes-He-Does-Not. He has no sense of what is right and proper. He has no sense of duty . . .*

And Ptolemy Soter shook his head, for what Eskedi said was the truth.

Eskedi went on: *What qualities does Pharaoh need? He needs the talent to command affection. He needs the talent to communicate energy. But Keraunos does not command affection. He will capture the heart of nobody. The Pharaoh must have charm. He is Great in Sweetness. But Keraunos has no charm, and he is not sweet but sour.*

Truly, Eskedi said, *Pharaoh must have his harsh aspect. He must terrorize any man who opposes his will. Pharaoh must smash foreheads. Fear of Pharaoh must be throughout the land, so that nobody can stand up in his presence. Keraunos is like this, but he has only the negative qualities of Pharaoh.*

For Eskedi, Keraunos was the hot-head so despised of the wise men of Egypt. He was like the *puraustes,* the moth who gets himself singed in the candle flame, and he troubled the heart of this young High Priest.

Eskedi became urgent in his words, saying, *The hot-mouthed man is like the young wolf in the farmyard. He dims the radiance of the sun.* And he said, *The boat of the greedy is left in the mud, while the barque of the silent man sails in the wind.*

Ptolemy thought hard. Mikros, to be sure, had got the habit of idleness, but he had also the habits of a scholar. He had achieved *arrepsia,* balance of the soul. He was unwarlike, he was peaceful. He was shrewd, and full of sense, like his father, whereas Keraunos, in truth, was the opposite.

Mikros had been brought up in the shade, because his fair skin made him burn up in the sun. He had grown up rather too soft, unlike Keraunos, who was a hard man. But Keraunos was too hard, and a hard man would do great damage to Egypt.

Soter fretted about Mikros, who had hardly heard an enemy bugle, let alone lifted his sword in battle, but there was time enough, he thought. Mikros was still a young man. It troubled Soter that Mikros was so unequal to violent exercise, so very unwarlike, but then again, the Egyptians hated war. They wanted a pharaoh who preferred peace.

Ptolemy thought of the treatises upon kingship that Demetrios of Phaleron had made him read, and he said, *A good man is stronger than himself. He is able to control his appetite for food and drink, for sleep and aphrodisia. But Keraunos does not control his desires. He is a man out of control.*

He said, *A king needs to be a man who is the honourable master of his pleasures, not the shameful slave of them.*

Ptolemy listened for a long while to what both Demetrios of Phaleron and Eskedi the High Priest said, but the last words of Eskedi were what lodged in his thoughts as he tried to sleep that night: *Do not start a fire if you cannot quench the flames; do not set in motion a train of events which you may not be able to stop.*

And he could think of nothing, all that night, but the fact that Ptolemy Keraunos was by his nature *mad* on war—war-mad—the kind of man condemned by Aristotle as less than human.

As for the thoughts of the wives of Ptolemy about the succession, the voice of Eurydike—absent at Miletos with her daughter—was not heard except through Demetrios, but she could support no other man than her own son, and privately expressed her horror that Ptolemy could even think of choosing another.

Berenike, she favoured, of course, Ptolemy Mikros, for she was his mother, and she knew in her heart what would happen when King Ptolemy died if Keraunos were to be King in his stead: yes, Keraunos would have Berenike murdered, and her son Mikros murdered also, and she spoke of her fear to her husband, who knew that Mikros would do the same to Eurydike, and to Keraunos also if he, Mikros, were to be King. He knew that whatever happened, one of his sons—of his body, his own flesh—was fated to die.

And the other sons—those who were not even thought of as heirs—they must die also. For had he not brought up Keraunos to think like this—to see in the murder of his siblings the only way he could survive as King?

What, then, would Soter do? Would he not choose for his heir the son of the woman he loved, Berenike, and send away mad Eurydike for good, and her mad son Keraunos with her?

In the end it was an easy choice: between the wild-tempered, dark-haired Ptolemy Keraunos, whose eyes were rather too close together, and the grace and talents of Ptolemy Mikros, an Apollo with hair like butter, a young man who looked very like his father. The choice was, yes, between brutality and intelligence, between vice and virtue. Really, there could be no question of Egypt being ruled by a brute like Ptolemy the Thunderbolt.

And how would Soter justify such a decision? To be sure, the best of reasons was that a king must take his example from the gods, and so he pointed to Kronos, last born of the Ouranides, and to Zeus, youngest of the Kronides, and he pointed to Ptolemy Mikros, the youngest of his three legitimate sons.

More royal, he said, *and more divine, is the blood running in the veins of the lastborn offspring . . .* And so he said, *Mikros shall succeed us, Mikros shall be co-Ruler.*

The battle for the succession, to speak the truth, was fought and won in the *gynaikeion,* between the two women who battled for the title and position of King's Mother. Both Berenike and Eurydike had everything to lose, even their lives. If Berenike's son Mikros were to be King, she would be the Great Royal Cow Who Dwells in Nekher, the Great Royal Mother, and her days of glory would continue. But if Eurydike's son Keraunos were to be King, Berenike would be dead, dead, and it was unthinkable to King Ptolemy that Berenike, his beloved, should not be Queen Dowager after he had gone down to Hades, or to wherever a Pharaoh of Egypt might go to in the Afterlife of the Egyptians.

Thus it was that in place of his eldest legitimate son, his rightful heir, Ptolemy Soter came to choose his favourite son, the son of his favourite wife, and in spite of that son being not thin in the flesh, not warlike, and not at all trained up or ready to be a king or a pharaoh or a living god.

And many of the Greeks thought even that Ptolemy Soter had taken leave of his senses to do it, for that Ptolemy Keraunos was handsome, popular, manly, whereas, in truth, Ptolemy Mikros was not, and the army of Soter was not much pleased to hear of their new Commander-in-Chief. For it was Keraunos they looked up to, Keraunos who rode out every morning with them, while Mikros lay in his bed, sleeping late. Ptolemy Mikros *never* trained with the phalanx.

Berenike—what did *she* think just then? Did she think that she might rule through Mikros her son? Perhaps. For all her gold and jewels and splendour, she was a tough, ruthless woman, who delighted to wear the vulture—that was abhorrent to every other Greek—upon her forehead; who had trained herself up to stop at nothing in order to have whatever she wanted. And now she had got it: now Berenike had everything.

This was the hour, then, of the great triumph of Berenike, Berenike's mighty victory, and when she was on her own, in her private chamber that night, Berenike danced, Berenike laughed, Berenike sang, for the future belonged to Berenike—all of it—and of this momentous decision of Ptolemy, Eurydike his spurned wife, still away at Miletos, in Ionia, knew nothing.

3.21

Bronze Nails

When Ptolemy Keraunos saw himself in his dream having *aphrodisia* with a pig, he knew that things must be as bad as bad can be, for such a dream meant that a man must be deprived of all his possessions.

But at the same time Keraunos laughed, for to seek meaning in a dream—well, it was as much nonsense as believing in the gods.

Even so, it was the next morning that King Ptolemy called Keraunos to his side and told him what had been decided about the succession, and Soter said, *You could not be too quick in departing. Make haste and be off.*

Keraunos just stared at his father as if he could not believe the words. He tried, then, to call Soter *Patridion,* Papa, as if to plead with him, saying, *I am the eldest of your sons . . .* as if he would make Soter change his mind. But Soter's mind was made up and he would not now change it.

Go to the harbour, he said, *the trieres is waiting to take you away . . .*

And when he saw that Keraunos, even Keraunos, would weep soon, he said, *Don't make bad worse,* and he put his hands upon Keraunos's shoulders and looked into his eyes, and he said, *As soon as I am dead . . . Mikros will be your enemy.*

Mikros is my enemy already, said Keraunos.

When I am dead, Soter said, *your brother will be sure to try to kill you.* And Keraunos saw the tears in his father's eyes, for he did not hate this son of his, wayward though he was, but loved him.

Let him try, Keraunos said, and he laughed the desperate laugh of one who knows he has lost every thing.

Where must I go? Keraunos said. *How shall I live, out of Egypt?* And his father explained about the money that was to be paid to him for so long as he kept away from the Two Lands.

But Keraunos did not want to quit Alexandria, and it was still his thought that he was himself the man who should be the heir of his father, and he asked for a few hours to gather his belongings, but instead he galloped his horse about the city that afternoon, during the siesta, trying to stir up his friends and supporters and even the army of Egypt to revolt, so that not only his brother Mikros but even the King his father might be a dead man that very day.

It was Eskedi, High Priest of Ptah, who hurried to speak urgent words to King Ptolemy about this son of his, saying, *Now that he knows his fate, he shows himself in his true colours. He flips his tail like the young crocodile. He draws himself up to strike. His lips may be sweet, but his tongue is bitter, a fire burns in his belly* . . . And he urged Ptolemy to put Keraunos upon the *trieres* at once, before he could have his revenge upon his younger brother—that Mikros who, if they should fight, would not be quick to defend himself, but would most surely be knocked down, beaten, murdered.

And yes, upon seeing Mikros in the distance Keraunos screamed at him: *I am going to kill you now, this very afternoon,* and he called him *skubalon,* filth, and worse things, and when he came close, he had to be held by the arms by his friends, for fear that he should strike his brother.

The army of Ptolemy Soter proved, however, loyal to the King and they were pleased to deliver up the son to his father, trussed and bound like a prisoner of war.

Ptolemy told Keraunos again that there was no longer room for him in the city, and that the *trieres* was waiting in the private harbour to take him away, and that he would be a fool, if not a dead man himself, if he tried to return.

Behind the closed doors of his father's chamber Keraunos raged. The Pharaoh heard him for a while, but few of his words made sense, and when he clapped his hands the bodyguards carried this youth away, kicking, and he shouted his abuse even at his father as he went.

From the high terrace of his palace Ptolemy watched the great ship weigh anchor, and her two hundred oars rose and fell as one, like the wings of a giant vulture, and he watched until the sail was nothing but a black spot upon the horizon. Only then did the tear escape from this King's eye regarding the son who had failed him in every respect, the son who, no doubt, must still cause trouble, but whom he could not find it in his heart to put to death, for he was innocent, as yet, of any crime but the *aphrodisia* upon his sister.

Also upon that *trieres* were Meleagros and Argaios, the other sons of Eurydike, who went with their brother to Thrace, seeking their fortunes. For it was clear to all men at the court of Ptolemy that none of this woman's sons was safe, but that they posed a threat to the stability of Mikros.

Ptolemy brushed that tear away, angry, and returned to Egyptian business: petitions, decrees, *prostagmata,* the corn supply, the prospect of never-ending war with Syria and the House of Seleukos, and he wiped out the thought of Ptolemy Keraunos from his heart, as the scribe wipes out a mistake in his papyrus. To such children as remained still in Alexandria he said, *Thou shalt regard Ptolemy Keraunos like him that thou knowest not,* and nobody spoke the name of the Thunderbolt in the Residence again.

Keraunos had never drunk from the River, for he had seen the natives throw their filth into it. No, Keraunos had drunk nothing but wine, undiluted wine, in Egypt, and he would not come back. Keraunos fell, then, from favour, and with him fell his great supporter, Demetrios of Phaleron, who had spoken so warmly of Keraunos that things could no longer continue for him as before. What happened to this wisest of men nobody could say for sure, except that there was a story put about that he travelled up-River on some mission, or thought, perhaps, to make good his escape across the desert from Koptos to the Red Sea, and thence to India, but that he fell asleep under a palm tree in the heat of the day, where he was bitten by a serpent.

Indeed, this unfortunate death of Demetrios of Phaleron was commemorated in a poem by one of his fellow scholars in the Mouseion:

> An ASP that had much poison,
> Not to be wiped off,
> Darting no light
> But black death
> From his eyes,
> Slew wise Demetrios.

Not a very good poem, perhaps, but it was all that was left of him apart from bright ideas. So much for wisdom, and for wise advice, and for cleverness of speech, none of which things saved the famous Demetrios of Phaleron from going down to Hades like everybody else, and rather earlier than he had planned.

No sooner had Ptolemy Keraunos been got rid of, and Demetrios of Phaleron conveniently sent up-River, who should appear once more in Alexandria but Eurydike, who took up her residence as before in the palace of her lawful wedded husband, as was her right.

What will become of Eurydike? Berenike asked the Pharaoh.

Perhaps she will be well pleased to go back to Miletos for all time, he said. *Eurydike may do as she wishes. She is not a prisoner here,* he said, and he spread his hands, and sounded a little as if he did not care what became of this wife of his, but had more urgent matters to think about.

But it was the private thought of Berenike that the niece was bound to make trouble behind her back, agitating on behalf of her son Keraunos, for him to have the throne. And to be sure, she knew that Eurydike was quite capable of having Mikros stabbed or poisoned, and perhaps Berenike too, if it meant that Keraunos could come home and be King after all. In truth, Eurydike was now a dangerous person to have wandering about the palace, and so worried was Berenike about what the niece might do that she gave orders for her to be watched at all times, and asked for a daily report of who she spoke with.

In spite of the guards outside her apartments, Berenike began now to bolt her door by day as well as by night, to keep Eurydike and the agents of Eurydike from creeping up on her unawares. It was a situation that could not be allowed to go on for very long.

When Keraunos was sent away, Demetrios of Phaleron had left for Eurydike upon her return from Miletos his message of warning, to be on the watch for knives, for poison, for unfortunate accidents upon the staircase, and the result was that the Eurydike who came home to Egypt became so fearful of murder that she had her most trusted waiting-woman taste her every dish of food.

In the meantime, what was Eurydike really doing? In her bathroom she stuck bronze nails into an image of her nephew, the Prince Ptolemy Mikros, made out of old bits of soap and candle wax: two nails in his two eyes, two nails in his two ears, two nails in his two nostrils and one nail between his legs—nails, in fact, in every part of Mikros's flesh. And she floated the image of Mikros in her bath, and held it under the water, and hid it afterwards beneath a loose tile in her bathroom floor.

When Eurydike heard that Mikros had caught a chill, she sensed success, but it only made him sneeze, and a sneeze, as every Greek knows, is nothing but a sign that Good Luck is his, a sign from Zeus, and Mikros did not oblige Eurydike by departing this life.

Eurydike even abandoned Greek magic for Egyptian magic, half-learned from her waiting-women. She rubbed her hands with incense. She rinsed her mouth with natron. She gabbled the holy words of Ra in a language she did not understand, in order to force the god to give her what she wanted: the death of Ptolemy Mikros, and the appointment of her son, Ptolemy Keraunos, as heir to Egypt in his stead. But in spite of Eurydike bathing seven times a day for three days and painting the figure of Maat upon her tongue with green paint, her magic had no effect, for the words she spoke did not make sense. The magic, for Eurydike, had stopped working some time ago.

Mikros was indeed surprised to be named the heir of his father, for he had not been raised to see himself as the future King of Egypt. In his heart Mikros laughed. He thought Keraunos deserved what he got: nothing. He thought Keraunos a born idiot, beyond help, a fool, who could not control even his own *rhombos*.

Mikros, to be sure, had not had the extra tuition in economics and mathematics, let alone the extra lessons in strategy and tactics that his brother had. By no means. It was always Keraunos that enjoyed the *kudos*, every sign of favour, whereas Mikros had often been left to his own devices, and to think of himself as of lesser importance, a boy whose future might lie in the governorship of Cyprus, or as Epistates of Libya, but not as a king, let alone a god in his own life time.

But the day after Keraunos vanished for good, Ptolemy Mikros was associated upon the throne of his father the Pharaoh. And this was no new thing, but common practice among the Pharaohs of old, for it made sure that, when a king died, there would be no question about who must follow him, and the bath of blood that was always a possibility even in Egypt upon a new king's accession, would, in theory, not come to pass. Every thing, then, would be well. King Ptolemy could now enjoy his old age without worry. Ptolemy Mikros would worry on his behalf.

Not long after this, Ptolemy Soter sallied forth one last time in his *oktophoros,* upon ritual business, to anoint with the little finger of his right hand the jewelled statue of Ptah with incense, and when he returned to the Residence, he was told that Eurydike's suite of rooms in the *gynaikeion* was empty and deserted. So astonishing was the news that Ptolemy clambered up the staircase to see with his own eyes that what he was told was the truth. And yes, he found room after empty room stripped of the golden fittings, and there was no noise here of women's voices, no noise of the clanking loom, just the *slap slap slap* of the bare feet of the dwarfs running away from him down the corridors, and the dwarfs' shrill laughter in the distance, and then the silence.

Ptolemy stepped, of course, in the *skubalon* that was left upon the mosaic floors, as if to tell him what she thought of his royalty, of his kingly treatment, of his insincere attentions, of his princely marriage; and he cursed, but knew that in ousting the Thunderbolt and allowing the departure of his mother, he had done only what was right.

Some reports said that Eurydike had fled by ship to Byblos, in Phoenicia; others that she had taken a string of camels along the Roads of Horus, by way of Gaza, Tyros and Sidon, going the long way round to Miletos, for that in truth she was afraid of the sea; or that without any escort she had made her way back to Miletos direct, risking even the attentions of the pirates.

At all events, the stories agreed that Eurydike journeyed again to Miletos, and that she stayed there until the day came when she went down to Hades.

Ptolemy Soter thought only of the beautiful Berenike, his Queen, the Mistress of Happiness, She at Hearing Whose Voice the King Rejoices, Lucky Berenike, and of what might have become of her if he had let the succession go to Keraunos. Yes, he could see Keraunos *murdering* this stepmother of his, the moment his father breathed his last. And Berenike did not deserve, he thought, such a dreadful fate.

Yes, indeed, the one great reason why he had chosen Ptolemy Mikros was that he was the son of Berenike, Fair of Face, his Great Royal Wife, his beloved—the one that he loved.

Eurydike, a woman still of only some forty-eight years, and still not having lost all her charms, might well have married a fresh husband at Miletos, for there were many men there who approached her with generous offers. Eurydike did not lack riches in her own right, as the daughter of Old Antipatros, Satrap of Macedon. But her suitors were not princes—not even rulers of minor kingdoms—and she refused every one of them.

If my paps could give suck, she said, *then I might perhaps come to another marriage bed with unfailing feet . . . but age has put a thousand wrinkles upon my flesh . . . Eros is in no haste to fly to me with his gift of pain.*

The first husband of Eurydike had already showed her ingratitude enough. She really had no wish for the burden of further troubles.

No, Eurydike put her hopes now in the poor girls of Miletos, and she gave them dowry money so that they might become wives rather than whores, and so that they might have their independence. Eurydike's own hopes had come to nothing. *Perhaps,* she said, *the marriage of another woman might be made a success where my own marriage has failed.*

In Thrace King Lysimakhos welcomed Ptolemy Keraunos, his half brother-in-law, whose dubious reputation he did not know about. But Arsinoë Beta refused to meet Keraunos. She complained of a pain in her belly, and pretended that she was confined to her bed in the *gynaikeion,* a place where, of course, Keraunos could not set his boot. But the truth of it was that she did not wish to look upon his face.

No, it was Lysimakhos who heard the story of Keraunos, and how his royal father had most unjustly banished him from his rightful kingdom.

Lysimakhos found that he liked this Keraunos, his half-brother-in-law, and he passed on this man's message to Arsinoë Beta.

Tell my story to my sister, Keraunos said. *Ask my sister for soldiers and money. Beg her to help my cause.*

Arsinoë Beta gave her brother hired soldiers, then, and many talents of gold, to make him go away. They sent each other scribbled messages, but at length Keraunos grew, as usual, tired of waiting and went on his way.

And what did Arsinoë Beta do, this most powerful of women, this richest of women, whose husband did every thing she asked of him? She gave her brother every thing he asked of her, more money and more soldiers, because she believed that as the eldest son he deserved to be Pharaoh of Egypt.

It was now that the thought flashed through the heart of Ptolemy Keraunos that if he were to *marry* his own sister, this Arsinoë Beta, he might with her help murder Lysimakhos and become King of Thrace; that he might with her help indeed oust his half-brother from Egypt as soon as Ptolemy Soter died, and then be King of Egypt, because, as he said, the old man did not look like to live much longer.

Some days afterwards, having become a little tired of Thrace, and of fishes, Ptolemy Keraunos appeared on the threshold of his mother's house at Miletos, armed and grinning. Eurydike thought too late about the wisdom of letting him step through the door, for the truth of it was that she was afraid of him, afraid of his violent temper, because living with this man was indeed like living with the thunderstorm under her roof.

But Keraunos did not show his mother violence, nor his widowed sister Ptolemaïs either, but offered his protection, and gave them guards for the house, for that these women were the wife and daughter of a king, and because he had raised for himself now his own army of hired soldiers, paid for by his sister Arsinoë Beta's great wealth, and he now took his position at the head of it, his rightful position, and he led his mother to the street door, to show her the column of thousands of soldiers lined up silent outside, all of them wearing his purple livery, and when Keraunos raised his arm they shouted his name, and the battle cry, and they stretched into the distance as far as Eurydike could see, and every man was armed with sword and shield for the campaign that would make Keraunos King of Egypt.

Now his father and all the House of Ptolemy should see what Ptolemy Keraunos, the Thunderbolt, was made of; *now* they should see what great victories he could win; *now* his father should see what sort of heir he had rejected.

Eurydike caught her breath when she saw the army of Keraunos, and he swore to her, then, that he would make himself King, even if it meant that between them they must kill his hated father, but that when he did so, she, Eurydike, should be Mother of the Pharaoh, the Great Royal Mother, and he laughed that hyaena laugh of his; and Eurydike did now a thing that she had never done before—she embraced him, and covered his neck with her kisses.

3.22

The Lighthouse

In Egypt there would be peace, for a time, until Ptolemy Keraunos, perhaps, made the best of his way across the Great Sea and managed to attack his homeland. But for the moment the soldiery stood idle, and the work that continued upon the Pharos was helped by the foot soldiers who had no other employ, labouring on Pharos island, with the purpose of finishing this wondrous monument lest Ptolemy Soter should go to his tomb without setting the taper to the great light himself, with his own hand, and seeing the end of that which he had begun.

The Great Lighthouse already cast its long shadow, and the shadow grew steadily longer, and Ptolemy would stand at his Window of Appearances, from which he distributed, from time to time, the Gold of Valour, or, at the New Year, gifts for his ministers of state, courtiers, first friends, second friends—and watch the Pharos, as he said, *growing*.

Some times he would send the queue of petitioners away, every one of them, that had stood on his great staircase for months upon end without seeming to grow any shorter, and say that word that no Greek is ever supposed to say: *Tomorrow*. The reason for it was his wish to make the ascent of the Pharos, in order to urge on the workmen, and see the progress, and look again at the view of the illustrious and most illustrious city of Alexandria, and to check once more whether a man could, or could not, see as far as the Great Pyramid of Memphis from the top of the Pharos.

Ptolemy climbed the inside staircase, up which, day and night, a procession of donkeys would carry the fuel with which to feed the great flame, and up which, just then, a procession of donkeys carried blocks of stone, and scaffolding, and every necessary thing to finish the third and topmost storey.

The Pharos was almost finished. In the metal workshops of the city there existed already the prototype of the great statue of Poseidon, who would stand on the top, and the great letters of lead that spelled the name of SOSTRATOS OF KNIDOS, without whom there would have been no Pharos, and that would be fixed, in due time, to the side of the second, or octagonal storey, with a promise that the letters should face the landward side rather than the seaward side, so long as Sostratos found the last remaining instalments of the eight hundred talents the Pharos had cost to build.

Ptolemy looked and looked, and he was well pleased by every thing he saw. He only hoped and prayed that the gods would not take him before that glorious day when Alexandria ceased to be dark during the hours of darkness, for he had been assured that the sight of Alexandria *lit by night* would be the most astonishing sight that the world, the *world* had ever seen, for no other city had any thing like it.

Alexandria was set to be the greatest, most famous, most lucky city of all time. Athens was nothing compared to it, Pergamon little more than a village. The much-puffed Seleukeia-in-Pieria—well, it was built of mud brick, hardly better than the cities of the Egyptians.

3.23

Bride of Hades

All these years, throughout the crisis over the succession to the throne and the troubles with Ptolemy the Thunderbolt, the youngest child of all Ptolemy Soter's children, Philotera, had remained at home in Egypt, unmarried.

Every time one of her older sisters or half-sisters was married, it was supposed to be the duty of Philotera, as the youngest, to make ready the bridal bed, a Greek custom that added sanctity to the marriage. But since not one of her sisters had been married from home, Philotera had never performed this service. The fact was that this girl had never been to anybody's wedding ceremony, except that of Mikros to Arsinoë Alpha, so that it seemed to her, some times, as if a wedding was some thing that was forbidden.

As for her own marriage, that was a thing that Philotera never dreamed of, and when she was asked about it she said that her only wish was to be the maiden priestess of Artemis.

All happened, of course, as had been planned by the Fates at her birth, and it was the fate of Philotera to know not a man, not even her brother Ptolemy Keraunos, and she would never know the experience of childbed.

Philotera had heard the screams of palace women as they gave birth to their children. She had been told what it was that a woman must undergo in order to become a mother, and she had no wish to suffer such torments.

From time to time her sisters had written letters to her from Thrace, or from Syracuse, or from Cyprus, saying such things as: *Do not marry. Never. Marriage is dreadful. It is madness.* So that Philotera was fixed in her dislike for the idea of wedlock.

When Ptolemy her father warned that a woman who refused to marry would be condemned to carry leaking jars of water in the Underworld, Philotera said she did not care. She said she would prefer to carry water like this, for she did not like men, and had no wish to bear children.

And when King Ptolemy said to her, *It is the greatest of misfortunes to die unmarried,* she raised her voice to speak her last word upon the matter:

I would rather stand in the phalanx of your army in battle three times than give birth once.

Ptolemy threatened her with a whipping, for disobedience to him, but she said that one month of whippings would not make her change her mind, and Ptolemy stopped trying to persuade her.

Philotera, without experience of life, and insensible, so it seemed, to the assaults of Eros the Boy, would never be any man's ripe young wife in this world.

But, Philotera, ever in a condition of *anerastia,* ignorant of love, and unlovely also, was happier than any of her sisters, and perhaps happier than any other member of her family.

As God's Wife of Ptah, an office that was bestowed often upon the daughter of the Pharaoh, and as a priestess of Ptah, she was in fact barred from marriage, obliged to stay a maiden, and she would adopt the daughter of the next king as the heiress to her office.

And yes, it was the thought of Eskedi, High Priest of Ptah, that to allow a Greek girl to do such a thing would be good, very good, for the relations of the Greeks and the Egyptians, and would draw both nations closer together.

The Princess Philotera would pass the rest of her days going back and forth between the temple of the Egyptian god and the temple of the Greek goddess, as priestess of both. She spent her life rattling the *seistron* for the gods of Egypt to ward off evil spirits. She wore the spotted leopard-skin dress of a priestess of Egypt.

Philotera would be the bride of no living man. It was her fate to be the bride only of Hades, in the Underworld, but Philotera did not lead a life that was unfulfilled. By no means. Philotera smiled better than any other member of her House.

Of her sister Theoxena, it was said that after her return from Sicily and the death of her beloved Tyrant, she never smiled again. Theoxena began to walk about while she was still asleep, wandering in the labyrinthine corridors of the Residence night after night, until the family, fearing that she should walk over the parapet of the terrace and fall to her death upon the pavements of the Great Harbour hundreds of cubits below, tied her limbs to the bed at sundown.

Latterly, Theoxena seemed not even to know where she was, but babbled by day about Syracuse, and when she took to walking right out of the Residence during the siesta, and was found halfway down Kanopic Street in a state of confusion—reported to have exposed her *bolba* in an indecent manner in the *agora,* they took to tying Theoxena up during the day as well.

To be sure, they looked after Theoxena as best they could, and Philotera brought her her food when she was not busy at the temples, but really there was no mystery about what became of Theoxena: she went mad, for she was, after all, her mother's daughter, and she lived out the rest of her time locked in some out-of-the-way chamber.

Assuredly, the prison of mad Theoxena was in a retired part of the Residence, so that visitors should not hear her howling, and so find out the saddest secret of the House of Ptolemy. Theoxena had every thing she could wish for, and her tapestries delighted the poor women of Alexandria, to whom they were distributed, because the ex-Tyrantessa could no more be trusted with the needle, but must sew with just her teeth and fingers.

The two sons of Theoxena were grandsons of King Ptolemy and could be given nothing but the best Greek education. At the age of eleven years the elder boy, Arkhagathos, was enrolled in the most illustrious of the city *gymnasia,* and he began to develop the taut muscles and fine weapon skills of a Greek warrior. He had the proper training in strategy and tactics, geometry and mathematics. He drilled with the phalanx and rode with the mounted troops in his turn. He was a boy who might, if all had gone well with him, have fought in the armies of Egypt beside his Ptolemy cousins; who might have played his part as a *strategos* in the victories over the enemies of the Two Lands.

At eighteen Arkhagathos was initiated as an *ephebos* and swore the oath of loyalty to King Ptolemy. At every stage his progress was watched and approved by Ptolemy himself, who smiled upon this son of Theoxena—and by the officials of his Greek court.

All those who watched Arkhagathos so hard thought, however, but the same thing: that the blood of mighty Berenike did not course through the flesh of this young man; and that he was a grandson of the disaffected Eurydike, the son of mad Theoxena; and that he was of the lineage of that morally most dubious Agathokles of Syracuse, and that all would not go well for this boy and his brother, for that their days were numbered, just as the days of Theoxena had been numbered.

Aye, the one sure thing was that the sons of the Princess Theoxena would not be let to live for long, for the older Ptolemy became, the more dangerous became the thought of these grandsons, whose names were near the top of the List of Troublesome Relations.

Mikros watched Arkhagathos and Agatharkhos also, for it was, of course, Mikros who must find either useful employ for them, so that they did not threaten his position, or cross them off the List of the Troublesome altogether.

3.24

Nightingale Flesh

Ptolemy, Old Ptolemy, grew older. He had named his heir, and after that, really, Mikros thought his father might do what any man who has fulfilled all that a man can do—and more, much more—and just die, so that he, Mikros, might be Pharaoh instead. But Ptolemy Soter did not die, but went on and on, living for ever indeed.

The Greeks mostly think that if a man lasts to seventy years old he has done well, very well. To live beyond seventy was to command awe, though, as if he had been forgotten by the gods, and was blessed with immortality; but Ptolemy was now over eighty.

Ptolemy Soter—he was heavy now in his legs, slow, and then slower still. He trembled in his lower lip, and his trembling hand spilled his food as it tried to reach his mouth. This aged man was dried up, burnt by the Egyptian sun, his face like a ripe chestnut.

Ensconced with the *Dioiketes,* his First Minister, wrestling with problems of peace, Greek problems, Egyptian problems, priestly problems, Ptolemy fell now sound asleep by day, snoring even upon his throne of gold, and so often did it happen that the *Dioiketes* spoke with Eskedi, and between them they did what they could to relieve the old man of the burden of his office, and pass the weight on to Mikros instead.

Old age, Ptolemy said, his voice wavering, *it is like straw, worth nothing.* He laughed a little, then, but they saw that he was ripe for death, and made what arrangements they could. But Ptolemy went on living.

Month by month Mikros took on more and greater control of the business of government. His father did such work as he was capable of, tasks of his own choosing. And Mikros was careful not to give direct orders of any kind to his revered father. Ptolemy, as always, voiced his thoughts on Egypt's affairs, but now, as with the opinions of women and children, whatever he said, it was quietly ignored.

And Mikros gave many orders, and arranged many things, of which his father was told not one word, already doing much as he pleased with the kingship, even before he was sole ruler.

The Old Ptolemy lay awake now most of the night, thinking about the past, trying to forget, trying not to remember, and the physicians fed him nightingale meat to help him sleep.

He chewed his way through basket upon basket of nightingales, and slept, or tried to, with his head upon a pillow stuffed with nightingale feathers, though he complained that it was useless. Latterly he stopped trying to sleep, but sat up writing by the grim light of a lamp fuelled by *kiki* oil, setting down on papyrus, in his own hand, something of his history. Even so, he had never got beyond the crossing of the Hellespont at the outset of the Asian campaign, but sat thinking, chewing the end of his reed pen.

Some nights he would dream the dream of the eagle perched upon his head, its talons digging into his scalp, and the dream so bothered him that he woke up.

Worried about what such a strange dream might mean, he asked, as usual, the oneiroscopist, the interpreter of Greek dreams, who knew that the eagle dream meant the death of the dreamer. But he did not dare tell the Pharaoh such a thing. No, he told him that the eagle meant life, prosperity, health, and Ptolemy was comforted, and slept a little better, though he did not stop dreaming of eagles.

As always, he was surrounded by his multitude of women, women younger than Berenike his wife, who made their exercise for his *rhombos* every third afternoon, even when he was eighty-two years old.

But as Ptolemy said himself, *What is a Pharaoh good for, if he may not satisfy his every wish?*

And he made it his habit to chew rocket seeds with pepper and syrup in order to promote tumescence, and the pepper made him sneeze, which to a Greek could never be anything but the best of omens.

At times, then, Ptolemy knew total peace of mind.

All the same, Death lurked close by, waiting to take him. A palace guard who looked as if he might be good for thirty years' more duty dropped dead at his post. The palace washerwoman, who had borne ten children and looked fit to be delivered of ten more, fell dead into her tub. In Egypt most mothers did not survive childbed. Most children died in infancy. Even a Greek princess might expire at the ripe age of twenty-five. Life was brief for most of Ptolemy's subjects.

When Ptolemy reached the age of eighty-three, it was an excuse for great celebration, and there were processions of troops and horse and singing children along Kanopic Street, and great games at the hippodrome, and the entire population of Alexandria feasted and drank to excess for three days at Ptolemy's expense, and it seemed impossible that this King should ever go to the stars, or to his tomb in the West.

He will live to one hundred and twenty, they chanted up at Memphis, *like the Ethiopians,* and it was not mere politeness.

Ptolemy himself was often weary, thinking of Achilles's rejection of old age without fame, in favour of an early death with glory. Ptolemy had old age *and* glory, and had outlasted the wars and hardships of his youth as if by some miracle of the gods. *Better,* he thought now, *to die young in battle than to put up with the living death of an old man.*

Some times he thought of the Sibyl, who asked for everlasting life but forgot to ask for everlasting youthfulness, and he knew how the Sibyl must have felt.

Some times he thought of Sophokles: *Never to have lived is best . . .*

And some times he thought of Alexander, gone in a blaze of glory forty years ago, and he lost himself in his past.

He went more often to sit beside the body at the crossroads of the capital, and he poured more solemnly the libations of milk and honey and undiluted wine for his dead friend, gazing upon the waxen face that both was and was not Alexander, and he wept for the long-lost life of his General. He talked to the corpse, the guards said, though he never got an answer—told Alexander all his troubles, all his secret thoughts, and every last thing about the House of Ptolemy, savoury and unsavoury alike. Yes, Egypt was in safe hands, he said, everything would be all right . . . Some days, though, he would rage at the dead man for his stupidity in leaving them all to fend for themselves. They had needed Alexander to stay alive, not to leave them in a mess that took half a century to clean up.

There were days when Ptolemy swore by Zeus and Pan together that the eyelids of Alexander fluttered, that his upper lip twitched, as if he was about to say a few words, though he knew for sure that Alexander's eyelids were sewn up, and that his lips were drawn so tight with papyrus thread that the man could not have twitched an eye or spoken a word if he did wake up, for Ptolemy had seen to these things himself.

No, Alexander, Great Alexander, was dead, and although the

prostagma was still upon the statute books—that nobody, under pain of a beating upon the soles of both feet, should speak of this man as a dead man, because he was not dead, only asleep, and would, in fact, be living for all time—Ptolemy knew now and at last, that he would not, not ever, not by Greek magic or by Egyptian spells, not by wishes or hopes or by interminable prayers to the obscurest Egyptian gods (whose names no Greek could so much as pronounce), and not either by prayers to the entire pantheon of the gods of Hellas (who did not in any case really exist except in a man's imagination), that not only not in Ptolemy's life time but also not in the life time of any one of his successors either, right down to the very end of all time and the last full stop of history, would Alexandros son of Philippos ever draw breath again.

3.25

Vulture Beak

And Berenike? What of the Queen? Still she remembers nothing, for she has willed herself to forget her past, as surely as Ptolemy cannot forget. This toughest of tough women—she does not dream troubled dreams of blood and eagles. Berenike dreams only of glory, and she sleeps sound, for she has no burden of state business to keep her awake. By no means: Berenike has no need of nightingale meat, not one mouthful.

In these last years of her life as Queen her son Magas of Kyrene minted quantities of gold oktodrachms stamped with the face of his beloved mother. Berenike was pictured not as a young goddess but as an aged woman, with an elongated nose, hooked and pointed at its end, not unlike the beak of the vulture that, as Queen of Egypt, she wore so often upon her head.

She looked bored upon her coins, and her hair—the careful arrangement of her hair, its perfect tight curls—it was like nothing so much as a wicker basket lying upon its side. In all her years as Queen this woman never so much as cooked a meal. From time to time she had, perhaps, walked up and down the mosaic floor, when the click of her golden sandals was the only sound that could be heard in the *gynaikeion*. Berenike was the Queen, and it was the duty of a queen to do nothing, except be a living goddess, a living symbol of terrifying power. And Berenike *was* terrifying.

In her old age there were days when Berenike prayed for death to come quick, but neither Anubis nor Hades visited her, for the day appointed by the Fates to be the last day of her life was not yet come. She lived on, and the corners of her mouth seemed to be set permanently down.

Had the artist made the bird-beak of Berenike's nose on purpose like that of the vulture, or did he merely engrave what he saw?

Yes, to be sure, this nose of hers was just like the vulture's beak. And yes, this woman was ready to rip flesh like the rest of her family, like the vulture indeed. She showed the same sureness as her husband that their dynasty would last for all time. And like the vulture she watched over it, to make sure that it was so, waiting, waiting.

Of the rest of the family there was only one member still in Alexandria of the generation of Ptolemy Soter, for there had only ever been one relation: Uncle Menelaos, Soter's younger brother, the useless brother who lived in Egypt only because he had no other place to go.

Menelaos was nearing eighty years of age himself, and no longer able to control the trickle of saliva from his mouth, but he insisted on offering his brother the best of his advice about affairs of state.

Menelaos, to be sure, deserved a little respect. He had been present at the founding of the city, and he had his residence within the palace walls, his household of slaves, his sinecures and ceremonial duties. Menelaos would never be a god himself, and no man who lost an island could be a hero. No, he deserved some respect, but not much, and Ptolemy never forgave him, even when he got back Cyprus for his own possession, because a Greek, even a Greek famous for kindness and generosity, simply does not forgive anybody for anything.

Ptolemy Mikros, he took the best advice of Uncle Menelaos not very seriously. He showed the old man the deference due to his age, but in private he said, *Uncle Menelaos is an old dribbler*. Menelaos had achieved nothing in his long life that was worthy of honour, except to walk in the procession of the Cult of the Divine Alexander, carrying the wicker basket—the only office he was capable of filling, some said, because all the Priest of Alexander had to do was to hold the basket in the procession; and even so, Menelaos always dropped it.

Really, Menelaos was almost as great a disgrace to the House of Ptolemy as Keraunos. So that Mikros wondered, Should he get rid of

Menelaos in the night of blood that must follow his accession? Or should he allow the dribbler to die of old age? Really, Mikros could not think that his uncle was much of a threat to security, and yet, one never knew who might be plotting until it was too late.

Yes, it would be a simple matter to have the old man put under house arrest; to give out the news that he was unwell.

The day would soon come when Menelaos could be made to disappear. Then he would announce that he had choked on a fishbone, and order three full days of public mourning, and carry the libations of milk and honey and undiluted wine to the tomb himself.

So inoffensive during his life time, Menelaos could cause no trouble afterwards, for that he had lived out more than his full span of years, and such a man was guaranteed to come back to haunt nobody.

Some nights Mikros thought such thoughts, but Mikros was really an honourable prince, a *kalokagathos* if ever there was one, a man of perfect purity of soul, and he pushed these thoughts out of his heart in disgust and raised his arms in prayer to the gods of Greece, in order to be forgiven.

3.26

The Dream of Eating the Stars

When they sent to tell him of an old woman at the palace gates, asking for Ptolemy son of Lagos—a woman with limbs twisted by leprosy, a woman with white hair, and bent almost double, hardly able to walk— Ptolemy asked what were her words.

Tell Ptolemy I was the famous Thaïs, she said, they said.

But he shook his head, saying, *They all say that; they cannot all have been Thaïs . . .* and he refused to see her.

Give her a loaf of bread, he said.

As usual, the strange woman at the gates unsettled him, started him thinking again about the past that he would rather forget but could not help but remember. Thaïs—where now, he wondered, was the golden brilliance of her famous beauty? Where now were her disdainful brow and proud spirit, her slender neck, the rich gold clasps of her haughty ankles? Now, surely, her hair must be unadorned and unkempt, and rags must hang about her feet. *She must,* he thought, *by now be just like the woman at the gate,* almost as old as himself, but poor. Such was the end of whores. If, indeed, she was still alive.

He looked out of his high window, and his eye caught the eye of this woman, looking up, waiting, and he knew that it both was and was not, could not be, her, and he turned away, and the bull's tail that hung always between his legs swung with violence. Sand blown in from the desert made his eyes water.

He sent down even so a purse of gold oktodrachms after the woman, coins with his own face upon them, and his title *Basileus,* and his name, Ptolemaios. Above every other thing, it was the thought of Thaïs, the lost Thaïs, and what might have become of her, the first woman he ever loved, that kept him awake by night.

Ptolemy lay sleepless as a donkey in a thorn bush, as he said, night after night, thinking not of today but of yesterday, against all his philosophical principles. When he complained of it, his physicians increased the dosage of nightingale flesh for sleeplessness, so that he fell asleep now in the middle of audiences with foreign ambassadors, or during the Council of State, and it led Eskedi to suggest that it might please Ptolemy to hand over the whole responsibility of government to Ptolemy Mikros.

But Ptolemy refused. *Not yet,* he said.

Ptolemy slept less and less, and then when he did sleep he would wake up screaming the *Alalalalai,* and at dawn his face would often be wet with tears, for it was the hour for the burial of the dead, and he thought of his friends gone to Hades.

Seeing the old man troubled, Eskedi suggested, *Let him write down what he remembers. Let him put down his thoughts upon papyrus. Let him forget by remembering.*

So that Ptolemy restarted his History of Alexander, which he had, in fact, been trying to write these forty years. For some hours each day, and often during the dead hours of the night, he would sit with the reed pen in his hand, writing.

When the sleeplessness improved only a little, Eskedi spoke with Queen Berenike, and with Mikros her son, to ask what might set his troubled heart at peace. And the wife thought, and the son thought, that the one thing Old Ptolemy missed most as Pharaoh was the companionship of his old comrades; that he suffered most from the *aloneness* of power.

And so the Queen, the Prince, the High Priest—they asked the old man what would please him most, and between them the suggestion came forth that he might like to go back to being ordinary.

In fact, it was so arranged that the thought was the idea of Ptolemy himself: that what would please him most would be to go back to drilling with the ranks, to go back to shouldering his *sarissa,* and be part of the great phalanx of foot soldiers once again.

Even Berenike, who might formerly have laughed such an idea to scorn, said, *Let him go back to being a common soldier if he wishes it,* because what it meant was that her own son, Ptolemy Mikros, could put on all the panoply of the Pharaoh. It meant that Mikros would be king in all but name, and it was the beginning of the triumph of the widow from Macedon.

A co-regency, it was, to keep strong the authority of the Pharaoh at that most dangerous of times, the changeover between two reigns. But it was no new thing. By no means. Rather, it was the ancient Egyptian custom to set the son upon the throne beside his father, and the Pharaoh Ammenemes started it, or, as some said, Piopi the First, hundreds of years previous, when that Pharaoh had said, *Crown him as King, that I may see his beauty whilst I am still alive,* and called the chamberlains to fasten the crowns upon his head.

Eskedi, High Priest of Ptah, made every arrangement. It was not some new idea of the Greeks, who, in truth, did not dare to meddle with such high matters—or at least, not yet.

The day came, then, when Ptolemy Mikros showed his face wearing the Double Crown called the Great One and with the *Ouraios* serpent sitting upon his forehead, and became to every appearance King of Egypt; and Ptolemy Soter quit wearing the *khepresh* crown all day, but was a retired Pharaoh, and Berenike almost died of delight to see her son, her own son, a king and a living god.

Ptolemy Soter now enrolled himself anew in his own palace guard, and went back to drilling with the phalanx each morning, before the heat of the day grew too fierce. He shouldered again the *sarissa,* or lance, of Macedon, with the young men. He marched down Kanopic Street in the parade of the veterans of Alexander, and he was only a little out of step. He joined even in the classic exhibition of marching and counter-marching, the silent show of Macedonian power, that had so impressed the barbarians on the borders of Thrace when he was a young man. He sang the Paian to Apollo, and the Greek songs of war, and the marching songs, even in the wine shops of Alexandria with the veterans, and he staggered home up Kanopic Street in the early hours with the other old men, shouting the *Alalalalai,* and he smiled his old smile, not the half-smile of the Pharaoh.

No, Ptolemy had never wanted to be a *strategos*. He had never sought high command, but it had been thrust upon him. Now he found again the delight to be got from drinking with his fellow men, and the good that came from talking over past times.

And no, nobody thought the worse of him for any of it. On the contrary, it was the greatest honour he could possibly pay to the common soldier, without whom no battle in all of Greek and Egyptian history together was ever won.

Moreover, although it was unthinkable that Pharaoh should wander the streets and be again a private citizen, this was what Ptolemy now did at Alexandria—and the Greeks loved him for it all the more.

Ptolemy would go *on foot* into the gardens of his great white Residence. He passed hours staring at the Great Sea, the *grey* sea, out of which his Pharos rose. He would speak with the tunny fishermen beside the Harbour of Eunostos, the Harbour of Happy Returns. He sought out the old soldiers with whom he had marched across the Paropamisos, or Hindu Kush, and the terrible Desert of Gedrosia, and they told their tales, and laughed and shed their tears together, and remembered the dead, and Ptolemy pressed his silver tetradrachms into their palms, and the coins had upon them his own beetled brow and jutting chin, his wild curly hair, and his own name: PTOLEMAIOS.

Wherever Ptolemy went, the ripple of applause followed him. In the *agora* the Greek tradesmen prostrated themselves before him in the golden dust, and beat the ground with their fists, until Ptolemy made it plain that the prostration was unnecessary, not now that he was not quite King of Upper and Lower Egypt any more.

Ptolemy had lived beyond his time. One by one his contemporaries passed away, and he outlived all of them, except Menelaos the brother. He was waiting, now, waiting for Hades to take him, waiting to be reborn in his tomb in the West, waiting to make his journey to become one of the Imperishable Stars. He was making his farewells.

When the marching became difficult, because of his infirmity, Ptolemy the Ever-Living would pass the days in the Residence, seeing nobody but ghosts, looking all morning out of his windows at the Pharos, thinking, *Nearly finished,* and looking at the glory of his Great Harbour, watching the ships come and go, the oars rising and falling in perfect order, like the wings of the eagle.

The afternoons he passed writing, or trying to write, but he was wide awake long after midnight, shuffling about the corridors, thinking, thinking.

One time he consulted the Homer Oracle, to find how many days he had left, only to be delivered words that seemed to apply more to Keraunos, the disgraced heir: *Master your great passion. You should not have a heart that does not forgive.*

But the Greeks know nothing of forgiveness. A Greek will always choose revenge. And no, he would not forgive Keraunos for his stupidity, for his wildness, for the way he acted like a regular barbarian. Above all, he could not forgive the *aphrodisia* upon his own sister, that would like as not prove fatal for the House of Ptolemy for generations to come.

Sometimes Ptolemy raged about these things; sometimes he chewed nightingale; sometimes he slept, sometimes he did not sleep. He would sleep the long sleep, the bronze sleep, he thought, soon enough.

On the days when to live seemed almost more troublesome than to die, Ptolemy thought he might fly to the stars upon the whirlwind and not mind it at all. But it was not to happen yet: the day appointed by the Fates—the Three Sisters, Klotho, Lakhesis and Atropos—for Ptolemy to end his life, had not yet dawned.

Death, whom this Ptolemy had urged to come quick so many times—while slicing up his enemy upon the field of battle, or as King of Egypt with the power to send a man down to Hades with a single word—Death would be a long time coming to Ptolemy.

He had time enough left to write more of his memoirs, his History of Alexander; he had time still to set down every thing he could remember, in spite of his trembling hand. And when the ague, the marsh fever, fell upon him—and it was still a regular, a frequent thing—he trembled so much that the words he scratched upon the papyrus nobody could read but himself, and he murmured: *Old age has its cruel hold upon me now . . .*

The time passed and the time passed and Ptolemy dreamed that winged ants were walking into his ears, and he knew that the dream meant perilous voyages.

He dreamed of eating the stars, and he knew that while eating the stars signified Good Luck for astronomers, to other men it meant death.

When he dreamed again of the eagle perching upon his head, Ptolemy again asked the opinion of the oneiroscopist, and this time he was told the truth.

The eagle perched upon a man's head, said the interpreter of dreams, *means the death of the dreamer, for the eagle kills whatever he grasps in his talons.*

And so Ptolemy began to make ready for his last journey, the short voyage in the Boat of Charon across the River Styx to Hades. In case he did not wake up, he practised going to bed with the obol upon his tongue, the coin to pay the ferryman, seeing how it felt; wondering if a dead man might not swallow the coin in spite of himself.

So much for the Greek way of dying. But he knew by heart, now, also the correct words of power of the Egyptians, and he whispered them as he lay in his bed, eyes closed, taking what might be his last breaths: the relevant chapters of the *Book of Coming Forth by Day*:

> *I am Yesterday; I know Today . . .*
> *Who then is this?*
> *Yesterday is Osiris . . . Today is Ra . . .*

Old Anemhor, and Eskedi after him, had seen to it that Ptolemy was well briefed. He would take no chances regarding the Afterlife; he wanted the best of both Otherworlds, Greek and Egyptian, but refused to commit himself to what manner of funeral rites he wanted, so that— when the end came—they might, perhaps, give him both, or at least decide for him, because, to be sure, this man who was not quite a Greek and not quite an Egyptian either could not make up his mind about it.

Some days, when Eskedi, High Priest of Ptah, came to talk to him, he wavered, refusing to acknowledge the Egyptian rite.

We are a Greek, he said, *not an Egyptian . . .* And he saw the horror upon Eskedi's brown face, because for Eskedi to bury the Pharaoh according to the custom of Egypt—brain hooked out through the nostrils, body steeped seventy days in dry natron, soles of the feet removed and replaced with gold, eyes replaced by two white onions, the golden finger-stalls, thousands of cubits of bandage, topped by the golden mask—it was the most momentous task of his priestly career, of his whole life, and his very reason for existing.

Eskedi breathed with patience. He adjusted his leopard-skin mantle, sat down beside Ptolemy, and began the lesson of lessons once again, the Instruction for Conduct in the Afterlife.

He explained, yes, how the whole of Chapter One Hundred and Twenty-five of the *Book of Coming Forth by Day* was written by Thoth in order to shrive Ptolemy of his sins; how it had been written for him upon papyrus; how it must be placed between his knees inside his coffin of beaten gold.

But all Ptolemy said was, *You have told us that Pharaoh can commit no sin . . . The Pharaoh can do no wrong . . .* as if he wanted to make fun of the High Priest of Ptah.

At this Eskedi became urgent in his speech, telling Ptolemy again and again how the papyrus was his indispensable Guidebook to the Underworld: that Ptolemy should not think that he might go there without it, and that without the embalming after the manner of the Egyptians his *Ka* would not, could not, live, and Ptolemy would not, in that case, be Ptolemy the Ever-Living, but would be a dead man in the Afterlife.

But Ptolemy, in his half-understanding, was content. He faced the unknown with composure. He was quite ready to undergo the Weighing of his Heart in the Scales. He had been led to view Thoth the Ibis, who writes down the Judgement of the Gods, as his personal friend. Then he said he was not, in any case, going to die just yet, that he was not ready to go, and he sat up with the agility of a man half his age, swung his legs over the edge of the golden bed, waved the High Priest and his leopard spots away, and sat down to pen a further chapter of the great History.

No, Ptolemy was not ready for the Great Strider, the Swallower of Shades, the Breaker of Bones, the Eater of Blood, the Announcer of Combat, or any of the other demons he would face in the Afterlife. And no, he did not need, just yet, the dead man's Guidebook to the Underworld.

Ptolemy the Ever-Living wanted to live a little longer.

3.27

The Wet Nose of Anubis

The family saw things different: that he could not last many more days, and that the dying man was their messenger to the Underworld, and they busied themselves writing their Letters to the Dead, after the curious custom of the Greeks, which they would hurl upon his funeral bonfire as the latest courier to the unseen world, sure that Ptolemy could have no last rites but Greek rites.

The daughters mouthed the messages they would whisper at the moment of the last kiss, into the dead man's ears, when they believed they might make contact with those that had gone before them.

Berenike made ready her message for her kinsman Antipatros (*A Queen*, she wrote, *a Goddess . . .*) and a message even for Philippos, her first of husbands (*Impossible riches . . .*); and Theoxena rehearsed words that she would whisper for the dead Agathokles of Syracuse (*Not happy, but I shall join thee soon . . .*).

This custom was new to them. They had not looked upon the dead. They had no experience of death. In this family, relatives did not die, but simply disappeared. Thaïs had vanished. Their grandparents might as well have never lived. Nobody these children knew had ever died and had a funeral. It was as if at the court of King Ptolemy death, apart from the death of the Sacred Bull, did not exist.

This state of affairs was about to end.

Ptolemy himself prayed to Phoibos Apollo for a peaceful passing; not to be burned up *alive* on his pyre, but to be properly dead. Such things every Greek worried about, but now the uncertainty of death came close, he found that the gods of Greece were real after all, and a comfort to him in his last hours.

Eskedi, High Priest of Ptah, came often to talk to him, and he saw this aged King, his flesh wrinkled like the shell of a walnut, his limbs heavy, his eyes misty with age, and he said, *Behold now, His Majesty—Life, Health, Strength, to him!—has become old. His bones are like silver. His limbs are like gold. His hair is like sappheiros . . .*

And he said, *You shall not perish, your members shall not be destroyed. You shall not be wiped out for ever and ever. May you live.*

And Ptolemy was grateful to him.

He set about making ready for death, after the custom of the Greeks. He took the ritual bath. He settled his affairs. He prayed the prayer to Hestia, goddess of the Hearth, and the prayer for a safe crossing of the Styx. And he said his last words to his officers of state, his ministers, his generals and admirals, to his friends, and to the family—those members of it that were left in Egypt—who loitered beside the bed and clasped his hands, and said their *Fare thee well, Ptolemaios, even in the House of Hades.*

Then he ordered them all out of the chamber, so as not to see the moment of his passing. But the family refused to budge, believing that at his death a man's soul is raised to a higher plane of consciousness that enables him to prophesy the future. Thus the dying Patroklos had foretold the death of Hektor; thus the dying Hektor had foretold the death of Achilles.

All Greeks expect a dying man's speech to be memorable, and they wanted to hear what Ptolemy would say. Yes, they wished above all to know what would become of the House of Ptolemy in Egypt without him, and to the Greeks abandoned in a foreign land. They had, every one of them, a burning desire to know what might happen next.

The heir, the Prince Ptolemy Mikros, bent over his father and looked into the staring eyes, knowing that so long as he could see an image reflected in the pupils the old man would live. But the truth was that, like all heirs to thrones, he wanted his father to die.

Beside the bed sat ever the old Queen, Berenike, with the hem of her *peplos* stuffed into her mouth to stifle her sobs.

A man loved from the heart by Zeus, she murmured, *is worth many armies.*

Berenike would receive the last breath of Ptolemy, as was her duty. She would cease to be the Great Royal Wife and become the new King's Mother, with the burdensome title of the Great White Cow Who Dwells in Nekher. She found it unspeakable in the extreme for Berenike, Beloved of the Vulture, who smiled beneath the Vulture Tiara, to take on the form of the cow, a beast sacred to the Egyptians but disgusting to every Greek, a creature that was pleased to stand in her own filth, and stupid beyond belief.

But the life of Berenike would change little. She would never stop being bored by the sight of gold, which she said now was like *skubalon,* like filth. She would never stop being bored of finery, bored of being royal, bored of being carried everywhere in her electrum-plated litter when, really, she would prefer to walk, and bored above all by her life of high pretence.

Berenike thought often that she would be pleased to slap her laundry upon the rocks, like the native women she watched from her high windows, a useful occupation which in times long past she had found quite satisfying.

It was in the season of the dogs going mad that King Ptolemy Soter arrived at the day that was fated to be the day of the Scissors of Fate, when the thread of his life must be cut, and the day was hot.

Ptolemy lay now gasping for his breath, like a fish upon the mud bank, and he wore still about his neck and wrists and upper arms the Greek talismans that he had worn all his life and sworn never to take off, that were now cased in gold or leather because there was little left of them but dust. And he did not stop, even upon this day that was his last day, from fingering the *phallos* amulet that brought him the best of luck.

Towards the end of the morning Mikros took his father by the hand, so that he should feel no fear in his heart. When he went quiet, they hoped that he might be dead, and Mikros placed two fingers over his father's wrist, seeking the beat of his pulse, or the lack of it; but the pulse was busy, like ants running under the skin.

At the Hour of Perfuming the Mouth, with the sun at its height, they fanned the old man with palm-leaf fans, and he moved to hide his face, thinking to pour out his spirit into Charon's boat, and he seemed to fall once again into the sleep from which there is no awakening. But the fingers of Mikros felt yet the ants running through his wrist.

So many times they thought he had left them. So many times they tried the unbeatable test for death that was the finger touched upon the eyeball, and when at last there was no response when the Prince Mikros poked the finger, Berenike closed the dead man's eyes, and drew his legs down straight, and gathered up her breath for the howling.

But Mikros furrowed his brow. *Ants . . .* he murmured, and Berenike sighed a long sigh, and they tramped all of them from the chamber and left him—in truth a little exasperated that he would not die but kept them waiting—and sought refreshment: olives, and dough dipped in honey, and undiluted wine, that was the breakfast of the Greeks.

At first the half-dozen dwarf slaves they left with Ptolemy thought he was just resting. Then they thought he just slept, although his chest moved not, and the labour of his breathing was no more.

Do not disturb, they said. *Do not touch.* And for the moment this Pharaoh was, like Alexander, neither quite alive nor quite dead.

A bluebottle landed upon the stubble of his scalp, and stood flexing the limbs, making ready for the feast.

One of the dwarf slaves that cared for the King's wardrobe now slipped his bare black feet into the golden sandals of the Pharaoh and tried a few steps across the mosaic, showing his white teeth to his friends.

A second bluebottle alighted on Ptolemy's head, and a black cloud of Egyptian flies hurtled past the closed shutters of the Window of Appearances, where he had shown his smiling face for the last time.

A second dwarf slave, who looked after the regalia, picked up the crook and flail of gold and *sappheiros* and held them crossed over his chest, laughing his high-pitched laugh: in the pause between two reigns even a dwarf slave might be a king, and his white teeth flashed in a face that was like night.

In another part of the Residence a fresh cloud of flies effected their entry and rocketed down the passage towards the sour-sweet smell of death.

One by one the personal possessions of this King moved upon his bedside table of ebony and ivory and gold—the fly-switch of gold, the golden Eye-of-Horus bracelet, the bull's tail that had flicked between his buttocks twenty-two years—and adorned in turn the flesh of his body-servants. The high shrill laughter escaped their dark lips, and they were kings for a further moment.

Ptolemy stirred not. Some dark liquid trickled from his mouth and dripped on to the mosaic floor. Now a deep stillness reigned, and the slaves seemed to hold their breath, waiting for others to do what they could not do themselves: end the old era and begin the new.

Afterwards they swore, yes, the soul of the old man flew out of his mouth with the very noise of a pheasant flushed from cover, and they mimicked the squawking of it; but the truth was that Ptolemy died quiet, and nobody noticed his passing.

Apollo had granted this Greek the greatest gift within his power: a peaceful death.

When the royal family wandered back into the chamber they squeezed the body of Ptolemy with their hands, to force the soul out of him, after the custom of the Egyptians, and Mikros swore that he had seen his father's soul fly forth from his lips in the form of a raven.

It was a fiction. Everybody knows how the Greeks love to tell lies.

The truth is that a dying man will always see things, and Ptolemy saw things in his last hours that no living man could explain to him. He saw in the distance Anubis the Dog-head walking towards him through the succession of connecting chambers, and it was Eskedi, of course, the High Priest of Ptah at Memphis, wearing upon his head the jackal mask, and he was Anubis, Pharaoh of the Underworld, and Ptolemy knew that the wearing of the dog mask was the sign of the hour of his death.

Eskedi knew, in his turn, the horoscope of this King, that the hour had come for this Pharaoh to go to the sky; for him to become indeed one of the Imperishable Stars.

To the priests of Egypt the passing of the Pharaoh is never a surprise. From the beginning they know that a child will live so many years, months, days, for death is no accidental thing, but part of the great plan of the gods, like everything else in his life.

Black Anubis took this Ptolemy by the hand, and the hand of Anubis was lean, black, soft, furred like the leg of a dog, and for Ptolemy, who had waited so long, wondering how many days, here, at last, was his answer, for the wet nose of Anubis now pressed into his shoulder, nudging him forward. The paw of Anubis pushed into the flesh of his back, making him walk, and Anubis the Jackal, the Supervisor of the Secrets, led Ptolemy away. Anubis: the inside of his ears and the collar round his neck were of gold, and his eyes were white, like calcite, with pupils black, like obsidian, outlined with gold; his eyebrows were of gold, and his claws shone like silver, pressing into the flesh of the hand of Ptolemy, sharp, and the ears of Anubis were pricked, upright; and he knew that Anubis was the god, that Anubis was real, from his gentle growling, and from the fact that the dog's hand and arm were hot, hot, like living flesh, and for that his nose was wet, and his dog breath was hot upon the back of Ptolemy's neck, and the wet nose nudged him onwards.

Eskedi told the family then, *Yea,* he said, *the scarab beetle flies during the hottest hour of the day in Egypt, and for this reason he is associated with the Sun god, with Ra.*

Mikros, Berenike, and the rest of them, looked at Eskedi, with curiosity, perhaps understanding, perhaps not.

The dead King, Eskedi went on, *flies now like a bird, alighting like the beetle upon the empty throne in the celestial boat of Ra.*

Aye, when the soul of this Pharaoh left his body, it flew upwards with a wild squawking, with a frantic beat of wings, like the duck in the papyrus marshes, and it was the veritable *Ka* of Ptolemy, like a human-headed bird, and it flew round and round the room like a sparrow trapped in the house that cannot find her way out; and Eskedi, High Priest of Ptah, the Master of Secrets in the Secret Place, opened the shutter of the Window of Appearances wide, to allow it to pass through, and the soul of Ptolemy the Ever-Living was gone.

3.28

The Red Feast of the Dead

As soon as they were satisfied that the ants had indeed stopped their running and the last breath was out of his body, Queen Berenike did what the wife of every dead Greek man must do, and took off her jewellery of gold. She pulled off her vulture finger-rings, her siren earrings, her heavy vulture-necklace of gold and every august costly stone, her golden anklets, and she put on instead the black earrings, the necklace of beads of jet, the bracelets of plainest ebony. She changed her white linen dress for the black *peplos* and the black sandals of mourning.

She smeared then the black mud of the Nile upon her face and hands and breasts and she felt it was disgusting, filthy, and her grief would be false grief, for that she felt now nothing for this dead man, in spite of history saying that hers was a love-match. Her love was dead love, that had been cold a score of years, and some said *never hot.*

Berenike gathered herself for the wailing, and Eskedi, High Priest of Ptah, threw open the double doors of cedar wood and gold inlaid with ivory from the Land of Punt, and he spoke the dread words to the door-guards: *The Falcon has flown to the sky . . . and the King his son is seated upon the throne of Ra in his stead.*

The long long silence broke then, with the *slap slap slap* of bare feet upon the mosaic floors, and it was the feet of the palace dwarfs running, and at once the howling started up, the dreadful ululation of Berenike the widow, and it was echoed and magnified not only by the native women of Egypt but also by the women of Greek blood, that shrill howling that makes every man's hair stand up upon the back of his neck, and a shiver run down every man's spine in spite of the heat; the wailing that the women always set up when anybody died, but that was more specially shrill upon the death of Pharaoh.

The wailing raced across the colonnaded Greek courtyards and out through the Greek gates into the Greek city, swift as a flame in dry grass, down Kanopic Street and the Street of the *Soma,* or Body, of Alexander, into the native quarter called Rhakotis, across the Heptasta-dion to the still-unfinished Pharos, out through the Gate of the Moon and along the Canal to Kanopos, and up-River to Memphis; and then rapid as the plague the wailing flew south to Heliopolis and Hermopolis, Hierakonpolis and Apollonopolis, to Philai and Syene and the borders of Egypt, on and on, into Nubia and the Land of Punt, the spice-bearing country, with the news that Ptolemaios the Greek, Ptlumis, King Ptolemy, Beloved of Amun, Living for Ever, was dead, until it seemed as if every woman in Egypt wailed with one voice.

Disaster had befallen Egypt and there would be chaos in Heaven until the successor of Ptolemy was crowned: a brief reign of the eternal Trouble-Maker, Seth, who was the embodiment of all Evil, until the coming again of Osiris, and his son, the Living Horus, in the form of the new Ptolemy, the Ptolemy who would be called Ptolemy Philadelphos, the Sister-Loving One, whom for the time being they knew, all of them, as Mikros.

Loudest of all the wailing women was the Queen. Berenike howled, like the wolf, like the jackal of the desert. She howled for her dead husband, and for herself left living without him, and for the uncertainty of her future, and for the bloody purge of all relatives, which she knew must come at once; but she howled most of all for the beginning of the end of her time of glory in Egypt, knowing that it could not last.

Away at Miletos the self-styled ex-Queen Eurydike of Egypt woke in the dead hours of the night, only halfway through her dream of a sumptuous palace life in Alexandria that was now lost, screaming and shivering, in spite of the heat.

Yes, Eurydike sensed what must have happened, without having to wait for the news, and she put on at dawn not the white *peplos* and gold jewellery of a woman who was almost a queen, but the black *peplos* of mourning for the dead man.

As for Ptolemy Keraunos, the Thunderbolt, her son, the Prince who should that day have been the new Pharaoh, who was then some thirty-six years of age, when the messenger reached him with the news of the King his father's death, his face did not change. He said nothing, no, not one word, but his lip curled up in a sneer, and he spat his spittle upon the ground. It was only when night fell that this hardest of men gave in to his feelings, and only under the blanket of his bed, where no man could see his face, that he might have wept for the death of his father, and for the loss of every thing for which he had yearned.

Back in Alexandria the howling went on without stopping for seventy days and seventy nights, which was the length of the embalming process, until the burial of this great King had been accomplished— caterwauling for a Pharaoh who was not even an Egyptian.

In the Residence all work came to a stop. No business was done. No food was cooked. Nothing happened in the Residence for seventy days but the endless shrieking of the women.

The succession, at least, was secure, and King Ptolemy Soter died, surely, a happy man, but in the immediate chaos that followed his flying to the sky the great concern of those who outlived him was what to do with his earthly remains.

Aye, Thoth asks it also: What would they do with him, this Greek King dead in a far country? Normal Greek practice would be to have the corpse exposed at the laying out, upon a couch, and let the Greeks file past him to pay their last respects, which was what had been done when Alexander died. So they came, then, *every soldier of his army,* and wept tears for him not living longer. They kissed his still-warm lips and stroked his hot stiff fingers, and whispered their messages for the dead into the whorled crevices of his ears.

Meanwhile, this Greek family of his argued with the Egyptians about what were his last wishes, and the voices rose and fell, Mikros and Berenike, Philotera, Arsinoë Alpha, Eskedi and the High Priests of Heliopolis and Hermopolis and Thebes, arguing, late into the night.

Mummification after the manner of the Egyptians was not what this Ptolemy had wished for. He had seen the earwigs scuttle up dead Alexander's nostrils. He had watched the larder beetles march in and out of Alexander's stoppered ears, and he had wanted none of it.

Burn me up, he had said, *for I have no desire to last for ever, like Alexander.* And the Greeks swore he had said it, over and over again, until Eskedi spread his hands, turned upon his heel, and the leopard spots moved fast down the corridors of power, and it was the first and last time they saw him run.

The serving women washed the flesh of Ptolemy, and anointed him with olive oil, and dressed him in a fresh white tunic, and laid his purple cloak upon him, treating Ptolemy in death like the heroes of Homer, for the world of the Greeks, like that of the Egyptians, was a world where nothing was meant to change, but every thing must be done according to tradition.

They garlanded him with white flowers and laid him upon his bier in readiness for the journey to the pyre, Greek-style. For two days the family sat up with him, to make sure, doubly sure, the old man was dead, watching for the last flickerings of life, so that they should not burn him up still living, and yes, staring at his smile. For if the corpse wore a smile, it meant that he must draw after him another member of the family. And Ptolemy did smile. He grinned even in death that mysterious smile, that half-smile of a pharaoh. And for all the pummelling that Berenike gave his fat cheeks the grin was set hard, like Egyptian plaster, and would not go away, as if he might draw after him not just one, but all of them; as if there must be repeated deaths, deaths many and violent beyond any man's imagining.

And, Thoth knows, it would be so.

On the third day, before sunrise, the procession moved out of the gates of the Residence and they carried his body to the beach east of the city of Alexandria, when, after years of silence and being told to be quiet, the Greek women came into their own.

Queen Berenike, the chief mourner, stood by the head of the dead man and began the *klama,* the song of mourning, lifting her voice in praise of her husband. Her knees stiffened, her hair fell in disorder, her veil she stretched across her two shoulders, holding one end in each hand, working it up and down in a sawing movement in time to the slow beat of the dirge.

Berenike struck her breast with her two fists. She clawed at her cheeks. The dirge went faster and faster, until it was a meaningless gabble of Greek, and at the last it was nothing but shrieking, wholly without meaning, until Philotera and Arsinoë Alpha took up the song for her.

Berenike tore out her hair in handfuls and flung it upon the bier, just as Achilles and the Myrmidons had cast their hair upon the bier of Patroklos. Berenike staggered like a drunken woman, her hair in a tangle over her face, her cheeks criss-crossed with tears and blood and the deep scratch-lines that would never disappear.

The waiting-gentlewomen, who knew Berenike better than anybody else, thought she overdid the wailing, that she was not utterly sincere in her grief, and the tongues clicked for some days afterwards.

As for the men, Mikros, Uncle Menelaos, the bastard sons of Soter whose names nobody could remember, and Lagos and Leontiskos, sons of Thaïs, about whom everybody had forgotten—they were uncomfortable amid this public and uncontrolled grief. They fixed their eyes upon the ground, thinking of the night of the knives that was to come, and shifted their feet in the golden sand.

And so they burned him up, in a wall of flame, and the smoke flew into their faces and made their eyes water.

In the absence of Keraunos it had to be Mikros that gathered up the bones after the burning, washed them in gleaming wine, and wrapped them in soft cloths of purple embroidered with golden thread by the women of the House, and placed them in the proper *larnax*, or box, of gold, after the custom of the Greeks, and then they lodged what was left of him beside Alexander, in the great Tomb, or *Sema*, upon Kanopic Street, at the crossroads of his city.

Year upon year for three hundred years, the House of Ptolemy would keep the day of the birthday of the dead Ptolemy Soter, and walk in solemn procession to the Tomb, bearing the proper libations of milk, and honey, and undiluted wine. They poured out the liquids according to their religious duty, as if a man beyond the grave might benefit from having whole amphoras full of wine tipped into the cracks between the stones of his last resting-place.

In latter years they would argue about the founder of this House, having forgotten not only how they had disposed of the first Ptolemy, but even also where they had left him. To be sure, the day would even come when they did not know whether this King was burned as a Greek or buried as a Pharaoh, inside the triple coffin of solid gold, wrapped and bandaged in death just as he had been wrapped and bandaged at birth, so that he finished up just exactly how he started.

Nobody forgot, however, what was done immediately after the funeral of Ptolemy Soter. By no means. This they remembered for ever, because they all trooped back to the Tomb after the proper number of days, to eat the *Thanatousia*, the Banquet of the Dead, the funeral feast of the Greeks, at which every last foodstuff was *red,* for they ate upon this sad occasion all the foods that were forbidden to be eaten at any other meal, gorging themselves upon tomatoes, and raspberries, and strawberries, and red mullet, and crayfish, and shrimps, and lobsters, and bacon, and beetroot, and cherries, and cranberries—stuffing their Greek faces with the foods that were the colour of blood.

For in Greece *red* is the colour of death.

Thoth says it: To speak true, the family of Ptolemy *liked* the *Thanatousia* better than any other meal, and the Red Feast of the Dead was the one thing that made a death in the family something to look forward to, something to be remembered afterwards, so that some of these Greek folk would even pray for a fresh death in the family; so that they might once again be allowed to eat lobster and strawberries, with the red juice trickling down their chins. And so it was, yes, year upon year, generation upon generation, for there was death after death, death upon death upon death to come in this family, and every time it was the same: their lips and chins were red, and their Greek garments of whitest linen were stained red and splashed, as if with blood.

For the House of Ptolemy death was almost a welcome event, not so much the cause of sorrow and grief, but of a quiet rejoicing.

Indeed, to the Ptolemies death would come often.

3.29

Makers of Trouble

When they were done with last rites, there was the problem of what must be done with the Trouble-Makers, and at the top of the list of difficult people was Uncle Menelaos, brother of Ptolemy, who dribbled still in his high apartments, but must be the first suspect, even so, for treachery.

For some hours the new Pharaoh, Ptolemy Mikros, paced about the mosaic, looking at the dolphins and tridents, thinking what must be done. Menelaos might die soon enough, of natural causes. He presented, in truth, no threat to security. But there was the matter of his sons, whose names nobody in after years could name, and the sons of those sons also, and the problem was that the sons and grandsons could not be killed off without killing also the grandfather.

Mikros—did he not despise this uncle of his, the dribbler, whose pleasure was always to tell him what he should do? This man, the high point of whose military career had been the loss of the island of Cyprus?

Mikros wondered if he might make it possible for Uncle Menelaos to have some accident with his bronze razors.

Should he, he wondered, hurry Uncle Menelaos along the road to Hades?

But no, Mikros had his doubts. He was a king of the highest honour, who told the truth at all times. And he put away his dark thoughts and sent Menelaos a basket of figs, as a gesture of goodwill.

Down at Memphis, the word was that Menelaos was still alive, living, yes, in his old apartments at Alexandria.

Up at Alexandria the word was that Menelaos was enjoying a well-earned retirement up at Thebes, where the climate was more healthy, more dry.

Winged Rumour spread her stories: Menelaos had fled Egypt, she said, as soon as the old King passed away. Gentle, kind Menelaos, they said, was got rid of when his nephew came to the throne, and his devoted wife with him, and their sons, trained from early youth to be *strategoi* in the army of Egypt, and his grandchildren also, usurpers all of them, a rival dynasty waiting their moment to seize power: the very embodiment of Trouble.

Ptolemy Soter had warned this son of his to do the deed and do it quick, to waste no time. The Night of the Short Sword, he called it, when the new King must work through the list.

Mikros heard the old man's voice still, loud and clear: *To be safe, every one of them must be put to the sword.*

And when Mikros had pulled a face, he had become urgent in his speech: *If you do not cut down every relative, it will be your fate instead of theirs, and Ptolemy Mikros will set his foot in the House of Hades fifty years early.*

Soon the official line emerged: that Uncle Menelaos ate too many unripe figs and choked to death; that it was his own stupid fault—though in truth the only crime of this most inoffensive of old men (apart from the loss of Cyprus) was to be the brother of a king.

As for the family of Menelaos, there was talk of dysentery, snakebite, fishbone in the throat; of some dreadful fever ripping through his sons and grandsons, one after another, resulting in their sad death.

Counter-Rumour, of course, said that the fever was Mikros himself. But no, Mikros was Pharaoh, a man of the highest honour, who knew how to keep his hands clean, and his reputation also.

Whatever was the truth, no member of the House of Menelaos survived, and there was no memory of what became of them all. They were among the disappeared, as surely as if someone had worked the Spell of Invisibility upon them.

Swift Rumour murmured also of the murder of Argaios, half-brother to Mikros, the son of Eurydike. They said Argaios was executed for conspiracy. And yes, it was just as Eurydike had feared: that the family would resort to killing each other in order to feel safe.

Ptolemy Mikros performed the proper rites of purification: he tipped the bowl of piglet's blood over his two hands. He emptied a bowl of piglet's blood over his head. To be sure, he had not lifted the sword himself, but in spite of the technicality over the blood-guilt, in spite of not being strictly guilty of any crime, but only, as it were, of having commissioned it, Ptolemy Mikros felt guilty, and his guilt would not go away from him.

For, to be sure, to the Greeks a murder in thought is as much as a murder in deed.

In Alexandria the Greeks had created a city where every thing was allowed; where no thing that a man might want to do was forbidden—which meant, perhaps, all the bad things as well as all the good things that a man might do.

It was the crime of Argaios simply to exist. His conspiracy consisted in being the living brother of King Ptolemy, and a son of the unstable Eurydike, and he had lingered too long at Alexandria with too little to do.

It was, all the same, Ptolemy Mikros—this Ptolemy—that would found the illustrious and most illustrious city, up in the district of the Lake of Moeris, that he named Philadelphia, or Brotherly-Love. Mikros the Unwarlike—yes, to be sure, he was making good progress.

What, though, of the rest of the family? Eurydike stayed at Miletos in Ionia under the protection of her most warlike son, Ptolemy Keraunos. With her, at length, dwelt also her widowed daughters Theoxena, and Ptolemaïs—*Three madwomen together,* as they said—for that Alexandria was a city where they could no longer reside in safety, or in their former luxury, or, indeed, feeling in any way comfortable, because of the danger of the knocking upon the door after the hours of darkness. For it was the thought of Mikros that even a sister might resort to poison, to knives; that even a sister could order up a murder if she offered enough money, and he fancied that even these crazy sisters of Ptolemy Keraunos supported his cause. And maybe he was right.

As for the two young sons of Theoxena, who remained in Egypt, the elder boy was that Arkhagathos who was later married to Stratonike, a daughter of Demetrios Poliorketes. When his mother came home to Egypt, he was some ten years of age, a prince with no future; but by the time he was twenty-one years old, he was made *Epistates,* or Governor, of Libya, and the purpose of it was to get him away from Alexandria, where he might have caused trouble.

Arkhagathos was, then, sent up-River, whence, if he did not die of some fever, he might perhaps return some day and be useful to the Pharaoh his cousin, or he might be quietly murdered himself when the time of the disposals came, or as soon as he was reported to have put a foot wrong.

Up-River, to be sure, Arkhagathos felt he might behave just as he pleased, and he devoted his time not only to his duties, which involved the hunting of elephants of war for Ptolemy Mikros, but also to the pleasures of the flesh. Arkhagathos thought that in Libya nobody watched him, but the truth was that he was carefully spied upon by the agents of Ptolemy, and that his every action, good and bad, was reported to the Residence.

Beyond the fact of his sojourn in Libya, nobody could say what became of this youth, except that he stopped appearing in the archives at just about the time of the crowning of Ptolemy Mikros.

Thoughts of Thoth: Really, it is not hard to guess what happened to this boy.

Of the younger brother, Agatharkhos, less still was known, and he suffered the worse fate, in that nobody would so much as remember his name, let alone what was his history, and it was bad because, for the Egyptians at least, for a man's name to be forgotten means that he has no existence in the Afterlife.

So much, then, for the family of Theoxena, a girl who started her adult life with great hopes, and ended it in disaster, without a husband, without heirs, and without her happiness, for how can such a woman be called happy?

Often Theoxena would start the tale of her days in Sicily for any woman who would listen, saying: *I had a husband years ago . . . the bravest and best of our race . . . a lion-hearted man . . .* But she could never finish her story for weeping, not once, not ever, and the women suspected the truth of it was that, love him though she did, and mention it though she did not, her Agathokles treated her with his usual cruelty.

What did the great Solon say? *Call no man happy till he is dead; he is at best lucky.* And he might have added *and no woman.* But Theoxena was not even lucky.

3.30

The Great White Cow

The wife of Ptolemy Mikros, Arsinoë Alpha, daughter of Lysimakhos, was delighted to be the Queen of Egypt, and to wear the Crown Jewels of the Two Lands, and she delighted also in the adoration that fell upon her as the young wife of the Living Horus, the Falcon of Gold, the Son of Ra. Arsinoë Alpha—she smiled almost automatically the smile that the Queen of Egypt was meant to smile, vague, and mysterious, for she was herself, in truth, a vague young woman, whose thoughts tended to be vacant thoughts, but certainly not thoughts of ships of war, or of geometry, or how best to muster an army of hired soldiers, for she had not been given an education in any subject but weaving and tapestry and sewing, and to tell the truth she could not so much as go from *alpha* to *delta*. No, Arsinoë Alpha knew *nothing* of any thing outside household affairs. But none of that mattered one iota to Ptolemy Mikros at the time of his marriage.

Nevertheless, Arsinoë Alpha counted herself very lucky, and she had every thing she desired. She was surrounded by her waiting-gentlewomen, and the *gynaikeion* at Alexandria was loud with the chatter and laughter of young women that were beautiful, like the goddesses to look at, and there was nothing to spoil their contentment.

Arsinoë Alpha passed her time either at Memphis or at Alexandria, depending upon where the court of her husband then was. She did not, to be sure, set eyes upon this husband of hers every day, but she knew that the business of a king is burdensome and unending. She had learned from Arsinoë Beta, her stepmother, how a queen must comport herself, and while she lacked the interest in military matters that the other Arsinoë had, she was eager to involve herself in Egyptian affairs where she could be of some use, and where she understood something of what went on. So Arsinoë Alpha oversaw a fleet of merchant ships that plied in her name up-River and down-River with cargoes of grain, and bananas, and olives, and amphoras full of oil, or wine, and she made sure that the merchant fleet brought in a profit for the Treasury of Ptolemy Mikros.

Arsinoë Alpha ran also the royal manufactory of perfumes and unguents, encouraging always the never-ending search for a mixture that would keep a Greek woman's perspiration to a minimum and at the same time scare off the flies and biting insects of Egypt that liked so very much to land upon her with intent to attack her flesh.

The work of Arsinoë Alpha, then, was not man's work, but war against the flies; but always her meaning was to enrich the coffers of her husband. Her every undertaking was for the greater glory of Ptolemy, for she was the Great Royal Wife, and the King's Wife was not a woman who sat about all day doing nothing. Arsinoë Alpha, Mikros ensured, would *not* become like *Eurydike*.

Queen Arsinoë travelled with King Ptolemy Mikros when temple ritual demanded her presence at his side. She became skilled at playing the *seistron*. Up-River she put on the costume of Isis, the Great Goddess, Great in Magic. She wore the cow's-horn headdress of Hathor without complaint, and the near see-through dress of a living goddess, and she smiled ever the vague smile of the Queen, and she was happy, more than happy, with her new life. In return, Mikros felt that never in his life time had he been so happy, and in his heart he thought it possible that—madness though it was—he loved this wife of his, this beautiful Queen, who wore the Vulture Tiara with such grace.

Arsinoë Alpha might have lived her uneventful existence in Egypt for the rest of her days, but, as it happens, Fate had decided otherwise.

Thoth knows that upon the horizon there was worse trouble for this man and his wife than any trouble they had known in their lives before, and that the cause of it was another woman, and that her name was also Arsinoë—Arsinoë Beta, the other Arsinoë, the woman whom Arsinoë Alpha had thought never to see again in all her life time. For no, the happiness of Arsinoë Alpha would not last for ever, but was fated to come to a dreadful stop.

What, though, of the Old Queen? What had become of Berenike, the Queen Dowager, born some seventy years previous? In these days she would speak most often of the beauty of Greece, of Macedon, her birthplace, for she wished above every other thing for everlasting peace with Macedon, so that she might go home and die in her own country; so that she might die a cool death, instead of dying in the heat of Egypt that was, as she said, like nothing but a fire-box.

But Berenike knew she would never go home to Greece, not now. No, she must stay where she was and sweat it out.

In summer she would have herself driven in the *harmamaxa*, out to the Spouting Rocks, east of the city of Alexandria, with her grandchildren and their nurses, and the instructor of swimming, and they would disport themselves in the Great Sea, because seawater was supposed to be healthy.

To have the skill of swimming, Berenike said, *is so important.* And she drew attention, as her late husband had done, to the curious fact that great Alexander himself was unable to swim, quite unable to do it. And so it became the family tradition for every Ptolemy to learn this art, and to pride himself upon doing something that Alexander had been unable to do, and to learn to do the dog-paddle as well as Berenike.

For Berenike, clever Berenike, swam very well, and in her bathing-dress, shapeless and diaphanous, the Great White Cow That Dwells in Nekher looked like nothing so much as a great sea-monster. And when she floated herself upon her back, she would blow out great spurts of water, very like the whale who some times made his appearance even in the Harbour of Eunostos, the Harbour of Happy Returns.

But Berenike did not, in fact, long survive her husband, and it was just as well she did die, because if she had lived, she would have died for shame at what was going to happen next in the House of Ptolemy, of which Thoth will speak more below. Do not, Reader, quit reading.

Upon the death of Queen Berenike—who became Berenike *Alpha* to distinguish her from the next Queen Berenike to come along—the tears of her son Mikros were like the tears of the crocodile. He felt, in truth, no sadness at the death of this woman, for that she had kept her distance from him most of his life.

Did Berenike abandon this boy to his nurse, and show him but small affection? She did. Not once after he reached the age of seven had she embraced him and lavished her kisses upon his head. Not once had she told this son of hers that she loved him.

Why so? Queen Berenike was good at smiling, good at every pretence, but she had closed that heart of hers against the arrows of Eros, the Wild Boy. Her heart was tough, like a boot of leather, and she did not feel the pangs of love after the failure of her marriage to Philippos of Macedon, but had learned to make believe, in order to have what she wanted. It was a question of survival, of a woman doing as well as she could for herself and for her children. And surely, few women in the history of the world did so well as Berenike, who, though of quite ordinary birth, ended up a queen and a goddess and the richest woman alive.

Even so, she was proud for Mikros her son to be Pharaoh.

Some men said that the coldness of Arsinoë Beta came from Berenike her mother—a woman who was beautiful, but with a heart like a rock, for that her life had been spoiled, ruined, before ever she came to Egypt, by that Philippos whose name and fate were too terrible for her ever to mention.

To his elder sister, Arsinoë Beta, Queen of Thrace, Mikros sent then the message, laconic, after the manner of the Greeks, none of whom would waste six words where two would do: *Mother dead.*

As it happened, Arsinoë Beta knew already. She had woken in the night with the tears flooding down her cheeks for no good reason that she could think of, and nothing to do with the handsome Agathokles. And yes, she had seen the pale figure of Queen Berenike standing at the foot of her bed of beaten gold, face like thunder, and when she sent to ask later, it was the exact hour of her passing.

In the women's quarters there were stronger bonds of affection. If this cold, fierce Arsinoë Beta ever truly loved any member of her family, she had loved her mother, to whom she owed the greatest debt of thanks, for Berenike taught her every thing she knew about magic, and spells, and potions against all manner of illnesses, and about poisons, and how to dispose of a man who was, for whatever reason, unwanted. Berenike was a survivor, and Arsinoë Beta owed her ability to survive to her mother.

They burned the old Queen wearing her finest purple *peplos* and all the jewels she possessed, like any other noblewoman of Macedon, except that there were very many jewels, all of the greatest splendour, and they were Egyptian jewels: vulture collars, snake bracelets, and Horus Eyes, and necklace upon necklace of genuine costly stones.

Or at least, she wore her jewels to the bonfire, and before the flame was kindled they took them all off her, because this degree of finery was too good to go up in smoke, and Arsinoë Alpha wanted it for herself.

With the bones of Berenike at least they buried the two amphoras of oil, and the table of offerings for the funerary feast in the Greek style, and the food to go with it: Greek olives, and dinner loaves, and goat cheese, and dates, and amphoras of wine—the simple fare of Macedon. There were garlands of white roses and narcissi, and the offerings of incense burned up at her funeral rites were more than all the temples of Egypt used up in an entire year. If Berenike was not quite loved, she did, at least, earn the respect of those she left behind.

· · ·

Thus, anyway, the second King Ptolemy, with every relative of his who might possibly rise up and push him off his throne got rid of, sat now safe upon it, and he was pleased with what he had done, most pleased.

Every thing now seemed to be well in Egypt, and this new Pharaoh settled down to begin his rule of peace, and wealth, and glory. *Life! Prosperity! Health!* unto His Majesty.

In the meantime, everything was not quite so well in the Palace of King Lysimakhos of Thrace, but there was trouble, bad trouble, and there would be more, and worse trouble, and the cause of it was the Queen, Arsinoë Beta.

Yes, for Arsinoë Beta there was saved up all the trouble in the world, for her horoscope had long years before foretold it: terrible trouble, and horrors such as would make the hair stand up on end like horns.

Part Four

ARSINOË BETA

Handsome Agathokles

Arsinoë Beta held from Lysimakhos the fief of Ephesos, and in that city she issued coins in her own right—tetradrachms and oktodrachms of gold—that had her image upon one side. She gave orders that she must be shown looking young, queenly, round of face, and veiled—the epitome of a Greek queen; a woman who had achieved already by the age of twenty-two years every thing that a woman might achieve, short of being made a goddess in her own life time.

It was possible, by catching the sunshine upon her coins, to make the golden Arsinoë Beta seem to smile. But the truth was that, though she might smile upon the drachmas of Ephesos, she seldom smiled in the flesh, but went about solemn-faced, or frowning, as if she were angry.

Every letter that Berenike sent to her daughters in Thrace had ended with the same words: *For the rest, please do us a favour by taking care of your health.*

Lysandra had indeed been careful, and little good it would do her, but Arsinoë Beta ignored her mother's wise counsel and did just whatever she pleased, eating all the foods that were most bad for her. Mild pains in the stomach troubled her from time to time, but Arsinoë took no thought for them, and did nothing to change her habits of life. Some days the stomach trouble grew so severe that she had to take to her bed, but even then she did not send for the physicians of her husband, men she looked upon as little better than sorcerers and magicians. She liked much better to dose herself, for fear of being poisoned.

On the one occasion that Arsinoë did ask for the help of her own personal physician, that Dion who had been sent with her from Egypt, he remarked upon the swollen state of her belly, thought she must surely be once again with child, that it must be her time, and urged her to sit upon the royal birth-stool. But for all her screaming and straining Arsinoë was delivered of nothing but a thin black diarrhoea.

What did Arsinoë do? She went back to gorging herself upon roast meat, then she ate nothing but grapes for a month in order to make herself thin, so as to be more pleasing to the Prince Agathokles, and then as soon as she started eating she would become ill again.

To be sure, most of the time this Queen shat black pellets like goat droppings, and for the most part the griping pains in her belly did not leave her in peace.

Such was the beginning of the physical troubles of Arsinoë Beta, and her physical troubles did not go away; and her troubles in love grew, if anything, worse.

As the months and years passed by, the feelings of Arsinoë Beta towards the young Agathokles changed, so that as well as loving him she began also to hate him a little, and the truth of it was that she hardly knew what she was doing, for her love, like every love, was a kind of madness, and she was blinded by it from seeing any sense or reason.

She started to make complaints to Lysimakhos that Agathokles his son had made use of improper language to her, and that he had offended her by putting his hands inside her *peplos* and trying to fondle her breasts.

Lysimakhos found it difficult to believe that his son, a boy of perfect manners, would do such a thing, and for the time being he took no action, leaving the hatred of Arsinoë to grow, until it was her wish not only to see Agathokles punished, but to have him sent away from Thrace altogether, in order to stop his godlike beauty tormenting her day and night.

She hated and loved, now, in equal measures, and she offered Agathokles impossible rewards if he would only step inside her bedchamber; if only he would hold her in his arms and kiss her upon the lips. But Agathokles would always shake his head, and in private, among his friends, he spoke of his concern for the state of mind of his stepmother, and of his sorrow at her distress. He had no idea what words she had spoke to his father, and he breathed never one word to Lysimakhos about what Arsinoë was trying to make him do, knowing that this King would be sure to have his wife put to death, or at the very least divorced and banished, and in truth this boy wished his stepmother no harm. Truly, there was no guile in the heart of handsome Agathokles, who was one of the most virtuous young men that ever lived.

Thoth says, How very different the life of this woman might have been, if only she could have been married to the handsome son instead of to his horrible old father. But the fate of Arsinoë Beta was written from the beginning, and she could not change her fate any more than anybody else. Yes, the fate of Arsinoë Beta was harsh, as if she was fated to be not a woman at all, but, as it were, some poisonous serpent dressed up in a woman's clothes.

Alas, unable to talk Agathokles into doing what she wanted him to do, Arsinoë Beta began now to make experiments with the Greek magic she had learned from Berenike, her mother, and she set out to *force* him to fall in love with her, to follow her like an automaton to her bedchamber, and do there with his *rhombos* whatever she commanded, and to be her slave in all things.

Agathokles, of course, seeing the way matters were going, had long since taken the most elaborate precautions, working the counter-charm against the magic of any woman who tried to bind a man against his will. Agathokles was proof against all enchantment, and Arsinoë Beta, of course, knew nothing of it.

Did Lysandra, wife of Agathokles, know what were the feelings of her half-sister? To be sure, Lysandra had felt some sympathy for Arsinoë at first, married as she was to the old man—for LOOK! Lysandra had gotten herself married to a young man *two times over*—and as girls in Egypt they had not always been upon unfriendly terms. But little by little the pity of Lysandra ebbed away as she heard from Agathokles that Arsinoë Beta was becoming a real nuisance to him. Lysandra had some idea of what was going on, but short of killing her sister—and she would never do such a dreadful thing—she was powerless, powerless, except to tell Arsinoë to stop ogling Agathokles, to stop it, stop it, because it was disgusting, and to say that whatever it was that she wanted, she could not have it, for that Agathokles already had himself a wife, and that was Lysandra.

This most unsatisfactory state of affairs went on, then, on and on, and none of the parties involved did one thing to stop happening what was—if they had stopped to think about it—bound to happen.

For Arsinoë Beta began now to think, *If Agathokles cannot be mine, why, he shall not be anybody else's either . . .* And the thought came into her heart that she must rid herself of her tormentor, and that there was one way only of doing it. Agathokles might turn out to be proof against her magic spells, but he was not, she thought, proof against her poison. No, Agathokles was not one of the immortals yet, and she thought about how she might best murder this young man, whose only crime, surely, was to be handsome above every other man in the kingdom of Thrace.

Thoth shakes his head, again, and says, Why, though, should Arsinoë Beta want to do such a terrible thing? And his answer, of course, is this: That she wished above every other thing to be Queen of Thrace, Queen for ever and always, and yet she saw clear that her power must be limited to the life time of the old man who was her husband, Lysimakhos. The time must surely come, she thought, when her sister, Lysandra, would be Queen, and she, Arsinoë Beta, no Queen at all, but merely the stepmother of the new King Agathokles, when she would most surely be thrown out of Thrace, for she could not think that Agathokles would put up with her living under the same roof with him after all that she had tried to do. No, she thought it very like that Agathokles would have her put to death as soon as he came to the throne, for that in his eyes she was nothing but a trouble-maker.

Yes, if Arsinoë Beta could have Agathokles a dead man, it would mean that Lysandra could *never* be Queen of Thrace instead of herself. It would mean that Arsinoë Beta would be regent during the minority of her son, her eldest son Ptolemaios (of Telmessos), and then Queen Dowager, for if Agathokles were dead there was no other heir to Thrace but this son of Arsinoë Beta. To kill Agathokles, then, meant that Arsinoë Beta might cling to power even after the death of her husband.

One night, then, Arsinoë Beta went so far as to break open the seals of the papyrus parcel that she had carried with her from Egypt and kept hidden in her private chamber ever since, which was the parting gift of Berenike with inside it enough poison to wipe out the entire army of Thrace, and about which she had been told to say, if Lysimakhos should find it, that it was arsenic for murdering the flies.

When Arsinoë Beta looked upon her parcel she smiled, and she did not stop smiling, for she felt no longer helpless in the hands of her Fate, but powerful with the power of life and death—powerful beyond any living being. Thus it was that the thought in the heart of Arsinoë Beta that started off like a tiny seed began to swell and put forth shoots, and the root of the thought was that handsome Agathokles was going to die.

All the same, Arsinoë Beta knew, in this cold, or hot, heart of hers, that what she wanted so very much to do was *wrong*, and she sought now to find out what she must do, by asking the opinion of the gods, for she was truly in the very depths of despair about Agathokles, whom she loved.

She poured seawater into a golden bowl. She tipped green olive oil upon the surface of the water, and in the darkness of her chamber she bent over the vessel and spoke the question in her heart to which she wanted an answer. And then she pushed down the head of the young boy who must look into the bowl and tell what he saw there, the pure boy that had not yet known a woman, who was her own son, her youngest son Lysimakhos Mikros, about whose *rhombos* the feathers had not yet appeared.

Some days the attempts of Arsinoë to foresee the future by bowl divination were very slow to work, when she might burn a crocodile egg upon a flame in order to make it work faster.

Some times the gods seemed unwilling to come in for her, when she forced them, by mixing the bile of a crocodile with frankincense upon the brazier.

But at length, like every other person who made use of such spells as these, Arsinoë Beta was amazed, because she got the answer she was seeking, and her smile, that was so rarely seen, grew broader.

And Lysimakhos Mikros, what did he see? What did he tell his mother? He told her what he thought she wanted to know, and he kept quiet about the things he saw in the bowl of water that made him cry out. No, he did not wish to tell Arsinoë what he saw, for he saw blood, spilt blood, blood in the streets, blood upon the walls, and two young boys dead in his mother's arms, and he was afraid.

4.2

The Bloodlicker

It was some eighteen years after Arsinoë Beta quit Egypt that the region of the Hellespont was rocked by a violent earthquake, in which the worst damage was done to the city of Lysimakheia. Arsinoë felt her chamber tilt, and her golden furniture slid across the floor, and she screamed, for the Palace of Lysimakhos was proved to be not proof against all tremors of the earth, as she had feared.

The interpreters of omens said that the disaster was a warning sent by Heaven, a foretaste of the ills that were coming upon the Greek world, and they forecast grim ruin for Lysimakhos, and for his House and kingdom also.

Others calmly observed that the earthquake was not uncommon in the district of the Thracian Khersonesos; that there had been quakes before and there would no doubt be quakes again, but that the earthquake was a natural phenomenon and meant nothing, least of all the wrath of the gods of Greece.

The forecasts of disaster, however, were all of them fated to be ful-filled.

Not long after this last tremor of the earth Lysimakhos himself began to nurse a particular hatred for Agathokles, a hatred that was quite abnormal not just in a father but in any human being, for he saw now that there was some truth in the stories that Arsinoë Beta told him, and the thought came into his heart to do just what Arsinoë wanted him to do, which was to give her his permission to have Agathokles, his own son, done away with.

All this was in spite of having already named Agathokles as his heir, and in spite of Agathokles's undoubted abilities as a soldier, who had helped Lysimakhos win many battles; and when it was all over, no man could understand why he had done what he did, except to point out the fact that Agathokles had gone so far as to name a city Agathopolis, after himself, and that he had forgotten himself so far as to coin drachmas with his own face upon them, wearing the royal diadem of a king— which was something that Lysimakhos had not even done for himself.

Agathokles was perhaps, then, not utterly innocent of any crime: he was guilty of making some small claim to authority, and not, therefore, undeserving of his father's wrath, though nobody thought he needed to die for such a small thing.

When it was all over for Lysimakhos in Thrace, some men said that Arsinoë Beta's son, Ptolemaios (of Telmessos) had something to do with the end of Agathokles. Ptolemaios was then aged about fifteen, almost at the height of his physical powers, and as handsome as any boy could be, and he had, surely, everything to gain from involvement in his mother's plots, for if the heir to Thrace were dead, the obvious succes-sor was no other boy but this boy.

To be sure, then, this young Ptolemaios was most like to agree to do whatever his mother told him to do.

But what part could such a boy, a mere boy, have played in a killing? Did he make his friend Agathokles eat up the fatal dose of poison? Was Ptolemaios the unbolter of doors, the boy who let the murderer into the private apartments of this high prince? Assuredly, Arsinoë Beta would not sully her fair hand with a murder, but employ some other to do such a deed for her. Why, she thought, should not her son Ptolemaios do the murder himself? And she laughed her dry laugh, thinking to train the boy up in the way that he must go: able to look after himself, able to manipulate the Fates to his own advantage. Yes, she thought it was time the boy made himself useful—this handsome youth, this special friend of handsome Agathokles, who had, after all, free access to his person after the manner of Greek youths, and who was in any case often sought out by Agathokles in the dead hours of the night, without anybody taking any notice, or thinking the worse of either of them for what they did.

Yes, thought Arsinoë Beta, although Agathokles had taken every step to counteract sorcery and magic, even hanging up the muzzle of a wolf in his bedchamber, he could not protect himself from treachery by an intimate friend, a friend in whom he had put his trust.

To be sure, this Ptolemaios was *not* his mother's son in so far as his later career would show him to be a caring and responsible Tyrant of Telmessos. But on the other hand, as the son of his mother, the son of this domineering woman, he must do whatever she told him to do, or enjoy the sharp knife that was her tongue. And what Greek boy in any case could resist the thought of becoming a king if only one murder stood in his road? This was the custom of the Greeks, to seize power by whatsoever means they could get it; even if it meant killing their own kindred; even if it meant betraying the most sacred trust and the first rule of friendship.

The last time Arsinoë Beta tried to make Agathokles lie with her, he said, *Really, Stepmother, you should know that I prefer boys . . .*

But Arsinoë knew that the love Agathokles showed for Lysandra, his wife, was true love, and that he had seldom been interested in handsome boys apart from her own son—an interest that she had quietly encouraged, in fact, as a means of being able to get at Agathokles herself in order to kill him. But she knew that he was no regular *kinaidos* and she laughed in his face her mirthless laugh of disbelief, knowing that he made excuses, so that she should leave him alone.

At all events, what was certain was that Eros had clapped his wings of gold and flown away from Arsinoë Beta a second time, and she had nothing left now but hatred for Agathokles. She had even been heard to say, *I care not a splinter for the man.*

And so it was that the patience of Arsinoë Beta slipped away, and she came to issue her orders, and to make her plan of plans. She was seen upon the Seventh Daisios arguing with her son Ptolemaios, who sounded as if he really had no wish to do whatever it was that his mother had asked him to do, so that she raised her voice, and her words echoed round the courtyard of the palace: *Believe me, too much niceness is the highway to destruction.*

All that night of the Eighth Daisios Arsinoë Beta lay awake in tears, with the awfulness of what she was about to do weighing upon her soul, and she felt already a terrible sadness for that she had ordered up the death of the man she loved. But in the battle between hate and love, hate was the winner that night, for it was her last thought before the dawn that Agathokles could not be let to live one day longer, because she could not bear the thought of the torment of his terrible beauty, and she felt that by killing him she would be set free, at last, from the burden of all her troubles.

However, since this was Arsinoë Beta's first murder, she really did not know what it was that was coming to her, still less that, so far as trouble was concerned, this was but the beginning.

On the morning of the Ninth Daisios, the day that she had named to be the day of the death of Agathokles, Arsinoë Beta was still having her last doubts about whether she should do the deed or not, and she tried to make up her mind by asking for the divination by bones, so that she might, perhaps, set her seething heart at rest, and to make sure that every last omen was favourable.

The Priest of Apollo brought the lamb to the altar for her, and the lamb made much noise, struggling to leap out of the arms of the boy that carried it. Aye, this lamb was a lamb of loud voice, but he did not shout for long, for the usual rites of Greek sacrifice were quickly done, and the blood splashed into the bowl and the lamb was dead and his bones cleaned of the meat.

The Priest of Apollo held up to the sunlight the shoulder blade, and offered the bone to the diviner, for his scrutiny.

If the bone was white and the sun shone through it, the meaning was extreme poverty, and misery.

If the bone had black spots around the edges and only a small dark space in the middle, it meant the coming of disaster.

Arsinoë Beta held her breath, almost unable to watch for excitement, for the rushing of the blood within her, for knowing what was the future before it came; but she was given the answer to her question without delay, and the bone glowed red at the edges, and in the middle it glowed red, as it had to, for the sun shone through it. Arsinoë smiled then the smile that was not only with the mouth but also with the eyes, for it meant that she would indeed get whatever she wanted.

All that day Arsinoë Beta went about her business as in a dream, her limbs trembling. She tried to eat, but she spilled the food because of the tremor of her hands. She tried to sleep in the siesta, but her heart raced too much. She was too highly wrought to do any thing but think of what was to come.

That night, at the hour of lighting the lamps, Arsinoë gave the word to her agent, the man who may or may not have been her own son,

Ptolemaios—the man who would do whatever it was that she asked him, without question—and she gave him her bronze dagger with the hilt of gold, all jewelled—her agent, whom she trusted—and she spoke to him one word only: the Greek word *Ginestho,* which being translated means *Let it be done,* or *Make it happen.*

Many stories were told about the end of handsome Agathokles of Thrace. Some said that Arsinoë Beta first tried to give him the poison that she had carried from Egypt, but that, having passed seventeen years wrapped up in its papyrus parcel, it had lost its power, and had not the least effect upon his health. Others said that she did indeed offer him poison to eat, but that he had been in the regular habit of eating small amounts of arsenic for years, in order to render himself proof against just such an assault as this, as so many princes did in these uncertain times, knowing very well that to trust any man might cost him his life.

It was also said that Arsinoë Beta herself was in the habit of eating small amounts of poison, for the same reason, and that *this* was the reason for her daily vomitings, and for the appalling state of her health in later years.

At all events, Arsinoë Beta, they said, chose a night when Lysimakhos and Lysandra would be away from the palace, at the theatre, and she had given her waiting-gentlewomen, slaves, servants, eunuchs, leave to see the drama, and given her second son, Philippos, orders to beat the dogs, so that the noise of murder might be drowned out by their barking, and so that nobody might run to save the doomed Agathokles, who was kept in the palace himself under the pretext of a meeting with the agent of Arsinoë Beta, who may, or may not, have been her son Ptolemaios.

Some accounts, then, spoke of poison; others swore that knives were used. The stories differed in their detail: what they agreed upon was the fact of the death of the heir to the throne.

Agathokles squealed like the pig having his throat slit, and the squealing seemed to go on for hours, and the dark blood flew out of his golden flesh and spurted from many wounds, and splashed the white walls of his private chamber, and flooded the mosaic floor, and spattered the white linen of his golden bed. The body of Agathokles writhed, twisted and struggled, and he wrestled, all naked as he was, with his naked assailant, shouting, and squealing, and screaming with rage, and it was dark, dark, and he could not see who it was that attacked him with a bronze dagger, but he knew who he was. Agathokles, indeed, knew his killer, and he had been pleased to open the door to him. He had been pleased to fall upon the bed in a tight embrace with the man who killed him. At length the body of Agathokles went slack, and the fog of death came down upon his eyes, and he set off upon the journey that no man wants, down to the House of Hades in the cellars of the earth.

Agathokles—aye, it was the agent of Arsinoë Beta that lopped off the extremities of this most handsome of men, and severed now his beautiful hands, and hacked off his smooth bright feet, and sliced off even his necessity, and strung these bloody trophies around the dead man's neck and under his armpits upon a papyrus string, in order to stop the blood-guilt of the murder landing upon himself, and so that the ghost of Agathokles, his angry ghost, might be maimed, and thus harmless. It was the agent of Arsinoë Beta who licked up dead Agathokles's blood three times upon his tongue, and spat it out three times, as every murderer must do, and wiped his bloody dagger upon the head of Agathokles, upon his bright fair curls, in order to stop this man's ghost following him wherever he walked for the rest of his life time. And whether the agent of Arsinoë Beta was her son, her own son, Ptolemaios, or not, this Ptolemaios that night was sick in his stomach, vomiting in every corner, and he wept a flood of tears that did not dry up until dawn, and why should this be so if he, too, had not killed the man he loved?

In spite of her every precaution, however, the blood-guilt landed fair and square upon the head of Arsinoë Beta, not upon her son. She had killed the man she had so loved to hate, and she had imagined in her heart that to kill him would wipe him out of her thoughts for ever, for all time. But the truth of it was that she had passed so very many days and nights thinking about this young man that she could in no wise stop herself from thinking of him now that he was dead. By no means: to have killed him merely made her think of him the more.

When Lysandra returned to her unlit apartments and heard the dogs baying, she sensed at once that some disaster must have happened. Screaming for lights and slaves, she ran through the empty rooms looking for her husband. Alas, she would have nightmares about this dreadful evening for the rest of her days: about the blood-stained walls, the bloody floor, the bloody mangled linen of her bed. At last she came upon the body of her lord, a twisted heap of limbs, and he lay with a cold, bleak look upon his face, without a garment upon him, and the thought that she had not been at his side when he drew his last breath would haunt Lysandra always. Lysandra—her screams were dreadful, unlike the grief of most Greek women, for she had loved this husband of hers as much as Arsinoë Beta had done, and more, and her love was no make-believe, but real. For yes, Eros had been busy, very busy, among the women of this family.

The first thought of Lysandra was that this deed was the work of her half-sister, for nobody else in the palace could have wished for so hideous a crime as the butchery of her husband, a man who in all his life time never spoke an angry word. And so Lysandra blackened her face at once, and fled to the harbour, in disguise, and somehow she took ship for the court of King Seleukos at Seleukeia, in the north of Syria, and she had her infant children by her.

With Lysandra went also Alexandros, the son of Lysimakhos by his Odrysian concubine, and these two begged Seleukos to make war upon Lysimakhos, in order to avenge the murder of Agathokles.

Arsinoë Beta? She laughed a high-pitched laugh, for that she had indeed done what she had planned to do, and her laugh was like the laugh of a mad woman. But Arsinoë Beta would not laugh for long.

Ptolemaios her son? Assuredly, this youth was covered in sticky blood that he could not wash off. Of a certainty he took six baths that night. To be sure, he wept and retched all that night, and his mother said it was for the death of his Uncle Agathokles, whom he loved, which was, perhaps, the truth. Ptolemaios recovered. After a day or two he began to smile again. The Macedonians, they say always that the first man a man kills is the most difficult. No, no, Ptolemaios was soon smiling once again: he would be the next King of Thrace.

As for Arsinoë Beta she put her bronze dagger with the hilt of gold, all jewelled and bloody, back in the bottom of her jewel-chest, as she said, *for the next murder.*

4.3

Blood of the Piglet

As soon as she looked into the staring eyes of dead Agathokles, Arsinoë Beta wished with all her heart that she had not done what she had done, and she knew that she would never be rid of the image of this man lying in the pool of his own blood, his handsome body smashed and broken. She vomited up her last meal when she saw Agathokles dead, and she would never after, in fact, be free of vomiting up her food, as if she had been cursed with the curse of not being able to keep down her food, that was, surely, the worst curse that might fall upon any man or woman.

When she was able to sleep—and often she did not sleep—she suffered from nightmares in which the dead Agathokles followed her, all dripping with blood, and tried to place his hands around her neck to throttle her. In her waking hours she wished that she had never ordered this deed, and yet, of course, there was no good that regret might do; there was nothing in the world that would bring back her dead man to life, short of a miracle, but it was too late for miracles.

What, indeed, could any murderess do, but pray to the gods of Greece for forgiveness, and for mercy, and for an end to what now looked like to be her endless sufferings. But the prayers of Arsinoë Beta went unheard, unanswered. The gods of Hellas took no notice of her lavish offerings and daily sacrifice, and she would not know one day's peace for the rest of her life, but the torment would go on, and on, and never stop until the day she herself was dead.

With Agathokles no more there came the immediate problem of what to do with his corpse. On the one hand it was the first thought of Arsinoë Beta to have this article cast out for the dogs' and birds' feasting, as only what he deserved for plotting against his father and thwarting the wishes of his stepmother. On the other hand, Lysimakhos felt he must do a father's duty by this son of his, whatever crime had been committed, and he said to his wife that whatever Agathokles was guilty of, he must give him honourable Greek burial. It was also, perhaps, the wish of Lysimakhos to make his wife suffer a little, for that it had been her thought to dispose of his son, and the truth was that when Lysimakhos looked upon this son dead he could not but shed tears for what had happened. Now, however, he came to his senses, cursing himself for having done nothing to stop it. And so Lysimakhos thought it would be a goodly thing to give Agathokles the full Greek funeral rites.

Perhaps it would be well . . . Arsinoë murmured, dreading the thought of it.

But what woman, Lysimakhos asked, *will lead the weeping for my son? Not Nikaia his mother, for Nikaia is dead . . . Not Lysandra, who has run away . . . Nor Arsinoë Alpha his sister, who is in Egypt . . . Who shall sing the klama for Agathokles?* he said, looking hard at Arsinoë Beta. And his dog growled at her, then, as he had done these twenty years.

And Arsinoë just stood there, aghast at what he must say next, and Lysimakhos said, indeed, what she had thought he must say: *Surely,* he said, *the work of leading the mourning must fall upon yourself.*

And so, yes, the stepmother of Agathokles, Arsinoë Beta herself, would have to be his chief mourner, the woman who began the weeping at his funeral.

But how, Arsinoë thought, how could she lead the weeping for the man she had herself killed? And her heart turned over inside her breast, and the awfulness of what lay in store for her swept through her body so that she trembled from head to foot at the thought of what she must do, for she had never imagined that she would have to weep for the man she hated, and she was afraid that no tears would fall, so hard had she made her heart against this man.

The morning came, the next day, at dawn, the third day after the murder, the awful day upon which the body must be burned, and Arsinoë Beta had not slept one moment, but lay awake fretting. In the end, though, it was not a difficult thing for her, because she had loved handsome Agathokles with a crazy love, and it was real and true, and such a love, such a tremendous love, made the lamentation easy for her, and her hatred disappeared.

In the procession to the funeral pyre built for him upon the beach, she felt weak at the knees and her head swam, as if she must collapse from the strain, but her waiting-women held her up as they sang the sad songs, walking beside the bier that had handsome Agathokles stretched out upon it, washed clean of all the blood, lacking his nose and ears, but with his cold face looking, if that were possible, even more handsome dead than alive.

At first Arsinoë felt as if her tongue was glued up to the roof of her mouth, as if it would not sing one note for her, but then she looked upon the dead face and the wailing just poured forth from her lips, and she sang for the first time the song of her love for Agathokles, of her hopeless and impossible love for him that she had never put into words before because her love was forbidden, and as she sang her voice soared high and shrill and beautiful in the wailing, like nothing anybody standing by had heard before, in an unstoppable flood, and at the start it made perfect sense, but after a time the meaning and the words ran out, so that Arsinoë Beta sang a wordless song of grief that was more beautiful than any song of lament any of them had heard before: like the nightingale it was, until her voice gave out altogether and the song ended with her groaning, croaking like the raven, and the waiting-women took up the song and the wailing for her.

All the while, as Arsinoë Beta sang, she touched the bronzed flesh of dead Agathokles for the first time without censure, stroking the soft smooth flesh of his forearms that were covered with golden hairs, and running her fingers through the hair upon his head, that was like the colour of a field of ripened wheat, and falling upon his bronzed neck, sobbing, with one hundred kisses, and with a torrent of tears, and for the first time she could behave toward her Agathokles like a lover, like one who had loved him even unto madness, and nobody knew of her guilt, nobody suspected the truth, for this behaviour was only what was expected and required of the chief mourner at any man's funeral.

And Ptolemaios of Telmessos? He shed no tears that day. He had recovered his senses. He would be King in Thrace after his father. He stood there with the men, looking awkward, shuffling his feet about in the sand, looking at the ground, and avoiding his mother's eye.

Truly, the iron heart of Arsinoë Beta banged in her breast as if it were split down the middle, and she prayed for the impossible to happen—that Agathokles might sit up and smile at her, and live again—although she knew very well that he was a dead man, and that however hard one might pray to the gods, most times the impossible does not happen.

And then they burned up Agathokles of Thrace in a wall of flame, and when the bonfire was cold, Lysimakhos made Arsinoë herself gather up the bones and wash them in sweet wine and wrap them in soft purple cloths and stow them in the *larnax* and carry them in her own hands to the tomb, and all the while, over her shoulder, behind her, she sensed that the ghost of Agathokles son of Lysimakhos walked behind her, accusing her for what she had done.

She had thought that to lop off this man's extremities would keep his ghost from her, for she knew that any ghost must haunt his murderer for the span of his natural life that was left to him, and she had calculated this to be almost fifty full years, or eighteen thousand two hundred and fifty days and nights exactly, for he was at his death still only in his middle twenties.

However, as it turned out, the ghost of Agathokles would haunt Arsinoë anyway, for so long as she lived, and it was all her own fault, and those who at length heard her story thought that she had but got what she more than deserved.

When the news about the Prince Agathokles was made public, the foremost citizens of Lysimakheia sent a deputation to express their sincere regrets at the death of so good a general, such a fine prince, such a handsome young man, who would not now be their King.

Lysimakhos replied to this fine tribute by indulging himself in the massacre of those who delivered it, and the word got about that he was just as mad as his wife.

The result of this unfortunate bloodbath was that the survivors and the army officers defected, every man of them, to King Seleukos of Syria, and urged that King to attack Lysimakhos, which was a thing that Seleukos already had in his thoughts, because he was jealous of Lysimakhos's reputation.

At the same time Philetairos, the treasurer of Lysimakhos's wealth, who had been shocked at the murder and who was suspicious of Arsinoë Beta, occupied the city of Pergamon on the Kaiokos, and surrendered both himself and what was left of Lysimakhos's treasure, through a herald, to Seleukos.

That King now marched his troops into Kilikia and Pamphylia, and town after town opened its gates to him. By the following year Lysimakhos had no choice but to counter-attack, and the battle that followed next would be the very last of the struggles between the Successors, the kings who had been comrades-in-arms of Alexander.

It was now the turn of Lysandra to begin plotting. Her *sister* had murdered her beloved husband, and she could not but think of taking her revenge.

Lysandra would, surely, kill Arsinoë Beta, would surely kill even with her bare hands, if she could get near her. Arsinoë, though, was too clever to let such a thing happen, but had herself guarded day and night by dozens of her hired soldiers.

No, Lysandra would take her revenge in a more subtle fashion. She thought that if she could avenge the murder, perhaps then Agathokles might come to her in her dreams not mutilated and covered in blood, but whole, and smiling. And so Lysandra worked against her sister every Greek spell she knew, every Greek spell of binding that she could remember.

The Princess Lysandra did not remarry, but hid herself in the *gynaikeion* in Seleukeia in Pieria, where she spent her days sticking pins into wax images of Arsinoë Beta, and it made her grief a little easier to bear.

It was perhaps, then, the magic of Lysandra that made Arsinoë Beta so very sick in her stomach, and to be sure Arsinoë Beta was herself convinced of it, so that she in her turn worked the counter-magic against Lysandra, and both sisters used the magic of Berenike, the most powerful Greek magic known to exist.

What was the end of the story of Lysandra nobody in Egypt ever knew, not even Thoth, except to suppose that she must have lost her wits, for how could any woman live through what happened to Lysandra and keep them? The last that was heard of Lysandra out of Seleukeia was that she used up her energy in railing against the sister whom she once had loved. And then there was a silence.

As for the infant children of Lysandra and Agathokles, boys of princely family would always present a threat to stability, wherever they were, and while Seleukos might protect the interests of Lysandra while he lived, things would be different after he was dead.

In matters such as the survival of the male children of exiled royalty, it makes sense to think the worst.

Arsinoë herself took every precaution, in spite of having only commissioned a murder. She followed the course of action laid down by Zeus, who heartily abhors the killing of any man, but who will still be pleased to befriend a killer if she makes amends. And so Arsinoë set about performing the rites by which she might be pardoned if she sought asylum at the sacred hearth.

She took a sucking piglet from a sow with dugs still swollen after littering.

She held the piglet squealing and struggling under her left arm.

She slit the piglet's throat with the knife.

She let the blood splash all over her hands, and she called upon Zeus the Cleanser, who listens to every murderess's prayer with friendly ears.

And she prayed then the prayers to Zeus, in the hope that she might make the loathsome Furies leave her alone, and that Zeus might once again smile upon her. But even as she offered up the proper prayers, she thought that Zeus had never smiled upon her yet, and she began to think that he never would.

In this matter Arsinoë Beta was, perhaps, right, for the Furies, those three daughters of Night, dressed in black, with snakes for hair, whose purpose was to avenge blood-guilt, did not, would not, leave her, and as for obtaining her peace of mind, the business with the piglet was a bloody waste of time.

4.4

Arsinoë Hard-as-Nails

Arsinoë Beta next tried to go back to living her normal life, behaving as if she had not done a murder and was in no wise responsible for the death of an innocent man; but this was, of course, an impossible thing for her to do, and the life of Arsinoë Beta was not normal, but full of strange imaginings and curious outbursts of weeping.

As for her relations with her husband, King Lysimakhos, it was whispered that he was only too well aware of what Arsinoë had been up to with regard to Agathokles, for the people who lived in that palace at Lysimakheia were the most spied-upon people that ever lived. But they said also that at the end of his life this Lysimakhos had nothing left to his name, because he had handed over his every last possession to his murderous wife: not only cities and fiefdoms but money in gold bars and rough lumps of gold, and all of his money in drachmas and talents.

This dreadful Arsinoë Beta, they said, milked her aged husband of every thing he had, reducing him to the position of a beggar.

Worse, because of all this, and because of *her,* his friends now abandoned him, and turned themselves into his enemies.

The end of Lysimakhos of Thrace came soon after, though it was not from old age or decrepitude, but in battle, as a result of the war that now broke out against Seleukos of Syria. In their glorious youth these two heroes had marched with Alexander. Now they were old men with silver hair: Seleukos was seventy-seven years old, Lysimakhos seventy-four, but both were still full of the fire of youth, and both had still their insatiable lust for power. Between them they had most of the Greek world in their hands, and yet they wanted more.

At Korupedion, near the town of Magnesia-by-Sipylos, in Lydia, the two kings drew up their armies for battle, and it was the very place where, according to tradition, the banquet given to the gods by Tantalos was held, in which Pelops was chopped up and put into the soup, and this was what Seleukos threatened to do to Lysimakhos now.

Although tens of thousands of troops faced each other, it was not the purpose of the two kings to let their armies solve the dispute, for they insisted upon fighting in single combat before the assembled armies. First, sword upon sword, then with the short sword, and daggers, and at the last with their bare fists, they slashed and clawed and screamed at one another, and the two armies stood silent, as if holding their breath, while the fate of half the world was decided. Then they roared and chanted, each army urging on its leader, until, in the end, only one of the two aged men was left standing, and the King who waved his sword in the air in answer to his cheering troops was Seleukos, for Lysimakhos was sprawled upon the ground, turning the earth all about him scarlet.

For some reason the body of this King was not taken up for burial as it should have been—perhaps because his men fled at once—but lay where it fell for some days, and they told a story that Firetail, the dog of Lysimakhos, refused to leave his master's side, but sat on the field of battle, howling, and so starved himself to death there, the only mourner.

As for Seleukos, he rejoiced, and he crossed over into Macedon in order to claim for Syria the spoils of victory. However, in his delight, Seleukos so far forgot himself as to become boastful, saying, *This is not the achievement of a mortal, but the gift of the gods.* But, aged though he was, and wise also, he did not know the future, or that he must shortly himself be an example of the frailty of the human condition.

As for Thoth, who knows all, Thoth asks, Was this the Truth? Or not the Truth? For a different account of Korupedion said not one word of single combat, but held that Lysimakhos was sent to his death by Malakon of Herakleia Pontike, a soldier in the army of Seleukos, who struck him down with a shield.

Nobody, at least, disputed the fact that Lysimakhos was dead. But who should succeed him? This unlucky man had buried, by reason of plague, measles, stillbirth, stoppage of the guts and so forth, some fifteen of his own offspring. Agathokles, his son and heir, was already dead. Now Lysimakhos was dead himself, and it was the finish of the rule of the House of Lysimakhos over the Kingdom of Thrace, and all his thoughts of founding a dynasty that must last for all time were but as a hot wind.

It was told also that Ptolemy Keraunos, the famous Thunderbolt, who found himself fighting in the army of Lysimakhos, was taken prisoner at Korupedion by Seleukos, who showed him much kindness, remembering that Keraunos's father, Ptolemy Soter, had shown great generosity towards him when he was a hostage at Alexandria some years before. And so, of course, these two knew each other from of old, when Keraunos was no more than a boy.

. . .

Arsinoë Beta, the Queen, she waited to hear the outcome of the Battle of Korupedion in the nearby city of Ephesos, or Arsinoëia, which was her own possession. When she learned the news, and that it was the worst news that could be—that her husband the King was dead, and the armies of Thrace defeated—she shed not one tear. She did not rip open her *peplos,* expose and beat her breasts with her fists for grief. She did not wail, or gnash her teeth, as a Greek widow was meant to. No, she had no time to attend to funeral rites for a man she had not loved, but put into action at once the plan for her own survival, than which no other thing was so important.

Things were all up for Arsinoë Beta now in Thrace, and she must think rather to her own personal safety, for the troops of Lysimakhos had every man deserted to the camp of Seleukos, so that she was no longer safe even in her own city, but feared that she too must now be put to death; and so she set about making her escape.

Even so, for a Greek to neglect the rites of burial, it was the most grievous crime against the gods that any man or woman could commit.

Thoth asks, Was this Arsinoë Beta a woman utterly lacking in all human feeling, apart, perhaps, from feelings of lust? Some have thought so; some have said it. Thoth will record the Judgement of the Gods when the heart of this Queen is weighed in the Balance, against the Feather of Maat, the Feather of Truth. It is not for man to judge the dead.

But what did Arsinoë Beta do? When Menekrates, the Seleukid commander, took Ephesos and gave the order for this Queen to be hunted down and put to the sword, and the troops ran through the streets after dark, seeking her, and there was no noise in that city but the noise of hurried footsteps and the noise of the running boots of the men of Seleukos, Arsinoë had little choice but to flee as swift as she could. She thought of the wise words of Berenike her mother, and she dressed up one of her loyal waiting-women in her royal robes of purple, and sat this trembling woman in her own chair, in her own *oktophoros,* or litter, and sent this vehicle carried by eight men towards the harbour, telling them to *run.*

Arsinoë Beta now took soot from the brazier and blackened her own face, and put on the dirty rags of a beggar. Barefoot, she slipped through the streets that were busy with Syrian troops, looting and burning, and raping whatsoever women they could lay their hands upon, and all the time hunting for Arsinoë herself, and she managed, in this disguise, to reach the harbour of Ephesos, where one of her own ships rode at anchor, ready to carry her away to Macedon.

Indeed, it was a goodly thing to be so very strong, so very hard, as this Arsinoë Beta, who thought nothing of saving herself at the expense of her waiting-gentlewoman, who, of course, was slain upon sight, butchered and cut to ribbons by Seleukos's men. Yes, Arsinoë Beta— was she not harder than hard, as hard as iron? Yes, she was, and it was a goodly thing to be as hard as iron, until a *magnet* such as Agathokles walked by, when Arsinoë Beta would be attracted. It had happened once, twice, and it would happen a third time, for her gods had not yet finished their games with Arsinoë Beta.

But what did this hardest of women do now? She had yet her presence of mind where her wealth was concerned, and her organizing skills had not deserted her, for she managed to take with her the immense riches she had gathered in Thrace, and her three sons also: Ptolemaios, Philippos, and the Lysimakhos they called Mikros to distinguish him from his father. This unhappy family now took ship for Kassandreia, another of the cities that belonged to this Queen, that lay across the Aegean Sea, upon the western peninsula of Khalkidike, not far from Pella, and which was the richest city in Macedon, a place where the husband of Arsinoë had been worshipped with divine honours even while he lived. The position of Kassandreia upon a narrow isthmus of land made it easy to defend, and it was the thought of Arsinoë Beta now to barricade herself inside her citadel and fight off her every enemy.

Thoth asks, How could this Arsinoë, a mere woman, achieve such things? But the answer is that she was a woman of very great personal wealth and power, and she was her father's daughter, the true heir of Ptolemy Soter, and Thoth says it again: she was cunning as the vixen. Her riches meant that for her to hire an army of tens of thousands of soldiers was as easy as buying a loaf of bread. To have a ship ready so that she might make her flight from Ephesos was merely the kind of thing this Queen had come to expect. Arsinoë Beta was not only very well able to look after herself, but also clever above all other women, and most men, and she was the model and example to all the women of the House of Ptolemy that came after her. For she had been taught by Berenike, her mother, how to survive, and her mother's great lesson was that a woman must *never* give up trying, *never* give up hope, *never* accept defeat, but go on fighting.

Truly, this woman was just about as sharp as the eunuch-maker's knife.

Uppermost in the thoughts of Arsinoë Beta was the matter of what to do about the kingship of Thrace. The natural thing would have been to get her eldest son, Ptolemaios, proclaimed King straight away, and to make herself the regent for this boy, who was about seventeen years old, but quite lacking the wisdom or experience needed to be sole ruler of a nation in the middle of the gravest crisis.

To be regent herself would mean that Arsinoë Beta could hold on to her power, but for the moment she did nothing, nothing, but waited to see what might happen.

Thoth asks, Why should this be so? And the answer is that in truth no Greek would do any thing without first finding what was the will of his gods. No, they would not so much as go out of the door of the house without looking for good and bad omens. Arsinoë Beta paused, then, because she must first send to the oracles for guidance. She worked also her spells of divination. She spent long hours with Lysimakhos Mikros, her youngest son, making him stare into bowls of water with oil floating upon the surface in order to tell her what he saw there concerning the future. She questioned her soothsayers about the flight of birds and the state of the entrails of sacrificial beasts. But for all her trying, she could get no favourable sign for what she wished to do, and the truth was that her thoughts were troubled all the while by the murder of Agathokles, whose ever-present ghost wrought havoc with her sleeping habits, and she was followed wherever she went by the three women in black, whose hair was not hair but snakes.

Strong though Arsinoë Beta was, she was not a man, and not a *strategos,* and had not the practical experience of war, and though she might yet ride into battle, this was quite different from having thousands of hired soldiers take their orders from a mere woman. No, she saw the need for some strong man to rule Thrace, some strong man who might also be her husband—and this time she would choose him herself. But just then she could see no man strong enough for her liking, or young enough either, for to be sure she had had her fill of old men.

For the moment Arsinoë Beta tried to secure the empty thrones of Thrace and Macedon for her son Ptolemaios. But in doing this she managed to attract the attention of the strong man who was Ptolemy Keraunos.

Thus it came about that for Arsinoë Beta every thing began to slide into confusion, and it felt to her as if the earthquake was upon her again, with the furniture crashing across the floors of its own free will, and the ceilings falling down upon her head, and everybody screaming, including herself, and smoke everywhere, and dust, and tumbling masonry—except that the earthquake was shaking not her house, not her palace, but her *life* to pieces.

4.5

Keraunos Kills

What, then, had Ptolemy Keraunos been doing all this while, apart from seeking to make himself King of Egypt? After the Battle of Korupedion he was the prisoner of Seleukos, who continued to treat him with kindness, allowing him as much wine as he could drink, and his food, and every goodly thing that the son of the late King of Egypt deserved. But he did not keep Keraunos in a cage, like the unfortunate Demetrios Poliorketes. By no means: Keraunos was the *friend* of Seleukos, not his enemy.

Seleukos, however, had now no rival for the supreme command that had belonged to Alexander, and all of Asia having fallen into his hands, he was keen to sit back and enjoy his successes.

To Ptolemy Mikros, the new Pharaoh of Egypt, the situation looked grave, for he had heard that his half-brother Keraunos was still in the train of Seleukos, and that it looked as if Seleukos would help Keraunos in his claim to the throne of Egypt. And so this new King Ptolemy began his reign fearful that his kingdom would shortly be taken away from him.

Mikros, for the time being, did nothing but wait to see what should happen next—much as his full sister, Arsinoë Beta, was doing at Kassandreia. He had taken no part in the Battle of Korupedion, being, in spite of his name, still most unwarlike, but he watched how matters unfolded now with alarm. He lay awake at night, just as his father had done, as if he had inherited Soter's sleeplessness along with his kingdom, but he refused the diet of nightingale flesh. By day he sent to the Oracle of Zeus-Ammon in Libya to find out from the god what he must do. He had his dreams explained by the oneiroscopists. He spent hours seeking to discover what must happen in the future. But always Mikros would find it easier to do nothing. At last, though, he gave the order for Egypt to make ready to fight an invader, and when he thought of the fact that his rule over Egypt had been but brief, he wept, because the

one certain thing in these uncertain times was that the troops of
Seleukos and Keraunos joined together would be sure to defeat him.

King Seleukos of Syria, however, dreamed of nothing more violent than
making his journey home to Macedon, so that he might enjoy a peaceful retirement. He really had no thought to become involved in fighting
yet another war. He had really no wish to go to the trouble of invading
Egypt either, which was a notoriously difficult, dangerous and expensive business, as Antigonos One-Eye, Demetrios Poliorketes and
Perdikkas had found out before him. Seleukos did not want to waste
the last of his energy fighting so that the volatile, hot-headed, unreliable
Thunderbolt might be made King of Egypt.

Seleukos had watched Keraunos the boy, while he passed the
months waiting to be restored to his Satrapy of Babylon, and he knew
Keraunos better than most men. To be sure, he *liked* Keraunos, but he
did not trust him, and his suspicion was justified. Seleukos saw, as
everybody else had seen—apart from Demetrios of Phaleron—that
Keraunos would not make a good ruler, and that if he were to be King
there would be nothing but trouble for everybody else, because if the
truth were told, Keraunos had really not a clue what he was doing, and
did not *think* what he was doing, but behaved in all things like the pig in
the roses, charging blindly about, doing damage. Keraunos lacked all
foresight; he lacked all imagination.

Seleukos now sent his best regards to Ptolemy Mikros in Egypt and
gave his opinion that he, Mikros, was the best heir to Egypt, and told
him that he was not going to fight on behalf of Keraunos. *To be sure,* he
wrote, *Keraunos is our friend, but Mikros is a better friend.*

Old Seleukos then made what was perhaps the most foolish mistake
of his life time, because he now told Ptolemy Keraunos his private
thoughts.

We are going home to Macedon, Seleukos said. *We are too old to fight
another war,* he said. And he watched the face of the Thunderbolt grow
very like thunder. *We have no strength left to fight for a young man,* he
said. *Keraunos will have to fight his own battles.*

The face of the Thunderbolt showed his bitter disappointment, and
a shouting-match followed, even in the Palace of Seleukos, in which
Keraunos told the old man what he thought of him, this King who was
ruler of all Asia, master of half the world, and the greatest of the Successors of Alexander (after Ptolemy). But Keraunos's screaming only
served to confirm Seleukos in his opinion.

You have not the manners, he said, *to be a monarch. And that is why you are not King of Egypt now.*

The shouting and screaming grew louder, until Keraunos began to prod Seleukos—King Seleukos—in the chest with a finger, and his screaming sounded very like that of a maniac, and the guards held his arms because he was breathing so hard, and led him away, marching him backwards, before he should do Seleukos some injury.

Locked in a store-room for the night, on his own, Keraunos brooded and raged, but when they let him out, he did not take steps to remove himself from Seleukos's court, and Seleukos did not send Keraunos away, but let this madman go on living under his roof as before. The only difference was that the matter of *Egypt* was never mentioned again.

Keraunos calmed himself a little. He did not raise his voice. He did not show temper in public. But he began to nurse a deep hatred for the King of Syria, showing, in fact, just the same violent change-about in his emotions as his half-sister, Arsinoë Beta, had shown with regard to handsome Agathokles.

It was now Keraunos's turn not to sleep by night, and he lay awake and angry, muttering to himself, worrying about how he might now get for himself his rightful throne of Egypt and be a king. He resented most of all the fact that Seleukos had given his promise, his solemn word, to help him, and he arrived, at length, at the thought that there was one thing only to be done about the treachery of Seleukos, about Seleukos's betrayal of his cause, and he went about with his face set grim, his heart made up that he must kill him.

In the summer time of the year in which Ptolemy Keraunos was thirty-eight years old, Seleukos crossed the Hellespont into Europe, and Ptolemy Keraunos was still marching beside him, still enjoying his allowance of wine, and now laughing and making jests with Seleukos as if nothing had happened to stop him being his friend—to every appearance his faithful ally; as if he had forgotten how very badly Seleukos had let him down.

The greater part of the phalanx of Seleukos was quartered in Arsinoë's one-time city of Lysimakheia. Not far from here, on the Thracian Khersonesos, but some distance off the military road, there lies a rough heap of stones called Argos that tradition said was an altar raised by the famous Argonauts, or by the host of Agamemnon, or in memory of the fallen in the Trojan War.

Whatever it was, this heap of stones was old, and Seleukos, ever curious about the glorious history of the Greeks, turned his horse off the road so that he might see this so-called Altar of the Argonauts, and only a few of his personal bodyguards went with him, one of whom was Ptolemy Keraunos, who had not had his sword taken away from him, but went fully armed, because he was the son of a king, and Seleukos's *friend*, and was there to protect him.

When Seleukos got down from his horse and bent over to look at the ancient monument, and to hear the story made up about it by the local guide, Ptolemy Keraunos was close by the side of this King, his aged benefactor, his friend, and he took the old man's head by the hair with his left hand and pulled it back, and with his hunting knife in his right hand he slit the throat of this King from ear to ear.

The blood of Seleukos flew out, splashing the face and arms of Keraunos himself, who stood over his groaning victim like some wild beast, showing his teeth in a mirthless laugh; as if to say that any man who came near him to avenge this crime would suffer the same fate.

Yes, Seleukos was slumped upon the ground, and Keraunos thrust him through and through with his short sword, his *kopis,* to make sure the old man was properly dead, to make sure he did not come back to life to be his accuser; and his sandals stood in the pool of Seleukos's lifeblood, and he did not so much as notice.

Having done his long-planned murder, Keraunos took off the diadem, the strip of white cloth that was the mark of the kingship, from the old man's head, and tied it, bloody though it was, round his own head. He then leaped upon his horse and galloped back to the army barracks at Lysimakheia, with a royal guard waiting upon him, and he whooped as he galloped, like some idiot, and he spun his horse, making him dance and perform tricks as he went, and the great grin never faded from his face for one moment.

Keraunos rang the alarm bells in the camp, called the troops together, and addressed them, shouting: *The King is dead . . . King Seleukos is no more . . .* and he suggested that there was only one man who could be King in his room, and that man was himself.

The army, taken by surprise, and fearful of what Keraunos might do if they showed that they did not want him to be their King, and that he might order their massacre, had little choice but to put themselves at his disposal, and they elected him King of Macedon on the spot, by the usual show of hands. And yes, they carried him then shoulder-high round the army camp, cheering him, as if they did not know that they had elected a killer; as if they felt nothing for the spirit of Old Seleukos.

But the truth was that the men were dazzled by this strong young man, who had more fire in him than the aged Seleukos, and they were, most of them, hired soldiers, so hardened by unceasing war that they cared not much who was their King so long as he paid their wages. And in any case, Keraunos, who knew well that such men would change sides and swear to be faithful for all time to whatever general offered the most money, at once tripled the daily pay from four obols to twelve and that was the first reason why they raised their hands and shouted for him.

Ptolemy Keraunos, then, was a king, and his plan was to invade Egypt, with the army of Seleukos behind him, and to oust his half-brother, Ptolemy Mikros, from the throne and make himself King of Egypt in his stead. For, just as his half-sister, Arsinoë Beta, had a burning desire to be a queen, so Keraunos was hot to be a king, and he was urged on by the thought of the injustice, for he held that Egypt was his by right, as the eldest legitimate son of his father.

All of this fine campaign, however, came to nought, because Antiokhos son of Seleukos came hurrying to avenge his father's murder as soon as he heard the news, and if Keraunos wanted to march on Egypt by way of Syria, well, he could not, because he needs must cross the very heart of Seleukos's former kingdom, where the entire population boiled with rage, hot to punish the killer of their fine King, and wanted very much to tear his flesh in strips, and hang him up in the sun for the crows to peck out his eyes.

And if Keraunos wanted to take the other route to Egypt, and go by sea, well, he could not do that either, because he needs must sail past the fleet of Mikros his half-brother, who was fully master of the sea. And it so happened that Keraunos did not have any ships of war, nor even a transport ship to his name, no, not one.

What, then, would Keraunos do? If he could not lay his hands upon Egypt, for the moment, he would, he thought, seize hold of the throne of Thrace instead, that had been empty since the death of Lysimakhos. So, he turned his face towards Macedon and he tried to carve out for himself a European kingdom.

No, he could not be King of Egypt just yet. In the meantime he would be a king elsewhere. He was, he thought, born to be a king. He really had an urgent need to be king of somewhere.

Thus, at any rate, ended the life of Seleukos Nikator, the Conqueror. He had marched with Alexander. He had been Satrap of Babylonia. He had founded the great cities of Antiokheia and Seleukeia on the Tigris.

He was truly the greatest king of all the kings who came after Alexander (apart from Ptolemy).

On the one hand the whole Greek world, as might be expected, cursed Ptolemy Keraunos for sending down to Hades the man who had shown him generous hospitality at a time when he had no home of his own. And all the Greek world praised Seleukos for a most religious and right-dealing monarch. On the other hand, was not the murder of Seleukos the revenge of Keraunos for the death of his sister's husband, Demetrios Poliorketes, his brother-in-law? Perhaps, though Keraunos and Poliorketes had never met but once, at the Battle of Salamis, when Poliorketes had taken the family of Ptolemy prisoner.

When Seleukos met his fate there were three men struggling for mastery over Macedon: Keraunos himself, Antigonos Gonatas, or Knee-Cap, the son of Poliorketes, and Ptolemaios (of Telmessos), who had sailed with his mother, Arsinoë Beta, to Kassandreia, and who also thought himself fit to be a king.

The stories that reached Egypt by way of the fishing fleet were confused about what things happened next.

First, there was word of a sea battle between Thunderbolt and Knee-Cap, in which Knee-Cap was thrashed, but which could not be the truth because the Thunderbolt had no ships of war.

Second, there was some talk of a treaty of peace between Knee-Cap and Thunderbolt, which seemed most unlikely, because it was common knowledge that Keraunos much preferred to make war.

Third, there were rumours of a full-scale battle between Keraunos and the young Ptolemaios, who was supposed to have been helped by one Monounios, an Illyrian chieftain.

And then there came a preposterous tale that Keraunos had gotten himself married to his own half-sister, Arsinoë Beta, which every man in Alexandria scoffed at as an idle story, because to do such a thing was an insult to the gods of Greece, an affront to nature, and something that not even Ptolemy the Thunderbolt would dare to do.

But this was just what Keraunos was planning, and the truth was that this man could not care less whether a brother-sister marriage would offend the sensibilities of the gods of Greece.

No, Keraunos went about saying quite openly, *I shall do what I like. I shall do just what I please. No man shall tell Ptolemy the Thunderbolt what he must and must not do, nor any god.*

4.6

Flesh of the Sister

Thoth says, What thought was in the heart of Ptolemy Keraunos? What did he think he was doing when he proposed marriage to his own half-sister?

Thoth's answer: It was his heart's thought to win over her three sons, the children of Lysimakhos. If he could adopt these boys as his own sons, they would not, could not, try to work against him, out of respect for the fact that he was, at least in name, their father. And no, they would not then resist his take-over of Thrace.

The Thunderbolt wrote now a letter to King Ptolemy Mikros, his half-brother, and said he was putting to one side his anger at the loss of Egypt. And he gave his word that he would no longer seek to make himself King of that country, for he had more honourably, he said, gained the throne of Macedon from Seleukos, who had been his father's foe.

Keraunos told Mikros what a fine Pharaoh everybody thought he was, trying to turn him into his friend, for he was afraid that Mikros would join forces with Antigonos Gonatas, or with Antiokhos son of Seleukos. And Keraunos really did not need a third enemy.

Thoth says, What, though, was in the thoughts of Ptolemy Keraunos in these uncertain days?

Keraunos thought, *Enough of Seleukos, enough of the past . . . Keraunos is the future.* And he thought of his sister, the murdering Arsinoë Beta, the widow who sat in her citadel of Kassandreia with a heap of gold oktodrachms, thousands and thousands of talents, more wealth than she knew what to do with.

Keraunos, then, ever a man to act first and think afterwards, sent the fatal letter to this sister of his, saying, among other things:

> *I should be happy to make you Queen of Macedon . . .*
> *I should be quite happy to adopt your poor fatherless*
> *children as my own sons . . .*
> *I should be quite pleased to guarantee the throne of*
> *Macedon (after my death) to the eldest of your sons,*

For he knew very well that Arsinoë Beta would not be able to refuse such an offer.

Keraunos now, like some new Alexander, rolled his siege-towers and engines of war up to the walls of his sister's city, surrounded Kassandreia with his army of hired soldiers on triple wages, and settled down to starve her out.

However, the truth of it was that Keraunos had not the patience or the genius of an Alexander, and he quickly grew tired of sitting about day after day, doing nothing but waiting for his sister either to surrender, or to accept his proposal of marriage. He tried next hurling great rocks, hot sand, rotten fish, from his siege-machines, but he failed to dislodge this sister, who sent out a message saying. *We shall never surrender, so you may as well go away.*

She also wrote, *Why should I wish to marry a brother who hurls rocks at my city?*

The first thought of Arsinoë Beta was, of course, that all his life his promises had been worthless. He was like the parrot from India, who could speak a few Greek words but did not know what it was that he said. And so the other messages of Keraunos she ignored, and when he sent her presents of golden earrings and glittering jewellery, she sent it all back to him.

In his tent of leather in the temporary camp Keraunos worked now the spells of love and binding that he had learned from his Greek tutor, from his Greek nurse, and from Eurydike his mother. He took three live fishes and put them in a row upon a gridiron over the fire. While the fishes cooked, he hit them with two small sticks and spoke the words of power: *As these fishes gasp, so may the maiden whom I love pant with longing.*

When the fishes were burned to cinders, Keraunos took a mortar and beat them to a fine powder, which he mixed into a potion and sent to his sister at Kassandreia in a stoppered bottle, and his message said, *Drink, it is the latest cure for the dyspepsia.*

But Arsinoë knew what it was, what Keraunos was trying to do, and she refused to touch this black, fishy liquid. It was a spell she had tried herself, and it had not worked upon Agathokles either. Really, Arsinoë Beta was far too clever to be tricked like this. It had long since, in any case, been her first thought always that any gift meant to be taken by mouth was sure to be poisoned.

Yes, she suspected Keraunos's criminal intentions from the beginning, and she voiced to Dion, her *apokrisiarios,* her private secretary, her deep distrust of her brother.

Keraunos, however, did not go away from Kassandreia. He sent his word of honour that he would share his kingdom of Macedon with her sons, against whom, he said, he had taken up arms not because he wanted to steal their kingdom from them, but because he wanted to give a portion of it to each of them as a gesture of goodwill.

Arsinoë laughed when she read the message. Really, she had not thought Keraunos was quite so stupid.

Keraunos stepped up his assault upon his sister's affections. He told her she might send her ambassadors to receive his oath, if she wished, and he promised to bind himself in their presence, before the gods of Greece, by whatever words Arsinoë cared to mention.

Arsinoë laughed a second time, and it was a rare occurrence, but she felt also the stirrings of temptation.

At the same time, though, she really did not trust this brother, nor did she quite know what was the best course of action. She was afraid that if she did send her ambassadors she would be tricked by some false oath; but that if she sent nobody she would provoke Keraunos's wrath, and a fresh military assault. She had seen her brother's fury in the past. She had been a witness to his cruelty, what he was like when he did not have his own way. She was well aware that Keraunos was capable of razing Kassandreia to the ground with herself and her three sons inside it, and that he would laugh as he watched her city burn, for that he loved above all things to destroy.

And then she wondered whether her three sons might not be better protected by a strong father like Keraunos from the other kings who were surely about to invade her territory. Beginning to waver, she sent Dion, who was now one of her most trusted friends, on an embassy to Keraunos, to see what might be gained by talking to him.

Ptolemy Keraunos smiled his smile, showing the front teeth, the grinners, like a man who is about to have what he wants. He withdrew, then, his engines of war, his siege-machinery, sappers, battering-rams, bolt-throwers, his archers, guards, spies and camp-followers, and made his troops retreat until they were out of sight of the city of Kassandreia, and told them to await further orders.

The following day he led his sister's ambassador into the Temple of Zeus-Ammon that stands upon the promontory of Pallene, a place held in high honour by all Macedonians. He grasped the altar with his two hands. He touched the images of the god. And he swore with—for him—unheard-of oaths, that he sought a marriage with his half-sister in true sincerity. He promised that he would allow her the rank and title of Queen of Macedon, that he would not dishonour her by taking any other wife but her, so long as he lived. He vowed next that he would have no children but her children, and that he would have nothing to do with whores, or flute-girls, or animals, ever again, and he swore it by all the gods of Hellas.

It was an astonishing forswearing of every thing that anybody who knew Keraunos would have wagered he would never be able to give up, for he had never shown one iota of restraint in such matters before.

Even more astonishing was that all the time he swore, he had not seen the face of this half-sister of his for twenty years, except to see her waving in the distance, shaking her fists at him from the top of the city walls.

How, then, Thoth asks, did it happen, what happened next? Had Arsinoë indeed been driven mad by her love for Agathokles, and then by his ghost? What had got into the heart of Arsinoë Beta that she should do this foolish thing that she was now planning to do? Thoth shakes his head in dismay, and has no answer.

But Ptolemy Keraunos knew how the mind of his sister worked, and that the only thing she thought of was what she had lost: the condition of a queen, and the power of a queen, and the glory of being a queen, and the title of Queen. If she could not be Queen of Thrace, she might make do with being Queen of Macedon, especially if it meant that she might also some day be Queen of Egypt. For Arsinoë Beta very badly needed to be queen of somewhere.

At night, when the ghost of Agathokles kept her awake, Arsinoë Beta lay in her bed thinking about this great new trouble in her life: whether she should, or whether she should not, be married to her half-brother.

In her heart she knew that to do such a thing was an offence to the gods of Greece, just as to be a murderer in thought was also, and the voice within her heart told her that she must not think of this marriage, for that it would be utter folly, complete madness.

But there was also a second voice within her heart, telling her that to marry Keraunos was really not such a great thing, not such a great calamity as she might imagine.

She tossed and turned in her bed all night, night after night, turning over and over the thoughts of her heart, and when she could bear the turmoil no longer she sent her private secretary, Dion, as usual, as always, to the Oracle of Klaros at Didyma in Ionia, to ask the opinion of the gods.

And sure enough, in due time, he came back with the answer that she wanted: *To marry a brother is no great wrong,* and Arsinoë Beta was from then onwards filled with joy.

When they met at last, upon neutral ground, for face-to-face talks, Arsinoë Beta was struck silent by Keraunos's glowing appearance of health. He was bronzed by the sun. He was lean and muscled. Although he was in the thirty-sixth year of his age, he looked as if he was barely twenty years old. His sulky temper had vanished. He smiled and made jests, and was quite the Keraunos she had *liked* before he grew up, before his complete nastiness came upon him. He was, she thought, almost like the gods to look at, and she found herself unable to stop from staring at him. And yes, the eyes of Keraunos locked with her eyes, locked together as the two of them tried to stare each other out, just as they had done when they were children in Egypt. Always it is dangerous to look so hard into the eyes of another, but this time Arsinoë Beta did not break the stare and run away blushing but stood her ground, thinking *Real gods do not blink,* and remembering how it had been between them upon the couch of gold in the hot afternoons of her youth, long ago now, and of how she had loved this brother of hers in spite of his cruelty.

Arsinoë thought, then, that her brother's sworn words had to be sincere, and that he was indeed a changed character.

And he pleaded with her, saying he needed her expert military knowledge, her skills in strategy and tactics. He said he badly needed to take her advice upon so many matters, and she was flattered by his words, and the thought that her services were required by *Macedon* began to sway her heart, and the very handsome good looks of Ptolemy Keraunos began to sway also her womanly feelings, and she quite forgot the solemn warning of Berenike her mother, who had said, *Never allow yourself to fall in love . . . To fall in love is nothing but madness.*

But it is never to be forgotten that this love of Arsinoë Beta was no new thing. She had known these feelings for him before, long before, and it was as if her love had been sleeping these twenty years and more, but now woke up, like the fanned embers of a dying fire that spring into new life with a bright flame, and thus it was that Arsinoë Beta herself took fire, was caught once again by the golden arrow of Eros, and she felt a roaring in her ears as of a wall of flames, and she was burning again, burning.

When Ptolemy Keraunos made so bold as to now kiss this sister of his upon the lips, it was a kiss that went on for so very long that she gasped for breath. It was a kiss so fierce that her brother's spittle trickled into her bosom; so violent that his teeth drew blood from her mouth. But Arsinoë Beta hardly noticed these things, these ill omens, for Ptolemy Keraunos was *young*, still young, and he was hot, burning hot, and so unlike the cold old Lysimakhos, and he was willing, unlike the late lamented Agathokles, and it was fully twenty years since Arsinoë Beta had been kissed by any man she had any feeling for. In fact not since her brother had kissed her last had she felt a passion like this and had her passion returned. Keraunos indeed made the iron heart of Arsinoë Beta beat like the hammer, and she failed to heed the warning, and that heart of hers felt so hot that she feared it would melt.

Arsinoë Beta fell in love, then, and she was blind, but love had not blinded her waiting-women. If Keraunos was indeed in love himself, this was the next best thing to insanity, and many said that Keraunos was already mad. If he were to be doubly mad, things would only get worse. And they were fearful for Arsinoë herself, who had only once before showed such high emotion, with regard to Agathokles, and with dreadful results. Was she, her women wondered, so blind that she could not see the real Keraunos, who was incapable of changing his boorish habits of life; who was still, underneath his pretence, the same pig-in-the-roses that he had always been?

The women voiced their fears, saying, *Let him not lie too heavy upon your soul; take not too much thought for him.* But Arsinoë was determined. She wanted above all things a fresh husband. She had slept alone in her bed without love for twenty years, and twenty years was long enough. Eros the Boy had struck Arsinoë Beta deep with his arrows of gold a third time. She thought the third time was the lucky time, and she saw nothing but a golden future ahead of her. And perhaps Keraunos had even made sure of it, fixed her blindness, conjured up her love, by the working of his own private magic—Keraunos, whose heart was as full of evil thoughts as it had ever been, but of which Arsinoë Beta now suspected nothing.

Blind Arsinoë, then, said yes, and made the arrangements for the marriage, and they named the day upon which she should become Queen of Macedon. She asked for only one favour, which was that she must be married before the entire assembled army of Macedon, as her witness.

Two days before the marriage Keraunos sent a message scratched on papyrus in his own wild hand:

Nothing, truly, will be dearer to me than to protect you for the rest of your life. Lay this to heart—nothing painful shall befall you, but every care will be taken by me to see that you are untroubled. For me swearing truly, may things turn out well, and for me forswearing, may the women of my House bring forth monsters.

Thoth says it again, There is no liar like a Greek liar, but Arsinoë Beta thought her brother wrote nothing but the truth, and the flame of love had warmed her heart of metal so that love was the only thing she thought of. But Keraunos did lie, and his House would indeed suffer the consequences.

Arsinoë Beta—she called herself happy, even if her happiness was next to madness. The citizens of Kassandreia were happy, because there must now be an end to the assaults of Ptolemy the Thunderbolt upon that city. But not everybody rejoiced on account of the coming marriage and least happy of all was the eldest son of Arsinoë, the Prince Ptolemaios, who was now about seventeen years of age, and who suspected that the intentions of his half-uncle were less than honourable, for he had heard many stories from the hired soldiers.

I warn you, Mother, he said, *there will be treachery at the bottom of it. You would be crazy to wed a man like Uncle Thunderbolt.*

Arsinoë laughed her rare laugh. *We shall not be told what to do by our own children,* she said. *You have never met your Uncle Thunderbolt,* she said, *so how may you be a judge of his character?* And she ignored her son's words of advice, much as Keraunos ignored advice, for her mind was made up, and she would not now change it for any reason.

All will be for the best, she said, and she ordered the wedding feast to be made ready. For yes, she was so sure of the future that she forgot that no Greek must so much as speak the word *tomorrow* for fear of tempting the fates. Arsinoë and Keraunos—they would be happy, a god and a goddess together, and their children gods and goddesses after them, for she saw herself now even as the next Queen of Egypt also, and she doubled her daily sacrifice of a goose to Aphrodite, Bringer of Wedded Happiness, in order to make it happen.

Up in her private apartments, high above the city, Arsinoë snapped at her son Ptolemaios day after day, and told him not to sulk, not to be so suspicious, and promised him that all would be well, and that, besides, her marriage was the one sure means of stopping a renewal of the Siege of Kassandreia.

But this was what Ptolemaios was worried about: that the purpose of Uncle Thunderbolt was not wedded happiness but further violence, and he made his decision to flee from Kassandreia, fearing the worst, the very worst; for the one great lesson he had learned from his late father, Lysimakhos, was that a king must trust nobody, not even his own mother, and certainly not a man like Ptolemy Keraunos, family though he might be. But, alas, Thoth says, it was indeed *because* Keraunos was family that he should not have been trusted.

On the eve of his wedding day Ptolemy Keraunos dismissed his aides and sat down at the military folding table that he used for looking at maps and charts of Macedon (of which country he had no great knowledge), and fashioned an image out of wax. After a time the wax took shape in his hands, and it was of a woman kneeling upon her knees, with her hands bound behind her back. He pierced the wax with nails of copper: one nail thrust in the top of her head, one nail in each of her ears, one nail in each eye, one nail in each nostril, one nail in her mouth, one nail in each breast, one nail in the belly, one nail in the *bolba*, and one nail behind—thirteen copper nails, and he smiled at his handiwork. Upon a lump of lead he now scratched the words: *I pierce such and such a part of Arsinoë Beta in order that she have no one in mind but me, Ptolemy.*

When he thought of what he had planned for the next days he laughed his lunatic, hyaena laugh, and crowed like the cockerel, and called for wine, more wine.

On the eve of this marriage, that night, Keraunos slept sound, and he dreamed the best of all possible dreams, which was the dream of eating human flesh, and it happened that the flesh was the flesh of his sister, and it meant nothing but Good Luck.

As he rode into the city of Pella to be married, Keraunos showed his front teeth, the grinners, and hummed the battle songs of Macedon, sure in the belief that this day would be a good day, an auspicious day, and he sang aloud the Victory Paian to Apollo, Lord of the Silver Bow.

Upon a different road Arsinoë Beta also made her way towards Pella in Macedon that morning. As the city came into sight, her procession of attendants was met by men on horseback riding out of Pella, and they were the messengers of her brother, bearing gifts, and among the gifts was a *lekythos* of gold with the image of Eros holding a cockerel, and the Eros had the face of Keraunos himself.

He sent also a golden *krater,* or bowl, that showed a pair of griffins fighting, and the faces of the griffins were the faces of Arsinoë Beta and Ptolemy Keraunos.

Omens, perhaps, of what was to come, but Arsinoë Beta was still blind. She had lost her sense of balance. She did not think about *Moderation in all things.* She had forgotten about *Think what you are doing.*

With these gifts Ptolemy Keraunos sent his last message, promising her, *While I live and see the light upon earth, no man will lay violent hands upon you.*

It was, for once, the truth, for his purpose was to lay violent hands upon others.

4.7

The Bloody Wedding

The lucky dream of Ptolemy Keraunos was not, however, the only dream he saw on the eve of his wedding day. He also dreamed disturbing dreams. To be sure, he knew that the most dangerous dream in the world was the dream of defecating in the *agora,* or upon the street, or in his bath, and he dreamed all of these things one after another that night, and they meant, all of them, the same thing: the wrath of the gods of Greece, and most improper behaviour, and extraordinary loss, and that the dreamer would be an object of hatred. Keraunos knew all of this, and yet he was heedless of the warning. He laughed again his hyaena laugh. The gods could do as they pleased. He was Ptolemaios Keraunos, the Thunderbolt of Thunderbolts, the next Pharaoh of Egypt, Living for Ever, and he would get what he wanted without the help of the gods, by his own efforts.

Such was the terrible hubris, the overweening pride of this Ptolemy, but he seemed not to know what every Greek knows: that pride does not go unpunished, that pride cannot go unpunished.

As for Arsinoë Beta, the night before her marriage she dreamed of fire: of ceilings on fire, balconies on fire, lintels on fire, of a palace all in flames. And what did it mean? It meant the loss of property, the death of children. But in the morning Arsinoë laughed, just as Keraunos laughed, and thought no more about it. Really, she did not believe the old-fashioned nonsense that every dream is an urgent message from the gods.

So sure was she that what she did was right that she sent one last letter to her betrothed: *Arsinoë, to her Brother, Keraunos, greetings. You must know that I do not see the Sun because you are out of my sight, for I have no other Sun but you.*

Ptolemy Keraunos, who saw himself as the next Son of the Sun, laughed his hyaena laugh for a long time.

For the ceremonies of the marriage this bridegroom stuck a black-handled knife inside his belt. The bride put the usual open pair of scissors inside her left shoe, and the purpose of these objects was to cut off all evil influence. Alas, neither the knife nor the scissors would have the least effect.

For the ceremonies Arsinoë wore the usual wedding garment with the Herakles Knot that her husband must untie that night. And at the *Anaklypteria,* the Festival of the Unveiling, when the bride must take off her maiden veil, Ptolemy Keraunos hardly troubled to look at his sister. She was, for one thing, no longer a *parthenos*—he had seen to that himself. She was just his sister, and he had seen her before. He knew only too well what she looked like. She was thin—thin like the starving jackal of the desert of Libya—and her heart was hard, like the rocks of the desert.

On this day however Arsinoë Beta was at her most generous, and she gave to this brother of hers the wedding suit of golden armour that was what a princely husband must have, and it was heavy golden armour of the finest Thracian workmanship.

As a boy, Keraunos had made Arsinoë Beta the proper gift upon the anniversary of her birth, but his gifts had been horrible gifts, chosen not so much to please as to annoy her, though she had loved them even so: his frogs, his snakes, his scorpions. What would he give her now—now that they were to be husband and wife? Something special, he thought, but something unpleasant, for this woman in truth rejoiced in nasty things.

So, yes, after much trouble getting his hands upon it, and after much difficulty with the transport, and after much trouble with keeping it still while the finishing touches were made, he gave her for her wedding gift: a crocodile, a young crocodile of the River Nile, who was one and a half cubits long, and who wore about his ankles circlets of gold of the Egyptians, and earrings of gold in his ears, and who had every august jewel of Egypt and every costly stone embedded in his armoured flesh, so that as he crept about he glittered in the sunshine—a bejewelled crocodile upon a jewelled leash, like the tame crocodiles of their childhood at Memphis; a crocodile who was not safely dead but dangerously alive, and it was, Keraunos thought, the beast of all beasts that was most like unto herself—glittering, yes, but very nasty, and very like to kill.

It was Keraunos's thought that Arsinoë would be blind to the meaning of his gift, and he was right. She was pleased, very pleased with her crocodile, and when she saw him she squealed with delight, and embraced her brother with many kisses. And, truly, Pella had never seen the like of it, neither the crocodile, nor the sight of a brother married to his own sister.

This marriage, then, was celebrated with the greatest magnificence, and with the pretence of general rejoicing, and with music in the streets, and dancing, and drums and trumpets, and processions of singing children, all witnessed, as Arsinoë had insisted, by the entire grand phalanx of the army of Macedon, numbering sixteen thousand three hundred and eighty-four men exactly.

At the end of it Keraunos tied the diadem round his sister's head and saluted her as *Basilissa,* Queen, and kissed her upon both her cheeks. The heart of Arsinoë Beta beat high. She was dressed in white, with wedding shoes of white felt, and garlanded and crowned with wreaths of scarlet flowers, and anointed with the most costly perfumes of Syria; and the open scissors in her shoe bothered her all day.

This bride and groom acted out every Greek ritual, not forgetting the quinces sacred to Aphrodite, Bringer of Wedded Happiness, that must be eaten as part of the ritual: hollowed out quinces, filled with honey and cooked in a case of pastry that melted in the mouth, and the honey trickled down their chins, and they licked up the sweetness, kissing each other upon the lips all the while.

In his youth Keraunos had said always, *Singing is for Kinaidoi,* but at his wedding banquet he was persuaded to sing himself, and he sang the wedding songs of Macedon, the Swallow Song and the Crow Song, and the feasters applauded him, and Keraunos smiled a genuine smile. He was, in fact, good at singing.

That night, outside the door of the bridal chamber, a choir of singers sang the hymeneal songs whose purpose was to drown out the nightingale wailing of Arsinoë Beta as her marriage was consummated, and to drown, perhaps, her screams, as Keraunos twisted her arms and sank his teeth into her neck, and slapped her and pinched her, and hurt her, just as he had done when they were little more than children, at Alexandria.

In her excitement the heart of Arsinoë Beta hammered so hard that she could hear it, and just then she felt that she had got back every thing she had lost before ever she had sailed away to Thrace, and she thought that on that night she was happy as she had never been happy before. But what Arsinoë Beta did not then know was that this marriage of hers was fated to last but one day and a half.

What Arsinoë Beta did next was perhaps the most ill-advised thing she did in all her life time, for she said now to this husband of hers that it was her purpose to make over to him as *his* wedding gift her city of Kassandreia, and she invited him to visit her there so that she might hand the keys of it to him, and told him that the next day she planned to go on ahead of him to make ready for his welcome.

The government of cities, she said, *is not woman's work. A woman's work is to bring forth heirs, and to raise up her children.* For it was her purpose to have further offspring by her half-brother.

She decreed then the day of Keraunos's coming to Kassandreia a public holiday, and ordered every house and temple, every public building, to be decked with garlands of scarlet flowers. She gave orders for one hundred oxen to have their horns gilded for the sacrifice, and the entire city would feast upon them at Arsinoë's expense.

Flowers were sent to Kassandreia in their thousands, and Arsinoë emptied her wine cellars for this feasting, and had to hand every delicacy for a banquet of surpassing magnificence, including all the forbidden red foods that she knew Keraunos loved so much, and she ignored as childish nonsense the fact that to eat the red food at any banquet but the funeral banquet was the worst of ill luck. Yes, the citizens of Kassandreia would feast in the streets, and the kitchen slaves of this Queen spent hour upon hour slapping octopus upon the rocks in readiness for her great day of celebration.

At dawn on this fateful day, when Ptolemy Keraunos was due to make his appearance in Kassandreia, the other Ptolemy, whom they later called Ptolemaios of Telmessos, now about eighteen years of age, took the fastest horse from his mother's stables and galloped westward, towards Illyria, where he thought to take refuge with Monounios, the chief of a barbarian—but Greek-speaking—tribe, whom he knew from having entertained him some years previous during a trading mission to Thrace, and whom he regarded, rightly, as his friend.

When the cloud of dust that was the entire army of Macedon was sighted in the distance, the other two sons of Arsinoë Beta, Philippos, fifteen years of age, and Lysimakhos Mikros, thirteen years—boys remarkable for handsome good looks—rode out from the gates of their mother's city upon white horses, with a mounted guard of troops, in a formal procession of welcome for their Uncle Thunderbolt who was now also their stepfather.

The Thunderbolt wore still his white *khiton* and he was garlanded still with flowers, but he wore also his cuirass of gold, his golden helmet and greaves of gold, that were the wedding gifts of Arsinoë Beta, and although his flesh was sleek with unguents and he was plastered from head to foot with myrrh, he carried also his gilded shield, and his sword with the golden hilt, and the *kopis,* or short sword. Aye, the dagger was still in his belt, as if for battle, and he murmured under his breath the prayers to Ares, god of War, and his eyes shone with amusement, for he was in a very good temper.

Aye, Keraunos that so famously held the gods of his own country of no account, was saying his prayers, and, Thoth knows, it could mean nothing but the worst of trouble.

The first words he spoke were, *Are there not three boys?* For he missed at once Ptolemaios, the eldest son, the heir.

But Philippos said, *Our elder brother is unwell. He has eaten too many unripe dates . . .* For he did not dare tell Keraunos that, suspecting foul play, this Ptolemaios had fled.

The stepfather embraced his stepsons and nephews, who wore new white tunics, and crowns of golden oak leaves. He was a man they had never before set eyes upon in their lives, except in the distance, and they had never yet spoken to him one word, but this man now kissed them upon their cheeks and arms and even upon their lips, as if he had known them since the day they were born. He hugged and squeezed these two boys quite beyond the warmth of real affection, and persisted in kissing them for some time, so that Arsinoë Beta, watching from the battlements, wondered what he thought he was doing. But her doubts were momentary, for Athene had endowed Keraunos that day with such magic charm that all eyes were turned upon him in admiration, this King, and nobody was more charmed by him than Arsinoë herself. She had never seen Keraunos looking so bronzed, so handsome, or so desirable, and she ordered the gates of Kassandreia to be thrown open so that he might ride into the city.

Keraunos rode, and his army rode and marched behind him, fully armed, with breastplate, greaves, helmet, sword and shield, every man of them, but with orders to look harmless, to show the teeth; and the people of Kassandreia welcomed them with applause, with cheering and whistling, and there was much beating of drums and much blowing of trumpets and flutes, as Kassandreia went wild to welcome the new husband of Arsinoë Beta.

However, as soon as the tail end of the column of troops passed inside the walls, Keraunos began to wave his sword above his head, and to shout and scream orders, and what he ordered was for the city gates to be closed and barred so that no man might escape, and for the citadel of Kassandreia to be seized. To Arsinoë Beta, who had come down from above to greet him, he screamed, *In an instant your dark blood will drip from my sword.*

There was uproar in the crowd, and the alarm bells were rung, but it was too late, for Kassandreia was the victim of a trick. Every man was in the mood for making festival, and not one of them carried his sword or any protection for his body. And yes, the drinking had begun before dawn, for Keraunos had sent to the city his gift of one thousand amphoras of the finest wine, on purpose, so that no man would be in a fit state to defend himself.

The massacre of Kassandreia began—men, women and children alike—and there was blood on every street, and blood flowing in the streets, and the dead would lie where they fell, because there was no man left alive to bury them.

Arsinoë Beta turned and ran, as if to retreat to the safety of her private chamber, and her sons were with her, but they were pursued by soldiers detailed to take care of them, and upon the staircase these boys were run through by many swords, in the lap of their mother, as she held them to her and embraced them, pleading with the men of Keraunos to do what they would with her, to kill her if they must, but to spare the lives of her children.

The blood of Philippos and Lysimakhos Mikros splashed upon the white wedding garment of their mother, and upon her wedding shoes of white felt, and she wailed and shuddered as she saw the black blood pouring from their many wounds, and all the while Ptolemy Keraunos her brother and husband stood there grinning, looking on, and brandishing his sword of gold, as if he meant to kill his sister also.

Arsinoë howled at him, then, *No man will keep the dogs away from your body. Not even your dishonoured Mother will lay you upon the bier and mourn for you, but the dogs and birds will share you for their feast and leave nothing.*

She screamed, *I shall not rest until I have let Hell loose upon you.*

But Keraunos yelled back at her the words of the Homer Oracle that he had consulted that very morning: *You will not kill me, since I am for sure not subject to Fate.*

Arsinoë screamed on: *The vultures will eat you here . . . The quick-running dogs will feed upon you . . .* And the curse flew from her lips and could not be taken back. For a long while her eyes were flooded with tears and the words stuck in her throat. Her sons lay dying in her arms, but Arsinoë herself Keraunos did not butcher, for she was his wife, and even Keraunos shrank from making himself a wife-killer, and it might even have been that Keraunos did, in truth, retain the vestiges of affection for his sister, and that he shuddered too at the thought of becoming a sister-killer. In truth, though, perhaps Arsinoë Beta owed her life to Keraunos's fear of vengeance from her full brother, Ptolemy Mikros, King of Egypt, the man who, though assuredly he had not much wanted it, found himself the most powerful man upon earth.

Keraunos wanted this sister of his to suffer, and she would suffer the more by being let to live. To kill her would merely bring her suffering to a stop, and he wanted more than any thing else to punish her for betraying him to their father, for blabbing the secret of their forbidden *aphrodisia,* and for breaking the oath she had sworn not to breathe one word of it to any man. For yes, it was all the fault of Arsinoë Beta that he had been banished from his rightful kingdom and was not now King of Egypt himself.

Now he had his revenge. Now she should know what was the anger of a Ptolemy. Now she might think twice before ever she came near to trouble him again.

And so it was that Keraunos allowed Arsinoë Beta, his wife and sister, to escape, and the marriage of one day and a half was at an end.

Thoth asks, What of the hired soldiers, the famous hired soldiers of Arsinoë Beta? Did they not lift the sword to help her? But no, the hired soldiers were busy drinking their wine, and making ready to swear allegiance to Ptolemy Keraunos in order to save their skins. No, no man in Kassandreia ran to help Arsinoë in her hour of torment, and no man raised so much as a finger against Keraunos to stop his terrible crimes.

Keraunos himself had work to do: half the population of his sister's city remained to be put to the sword. There was treasure to be looted, women to be raped, and the marriage feast stood ready for the eating, for there is nothing like a massacre to give a madman an appetite. Keraunos, then, gorged himself, and the juice of the forbidden red fruits ran down his chin, and he laughed, for the marriage feast of Arsinoë Beta had turned into a funeral feast.

When they wearied of slaughter and feasting, Keraunos's men danced the dances of the Greek wedding, and an all but naked Keraunos ran about the city that was his new possession, screaming with laughter like a lunatic.

Somehow Arsinoë Beta reached the harbour of Kassandreia and boarded one of her swiftest-sailing *triereis* without suffering injury, and her waiting-gentlewomen went with her, manhandling the chests of jewels and money on to the ship, a procession of weeping women, and no man of Keraunos lifted the sword to harm them.

What, then, became of the jewelled crocodile, her wedding present? For to be sure she did not carry this beast away with her to exile. By no means. Such a creature was far too precious to Keraunos to lose, and he carried the jewelled crocodile with him now as his talisman, wherever he went.

From the battlements of the *akropolis* of Kassandreia Ptolemy Keraunos yelled to the departing Arsinoë, *May your journey be rough,* and the journey was rough, and as usual she was seasick.

What man can feel sympathy for a woman such as Arsinoë Beta? Was not every thing that befell her only what she richly deserved? For, to be sure, the Furies, the maidens with bloodshot eyes and the hair of snakes, did indeed follow her wherever she went, and she did not escape the horrid attentions of the brass-clawed, brass-winged women who clanged about her until the day she died.

At length Arsinoë came, in difficult seas, to the island of Samothrake, which Lysimakhos her late husband had used as his naval base, and where she hoped she would find sanctuary and a kind welcome.

She came, then, to the high altar of Zeus Xenios, Protector of Suppliant Strangers, the famous place of refuge, where no enemy would be able to touch her, and she prayed that, with the help of the gods, her one surviving son, Ptolemaios, might flourish. She sat here holding a branch wreathed with white wool, by the statues of the gods, praying the prayers of supplication:

O Zeus, take pity on my woes, before I succumb to them entirely . . .

And Zeus did, this time, take pity upon Arsinoë Beta, for no woman, whatever crime she is guilty of, deserves the murder of her children.

On Samothrake Arsinoë Beta sent, as always, to the Oracle, saying: *God, Fortune. Arsinoë asks Apollo whether it would not be better for her to sail to Alexandria.*

But Apollo's answer came back: *Not to do it.*

She stayed where she was, but after a while she sent again to the Oracle to ask: *God, Fortune. O Apollo, will she fare better by departing for Alexandria?*

But the answer came back: *To dwell there and hold on.*

The third time she sent her question to the Oracle she said: *For Good Fortune. Arsinoë asks of Apollo, Will it be better and more good for her staying at home?*

But for the time being the gods would not let her go.

Arsinoë Beta, whose heart they always said was just about as hard as flint, showed at this time in her life the same feelings as any other woman and mother. She vowed that if her wish was granted she would dedicate a giant pair of silver ears to the god. She promised that if only she could escape from Samothrake she would dedicate the largest temple ever built.

She waited with patience for the sailing season, but the winter was hard, with heavy rains and deep snow. She passed day after day staring at the granite mountain from the top of which Poseidon had gazed upon the plains of Troy.

She lived upon goats' flesh and dried fruit, and she planned also the design of the rotunda that would be called the Arsinoëion, after her, that was to be the thank-offering for her safe deliverance from Kassandreia, and for her finding some safe haven, and for her revenge upon her brother Keraunos, if only she could have it. The Arsinoëion was to be the largest circular building ever built. And why? Because already every thing the members of this family did had to be bigger, and better, than any thing done by anybody else.

Arsinoë Beta mourned, to be sure; there was no end to her weeping, and the fear of her waiting-women was that she would harm herself, but at the bottom of all the grief was this tough woman, who had been raised never to admit defeat.

One night, at the time of her worst despair, she called up the gods by some Greek spell of hers, in order to ask a question: *Could you bring yourselves to give me your solemn oath that you will not plot some new mischief against me?*

But the gods said no, there would be no end to the trouble that was coming to Arsinoë Beta, or indeed to the trouble that she would cause. The family of Arsinoë Beta would enjoy three hundred years of trouble, three hundred years of the gods' mischief.

And so she busied herself once more with trying to alter her own fate. She believed in the gods when it suited her, making the proper prayers and sacrifices, and when it did not suit her, she did not. Often she would behave as if the gods and goddesses of Greece did not exist at all, for she was, in many respects, just like her brother Keraunos, a law unto herself.

Ptolemy Keraunos, he knew what his sister would be doing in the way of magic, spells, meddling, whispering over wax images, and he was careful to take the proper retaliatory action, working the most powerful magic that he knew against her.

One who has been bad to you, he murmured, *whom you must punish . . . all you have to do is to write her name in red ink, some words from the Book of Words, then burn the papyrus. And as the papyrus burns, so will she break.*

And yes, just as Arsinoë Beta had burned with love, so also she would be broken.

Just now, though the magic of Arsinoë Beta was, Thoth knows, powerful enough, it happened that the magic of Keraunos was stronger still—so powerful that it would continue to do its work for years after his death; a magic that would, in due course, utterly destroy this sister of his.

Ptolemy Keraunos was feeling pleased, very pleased, with what he had done, and it pleased him still further now to take possession of all the European territories of Lysimakhos. Successful though he was, for the rest of his short life he was followed by two white-faced youths with hair the colour of straw, whom he saw, waking and sleeping, wherever he went; whom he caught sight of looking at him out of every cart and every wagon, or sitting opposite him at table while he ate his food, or marching in the phalanx of his army, or standing in the doorway of his leather campaign tent; and he could not shake them off.

Ptolemy Keraunos laughed at the so-called haunting, for really he had no belief in phantoms—none whatever. But he became, as a result, more violent in his everyday life, more short-tempered with his generals, and he slept ill. His enemies he slaughtered as if they were wild beasts, and it gave him the greatest pleasure to cut down the youngest and most handsome of soldiers, the ones with pale hair and the faces of his two nephews, Philippos and Lysimakhos Mikros, young men who had died innocent of any crime.

Keraunos saw too out of the corner of his eye the Three Sisters with the wings and claws of brass—Aye, the Furies—whose task it is to torment those who have offended the gods of Hellas; but Keraunos laughed even at the Furies, and he hurtled blindly onwards, still the same pig-in-the-roses that he had always been, trampling underfoot every thing that stood in his path.

Any man of sense could see that Keraunos would die a violent death sooner or later. Every man saw this except Keraunos himself, who truly believed that he lived a charmed life, that he was lucky, born lucky, and not subject to the natural laws that govern the behaviour of other human beings.

Every thing, however, that happened to Ptolemy Keraunos was fated to happen. Nothing that happens in the whole world happens by chance. All is in the hands of the gods—Thoth swears it. And what would happen to Keraunos next would involve the spilling of still more blood, this time his own blood.

4.8

Thunderbolt and Lightning

Not long after the massacre at Kassandreia the curse of Arsinoë Beta upon her brother began to take hold upon him, in the form of the army of the Keltoi, or Gauls, who now swept down out of the north lands with the purpose of capturing for themselves the kingdom of Macedon.

Ptolemy Keraunos had been sitting for just two years upon his throne when the actual approach of these Gauls was reported upon the road to Pella, only a handful of days away. The kings of neighbouring territories heard the news with dread, and sent their ambassadors at once to try to buy off the barbarians with sacks of tetradrachms and every goodly gift of gold and silver. Keraunos alone heard of the coming attack without nervousness, and he marched his army out of Pella in person and with great delight, in order, as he said, to take a look at his new enemy. And he marched with only a few thousand ill-armed, ill-drilled, ill-trained troops, as if he thought to handle a full-scale invasion as easily as a murder.

The Dardanians now kindly sent word to Keraunos that they could lend him twenty thousand troops, if he wished, as reinforcements, to help him fight the Gauls. But Keraunos howled with laughter, and he sent a messenger to say that his men were the sons of men who had marched with Alexander, and that it would be all over for Macedon if, having conquered all of Asia, they must now rely upon the feeble Dardanians—upon barbarians—to help defend their frontier. For these people were so utterly wild that they dug caves beneath the dunghills to be their dwelling-place.

And so Keraunos went without the help of reinforcements, which in truth he badly needed.

The chief of the Gauls, one Bolgios (or Belgius), whose name, by chance, happened to mean Lightning, sent Ptolemy the Thunderbolt his ambassadors, with a generous offer to spare his territory in return for a very large payment of gold.

Keraunos laughed at Bolgios's proposals for peace, and sent a second messenger to say that he would never hand over so much as one quarter obol, and he demanded that the Gauls hand over their leaders to him, as hostages for their good behaviour.

Now it was the turn of Bolgios to laugh, and he gave the order for his hundreds of thousands of Gauls to swarm down into the plains of Macedon, where Keraunos was camped in a state of some disorder and confusion, with his tents put up the way all Greeks put up their tents, not in straight lines but at random, and not ready to fight a pitched battle with anybody.

The Dardanian King was reported by the ambassadors to have said that the famous kingdom of Macedon looked as if it would shortly fall by the rashness of a youth, just as it had risen. Keraunos took no notice.

Though Ptolemy Keraunos was no youth, being now more than forty years of age, he had still the marks of immaturity upon him—haste, recklessness, impulsiveness—and he was quite fixed in his thought to fight this battle without outside help, without a full complement of troops, trusting in his personal battle skills alone. Alas, Keraunos did not think hard enough about how many men he would need to beat the numberless hordes of Gauls who now lurked in the woods, roaring their songs of battle, making ready to hurl fire at and slice up the army of Ptolemy the Thunderbolt. Alexander might have won his usual victory in such circumstances, but Keraunos was, alas, not Alexander.

Keraunos was indeed a man of action, but he lived in and for the moment, like his father before him. He did not have the ability to think far ahead, and the past and the future meant but little to him. He was, to be sure, very good at one-armed combat, but he had really not the genius to be a general, and had only ended up as supreme commander because of the accident of his birth, and, of course, because he had butchered Seleukos. Formerly he had had always some senior officer to tell him what to do, but Keraunos hated like Hades to have to take another man's advice. He hated having to do what he was told, like an unruly child. And so, no, he would face his enemy alone, whatever the cost. He was a king eager to exercise full personal command, like his hero Alexander. He was keen to give every order himself, and to take all the credit for the victory afterwards.

Worst of all, Keraunos did not realize that in the thick of hand-to-hand fighting, however brave he is, a commander cannot see the battle as a whole, and he told his generals that they did not know what they were talking about. He thought he knew every thing about war, but he was wrong: the person who should have been at his side, helping him, was his half-sister and wife, Arsinoë Beta, who might indeed have won a famous victory for her brother. But Arsinoë Beta was still upon the island of Samothrake, and she would hardly help this brother now.

The Greeks liked always to say that the Gauls were madmen, for they lacked all *dike,* or right action, and were the embodiment of wrong-doing. Aye, the Gauls were famous for eating alive any sucking child that fell into their hands, and notorious for savagery, for rapes and for mutilations, and for other hideous crimes of war upon men and women alike, and they did not even trouble to bury their dead. When the leaders of these barbarians were taken prisoner, they would always refuse to surrender, but preferred to kill themselves, which to the Greeks was shameful above all other things, the behaviour of cowards. And yet, the Gauls were not cowardly, for they fought regardless of their wounds and showed a bravery in battle that astonished every man that saw it.

The Gauls, then, lacked every kind of civilized behaviour, and in that they were very like Ptolemy Keraunos himself.

Before he retired for the night Keraunos amused himself by looking up the Homer Oracle, to see what it was that the gods wanted him to do, and the Oracle said: *You lunatic, sit still and listen to the words of others.*

But Keraunos was not capable of sitting still for one moment, and he did not mean to take the advice of a mere oracle.

This night before the battle Keraunos hardly slept because of his excitement, but when he did sleep he dreamed the dream of eating books, a dream that will admit of only one interpretation, that is: *sudden death.* In fact, Keraunos dreamed that he was eating that most blood-stained of books, the *Iliad* of Homer, scroll upon scroll of papyrus, for that it was made of pastry; but he could not think that this had anything to do with his own death.

He put the thought out of his heart. Men died, to be sure, in every battle, but he believed that it was his personal fate not to die at all, but to be Pharaoh in Egypt, Ptolemy *Aionobios,* Living for Ever.

In the morning he strapped on the golden armour that was the wedding gift of his sister, and he fingered again and again his Egyptian necklace of magic talismans, the *Baraka,* or Bringer of Luck, for his great victory over the Gauls, and he had no mind but for the grim clash of war. He would go to battle wearing gold, like a girl, poor fool, and it would not save him from a miserable death.

While his men ate what might be their last breakfast, of bread dipped in undiluted wine, and sausages, Keraunos shouted, *Breakfast well, for tonight we dine with Hades,* and he laughed his hyaena laugh. As the men made ready for the fight he shouted, *Put a good edge to your sword, give a good feed to your swift-footed horses, and cast a good eye over your chariots, so that we can run the trial of hateful Ares all day long.*

As it happened, the only Greek to dine that night with Hades would be Ptolemy Keraunos himself. This man thought he was lucky, born lucky, lucky for ever, but the Luck of Ptolemy Keraunos had run out, for it was the day appointed by the Fates to be the day of his death, his *termia hemera,* and he did not know it.

When the Gauls started to move out of the woods Keraunos's friends urged him again to wait for the Greek reinforcements, who were on the road from Pella, but had been held up by torrential storms of rain. But Keraunos was so hot now in his desire to smash the barbarian that he ignored his friends, as usual, and ordered the attack.

We do not like waiting, he said, and he screamed the battle cry, the *Alalalalai* of Macedon, and it was taken up by the men, as if to say that they were ready to fight, eager to be started.

Keraunos that day followed the example of Philip, father of Alexander, who had always drunk wine before riding into battle. Why, Keraunos thought, should he do any thing different? And he ordered the extra ration of wine for every soldier, then doubled and tripled it, because of the triumph that was to come, and to urge them on.

The troops of Keraunos eyed the woods where the naked barbarians were gathered in their very many thousands, shouting in perfect rhythm the blood-chilling songs that fired up their spirits for the clash of battle—men who wore their yellow hair stood up on end, in spikes, and whose muscled bodies were painted blue from head to foot, and who howled a war cry that was more spine-chilling even than the *Alalalalai* that Keraunos's men now did not shout, because they were a little drunk, and because Keraunos had forgotten to give them the order, and because they were already as if hypnotized by the roaring of the barbarian.

The braying of the *karnyx*, or war trumpet, of the barbarian started up, the war horns' harsh cry, and the Gauls rushed then upon Keraunos's men with all the unreasoning fury and passion of wild beasts. They slashed with axe and sword, and nothing they did that day conformed with the proper rules and sacred laws of Greek warfare: they did not line up in their ranks; they did not give fair warning of when they would strike; they did not attack from one direction, but seemed to come at the Greeks from all sides, like a million nests of hornets. Keraunos screamed with delight to see it, but his voice, as he barked his orders, was drowned by the uproar, and so the blood began to fly. And yes, the barbarian chariots ran rings round the soldiers of Keraunos, and when their swords were gone they kept on fighting, with their bare hands, and with their teeth.

As for Ptolemy Keraunos himself, there were three different traditions regarding what became of him.

The first version said that as the men of the phalanx surged forward Keraunos was knocked off his elephant, and that the barbarian hacked his body to bits. His head, they said, was separated from his body, his arms wrenched out of their sockets, his legs pulled off like the legs of a fly. His necessity they cut off and stuffed between his teeth.

The second version said that Keraunos suffered one or two flesh wounds, was taken prisoner and tortured, while the Gauls fought among themselves to take their pleasure of his handsome body in a manner too disgusting for Thoth to relate. Then they took off his head from his body, stuck it upon the end of a Greek javelin, and carried it in triumph round the field of battle, so as to strike terror into the troops of Macedon, who saw that their King was no more, lost their nerve, uttered with one voice a great groan, and fled.

The third version seemed to suggest that no pitched battle took place, but that Ptolemy Keraunos faced Bolgios alone. For it was the custom of the Gauls, when they had made ready for battle, to step out before their enemy and challenge the bravest man to fight in single combat.

It was Keraunos, then, who screamed at Bolgios, *As one thirsting for a drink, so I desire to fight with you,* though this non-Greek-speaking barbarian understood not a word of it.

Keraunos heard the *bar-bar-bar* of the barbarian, and he laughed. He found it amusing that these savages had thought to defeat the power of

Macedon, and the noise they made—it was indeed like the twittering of the swallows.

As Keraunos jumped about upon the spot, waiting, eager to fight, one of his friends held his arm and said, *It is not a dance he is inviting you to join, but a fight to the death.*

Keraunos laughed again, and stepped forth. He was not, at this stage, quite sober. But who other than Keraunos could be the bravest? It was, he knew, what Alexander would have done, and it was his chance to prove himself as good as Alexander, if not better. All he could think was that his half-brother, Ptolemy Mikros, would never have dared to do this, and that in itself was all the more reason for Keraunos to fight alone. And yet Mikros was the wiser man.

This fierce swordsman, this powerful creator of panic, this Thunderbolt, now danced forward to face Bolgios, who was the tallest of men, and stood stark naked but for a collar of gold about his neck, with his sword of iron and shield of leather, and tattooed blue from head to foot, bright blue. Bolgios was younger than Keraunos, and lighter upon his feet, with the stoutest of muscles all over his body, and he was greased all over, but not dusted with sand as a Greek would have been, so that Keraunos could get no handhold upon his flesh for he was all slippery. This giant towered over Keraunos, roaring at him, laughing at Keraunos and mocking him, so that he threw himself upon the Gaul not with a cool head but in a raging temper, and screaming. Thus Thunderbolt battled with Lightning.

Ptolemy Keraunos strove hard, indeed, but he was weighted down by his sword of gold, his golden shield, his golden breastplate, his golden greaves, his boots of crocodile leather, and by his helmet of gold, that had in the top of it white ostrich feathers, which were the first thing that Bolgios sliced off.

Keraunos had grown a little heavy from too much feasting, and was a little slow also in his movements; whereas Bolgios danced around him, light upon his bare legs, without greaves or soldier's boots, leaping into the air and knocking Keraunos to the ground time after time with his flying feet. And then he stood himself upon Keraunos's chest and hacked at his arms and neck with his sword, and all the while the Gauls roared their song of praise for the mighty deeds of their ancestors, and the song in which they boasted of their great successes and reviled their enemies, and the rhythmical chanting and roaring that came from these painted savages was meant to strip the Greek of his proud, bold spirit before ever the single combat began, and it did so.

These brave hired soldiers of Keraunos—most of them were not flu-
ent speakers of Greek, and they had not the words of the Greek battle
songs by heart. They had not been trained by their master to chant
together, so they did not howl on his behalf, to encourage him, but
stood silent, watching. No, there can be no doubting the truth of what
happened: Bolgios stabbed Keraunos in the mouth with the pitiless
bronze, and the blade of his sword passed right through and up under
the brain, smashing the white bones. His teeth were knocked out and
his eyes flooded with black blood: wide-mouthed Keraunos screamed
his last battle cry then, spurting a well of blood through his mouth and
nostrils, and the black fog of death covered him over.

How many times had Ptolemy Keraunos stripped the bright armour
from the enemy dead? How many times had he severed ears and fingers, heads and *rhomboi,* as his trophies of war, and laughed his hyaena
laugh? Many times. Now it was the turn of Keraunos himself to suffer
the indignities that he had so often visited upon others.

The Gauls helped themselves to Keraunos's own bright armour, and
left him naked and bloody upon the field, deprived of all funeral lustra-
tions, to await the fulfilment of his destiny. And yes, whatever was the
truth of it, the ending was most disgraceful, for the soldiers of Macedon
turned and ran away. A few saved themselves, but most were taken captive, treated shamefully and sold into slavery, or cut to ribbons by the
sword.

While the war horns of the Gauls still echoed in the plain, the barbarians fucked the dying, male and female, soldier and camp-follower
alike. They fucked the already dead. And then, worse still, they committed sacrilege against the gods of Hellas by ravaging and defiling the
sacred precincts, altars and temples, omitting no disgraceful act
towards them. As they withdrew to the north they looted and ravaged
and slaughtered still more, and they set every farm building and every
field of corn on fire, so that the frontier of Macedon blazed from end to
end, and a black cloud hung over the land for days.

It was, indeed, the kind of behaviour the great Alexander had been
pleased to indulge in throughout his Asian campaign. For a change the
Macedonians were on the receiving end of their own treatment.

And Thoth says: Who is to say that they did not deserve it?

What, though, of Ptolemy the Thunderbolt, who lay where he fell,
with night coming on, abandoned, his golden armour gone, his bright
tunic, even his undergarment stolen from him?

His eyes went first, to the crows, for the eyes are always the crows'
preserve. Then went the soft, fleshy parts, that had always got Keraunos

into trouble. What was left of him, the scavenging dogs and the birds of carrion that make war upon corpses tore up at their leisure, and the tails of the dogs thumped upon the bloody ground, and the air was heavy with the beat of vulture wings. Before the next sunset the scattered bones of Ptolemy Keraunos, a king and the son of a king, were picked clean by the dogs' and birds' feasting, in accordance with the forecast of his horoscope.

This was no hot-headed youth, for although he looked no more than thirty years, and acted, some times, twenty, he was at his death forty or forty-one years old.

Now the Gauls have a strange belief that all the virtue of a slain enemy dwells in his head, and they persist in their belief that the severed head will continue to *live,* long after the body to which it had been fixed has died.

And so the *head* of Keraunos was not left upon the field, because it pleased these Gauls to come back later and pick it up, and they carried it home with them, stuck upon the end of a spear. Bolgios admired very much the savagery of his opponent, who, in spite of being drunk, or because of it, had fought with the spirit of a Gaul, and he went to the trouble of embalming the severed head in cedar oil, and it was the greatest tribute that a Gaul can pay to his enemy.

When the embalming was done, Bolgios decorated the head of Keraunos with gold and kept it in a chest, from which he would bring it out upon special occasions, showing it to strangers with pride, as a badge of his military prowess, and he refused till the day he died to part with it, even when offered its weight in gold oktodrachms.

At certain festivals of the Gauls Bolgios would carry out this great treasure and make use of it as a cup for pouring libations to his gods. Sometimes he would place the head upon a pillar, and by pouring a little water into the mouth make the severed head speak a few words, albeit in Greek, a tongue that the barbarian, by definition, was at a loss to understand.

By the pouring of undiluted wine into his mouth Keraunos could be made to move his blackened lips, and even to sing for the Gauls a line or two of the Swallow Song of the Greeks. In certain lights the artificial eyes of Keraunos, made of some costly stone, replacements for the eyes lost to the crows, were seen to sparkle with something approaching amusement.

The head of Ptolemy Keraunos, then—filthy, unshaven, haggard, caked with dried blood—would sing, just as the severed head of Orpheus sang, that made even the trees and rocks move.

Some nights the head of Keraunos could be made to lament, or to reply to simple questions, or to give its advice upon every important decision. But most important of all, it was held to fertilize the crops of the Gauls, and to repel every invasion of the Macedonians.

Ptolemy Keraunos, then, would live for ever, though not quite as he had hoped; even as his half-brother, King Ptolemy Mikros, the new Pharaoh of Egypt, would live for ever.

This last relic of the Thunderbolt ended up, therefore, as a family heirloom among the barbarians, who valued his courage, in truth, more highly than did his own people. Since Keraunos was very like a barbarian, it was not, perhaps, an unfitting end.

Some men saw the death of the Thunderbolt as but the revenge of the gods of Greece for the murder of his two nephews, whose blood cried out for vengeance; others saw it as no more than the working out of the curse, or the magic, of his half-sister, Arsinoë Beta. Others again thought of the words of Herodotos: *There is nobody that hath not misery as an ingredient of his fate.*

What, though, of that famous jewelled crocodile of the River? When Keraunos was killed, the Gauls helped themselves not only to his armour but also to his armoured friend. The jewels they prised out of his skin with their hunting knives. They stripped off his scaly coat to turn into leather breeches. His flesh they ripped up, for they were hungry.

Reader, they ate him.

Thus, at any rate, ended Ptolemy Keraunos, the famous Thunderbolt, the boy that was born to be dogs' meat.

4.9

Greek Ghosts

Who, then, ate the pease pudding, the funeral dish, for the dead Ptolemy Keraunos? Nobody. Who, then, gorged themselves upon the Red Banquet that Keraunos had so loved to eat, so much that he became a lover of death? Nobody. Nobody.

What of Arsinoë Beta, that half-sister and sometime wife of his?

What did she think and feel upon learning the news of her brother's death? Nothing. She felt neither joy nor sadness, just the usual numbness that a mother feels who has had her two sons murdered in her lap, and cannot forget it, or them. Arsinoë Beta felt nothing.

All the same, it is the Greek belief that the ghost of a man dead before his time must wander about, and wreak evil until the years of his natural span of life have been used up. And so the ghost of Ptolemy Keraunos was due to walk thirty years, for the remainder of Arsinoë's days upon earth, and the truth of it was that he came to her sure enough, so that she did not know one day when her half-brother did not haunt her, with the black skin and shabby grey clothes of a Greek ghost, and she would not pass one day or one night in which he did not burst into her chamber like a centaur, just as he had done when he was a youth, and crouch naked and bold upon her chest and hold her ears with his two hands and kiss her with the *khutra* kiss, the handle kiss, and he would place his two hands upon her two breasts and squeeze hard, so that the nails of his fingers hurt her, and he would bite her chin so hard that she cried out, and she did not know whether it was for pain or pleasure.

In her sleep she would scream at this brother, *May the quick dogs feed upon your flesh.* But his ghost, all bloody, mounted her regardless, and he would never leave her alone. She had pleaded with the gods of Greece at a quite young age for Keraunos to be at her side for ever. This prayer, at least, had been heard, and answered.

Neither, of course, did Arsinoë Beta know one single night that was free from the ghost of handsome Agathokles, who came to her, bloody and beautiful in death, lacking his hands and feet and other body parts, to accuse her for his most untimely murder.

Nor, of course, did Arsinoë Beta know one day or one night without she saw also the ghosts of her two murdered sons, the Princes Philippos and Lysimakhos Mikros, who followed her across the Great Sea even to Samothrake, and she was haunted ever after by their screams, by their adolescent voices, neither high nor low, but goatlike, husky, in the middle of breaking into adulthood. She saw, day and night, the image of their young limbs, bronzed from their exercise in the Greek *gymnasion,* striped with their own blood. She saw their young faces, half-horrified, half-surprised, and she relived their murder in her dream, as if she was guilty also of having done that deed herself.

For the rest of her days Arsinoë Beta would wake in the night, screaming, dripping with perspiration, long before the hour for rising, and who will be surprised at that? For there were now four ghosts in the life of this woman, so that in the night time her bedchamber was rather crowded.

Thoughts of Thoth: Arsinoë Beta, surely, she should have foreseen her future—a life time of sleepless nights, and the unending horror of looking at her past. Some men find it in themselves to feel for this hard woman some degree of pity, for that she had outlived her own children. But for the most part the Greeks shrug their shoulders: it was her fate. What happened was the will of the gods. And Arsinoë Beta, if she wanted to change her fate—she was clever enough. She should have had the wit to see what was coming to her.

It was the sure fate of Arsinoë Beta upon the one hand to enjoy glory, riches, power; and upon the other hand the gods of Greece that were so jealous, they could not find it in themselves to allow her to have every thing; and the one thing that they denied her was *happiness*.

Nobody, then, should have been surprised that this queen was a sick queen, and nobody needed to search long for the real reason behind her everlasting sickness: it was, to be sure, the revenge of the ghosts and the vengeance of the gods, and death alone, perhaps, would bring her a happy release from her torment.

For the moment her one consolation was that the fifth ghost, that of Old Lysimakhos, kept himself away from her, for this man had fulfilled his allotted span of years, and was not obliged to *walk*.

But Arsinoë Beta, though she was physically weak, had very great strength of will, very great strength of purpose, and very great cleverness, and none of her misfortunes brought her even to think of taking her own life. She was too strong for that, and she would wreak much more trouble in the nine years that were left to her upon earth, before she arrived at that day fixed by the Fates to be the day of her own death.

In that year of the first swift rumour of the coming of the Gauls, Year Three of King Ptolemy Mikros, son of Ptolemy Soter, when Eskedi son of Anemhor was High Priest of Ptah at Memphis, there occurred the death of Apis, the Sacred Bull of Ptah, who was the Calf of the Cow called Ta-nt-Merwer, in the twenty-second year of his age.

Eskedi and Neferrenpet wept, and all Egypt was head on knee for Apis dead. The new King Ptolemy moved at once to underwrite the expenses of his funeral, and in due course the twenty-nine days of his funeral rites were accomplished, and the mummified and bandaged bull was dragged upon the usual sled to the desert plateau west of

Memphis and buried in the *nekropolis* of the Apis Bulls with the greatest ceremony imaginable.

Eskedi wept. Neferrenpet wept. Padibastet and Nefersobek wept. Khonsouiou, brother of Padibastet, wept also. All work in every part of Upper and Lower Egypt came to a stop while this burial was attended to.

This most sad loss was seen as a forewarning of some very bad thing that must be about to happen, and the news of the death of Ptolemy the Thunderbolt, that was to many of the Greeks in Egypt still the rightful Pharaoh, came to Alexandria not long after.

There was, however, more mourning in Egypt, more lavish ceremony, more splendid ritual, and more heartfelt grief, even among the Greeks, for the dead Apis than there was in all the Greek world for the dead Ptolemy Keraunos.

In point of fact, when the news of his half-brother's death reached Ptolemy Mikros in Egypt, he allowed himself to forget, for a moment, the dignity of his great office, and he removed even the *khepresh* from his head, even the blue leather helmet-crown, the Crown of War, and threw it high into the air, even in his Hall of Audiences, even before hundred upon hundred of Egyptians, and let out a howl of delight.

There is no such thing, he said to Arsinoë Alpha, his wife, *as accident: all is sent by the gods.*

And he spoke the words written by Herodotos the Historian: *Men's fortunes are upon a wheel, which in its turning suffers not the same man to prosper for all time . . .*

For with the threat of Keraunos's invasion gone away, King Ptolemy Mikros would now surely prosper, and turn his thoughts not to war, but to the glory of Egypt as a peaceful trading nation.

After the death of Ptolemy Keraunos there followed a time of great uncertainty in Macedon, with many candidates claiming the kingship, who lasted as king for a short space only, and then found themselves driven out.

First of these was Meleagros, the almost forgotten son of Ptolemy Soter, and Keraunos's younger brother. But Meleagros was not quite made of the stuff of kings. He had lived his life in the shadow of the Thunderbolt, always outwrestled, outboxed, outwitted, outeaten and outshone by the boy who thought it was his fate to be Son of the Sun, the Son of Ra. Meleagros, like Keraunos, was a man born to lose, and he lasted only sixty days as King of Macedon, when he was thrown out as *inadequate*. What was his history after that, nobody could, or would, speak of it.

After Meleagros came Antipatros, a nephew of Kassandros, who ruled Macedon for forty-five days exactly, and earned in consequence the nickname of *Etesias,* after the Etesian Winds, that blow for forty-five days and then come to a sudden stop. Neither Meleagros nor Etesias could offer proper resistance to the Gauls, despite their training with the crack regiments of Macedon. The Gauls, then, carried on ravaging and laying waste the Greek lands, and all Greece wailed in lamentation.

After Antipatros Etesias came a general of Lysimakhos, called Sosthenes, a man not of royal blood, who refused to take the title of king. Sosthenes regrouped the remnants of the army and waged a war that kept Bolgios occupied while the Macedonian heralds went in search of Antigonos Gonatas, Knee-Cap, to beg him to come back to Macedon and seize the kingship—though to do this he would also have to save Macedon from the Gauls.

Next after Sosthenes came that Ptolemaios who was the one surviving son of Lysimakhos of Thrace and Arsinoë Beta, but this boy of nineteen years was no match for the combined forces of Bolgios and all the Gauls either.

Sure, it was the fate of this boy to be a king, but, clearly, Fate had not meant him to be King of Macedon. Perhaps, he thought, he might yet become King of Thrace.

At the last they made the famous Pyrrhos of Epeiros the King, a man the world would hear more of at a later date. Between them these five weak kings ruled Macedon for a total of three years.

One person remains unaccounted for at this point in Thoth's story: What of Eurydike, the mother of Ptolemy Keraunos? For this King had established his mother at Kassandreia during his brief rule over Macedon, where she enjoyed, at last and after all, the title of King's Mother, and insisted always upon being addressed as *Basilissa.* Did Eurydike not grieve upon the death of the Thunderbolt? If so, there is no record of it. But what mother could not weep for a son who dies before she does?

Still a young woman, this Eurydike might have married herself to a fresh husband, but she preferred to keep her independence; to have all of her life under her own control.

The last that was heard of Eurydike was that she ruled at Kassandreia with the help of her hired soldiers, many of whom had once been the hired soldiers of Arsinoë Beta. Eurydike, like her son, preferred to pay for a man's loyalty—men who would guard her, fight and kill anybody, so long as they were paid to do it. For yes, she had learned the great lesson that every ruler must learn: that she must trust nobody.

She kept up the good works that she had begun in Egypt, sending purses of gold oktodrachms to the poor girls of Kassandreia and Miletos as dowry money, so that they might be married, and so avoid the descent into slavery or concubinage. For such acts of generosity Eurydike, for perhaps the first time in her life, was loved.

When her time came she would be buried by the hands of strangers, among them the poor women she had helped, and who returned upon the anniversary of her death each year to pour out the proper libations of milk and honey and undiluted wine at her tomb.

Although it was common knowledge at Miletos and Kassandreia who Eurydike was, what she had been, she was never heard to speak the name of her husband. For this woman Ptolemaios was a name rather for curses and execrations, to be avoided like Hades. She knew, as so many others did not know, that the family of Ptolemy, even the very name of Ptolemy, was unlucky, for the horoscopists had told her so, and that the House of that fine husband of hers was due for three hundred years of bad luck.

Part of Eurydike rejoiced to have gained her freedom, and part of her was relieved, for that she and her daughters no longer quite belonged to the unluckiest family that ever lived.

With Ptolemy Keraunos dead, his brother Mikros in Egypt felt safe, for the time being. He slept easy in his bed of beaten gold decorated with the feet of lions and the heads of sphinxes.

Mikros devoted his hours now to the art of peace, and to furthering the glory of Alexandria and all Egypt. Ignoring the dangers of hubris, he allowed himself to boast that his reign would be the most glorious in the whole history of the Two Lands. In this boast, however, he was not far short of the truth.

As for war, and the threat of war, he was indeed safe, as Eskedi, High Priest of Ptah, said, *until the next time.*

4.10

The Homecoming

Arsinoë Beta, having waited some months upon the island of Samothrake—for fair weather and the return of the sailing season, and the right wind—at length happened upon a *trieres* bound for Egypt and set off for home with her Thracian waiting-women, keeping secret the matter of who she was, what she had been, and uttering not a word of the terrible things that had taken place at Kassandreia.

As she stepped on board ship, her friends said to her, *May the gods give you the joy of getting home again,* and she swallowed, as usual, the green lizard seasick cure, and as usual the green lizard had no effect, so that before ever the sail was hoisted the *nausiasis* came over her, and she sicked up her guts over the gunwales all the way to Alexandria.

When this former Queen was safe in the Harbour of Eunostos, the Harbour of Happy Returns, she revealed to the captain of the *trieres* her identity: *I am Arsinoë,* she said, *the sister of King Ptolemy,* and she wanted him to send a messenger to fetch this brother of hers to welcome her.

But the captain laughed in her face, and did not believe a word she spoke.

Neither did the harbour master believe Arsinoë's story, for, as he said, her women were all foreigners.

Nor did the Chief of Guardians at the gates of the great white Residence of the King, the sight of which, glittering in the sun, all marble pediments and porticoes and Corinthian columns, brought Arsinoë the most profound relief.

But no, Arsinoë Beta had quit the city as a girl of fifteen some twenty-one years previous, so that she gasped to see the wonder that was the nearly-finished Pharos towering over the harbour. Nobody in all of Egypt had thought to look upon this girl's face again, and those who knew her character only too well had been pleased to see the back of her, so that Arsinoë married was as good as Arsinoë dead and forgotten.

It should have been no surprise, though, for this Queen not to be recognized, for she did not look like a princess of the House of Ptolemy.

Her *peplos* was torn and stained with blood. Her once-yellow hair was dishevelled, and the shock of the events at Kassandreia had turned it grey. She had still a good deal of her wealth about her, in jewels, and gold, hidden in her baggage, but she had no possessions other than the blood-splashed white dress she stood up in, that she had refused to change since the day of the murder of her children, and the papyrus parcel of poison that she had taken away with her, that she refused to believe had lost its power, thinking she might have need of it back at home.

Arsinoë had desired to make a dramatic return, but she had arrived ahead of her story, and although the news of the death of Ptolemy Keraunos had flown across the Great Sea, the fate of Arsinoë Beta had been held up by rough seas and garbled by swift Rumour.

When the harbour master at last hauled this woman before her brother, all his dogs growled and barked at her, and with good reason. King Ptolemy knew her only by her voice, for she had torn her cheeks with the nails of her fingers, and the bloody scratch-lines remained as they were, because she did not wish to hide the signs of her ordeal with cosmetic paints, in order to gain the sympathy of her family. And, of course, it was over twenty years since Ptolemy Mikros had seen this sister.

I did not know your face, he said, for she was not the apple-cheeked Arsinoë he had said farewell to at the age of nine years.

When she met Philotera and Theoxena, she embraced them with tears, and said, *I warn you that your tears will flow soon enough when you have heard my tale, for the list of woes which the gods have sent me is a long one.*

And when she had finished telling, her sister Philotera said to her, *Arsinoë, you have wept too long. Enough of this incontinent grief, which serves no useful end.* And she suggested that Arsinoë make the sacrifice that every traveller must make upon landing, whereupon Arsinoë began to wail, *My hands are unwashed and I am ashamed to pour out gleaming wine to Zeus like this; and no one can offer prayers all spattered with blood and filth.*

So they heated the copper over the fire and made the water warm for her to bathe, in spite of the custom that women of Macedon might bathe only in cold water.

Arsinoë Beta wept so many and such bitter tears that her flood of womanly emotion surprised her family, who remembered a girl who, like Herakles, never wept, and that the Arsinoë who had gone away from Egypt had been tough as a dog leash, quite lacking female feelings.

She has changed much, they thought, but they wondered too whether she did not weep tears like the crocodile, at the same time trying their best to make her smile, which was, to be sure, at the best of times never a simple thing, saying, *Let not death sit heavy upon your heart . . .*

When they had had bathed Arsinoë and dressed her in fresh clothes, she made her sacrifice to Zeus, Protector of Persons Landing, and to Apollo, god of Happy Landings, and her joy was real, for there is, as the Greeks say, no sweeter sight for a woman's eyes than her own country.

Next of all, Arsinoë Beta asked for the recipe to disguise grey hair, that was made up of the blood of a yellow cow, and the fat of a yellow snake, and the yolks of a dozen canary eggs, and she managed to restore to her hair something of its former golden glory.

In the year of the return her brother the King reopened the Great Canal that had been dug by Darius, King of Persia, and by the Pharaoh Nekau, and the third and topmost storey of the Pharos, or Great Lighthouse, of Alexandria, was finished.

Arsinoë Beta did every thing that she ought to have done. She made lavish daily sacrifice to the gods of Greece, all of them. She sent often to the Oracle of Zeus-Ammon in the desert of Libya, to ask why it was that she could not have that which she most desired: to be rid of the horrible ghost of handsome Agathokles, that had not stayed in Thrace, but followed her to Samothrake, and now to Egypt, and that hung about her, day and night, waking and sleeping.

Yes, she had even stood under the shower of piglets' blood for half a morning, but Agathokles did not, would not, leave her alone.

Some nights Arsinoë Beta just sat in bed screaming, screaming. She took to bathing herself daily even in the Great Harbour of Alexandria, or from the beaches east and west of it, or at the Spouting Rocks, because to bathe made her feel clean; to bathe made her crime seem less, the burden of evil upon her seem not so heavy. He was ever in the water with her, though, even the ghost, the bloody ghost, of handsome Agathokles, naked and dead, doing the dog-paddle beside her. In the end there was nothing to be done but to put up with this ghost, because it was clear to her now that Agathokles was *never* going to go away.

She was tough. She decided that she would *not* go mad like mad Theoxena. And at length she rather liked to have Agathokles follow her about the palace. She decided that she was, in fact, rather pleased to have the company of Agathokles, and to see him standing at the foot of her gilded bed, and she said never a word to Ptolemy Mikros about the haunting.

Agathokles the Ghost was, even in death, very like the gods to look at, and so Arsinoë Beta began to see the ghost as her personal triumph, wherein after all she had got what she most wanted: for this Agathokles to be at her side for always.

Some nights she would murmur in her sleep, when she could sleep, *A ghost is as much as a husband.* And for the time being he was all the husband she had. In the half-dark before the sun came up, or in the wolf light that was ever after the hour of his murder, she was able to persuade herself that the ghost of Agathokles smiled at her a little, and sparkled his eyes on purpose, and her love for the dead man was no less than her love for him living, and did not leave her, so that Arsinoë Beta was, for perhaps the second time in all her life, almost a happy woman.

The other Arsinoë in Egypt, Arsinoë Alpha, was most definitely *not* happy.

Thoth says, Imagine it if you will: it was Arsinoë Beta who murdered this woman's beloved brother, and now Arsinoë the murderess, the one woman in the world whom Arsinoë Alpha never again wanted to set eyes upon, unless it was to dance at her funeral, was back in Alexandria, living in the same Residence, and if she did not refuse to have it, upon the point of moving into the *gynaikeion* with her, to share her days and boss her in every matter, and make her life miserable all over again.

What would Arsinoë Alpha do? Would she not try her best to rid herself of this hated stepmother, that had come like some homing vulture to roost in the palace that had said farewell to her?

And what of Arsinoë Beta? Would she not try to kill Arsinoë Alpha, before Arsinoë Alpha tried to kill *her,* as revenge for the death of Agathokles her brother?

Arsinoë Beta—she would do now a most dreadful thing with regard to Arsinoë Alpha, and she was indeed a snake, a very snake for guile, and for venom, and it was almost as if she was gathering herself up to strike, making ready to spit forth poison anew, like the cobra of the Egyptians, but biding her time, waiting for the right moment, waiting, waiting.

For his part, what would Ptolemy Mikros do about the two Arsinoës, who must live, somehow, at peace even under his own roof? Mikros always found it easiest to do nothing, and for the moment, thinking that these women's concerns would sort themselves out, and were none of his business, he did nothing now.

When Arsinoë Beta had had some days to grow accustomed to her new life in Egypt, Mikros sat alone with her in his private chamber and asked about the rumours that he had heard.

But Arsinoë Beta frowned and held up her two hands. *Look,* she said, *my hands are clean. I am not a part of this crime.*

In his dream Mikros had seen these hands of his sister all bloody, and he knew in his heart what must be the truth.

When he questioned her about the death of Agathokles a second time, she looked him in the eye.

I did not kill Agathokles, she said, which was the truth, for she had only ordered this deed, and technically was not guilty of any wrong-doing.

I am not the murderer, she said, *I loved Agathokles as a brother-in-law . . .*

Mikros wondered if she was not a born liar, like Keraunos.

When hysterical letters from Lysandra arrived, at length, from Syria, accusing Arsinoë Beta of dreadful crimes, Mikros knew for sure that Arsinoë Beta lied. And when the letters stopped, he did not know what to think.

All the same, it was not the purpose of Ptolemy Mikros to send Arsinoë Beta away again. She was already proving herself much too useful to him for that. No, he wished to ask for her thoughts upon both foreign policy and upon every detail of home affairs, for she showed herself at once to be the most clever of women. Mikros knew that whatever he asked the sister, she had the answer; and he knew also that whatever he might ask his wife, she would know it not. In the meantime Mikros would, he thought, seek out a fresh husband for his sister, so that Arsinoë Alpha his wife might perhaps be left to live in peace.

But while he asked for her wise thoughts, he knew very well that this murderous sister of his was quite capable of killing him while he slept, just as she had killed Agathokles, and he kept her at arm's length, and suggested that she might like to wear the near see-through dress of an Egyptian princess, so that he could be sure she did not hide a knife beneath her clothes, and of course, she was delighted.

Arsinoë Beta, however, had no thought to kill her brother. It was his wife she must get rid of. On the contrary, it was in Arsinoë Beta's interest to do every thing in her power to keep her brother alive.

When Mikros next asked Arsinoë what had become of Lysandra she looked at him as if she really did not know the woman of whom he spoke. She spread her hands. She shook her head. She had no knowledge, she said, of the fate of that woman, who had taken from her the man she should have married herself. Arsinoë Beta really cared little what had become of Lysandra, the sister she had come to loathe.

Although Mikros sent out his messengers, his scouts and spies, to find out the fate of Lysandra, his beloved half-sister, she was not heard of again.

Mikros knew Arsinoë Beta well enough, although he had not seen her face for half a life time. To be sure, one part of him loved this sister, truly loved her as his full sister. But another part of him truly detested her. And he swore now a great solemn oath that in all the rest of his days he would never trust Arsinoë Beta, because having her back again as part of the family was really very like having a poisonous snake living under his own roof.

What, then, *had* been in the thoughts of Arsinoë Beta, this most powerful, scheming woman, who was wealthy beyond belief; who could not stop herself even from killing the members of her own family? What had been her thoughts as she hung retching over the side of the *trieres* on her voyage home from Samothrake?

She had thought, *If I can get home to my brother, the King of Egypt, he will marry me himself; I shall make him do so.*

And the fact that Ptolemy Mikros, Pharaoh of Egypt, was her full brother, and already married to a wife, who happened to be the other Arsinoë, Arsinoë Alpha, daughter of Lysimakhos, sister of the man whose murder she had herself arranged, had nothing to do with it. Nor was the thought of the other Arsinoë living in the *gynaikeion* a problem either, for Arsinoë Beta had already made up her mind that she was going to *get rid of* Arsinoë Alpha as well, as soon as she could manage it, for there was no way she could live with that woman again, locked up in the same *gynaikeion*, not after what had happened, because one of them must surely murder the other, and also because *Arsinoë Alpha had exactly the same face as handsome Agathokles.*

Yes, Arsinoë Beta had all her life done just whatever she pleased, and nothing was going to change. What did she want, now, then? She wanted power in Egypt, and she would get it.

When Mikros asked yet again about Lysandra, and about what had happened in Thrace, Arsinoë Beta snapped at him, saying, *What do you care about Lysandra, she was only your half-sister, the daughter of mad Eurydike?* For she would stop his questioning if she could.

Mikros pushed out his lower lip, as if, perhaps, he had not quite thought about what he was saying.

Are you not, Arsinoë went on, *in truth pleased to be rid of that woman, who would only stir up trouble for you if she were here in Egypt?*

Mikros raised what would have been his eyebrows, if they had not been shaved off and plucked out to make him pure in the temple of the Egyptians, the purest of the pure.

But what did happen to Lysandra? Mikros said. Truly, he wished to know, even if only out of curiosity, whether Lysandra was dead or alive. In truth, he had been fond of Lysandra, whom, to be sure, he had seen seldom, but who was not so full of poison as Arsinoë Beta.

What did you do to Lysandra? he shouted, feeling in his heart that there must be treachery to be discovered, and it was the first time in his life that he had shouted at this sister of his. And also the last.

So that Arsinoë Beta changed the subject.

Did you hold the Funeral Games for our dead father? she asked him, all innocent, as if she had just then thought of it that moment, and not been planning all night to ask it.

Mikros opened his mouth for speech, but the words did not come forth.

Arsinoë stared, wondering whether this brother was not just as useless as their Uncle Menelaos.

Mikros spread his hands. He stammered, *I did not . . . There was no . . . How could we . . . There was no easy way of . . . I really did not know . . .*

Arsinoë Beta fixed him with her hard eye. *Did you,* she said, *or did you not, hold the Funeral Games for Ptolemy Soter?*

No, he said, *we did not.* And he folded his arms. Then he took off the *khepresh,* the War-Crown, and scratched the scalp from which every last hair had been removed.

There was the threat of war, he said. *We were fearful of an invasion by Keraunos and Seleukos . . . we were uncertain of the proper procedure . . .*

And, indeed, there had never been Funeral Games for any member of this family before.

Arsinoë Beta laughed her cold, hard laugh, as if she thought this brother of hers was as good an idiot as the famous Philippos Arrhidaios. *Well,* she said, *we shall have the games now. And because you have not the least idea how to organize a games, I shall do it myself.*

She saw the Funeral Games in her thoughts then and there, and she saw the torch race, using lighted torches as batons in the relay, by night, and it was then that Arsinoë Beta had her great thought.

Why, she said, *we must light up the Pharos also, upon the same day—with the Funeral Games lasting for the hours of daylight, and light up the Pharos by night, in honour of Ptolemy our father, who did not live to see this great monument of his completed.*

Mikros resisted a little. He said that the Pharos was not quite finished still; that the great bronze statue of Poseidon that must stand upon the very summit of the Pharos was still not yet done . . . but he could find no very good reason why the Pharos should not be lit at once, for the third and topmost storey was nearly ready.

And so Arsinoë Beta took charge for the first time of a thing that was, in truth, the business of her brother the Pharaoh.

Arsinoë Beta, that had the ability to conjure up armies of thousands of hired soldiers, was well able to manage a procession through the streets, and she gave the order for the entire army of Ptolemy Mikros to make ready to march, under full arms, every man of them. She sent out the *prostagma* for every native Egyptian priest to present himself on the appointed day, ready to march also.

Sure, the stomach troubles of Arsinoë Beta melted away for the period of her business with the great procession. She carried about lists of athletes, and orders to merchants of wine and olives, and suppliers of fishes and oxen and every last Greek delicacy, for it was her plan for all Alexandria to feast all night at her brother's expense.

She called up the runners for the foot races, and for the races in armour, and for the endless horse races, and the winner of the most races was to have the pleasure of lighting the fire upon the sacrificial altar, where there would be a great sacrifice of one hundred oxen to Zeus.

She laid plans for chariot races in the hippodrome, donkey races, camel races, ostrich races, race after race after race, and all Alexandria practised running before dawn or after sundown, in the coolest parts of the day.

All this time, of course, Alexandria had been sending the best of her athletes across the Great Sea to Greece, to Olympia, to compete in the Olympian Games there, and now also Arsinoë sent out her invitations to every athlete in the Greek-speaking world, to come to Egypt and race for the greatest prizes that had ever been offered in any games since games began; to celebrate the admission of Ptolemy Soter himself into Olympos, and the games were called the *Ptolemaieia*. Aye, these games were to be equal even to the Olympian Games of Greece, but better, with bigger prizes, and with every last thing done on the very grandest scale, and every last thing was the work of Arsinoë Beta herself, that could turn her hand to any skill; who was more clever than one million goddesses.

On the great day of the celebration Arsinoë Beta put on the elongated paint-stripe of the Egyptians at the outer corners of her eyes, because she wished now to be a woman of Egypt as well as a woman of the Macedonians, or a Greek woman; because it was now her desire to be *loved* by everybody in Egypt.

How would she make herself beloved? Why, by smiling instead of scowling. Why, by riding herself in the ostrich race, a thing that no woman, let alone the sister of the Pharaoh, had ever done before. Why, by racing camels herself. Why, by entering her chariots in the chariot races in the hippodrome and, contrary to all Greek custom, driving the chariot herself, and contrary to every man's expectation, winning. And why, by throwing sackfuls of golden dekadrachms to the crowds wheresoever she travelled. To be sure, the ghosts still followed this woman, but, rather like Ptolemy Keraunos, she feared nothing. Arsinoë Beta was changing. She was trying her hardest to live for now, for the present moment, like her late great father Ptolemy Soter, and to forget her terrible, terrible past. Furthermore, she went about being pleasant, nice, kind, friendly, which, by Zeus and Pan and all the gods of Greece, she never had done before.

And why? why? Because she wanted power in Egypt.

So the Funeral Games and the Games that were called the Ptolemaieia merged into one great Games, and they took place all that day, and they were much like any other games anywhere else, Reader, and you may imagine the Games for yourself, as you please, except to picture, if you will, a Games greater and more wonderful than any thing ever seen before or matched since. What is more important is what happened at dusk: for at dusk the torchlit procession of the army, tens of thousands of soldiers, followed by hundreds and thousands of Egyptian priests, and singing and chanting children, made its way, marching, from the palace quarter in the east, along the great processional way of Kanopic Street, and across the Heptastadion and the harbour to the mighty Pharos in the west, and every soldier, every priest, and every child, held a torch, and every soldier, priest and child sang, so that Alexandria glittered and sang from end to end. Bands of music played: trumpets, horns, pipes, drums, and all Alexandria lined the street to see the procession pass, and it was the first time that the broad street had been used for its proper purpose. Every Alexandrian sang the praises of King Ptolemy, and of King Ptolemy Soter his father, and they sang the praises also of Arsinoë Beta, who had organized every thing. Arsinoë Alpha, the Queen, just stood by with her mouth open to look, almost unable to believe what she saw, and Arsinoë Alpha had done not one thing to help except drip with sweat under her crown and try to look beautiful.

Ptolemy Mikros himself climbed the stairs inside the great Pharos, with his wife Arsinoë Alpha at his side, and the wife clung to him, for she trembled at the thought of walking up higher than anywhere she had walked before. It was left to the intrepid and wonderful Arsinoë Beta to ride upon the hydraulic lift to the top of the Lighthouse, slung in the great wicker basket there, and like a *snake in a basket,* and she was winched up by the mechanism that was used to raise the fuel to the top, where the light must burn, and where all was ready, waiting for the spark.

Arsinoë Beta had never in her life time risen so high as she did in the air upon this day, but she displayed not one sign of fear. She had no fear of flying. She was quite untroubled by the thought that if the stout ropes broke she must crash to her death hundreds of cubits below. She rode in her basket, with the tongue flickering in and out of her mouth like a tongue of flame, like a snake's tongue, and her snake's face was smiling, and she was waving to her trembling family as they climbed the stairs, and she was at the top before them, smiling like nobody who saw her had ever seen her smile before.

Mikros, on the other hand, did not much like to be high up. Mikros—his head swam. His palms felt damp, and his tunic sweaty above the normal, and every step of the staircase felt slippery unto him, and his knees, well, as if they might give way beneath him. He did not care to look very long at the great spectacle of his city of Alexandria all spread out before his eyes. He did not much care to look down, for fear of falling. And when his *Dioiketes* made some remark about Sostratos of Knidos, who had made the Pharos possible—and who was there, by the great light to see it lit, waiting—Mikros did not speak, no, not one word, for fear of his voice shaking.

Sure, it was not Sostratos himself who must light the light, but Ptolemy Mikros, the King, the Pharaoh. But truly, Mikros, his hands shook so, when Sostratos was graciously pleased to offer him the taper, and Mikros looked, really, as if he did not know what to do with himself for fear of being so high up in the sky.

Arsinoë Beta, however, why, she almost danced about in the confined space at the top of the third and topmost storey of the Pharos, danced for excitement, for joy, and, out of all previous reports of her cold character, she never stopped from smiling. And no, Ptolemy Mikros did not light the light, because Arsinoë Beta now grabbed from Sostratos the taper, and set fire to the fuse herself.

Sure, she screamed, *Stand back!* It was Arsinoë Beta that *took charge.*

And so the fuel went up with a rushing noise that made every man's and every woman's hair stand up on its end for being so loud and so sudden, and with the greatest imaginable roaring; and the royal family of Egypt felt that wall of flames hit them, and it was just like the wall of flames that goes up at the lighting of a dead man's funeral pyre, only with ten, twenty times the noise and force, for the Pharos was to be— had to be, indeed—the very greatest of lights that had ever been seen.

Sure, the royal family of Egypt—Ptolemy Mikros, Queen Arsinoë Alpha, Arsinoë Beta, and the infant princes Ptolemy and Lysimakhos— they were lucky to escape with only the singeing of their eyebrows— those that had eyebrows to be singed. But the Pharos was lit, and the mighty roaring continued above their heads, and the flame was dozens of cubits in height, the very greatest beacon light ever, for it was reflected and magnified by the very greatest of mirrors, made of burnished bronze, and the result was that the House of Ptolemy retreated now from the heat and the intensely bright light, making their trembling way down the stairs, and Arsinoë Beta went down as she had gotten up, in the basket, and was there ahead of every one of them and did not tremble in the slightest, just as cool as a snake about to strike.

After a while those at the top of the Pharos became aware also of a different kind of roaring, that came not from above their heads but from below, upon the earth, and it was, yes, the mighty roaring of the entire assembled populace of Alexandria gathered there to see the magic. All Alexandria screamed and whistled for delight, for the city was lit up, bright as day, and no one had ever seen the like of it before.

Better still, best of all, no ship after that night ever crashed upon the Hogsback Rock at the entrance to the Great Harbour, so that the greatest achievement of Ptolemy Soter—Saviour, Saviour of Sailors at Sea, Saviour of Alexandria, Saviour of Egypt, the founder of his House, the revered and mighty ancestor of all—was complete, and utterly wonderful. His city was complete, his Pharos was complete, and the first of the Books of Thoth, the Forty-third Book of Thoth, is complete.

Esteemed Reader, Pupil-of-Thoth, there is more, much more. Be patient. Thoth has not finished writing.

For the time being, let it be enough to say that the Pharos or Great Lighthouse of Alexandria would not fail to illuminate the illustrious and most illustrious city of Alexandria for one thousand years of nights. Thoth swears it.

SO IT ENDS, well and in peace.
For the spirit of the Treasury Scribe Phibis
of the Pharaoh's—Life! Prosperity! Health!—Treasury.
Copied by the Scribe Spotous, son of Osoroeris,
Prophet of Amen-Ra, Prophet of Min-Amun,
Prophet of Khonsu-Thoth, Priest of the First Class,
the owner of this papyrus.
AS FOR ANY MAN WHO SPEAKS ILL OF THIS BOOK,
THOTH WILL FIGHT HIM.

Glossary

Agathos Daimon: Gk., the Good Spirit; the divinized lucky house snake of Alexandria; sometimes personified as Thermouthis.

agora: Gk., market place.

akropolis: Gk., citadel.

Alalalalai: Gk., the battle cry of the Macedonians, offered to Enyalios, an epithet of Ares, god of War.

Ammon: Gk. name for the Egyptian god Amun (Amen), who was identified with the Greek Zeus as Zeus-Ammon. He is shown wearing curled ram's horns.

Amun: Lord of the Thrones of the Two Lands; supreme god of the Egyptians.

amphora: Gk., tall two-handled jar for transporting wine, oil, etc. Also a liquid measure: 1 amphora = 72 pints.

andron: Gk., the men's quarters of a house.

Ankh: Eg., the symbol of life.

Anubis: Eg., son of Osiris and Nephthys; god of the Dead, god of Embalming; protector against all evil. He is shown as a jackal, or jackal-headed man.

Aphrodite: Gk. goddess of Love, Beauty, Fertility; the Greeks made her equal to the Egyptian Hathor; at Rome she was assimilated as Venus.

Apis: Eg. the sacred bull of Memphis; the Living Image of Ptah. Known to the Greeks as Apis, or Epaphos; to the Egyptians as Hap.

apokrisiarios: Gk., secretary.

Apollo: Gk. god of Music, Prophecy, Healing and Medicine and Archery.

Ares: Gk. god of War; the Mars of the Romans.

Artemis: Gk. goddess of Fertility and protector of women in childbirth; the maiden huntress; daughter of Zeus.

Asklepios: Gk. god of Health; Lat. Aesculapius.

Athena, Athene: Gk., the maiden goddess of War, and patroness of arts and crafts; the personification of wisdom; Lat. Athena or Minerva.

Atum: Eg. Sun god and creator of the Universe; Lord of Heliopolis.

Basileus: Gk. title, roughly equivalent to King.

Basilissa: Gk. title, roughly equivalent to Queen.

Bast, Bastet: cat goddess of the Egyptians; daughter of Ra.

chendjyt: Eg., the pleated loincloth, or kilt, of the Pharaoh.

cubit: Gk., measure equal to 18 or 20 fingerbreadths (about 18 to 20 inches).

dekadrachm: Gk. ten-drachma coin.

dexiosis: Gk., handshaking.

Diadokhoi: Gk., the Successors of Alexander.

diekplous: Gk. battle manoeuvre in which the ships sailed through a gap made in the enemy line and attacked the fleet from the rear; lit. "sailing-through."

Dioiketes: Gk., Chief Administrator of Ptolemy in Egypt; First Minister, Vizier, and Minister of Finance.

Dionysos: (Dionysus) Gk. god of the Vine and Wine; god of Frenzy; Lat. Bacchus.

drachma: Greek coin equal to six obols; 6,000 drachmas make one talent. Also a measure of weight: one drachma = 4.36 grams.

Eileithyia: Gk. goddess of the Birth Pangs; daughter of Zeus and Hera.

ephebos: Gk., ephebe; a youth aged seventeen or eighteen.

epistates: Gk., governor.

Epithalamion: (Epithalamium) Gk., wedding song or hymn.

Eros: pl. Erotes; Gk. god of Love and Fertility; the son of Aphrodite.

faience: Eg., glass paste, blue or blue-green in colour, used for beads and jewellery.

Fates: Gk., a trio of goddesses (Klotho, Lakhesis, Atropos) that ruled people's destinies and was stronger than the gods.

Furies, or Erinyes: Gk., also known as Eumenides, "the Kindly Ones"; avengers of crime, especially crime against the ties of kinship. They are represented as winged women, sometimes with snakes about them.

gymnasion: Gk., place of exercise for males, designed to fit the *epheboi* for military service. The *gymnasion* at Alexandria was sited at the centre of the city, close to the *agora*.

gynaikeion: Gk., women's quarters of a house, where males were forbidden access after the age of seven years.

Hades: brother of Zeus; Gk. god of the Underworld, who ruled over the dead with his wife Persephone; also known as Pluto.

Hathor: cow goddess of the Egyptians. She is the symbolic mother of the Pharaoh, who is called the Son of Hathor; Hathor is shown either as a human female, upon whose wig sits a crown of cow horns and a solar disc; or she may be shown as completely cow-like. She is the daughter of Ra.

Hellas, Hellenes: Greece, Greeks.

hemiobol: Gk., half-obol coin.

Hephaistos: Greek god of Fire, especially the smithy fire, and of smiths and craftsmen. The Greeks made him equal to Ptah of the Egyptians. Lat. Vulcan.

Heptastadion: Gk., the seven-*stade*-long bridge linking the city of Alexandria to Pharos island.

heqat: Eg., the shepherd's crook of the Pharaoh.

Hera: Gk., wife of Zeus; Queen of the gods; goddess of Marriage. Lat. Juno.

Hermes: Gk. god of Fertility and Good Luck; the herald of the gods, who leads the souls of the dead to the Underworld. Patron of merchants and thieves, oratory, literature and athletics. Hermes is shown with winged sandals, winged hat, and the staff (*kerukeion*) of a herald. The Greeks made him equal to Thoth.

heröon: Gk., a hero's shrine.

himation: Gk., cloak or outer garment, worn over the *khiton* or tunic, or worn sometimes by itself.

hippodrome: Gk., horse-racing track.

Horus: Eg., Har; the falcon god, Lord of the Sky; the symbol of divine kingship in Egypt. The Pharaoh is the Living Horus.

House of Life: the part of the Egyptian temple set aside for priestly learning and teaching.

hyparkhos: Gk., subordinate governor, or overseer for the Satrap.

Isis: Eg. goddess, More Clever than a Million Gods. She is a goddess of immense magic power, the symbolic mother of the Pharaoh, and mother also of Horus and wife of Osiris. She is called Clever of Tongue, Great of Magic, the Lady of Many Names.

karnyx: the war trumpet of the Keltoi, or Gauls.

kausia: the felt beret, or sun-helmet, of the Macedonians.

Keraunos: Gk., Thunderbolt; an attribute of Zeus; also the nickname of Ptolemy Soter's eldest legitimate son.

Khepera: Eg. Sun-god creator in the form of a scarab beetle.

khepresh: Eg., the blue-leather war helmet, or War-Crown of the Pharaoh, like a mortar-cap.

kherep: Eg., the sceptre of office of the High Priest of Ptah at Memphis.

khiton: Gk., tunic (chiton).

khlamys: Gk., the military cloak of the Macedonian soldier.

klama: Gk., the lament for the dead.

klepsydra: Gk., water-clock.

Koile-Syria: (Coele-Syria) region of Syria-Palestine—Hollow Syria, thus called to distinguish it from Syria between the Rivers (Mesopotamia).

komos: Gk., victory dance in honour of Dionysos, god of Frenzy.

kynokephalos: the dog-headed baboon or Ape of Thoth, in whom Thoth is incarnate.

Kyria (Kuria) Gk., Madam, Lady.

larnax: Gk., funerary bone-chest.

lekythos: Gk., bowl.

Maat: Eg. goddess, the personification of all the elements of cosmic harmony as laid down by the creator god at the beginning of time—Truth, Justice, Moral Integrity. She is shown as a woman wearing one ostrich feather standing upright on her head—the Feather of Rightness and Truth.

maenad: Gk. word meaning "mad woman"—the votary of Dionysos, god of Frenzy.

Memphis: Eg. city, formerly called Ineb-hedj, or Mennufer, the city of Menes, the first Pharaoh; sometimes also called White Walls. The Greeks called this place Memphis.

Mikros: Gk., Small One.

Min: the Egyptian fertility god of Koptos; the Pan of the Greeks.

mina: Greek measure, equal to one pound weight of silver, or 100 drachmas.

Moeris: the lake to the south of Heliopolis. The Egyptians called it Mer-wer; modern Fayyum.

Monophthalmos: Gk., One-Eye; nickname of Antigonos of Macedon.

Mouseion: Gk., Temple of the Muses, or Museum.

Muses: Gk., the nine daughters of Zeus and Mnemosyne, usually named thus: Kalliope (epic poetry), Klio (history), Euterpe (flute-playing), Melpomene (tragedy), Terpsikhore (dancing), Erato (the lyre), Polyhymnia (sacred song), Ourania (astronomy), and Thalia (comedy).

Nakhthoreb: the last native Pharaoh of Egypt before the rule of the Persians. The Greeks called him Nektanebo, or Nectanebo II. He reigned 360–343 B.C.

natron: Gk. *nitron;* a hydrated carbonate of sodium used in the embalming rituals of Egypt.

naumachia: Gk., sea battle, or mock sea battle.

nausiasis: Gk., seasickness.

Nefertum: Eg. god, the son of Ptah and Sakhmet. He is the god of the primeval lotus blossom, the blue lotus out of which the Sun rises each day.

Neith: Eg. creator goddess of Sais; Mistress of the Bow, Ruler of the Arrows. The Greeks made her equal to Athena.

nekakha: Eg., the flail or scourge of the Pharaoh.

Nekhbet: the vulture goddess of Upper Egypt.

nemes: Eg., the red-and-white-striped headcloth of the Pharaoh.

Nephthys: Eg. funerary goddess; sister of Isis and mother of Anubis by Osiris.

Nike: Gk. goddess; the personification of Victory.

obol: Greek coin; one sixth of a drachma.

odeion: Gk., council-chamber.

oktodrachm: Gk., eight-drachma coin.

oneiroscopist: interpreter of dreams (Gk. *oneiros* = dream).

Osiris: Eg. god of the Dead. He is the husband of Isis, the Great God, the Mighty One.

Osorapis: the Egyptian form of Sarapis; the sacred bull of Memphis worshipped as a bull after his death.

Ouraios: Gk. form of the Latin uraeus: see "Wadjet."

paian: Gk., song of triumph or thanksgiving esp. to Apollo or Artemis.

Pan: Gk. god of Flocks and Herds and Fertility; patron of shepherds and herdsmen; the Min of the Egyptians.

parthenos: Gk., maiden.

peplos: Gk., woman's dress.

phalanx: Gk., the formation of the heavy-armed foot soldiers in battle, consisting of 4,096 men. The Grand Phalanx numbered 16,384 men.

plethron: Gk. measure, equal to 100 feet.

Poseidon: Gk. god of Earthquakes and Water, later a god of the Sea and associated with horses; brother of Zeus and Hades. Lat. Neptune.

prostagma: Gk., order, decree.

prostasia: Gk., leadership, governorship.

Ptah: the Egyptian creator god of Memphis; Gk. Hephaistos; Lat. Vulcan.

Punt: the South Country, perhaps the modern Somalia.

pylon: Gk. name for the gateway of the Egyptian temple.

Ra: (Re) the creator Sun god of the Egyptians at Heliopolis; shown as a falcon with the Sun disk on his head. The Greeks made him the equal of Helios.

Rhakotis: the native quarter of Alexandria. The word means "Building-Site" and was used by Egyptians who would not speak the name of the city of Alexandria.

Rhinokolura: penal colony on the north-east borders of Egypt: lit. Gk. nose-cutting.

rhombos: Gk. magic wheel; *phallos.*

rhyton: Gk., drinking vessel.

Sakhmet, Sekhmet: the Egyptian lioness goddess of Memphis; wife of Ptah and mother of Nefertum.

Sand Dwellers, Sand Rovers: the Bedouin.

sappheiros: Gk., the costly blue stone known as lapis lazuli.

Sarapis, Serapis: god of combined Egyptian and Greek characteristics. From Zeus and Helios he draws his aspects of kingship and Sun god; from Dionysos, fertility in nature; from Hades and Asklepios his connection with the Afterlife and Healing.

sarissa: Gk., the lance of the Macedonians, 12 or 14 or 16 cubits or 18 to 26 feet in length.

satrap: old Persian word meaning provincial governor, or governor of a province.

Satyr: Gk., a half-bestial spirit of the woods and hills, attendant upon the god Dionysos. Satyrs have a human body but goat's legs. They are lustful and like to chase nymphs.

seistron: Gk., sacred rattle used in Egyptian temples to ward off evil; Lat. *sistrum.*

Selene: Gk. goddess of the Moon, identified with Artemis.

Sema, Soma: Gk. *sema,* tomb; *soma,* body—the name given to the burial place of Alexander at Alexandria.

Seth: Egyptian god of the desert; the embodiment of disorder; brother of Isis.

Shai, Shay: Eg. god of Fate or Destiny, appearing in snake form. He merges with Agathos Daimon under the Greeks.

Shu: Eg. god of sunshine and air. He is shown as a human with a feather on his head.

Sobek: the Egyptian crocodile god, symbolic of pharaonic might, his great skill at snatching and destroying make him a fine manifestation of royal power.

Sokar, Seker: hawk god; patron of the *nekropolis* of Memphis. He is shown in human form with a hawk's head.

Soter: Gk., Saviour, or Deliverer from Danger; a title of Zeus, also bestowed upon Ptolemy I.

stade or *stadion:* Gk. measure, equal to 600 feet; also the name for the Greek running-track, and for the foot-race that was one length of the *stadion.*

strategos: Gk., general; also military governor.

Syene: city of Upper Egypt, the ancient Egyptian Yebu; modern Aswan.

talent: Gk. unit of weight and money, equal to sixty minas or six thousand drachmas, or 36,000 obols. One talent weight was perhaps 84 pounds of gold or silver.

Thanatousia: the Gk. Feast of the Dead.

Thebes, Egypt: to the Egyptians this city was Waset, or the Southern City; to the Greeks it was Diospolis—City of the Gods—or "Hundred-Gated" Thebes. The modern Luxor, or Karnak.

Thermouthis: Name given to the lucky house snake of Alexandria, who was also the Agathos Daimon, or Good Spirit. Thermouthis was seen as the messenger of Isis, if not as Isis herself.

trierarch: Gk., commander of a *trieres*.

trieres, pl. *triereis:* the Gk. oared war-galley; Lat. *trireme*.

Tykhe: Gk. goddess of Chance, or Luck. Lat. Fortuna.

Typhon: Gk. counterpart of Seth. The Egyptians liked to see the Greeks as Typhonians, as the personification of Disorder.

Wadjet: The cobra goddess of Egypt. The *ouraios* or *uraeus* cobra is the symbol of sovreignty the Pharaoh wears on his forehead—it is Wadjet rising up in her anger to spit flames in defence of the monarch. Wadjet, or Udjat, is the tutelary goddess of Lower Egypt. Her southern counterpart is Nekhbet the Vulture.

Zeus: Gk. King of the Gods, the father of gods and men. He is the supreme ruler, who controls thunder, lightning, rain, and who upholds justice, law and morals.

Zeus-Ammon: Gk., renowned oracle in the desert of Libya; the modern Siwa.

Greek Measures

4 fingerbreadths = 1 *palaste,* or palm of the hand.
12 fingerbreadths = 1 *spithame,* or span of all the fingers.
16 fingerbreadths = 1 (Greek) foot (*pous*), or 4 palms.
18 fingerbreadths = 1 *pygme,* or short cubit, the distance between elbow and knuckles.
40 fingerbreadths = 1 *bema,* or step.
96 fingerbreadths = 1 *orgyia,* the length of the outstretched arms, or one fathom.
1,600 fingers or 100 feet = 1 *plethron.*
9,600 fingers or 600 feet = 1 *stadion* (*stade*).
288,000 fingers, or 30 *stades* = 1 *parasang.*

Greek Money

6 obols = 1 drachma
100 drachmas = 1 *mina* (also one lb. weight of silver).
60 minae = 1 talent, or 6,000 drachmas, or 36,000 obols.
An ordinary Greek soldier earned 4 obols a day.
At one drachma per man per day, one talent would pay the crew of a *trieres* for one month.
A sculptor at the height of his career might earn two drachmas a day.
The best of flute-girls might command two drachmas for an evening's entertainment.
Two hundred drachmas might buy a good slave.
Two hundred drachmas was also the standard ransom for prisoners of war.
A mina concubine cost 100 drachmas a time, or 600 obols—150 days' pay for an ordinary soldier.
An obol whore could be had, then, for a quarter of a man's daily pay.
Strato of Lampsakos was paid 80 talents to tutor the young Ptolemy Mikros. This sum represents 1,972 years' pay for a common soldier.
As for the Pharos, or Great Lighthouse, at 800 talents this cost the equivalent of one common soldier's pay for 19,726 years.
It would take the common soldier 9,000 days, or nearly 25 years, to earn one talent; yet Alexander handed out talents to his veteran soldiers as a tip or bonus.

AKHENATEN
Dweller in Truth
by Naguib Mahfouz

Nobel laureate Naguib Mahfouz brings us the story of Akhenaten, or the "sun king," whose monotheistic beliefs eventually earned him the epithet "heretic pharaoh." Narrating the novel is a young man with a passion for the truth, who questions the pharaoh's contemporaries—including his closest friends, his worst enemies, and finally his wife, Nefertiti—years after the king's death in an effort to record a history free of bias. As each contributes their versions, Akhenaten emerges as a charismatic enigma whose character encompasses all of the contradictions his subjects see in him.

Fiction/Literature/0-385-49909-4

FUNERAL GAMES
by Mary Renault

Alexander the Great died at the age of thirty-three, leaving behind an empire that stretched from Greece and Egypt to India. As the King's only direct heirs were two unborn sons and a simpleton half-brother, every long-simmering political faction exploded into the vacuum of power. All vied for the loyalty of an increasingly undisciplined Macedonian army. No one, it turned out, possessed the visionary leadership necessary to keep the great empire from crumbling, but Alexander's legacy endured to spread to worlds he had only seen in his dreams.

Historical Fiction/0-375-71419-7

THE CRUSADER
by Michael Alexander Eisner

Francisco de Montcada, the young Spanish heir to a vast family fortune, returns from the Crusades a gaunt shell of a man, rendered speechless by the horrors he has witnessed. As his friend Brother Lucas draws out his story, Francisco relates a gripping tale of fierce battles, cruel betrayals, and religious zealots. A first-rate novel of disquieting contemporary relevance, *The Crusader* captures with impressive style and historical authenticity the ghastly deeds men pursue in the name of God.

Historical Fiction/0-385-72141-2

CREATION
by Gore Vidal

Cyrus Spitama, grandson of the prophet Zoroaster and lifelong friend of Xerxes, spent most of his life as Persian ambassador for the great king Darius. He traveled to India, where he discussed nirvana with Buddha, and to the warring states of Cathay, where he learned of Tao from Master Li and fished on the riverbank with Confucius. Now blind and aged in Athens—the Athens of Pericles, Sophocles, Thucydides, Herodotus, and Socrates—Cyrus recounts his days as he strives to resolve the fundamental questions that have guided his life's journeys: how the universe was created, and why evil was created with good.

Historical Fiction/0-375-72705-1

KING HEREAFTER
by Dorothy Dunnett

In *King Hereafter*, Dorothy Dunnett's stage is the wild, half-pagan country of eleventh-century Scotland. Her hero is an ungainly young earl with a lowering brow and a taste for intrigue. He calls himself Thorfinn but his Christian name is Macbeth. Dunnett depicts Macbeth's transformation from an angry boy who refuses to accept his meager share of the Orkney Islands to a suavely accomplished warrior who seizes an empire with the help of a wife as shrewd and valiant as himself. She creates characters who are at once wholly creatures of another time yet always recognizable—and she does so with such realism and immediacy that she once more elevates historical fiction into high art.

Historical Fiction/0-375-70403-5

VINTAGE AND ANCHOR BOOKS
Available from your local bookstore, or call toll-free to order:
1-800-793-2665 (credit cards only).